To Harry,

I reckon the [...] of Finn in u

I hope you enjoy following him.

Myk

July 12th 2021

*Books by the same author*

The Diary of Nicholas Oldman (Books 1, 2 and 3)

Twisty!

**The Last Teabag**

# SEARCHING for SAM

By

M. G. Atkinson

4th Edition

First published 2017

Copyright © Michael G Atkinson 2016/2017/2018
The moral right of the author has been asserted.

Cover knife by, Philip Drury.
flip_fury@hotmail.com

Cover design and render by, Myk.
Special thanks to Brusheezy.com

With a very special thanks to;
my aunt, Jennifer Lemm, who once again, found
those errors and typos with her eagle-eyed proof-reading
and magnificent editing, I couldn't have done it without you.

All rights reserved.
No part of this publication may be reproduced,
or transmitted in any form or by any means,
without the prior permission of the author in writing,
nor be circulated in any form of binding or cover other
than that in which it is published.

All characters in this publication are fictitious and
any resemblance to real persons, living or dead,
is purely coincidental.

eMail: myk.atkinson@ntlworld.com
Facebook: http://www.facebook.com/mgatkinsonauthor

ISBN-13: 978-1979802567
ISBN-10: 1979802564

Dedicated to:
The slaves of the world. Your day will arrive.

# Foreword

Just a few words, to point out and clarify a point or two. I promise, I won't keep you long.

Firstly - because it is a quick point - the word *Geis*.

This is an old Celtic word pronounced *Gay-sh* and is a very complicated kind of oath or as often is the case a taboo. For example; an Irish King, when crowned in front of his province may be held under *Geis* to never turn a Smith away from his halls and never hunt boar on the last Sunday of the month. (I made that up but there are many other, far stranger, *Geis*.)

To break your *Geis* is to invite certain doom, and often that doom is in the form of some magical affliction or malady. I'll say no more, you can find plenty of information if you really wish to look further.

But...<rubs hands together and grins> I now lay this *Geis* on you, my poor, unfortunate reader – and believe me, the Faery *are* listening.

Your *Geis* is to read the Prologues and Epilogues of the novels which you read.

Which leads onto the next point in this silly, little foreword.

I visited a lady in her late-sixties (age relevance will become apparent in a sentence or two), who had kindly offered to read my novel before I released it.

She asked me a question about something which hadn't made sense and I told her the answer to that question lay at the beginning, maybe even on the very first page of the Prologue. And this is what she said;

*"Oh! Well. I don't read the Prologues or the Epilogues."*

And I understood completely where she was coming from; there really was a day when Prologues and Epilogues and Forewords were very detached from the storyline and the main 'meat' of the novel and thus we just sniffed and turned to good old Chapter One.

So, dear reader, the Prologue is almost like the opening scene of most modern films; a sharp look ahead at the things to come before they roll the titles and credits.

Similarly, the Epilogue is now, more or less, one of two things - or both, like this novel - a way to tie up the loose ends and/or leave you with a hint of something else to come; an ending with possible new beginnings, just like the end of a great film.

Your *Geis* isn't that hard after all and I'm sure the Faery won't come down on you too harshly if you do break it. Or will they?

And finally and more seriously, slavery.

Slavery is a very real and very frightening thing which is happening in our world, our countries, right now. My research has led me to untold stories, un-listened to is probably a better way to say that.

I am not going to depress you but I would like to share something about the process of writing this novel, if I may.

*Searching for Sam* is a fiction, we've got that straight at the beginning, Finn is also a fiction. But Finn wanders around a landscape which is based upon real things, real happenings, real evil. I am refraining from saying real events; these exact scenarios and situations which I have placed Finn in may well exist but mine are fictional for the sake of the story and for the sake of how Finn deals with them.

Now, I won't say I have secret sources and things like that because I don't, I use the internet and I read everything, as many sides of the coin as I can get, all of the angles as far is humanly possible. And the internet is full of nightmares.

I would recommend reading a brilliant article I found on the internet explaining and revealing the other side of our friendly, information, communication super-highway, a place referred to as the Dark-web.

I had never heard of this Dark-web until two years ago. I can't plug the article here, but you can use a search engine and find it yourself. It is very good reading.

Well, that's it, read on and I sincerely hope you enjoy.
Michael.

# One

# Finn

# Prologue

*A breath before death,*
*Afore the eye which flutters shut,*
*Hold my gaze and see that which is hidden.*
*Take my secrets back to the green-isle under the blue sky.*

*Take my secrets back,*
*And I will be by your side before the new dawn.*
*Upon lawns of running green.*

*Take my secrets back,*
*And never again shall we part.*

*Take my secrets back.*

\* \* \*

Seven Years ago.

Bright, swinging streetlights washed the long, dusty street in a dirty, yellow glare. It was quiet in the small Mexican town and business was slow as the clocks ticked on past midnight.

A twelve year-old girl sat perched on a wicker-basket, her small frame hardly making the thing sag. Business was slow, she wanted to go home.

She looked up and could just make out her pimp standing in the shadows, watching and waiting. She couldn't go home, not yet, not until she had made another hundred dollars at least.

She willed the taverna to close and the men to begin their boozy marches back to their homes. Any one of them would be better than having her pimp using her. He would. If she didn't get another customer, he would.

She could feel his eyes on her, touching her beneath her short skirt and tight vest. He *would* use her, he had promised her, if she didn't make enough, he would.

Tears welled up in her green eyes. She fought to control them; she must not let her makeup run.

They didn't like it when you cried. Well most of them. Some of them wanted to see tears and pleading, but that was all part of the game. Her pimp would *make* her cry, would hurt her on purpose.

The tears threatened to come again and she sobbed. She just wanted to go home.

A man came walking briskly down the street.

The girl raised her head and her smile and waited.

The man drew near and looked at her. He clearly hadn't been drinking, but she was desperate and had to try.

'What's the hurry, mister?' Her smile was radiant.

The man slowed a little but didn't stop.

'If you like what you see you can come in there with me.' She said, and nodded behind her to the deeply shadowed doorway. 'I'll show you a good time, mister.' Her eyes twinkled.

The middle-aged man looked suddenly embarrassed and then afraid. His eyes widened and he dropped his gaze as he passed her.

'You can do anything you like for-for fifty dollars, mister!' She pleaded as he strode away.

Her eyes brimmed and her smile fell as she looked down to her knees, casting a fearful glance up the street to where her pimp stood. He wasn't there. Probably gone for a piss in the ally.

She thought about just running, running home and locking the door on the night and her pimp. But she knew she wouldn't; she needed the money, her family needed the money, but more than they needed the money, they *didn't* need to know that their little Gabriella sold herself to get it.

She shot another furtive look up the street. He still wasn't there. Damn him! She hated him. She hated him more for forcing himself on her as her pimp than she did for just forcing himself on her. She had to work twice as long and hard to make even half the money she used to make when she was just by herself.

She looked down at her bruised thighs. They used to be bruised from playing after school.

The hurried man continued his trot for his own home, his own wife and children.

Gabriella watched his back as he went.

That was her father. If she had been someone else, another twelve year-old girl, and her father had passed just then, he would have done exactly the same thing. Coward.

She continued to stare at the man's back.

She hated him almost as much as she hated her pimp. His cowardice, his weakness. He should stand up for her, be there to take care of her. How could he walk past like that? Like she had a disease and he would taint his good soul with her filth.

He was worse than the men who paid her to let them do things to her. *They* didn't care. As long as they got what they wanted from the world, they didn't care and were honest enough to admit it.

But *he* was one of those who were supposed to care; those who had children of their own and were genuinely outraged. On the surface and in front of others of the same mind at least; underneath they were all the same; spineless do-gooders who hid themselves behind a façade of moral-righteousness while they did very little other than whine at their breakfast tables as they read the daily horrors in the newspapers.

She spat on the ground hatefully as he disappeared around the corner.

Back up the street, the corner where her pimp usually sat was still empty. What was he doing?

She stared hard into the shadows to see if he was standing against the wall and just watching, staying almost invisible in the deeper shades.

Then she suddenly felt afraid. A shiver ran through her, the shadow undulated. Or did it? Her eyes were playing tricks on her staring into the blackness like that. But she could have sworn that there had been a subtle shift in the shadow, a movement of something deeper than the shadow itself.

Her heart was hammering. Why was she afraid? He was brutal, yes, but she had never felt as afraid as she did now. She felt there was a presence in the shadows watching her and it wasn't her pimp.

*Stupid! Stop it, it's just him trying to make you feel more afraid than usual. Bullying jerk.*

Something glittered briefly, a flash of dull metal, and then a ragged ball came rolling out from the alleyway.

It crossed the full length of the pavement and dropped into the gutter, rolling down the street a little before coming to a halt.

What was he doing? Going through the trashcans and throwing the rubbish out for her to see?

She looked closely at the ball, the strange, angled edges and lumpy shapes made no sense; it was just a lumpy thing. A dark, lumpy, round thing-

Her breath caught in her chest and her eyes suddenly widened.

A dark, lumpy, round thing with open eyes.

As her mind finally made sense of the mess of shapes, the young girl's skin throbbed with the buzz of shock at the sudden realisation of what she was seeing.

His eyes were half lidded but he still stared at her nonetheless, hard and leering almost; *where's my money?* They still said.

The shadow drawn across the alleyway throbbed again as something moved beyond its edge.

Gabriella could still feel the attention of something inside firmly fixed on her. Waiting. Waiting for her.

She stood up ready to run in the opposite direction but couldn't tear her eyes away from the shadow. Something was there and it was waiting for her, she should run and keep running but she had to know.

Her pimp probably had many enemies, probably deserved to die a thousand times over, but the thing in the shadow was waiting for *her*; it hadn't killed him for its own reasons, it had killed him for her.

Before she knew what she was actually doing the young girl had stepped out into the road and was halfway across.

She gingerly stepped around the staring head and then stopped in front of the alleyway, huddling her arms to her chest and peering into the darkness. 'Thank you.' She whispered.

From the right-hand side of the alleyway a darker shadow detached itself from the wall and walked a step closer.

Streetlight filtered through the deep shade, casting a pallid line of light across the eyes of a tall man.

His bright-blue eyes stared at Gabriella, the bluest eyes she had ever seen, bluer than the bluest sky. Lightning-eyes she thought.

He took another step forward, staying close to the edge of the shadows. His left hand hung by his side clasping a long, steel blade, its edge darkened.

Gabriella stood frozen, mesmerised by those piercing, blue eyes as the man took another step closer and another step; long, slow, silent strides like the pad of a prowling cat.

Her mind cried out again for her to run away but she couldn't find the will to move her arms or legs, all she could do was look at those eyes as they came closer and closer.

He was right in front of her now, right at the very edge of the shadow.

The man raised his arm slowly and reached for Gabriella's face, frowning as he stroked her cheek gently. Then quite suddenly his face relaxed and his eyes softened as he quietly spoke.

'Ah! There you are.' He said, his blue eyes filling with tears. 'There you are.' He repeated, and leaned forward and embraced the small girl.

Gabriella released herself to it and all of her fear dropped easily away with that one, single embrace.

She sobbed quietly. 'Thank you.' She whispered again.

The man held her tightly for a moment more before slowly releasing her and then stepped past her into the street.

'Go home, child.' He said as he walked away. 'Go home and be safe.'

Gabriella kept her back to the street as the tall man disappeared into the night, his steps quickly fading to silence.

She wanted to run after him, thank him some more, ask him why he had helped her, but it seemed that the right thing to do was to let him go; the less she knew about him, the better for him.

She looked down and saw the shadowy form of her pimp's, headless body laying on its back a few steps away. His shirt was ripped open she saw, and there was a pattern of wounds on his bare chest.

*Just leave, go home to bed and forget about it.*

But she wanted to know what the pattern was, she had come this far, she had to go all the way to the end now.

She took a small step closer and peered into the gloom of the alley, trying to get a better view of the seemingly random lines. And then she had it, they were letters.

*Go home, child.* The tall man's words echoed in her mind.

She took another step and leaned a little forward, standing on the tips of her toes.

The letters spelled out a single word; *Finn*.

## Chapter One

Today.

Early morning sunlight and wet streets; bright, flaring sunlight gilded the wet, stone flags.

Shelby looked down from his sixteenth storey office and sipped his coffee, marvelling at the golden wash. Everything looked so clean after the rain, leaving his spirits lifted and restoring his confidence in the world a little.

The world Graham Shelby knew was much darker than the view from his window.

It was almost certain there were seven serial-killers roaming the planet, but according to his contacts within the FBI it was speculated that there could be as many as thirteen serial-killers hiding somewhere amongst us.

Shelby had the task of catching one of them, a task he had been undertaking for the past seven years without so much as a hair or fingerprint to work with. Only bodies and a sterile crime-scene were left behind by this killer. Until now.

The hairs on Shelby's nape prickled as he thought about the package lying on his desk. Arrived this morning, had been expected to arrive all week, but until it was actually delivered he didn't dare entertain the idea that it was real. Now that it was here he found he was actually afraid to open the damn thing.

Seven years without a single clue to the identity of the killer calling himself, *Finn*, not a single scrap of anything and suddenly he had a package which just might hold a picture of the man. An actual picture!

Shelby shuddered. It was like waiting to see a long, lost relative for the first time. Or was it more like being released from prison after years inside? A bit of both maybe.

He sipped more coffee and refused to listen to the insistent nag of the package at his back. I've *waited this long,* you *can wait for me,* he was thinking.

He caught his own eye in the reflection of the window, seeing his own, frowning brow and the questions beneath.

*Why now? Why has he slipped up now?*

His reflection didn't answer, but then again it didn't need to; Finn hadn't slipped up, he *wants* to be seen but why?

The man wasn't egocentric at all. He was brutal, bloody and to the point, meticulous in the execution of his crimes, but he wasn't a show-off; he didn't leave cryptic messages to taunt the police, didn't make contact afterward, didn't collect trophies from his victims. His only calling card was the word *Finn,* carved somewhere onto the bodies of his victims.

A sudden flash of guilt washed across Shelby's chest; *why couldn't you just stay hidden, you selfish bastard?*

He sighed deeply as old conflicts came rushing to the surface.

Finn was complicated. His *modus operandi* was brutally extreme in most of the cases but his reasons were quite apparent and even admirable; he was targeting the underground sex-industry.

Every case saw a child or a group of children or young men and women all being freed from some horrendous, perverted bondage.

The abuses and horrifying crimes committed against these young human-beings became more apparent when witnessing the crime-scenes which Finn left behind. The man must have seen things which can only be imagined in the darkest of nightmares.

But Shelby was sworn to capture him, put a stop to his crusade of wiping out the real villains and freeing the innocent, and he didn't like it one bit; something just felt completely out of whack.

*Why couldn't you just stay bloody hidden!*

He finished his coffee and crossed the room to the percolator, avoiding his desk and the glaring package sitting on its polished top.

He refilled his cup and then took another from the bright-pink cup-tree - a gift from his wife and one which was completely out of place in his modern office, just as she had intended - and filled that one as well.

Just as Shelby replaced the coffee pot onto its hotplate the door opened and his long-term partner at Interpol bustled in.

'Morning, Gray.' She said, striding over to her desk and dropping her handbag on top.

'Morning Soph, coffee's on.' Shelby replied, raising her cup.

Sophie Bollinger had been partnered with Shelby for six years, she had been neck-deep in the Finn case right from day one.

'Is that what I think it is?' She asked as she passed his desk, nodding at the package.

'It is.'

'And why haven't you opened it yet?' She took her coffee and sipped it, looking Shelby in the eye.

'Because I thought I would wait for you and we can do the honours together?' He replied and looked away, stirring his coffee some more.

'Liar.' She prodded him in the arm. '*You* don't want to know for the very same reasons *I* don't want to know. Damn it! They should give the man a bloody medal and get him to school us on how he gets so deep into these underground sex-networks.'

'We still have a sworn job to do, Soph, it doesn't matter what we think or how we feel at the end of the day does it?' He replied, looking up.

'Well, I would have to disagree there; it's our empathy to our cases that makes us better able to understand them *and*,' she raised her eyebrows to emphasise the point, *'and* gives us a truer perspective of what justice really is. Especially the Finn case.'

She softened her gaze then and sighed. 'You know as well as I do that I will do everything I can and not an ounce less to bring Finn in, but now that we have that,' she nodded at the package again, 'we have to start being honest with ourselves; there is a moral justice to be faced, Gray, and not just Finn's.'

Shelby pondered his partner's words and slowly nodded. 'It is the very morality of it which is making me hesitant to open the damn thing, but we still have a duty to perform which is steeped in moral justice; the protection of life. And not just the potential victims, but Finn's as well.'

He looked at Bollinger and waited for his words to sink in then added quietly; 'How long can it be before he gets caught by the wrong people?' He said. 'What do you think will happen to him if he does get caught? It doesn't bear worth thinking about, Soph, we have to bring him in one way or another.'

'And then?' Bollinger asked.

'And then I don't know, but I will promise this; he will be brought here, back to London HQ, and we can at least hold him on safe ground. After that? I have no idea. But you are right about one thing; there will be a reckoning at the end of all this.'

He sipped his coffee and then smiled. 'As long as you're with me, Soph, I'm sure we'll both make the right calls.'

Bollinger chugged down the last of her own coffee. 'Then let's get cracking shall we?' She said, and dropped her cup next to Shelby's.

The pair of them turned and faced the desk where the package still sat waiting for them.

Bollinger gently elbowed, Shelby. 'You can do the *honours* then.'

He took a deep breath and then strode to his desk, snatching up the well-travelled, brown-paper parcel and tearing the top edge open. He tipped it up and two CD's and a hand-written cover-note fell out.

*To Inspectors G. Shelby and S. Bollinger,*

*I am enclosing 2 copies of the images retrieved from the computer from the Cafe on Beyaz Gemi street.*

*I hope you will find them of some use.*

*We will keep you up-to-date with our findings and hope to hear of your own once you have looked through the contents.*

*I must warn you that there are over 6,000 images. Fortunately they are in separate and dated folders, each day holds 288 images.*

*Best regards,*
*Captain Babacan Demir.*

Shelby whistled. 'Looks like we've got our work cut out for us. Six-thousand images! Christ! Don't we have lackeys for this sort of thing?'

Bollinger scoffed. 'If only.'

She picked one of the CD's up. 'I'll take the front half, you take the back, and we'll meet back here when we have a picture of our man, Finn.' She said, and strode off to her desk and waiting computer, still chuckling.

Shelby sat down behind his own desk and pulled his monitor around to face him. After pushing the CD into the drive he sat back and waited.

Bollinger was already sat with folded arms, waiting for the same program to start up and read the disc. 'Tell me again, Gray, how it's a good thing that our super-powerful computers are slowed down by sixteen security-filters and several firewalls.'

'It's a good thing, Sophie, that our computers are passed through several *uncrackable* firewalls and *eighteen high*-security filters.'

'Sorry; *eighteen high*-security filters.' She responded sarcastically before adding; 'if they're uncrackable, why do we need several? Surely one uncrackable firewall would do the trick?'

Shelby peered over the top of his monitor at her. 'Passive dongles and onion layers, Bollinger, finger-press traces and worms.'

She guffawed. 'God, I love it when you talk gibberish.' And then laughed whole-heartedly.

Shelby's monitor pinged musically to alert him to the computers now-ready status.

Bollinger's played the first few bars of *Albatross* by Fleetwood Mac.

Shelby peered over his monitor at her again. 'What happened to *Avenues and Alleyways*?' He asked.

She shrugged. 'While it had an obvious meaning and connection to the job I found the wide open spaces and unrelenting, restless flight of the Albatross to be more fitting.' She answered.

Shelby just stared at her. 'Well that was pretty deep, Soph. For a slow computer.'

She just smiled and carried on clicking away with her mouse, opening the folders where the images were placed.

The pictures were taken with a low-resolution web-cam and were small and not of the best quality.

It was difficult to make out any serious detail, the compression ratios sometimes blurring features beyond recognition, but on the whole the images were good enough to make out enough detail to see individual faces and people.

The camera was placed in the front window of a Turkish café on a busy street and the view gave a wide shot facing north up the street.

In every shot there were people and vehicles passing the window from both directions and on both sides of the road.

The people on foot were a mix of locals and tourists, the tourists clearly marked out by their western skins and clothes.

Seven years of working the case, nineteen different crime locations worldwide with a body-count of thirty-nine and all they had gleaned from that was they were looking for a tall man with blue eyes, dressed in black and always carrying weapons ranging from pistols and knives to hatchets and clubs. And that was it. Everything else was missing; no other details except he always carved his name into his victims and the children he saved all said the same thing; he told them he had been looking for them and then released them to go home.

Two hours passed by and Shelby had to raise himself from his chair and stretch.

Without asking, he made them both more coffee, placing Bollinger's on her desk.

'Have a minute to stand and stretch, Soph, clear your eyes.' He said.

She sat back in her chair and ran her fingers through her blonde hair. 'Everyone I look at is beginning to fit the description.' She said, as she sighed, pushing herself to her feet.

She picked up her coffee and took a place by Shelby's side in front of the windows and looked out over the city.

The silence between them was loaded with a mixture of trepidation and frustration.

Each time they brought a new image up to be scrutinised they felt a subtle excitement that *this was it*, they would spot him in this image, but after going over every pixel and not finding anything they were left sighing and feeling deflated, while at the same time they were also guiltily pleased.

Two hours of this emotional see-saw had dripped by; up and excited, down and deflated, back up and pleased, load the next image.

Crawling, mid-morning traffic streamed slowly past below in the streets. Like the images, it was hard to make out much detail from up here, the vehicles all travelled at the same, slow pace in both directions. If you stared at it for long enough it began to look like a conveyor-belt with different coloured boxes rolling along it.

Every now and again though, a single shape and colour would stand out, usually a bigger vehicle like a van or a bus.

Bollinger scoffed and shook her head. 'Even the traffic's beginning to look like a puzzle.'

'One or two occasionally standing out more than the rest?' Shelby said, looking at Bollinger and sipping his coffee.

'You're seeing it too.' It wasn't a question. She laughed again.

'It's because we've just come away from performing that very task; searching for the thing which stands out. We're a bit *programmed* at the minute.'

He tipped his cup. 'The coffee will sort us out.' He said, 'And if it doesn't it will at least make us work faster.'

'Oh! Great! I can fail to find Finn faster.' She said, and scoffed. 'Say *that*, twenty times, quickly.'

'See? The coffee is working wonders already.'

Shelby finished his own and then went back to his desk.

Bollinger lingered at the window, mentally reciting *'fail to find Finn faster'* over and over in her mind.

'Stop trying to say *fail to find Finn faster*, Bollinger, you'll drive yourself mad and end up reinforcing your will to fail.' Shelby muttered as he opened another image.

Bollinger quickly finished her coffee and sat back behind her desk. 'I lost it after the ninth time.'

'Unlucky. I managed twelve.'

'You've had more coffee.'

Shelby smiled but said nothing.

The images slowly flowed past the eyes of the two Inspectors, a series of moments separated by five second intervals. The same people and same cars were often in more than one consecutive capture.

Bollinger studied the picture of a man, a local by his dress, who had been in the last four pictures.

She flicked through the other images ahead, he was in twenty-nine of them altogether.

In the first thirteen images the man just stood holding his cup before placing it down on the café's window sill. He then stood looking across the street before picking his cup back up and moving back the way he had come. Odd.

Bollinger flicked through the images again to try and see what the man had been looking at for the two minutes he had been standing there.

Nothing stood out. He was deeply in the shade of the café's parasol and she couldn't make out any details of the man himself, only his cup was brightly lit being now perched on the sill in front of a small, burning lamp.

His cup.

'Oh! Shit!' Sophie breathed. 'You'd better take a look at this, Gray. Oh! Fucking Hell!'

Shelby was up like a shot. 'What is it? What have you got?' He said, as he sidled up to her, peering intently at her monitor. 'What am I looking at, Soph?'

He scanned his eyes around the picture, flicking from one detail to the next, dismissing the people he saw before moving on to the next detail which caught his eye.

Eventually he spotted the polystyrene cup on the sill and almost dismissed it before catching the black smudges on its edge.

'What's that on his cup?' He said, frowning and trying to make out the blurry lines.

Bollinger dragged her cursor over the top of the cup to highlight it then pressed a key to make it bigger.

She sat back with a blank look on her face and just stared.

A word had been written in faded, black ink; *Shelby*.

Shelby slowly straightened himself up, never taking his eyes from his name on the cup.

The rules had just changed and although it seemed at first that Finn was threatening him, Shelby thought it was something else.

'What does it mean, Gray? How does he know your name?'

'I don't know,' Shelby answered. 'But keep looking, I expect we will find some more cups with messages on them.'

Bollinger opened more images and sure enough on the images from the following day, at almost the same time, Finn returned. This time his cup had *Afghanistan* written on it.

The next day was exactly the same only this time there were two words; *March April*. And then nothing. After searching the rest of the images they found no more Finn or cups with words on them.

'*Shelby. Afghanistan. March April.* I think our friend is trying to tell you something.' Sophie remarked. 'He's going to do something around that time in Afghanistan if you take it literally and he wants *you* to know.'

Shelby paced the room. The rules had been changed beyond recognition now.

'I think it's something else,' he eventually said. 'I think your right about he's planning something in Afghanistan around those months and I also think you're right that he wants me to know, but I get the feeling he actually wants our help with whatever it is he is planning on doing.'

He stopped his pacing and looked levelly at Bollinger.

'You can't be serious!?' Bollinger looked thunderstruck. 'But he would have to have some level of trust wouldn't he? Why would he trust us?'

Shelby began pacing again. *Why* would *you trust us? Afghanistan? What the hell is in Afghanistan?*

He stopped pacing again. 'I don't know why he would trust us, but I would be willing to bet that whatever it was that set him off in the first place is now coming to a head; whatever fantasy he is living in is coming to some natural end. I don't care what Appleby and his psyche-tests say; Finn isn't your textbook, psychopathic serial-murderer. We both know it.'

Bollinger nodded her head slowly in agreement.

'Whatever it is that is driving him hasn't escalated at all,' Shelby continued, 'he hasn't become any more or any less brutal in dealing out his retribution.'

He said, picking up his pacing again. 'And now we find out that he knows us, is trying to make contact with us. If he *was* the textbook psychopath, I think you and I, Soph, would have had some kind of run in with him by now. At the very least I think he would have left a memento of one of his hits for us, something he could gloat about.'

'But he hasn't.' Bollinger finished for him.

'But he hasn't.' Repeated Shelby, sighing as he came to halt again. 'Probably the very reason why we haven't had any luck at all in tracing him; because he's something *other* than a psychopath.'

He sat his big frame on the edge of his desk and looked down at his feet. 'You know the protocol now, Sophie.'

He looked up at his partner. 'A personal contact has been made which could be perceived as a threat, I'm supposed to report it and then distance myself.'

'But you're not going to are you?' Bollinger asked quietly.

Shelby shook his head. 'I can't. Not after so long.'

He paused for Bollinger's protest but she simply waited to hear what he had to say.

'I can't say I know Finn, but I do know that this is not a threat.' He continued, pointing to the image on the screen. 'If we ever had a chance of bringing him in, this is it.'

Bollinger studied her partner, looking for any signs that would tell her he was making a mistake. He wasn't, she felt exactly the same thing; this was a chance they couldn't miss and they must not let anyone else in.

'Well, I suppose we had better start opening *our* avenues and alleyways of research into Afghanistan.' Was all she said.

## Chapter Two

*The cave again. Dreaming again. And I know I'm dreaming. Again, again, again.*

*I can feel her at my back; her hazel and amber eyes set into her perfect, silver face; a she-wolf of tremendous power, staring and waiting for me to move.*

*Water drips down the walls, my naked body is drenched in my own perspiration as I stay crouched on my haunches, curling my arms around my legs and making myself as small as possible.*

*I can see the place I want to get to. The curtain of water cascading past the archway blurs the beyond to an unrecognisable wash of hues and bright colours, but I know that is where I need to get to. If only she would let me.*

*I hear her rumbling growl rise in her throat, a deep, unsatisfied sound which sends my blood cold. She knows what I am thinking.*

*I try to cast my mind away from the archway but it's too late; I have displeased the she-wolf. All I can do now is close my eyes and wait for the rending claws and tearing teeth to set upon me. All I can do is wait and scream.*

Grinding gears and the heavy rumble of a passing truck in the street, vibrated through the tiny hotel-room. The man on the bed sat bolt-upright, panting heavily and staring around with wide, wild, lightening-blue eyes.

He turned his head sharply to look out of the window, listening to the rumble of the truck as it passed away into the night while his chest heaved and the sweat dripped from his chin.

The truck faded to silence, Finn turned away and swivelled his legs over the edge of the bed and sat with his head down and eyes closed, pushing the last of his nightmare from his waking mind.

She had set him another task. But did she know? About Shelby and Afghanistan? Did she know what he was planning and why?

He thought not, or at least if she did she wasn't bothered by it. As long as he completed her own tasks she wouldn't care. In fact she would be pleased about Afghanistan, wouldn't she?

He ran his scarred hands over his equally scarred face and head, wiping the sleep away and pulling his long, blonde hair back. He sat up straight and looked around.

Another room in another city, another country, but the same room nonetheless.

It didn't matter where in the world he was, the rooms in the red-light districts where he usually stayed were all the same; same gaudy colours, same boxwood end-tables, same leering paintings and always the same over-used mattress.

Home for the past seven years.

It was still dark outside. He had another task to do while he was still in Turkey; he had to find the girl who the she-wolf wanted. He would do it tonight. She was never wrong when she sent him to these places. Never.

How many had she sent him to find and bring home? How many had she seen him kill to get to the ones she wanted to be found? How many more?

The faces of the dead were never far from Finn's minds-eye, the one part of his *geis* to the she-wolf which he truly hated but embraced all the same; a reminder of the hurt he had caused her.

*I'm sorry.* He said to her in his mind.

He was acutely aware of her pain, a pining of such deep loss which only mothers felt at the loss of a child.

'I'm sorry.' He whispered aloud.

*Go and find her!*

Finn flinched as the roaring command flashed across his mind.

*Go!*

He slowly raised himself to his feet, the shaft of streaming streetlight, filtering through the half open curtain bathed his naked body in a pale warmth as he rose through it.

Silvered lines criss-crossed his body and arms and legs; a map of scars punctuated here and there with red lines and puckered circles of the more recent additions.

The fourteen bullet scars were connected by a myriad of knife cuts and slashes, like connecting roads between towns and cities, making the cartographic illusion complete; Finn really did have a map of violence cut into his skin.

A few of the wounds should have killed him, but *she* wouldn't let him die. She was always there to claw his eyes back open, rake and slash his body until he woke up.

Healed him with pain.

He turned to the small, wooden chair by the bed and retrieved his clothes.

On the outside the shirt and trousers looked to be ordinary, black clothing, but Finn had, had these garments specially made in Russia by a company who catered for the *underground* security-industry.

Both were fire-resistant to the point that nothing short of a flame-thrower would ignite them, they were completely water-proof, tear-proof and were not easy to grab hold of in a fight.

But most importantly; they were lined with a criss-cross webbing of carbon-fibre and were incredibly hard to stab through. A bullet could still penetrate, but much of the energy would be absorbed, lessening to some degree the damage which it caused.

*She* had insisted on him seeking them out and acquiring them. He couldn't find the girl if he was dead now could he?

He sheathed two daggers in cleverly concealed scabbards just beneath his armpits, one on either side, he wouldn't need his pistols tonight.

Finally, he covered all with a dark-gray, casual jacket which he had bought the day before along with the black baseball cap to finish off the illusion of normal tourist.

Years of doing these tasks had honed his evasive skills to a sharp edge and evasion began the second he set off.

He didn't use the door which he kept locked with its '*Do Not Disturb*' sign in place. Instead he used the window in the dirty, en-suit bathroom.

The grit and refuse crunched beneath his feet as he dropped to the ground, the smell of yesterday's business lingered on the hot, thick air, sickly sweet.

Finn ignored it and strode further into the gloom of the alley he had dropped into, making his way along the darkened backs of the buildings along this street.

Every other building was occupied by inconspicuous bars and well-hidden sex-dens, while the rest were either a hotel of some sorts, or just a brothel in a house, but all had that same seedy appearance on the outside, while inside, seedy often turned to sick and sinister.

Finn marched his way quietly down the back ally, keeping well away from the fences and walls which marked the boundaries of the buildings.

Piles of refuse sacks lay scattered at the base of most walls and some even had the odd mattress or broken furniture piled up ready to be taken away by the garbage collectors.

By the size of the mounds though, it didn't look like collection-day had been for quite some time. Finn could hear the distinctive scratching sounds of rats nesting underneath.

At the end of the narrow, dirt track the main road cut a path from left to right, but straight ahead was another track leading away from the buildings; a meandering path which followed no discernible direction and didn't seem to lead to anywhere of significance.

Finn stood in the shadows at the corner of the last building and watched the road. It was quiet and only dimly lit but had a view from all around.

He waited for five minutes until he was satisfied that nothing was stirring and then crossed, disappearing down the dark path ahead.

High weeds and bushes choked the sides and threatened to encroach onto the well-worn track.

Finn brushed overhanging twigs and long, loose grass from his path as he walked past and had to duck more than once under the hanging boughs of the small, scrubby trees which grew all around the hills and wild-lands out here on the outskirts of the city.

Twenty minutes of walking and he found himself looking at the dim glow of a single bulb hanging over the doorway leading into a small, steel shack. A thin, white smoke filtered up from a tiny pipe protruding through the flat roof.

The thing was nothing more than a storage unit or goods container, secreted, no doubt, by the entrepreneur who peddled in innocent, young skin.

Finn took a glossy flyer from his pocket, one of thousands handed out daily to tourists.

This one advertised a bar which also served English food. On the back the man who had given Finn the flyer just a few hours ago had drawn a crude snake with a sword standing behind it. He had told Finn he must show the snake to the man on the door of the shack and once inside he would be expected to pay up-front.

Thirteen seconds after that conversation and the pimp lay buried beneath a heap of refuse behind the bar where he sought out potential customers; a single stab with a long stiletto had seen him gasp his last, disgusting breath as his heart was pierced by the steel blade. Finn had cut his mark into the dead man's forehead before covering him up.

He watched the door and the shack intently. She was there, right behind that door, just a few more feet and a quarter of an inch of steel before he saw her again. His heart hammered in his chest.

*I'm coming, daddy's coming.*

Finn stood motionless, staring at the door from his place in the shadows.

Finn the bringer of justice, the rescuer of the helpless and the weak, fought with the man in his mind, the man who screamed when Finn killed.

*Damn you! Leave me be!*

The man was strong, almost as strong as he was, and battered and assaulted his senses trying to get out and stop him from doing what he had to do.

But it always ended the same way; the man sagged and wept and yielded with pleas. *Don't kill them. Please don't kill them.*

Glazed, blue eyes suddenly narrowed and focussed, the task must be completed or he would be damned forever.

*Damn you!*

Pain suddenly lashed across his mind.

*Go! Go now! Find her, bring her home. Go! GO!*

The man fled and Finn hissed as the command seared through his head and body, stiffening as every nerve-ending seemed to suddenly fire at once.

He stood for some seconds, muscles taught and trembling with shock.

*I'm sorry.*

The pain subsided. Finn wiped away his tears and then in the blink of an eye transformed instantly into the tourist he needed to be to gain entry into the shack.

No one would have ever guessed that only moments ago the man had been deep in the throes of a violent, mental anguish.

Even as he approached the door he could almost smell the corruption inside, the smell of dark hearts and fearful innocence. It made him want to gag.

Such darkness had no place on this earth, no right to claim the good and the pure to fulfil its own need to bring all things to decay.

Finn found the darkness in his own soul, his fire to their fire, and embraced it, filled his mind and heart with it and then knocked on the door.

Sounds of someone raising themselves from a seat came to Finn's ears. A second later and a small, square hatch was opened and a large, frowning face appeared in the opening. The thug said nothing and just looked hard at Finn.

'I-I was told to show you this.' Finn said, acting his part of nervous, first-time tourist. He held the flyer up for the man to see.

The man looked back at him, still scowling almost. 'Cash?' Was all he said.

Finn reached into his jacket-pocket and produced a substantial roll of money.

The man's face instantly changed to one of congenial host. 'Welcome, sir! Allow me.' He said, through a mouth full of gold teeth.

The small hatch closed and a bolt was drawn back from the top and bottom of the door. It opened and a warm, spice-scented air flowed out from around the big, grinning thug. He gestured with his hand for Finn to enter.

Finn stepped through the door and walked inside. Behind him the clang of metal on metal gonged out as the thug closed and bolted it again.

Almost instantly the smell of garlic and old cheese, that odour of unwashed bodies and stale air, came to Finn's nose. The spicy scent did little to mask out the offending odours once the door was closed again.

Further in and a dirty, blue piece of rough cloth had been hung from one side to the other on a sagging, yellow rope, effectively shutting out the back of the container.

In front of the curtain and to the right sat an old woman behind a small, round table which had an assortment of glasses and bottled liquor spread across its top. A single bowl of flaccid, bruised olives finished off the tardy attempt of *complimentary extras.*

The old woman looked utterly cowed, her head down and her gaze vacant; years and years of living as a *thing* and not a person. Finn had seen that look many times before.

On the other side, almost opposite the table and the woman, a battered, leather settee had a tall, greasy man lounging across it. He was staring at Finn, a knowing look on his sneering, vulture-like face.

The big thug walked past Finn's shoulder and stood in front of him, glancing at the roll of cash still in his hand. 'You know you pay in advance, right?' He asked.

'Y-yes, of course. Could I-could I see first?' Finn asked nervously.

The thug just stared for a moment and then suddenly smiled brightly. 'Of course! Of course!' He said, slapping Finn on the shoulder.

He turned to the old woman and his scowl immediately returned. '*Buraya getir!*' He barked, and nodded in the direction of the curtain. '*Bring it in.*' Finn's English mind translated.

He watched as the old woman flinched at the order and then raise herself as quickly as she could, disappearing behind the blue curtain.

Once she had gone, he turned his attention back to the thug and the greasy man.

The old woman sighed as the curtain fell closed behind her. Just to be out of sight felt like a freedom in itself and she relished these moments when she wasn't in the focus of her tormentors. Family, both of them, but tormentors all the same.

She shuffled forward on limping legs and approached the girl sitting on the floor.

She had only been brought in a few days ago and still had that look of numb shock on her tiny face.

The old woman thought that was a good thing, she would be better off being numb, poor creature.

She stroked her hair and spoke to her in soothing tones and then coaxed her to her feet.

The old woman didn't know exactly how old the girl was, but she couldn't have seen more than eight summers.

She held her tightly, telling her to be brave again as she continued to stroke her hair and embrace her small frame.

The girl was unresponsive, her eyes simply stared straight ahead while her face showed no emotion whatsoever.

The old woman stood up straight and took the girl by the hand, leading her to the curtain, she herself falling into the submissive role she had been in moments earlier.

Pulling the girl along she opened the curtain and steered her through into the room beyond, easing her forward to stand in front of Finn.

The old woman didn't raise her eyes as she stood at the back like a servant or slave of ancient times. But she knew something was wrong; she could smell blood.

Finn stood before the girl, panting, his twin blades in his hands and the bodies of his victims laid at his feet where they had dropped without a struggle.

He took a step forward and lowered himself onto one knee, staring wildly into the face of the child.

*Is it her? Is that you? Is it?*

His eyes suddenly calmed and he sighed as tears began to run freely down his cheeks. 'There you are! I've been looking for you.'

He reached for the girl, taking her by the shoulders, peering into her small, brown eyes. 'I found you.' He said.

And the girl focused on his gaze and her lips quivered as she tried to smile bravely.

He embraced her tightly then and she held on to him, shaking as her screams and her pain were released, the fragile dam of emotions shattering now she knew that she was safe.

The old woman raised her head and saw the bodies of her nephews. She spat in the direction of the thug and then looked at Finn, a calm fear of readiness in her stance and stoically raised chin.

Finn merely smiled. 'I give you your power back, old one.' He said, respectfully and nodded, dropping his gaze a little. 'Whatever time you have left, live it as a free human-being under the stars.'

The old woman said nothing but her heart lifted and leaped, a feeling she hadn't felt for years beyond count it seemed; free under the stars, he had said. Free under the stars.

Finn stood up, lifting the child with him. 'It's time to go home.' He whispered to her, kissing the top of her head.

Looking at the old woman he asked; 'Do you know where?'

She nodded.

'And has your power returned?'

She nodded again.

'Then begin your life, old one, and go home too.' He said, as he passed the child over into her waiting arms.

He stood back and watched them both as they wept together and then silently he turned and opened the door and walked out into the night, never to be seen by either of them again, but never forgotten.

## Chapter Three

Saied Faraz was a rare man in more ways than one. Firstly, he was born with his heart on the right-hand side instead of the left and secondly, he was the only victim ever to have encountered Finn, and live.

Both rarities were inextricably bound; should Faraz have been born with his heart in the usual place, the knife which Finn had plunged through his back several times would have killed him. Instead it punctured his lung and did little else other than skewer the obese layers of fat together.

He lay sweating on his hospital bed, the wounds on his face where the maniac had cut him were driving him mad. From right jowl to his left temple and ear, the word *Finn* was carved to the bone in his prodigious face, leaving one eye blinded by the attack.

Half dazed by the drugs in the drip he struggled to open his remaining eye, the bright lights making it sting and fill with tears.

Through the blurry wash he could make out someone sitting in the visitors chair at the foot of the bed.

He raised his head groggily, fumbling with the tubes attached to his arm as he wiped his eye clear.

A man he had never seen before sat there looking at him seriously.

He sagged with relief when he saw it wasn't the maniac by the docks. Police by the looks of him. English police. Something else was going on.

The grey-suited man sat with his legs crossed and his expensive overcoat laid across his lap.

Middle-aged and short-cropped hair; a detective then.

Faraz squirmed inside at the thought of talking to the police, but this wasn't about his business with the Malas brothers, it couldn't be. No one knew he was in hospital except the people who must have worked on him when he walked in.

The man stood up and walked to Faraz's side, standing over him and looking down. 'I'm glad you are making a good recovery, Mr Faraz.' He said.

He produced a black wallet from his inside pocket then and flicked it open for Faraz to see. 'Detective Brown.' Was all he said, before whipping the wallet away again and stashing it. 'I think you already know that you have had a very lucky escape don't you?'

Faraz scoffed. 'I wouldn't call *this* lucky.' He said pointing to his face and blinded eye.

The detective sniffed and put his hands in his pockets, appraising the man on the bed for a moment. 'How would you feel if I told you that the man who did this to you has done it at least thirty-nine times before and until now has never left anyone alive?'

Faraz looked shocked. 'You're not serious?'

'Deadly.' Said Brown. 'He's been killing all over the world for the last six or seven years and now he turns up here, in Turkey.'

The detective raised his eyebrow and stared at Faraz, waiting for him to squirm.

'But-but why attack me? Is he a lunatic or something?' Faraz asked. 'What if he comes back?!'

Detective Brown continued to look hard at the man and then suddenly he relaxed. 'Oh. I wouldn't worry about him anymore.' He said, smiling brightly.

Faraz noticed that the smile didn't reach the man's eyes. 'What do you mean?'

'We think he's already left the country, or is at least trying to.' Detective Brown answered. 'We think he might be heading over the border to Iran and then on to Afghanistan.' Brown waited again, looking for a reaction in Faraz.

'W-what-' began Faraz.

'Don't!' Barked Brown, suddenly.

Faraz flinched.

Brown leaned forward, bringing his face close to Faraz's good eye. 'Don't. Lie. To me.' He said quietly, searching Faraz's face and running his gaze across the man's wounds.

He abruptly stood back up and sighed loudly. 'Made a pretty mess of your face didn't he?' He said, the false smile back in place.

Faraz thought the man was mad and suddenly felt very afraid again. 'What do you want?' He said, quietly, never taking his eye away from Brown.

The detective cocked his head to one side and thought for a moment.

'Um. I want everything, Mr Faraz, simply everything.' He eventually said, smiling still, his eyes twinkling insanely. 'But from you I only want the truth; tell me everything you told your attacker.'

He leaned forward again and this time his face was blank and his eyes cold. 'And remember; if you still value your one, good eye *don't* lie to me.'

Faraz began to sweat, his heart thumping in his chest. He squirmed as his newly-refilled lung burned each time his chest heaved too quickly.

Brown smirked and then stood back again. 'In your own time, Mr Faraz.'

The detective turned and picked up the chair at the foot of the bed, placing it at the bedside and then sitting down again. 'Whenever you're ready.' He smiled.

Faraz didn't know where to begin. Lie after lie kept on formulating in his head, but just looking at the man sitting by his side made him think long and hard before opening his mouth.

'Well, err-I mean, you obviously know about the Malas brothers and, err-' he stumbled for his words, the anaesthetic in his drip not helping. 'Operation?' He finally said.

Brown nodded. 'Go on.'

The man knew about the Malas brothers. What did that mean? Faraz probed a little. 'Well if you know about the Malas' then you know that I work for them? I don't think they will be very pleased that you are interrogating me like this.' He said, trying to show more backbone than he actually had.

Brown just gazed at him, remaining relaxed in his seat, a small twitch of a smile playing at the corners of his mouth. 'To be truthful, Mr Faraz,' he eventually said, 'I think that the Malas' would be very, very pleased to hear of my visit to you. In fact, I would go as far as to say; they would be almost *ecstatic* to hear anything at all, ever again.'

Brown sniggered when he saw the look on Faraz's face.

'Wh-what do you mean?'

Brown leaned closer again. 'They're dead, Faraz, killed by the man who did that to you.' He answered cheerfully, nodding at Faraz's face. 'And not just them either; everyone in that building the Malas' ran their *operation* from. Everyone that is, except the children.'

A cold rush of dread and shame ran through Faraz's stomach, that sinking feeling of being caught doing something dirty.

Brown just continued to look and watch Faraz squirm in his guilt; good.

'He killed them almost straight after he ran into you, Faraz.'

He leaned forward. 'What else did you tell him?'

Faraz looked shocked. 'What? Wh-what do you mean? I-I didn't tell him anything! I didn't know, you have to believe me.' He pleaded. 'He was just a sailor docked for a few days and wanted some action that's all, I swear! I just pointed him to the Malas place.' He stared wildly with his one eye. 'I've sent many sailors there before, how could I have possibly known?'

Brown studied the man's face. He wasn't lying, he'd had no knowledge of who or what Finn was.

'I believe you, Mr Faraz.' He said, and leaned back in his chair again, crossing his legs.

Faraz sighed and breathed deeply, wincing through the pain in his chest.

Brown steepled his fingers and studied his subject. 'Did you tell him anything else?' He asked seriously.

Faraz looked puzzled for a moment before replying. 'Anything else? There was nothing else *to* tell him. I just pointed him in the right direction that's all. I swear. What else *could* I tell him?'

Brown studied Faraz again deeply and then suddenly stood up.

Faraz flinched once more.

'You've just lied to me, Mr Faraz, if I'm not mistaken - which I'm usually not,' he said, producing a pen from his breast pocket.

'I'm going to use this pen to remove your eye, as I promised I would if you lied to me. I didn't say you would lose your eye if I *caught* you lying, I said you would lose it if you *did* lie, which you have.'

He waved the slim, silver pen around in front of Faraz's face to punctuate his words. 'The difference is quite apparent but admittedly subtle, so, in the spirit of fellowship, I will forgive your error, Mr Faraz, this time, and put it down simply to the language barrier.'

Faraz's eye tracked the pen as it flicked around in front of his vision. 'Y-yes, yes, that's it; language barrier.' He said. 'I-I forgot that's all, you see?'

'You forgot? What did you forget?'

'I forgot to mention that I told him he could get anything from anywhere from the Malas brothers, that they regularly shipped in err- new *goods* from over the um, border.'

'By "the border" you mean the Iranian border?' Brown asked.

Faraz nodded. 'Yes.' And then sighed as he watched Brown return the pen to his pocket.

'And by extension you also told him that much of the *goods*, as you put it, come from Afghanistan?' Brown smiled.

Faraz relaxed and nodded, the man didn't seem to be bothered

'There! That wasn't too hard now, was it?' Brown said.

He turned and casually examined the drip-bag standing next to the bed, flicking the line and watching the slow droplets plop into the flow-well.

'I think I have everything I need now, Mr Faraz.'

His fingers found the small lever controlling the flow and turned it until it was fully opened. 'I'll let you get back to your rest now, you look like you need it.' He said, earnestly, looking down and smiling again at the prone man.

Faraz began to protest and tried to pull the tubes from his arm.

The cold, creeping anaesthetic slipped easily into his veins and found the small muscles in his hands first. His fingers felt suddenly detached and useless and very quickly the feeling spread all the way up his arm until it entered his heart.

His good eye stopped seeing well before its lid closed.

Brown watched as the man fell fast asleep and then turned the drip back to its original position.

He took a small, leather case from his pocket and opened it, selecting a screwdriver from inside.

Turning to the ECG monitor he began humming a tune as he unscrewed the front panel.

The panel came away easily, revealing a network of wires and circuitry.

He peered closely inside and then traced a red wire from the speaker on the front until he found its connection on the circuit-board behind.

He pulled the wire from its plug and then stood back smiling to himself, a job well done.

Clapping his hands and rubbing them together in that universal show of *let's crack on,* he turned his attention back to the still-sleeping Faraz.

He continued humming on the job as he pinched Faraz's nose with one hand and covered the man's mouth with his other, keeping one eye on his watch.

After half a minute Faraz's body began to heave as his unconscious survival-instincts began to revolt. Soon the whole bed was vibrating as Faraz thrashed under the deadly grip.

Brown had to lend his whole weight to stop him from breaking free. 'Oh! Steady on now.' He chuckled.

Slowly the trembling and thrashing began to subside and then trickle to tiny spasms.

Brown held on, counting the time away and after three-minutes; 'Three, two and one!'

He stood up brushing his hands together, a grin of satisfaction spread across his face.

The ECG monitor was flat-lined and the alarm was flashing but the usual high, piercing sound which alerted the nurses outside remained silent.

Brown quickly screwed the front panel back in place, humming the same non-descript tune.

After a final check that the ECG monitor looked to be back as it was, Brown turned his attention to Faraz, picking up his arm and feeling for a pulse. He couldn't feel anything.

'You could do with losing a few pounds.' He said, not being convinced he would feel a pulse through the fat even if Faraz *was* alive.

He leaned over and listened to the man's chest instead.

He closed his eyes and smiled; there was nothing like the emptiness of a body freshly relieved of its soul. Nothing.

Brown breathed deeply in and out, revelling as he imagined the energies leaving the dead man and entering him, joining and filling his own soul with more power, more energy.

Once he was satisfied that Faraz was dead he stood back up and straightened his jacket, sighing deeply as he always did at the end of a successful task.

One, final thing to do before he had to report back.

With a friendly pat for the dead man's prodigious stomach, Brown walked out of the room and made straight for the nearest stairwell.

He checked the way was clear before slipping through the door and making his way to the basement.

A dull rumble told him he needed to make his way to the western rooms while arrows and signs on the wall told him the same; *Boiler rooms.*

The air grew suddenly hot and the rumble became louder; just beyond a double-door lay the furnace.

Brown quickly ducked inside and opened the chute which fed the flames. He pulled the ID wallet he had shown to Faraz from his pocket.

'Good-bye, Detective Brown.' He said, and chuckled, dropping the whole wallet containing the false identification down the chute.

He peered after it as it fell and waved a sarcastic farewell. 'It was fun while it lasted.'

He turned his back on the furnace and stood motionless in thought, bathed from behind in its glow.

His next job was to report back and after that he suspected he would be given his most difficult task yet; killing the man called, Finn.

He knew of Finn, had followed his story as closely as anyone could given that the man was a genius when it came to covering his tracks; he was a god in his own right.

That thought seared coolly across the mind of the man masquerading as detective.

*Only a god can kill a god.*

Could he do it though? Could he end a legend?

The prize taunted and tempted him; the glorious energy he would receive if he *did* kill Finn, the strongest life-force he could get.

But why kill him if he was the same? Why not be gods side by side and listen to the prayers of their disillusioned masters together?

He stood and smiled and his eyes gave away only a hint of the madness within.

'*Que sera, sera.*' He said, loudly as the furnace flared suddenly behind him, adding its molten boom to the menacing echo of his voice.

## Chapter Four

A *Monet*. A genuine, *bona-fide Monet* and Shelby was looking right at it.

He felt staggered when he thought of how much it must be worth. And here he was standing in front of it and breathing all over it.

He tried to keep his mouth closed while his wide-eyes scanned every brushstroke of the familiar painting from Monet's visit to Venice in the early 1900's.

Shelby had no idea of the exact title of the piece but there was no doubt about its location with its handful of gondolas in the view.

'You've had your nose pressed up against my Monet for the last fifteen minutes, old man.'

Shelby jumped and whirled round to face the man who had spoken.

'Anyone would think you were planning on stealing it.' He continued.

'Kevin!' Shelby said, and stepped forward to greet his old friend. 'It's good to see you.' He added, beaming and pumping the proffered hand. 'I couldn't believe it when I got your call. How long has it been?'

'Must be five years at least.' Said the man called Kevin, enthusiastically grinning back. 'We've got a lot of catching up to do, I'd say.'

He stood back and appraised his long-time friend. 'You know, you haven't changed a bit, Gray.'

'Oh. I don't know about that.' Shelby replied, tapping at his temples. 'I don't think I had this five years ago.' He said, indicating the peppering of grey in his dark hair. 'I see you don't have that problem.'

Kevin laughed. 'I've got a good hair-dresser.' He said, tapping his nose and winking.

He placed a hand on Shelby's shoulder then. 'Come on, let's have lunch, we can catch up while we eat.' He said, as he ushered Shelby toward the door. 'Margret's cooking up one of her specials.'

'Margret?' Shelby sounded surprised. 'You've still got Margret housekeeping for you? But she must be about a hundred by now!'

Kevin laughed. 'Don't let her hear you say that. I happen to know she has only just reached seventy. She simply *refuses* to retire and let me take care of her.'

He shrugged his shoulders. 'You know? There is no arguing with the woman.'

The two men left the drawing room, chatting eagerly the way only long-standing friends do.

Shelby had known Kevin Keys for almost thirty years. Inseparable throughout their university years, they had remained firm friends as they made their respective ways through their careers.

While Shelby had joined the London Mets and had progressed through the ranks until he was recruited by Interpol, Keys had followed his dream of becoming a politician, working for the betterment of the people and the country.

'*I'll build it,*' he used to say.

'*And I'll keep it safe.*' Was Shelby's reply.

Most things went the way Shelby wanted them to and he had always ended up better off as he climbed the career ladder, but for Keys the way had been littered with bad luck and back-stabbing partners who didn't give a damn about who they had to stand on to reach their goals.

It was nothing short of a miracle then, when Keys saw himself being offered a diplomatic post in Eastern Europe.

The sudden meteoric rise of the wannabe-politician to international diplomat was the talk of Westminster for months. No one could understand how the man had done it, but most of them knew how ruthless politics could be when in the hands of someone ambitious.

For weeks they were on the constant lookout for the fallout or victim but nothing came to light and people soon stopped talking about Kevin Keys.

And then he had begun to work his diplomatic miracles, just seemingly minor things at first until you looked at the bigger picture.

His charismatic approach to international business relations and trade-routes had seen a huge boom in production which spread from the eastern-continent right across to the west.

He gathered leaders and businessmen from all over Europe, some of them usually unwilling to participate if their '*enemies*' were present - and most of them *did* have some qualm or argument with one or more of their neighbours.

But Keys was relentless. He broke down barriers with simple logic and a little rhetoric, leaving his audience with little or no choice but to see the truth and wisdom in his proposals.

The final pearl in Keys' bag was the new trade-routes between Cyprus and Turkey.

The business-world had held its breath as it waited for an answer to Keys' request for both countries trade-ministers to meet, with the proposal of Turkey apologising for its part in the artillery attacks at the end of the second World war while Cyprus would need to forgive and shake hands, '*and see that it was the people of yesterday who made the mistakes on both sides, while the people of today are still being left to account for it all. My esteemed Madams and Sirs, isn't it enough yet?*'

A week later and both ministers had agreed to meet.

He now had two diplomatic-stations in Eastern Europe; his original in Greece and the other now in Turkey.

Keys sat at the small dining-table opposite Shelby, and they talked of the good-times while they ate. Margret had disappeared once she had served up the lunch.

Shelby crossed his knife and fork on his plate and sat back looking satisfied. 'Well that was an excellent hotpot, make sure you pass that on to Margret.'

He finished wiping his mouth and dropped the napkin onto his plate. 'I'm stuffed.'

'Yes, she does that to you doesn't she.' Keys replied, pushing his own plate away and tapping his stomach.

He poured them both coffee and then sat back again, his face becoming serious. 'I've got a confession to make, Gray; I didn't just ask you here for a casual catch-up.'

Shelby nodded but said nothing and just waited patiently.

'I know you've just come back from Turkey, another Finn hit.'

Shelby wasn't surprised Keys knew about Finn, they'd discussed the case a few years ago, but he was a little surprised that Keys had known about the latest hit so quickly.

He nodded again and kept his thoughts to himself.

'I wasn't in the country myself at the time, but Sean - you remember O'Keel don't you?' Keys asked.

'O'Keel?' Shelby thought for a moment. 'Oh yes, your driver isn't he?'

'Yes, amongst other things; he keeps his eye on things when I'm not around.

'Well, I have always had an interest in your Finn case, obviously, and keep my ear wired to the world's police so to speak.'

Shelby had his answer to how Keys had found out so quickly. 'Is that legal, Kev?' He chuckled.

'Well, I can't say it's *illegal*, I mean I'm good friends with the Turkish chief of police and *he* doesn't mind sharing things with me, so,' Keys shrugged, 'you know?'

Shelby just continued to laugh, shaking his head.

'Anyway, O'Keel called me when he heard of your arrival and I asked him to make his own discreet enquiries at the police station about the latest attack by Finn.

'I couldn't get there myself, I was tied up in meetings in Switzerland and still had another three days left.'

'I see. Well I can't say it wouldn't have been good to see you, but why would you send O'Keel to the station?' Shelby asked. 'I mean; if you already knew I was there, then you would know I would have access to everything that the police had.'

Keys looked a little put out, edgy even, thought Shelby.

'I'm going to be brutally honest, Gray; the Malas brothers were part of a conglomerate of traders who held shipping status and *I* invited them into a trade partnership.'

Shelby waited for the rest, the setup. When it didn't come, he said; 'And that's got you worried?'

'Of course it's got me bloody worried! I invited them in and they turn out to be part of a ring of slave-traders! But more than that, Gray, I think they were working for someone much higher up.'

Keys frowned and looked genuinely worried. 'O'Keel *did* find something at the police station.' He said. 'Something which you should have known about and seen for yourself.'

'Yes?' Shelby said, interested.

'O'Keel went inside and spoke with the detectives who had cleared the scene at the Malas place. They showed him the few bits of useless evidence they had collected. None of which showed anything of use in identifying Finn, but one of the detectives said there was a phone in amongst the other stuff; he knew it because he had bagged it himself.

'They looked through the bagged evidence numerous times and emptied their desks and drawers but couldn't find the phone anywhere.'

Keys paused while he sipped his coffee.

'Hm. That *is* interesting, Kev. What do *you* think happened to it?' Shelby asked.

'Oh. I know what happened to it, Gray; I've got it, or at least I've got what's left of it, but that's not what's worrying me.'

He leaned forward. 'When O'Keel reported back to me and I heard about the missing phone, I asked him to wait at the station until the chief arrived. He was to ask him to contact you immediately and also let you know of the missing phone.'

'Well that never happened, I didn't receive any messages once I'd concluded my own investigation, Kev, and I was there for three days.'

'I know and that's because O'Keel found the phone before the chief arrived!'

Keys sipped more coffee and sat back. 'If you remember anything about O'Keel, you would remember that he smoked.'

Shelby frowned, but nodded.

'Well, as much as the Turks like a cigarette or six the police-station doesn't allow smoking inside. O'Keel had to take himself outside to stand by the bins at the side of the building.

'As he stood there, a window opened and a uniformed arm came out holding a clear evidence-bag. The culprit upturned the bag and emptied out a lot of bits of plastic straight into the open bin O'Keel said. So he had a look and lo and behold! There lays a broken mobile-phone.'

Keys waited for Shelby to say something.

'So he gathers up the bits and gives them to you. Did he try and find out who threw them out?'

'As a matter of fact he did, but the window which had been used was in a corridor in the stairwell; anyone and everyone could have done it. Besides, I didn't want O'Keel to get himself in any trouble if you know what I mean?'

'Yes, of course and quite right too.' Shelby agreed. 'So what did you do with the phone?'

'I have it here. I could run it through the usual channels and get it looked at, but,' he paused, 'well, I would feel much safer if I handed it to you; it has almost gone missing once.'

'It will be safe with me.'

Shelby looked at his friend. 'There's something else isn't there?' He asked.

Keys seemed to think for a moment, trying to work out whether he should tell Shelby or not.

Eventually he said; 'I'm not sure it's anything, Gray. Maybe I'm simply fantasising about helping you with Finn.' He scoffed at his own words.

'Look, it's probably nothing but I remembered the time when you told me that you thought Finn was using the red-light areas to live in while he planned his next hit, so I asked O'Keel to go down to place at the edge of the city where I know there is a *vice influence*, you might say, and ask a few questions.

'Nothing turned up I'm afraid except one, small thing; an old man remembered seeing a tall man taking an ancient, mountain path which led to a now unused pass through the mountains leading to Iran.

'He thought it was strange that he would go that way when the new and modern road would serve him better, but then again, he also said that there was a small settlement of herders up there. So,' Keys shrugged again, 'it could just have been someone from there returning home. That's it. I told you it was nothing really.'

Shelby sat relaxed on the outside but his mind whirred into overdrive at the mention of Iran; Finn was crossing the border and was going to work his way across the country to the Afghanistan border.

So, the man had begun his journey. It gave Shelby an insight to how Finn had been travelling and why they had never managed to capture his image at airports and borders; he must be walking everywhere, planning his trips months in advance it seemed. Meticulous to a fault. How the hell could one mind plan so devastatingly accurately for seven bloody years?!

'It may be nothing Kev, but I will make a line of enquiry anyway; every little bit helps and you never know.' Shelby said. 'Why don't you get me the remains of the phone and I'll get it back to base for analysis.'

'You're a good man, Gray, I feel better already. Give me a minute, it's locked in the safe upstairs.' Keys rose to his feet and left Shelby to pour himself another coffee.

Something strange was happening in Finn's world, that place where he practised his cleansing, and it was now leaking into Shelby's.

It felt almost as if Finn's attack on the corruption and darkness in the world were causing it to shy away from him and flow deeper and deeper into civilised folds instead.

Someone, somewhere didn't want that phone to be found, a mobile phone with a traceable identification not to mention a call-log and camera.

That someone had a degree of power in high-places, which also meant that whoever owned the phone must also have high connections and was a victim at the Malas' building; Finn never left anyone alive once he was inside a place.

*What are you getting me into, Finn?*

Afghanistan was the key, he felt sure of it. Not just another target, but an enlightenment awaiting. For who though? An enlightenment for who? Finn? If so, why had he broken all of his rules and practically asked for help with this hit?

No, it was something else, something bigger, something which directly connected to the hit at the Malas' place.

*What are you getting yourself into, man?*

Footsteps padding down the hall announced Keys' return.

He placed a sealed, plastic bag containing an assortment of bits of broken plastic and circuitry on the table.

'I'm not sure what can be revealed, it looks like a total mess to me, but technology was always your game, Gray, if there's anything to be found I'm sure you'll find it.'

Shelby just looked at the bag of broken bits and sighed. It didn't look good. He could see a couple of unscathed chips on random pieces of circuit-board, they may still hold something, but on the whole it was looking dismal.

'Great. Thanks, Kev.' He said cheerfully, expertly hiding his disappointment.

He stood up and picked up the bag. 'I'd better get off now, I'll get cracking with this as soon as I get back. I'll let you know everything I find.

'Don't worry, Kev, nothing will come to light about your connection to the Malas, I promise. Even though I do think that it's not a problem anyway, so don't worry about it, eh?' He said, offering his hand.

Keys shook it. 'I'm glad we had this catch-up, Gray, it's a pity it had to come under such circumstances.'

'No matter what the occasion we shouldn't leave it so long next time.' Shelby answered, releasing his grip.

He allowed himself to be led to the front door where they shook hands again and said a final goodbye.

'I'll be here or at the office if you need me.' Keys said.

Shelby nodded and waved the plastic bag. 'Thanks again, Kevin, take care.'

Keys disappeared behind the closing front door while Shelby climbed into his car, throwing the bag onto the passenger seat and then just sitting motionless, staring at nothing over the top of the steering-wheel.

The damn rules kept changing. Finn, the bastard, kept changing them.

The phone at his side was much more than just about that crazy bastard now; it had implications which Kevin hadn't even realised.

The man behind destroying the phone, the top man who could control the police like that, would have only one reason to do so and that would be because the phone belonged to a victim and that victim was connected to him somehow.

Both of the Malas' phones had been found and were useless, the three other victims all had their phones accounted for and again they were useless.

Shelby searched his mind, retrieving a mental picture of what he had seen when he had arrived at the crime scene less than twenty-four hours after the attack had taken place.

*He walked a drab hallway with doors on either side, just another hotel corridor. At the end is a stair leading to a basement which has more rooms, cubicles would be a better description; flimsy stud-walls used as partitions with curtains drawn across their fronts.*

*Each room has a bed and a chair, an assortment of ropes and tethers hanging from hooks on the wall, full-wall mirrors and a shelf littered with both adult and children's toys. A small cupboard with towels inside and wash-basin above, sit at the side of each bed.*

*The first six rooms are empty, but at the seventh there is a pool of smeared blood outside the curtain.*

*Inside, the body of a middle-aged, Turkish man lays face-down on the ground, attacked outside before running in here,* Shelby thought.

*There is more blood pooling out from beneath him. He is completely naked. The word Finn is carved all the way across his flabby back.*

*The room directly opposite has another victim, this one with his head almost completely removed by the ferocious attack with the knife the murderer had used.*

*The body sat with its back resting against the mirrored wall while the head lay obliquely across the left shoulder and upper-chest. It was naked from the waist up but still had trousers on, flies opened and a flaccid, fleshy member protruding.*

*The spray of blood from the initial attack could be seen splashed across the back wall overlooking the bed; Finn had come in behind the man as he stood with his back to him and then had cut his throat as he stood there doing whatever it was he was doing that enraged Finn so much it had caused him to throw the man around and force him to the ground where he continued to hack and saw at his neck, left to right. 'Finn' was cut into the man's stomach.*

*The room next and one up from this one held the third and final victim down here. The Malas' were both upstairs.*

*The man in this room sat on a chair, a single stab-wound through his left eye the cause of death. He held a teddy-bear toy in his hands and a story-book lay at his feet, a trickle of blood from his damaged eye ran down his cheek like a single tear while smaller slivers ran down his forehead where he had Finn's mark carved upon it.*

*There was a pool of blood just inside the curtain, the place where Finn had started the attack on this victim.*

And pause.

Shelby felt something wrong about that, a square puzzle piece trying to fit into a triangle slot.

He thought about it again from the beginning; the corridor, the stairs, the pool of blood outside room one, the headless man in two, the man holding the bear. Why was he holding the bear?

Again. The pool of blood outside room one, the pool of blood under the first victim, the pool under the headless man, the pool of blood by the curtain in the last room with victim three. Victim three.

Shelby's eyes widened. Four pools of blood and only three victims.

The third man had no blood around the chair he was propped up in and the bear in his hands was just too dramatic to have been something Finn would have done. He had been moved there and had the toy placed in his already dead hands for effect. But why and by who?

His mind traced the attack as he now thought it could have occurred.

Finn had come down the stairs and walked straight up to the man who he then stabbed in the eye. The man was probably just loitering there or maybe worked there, but whatever he was doing he didn't have a chance or feel the need to defend himself and had gone down quickly and silently. *That* man had left the pool of blood outside the next victim's room.

Finn then moved into the room immediately to the left and had stabbed the fat man once in the back of the head and then cut his throat as he lay prone on his stomach.

Next he made his way to the room opposite and had cut that victims throat and almost beheaded him.

And finally he had moved to the next room up and had killed someone else right there, a fourth man, just inside the curtain.

Sometime between the time of the crime and the arrival of the first officers and detectives on the scene, someone had removed a body, missing his phone in the process, and then had carried the man with the eye wound to the chair in the room, furnishing him with the stuffed toy and possibly the storybook at his feet too.

Shelby looked at the phone again, staring at it hard.

*What the hell did you do, Finn?*

## Chapter Five

Firelight bathed the small, natural cave in its flickering glow, Finn's shadow danced around behind him as he sat staring into the flames.

The other man was quiet tonight, as quiet as the stars and the land all around.

*You don't listen anyway.*

'What's to listen to? *You* say the same things, *I* say the same things, we don't get anywhere.' Finn said aloud.

*Must find her!*

'I will.' He snapped.

The man's pain irritated Finn, made him want to slap his whining face and tell him to get on with it, but it was useless; *he* didn't listen either.

'We butt our heads more than stags in heat, man.' Finn muttered.

*But you know where she is!*

'Aye! And you know where *she* is; I can't break my bond to her and you know it. What good if we are both damned? Think man!' Finn retorted, frustrated.

A howl broke the silence of the night as though emphasising the point; wild dogs roaming the mountains.

Finn shuddered at the sound. *She* was never far from his thoughts. He had failed her once, he wouldn't fail again.

The man wailed in his head as Finn thought of his failure to the she-wolf.

'Be still, man! Damn you!'

But his cries only intensified.

'BE STILL!'

Finn pound on his temples with his palms, driving the man back as he surged forward with his misery and guilt, threatening to drown Finn and suffocate him with it until he was dead.

'Damn you! Damn you!'

*I'm coming, baby, daddy's coming!*

'SHUT UP! SHUT UP! SHUT U-U-UP!'

Finn held his head tightly in his hands and sobbed, his face screwed up in obvious pain.

*Must find her! I'm coming, Sa-!*

'NO-O-O!'

Finn's mind retaliated, fighting back with the strength of the warrior that he was. He would not fail her and he would not allow the fool to stop him when he knew it was the only way they would both get what they wanted.

In his mind he drew his long blades.

'*These* are not for you, but by Maeve's honour I swear I will use them on you if you try to stop me!'

The man stopped his wailing instantly, pulling away from Finn's mind and staying at the edge.

*You must find her*. He said quietly.

'I will, damn you, I will!'

He relaxed his grip on his head and opened his eyes. 'I must.' He whispered. 'For both of us, I must.'

*You don't have to kill them.*

Finn couldn't understand the man's reluctance to kill those who were responsible for the horrific crimes which Finn targeted.

'Yes, I *do* have to kill them; darkness such as there is should not be allowed to spread its vileness and evil so that it taints even our most innocent. Why can't you understand that?'

*I do understand, but you're not a god, you're a man and that means you are just another murderer.*

'And what is it called when a god kills?'

*Justice.*

'And what is it called when a man is *commanded* by a god to kill?'

The man remained silent.

'I am Finn of the Seven Spears and the Nine Northern Stars, my word is my bond. I have taken my fill of the three cauldrons and I will *not* be swayed from my *geis*.'

He dropped his gaze as he spoke the last words. 'I am not a killer by choice.' He said quietly.

He had, had this conversation before. Why couldn't the man understand?

Finn often wondered who he was, but never had the time nor the interest to find out. Sometimes he thought he knew him; like a memory misplaced, a déjà-vu moment of sudden understanding and then it was gone, leaving no trace. Just a strange emptiness in his mind remained.

Since those first two he had killed, the man had been in Finn's head, always pleading the same arguments and wailing for him to stop killing.

The first two; a bad affair. Finn had been stabbed twice on that occasion because of the man's, sudden appearance.

His mistress had sent him to the east-coast of England to find a girl who had been missing for several weeks.

Finn had found her, found the place in the seaside town where she was being held and had paid the house a visit.

Armed with a single Bowie-knife and the five hundred pounds to pay for "*something special*", Finn had knocked at the door of a smart house, on a tidy street, in the small hours of a cold, Saturday morning.

A tall, fat youth opened the door, his sneering, piggy face instantly giving Finn reason to dislike him.

'Yeah?' The Piggy said.

'I-err, I-I've come for something special.' Finn replied, holding up the roll of cash.

Piggy looked at it and licked his lips. 'It's a bit late though innit, mate?'

'Sorry. I-I wouldn't take long.' Finn shuffled and tried to make himself look more vulnerable; give Piggy some power to be generous.

The fat youth sighed. 'Okay, just this time though, innit?'

He opened the door and stepped to one side allowing Finn to pass through into a dimly-lit hallway.

He could hear the muffled soundtrack of a program on TV coming from the room on the left, the living-room, and further along he saw a shadow moving around in what he took to be a kitchen.

The place was spotless, lavishly furnished and adorned with expensive ornaments and pictures on the walls and shelves. Clean to a fault, Finn wondered if he had come to the right place.

The tidy, homely surroundings clashed with the dirty and vile image of a world where 'something special' meant something young and innocent.

'Nice house.' Finn said, looking around in feigned interest.

'It's alright I s'pose.' Piggy answered.

He then turned his attention to the doorway ahead leading to the kitchen. 'Mam? Mam!? Make another one, we've got a visitor.'

The shadow in the kitchen grew larger until a middle-aged woman appeared in the doorway.

The gaudy make-up and over-perfumed old flesh, the over-fluffed negligee and outrageous hairdo made Finn think of an actress from the fifties and sixties who had once seen stardom, but was now on the D list and having a hard time coming to terms with it.

The illusion was shattered as soon as she opened her vile mouth and spoke.

'D'ya want a cuppa now or are you going to have a shag first, love?' She asked, looking straight at Finn.

She stood against the doorframe and looked almost as if she were seducing it. The light, she knew, was flaring through her thin, pink negligee, giving Finn a good look at her prodigious body.

'Err-a-a cup of tea would be nice, thank you.' Finn replied, smiling shyly. 'C-could I have err, a look first?' He then asked Piggy.

The fat youth looked to his mother.

'You finish the tea and I'll take our guest up.' The woman said, stepping into the hallway and sidling up to Finn.

Piggy looked disappointed and turned away with a huff.

The woman took Finn by the arm and squeezed it warmly. 'Shall we?' She said, as she ushered Finn to the stairs. 'It's so nice to have such a handsome visitor for a change; the ugly bodies I have seen! Ugh! You wouldn't believe.'

Finn looked at her and frowned, but said nothing.

'I know what you're thinking, love; you thought you would be going in by yourself, but I can't have that now, you understand?'

Finn didn't, but nodded.

'Good.' She said, smiling and wrinkling her nose up at him. 'And if you need any, umm, help, I'll be more than glad to be at your disposal.'

She ran her fingers over Finns chest, drawing circles with her nails, suggestively.

The acrid perfume did little or nothing to blot out the stench of the woman now. The pungent musk of her lust and the corruption in her heart made Finn want to throw-up.

He forced his smile instead and nodded. 'That would be great.'

She sighed and shuddered as whatever sordid thought she was thinking ran through her mind, pressing herself against Finn and doing her damndest to make her wrinkled breasts ride up and spill over the top of her clothing.

She looked up at him like a first-time teen and fluttered her eyelashes. 'I hope you will be gentle with me.'

Finn could smell the woman's breath, foul like excrement and laced with alcohol and cigarette smoke.

She lingered a moment more before turning away and pulling Finn onward toward a door at the end of the upper hallway.

'She'll be asleep, of course; I have a ready supply of temazepam.' The woman chuckled. 'Dirty bastards are doctors, you know?'

They reached the door, the woman magically produced a key from somewhere beneath the folds of her skimpy garments and unlocked it.

She slowly pushed the door open and a dim, orange glow crept out, bathing her in a sickly, tanned light.

She pointed to the bed at the back of the room, the orange night-light standing on the bedside table illuminated the small bump laying beneath the Thomas the Tank Engine covers.

'Come on, darling.' The Hag purred, and took Finn's hand, leading him to the bedside.

A young girl's, sleeping face peeped from beneath the quilt which was pulled up to her chin. Her eyelids were fluttering as she walked the hazy, disorientating landscape of her drug-induced dreams.

Her hair was golden and draped around her head like spreading honey.

Finn's heart ached to find such innocence being forced into this sordid world of adult corruption; she looked to be only nine or ten years old.

The Hag stood at his side, smiling, mistaking the look on his face for one of satisfaction.

'Let's have a closer look.' She said, closing in on Finn once more and pressing her body up to his again.

*She pulled the quilt back and uncovered the sleeping girl, her pyjama's had a pattern of pink fairies upon it.*

*The Hag sighed satisfactorily. 'She's beautiful isn't she?' She said.*

*She reached for the girl's pyjama-bottoms. 'Let's just-!'*

Finn had seen and heard enough. His rage boiled over and he released it with one, swift motion of his left arm, his hand holding his knife, murderously.

The blade shot upward into the unsuspecting Hag's chest, piercing her heart and killing her almost instantly.

*She dropped to the floor and was silent.*

The silence on the outside was immediately replaced by the terrifying screaming and wailing which suddenly flashed painfully across Finn's mind.

He dropped his knife and clutched at his head, his jaw locked tight in a grimace of pain.

No-o-o! N-o-o-o!

The wailing continued; a man's voice shouting out a single denial over and over again.

Finn dropped to his knees then, tears of pain streaming down his face. His head felt like it was too small to hold so much noise, like it was trying to crush him and drive him out.

'Get out!' Finn pushed back, driving his will up against that of the man's. 'GET OUT!'

But the man was strong and pushed and pulled and screamed Finn into stepping back. He was winning, he was going to drive him out. Just too strong. Too str-!

Searing pain flared suddenly across his back. The screaming stopped instantly and he felt the man pull away, terrified.

Finn looked up to see Piggy standing in front of him holding his knife. He looked shocked and pale, his piggy, tight eyes now as round as plates.

Finn stared at him, realised that the pain had come from the fat youths attempt to stab him. By the looks of him though, it didn't seem as though the stupid Piggy had ever had any kind of serious confrontation before.

The two stab wounds on Finn's shoulders throbbed; as deep as the shoulder blade but not enough rage to create the force necessary to do any serious damage.

He could feel the warm blood trickling down his back and seeping into his waistband. He ignored it and the pain and stood up.

Piggy flinched and took a step back. 'W-what are you doing? What did you do to, mam?'

Finn just stared, his lightening eye's piercing Piggy's soul; a promise of righteous death.

The fat youth understood one thing if nothing else at all; he had to get away from this man, the man who had killed his mam.

Finn's blade dropped to the carpeted floor with a dull thud as Piggy turned and fled back to the stairs, moving surprisingly quickly for someone so overweight.

Finn picked up his knife and then loped after the youth, but before he caught up with him he saw the stupid, fat boy stumble forward in his haste to escape and fall headfirst down the stairs.

He listened to the rolling thud of Piggy's body bouncing down the long, hard steps and then come to a sudden, crashing halt as it reached the bottom.

From the top of the stairs Finn looked down; the fat youth was laid on his side, his legs twitching feebly while a hole the size of a golf ball in his forehead dribbled blood and brain-matter alike onto the expensive, Persian rug.

The corner table by the front door had done the job Finn had set out to do.

He walked back to the bedroom and the sleeping girl.

Replacing the covers over her, he sat on the edge of the bed and looked at her lovingly and stroked her hair. 'I found you.' He said, and kissed her forehead. 'Time to go home now, Puppy.'

He left the girl and walked back down the stairs. At the bottom, he picked up the telephone which had been standing on top of the killer table and dialled 999.

'Emergency services, which service do you require, please?' The tinny voice of the operator asked.

'All of them, come to where this telephone is.' Finn replied, setting the handset on the tabletop.

He could hear the operator's small voice asking for his name and then repeating; Hello? Hello? as he walked back out, into the night.

\* \* \*

Fire-nymphs disguised as sparks danced a jig in front of Finn's face, sharing his thoughts as he shared their fire.

His mind came back to the present, the two scars of his first task itched annoyingly.

They annoyed him because that was the only time he hadn't left his mark and the old wounds liked to remind him of that.

It wasn't because of the anonymity that he became annoyed, it was because it didn't feel neat. Like a tardy understudy or a simple essay in the beginnings, a piece to look back on and say *'God! Did I really do that*?' and wish that you had done it *'this way'* instead.

He leaned forward and threw more wood on the fire. A million, more, cavorting nymphs sprang upward and danced out their short lives even before the new wood had settled.

*'A fire in the hearth,*
*A pot on the fire,*
*A fish in the pot,*
*Cress in the fish,*

*Wind in the cress,
Breath on the wind,
A word on the breath,
A tale in the word,
Knowledge in the tale,
Power in the knowledge,
Province with the power,
Castle in the province,
Hearth in the castle
And a fire in the hearth.'*

Finn recited aloud as he threw on more wood. A bardic lay taught to him by-? By who? He couldn't remember. It vexed him that he couldn't remember his teacher, a woman he thought, but that was all he thought he knew.

He felt it was somehow important that he didn't know, some dark reasoning to forget his mistress, but no matter how hard he tried he couldn't work it out, his mind wouldn't let him focus on it for too long.

Everything he knew about being a warrior he had learned from her.

From her? Was it the she-wolf? He didn't think so; she was just too damned persistent and vicious when she wanted him to do her bidding and she knew she could just ask and he would do it anyway.

No, *she* meant to cause him pain, somehow it was linked to what he had to do in more ways than just her holding him to his *geis*.

She was there now, waiting in the shadowy parts of his mind, watching and listening to him.

She always kept him safe and he loved her, but she hurt him and used him and he hated her just as much.

She growled softly in his mind, a chuckle of sorts, warm and without an iota of malice.

She rarely spoke to him other than to tell him where to go and who to find, but occasionally she would whisper to him, caress his temples and sooth his mind.

Sometimes she told him she loved him and didn't want to hurt him, she was even sorry that she did, but it was necessary to keep him alive and on the right path.

He owed her, he had sworn an oath to her and had failed in its keeping. Not broken it so much, but had lost the treasure he was sworn to keep and protect. He would never stop looking until he had found it again.

The darkness outside the cave's small entrance suddenly filled with reflected light from Finn's fire.

A huge, pale dog stood just outside, its eyes filled with the orange glow of firelight and inquisitive intelligence. Its mastiff head sat on powerful shoulders and legs, legs used for running down quarry in the mountains.

Finn sat calmly, firmly attached to his place in the world and looked the big dog straight in the eye, showing his own, passive inquisitiveness.

*No enemy in here, old dog.*

The dog twitched its massive head from side to side, trying to understand what it was seeing and smelling.

The fire put it off from stepping right into the cave, as well as the man sitting inside. It knew Finn was dangerous but sensed no immediate danger and the aroma of the food Finn had cooked was also compelling it to have a closer look.

Finn sensed its confusion and understood what it wanted.

He opened his rucksack and pulled out a package of dried rabbit-meat, opening it and then tossing the lot straight to the dog's feet.

The hound immediately stooped its head and snapped up the meat on the ground, chomping it noisily.

Once he had finished he raised his head again and peered straight into Finn's deep, blue eyes with his own amber gaze.

Finn had no idea what was actually passing between them, but it felt a little akin to a kind of understanding.

The dog continued to stare for a moment more and then he sniffed the air once and simply turned away, heading back into the night.

Finn watched his muscled bulk fade into the gloom, another warrior out on the prowl. He wished him good hunting and then lay down on his bedroll.

Knowing the hound was out there made Finn feel easier about sleeping and he soon dozed off, his thoughts on the coming weeks ahead and his goal in Afghanistan.

## Chapter Six

Winter had passed, it felt good to bring the goats this far up the mountain again. The grasses were plentiful, sweet and fresh, fed with the finest rains and mists for the goats to fatten up on.

Salya unwrapped her pack and called to Rafiq to come and eat.

Even though he was ten and supposed to be in charge of the small herd now, her little brother was still incapable of doing anything without her help and approval.

Salya, at thirteen, was the eldest child of four, she being the only girl.

The goats were stirring and bleating, annoyingly close by, kicking up dust and grass which billowed down the slopes as they jittered to and fro.

She called for Rafiq again. 'It doesn't take that long to *whizz*, Rafiq, hurry up and come and sit with me and eat.'

There was no reply and no sound of anyone else up here other than the goats which were slowly getting closer as they ran left and right along the mountainside.

The girl stood up and shaded her eyes from the sun and looked out to the line of scrubby bushes which her younger brother had chosen to use.

'Rafiq? Rafiq? Come on, what are you doing?'

There was no answer.

'I'm not playing, Rafiq! Stupid. I'll tell father!'

No reply, no noise except the goats running came to her ears.

She turned around and saw that they were only a few yards away now. What was happening?

She turned back to face the bushes and took a step forward.

A sudden rush behind her startled her to turn, but she didn't get the chance to face the noise before a large hand holding a clear cup, clamped down over her nose and mouth while another grabbed her by the waist and held her tightly.

Her nostrils and throat and lips suddenly began to burn, her chest flared painfully as the vapours of ether seared her lungs, and then the world faded quickly to dark and quiet and then to blackness and silence.

She was awakened by the jostling and revving engine of the truck she was travelling in.

Her head hurt, throbbed with the remnants of the drug. How had she ended up here?

She next became aware of the pain in her wrists and belly. Her wrists were tightly bound together, the rope biting into her flesh and cutting off the circulation.

She fumbled with the knots but her limbs were too lethargic to do anything other than ease the bite a little and encourage the blood to flow back into her fingers.

Her belly flared again and this time she felt a stabbing pain between her legs and a searing ache in her hips and lower back. She had been raped while unconscious.

Tears dripped down her face but she didn't sob or cry out. Instead she turned her thoughts to her brother; was he here?

She searched through the gloom with eyes which were already hazy enough. She couldn't make out any details but she was sure there were other people in here with her.

Her eyes suddenly became heavy and she had to close them again, unable to fight the remaining drug in her bloodstream as it passed around her fuzzy mind.

A minute or an hour, maybe a whole week had passed, she didn't know, but when she opened her eyes again the truck had stopped and its engine was silent.

She could hear voices outside, distant and far away, men's voices, Afghani and Russian by the sounds of it.

Her eyes welled up again, she had been kidnapped.

She had heard the rumours, had, had the talks with her mother and father, had been warned to stay on the lookout and keep away from strangers, especially Russians.

She had been told and now she had been taken; stolen and violated. The pain in her groin flared sharply as she sobbed.

The voices grew louder and then the back of the truck was thrown open. Bright, fluorescent light flooded in causing a chorus of gasps to rise from everyone, including Salya, inside the truck.

She looked around; there must be at least twenty other people tied up the same way she herself was. Mostly children and mainly female, no one looked to be older than Salya at least.

She scanned the truck in the light until she found Rafiq. He was still asleep, tied to a pallet at the rear. Next to him and on the same pallet, was a younger child, a girl also still asleep.

The other children were all in various stages of waking up but all were sharing that same, bewildered look on their tear-stained faces.

'Stay strong.' Salya whispered to herself. 'Stay strong.'

*No matter what happens in life, Salya, stay strong and you will overcome it.*

Her father's words echoed through her young mind. He was always telling her to stay strong, he knew what a miserable life could be had by a young,

Muslim girl.

She was lucky she had a father like the one she had; he treated her no differently to her brothers and was unusually modern and tolerant with his wife, her mother.

She missed them, wondering if she would ever see them again.

*Stay strong, Salya.*

Grating metal being dragged across the floor brought Salya back to attention.

Two Afghani men were pulling a heavy, steel ramp up to the truck, hoisting it onto brackets set on the lip of the tailgate.

Another two, big men dressed in black uniforms then walked up the ramp and began hoisting the first children to their feet.

The way they handled the youngsters was the same way Salya and her father handled the goats.

'Up. Up.' They ordered neutrally, their Russian accents doing nothing to soften their commands.

One by one the children were ushered down the ramp, forming a huddle at the bottom. Some of them began to cry.

Salya, clutching her aching stomach and drew some of the younger ones to her and hushed them. 'Don't be afraid, be strong.' She whispered to them.

She looked around, taking in their surroundings; they were in a long storage depot, boxes and crates were stacked neatly in rows up and down each side. At the back, a small office with big windows was built straight onto the rear wall. The lights were on and a man and a woman were standing inside.

The huddle of children was marched away from the truck, slowly being led to the office. Once there they were told to sit on the ground outside and be quiet.

Almost immediately the door opened and the woman came out. She was dressed in nurse's whites and although she looked important, Salya noticed the downcast eyes and the submissive, sad look when she approached the children. Another slave.

She spoke to the first child she came to, a girl of around eleven or twelve. The girl stood up and went into the room with her.

Salya looked back to the truck, waiting to see her brother being brought out and led down here to where the rest were.

Two men stood at the back talking heatedly while a third man inside the truck dragged a pallet to the front.

He jumped down to the ground and then pulled two, small bodies from the pallet, their hands still tied together at the wrists.

He lifted them easily by their bonds, carrying them like dead meat still on the hook.

The way their heads hung down over their small chests and the flaccid emptiness of their oddly-swaying legs, told Salya that they were dead. Rafiq was dead. He had been hiding behind a bush and now he was hanging from a

Russian man's hands and was dead.

*Be strong.*

The two men at the back were still arguing when the door of the office was suddenly thrown open and a small, fat man came charging out, making a beeline for the two men

He began shouting and pointing to the two, dead children.

The two men stood with their eyes downcast.

Salya watched his wobbling face turn red and his bald head begin to shine as his blood pressure rose too rapidly. She couldn't understand what he was saying, but she could see he was clearly angry at the loss of the two children.

The big man who had removed the bodies, carried them out of the building through the large doors which the truck had entered by and then disappeared around the corner from sight.

*I'm sorry, little brother.*

Salya set her heart in stone then, she *would* be strong.

Atash Nazari stood trembling in front of the two Russians, his rage threatening to blow a major artery if he wasn't careful.

'Thirty-seconds, you sister-fuckers! Thirty! Not twenty or fifty, but thirty! Fucking apes!' He screeched at them.

Neither of the big men would meet his gaze; Nazari may look small, fat and weak, but he was their commander while they were here and he was utterly ruthless, commanding a respect from *their* superiors which far outweighed the respect their superiors had for *them*.

A nasty, small man with a complex to suit, the Iraqi ex-commander had fled to Afghanistan during the conflict with the Americans, being on their *Most Wanted* lists for crimes committed both before and during the war.

Nazari was an excellent commander and expert negotiator, he soon found the Russians still hiding in Afghanistan and offered his services to them.

It wasn't long before the Russian bosses back on their home-turf heard about Nazari; his knowledge of the land and its smuggling routes meant he soon became an invaluable asset to them.

Heroine was their usual business, but Nazari soon showed them a more profitable line of goods in people.

Acting on Nazari's advice, the Russian underground funded a project to build a 'hideaway' deep in the south-western deserts near the border-mountains; *Paradise Begins*, Nazari had called it once it had been completed.

Almost a third of the heroin which came out of Afghanistan came from this point and the movement of slaves was unparalleled anywhere else.

A hefty twenty-eight percent of the Russian mafia's profits came directly from Atash Nazari's *Paradise Begins,* and he hated to lose merchandise.

'Can you even count up to thirty, you fucking morons?' He shouted. 'Big children; forty-seconds, small children; thirty! No more, no less!'

He gave them a hard stare, leaning over and raising his eyes under their lowered heads. 'The next time it happens I'll have Hack give you a lesson in mathematics; I'll ask him to cut your fucking balls off and teach you to count with them!' He hissed venomously. 'Understood?'

The pair nodded their heads once and snapped off a clear *'Yes sir!'*

Nazari stood back and gave them one last, lingering, hard look and then turned away and waddled quickly back to the examination booth.

He walked past the children without looking at them or even acknowledging they were there. If he had, he would have seen that all but one of them had their heads bowed down in fear; Salya's eyes were set firmly on the fat, little man as he walked past.

Her young, innocent heart had never known any emotion other than love and happiness and the joys of childish discovery, but it now only had room for hate and she aimed every ounce of it at the fat, sweating man in front of her.

Her life on the mountains had furnished her with a keen sense of survival and freedom; she would not become a slave for anyone.

One by one, the children were led into the booth by the nurse where they spent ten minutes being examined and questioned about their health before being taken back out to sit and wait with the rest.

The nurse stood in front of Salya and offered her hand. 'Come.' Was all she said.

Salya ignored the hand and stood up, falling in at the nurse's side.

The young nurse instantly picked up on the girl's defiance and placed a soft hand on her shoulder, leading her to the door.

She quickly leaned down and whispered in Salya's ear. 'Be good, don't fight, or he'll hurt you.' Was all the warning she had time to give before they were walking through the door and standing before a smiling Nazari.

The nurse closed the door and stood behind Salya.

'Hello.' Nazari said. 'Don't be afraid, girl. What's your name?' He asked.

Salya thought about staying silent and defiant but the nurse had put herself in the firing line to get that simple warning to her.

'Salya.' She replied.

'Beautiful name.' Nazari said, as he always did. 'And how old are you, Salya?'

'Thirteen.' She answered.

'Good, good.' He said, dropping his gaze and writing something on a pad he held.

He looked up and smiled. 'Now, if you would take your clothes off please and let nurse have a look at you.' He pointed to a bed behind a curtain. 'In there.'

The nurse took Salya by the shoulder again and led her to the side of the bed. She closed the curtain and then began undoing the knots on Salya's top.

Salya pulled away and looked balefully at the woman, scowling.

Slowly she undid the knots herself and then with a cold look of defiance she removed her top and then her baggy trousers. She dropped the clothes to the floor and then stood in her underwear, waiting for the nurse to begin.

At sight of the red smudge on the crotch of the young girl's pants, the nurse stepped outside the curtain.

Salya could hear the woman whispering something rapidly to Nazari.

'Bastard! I'll fucking kill that, Azziz; he's supposed to watch his men.' She heard Nazari say. 'Go on, get out of my face and check her out for the rest.' He barked, annoyed.

The nurse returned and asked Salya to sit on the edge of the bed.

She did as she was told.

She was then subjected to a thorough examination of her head and mouth, eyes and ears, and then the nurse listened to her chest and felt her pulse.

'Lie down please.' She then said quietly, her eyes lowered.

Salya brought her legs up onto the table and lay down on the cold, vinyl cushioning. The white tiles above needed cleaning she thought. She focused on the tiles, their tiny pores like pitted fruit.

She could feel the nurse's hands removing her pants and then examining her, trying to be gentle.

Salya ignored it, looked at the pores, stared until she saw patterns and recognisable images in the seemingly random display of dots.

The white spaces between each tiny air-hole began to ooze the longer she stared. Like a white sheet of webbing or dripping, milky rivers flowing around small, perfectly-round, dark islands.

The pain she could almost feel from the nurses probing was nothing but an illusion, like the images in the tiles.

*I am strong.*

And then the nurse was asking her to sit up again.

Salya's eyes throbbed as they suddenly snapped back to their natural focus, while something in her mind shifted slightly. She knew what she had to do now.

She dropped to the floor and dressed herself and then allowed the nurse to lead her back out into the office to stand in front of Nazari. She had to do it now.

Salya looked up and waited until Nazari looked at her and then she smiled just a little, looked just a little shy and pensive.

Nazari blinked and licked his lips.

Salya dropped her gaze and stood waiting.

'You can go back out now, Salya. Nurse will take you to be cleaned up and then later you and I can have a little chat.' He said, and winked and smiled at her.

Salya flicked him a shy glance and nodded but she didn't smile back. That had been much easier than she thought it would be.

Once the last of the children had been ushered into the office and had been examined, they and Salya were all led away back through the main doors.

Outside, the sun was high and bright, everything was flaring hotly white.

Once her eyes became accustomed to the sudden brightness of the clear skies, Salya looked about her.

They were walking across a courtyard surrounded by high, stone walls. The gate at the entrance stood wide open and she could see that there were more buildings on the outside, lavish-looking, smart and modern, like the ones she had once seen in the big city.

Inside the compound the buildings were nothing more than oblong boxes with flat roofs, simple and effective. Salya noted that all the windows in the buildings inside the walls had metal bars covering their fronts.

They were making their way to a building which was larger than most of the others in the compound but not quite as big as the warehouse.

As the line began passing through the door, Salya looked back to the building they had just come from. Men were busy inside, unloading crates and boxes from other trucks which had arrived.

Looking past the warehouse and toward the back-wall of the whole courtyard, she watched the air rippling and waving, distorting the picture behind as a fire raged in an oil-drum at the side of the building.

She couldn't make out any details through the flames and shimmering air, but she knew that the man she could see standing behind the oil-drum was the same man who had carried her brother's body out.

*I* am *strong*!

She fought hard with the tears and grief which threatened to overcome her, but she steeled herself and set her goal firmly in her mind.

As she passed the threshold and entered the shower-block, Salya said her last goodbye to her little brother.

The children were taken to a large, white-tiled room and told to strip and wash under the overhead showers.

Two older females wearing nurse's whites and the usual downcast expressions of slaves, stood and waited for them and then handed out towels once they had finished.

Some of the older children, including Salya, helped the youngest ones to dry themselves off.

Wrapped in their towels the children were taken outside the shower-room and lined up against the wall while clean clothes were handed out to each of them by the two nurses.

Salya looked up to a door directly opposite her and her heart hammered in her chest when she saw the symbol of a toilet pinned in the middle.

Her plan with the fat man had been to gain nothing more than entrance to a modern lavatory which she assumed he would have in his own apartments. All she had to do was get him to take her there. But now she wouldn't have to go anywhere near the disgusting pig.

Seeing the white tiles in the office had given Salya the idea.

She tugged the sleeve of one of the women and then whispered to her.

The woman pointed to the door and nodded.

Salya quickly walked to the door and opened it and stepped inside another white-tiled room, this one with four cubicles; the toilets.

On one of the rare trips she and her family had made into the city, her father had treated them to a meal inside a big restaurant. He had marched them all off to the inside lavatories and made them wash their hands before eating. Salya had been amazed to see the porcelain sinks and toilets.

*Don't be fooled by their modern, western looks.* Her father had said. *They still open underneath and go into the ground, just like ours.*

She entered a cubicle and studied the toilet; it was just a porcelain seat standing on the floor.

She pushed it hard and it moved a fraction. Again she pushed with all her strength and the toilet slid away to the side revealing a small, round hole in the floor, exactly as her father had said.

Removing her towel, Salya rolled the clean garments she had been given into its folds and then peered down into the hole. The stink made her eyes water but she didn't let it hold her back.

Holding the rolled up towel to her mouth and nose, she leaned forward and dropped head-first into the pitch-black pipe beneath, sliding down the curved walls and coming to a halt with a slimy, stinking splash.

One, long sewage-pipe connected the whole of the compound north to south.

Keeping her mind from dwelling on the months and months of piss and shit she had just landed in, years of the stuff even, she peered back up into the cubicle and took a deep breath, removing the towel from her mouth and clasping it between her knees.

Reaching up through the hole, her fingers found the edge of the toilet again. Slowly, inch by inch, she manoeuvred the heavy porcelain back into place.

She gasped involuntarily with the effort and strain and then gagged as the stench filled her mouth and nose, her throat prickled and bristled with rising bile, but the damn thing eventually slid perfectly, stupidly back.

She had the towel back up to her face in a flash, holding it tightly over her mouth and nose, and then breathed deeply while she looked around.

Now she had to follow the pipe one way or the other but which way? Which way would the pipe drain out?

She decided to go left, away from the smarter buildings on the outside of the compound, reasoning that the sewage would be kept as far away as possible from the higher-class of people who must live there.

A few minutes later and Salya saw a dim glow ahead of her, bright daylight reflecting from the sides of the dank, curved pipe. She had been right to follow it away from the smarter buildings on the outside.

Turning the shallow bend, the young girl found herself at the opening, the spill sliding down a concrete slope to form a disgusting pool at the bottom which seeped away into the earth.

She stood there covered in slime and shit but free.

She breathed the clean air in deeply and then scanned the way ahead. She had to get away and under cover before dark or she would freeze to death when the temperature dropped in the night.

The gully of filth ran on ahead; the best chance she had of staying out of sight while moving away from the compound.

She looked at herself and sighed. What she wouldn't give to be able to wash first.

She slid down the concrete spill and then followed the gully, making her way to the mountains a few miles ahead. She would be able to hole-up for the night there and knew she would find water somewhere on the slopes. After that?

She looked to the sky.

After that she had to try and get home, wherever that might be.

As Salya disappeared amongst the rocks and boulders, the two nurses were frantically searching for her back in the shower-block, but it was more than three hours before the whole compound was alerted and the search for her spread to the outside and the VIP buildings.

The young girl had guessed correctly that the buildings outside were used by the upper-classes, but what she didn't know was that most of these upper-class people came from outside Afghanistan.

The compound held the children and the slaves and had a small barracks attached with usually no less than twenty, male guards in residence.

While the village outside was lavishly built and furnished to cater for a clientele who had both deviant and freakish tastes and plenty of money.

Anything which an aberrant mind could think of could be catered for here at the village known as, *Paradise Begins*. *Anything* at all for both male and female customers alike; there was always a ready supply of oil-drums.

## Chapter Seven

The tech-lab in the basement of the Interpol building was usually off limits; the weapons it employed in its war on cyber-crime, a closely-guarded secret.

Bollinger was very friendly with one of those secret-weapons, however, and she and Shelby were busy at a consol with the remains of the mobile phone from Keys.

'It's not looking good is it, Soph?' Shelby sighed.

It was late, he was tired and the bloody phone wasn't giving up anything after hours of prodding it with the latest software.

'Well we can't let Mac have a look.' Bollinger said, referring to the friend who worked down here and who had let them in. 'He's a good bloke and all that, but if we did find something he would have to log it and send it up to the relevant departments and before you know it, Appleby would be all over it.'

'Well I'm not getting anywhere with the damn thing so what do you suggest?'

Bollinger sat and stared for a minute, contemplating something; should she, shouldn't she? 'There *is* someone who might be able to help us,' she said after a moment's thought. 'You won't like it though, Gray.'

Shelby raised his eyebrow at that. 'Oh yes?'

'Have you ever heard of the group, *Code-8*?' She bit her lip, waiting for his reply.

He frowned. 'Well of course I have, it's the reason we have eighteen security-filters and several uncrackable firewalls isn't it? They're a gang of hackers.'

He looked at her, waiting to hear what she had to propose, but the thought was already in his head. 'You're not on about trying to contact them and give them a look at this phone, are you?'

She just looked at him, still biting her bottom lip.

Shelby looked back and made note of her little nervous display. He narrowed his eyes. 'You bloody-well know them, don't you?' He said, his finger pointing accusingly right at her.

Bollinger still said nothing, her eyes widened.

'Oh! God! Soph. What did you do?' Shelby asked, his voice tensing a little.

'I was seeing one of them for a few months.' She blurted out, breathlessly. 'I didn't know at first, honestly, Gray, and he didn't know about my job either.'

Shelby relaxed; was that all it was? He was worried for a minute that she was about to announce her own membership into the elite hacking-group.

'"At first"?' He replied, standing back and folding his arms, a tiny, tiny smirk at the corners of his mouth.

'What?' Bollinger said.

'You said you didn't know "at first", so what happened after you found out?'

Bollinger wanted to slap his silly, smirking mouth. 'Well what do you think happened? He bloody dumped me didn't he?'

Shelby's eyes continued to smirk. 'Oh. I see. I'm sorry about that.' He said.

'No you're not, you're an ass.' She huffed. 'Anyway, we wouldn't have made a good couple; he's a smarmy bastard and I'm always right, wouldn't have worked.'

Shelby chuckled loudly then, unable to contain himself.

'What? Why's that so funny, you git? I really liked him until I found out it was him who did the Kremlin hack.'

Through his laughter, Shelby managed to speak. 'Sorry. I'm not meaning to be insensitive, Sophie, but I can just imagine your face when you found out,' he slapped his thigh. 'And if that isn't enough; *his* face when *he* found out you were the law. You couldn't make this stuff up could you?'

He couldn't help himself and laughed loudly. Insensitive or not, it was just too funny.

Bollinger just stood back and scowled, but Shelby's humour was contagious and soon she was laughing herself.

'I must admit, now that I think of it, the look on his face *was* priceless when I showed him my ID.'

'I bet!' Shelby chuckled. 'Are you sure he would *want* to help us though? I mean he's bound to be on the lookout for a setup, surely?'

'Oh. He'll help; he knows just as you do that my word is sacred. I promised I wouldn't turn him in and I haven't and I won't. Neither will you.' She said, pointing.

'Scouts honour.' Shelby replied instantly and saluted.

'You were a scout?' Bollinger asked, unbelieving.

'No, but seeing as Interpol doesn't have a special salute I thought I'd use it.'

He picked up the remains of the phone. 'If your man can help us with this,' he held the phone up, 'then I'll help *him* with his next hack!'

Bollinger laughed.

'Great. Well, we can go first thing in the morning then, he lives in Hastings. I'll give him a call when I get home.'

\* \* \*

Low tides and high cliffs, the briny odour of the English Channel rising up the rock-face on the midday heat; Shelby breathed it in deeply.

The veranda he was standing on jutted out for several feet over the cliffs overlooking the channel, while behind him the small, white building it was attached to looked to be nothing more than a wooden beach-hut.

The man they had come to meet, Richard Harrison, was everything that Bollinger had told him he would be.

He was very intelligent but smarmy with it, not exactly sneering but definitely a little patronizing. He was classically handsome and clean but dressed like a slob; his neatly combed hair and clean-shaven face clashed wildly with his ragged, purple jumper with holes in the sleeves, the baggy beach-trousers torn at the knees and on his feet the odd socks and old trainers.

*Eccentric*, Bollinger had said. *Weird*, Shelby had thought when he had first met the man.

The one surprise in store for Shelby was the place Harrison called home.

He had imagined a house in the suburbs somewhere, a hidey-hole of a room at the back of a semi-detached maybe, but when they had pulled up outside the ornate double-gates of a large white-brick house at the very top of the cliff, he had actually whistled.

*Impressive! We're in the wrong job, Soph.*

Even though the view and the air agreed with Shelby, he was still a little peeved to be standing here by himself; relegated to wait outside while Bollinger persuaded Harrison to trust him.

He could hear them talking. Did they know he could hear them?

'I've been working with Graham for six years, Rich, give me a break will you?' Bollinger was pleading.

'Well, you will have to forgive me, my darling *Sophiella*-'

'Don't call me that.'

'Sorry; forgive me, my darling *Sophie*,'

Bollinger rolled her eyes and huffed.

'But I think the man looks very dodgy and untrustworthy, a little dishevelled and old-fogey-like. The sort that would shout "No! You're not having your ball back!" and then stab said ball with his gardening shears.'

'I'm right here you know?' Shelby said, without turning around.

'And a self-confessed eaves-dropper.' Harrison said, and gestured toward Shelby, making a face which said; *you see*? 'A curtain-twitcher, no doubt about it, how can I trust that, hmm?'

Bollinger sighed. 'You're still an ass. *Dick*!'

'Ah! I knew you would remember that. My dick I mean. I know you still think about us, Sophiella, the things we used to do right here.'

'Again; I'm standing *right* here.' Shelby said, loudly this time.

'And out there.' Harrison nodded, leering toward the veranda. 'Remember the squeaky board?'

Shelby felt a sudden, uncomfortable tingle in the soles of his feet and the palms of his hands.

He released the handrail and wished he could learn how to levitate. He was afraid to move in case he found the squeaky board.

Bollinger blushed very briefly before bringing her embarrassment under control. 'Knock it off and stop being a Dick and start being a Richard, will you?'

She walked up to face the grinning Harrison. 'We really need your help, Rich, and it's important. Life or death important.'

Harrison's grin lowered to a casual smile but his brow furrowed; the lowest his smile ever fell when things were serious. 'Okay, Sophie, no more games, I promise.'

Harrison turned to face Shelby's back. 'You can come in now. Sophie has convinced me you're okay.'

'Really?' Shelby replied sarcastically, and turned around, stepping straight onto the squeaky board.

Harrison grinned again, Bollinger blushed whole-heartedly this time and Shelby cringed inwardly, but stepped like a man into the room and pretended that nothing was amiss. Only *he* knew his left foot throbbed with the phantom caresses of Bollinger's, sordid encounter on the veranda with Harrison.

'So, what can I do to help you both?' The millionaire hacker asked, once he felt they were both comfortably uncomfortable.

Shelby produced the bag which contained the bits of broken phone.

He and Bollinger went on to tell him the story of Finn and what had happened at his latest hit in Turkey.

Harrison took the bag and studied the contents. 'That's an interesting combination of chips and wiring to have been given. Where's the rest of it?' He asked.

'In a rubbish bin outside a Turkish police station, I think.' Shelby answered, shrugging. 'But you're right; it is an interesting assortment, almost like these were *selected* to be given to us, but if they were, I don't know why, and if they hold anything, I don't know what.'

Harrison looked at Shelby with a newfound respect for the man. 'And what *do* you find when you use your own systems and software?' He asked.

'A lot of meaningless ascii, plenty of static, not a single header. In short; nothing. To be truthful, our software isn't quite as sophisticated as it could be.'

'And you think *my* software maybe sophisticated enough?'

Harrison smiled, the smarm right on the surface at having his ego rubbed.

'We can only find out, can't we?' Shelby said, and then pointed to the bag. 'It's in your hands now. If you want to help, that is? I've heard you can pretty much hack into anything; find the lead in there and you just may be saving a lot of lives.'

Harrison grinned and then laughed. 'Oh! I do love a good challenge. There is nothing like that moment when the glove is on the damn ground!' He dramatised. 'Watson! To the *Dick-cave!*' He said, and marched to the tall fridge standing at the back of the room.

Shelby looked at Bollinger and mouthed; *Dick-cave*, then sniggered stupidly.

Bollinger rolled her eyes and mouthed back; *he's bloody mental!*

The hissing sound of air being released made them both turn to see Harrison standing by an opening behind the fridge which he had revealed by pulling the thing round like a door on a pneumatic hinge.

A blue glow seeped up from a room beneath.

Harrison japed his way down the steps while Shelby and Bollinger stared in disbelief and quiet respect.

'Did you know about that?' Shelby asked, indicating the fridge-*cum*-secret-hideout door.

'What does the look on my face tell you?' She replied. 'Of course I didn't know.'

They quickly followed Harrison down the stairs and entered another world, a world with rows and rows of computers and monitors and wires and cooling systems, start-up systems, satellite gateways and several arcade machines from the eighties. At the centre of all stood an eighty-two inch HD screen.

Harrison was sitting in the seat in front of it, the bits of the broken phone lying in front of him. 'Ok, let's start with this.' He said, to his captive audience, waving a small, blackened chip around for them to see. He loved an audience.

He slipped a pair of magnifying goggles over his eyes and picked up the chip with a pair of tweezers. He brought it close to his face and examined it. 'Yes. Yes, look here.' He said to no one and not offering anything for anyone to see anyway. 'This last forked joint has been twisted together. Naughty.'

He took another pair of smaller tweezers and uncoiled the two tines at the end of the chip.

After some minutes of preparing the chip and straightening the rest of the connection-tines, he pulled a black socket from the front of the consol he was using. It extended on a retractable cable. The chip sat perfectly in the first series of slots in the socket.

'Right, here we go.' He said, turning around and grinning like a lunatic, still wearing his enormous, round magnifying-glasses.

His massive eyeballs flicked between them both and then finally settled on Shelby. 'If there's anything still on this chip this little program will rebuild it, but the other stuff that came in the bag will probably hold the keys to all of the CRC checks, I'd be willing to bet my glasses on it.' He said.

'What makes you so sure?' Shelby asked.

Without turning around, Harrison pointed to the big screen behind him. 'See that white, scrolling line?'

Shelby looked; a thin, diagonal line scrolled endlessly up the black screen, almost like the pause-loop of a video player.

'That's a file, or at least a part of a file, probably a picture or sound file; the chip is part of the media-control hardware.'

Harrison kept his owl-eyes on Shelby.

After a moment's thought Shelby spoke. 'So how does that memory-chip become so cleanly detached from its GPU? Shouldn't that be soldered somewhere directly underneath it?'

Harrison's respect rose even further for Shelby, the man had a good grasp on what he was dealing with. He wondered how much of a grasp.

He flicked his massive eyes to Bollinger. 'Does he ever talk *gibberish*?' He asked her.

'Oh! God, yes! Almost as much as you.'

Harrison laughed and turned back to Shelby. 'I'm impressed that you knew that the chip was part of the memory and not part of the core, and to answer your question; yes, it should be residing with the GPU. Whoever tried to destroy this phone knew what they were doing and were severing the very links from memory to chip and vice versa.'

Harrison beamed as he spoke.

'And that would keep all of the encryption matrices separated and useless.' Shelby finished.

'*Very* good. You should come and work for me, you have a firm grasp of the process.'

Harrison winked an enormous eye.

Shelby just stared at the man. The meaning of what he had just said to him slowly dawning. 'Well, I'll be damned! You're *Starlight!*' He said grinning.

Bollinger, who had kept quiet while the gibberish was flying around, stepped in.

'What's *Starlight*?'

'Not what? Who? Him,' Shelby said, pointing to the now chuckling Harrison. 'He's *Starlight*; *the* number one at the top of *Code-8*, its founding-father. You don't *ask* to join *Code-8*; *he* finds *you* and invites you in!'

Bollinger stared wide-eyed at Harrison. 'Is that true?'

'Well you don't have to bow or anything.' Harrison said, as he removed the glasses now.

She frowned and turned back to Shelby. 'And how do *you* know about this *Starlight*?'

'I keep my electronic-ear to the ground; you're not the only one with friends in the tech-lab, you know? And besides, I've always been fascinated with programming and hacking; Mr *I'm-too-smarmy-for-my-own-good* here is a legend in the techy-circles.'

Harrison scoffed. 'A legend. *Pah!* Legends are old and gone to the past, I'm a god out there,' he said, nodding at the world he was connected to through his huge monitor. 'Everlasting!'

'You're a cock, that's what you are.' Bollinger said, irritated.

Harrison laughed and pointed. 'Yes, but that's *Mr* Cock to you.'

Shelby coughed. 'You do know that there is a global reward being offered for information leading to your capture, don't you?'

'I know. Pitiful isn't it? Hack a few illegal bank accounts or a government's secrets and bang! They set the money-dogs on you.' Harrison said, seriously. 'How much is it at now, do you know?' He asked Shelby.

'One and a half million.' He replied.

'*Pfft!* Insulting!' Harrison looked genuinely hacked off. 'They recognise genius by holding out a handful of peanuts! Peasants and misers the lot of them.'

He turned to Shelby and Bollinger, his smile returning. 'I wouldn't bother with anything less than ten million if I were you.' He said winking. 'Now, let's get back to the task in hand.'

His magnifiers went back on and he picked up a piece of green circuit-board, bringing it close to his face. 'Hmm. This and-,' he picked up another piece of circuitry, 'this.' He said, dropping the pieces onto the desk in front of him.

He opened a drawer and brought out a small, black chip with wires attached. Each wire had a small crocodile-clip on the end.

After attaching four of the clips to different parts of the two pieces of circuit-board, Harrison plugged the black chip into the socket next to the memory chip which was still being read.

'And here we go.' He said, pressing a key on his keyboard with a flourish.

The big screen flickered once, Harrison clicked his fingers and pointed to the screen, grinning cockily. 'And done!' An image suddenly appeared. 'Well hello, handsome.'

Shelby and Bollinger both gasped and stared. *There* was the man they had been hunting for the past seven years.

The image was a little blurred but framed perfectly in the mirror in the background was a tall, blue-eyed man, and if that wasn't enough, they could clearly see the knives in his hands and the rage contorting his face.

'I don't think I would like to meet *him* on a dark night.' Harrison mused.

When he didn't get a reply he turned around.

Shelby and Bollinger were staring seriously at the image, lost in their own thoughts.

The last room where the victim with the eye-wound sat in the chair was immediately recognisable to both Shelby and Bollinger.

Two male children sat huddled on the bed, a look of complete terror on their small faces. Their eyes were wide and staring at Finn as he rushed in behind the man holding the camera.

As shocking as the image was, it was the form of the sprinting Finn which held Shelby and his partner's intense gaze. The look of fury was astounding; a terrifying glimpse into the human soul's darkest and most violent capabilities.

'We've got to find him, Soph.' Shelby murmured without taking his eyes from the screen.

Harrison's face dropped to a casual smile again as he frowned. 'I might be able to help with that.' He said. 'I think I may be able to retrieve the rest of it.' He said casually.

Bollinger dropped her gaze. 'The rest of it?'

Before Harrison could answer, Shelby spoke. 'It's a still-image taken from a video capture.' He said, his eyes still fixed on Finn.

Harrison nodded in agreement. 'I have a few tricks up my sleeve, I can give it a go.' He said.

Shelby turned his attention to Harrison, looking at him solemnly and serious. 'How long?'

'Give me forty-eight hours, but I make no promises; this phone has been tampered with by a *mediocre* expert.' He just couldn't bring himself to say it was actually a decent attempt at total obliteration of data.

'If the phone was also secure, that would cause a few problems, but there are places where data ends up *before* it's secured; it's those sources I'll be visiting.'

'Can you send me that complete file?' Bollinger asked, indicating the image of Finn. 'My email address at Interpol is-.'

'I know what it is.' Harrison said, his grin returning to full-on smarm.

Bollinger gave him a withering look.

'Oh. Don't be like that, what did you expect?' He shrugged. 'As soon as you told me who you were I came and had a look. No harm done.'

'You hacked Interpol?' Shelby looked stunned, his mind setting virtual fire to uncrackable firewalls and be damned with security filters.

'Only Sophie's computer. Honest.' Harrison sniggered. 'Why did you change your start-up to *Albatross*?' He asked her.

The two Interpol detectives simply stood with their respective arms folded in front of themselves while they looked down and stared at the grinning Harrison.

After a moments silence and once he realised they wouldn't be joining him in his smile, Harrison said; 'Right!' Clapped his hands together and rubbed them briskly like it was a cold morning. 'I'll be getting on then.'

He pointed to the monitor behind him and then turned away, resisting the urge to rub his neck where he could feel Bollinger and Shelby's dagger-eyes boring into his head.

## Chapter Eight

The mountains grazed away into the distance while the valleys and hills rolled along with them.

Salya knew the mountains. She stood and looked, shading her eyes to the high sun. She just wished she knew *these* mountains. She had no idea where she was.

From the time her eyes had been forced closed by the ether until they opened again in the back of the truck, Salya couldn't even begin to guess the direction they had taken, or how long they had been travelling.

After following the sewage culvert to the edge of the mountain's skirts she had looked back and wondered if she was going the right way.

She could have just waited until dark and made her way back along the mountain range that way, but what if they had come from the other direction? The direction she was heading?

In the end she had decided she had already started this way and was safe so carried on.

Going back and following the mountains into the east would have been the right way to go but would have been the wrong thing to do; of course Nazari had sent his thugs off back the way they had come to look for the girl, correctly assuming that she must be heading for home.

Luckily for Salya, she didn't know where home was.

There were hawks in the air. She watched them gliding expertly, circling the ground hundreds of feet below them. What she wouldn't give to be up there with them, afforded the view which they had.

She could see no reason to stray from the mountain range just yet; she was safe and dry and didn't go without food or water. But her yearning to see her parents and brothers again was strong and she couldn't feed that part of herself. She saw nothing hopeful before her to fill the need in her heart.

And then there was the hole where Rafiq should be, the place in her very soul where he used to be when he was alive. She felt she would never be completely whole again.

Revenge was always on the young girl's mind, revenge and the death of Nazari at her own hands.

In her nightmares, however, she was always helpless and afraid, a leering Nazari usually being the face which startled her into wakefulness again.

One of the hawks made a spearing dive to the ground.

Salya involuntarily sucked her breath in and held it; she never tired of watching these magnificent birds hunt. Some of them were big enough to take a lamb if you weren't careful, or so her father used to say. She had never seen it for herself but she could easily believe it.

With nothing more to spare than a metre of air between itself and its prey, the hawk spread its wings and air-braked, its huge, taloned claws flicking forward naturally as it caught the unsuspecting hare by the scruff of the neck.

It disappeared into the high mountain-grass and didn't rise again for another fifteen seconds. When it did, Salya breathed out as it took to the air, the limp form of the hare dangling beneath it.

The hawk flew away taking the body of the hare from Salya's sight. Thoughts of burning oil-drums filled her thoughts while tears spilled down her face as she turned away.

She made her way back to her small camp, the tears continuing to course down her cheeks and drip from her chin.

As she arrived back at the litter she had built up in front of the crack leading into a small cave, her tears of sadness and pain became tears of frustration and anger.

She would show that fat pig. If it was the last thing she ever did she would show that fat pig that he couldn't just kill her brother and get away with it. She would show him.

Sitting on a rock in front of the small fire, Salya's young frame cast giant, dancing shadows on the wall of the cave behind her as she stared into the flames and imagined how she would take her revenge.

* * *

*Hotter. The air is hotter, closer and more damp. The walls are streaming with water. Where it goes in this small cave, I don't know, but I'm too afraid to look around. She's sitting behind me, I can feel her, smell her. My she-wolf.*

*A child's laugh comes to my ears from a distance. Her musical voice is familiar but far, far away somewhere behind the curtain of water.*

*I dare not even look at it but she can't keep me from listening, I can't help but to hear.*

*'I could tear off your ears.' She says, without malice. 'But that wouldn't do any good now, would it?' She chuckles.*

*'I love you.'*

*'I know. I love you.' She replies, and means it.*

*The child laughs again, happily and whole-heartedly and startlingly close.*

*I flinch and without thinking what I'm doing, I look up.*

*Just beyond the veil of water cascading past the arch I catch a distorted, washy glimpse of a girl with blonde hair and wearing a blue dress.*

*'GET OUT!'*

*Pain sears across my naked back and I scream as her claws rake deeply through my flesh, flaying the skin from my torso in long, ragged, wet strips.*
'GET OUT!' The she-wolf is screaming. 'GET OUT! GET OUT!'

Finn woke with a start, disorientated and still carrying the fear and pain of the dream.

He scrambled to his feet, panting wildly and looking at his surroundings as though he had never seen them before.

Slowly his lightning-eyes unglazed and focused instead on the fire which had now gone out.

He sighed and shivered, bringing his breathing back under control. 'I'm sorry.' He whispered.

The she-wolf remained silent but not gone. There was a tiny warm-spot in Finns mind where she sat and simmered.

Her simmering felt different this time somehow. She hadn't shouted at him when he had apologised for a start, as more often than not she did.

He turned his attention to relighting the fire as he thought about that.

He was inside an abandoned herder-shack; an oblong, stone room with a roof of woven sticks, the small fire-pit being in the centre of the room.

There were hundreds of these places scattered all over Iran and Iraq, and though he didn't know for certain, he guessed there would be a similar story in Afghanistan.

A sign of the old ways slowly being replaced by the new and advanced ways; for every shack left abandoned in the wilds there would be a tower block in a city to replace it, a factory manufacturing modern, western goods for the herders and their families to work in, and a freedom replaced with a slavery wearing the façade of *modern society*.

Finn cleared the ash from the previous fire and then gathered up some of the charcoal from it. He built the fire up with the sticks he had collected a couple of days ago and then pushed the charcoal into the gaps between sticks. A flick of his lighter and the shack lit up brightly and the air quickly warmed up.

She was still silent. The child he had accidently seen beyond the watery curtain had something to do with it, he was sure.

He had never seen her before, he knew of no children with golden hair and who wore a blue dress. He knew no child save the one who the she-wolf had entrusted into his care, the one he had lost and now had to find again. So who was she?

'Who was that girl?' He asked, quietly.

A slap across his face with a clawed-hand made Finn flinch and recoil as though being attacked by an invisible assailant.

*Stay out of it!* She hissed in his mind.

'But who is she?' He persisted.

He flinched again, another clawing-slap.

*Stay! Away!* She growled, loudly this time.

65

Finn steeled himself. 'I need to know, Cait-!'

Before he could finish, the she-wolf attacked him with all of the ferocity he had ever felt before.

He crumpled to the ground, missing his fire by inches, and lay trembling and white-faced as the onslaught continued deep in his psyche.

She slashed and raked with steel claws and fangs, rabidly biting and chewing into his flesh.

The assault lasted for more than ten minutes and in his mind Finn had been reduced to a stretch of twitching meat, flayed from head to toe.

Several hours after his seizure, Finn awoke, his head pounding and only the vaguest of memories remaining about his ordeal.

He had asked her for something, had almost seen something. What? What did he see, what did he say? He felt he had been close to something, something he should know, something important, one of those missing things about his mistress.

And then like the minute after waking from a dream it was gone and Finn was left with a dull ache in his heart for some strange reason.

He looked at his fire. It had gone out again. How long had he been asleep?

No matter, he had to leave now anyway, the sun was on its way down again and he had wasted enough time.

He gathered his things together into his backpack and made one last check around the room.

Leaving the shack and the mental assault behind, Finn made his way down the mountain slopes, walking over the border into Iran.

Sixty miles away stood a small village he knew of, or rather a village that the she-wolf knew of; he had no idea how she knew but she always somehow did.

If he didn't stop he should be able to make it in around seven hours, arriving just before dark.

It was hot as it usually was, and dry.

Finn loped along at a steady pace, dressed in the whites of a peasant, keeping his temperature under control and avoiding perspiring. A trick of the mind his mistress had taught him.

Several hours passed by, he was still eighteen miles away, travelling along a dusty, orange road, when he spotted a dark shape on the shimmering horizon.

Half an hour later and an old man dressed similarly to Finn passed by on an old bicycle with a tattered, purple parasol attached to the handlebars.

He waved and gave Finn a toothless grin. 'Salâm.' He called, squinting through wrinkled, happy eyes.

Finn raised his hand slowly. 'Salâm.' He responded lamely, as the old man passed.

He stopped and turned, watching the ancient bicycle and the more ancient man as they wobbled off into the distance.

All around, the landscape was empty and hot and dry; the last place you would expect an encounter with a man on a bicycle with a parasol. Surreal. If he had stopped and offered three wishes for a glass of milk and honey, Finn wouldn't have been surprised.

He turned away and continued to follow the road toward the village, a small smile playing across his face as he mentally wished the old man a happy journey.

The miles dribbled away and soon the sun had almost gone.

Finn could see the village in the distance, half a mile away now, when he heard the distinctive bleating of a young goat coming from somewhere on his left.

Boulders and scree were gathered in piles at the feet of these mountains.

Finn caught the orange flare of firelight coming from behind a huge fall of rock a hundred yards away.

The goat cried out again, its machine-gun voice sounding as though it were coming from a well or deep place.

He raised his eyes to the heavens and sighed.

His aches made him look longingly to the village ahead and the food and rest he could have once he was there.

The goat sounded again.

But his heart ached more at the plaintive sound of the distressed animal. 'Fine.' He said, and sighed loudly, shrugging his big shoulders. 'Gods! Is there no peace for a weary soul?' He muttered to himself as he trotted up the scree.

He pressed himself through a narrow gap between boulders and came out onto a large shelf of flat rock. An old herder stood looking at Finn as he crouched at the edge of a sharp drop.

'Salâm.' Finn said, and touched his forehead.

'Salâm.' Repeated the man, and touched his own palm to his breast, a wary look in his eyes as he stared at the giant with blue eyes. He flinched as the goat below him bleated again.

'Can I help you, brother?' Finn asked, stepping to the edge of the precipice and looking down.

The crack ran away into a gloomy blackness, but twenty feet below where they were standing, a ledge jutted from the rock and on it stood the goat.

The man just looked up at Finn's scarred hands and face.

Finn could sense his unease.

Without looking at him, he raised his palm and said; 'Peace, brother.'

And again, without waiting for any kind of response or reply, he sat down on the edge of the drop and twisted himself around, lowering his legs until his feet found a hold.

Slowly, inches at a time, he climbed down carefully until he reached the shelf of rock and the goat.

Below him the blackness seemed to be never-ending but he could hear water running swiftly past, its gurgle oddly loud as it resounded up the rock-face.

He felt the man in his mind cringe at the thought of the drop.

Finn himself felt nothing for the height, fear held no sway over him, neither fear of death nor life.

*A man who lives in fear, lives in the world which his enemies have created for him.*

He thought it was his mistress who used to tell him that, teaching him what human fear really is and how it has been enhanced and utilized as a weapon by *those who would take everything*, as she put it.

*Fear is good, once it is back in its proper house.*

A warm nudge on his calf brought Finn back from his musings; the goat was trying to nibble his white, cotton pants.

Above him, the herder peered over the edge but still said nothing.

Finn picked up the small beast and straddled it across his shoulders, draping its legs around his neck and then tying them together using the ends of his rope-belt.

Steely fingertips bit into the rock, finding holds on even the tiniest of cracks and splinters.

Finn's strength seemed supernatural to the man above him. He watched astonish-eyed as the tall man crept back up to the top, vertically crawling almost, using nothing but the power in his wrists and fingers to keep from slipping back down.

That and the added weight of the goat were enough to see the man stay firmly on his knees as Finn pulled himself over the lip of the chasm to sit on the edge, breathing as relaxed as if he had just woken from sleep.

He untied the goat's feet and then let it slip to the ground behind him, smiling satisfied as he listened to its hooves clopping away back through the gap and to the safety of the open mountainside.

He kept the smile in place and turned to look at the man still on his knees and who was clearly afraid of him now.

'Peace.' He said again, trying his damndest to look friendly and unassuming, almost willing the scars on his face to disappear. 'I am Finn.'

He offered the man his equally scarred, big, callused hand.

After only the briefest of pauses the old man leaned forward and took it, clasping it in both hands and lowering his eyes slightly. 'Thank you for your help, sir,' he said. 'I am Davar.'

Finn made the same clasp with his own hands. 'Please, call me Finn.'

The man raised his head and looked Finn in the eye, the fear in his own now gone, replaced with a wondering respect for this gentle giant of a man.

'It will be dark soon, do you have anywhere to stay for the night?' He asked.

Finn nodded casually toward the outside. 'I am heading into the village.' He answered.

Davar looked suddenly astonished, his brow wrinkling as his brown eyes opened wide.

All of a sudden his face creased up as he laughed, almost causing himself to fall over backward as he wheezed.

'Forgive me, my friend.' He managed to say. 'I should let you walk into the village just to see the look on Habib's face!'

He slapped his thigh and chortled. 'Oh! The poor man would have a heart-attack!'

Finn chuckled. The old man was referring to his size and stark, blue eyes and scars; to these people he must look like one of the fair-haired giants from their fairytales.

The old man leaned forward and took Finn's hand and squeezed it. 'Do not be offended.' He said. 'I can see you are neither a giant nor a bad man, but it is plain to see that you have crossed paths with some great evil.'

He looked solemnly into Finn's lightning-eyes. 'Evil may leave its mark on our bodies, but it cannot taint our spirits unless we let it. I can see you beneath your scars, my friend.'

He squeezed Finn's hand again and smiled.

It had been years since Finn had experienced any friendly contact with another person. Years.

He struggled with the unfamiliar, warm emotions which he was both feeling and receiving, unsure what to do with them or how to react.

The old man could sense his discomfort and uncertainty. 'I would be honoured, Finn, if you would take your evening meal with my family and myself, and if you find the company pleasant there is a warm bed for you to sleep in and breakfast in the morning.' He said, letting go of Finn's hand and rising to his feet.

'Peace.' He then said, repeating Finn's own sentiment.

Finn looked away and thought for a moment and then slowly nodded. 'Thank you, that would be very welcome.'

The two men left the cave. The goat was waiting patiently for them outside.

Davar looked down at it balefully. 'You would be for the pot when we got back if I ate meat.' He said, as he pointed his finger, ticking the young animal off. 'I *still* might throw you in, so better be good!'

The goat blinked its staring eyes just once and then walked away. It stopped a few feet ahead and turned around and looking at them, waiting.

Davar pointed at it and looked at Finn 'We'll follow the guide home now, he's remembered where his bed is.' He said, his face creasing up into a huge grin.

\* \* \*

Davar's house was cool and spacious and comfortable. His wife, Hasti, was a gracious, robust woman who clearly wore the trousers when in the house.

His youngest son and his wife lived with them while they were building their own house.

Davar's youngest child, a daughter of thirteen, also lived at home.

On either side and at the back of Davar's house stood four more houses;

three for his older sons and their wives and children, and the fourth for his eldest child, another daughter who lived there with her own, two children.

Surrounding these houses were another nine houses, all occupied by one relative and their families or another.

The village which they were all a part of lay a further two miles away.

His hunger and thirst completely satisfied by his hosts, Finn sat with Davar on his porch overlooking the mountains to the west. The sun was behind the peaks now and their summits were sparkling orange and red like the molten ends of glowing pokers.

The youngest children had been ushered inside an hour ago while the older ones attended their chores before bed.

The whole evening had been one magical moment after another, Finn had never experienced this kind of family life, this closeness, this extraordinary ability to be on the same page and uniquely connected.

Or had he? His heart felt overwhelmed with something, a feeling which he couldn't quite put his finger on.

Smoke from the old man's pipe lingered past Finn's nose, a sweet, woody aroma.

'So tell me, my giant friend, what brings you to our little corner of the world?'

He looked at Finn, smiling lopsidedly with the pipe-stem still between his teeth.

Finn didn't know what to say, he just sat and stared back, looking bewildered.

It had been a long time since anyone had asked him why he was here or where he was going or what was he doing.

'I-. I'm looking for someone.' He eventually said, and looked away toward the setting sun.

Davar's years of herding and raising his family had furnished him with a quiet and subtle wisdom; the land had many tales to tell if you listened to it closely and people had as many more again of *un*told tales which only became apparent in their lack of words to your questions.

He could see that Finn's path had been cut out for him, his story already written by someone or something else, Finn himself held to it by some oath or honour.

'You have my greatest respect.' Davar said, removing his pipe and touching his forehead with his other hand.

He lowered his eyes. 'May the blessings of all gods and prophets go before you on your path, Finn.'

The two men sat in silence, a respectful moment passed as the sun's final rays disappeared behind the teeth of the mountain, leaving the bruising night to creep over the sky.

Davar's pipe-smoke began to drift once more as he took it up again. 'I have something which may be of use to you.' He said, turning to face Finn. 'A motorcycle which used to belong to my father.'

Finn frowned; a machine which the old man's father had owned must be a hundred years-old at least.

'It's a good one,' Davar said quickly, noticing Finn's look. 'A Suzuki!' He finished, and nodded his head proudly, sucking on his pipe like an expert of both pipes and motorbikes.

'You honour me.' Said Finn, happily. 'May I ask how your father came to own a motorcycle?'

Davar removed his pipe from his mouth and looked seriously at Finn. 'A man from out of town crashed into his grave and broke the stones. He left the motorcycle to pay for the damage and went away on half-dead donkey he acquired in town.'

Finn remained silent, his jaw tightly clenched to keep the smiles and the laughter in check, but he soon faltered and a tiny sputter broke through to the surface.

Davar slapped his thigh, wheezed and then laughed loudly. 'Two days later and the young man returned on foot; the donkey had dropped dead after a single day's ride!' He continued, wheezing deeply while the colour of his face began to lean toward the purple. 'A true story! I kid you not!'

And both men sat and laughed until they were equally purple and in tears.

An hour more passed by, mostly filled with the old man's tales of his youth and of his family, before Davar stood up.

'It is time for my bed now, my friend, I have enjoyed your company.'

Finn rose to his own feet and placed a hand on the old man's shoulder. 'Thank you for your hospitality, Davar, it has been a long time since I have been amongst friends.'

'You are welcome. Sleep well and we shall have more talk at breakfast in the morning.' Said the old man.

He turned and picked up his walking-crook and made to go through the door. 'We'll be up at the crack of goats fart.' He said as he disappeared inside.

Finn could hear him chuckling as he went.

After taking himself to his room, Finn lay down on the goat-fleece mattress and stared at the ceiling. *She* was with him.

*Davar is a good man.*

'They are all good people.' Finn replied.

*Perhaps.*

'I feel like I know them, or like I *should* know them. They remind me of something.'

*What do they remind you of, love?*

Finn paused and thought. 'I don't know. Life, I suppose.' He said.

He couldn't pin down what it was that the old man and his family reminded him of. He could feel something, something distant yet plain as day but covered by a thick blanket of dark smoke.

'Life.' He repeated, staring into a past which he couldn't see.

*Don't dwell on it, love, close your eyes and let me sooth you*. She purred.

Finn did as he was commanded and closed his eyes. Immediately he felt her taloned hands caressing his temples and the warmth of her fur as she pressed herself into his back. Her breath on the nape of his neck was like the softest down pillow.

Finn slept and for the first time in a long time he didn't dream.

## Chapter Nine

Shelby drew hard on his cigarette, his rare, dirty luxury.

Walking the busy streets had been supposed to empty his mind and take it off the task in hand. For a while at least.

The faces of the milling people did nothing but hinder his attempt to settle his mind. He resorted to a smoke instead.

He wondered at Bollinger's tenacity and ability to be so damned patient. She was still there, watching the drizzle of faces passing in front of her as the picture Harrison had gleaned from the phone was being scrutinized by Interpol's *facial-recognition* program.

Shelby was well aware of the software and the database which it had access to, but he had never seen it in action.

He remembered one of the lab-techs telling him about it, being excited about the amazing capabilities it possessed; it could track down practically anyone as long as they had a picture of themselves somewhere online.

He remembered the argument about the ethics of it.

'*Surely that's a huge breach on privacy?*' He had argued. '*Not to mention illegal on so many other levels.*'

'*The legality of it is a little bit hazy at the moment, but let's put it this way; if we have the means to trace a terrorist by searching for his or her face in the cyber-world then searching through everyone's images until we find them shouldn't really be a problem.*

'*We may look through, or rather let the software look through all of the images, but we are being specific in our searches to such an extent that we don't see anything else. We don't really have the means to look at everything without a decent enough sample in the first place.*' The lab-tech had argued logically.

Shelby took another pull on his cigarette and then dropped it into the gutter.

The only thing the lab-tech hadn't told him about the software was how bloody long it could take. He'd managed a good four and-a-half hours of sitting with Bollinger before his collar and feet had began to itch.

He checked his watch; four-thirty.

Turning on his heel he made his way back the way he had come, resisting the urge to light up another cigarette.

He was almost back at base when his mobile rang.

He stopped and fished it out of his coat-pocket. It was Bollinger.

'Soph?'

'*We've got a match, Gray.*' Was all she said.

'Okay, I'm right outside, I'll be up in five minutes.'

Shelby dropped his phone back into his pocket and walked up the stone steps to the entrance

*And here we go*, he thought as the sliding door opened and he stepped back inside.

There was a fresh cup of coffee waiting for him on his desk when he arrived. Bollinger sat behind her own desk looking at her monitor.

'I'm running the prelims now.' She said, while Shelby pulled his chair around and set it down next to hers.

He sat down and rejoined with the vigil at the computer screen.

The picture of Finn caught in the mirror at the Malas' hit was placed neatly above another photo of a smiling, blue-eyed, young man. The picture was from his organ donor-card, James Deere, the name stated.

'I can see the resemblance,' Shelby said, 'but it's far from perfect.'

'Eighty-two percent match.' Bollinger replied. 'And it was the *only* return.'

She looked with raised eyebrows at her colleague. 'That's just mental. It's like the man has no social background at all.'

'Well, that in itself actually does tell us something though, doesn't it?' Shelby pointed to the screen. 'James Deere there doesn't want to advertise his existence. Who else do we know does that?'

Shelby watched the space next to the two pictures, white text on the black background, scrolling up the screen; information collation and analysis. Nothing was showing up in the address or the details boxes.

'I would be willing to bet that if we did a search using the name James Deere, we would only come up with that single image.' He said quietly. 'Do we know where the donor-card comes from?'

Bollinger tapped a key and a small window popped open in the middle of the screen.

'Hartlepool. A blood drive, so it could have been mobile.'

'It's a start. I'll get on the phone to the blood-bank and see if they can shed some more light on James Deere.'

With a small shove, Shelby rolled the chair and himself over to his telephone while Bollinger left her desk and went to stand in front of Shelby's monitor.

'I'll run a separate search, Gray, look for James Deere; you're probably right, but we have to be certain that there really is nothing else.'

The pair of them felt they were actually moving forward for a change and the mood was high and positive.

Bollinger tapped the keyboard and fed the computer the information while Shelby tapped the phone-keys. They both waited as the phone at the other end of Shelby's line began to ring and the software in front of Bollinger began to initiate.

It felt a little more than coincidence then when a few seconds later the pair of them spoke at the same time.

'Hello?' Shelby enquired, as the phone was picked up.

'And we're off.' Bollinger said, as the software began to run.

Another three and-a-half hours disappeared in a slow, tedious dribble of more than apparent, frustratingly-long seconds.

They were no closer to finding James Deere's address than when they had started fresh-faced and caffeine-stoked all those hours ago.

'Well, at least we now know that this James Deere is more than likely our man, Finn.' Bollinger tried.

Shelby's mood was dark as thunder-clouds after hours of arguing with the blood-bank, and just after he had slammed the phone down for the umpteenth time the search had ended on his computer and the only result was just had he said it would be; that single image from a donor-card.

He knew Bollinger was trying to make him feel better but it wasn't working.

He stared long and hard at Finn's snarling face caught in the mirror.

He wanted to believe that the smiling man from the donor-card photo and Finn were one and the same, but you couldn't guess or hope or force the pieces to fit, not in this job

He had to know, he had to see the evidence for himself and be certain. More certain than the eighty-two percent the recognition software had given him at least.

It was now just after eight, they would have to call it a day. 'We'll have to sleep on it, Sophie, come back in the morning and look over it again.' He rubbed his face tiredly and ran his fingers back through his hair. 'I'm too tired and angry to think straight.'

Bollinger walked around the back of him and began to knead her thumbs into his neck and shoulders. 'We'll get there, we've moved forward more in the past week than we have in the six years I've been with you.' She said reassuringly.

Shelby sighed; Bollinger was good with her massages and had an in depth knowledge of the fine art of acupressure.

She pressed each thumb into the muscle just beneath his armpits, really working them in to reach the pressure point beneath. The pain could be excruciating but once she released after a few seconds he felt his ears throb as everything rushed onwards, like a damn of built up tension being released.

She continued to work like this on points along his upper spine and between his shoulder-blades until ten minutes later she released him and Shelby flopped back in his chair, a grateful smile spreading across his face.

'You're a genius at that, Sophie, a blooming genius. You're completely wasted working for Interpol.'

Bollinger smirked. 'Well, I hope you're not suggesting I'm a better masseuse than a detective!'

'Oh. I am. You are.' Shelby said, grinning and nodding his head guiltily.

She laughed. 'Right, well I'm only taking forty percent of that as a compliment, so unless you're going to invite me back for dinner you're in a lot of trouble.'

Shelby felt much better as he laughed with Bollinger, she was a very astute woman and would never let him go home to Rachel in such a black mood.

'You're on. I'll call Rach and let her know.'

He stood up and rummaged through the pockets of his overcoat hanging up behind him, looking for his mobile.

He threw his wallet and some tissues, a couple of sweet wrappers and three still-wrapped sweets onto his desk before he produced the phone.

While Shelby was waiting for his wife to answer her own phone, Bollinger picked up a sweet and unwrapped it, popping the sherbet-lemon straight into her mouth.

Shelby's open wallet caught her eye and she picked it up to look at the photo of Rachel in the sleeve.

She and Rachel had been friends since the first time they had met a month after she had been assigned to Shelby's office.

She smiled to herself as she remembered some of the good times and then her smile turned to a sudden frown.

Shelby's own donor-card was visible in the first card-slot behind the photo of Rachel. All Interpol employees had one, the agency had their own cards with their own motif next to the serial numbers at the bottom-left of the cards.

Bollinger rushed to her monitor and held Shelby's donor-card up to the image of James Deere's card. At the bottom left where the numbers were there was a motif of a flaring sun behind an inverted *A*.

The numbers were all attached to the blood-bank through various organisations, all of Shelby's enquiries had led to a dead end because he had given the *private* numbers of the organisation to search for and not the blood-bank's *own* numbers.

She turned to face Shelby, who was still talking to Rachel on the phone.

'Okay, love, see you in forty minutes. Bye.'

He turned around, smiling. 'She's loo-.' He stopped short when he saw the serious look on Bollinger's face. His shoulder's sagged.

'I've found something.' She said guiltily.

Shelby's shoulder's sagged further. 'Couldn't you find it tomorrow morning?'

He slumped to his seat. 'Go on then.' He said.

'You didn't get anywhere with the blood-bank because we were using the wrong serial numbers; we assumed that James Deere had a Joe-public donor-card when in fact, if you look closely at it, there is a tiny motif of the company who issued him the card, and *those* serial numbers will only match *their* records.

'Any serial numbers which that company uses with the blood-bank will be completely different.'

She folded her arms and waited for the pained look and the stress to creep back into Shelby's neck and shoulders.

'So all we have to do is trace the motif and we then have the company who issued that donor-card?' Shelby mused and stayed relaxed. 'That is a great bit of detective work, Sophie, I take it all back; you're a better detective than masseuse.'

Bollinger raised her eyebrows in surprise. 'Really? You're not pissed off?'

'On the contrary; you've found us a lifeline and a strong one at that.'

'But what about all the wasted time on the phone?' She asked, and not without reason; she knew full well how Shelby hated time-wasters and time-wasting.

'Not entirely wasted. We now know that we have completely exhausted that line of enquiry; anything which could have been gleaned from the blood-bank has been thoroughly scrutinized.' Shelby sniffed nonchalantly.

He wouldn't get wound up over lost time, it felt better to make the excuse and stay happy and focused.

Besides; a motif of a company would be something he could search for from home. He was hungry and the dinner which Rachel had said she was serving had set his evening up just perfectly. He wasn't going to waste it.

'Right. Make a copy of that motif and we'll go and eat while the food's still hot. We can use the laptop at home to search for it. Any company worth its salt will have a website and if it does we'll find it much quicker if we eat first.'

He stood up and retrieved his things from the table. 'Have you nicked one of my sherbet-lemons?' He asked.

Bollinger rolled the half-sucked sweet around her mouth, clacking it against her teeth and sucking noisily. 'No.' She said, as she bit down, crunching loudly.

Her eyes filled with tears as the sudden bitter-lemon sherbet exploded over her tongue. 'Why? Have you got some?' She said, through watery lips and scrunched-up face.

\* \* \*

Hartlepool. The only thing Bollinger knew about Hartlepool was its football fans were nicknamed the *Monkey Hangers*, a strange label if ever she'd heard one.

'You know why they're called the *Monkey Hangers*, don't you?' Shelby asked.

Bollinger couldn't bring herself to actually say the only thing which was *so* obvious that it simply couldn't be true.

'During the Napoleonic wars,' Shelby began when she didn't say anything, 'a French ship was wrecked during a storm and washed up on the Hartlepool beach, the only survivor? A monkey dressed in a French uniform.

'The local fishermen had never seen a Frenchman or a monkey before and thought they'd caught a French spy, so they executed the poor creature after it couldn't answer their questions.'

Bollinger just stared. 'Did you just make that up?' She asked seriously.

Shelby laughed. 'No. Honestly, that's how the legend goes of the hanged monkey.'

'Well that's just grim.' She said, grimacing. 'Poor monkey.'

*One hundred yards and you have reached your destination.* Shelby's sat-nav trilled.

'We're here.' He said, still laughing as he turned his car through the open, iron gates and parked outside the main doors of the building they had come to.

The search for the motif had returned almost instant results; the emblem belonged to a private hospital in the centre of Hartlepool, Rushcliffe Medical.

There was a nip in the air as they got out of the car and they both pulled their coats tightly around themselves, stuffing their hands into their pockets and darting up the tiled steps to the doors at the top.

The glass panels slid easily to one side with a small hiss and the warm air came rushing out from the foyer to meet them. An aroma of flowers tinged with the subtle edge of sterilizing bleach immediately filled their noses.

The foyer was modern and warmly furnished, its decor leaning towards the more radiating colours of the palette; deep ochre settees and chairs accentuated with red and orange cushions, sunflower walls with expertly placed lighting in the corners, casting radiating glows upward.

Thick, woollen carpets the colour of deep, burnt sienna spanned from wall to wall, and every wall was costumed with modern paintings.

The whole thing resembled a studio-apartment more than it did a hospital reception.

'Good afternoon,' Shelby said, to the woman sitting behind the oval receptionists-desk, 'we're here to see Doctor Anderson.'

'Do you have an appointment?' The woman asked, smiling professionally.

Her smile said she knew that they didn't have an appointment and unless it was God himself who had sent them they wouldn't be seeing Mr Anderson anytime soon.

'I called him this morning, he's expecting us.' Shelby replied, and showed his Interpol badge. *His* smile said, *'God sent me.'*

She didn't flinch or bat an eyelid. Well played, Shelby thought to himself.

'Ah, yes. I'll let him know you are here. If you'd like to take a seat.'

The receptionist gestured gracefully to the settee closest to them.

They sat down and waited for all of thirty-five seconds before the door behind the receptionist's desk opened and a small, middle-aged man, oddly resembling Albert Einstein, stepped through.

'Ah. Inspector Shelby, I presume?' He said, jovially as he walked around to greet them.

Shelby and Bollinger stood up, Shelby taking the hand offered by Anderson.

'And this is Inspector Bollinger.' Shelby greeted the doctor, gesturing to Bollinger by his side.

Anderson shook her hand as well. 'It's a pleasure to meet you both.' He said, his face creasing up as he smiled genuinely. 'Shall we go through to my office?'

He stood back, opening his arm and leading them back to the door.

'Could you ask Amy to bring some coffee and biscuits through please, Christine? And have Tony come down.' Anderson then asked the receptionist.

He led them through to a spacious office, but unlike the outside foyer, this room was almost like an Elizabethan drawing-room, blazing fire in the fireplace and all.

'Please,' Anderson gestured to the sofa and chairs surrounding the fire, 'sit, make yourselves comfortable.'

They removed their overcoats which were quickly snatched up by the small doctor and taken to a tall, antique coat stand.

Shelby and Bollinger sat down on the tanned, leather sofa.

Anderson sat in the chair which they both could see was *his* chair; a little scuffed and scratched and adorned with an array of Anderson-shaped dimples.

'How was the journey? It's a long drive from London.' He asked politely.

'It was okay,' Shelby replied. 'We had plenty of places to stop and recoup.'

'Oh. Good. I'm glad. I always use the trains myself, I think I am probably one of those people who fall asleep at the wheel! Bores the starch out of me, long-distance driving.' Answered Anderson.

A soft knock came at the door and then it opened. A young woman dressed in tidy, kitchen whites stepped in carrying a tray filled with a mountain of biscuits and four small cups behind. In her hand dangled a small urn of coffee. She set everything down on the coffee table.

'Thank you, Amy.' Anderson smiled at the housekeeper.

He leaned forward and took up the cups, filling them under the nozzle of the urn as the woman left the room.

After handing Shelby and Bollinger theirs he leaned back in his chair with his own, leaving the fourth cup on the tray.

'You were asking about James Deere. His best friend would be able to tell you more than I can, he'll be down in a moment. Tony, Tony Collins, he's our resident IT person. He and James were very good friends before-.' Anderson paused. 'Well you know, before he died.'

Shelby and Bollinger looked at one another. Only one of two possibilities remained; they were on the wrong track and James Deere was dead, or Finn had closed the chapters of James Deere's life and had begun a new one.

'How exactly did he die?' Bollinger asked.

Anderson frowned. 'Well I thought *you* knew that already. I mean I thought you were here to inform us you had found a body or something.'

He looked at them, bemused. 'Why are you here then?'

Shelby replied with a question of his own. 'You say he died but no body was ever found; how were you informed of his death, Doctor Anderson, what were you told?'

Before Anderson could answer, the door opened and the man from the donor-card photograph walked in, the man named as James Deere who they had just now been told was dead.

Shelby stood up and faced the man, causing him to stop in his tracks.

Anderson sensed the change in the atmosphere go from warm and friendly to cool and suspicious. He raised himself from his seat at the same time Bollinger stood up from hers.

'This is Tony Collins, I was just telling you about him.' Anderson said, sidling up to the man.

Bollinger stepped in front of Shelby, nudging him as she went. 'Too short.' She hissed as she approached the man called Collins.

She held the photo of the donor-card up for both Anderson and Collins to see. 'Why are you calling yourself James Deere?' She asked.

Collins took the picture with a suspicious look, his face suddenly becoming pained. 'Where did you get this?' He asked quietly and without looking up.

Bollinger shot Shelby a glance, he relaxed instantly; this wasn't their man, but it did go a long way to pointing at James Deere as being the man called Finn.

'I'm afraid we can't discuss our reasons with you, Mr Collins, but please help us understand why your face is on James Deere's donor-card.'

'It was a joke.' Collins said. 'Years ago now.'

He looked up at them all. 'People always said we were twins from different mothers, we looked so much alike. The only way you could tell us apart was when we were standing up; James was a good five inches taller than me.' He laughed. 'We took that picture and stuck it on his card and then let it get passed around the office to see if anyone would spot it was *my* face on *his* card.'

Shelby frowned in thought. 'Did you print the picture out and send it round, or was it in email?' He asked.

'Oh! No, we couldn't send it out using the network, I deleted the whole thing after we made one print of it. That's why I was shocked to see it.'

Shelby's heart hammered. That's why they had only found one picture; it had been hidden in a simple networked-printer's memory, a fluke, an almost magical piece of serendipity.

'Could you tell us how James died.' He asked, rather abruptly.

Collins handed the picture back to Bollinger and then picked up his coffee, sitting himself down in the chair opposite Anderson's chair. He sipped.

Shelby could see he was thinking hard and using the coffee to stall.

He sat down back in his own place and waited. Bollinger and Anderson retook their seats a moment later.

'Right.' Collins eventually said. 'Something's going on; *you* didn't know about James' death,' he said, pointing at Shelby and Bollinger. 'And you're definitely not here to do me for some kind of donor-card crime, and the look on *your* face when I walked in the room,' he continued, looking Shelby in the eye, 'was something akin to fear, you were at the ready at least. And to top it all, you did and thought all of that while thinking I was James.'

He dropped his cup to the table loudly. 'So why don't *you* start by telling *me* what the hell is going on?' He shouted, pointing angrily. 'James wasn't my brother, but he might as well have been. What's going on?' He asked again, clearly worked up now.

Shelby lowered his eyes and sighed.

Seven years he had been attached to Finn, seven years he had chased a demon, a shadow, a voice on the wind. He had forgotten that Finn was actually a man.

He had detached himself so much he had made him into a phantom even when he now knew he was real; the snarling man in the mirror was still a human-being, a soul lost somewhere with a past left behind.

'I apologise, Mr Collins. Please.' He said, and gestured with his hands for peace. He would be damned if he would tell the man to calm down. 'I really can't tell you anything much at all about our case but I do understand where you are coming from, so please forgive my insensitivity.'

Collins froze and then slowly relaxed, sinking back into his chair.

Without another word, Shelby pulled out the picture of Finn in the mirror and held it out for Collins to see.

He sat bolt forward again, snatching the picture from Shelby's hand. 'Oh! God! Oh! God!' He mumbled. 'That's James, that's James.' He was visibly shaking, his eyes disbelieving. 'Oh! Christ! Where did you get this?' He asked, looking up at them both. 'I don't care what it looks like in the picture, James is the kindest and most caring soul you would ever want to have on your side.

'I've seen that look for real, in town one night. A big feller punched his own missus to the ground, knocking her out. James went mental and leathered that man, gave him a right, old kicking.

'I can guarantee that whoever or whatever is in the line of his fire there is doing something that would enrage any, normal person.'

He sat back heavily, staring at the picture. 'Oh! Christ!'

Anderson, who had been silent all this time, sat forward himself now. 'So James isn't dead? And not only that, you're hunting him, Interpol are hunting for him, which can only mean he's done something really terrible.'

Shelby and Bollinger remained silent.

'I understand, I understand; you can't talk about the case.' Anderson said, waving his hands in submission.

Bollinger shrugged. 'You can tell us now, how did James Deere die?' She asked. 'Or not as the case seems to be.' She added.

'He committed suicide; threw himself into the sea, left a note here at reception.' Anderson replied.

'Why here?' Asked Bollinger.

'I assumed it was because he worked here; he was a nurse, one of our best. After the death of Samantha-.'

Bollinger held her hand up. 'Sorry; Samantha?'

'Yes, Samantha, his daughter. Poor girl. She died quite suddenly when she was only eight, brain aneurism.'

Both Shelby's and Bollinger's heart sank; a piece of the puzzle falling into place was always a rewarding and satisfying feeling but not when it was such a sad piece.

They were both thinking the same thing; this was the catalyst to Finn's appearance.

'I think we need to start from the beginning.' Shelby said. 'Tell us everything you know about James Deere.'

## Chapter Ten

Fifteen miles north of Hartlepool and the land rolled away, covered in lush, green forest, mainly pine and spruce.

Off the road and down a dirt track heading to the coast, brought you to a cluster of small houses; old fishermen cottages from the early nineteenth-century.

Shelby's car looked more than conspicuous parked outside one of them.

He and Bollinger stood on the path and looked at the tall hedgerow, a tall, cast-iron gate set into a perfect green arch stood closed and clasped.

Looking through into the front garden they saw everything was neatly pruned and the two, small lawns at either side of the stone path were neat and trimmed.

'So this is where he lived.' Bollinger piped up. 'I wonder who lives here now.' She wasn't convinced that coming here was of any use.

'I wouldn't have bothered coming here at all if I'd have thought someone was actually living here.' He said, sounding disappointed.

He had expected to find a run-down house, dislocated from its surroundings and forgotten. He was wrong. Strangely, he didn't feel wrong.

'You expected it to still be empty after all these years?' Bollinger asked.

'If there is one thing I have gleaned from working the Finn case, Sophie, is that nothing is going to go as expected.' He replied.

He scanned the front area and the small, unlit porch. 'I'd be willing to bet that if we try the door it will be locked and there will be no answer if we knock. I would also bet that we could sit on the doorstep all week and not see another soul come down that path. In fact, I would go as far as to say we could wait all month before we saw anybody come here.' He said, turning to face Bollinger again.

She stepped up to the gate and peered inside; Shelby had seen something. She stepped back.

'Two empty bird-feeders, a clear layering of the grass around the wheels of the bins where someone has frequently mowed but missed, indicating that the bins haven't been moved in a while, which by extension means there is no rubbish coming from the inside of the house, and lastly the upstairs windows all have their curtains drawn.' She said.

'Nicely said and quickly spotted.' Shelby replied. 'Let's get inside and look around the back.'

The gate opened with a squeak. They walked down the path, the silence was incredibly acute, like everything back beyond the hedge was in a time apart, speeding past while here even the air seemed to be locked motionless in a single, never-ending moment.

Absolutely nothing stirred, not a lark in the sky or a sparrow in the hedge; life had left this place, leaving behind only the frozen memory of a long-gone happiness.

Tony Collins had told Shelby and Bollinger the saddest story leading up to James' apparent death.

\* \* \*

'James 'Finn' Deere! If you don't get your cute, little arse in gear I'm going to sit in your chair and give birth to our daughter right here. D'ya hear me?'

Loud bangs and scraping sounds, drawers opening and closing - the wardrobe twice because he forgot the case.

'Oh! God, help me! I'm coming Caitlin. Where do you keep your damn underwear?'

'I don't need clean underwear right now, my stupid love, if we go any longer I'll only shite myself anyway, so get down here and take me to the damn hospital!' Caitlin shouted, her Irish accent making the command sound both beautiful and alive, as well as full of the promise of certain violence if he didn't get a move on.

James legged it across the wooden landing and leaped down the stairs, his piercing, blue eyes looking wild and round.

Under one arm he had a bra, a rolled up towel, and what looked like a slipper poking out of the end of it.

Under the other arm he held two pillows with her dark-green, satin robe hastily squeezed between.

In his left hand he had the other slipper, a toothbrush, a hairbrush and a shower-cap clenched in his big fist while his right hand throttled a raincoat, a bar of soap, a white hand-towel and a box of panty liners.

Lastly, tucked under his chin were his car keys.

'I'm ready. Have you seen my car keys?' He asked, breathlessly.

Caitlin laughed and stepped close to him, and picked the keys from beneath his chin.

'God, I love you, you big, blonde fool.' She said and kissed him on the lips.

Then pinching his cheek hard, she said, 'now get me to the damn hospital.'

She ended with a slap and turned to the door. 'Drop everything except the toothbrush and panty liners.' She called out behind her.

The small, sterile delivery room felt crowded, Caitlin wanted the peace to be alone with her baby.

James sat at her side as she lay propped up in bed. A screen had been pulled across her middle, shutting off the view of the two nurses and docto, who were still working on her behind it.

She couldn't feel anything at all now the epidural was in place. She had insisted that she wouldn't use it during the delivery, but afterward she had asked for it, the pain in her abdomen only lessening slightly once baby had been born.

She held her close.

James looked down at them both, Caitlin's Celtic, auburn hair flowing over her shoulders and covering their newborn-baby with a silky, dark-red blanket.

He leaned in and kissed them both.

'We did it, James, we made something magical. Oh! Just look at her.' Caitlin said, as happy tears streamed down her cheeks.

She turned her head upward then and looked deeply into James' eyes, caressing his cheek with her soft touch. 'Promise me, my love, promise you will take care of her always, no matter what happens, you must promise me, James.'

James wept. Caitlin knew something was wrong. He tried not to listen to the people working on his wife but he heard their voices all the same; alarmed and frustrated.

'Oh. Caitlin! I promise. I swear on old Maeve's grave herself; I'll always look after our precious daughter, I promise, but don't talk like that, hold on, love.'

His head drooped until it met Caitlin's.

'We have to name her after one of the grandmothers.' She murmured weakly, 'but I'll be damned if it will be mine; Katherine O'Connell was *not* a nice woman. No, we can name her after yours, she was so lovely to us was your grandmother, Samantha.'

Caitlin's hand slipped weakly back to the covers. The noise from beyond the screen became more frantic

James looked around. 'What's happening!?' He shouted.

Tubes attached to Caitlin's arms were trailing a path to the machines which were monitoring her, their electronic faces flashing red in alarm.

And blood. Blood where there should be clean, white sheets, blood up to the elbows of the doctor standing pale-faced behind, blood on the hands and smeared down the fronts of the two, masked nurses. Blood. Caitlin's blood.

'I'm sorry Mr Deere.' Was all the gaunt-faced, young doctor could say.

One of the nurses removed her gloves and walked around to stand in front of James. She made to lean in and take the baby from Caitlin's arms.

'James? Don't let them take Samantha.'

Her voice was very weak and far away now, but he sensed she knew exactly what was going on.

'Don't let anyone take Samantha away.' She said again.

James moved closer to his wife, blocking the path of the nurse. The look he gave her was all the prompting she needed to back away.

He turned and held them both close then. 'I'm here, Cait, we're all here, all three of us, and we're not going to let go.'

His eyes closed and the tears continued to spill down his cheeks.

He kissed her and stroked her hair and face, constantly telling her that he and Samantha loved her and would see her again. 'We will be together always, Caitlin.'

James could feel his wife's heart slowing, beat by slow beat. He felt it first fade and then flag and falter and finally stop.

Caitlin died in his arms, shrouded almost by his pure, unfaltering love while their daughter began her new life surrounded by the same arms and the same love.

He reached down and stroked her tiny cheek and ran his huge finger along the back of her hand. 'Always.' He whispered as he wept.

The seasons passed with the turning of the world, the years flowed by and Samantha grew to be a strong and healthy toddler and then an inquisitive and joyful eight year-old.

It had been hard for James at first. The empty spaces in their home which Caitlin used to fill were a constant reminder that he had lost something wonderful.

Over time though, the new spaces being filled by their daughter took more and more of his attention away from the sadness, focusing him instead on the happiness and joy which he knew in his heart Caitlin would have wanted.

From the very first day of her new life, James told Samantha of her mother, all of her developing years were filled with stories of Caitlin and her Celtic beliefs and background.

A historian at the university, Caitlin specialised in Celtic philosophy, but she didn't simply talk and teach the history of it; she lived it and held true to the Celtic way.

She was a fierce friend and lover, honest to a fault and true-spirited to all of her friends, and she believed deeply in honour and trust.

It was she who had taught James the way of the Celtic warrior and the very reason she had nicknamed him *Finn*; in Gaelic, Finn means *blonde warrior* and in Celt it means *fair*.

She also referred to him as *big, blonde fool* and *straw-head* from time to time, usually accompanied by a slap or punch or two.

From the sidelines she would watch people and point out to James why they were shackled to a fearful existence, telling him that *"It was a fault of man to be both ruler and slave at the same time; rulers of their own little domains and yet slaves to the fear which they themselves have created; the fear of losing everything, the fear of never having enough and the fear that someone else has more than they have."*

She called these people *half-souls*.

*Half-souls* were the people whose lives were in disharmony with their surroundings and their brothers and sisters, Caitlin explained, people who were so focused on surviving that they had forgotten how to live, their very souls were fragmented.

She showed him how to heal himself without the need to use any kind of prescribed drug, using his surroundings and his own mind as medicines instead.

"*Ninety percent of what your body and organs are capable of is hidden from you. Practically everything you need to heal yourself is already inside your body, or at least can be found anywhere around in nature to aid you, but it is your mind which has to tell everything what to do.*

"*Unfortunately most people have minds which are following the illusionist's hands rather than looking where the real magic is happening; within their own minds."*

And one of the greatest gifts she had given him was how to see beyond any veil or subterfuge simply by asking himself one, simple question when faced with any situation. *Who am I?*

"*Simple really, my love, it all depends on how you answer it;*

"*Am I that man who stands idly by while a man is beset by attackers in the street? Am I that man who sees a stricken creature and leaves it be to suffer in its misery? Am I the man who ignores the crying child?*

'*Or am I that man who is free under the stars, a friend and champion of the Universe who holds an honourable obligation to life itself, all life?*

'*Nothing can ever escape your attention if you always answer that, one question correctly, James."*

She shared the magic of the trees and of the flowers and of the small creatures which lived all around. "*Listen with your heart, love, listen and you will hear all of their tiny voices.*"

James and Samantha spent hours just sitting out on the back wall listening to the world hidden from their sight.

'I can hear the bluebells, daddy.'

'What are they saying, Puppy?'

'They're not saying anything, silly!' Samantha's laugh was as bright as sunlight. 'They're flowers.' She giggled loudly.

'Oh! Well! Pardon me!' James said. 'So what can you hear?'

Samantha stopped her laughing and looked seriously at her daddy, her best friend.

She studied his face, his lightning-eyes. He was her protector and she loved him and worried about who protected *him*. 'I can hear them watching us, daddy.' She simply said. 'Everything is watching out for us.'

She took his hand and then turned her attention back to the trees. 'Mummy's in the forest.' She said.

James frowned. 'What makes you say that, Pup?'

'She's in the trees and the grass and the flowers.' Samantha said, turning to gaze at him again, smiling happily. 'I can hear her sometimes. Singing. Singing my name.'

'Oh, she would sing your name, she was always singing, she had a beautiful voice. Her mother used to tell us that just before Caitlin was born she had stolen the voice of a faery, but instead of her mother gaining the beautiful voice, Caitlin had received it instead.

'To the day she died, Caitlin's mother couldn't sing two verses of any song without emptying the room.' James told the smiling girl.

They both giggled.

'Have I got a nice voice, daddy?'

'Oh. Samantha! You have the best voice of all because you were born with a faery-voice, just like your mother.'

James draped his arm around Samantha's shoulder and pulled her close, leaning down and kissing the top of her head.

'Just like your mother, precious.' He repeated in a murmur.

She wrapped her own arms around his waist and snuggled into him. There was no one like her daddy, no one gave cuddles as good as daddy did, she loved the sound of his beating heart, strong and alive.

'I love you, daddy.' She said, and yawned. 'I'm tired.'

James held her closer, dropping his head to rest on top of hers.

'I love you too, Pup.' He said. 'Very much.'

They sat together and watched the sun go down, listening to the sighing forest and singing bluebells while Samantha fell asleep. Fell asleep and never awoke again.

James took Samantha's death very badly and after burying her next to her mother he completely withdrew from the outside world.

He paced the home he had shared first with his best friend and wife, and then with their beautiful daughter, pacing and searching for something. Pacing and listening, searching and waiting, and poor James had no idea what it was he was waiting for.

The house seemed like a parody of his own, empty soul, a shell where the essence of life had once been but was now gone, leaving only a trace and a whisper of things that once were.

The sunsets and the bluebells, the pines and the spruce and the wind which passed through their boughs, the birds in the sky and the creatures in the fields; all were lost to James, nothing whispered to him, the trees didn't sing and he couldn't feel anything watching over him. He was lost and the world had no place for him anymore.

Six months after Samantha had died, a letter had arrived at Rushcliffe Medical, addressed simply *To reception*. It was James' suicide note. In it he said he could find no reason to carry on and then simply signed it with the letter J, but Tony Collins had said it was definitely James' handwriting.

The police searched for more than a week before a beach-comber came forward and handed in a pile of clothes and a pair of shoes he had found early one morning.

Inside the leather jacket they found James' wallet containing all of his identification.

They trawled the estuaries and combed the beaches for miles to the north and south but it soon became apparent that his body must have been washed further out into the harshest parts of the North Sea.

James Deere was pronounced dead, cause of death, suicide, and his case was closed.

Unknown to anyone, on the evening before his disappearance, James had curled up on the sofa again and had fallen into a troubled sleep.

He awoke in the small hours, his shirt clinging to his soaked skin. He had been dreaming, dreaming of somewhere dark and watery; a lair of some unimaginable nightmare beast.

What was it? James snatched at the fragmenting remnants of his dream. Something had been chasing him, a man, a giant who wanted to eat him, and James had escaped into the watery lair.

Cringing in a safe corner, hiding his eyes from the giant as he tried to force his massive body through the small crack of a doorway, and all the while something truly terrifying was already inside the lair with him.

He woke up at that point, his ears still ringing with something, a scream perhaps.

The moonlight filled the living room with a light which most would have found magical.

James sat up and stared for long minutes out through the window and straight into the face of the leering satellite, filling his eyes with its staring glow. They had loved the moon once.

'We loved you.' He whispered. Tears filled his already reddened eyes, flooded his lashes and spilled down his face. 'We loved you.'

His head dropped and his chest heaved as he sobbed. 'I'm sorry, Caitlin, I can't do it anymore.' His sobbing became a wail. 'I can't-anymore.'

He had tried so hard to carry on living, tried *so* hard! But he was outnumbered by the shadows of his happy past and couldn't find the beauty in anything in the present anymore. The beautiful things in his life had gone now, it was only right that he should go too.

He'd been thinking about it for a long time, the only thing holding him back was Caitlin's beliefs in life and the respect all humans, all sentient creatures, should have for it.

But he couldn't face another day of emptiness, a day filled with nothing but tears and heartache. He was dying anyway, piece by piece, he was fading away as his heart broke.

He lifted the half-empty whisky bottle from the floor and then walked heavily up the stairs.

After retrieving his fisherman's bowie knife he made to go into his own bedroom and lay upon their bed, but something made him turn the other way instead and go into Samantha's room.

It was untouched. In fact he couldn't remember if he had been up here since the day she had died or not.

Jezzy-teddy stood lopsidedly on one of her pink pillows staring at him. The furry toy would never feel her arms around him again and he was looking at James as if to tell him that.

Something fluttered inside James then, some tiny connection to the toy Samantha had named Jezzy-teddy and which she loved dearly.

He walked over to the bed and put the knife and whisky on the small table at the side.

Jezzy-teddy was still staring at him.

Lowering himself down to the mattress, James lay down next to the bear and stared back.

Instantly he could smell Samantha on the pillows and reached out, snatching the bear up and holding it close, as close as Samantha would have.

He closed his eyes and breathed in deeply and for the first time in months his mouth curled up into a small smile.

*I found you.*

His mind carried him away on the breath of his daughter as he fell deeply asleep.

When dawn arrived and the sunlight came streaming through the bedroom window, he flicked his eyes open and then sat up.

The whisky and knife were still sitting on the table, untouched.

He picked the blade up and felt its keen edge, his eyes boring into the polished metal, lightning-eyes reflecting back.

In the night as he slept, James Deere had slipped quietly away to search for Samantha.

Finn stared at his own reflection in the polished face of the blade and frowned as the voice in his head spoke.

*We have much to do, Finn of the Seven-Spears and Nine Northern-Stars.*

## Chapter Eleven

Richard Harrison sat back in his cockpit of a computer chair and for one, rare moment he didn't smile or congratulate himself or let his ego be rubbed up by his latest, successful hack. He simply sat and stared at his giant screen and wondered at the upside-down world he was living in.

It was very rare for Harrison to allow himself to be pushed toward anger. The video playing on the screen made him feel furious.

As promised, Harrison had found traces of what they were looking for after only a few hours, but he had told them it would take further programming of his software to keep the pieces coming in.

For the three days after Shelby and Bollinger had visited him he had been working endlessly on a new trace program, specially designed to look for the *e-Highway* routes which the image capturing Finn in the mirror had used.

At each stop which the program made in the trace, it picked up a few more bytes of data, seemingly just random numbers and machine-code, but once it had finished and Harrison had tirelessly pieced each fragment of code back together, eighty-seven percent of a video-file was reconstructed.

Harrison's program had wormed its way into over a million, different computers and proxy-servers.

It didn't matter that the camera-phone which was used to make the video was on a secured, private network; the servers and filters and the proxies which it used always left echoes of themselves; millions of tiny pieces of code scattered for thousands of miles over a virtual-highway.

Nothing was truly private or secure, it was just incredibly hard to find and difficult to reconstruct.

The video began again for the third time. Harrison was sure that he knew the man holding the camera-phone, the man caught momentarily in the same mirror which Finn suddenly appeared in.

"*Yes! Yes, just like that, Joseph, good boy.*"

The dark-haired boy in the video looked up and straight into the lens, a big smile on his face while his eyes were fearful, the way a slave might look at his master as he waited to see if he had done the right thing.

Another boy sat behind, also smiling but lopsidedly with drooping lids. This boy was clearly drugged.

"*Go and pick something from the shelf.*" The man said, panning the camera around to follow the half-drugged boy as he climbed off the bed.

The camera stopped, the man holding it purposely framing himself in the full-length mirror at the side of the bed.

He was naked from the waist up, his skin pale and his paunch of good living more than apparent.

His face was neat and clean-shaven, his brown hair was almost schoolboy cut, parted on the left and brushed over to the right.

As he stood there admiring himself the curtain behind him suddenly parted and Finn came bursting in.

The camera image blurred as the man tried to spin around and face his attacker, but only a second passed before the phone was dropped to the floor, face-down.

The image went almost black but the sound still could be heard, sounds of a choking, dying man.

The next sound was the shuffling of feet; someone moving around in the room, and then the distinctive, Irish lilt of Finn's voice said; *"You're safe now. I found you, you're safe."*

More shuffling and moving about, heavy footsteps, and then the quiet creaking of the bed as someone climbed off it came next and then finally the soft padding sound of bare feet walking out of the room.

After that there was another fourteen seconds of silence before the loop began again.

Harrison pressed a button on the keyboard sitting on his lap, freezing the video on the image of the man as he admired himself in the mirror.

He thought he knew him from somewhere. 'I know you, I'm sure of it, but from where, man?'

Those murmured words, words which if had remained unsaid would have seen Harrison's life go well beyond the seven minutes he now had.

'Very clever, Mr Harrison! Amazing! Simply amazing!' A voice said, loudly from the shadows where Harrison's old arcade-machines stood.

The man who had once called himself Detective Brown stepped from between two, large, gaming machines, brushing himself down with his leather-gloved hands.

'It was like watching a Maestro with an orchestra.' He continued to praise. 'You, sir, are a genius.'

'Thank you. Who the fuck are you?' Harrison responded, as he raised himself slowly from his seat.

'Oh! Don't be like that, Mr Harrison.' The man said, looking pained. 'Let's just say that I am a *friend*.'

'Really? I don't feel comforted by that at all so you'll forgive me if I don't welcome you with open arms.'

'Oh! And quite right too, I suppose; I didn't say I was *your* friend after all did I?' Chuckled the man. 'No, I'm *his* friend.' He said, pointing to the still-image of the half-naked man on the screen. 'And before we go any further, Mr Harrison, you must understand that the distance from where you are now to the door behind you is too far to run before I pull out my pistol and shoot you.' He shrugged as if to say *sorry about that*. 'So please let's not go down that path, eh? You have what I want, I'm going to take it and leave anyway,' he shrugged again but left the threat unsaid.

'Well. I never expected to come across a paedophile who had balls.' Harrison smirked as he said the insult.

The man standing before him dropped his fake smile and the look of the killer he was, was all that remained.

'I am not like him,' he almost hissed, 'I abhor the world that he goes to-,'

'Went to.' Corrected Harrison, staring hard.

The man blinked. 'Whatever. The difference is null,-'

'I thought you said you were his friend?' Harrison butted in again.

The man sighed. 'Rhetoric, Mr Harrison; purely by extension of the connections which the organisation I work for have to him, you see?' He said, the fake smile back in place.

Harrison had been trying to realign the control more in his own favour but he had it back now. 'As much as I would like to continue playing this game, time presses, so we will get to the nitty-gritty shall we?' He said.

He put his hand in his pocket and produced a Walther fitted with a short muffler, pointing it first at Harrison and then at the computer he had been sitting in front of. 'How many backups did you make of that?' He asked.

'If you were standing there you will have seen that I haven't made any copies of it yet, it's still sitting on the flash-drive there.' He replied, and nodded to the small, black stick which was wired up to the consol.

The man frowned. He was normally excellent at spotting a lie, or a truth for that matter. What Harrison had just told him looked to be both.

He pointed the pistol at Harrison again. 'I'll ask you again; how many backups are there?'

Harrison smirked again. 'I thought you saw what I was doing and understood it, a *maestro* you said. Well if you only understood half of what I was doing you would know that I haven't had a chance to make any copies.' He folded his arms, waiting to be shot.

The man just continued to frown and look at him.

Again it looked like Harrison was lying and telling the truth at the same time. It was true though, that he hadn't seen any attempt to make copies elsewhere. 'Very well, I'll take your word for it.' The man said. 'Unplug it please.'

Harrison sighed inwardly, he thought he was going to be shot as soon as the man came to the conclusion that he was telling the truth, which he was. Almost. *He* hadn't made any copies or backups of the video; the *network servers* he employed for his cyber-life had made automatic copies of everything. Just a little safeguard he had coded himself.

He unplugged the flash-drive and held it out to the man.

'You keep hold of it for now.' The killer said. 'Upstairs if you will.' He pointed the gun at the door behind Harrison.

Harrison turned and led the way back up to the living-area above.

At the top of the stairs he turned abruptly and walked backward, keeping his wary eye on the man with the gun.

'Please, Mr Harrison, you're making me feel guilty.' The pained expression returned. 'If I were going to shoot you, don't you think I would have done it by now?'

Harrison said nothing.

'Don't worry, I'll only shoot you if you try to do something stupid or don't do as you're told.' He said, casually. 'Over there please.' He continued, waving the gun in the direction of the patio overlooking the channel.

Harrison did as he was told and pulled the doors open and stepped out onto the wet boards.

The man stepped up to his side, the gun pointing at Harrison's chest. 'Now, if you don't mind I would like to see how far you can throw that drive out into the sea. Go on, give it your best lob.' He said, grinning.

Harrison turned to face the channel and then threw the small, black stick as hard as he could out over the balcony.

The two men watched as it sailed and then dropped, making the tiniest of splashes as it hit the water below.

'There! I feel better already, don't you, Mr Harrison?' The man said. 'Now, if you would be so kind and step up to the railing please.' The gun pointed the way once more.

Harrison took a step closer and then faltered. On any normal day he would love the view, and the drop lying underneath wouldn't bother him. Right now though, the soles of his feet were throbbing with the thought of the dreadful heights beneath them and a cold shard of terror made his heart beat too fast.

'Keep going.' The man and the gun encouraged.

He reached the rail and gripped it tightly with both hands; if the gunman was thinking of throwing him over he wouldn't go without a serious fight.

He flinched as he heard the man's footsteps on the boards behind him. They stopped and Harrison listened as the patio door was slid open again.

'I'll leave you now, Mr Harrison, I'll ask you to stay there with your hands on the rails and admire the view for, oh! Let's say, fifteen minutes, shall we?'

Harrison's relief was a flood of giddy emotions, the view was actually quite lovely. 'Fifteen minutes it is.' He answered, trying hard to sound as casual as he usually was.

'Goodbye, Mr Harrison.' The man chuckled and stepped back inside.

At his feet on the left, standing outside on the patio, was a trough of collected rainwater.

On the right stood another trough, this one empty. It was a wonder that Harrison hadn't thought about why the boards were soaked when there had been no rain for the past week.

The killer kicked the full trough over, splashing the water over the boards, allowing it to pool around the feet of the unsuspecting Harrison.

At the same time he flicked the switch to the lights outside and giggled stupidly as Harrison's body stiffened with his hands clasped tightly around the metal guard-rail.

The hacker's back arched unnaturally and it looked as though he were trying with all his might to stand as high as possible on his toe-tips and rip the rail clean off.

He shuddered and trembled and occasionally gasped, but apart from the singing electricity everything was quiet. Quiet enough to hear the seagulls and the hushing waves.

The man admired the view, it was a beautiful day.

He looked at his watch and then back to the now steaming and smoking form of Harrison. 'Ping!' He called gleefully and flicked the switch back off.

Harrison crumpled to the deck as every muscle in his dead body relaxed at the same time.

His hands were blackened and blistered, lines of livid red ran up and down his arms like rivers of blood running through charred skin. Blood trickled from his mouth, nose and ears.

'Excellent!' The killer said, clapping his hands together and rubbing them briskly. 'Now,' he said, quietly.

He turned and walked unhurriedly, whistling quietly as he went, making his way back down to the basement rooms and going straight to the circuit breakers again.

One of them had a six-inch, steel nail in the fuse slot and was blackened where it was making the connection.

He pulled it out, hissing as he did, and blew on his gloved finger; it was still very hot.

He let the nail drop to the floor and then replaced the proper fuse back in the slot, closing the box again and making his way back upstairs.

Now humming, he switched the lights on again, immediately causing the fuse to blow.

Finally he removed the wires he had running from the light socket to the handrail and replaced the bulb back in its slot.

He stood over the still-steaming body of the unfortunate Harrison and looked down, smiling.

'See? I told you I wouldn't shoot you if you did everything I asked. I am a man of my word if nothing else, Mr Harrison.'

With a final look at the splendid vista of the blue sky and grey-green channel, the killer buttoned his coat and went back inside, walking straight back out through the front door.

Instead of following the proper pathway back to the main house and then through the front gates, he disappeared amongst the hedgerows and made his way to the eastern wall. There he climbed over and dropped into the moorland at the top of the cliff.

A good day for a walk and a whistle he thought, as he made his way back to his car some four miles away. A good day indeed.

\* \* \*

"*The best laid plans of mice and men, often go awry.*" Harrison's favourite saying and usually accompanied by; "*well, I'm neither a man nor a mouse in the cyber-verse; I'm a god, and even a god needs a backup plan, my man.*'

Harrison had a backup plan for everything, it was one of the reasons he was so successful at staying out of the hands of the authorities.

Twelve hours after he had been murdered, seventy-two alarms were about to go off, seventy-two members of *Code-8* were about to receive an emergency signal straight to their mobile-phones, a coded message for them all to get to their workstations.

Every member had a single task to complete in the event of their leader's capture or demise.

They would clean the path which could lead to themselves and then re-establish a new network which cut him out entirely, ensuring the overall safety of *Code-8* and its cyber-elite members.

Some of the members had tasks which saw them withdrawing large sums of money from banks all over the world and then stashing it in safe locations until either the air cleared or they opened new accounts.

And one member had the task of contacting Sophie Bollinger.

Harrison may not have liked the fact she was an Interpol inspector, but he knew she was aware that he wasn't the *bad guy* and that if something truly bad happened to him, she would do everything she could to find out what, why and who.

Bollinger sat at her desk compiling a list of cleaners and cleaning companies in Hartlepool.

Yesterday's visit to James Deere's house had led both herself and Shelby to believe that someone was entering the building at least once a month and cleaning the place. Someone certainly was tending to the garden.

They hadn't entered the house to take a better look; they knew James hadn't been back there since he had left over seven years ago, but they did leave a note with their phone number written on it, asking whoever it was who was visiting to get in touch with them.

Bollinger's job at the moment was trying to speed things up a little by contacting the various cleaning services in the area.

As she copied the address of the seventeenth company she had found into a separate file her phone rang.

She picked it up and flicked the display open, the number was showing as withheld. She hit the cancel button and got back on with the task in hand.

She didn't need any insurance or double glazing, and she had never taken out a loan or entered a competition; callers who withhold their numbers were usually trying to sell you something.

It buzzed again. Same withheld status. She cancelled it again.

Her phone continued to ring for another ten minutes, every twenty seconds or so, and then stopped. She had twenty-nine missed calls, all with the withheld status.

Her email pinged. She opened it, a message from someone called *Fux Ake*.

*Answer your fucking phone!* Was all it said.

'Oh.' She murmured as her phone rang again. She picked it up. 'Hello?'

'*Fucking hell! Did you really think someone selling insurance would be so fucking persistent? Jesus! Harrison said you might be difficult to get hold of but he didn't mention you being thick!*' An angry, male voice shouted.

Bollinger held the phone away from her ear until he'd finished. 'Well, I don't suppose a sorry would help, would it?' She asked, once he had.

There was a pause, then the crackling, white-noise rush of a deep breath being expelled far too close to the microphone exploded from the ear-piece.

'*Fine! I'm sorry.*' The voice said. '*We're in a state of emergency right now and I'm a bit worked up.*'

Bollinger looked confused. 'I meant an apology from me to you for not answering my phone quick enough, but you know? You did fly off the handle and call me thick, so let's just say we're now both on the same page and get on with it. Why are you calling me and how do you know Richard Harrison?'

'*Something's happened to him, we don't know what, but the emergency alarm was blasted out to us an hour ago. We've gone through the procedures as Harrison set them and he isn't responding. It's my job to tell you that.*'

'By "us" you mean *Code-8*, I presume?' She asked.

'*Well who else would I be on about?*' The voice snapped back, irritated.

'And who are you?' She asked, ignoring his outburst.

'*You don't need to know that, all you need to know is that Harrison trusted you enough to be included in his emergency procedure. I've done my job.*' The voice said, still sounding irritated.

'I could just trace this call, you know?'

'*No you couldn't; you know Harrison, you know* Code-8, *you know how good we are. Your trace will take you well into the next century before it even returns the first digit of my masked number.*'

Bollinger was now getting irritated herself, the man was beginning to smack of Harrison's own smarm. 'So what else can you tell me about this "emergency"?'

'*Nothing. Like I've already said; my job was to contact you and let you know that something serious has happened to Harrison, that's all. I will say this though; the emergency procedure can only mean one of two things; Harrison has been kidnapped or he's dead. That's how serious it is.*'

Bollinger bit her irritation back then. 'Sorry,' she said, and meant it, 'I'll see what I can find out. How will I contact you if I do find anything?'

'*You don't. We'll know what you find if you find anything. Good luck.*' There was a click and the line went silent.

She flipped through the contact list on her phone and then auto-dialled Harrison's number. It connected and went straight to his message box.

'Shit!'

She dialled his house number. After several rings it too went straight to the answer-phone. 'Shit! Shit! Shit! Where the hell are you?' She mumbled to herself.

She dialled another number, Shelby's. 'Gray?' She said, when he answered. 'I've just had a call from a member of *Code-8*. Something's happened to Harrison, we've got to go back to his place in Hastings.'

'*What's happened to him?*' Shelby's phone-voice asked.

'They don't know, but an emergency alarm which Harrison had set up in case something ever happened to him was triggered, and I was part of the plan he put in place.' She said.

'*Okay, Sophie, wait for me there, I'll be back in around an hour. We'll go straight to Harrison's and see what's going on.*'

Bollinger bit her lip. 'I've got the worst feeling about this, Gray, it feels more than just coincidence.'

Shelby was silent for a moment. '*I hate to say it, Sophie,*' he eventually said, '*but I agree; our visit with the picture of Finn and now Harrison's alarm going off are somehow connected.*'

Although he didn't say it, Shelby was thinking about the man who had been powerful enough to order a policeman to destroy vital evidence. Was he powerful enough to reach out and destroy the evidence which they had given Harrison?

Shelby didn't think this was about the image of Finn, this was about something Harrison had found later on. He had promised he would look for more of the video and now it seemed as though he may have been successful. Like Bollinger had said, it was just too coincidental.

'I'll keep on searching for cleaning companies in Hartlepool until you get back.' She said. 'Bring me a sandwich up when you go past the *canty*, would you? I'll eat it on the way to Hastings.'

'*Okay. See you in an hour, Soph.*'

They hung up, Bollinger sat back in her chair and threw the phone back on the tabletop.

She just knew something really bad had happened to Harrison. If it had then it was a great loss on so many levels. Once past the man's incorrigible arrogance you discovered a human-being with a penchant for revealing great injustices, a little too cavalier for some people maybe, but his quest was never born of the need to make himself rich; it was as much to reveal the corruption and wrong-doings as it was to polish his own hacker's-ego, but never did he do it for personal, material gain.

A rare quality in a man nowadays, Sophie had often thought.

She brushed her hair back out of her face and sighed. They would know soon enough if something truly terrible had happened to her old flame.

In the meantime she kept her mind's wanderings in check and continued with her cleaning company list.

Here was another one, a small, private company by the looks of it, running from home. Out of all of her finds so far, this one was less than a mile from James Deere's house.

She put the number at the top of the list and then went back to the search page.

'What if?' She mumbled to herself.

She stopped her search again and sighed and went back to the number she had just found. It would be far too good to be true if she got a result from it, but it was very close to where James had lived, there may be chance that someone there actually knew James, Caitlin and Samantha.

She reached for her phone and dialled the number. After a short pause and a few rings it was answered.

'*Hello?*' The woman on the other end asked.

'Hello. My name's Sophie Bollinger, is that *Star Cleaning Services*?'

'*Yes, it is, I'm Gwen, how can I help you?*'

'Hello Gwen. I'm looking into buying a house on Sealcrest road, number forty-three.' Bollinger lied. 'I'll be wanting to hire a cleaner to come in maybe once a week, I see that you're just down the road from there.'

'*Forty-three? I know it, I clean there already, that's the Deere's place.*' The woman called Gwen said, sounding surprised. '*So he finally sold it then.*' She continued.

Bollinger couldn't believe her luck. 'Who sold it?' She asked.

'*Mr Deere. I'm not surprised really,*' she replied, '*he hasn't been back there for nigh on six or seven years at least, I'd say. Poor feller, I don't blame him.*'

'Are you sitting comfortably, Gwen?'

'*Um. Yes?*' Gwen replied, sounding puzzled.

'Good,' Bollinger said, sitting back in her chair, flipping her notepad open and taking a pencil from the jar of assorted pens and pencils on the desktop. 'Because I'm going to need you to tell me everything you know about Mr Deere and how you came to be his cleaner.' She finished.

## Chapter Twelve

Pale sand-dust billowed from behind the speeding motorbike, whipping past Finn's legs as he careered onward heading from west to east across the northern border of Iran.

Davar had, had the foresight to include a pair of children's swimming-goggles with the gift of the motorcycle which Finn was now wearing over the top of the white, cotton scarf he had tied around his mouth and nose.

As he had set off, after the warm farewells from Davar and his large family, Finn had suddenly understood just how easy it was for an ancient man on a peddle-bike with purple parasol to end up in a place like this.

He felt ridiculous with the pink, square, plastic goggles over his eyes. The four, small, yellow and white daisies stuck to the rims doing nothing to help the appearance. On the bright-side though, at least he could see where he was going.

Two days had passed. The motorcycle, being a four-stroke, handled the journey well.

Davar had given Finn two cans filled with extra fuel which he still hadn't needed to open just yet, but looking at the cracked fuel-gauge he could see the tank was now on its reserve.

Some distance ahead and way off to the left of the dusty road, Finn could just make out the dark shapes of shady buildings. He could rest there, but a small nag at the back of his mind told him to not approach it from the road.

Slowing down a little, he veered off straight into the north, making a line for the mountains ahead.

After thirty minutes of riding across the arid landscape he turned immediately right again, bringing the buildings back on line and making a slow beeline for them.

With just a few miles between him and the buildings, Finn stopped the bike and killed the engine. He sat in the seat and watched.

It looked like he was approaching a small settlement, only it didn't seem like there was anyone living there.

He un-slung his backpack and pulled a pair of hi-definition binoculars from one of the zip-pockets.

Bringing the lenses to his eyes, he scanned the buildings ahead. They immediately snapped into clear focus, the digital readout in the eye-piece telling Finn that the target was 4.2 miles away.

He was right; it was a village and it looked to be abandoned. Not an uncommon sight, but usually the buildings were in one stage of decay or another, or they were truly broken and left crumbling.

This place had all of its roofs still intact and even the stone wall and the small herders-gate looked to be undamaged. Maintained even.

*She's there.*

She had been distant for the past two days, quietly thinking in a corner of Finn's mind.

'It looks to be abandoned.' Finn muttered back, keeping the binoculars up to his eyes.

*You don't need me to tell you about surface appearances, Finn. She's there and you need to go and find her.* There was steel in her voice.

Finn dismounted the motorcycle and wheeled it over to a slab of grey rock, leaning the machine upright against it.

'I'll walk down and have a look.' He said, squinting into the dying rays of the sun. 'If she's there, I'll find her.'

*She's there.*

Finn shuddered as the steel in her voice gently stroked the nape of his neck. She was right, he knew she was right, she was always right.

He looked ahead again at the quiet village. On that premise that she *was* right, Finn wondered why someone was going to such great lengths to conceal their presence out here in the middle of nowhere. It could only mean trouble, whatever the reason.

He opened his backpack and removed his silenced pistols; a pair of Russian, gun-metal black PSS's which he slipped under his baggy, white garments and into their holsters on his protective shirt.

They came along with a complimentary knife, simply designated NRS 2, which went into its own, small scabbard on his left calf. The knife had a single shot capacity in the handle which could be replaced with a field survival kit if necessary.

Lastly, after concealing his twin stiletto blades in their sheaths on his hips, he fastened two, small grenades to his belt.

*Have you ever heard of overkill, my love?*

'Better to be safe than sorry; something doesn't add up down there, someone is trying hard not to be noticed.' He replied, while he pulled his belt taught and fastened it off.

He kept his local clothing over the top of his specialist clothing and then set off, loping gracefully, pulling the earth beneath his feet rather than moving himself across the ground. The difference was subtle but effective, a trick his mistress had taught him, one which had seen him run almost tirelessly for hundreds and hundreds of miles over the span of his wanderings.

Less than thirty minutes later and he was standing behind a rocky outcrop.

A hundred yards of open ground lay between him and the outer-wall. The ground had been cleared with a purpose; no one could approach without being spotted first.

The sun was dropping rapidly away on his right, its shadows drawing longer and longer.

A sudden flare of sunlight in the window of one of the abandoned buildings made Finn pull out his binoculars again.

He found the window and zoomed in. There, in the corner of the unglazed hole in the wall, sat a shiny, black camera.

'Someone's definitely at home and they're watching the door.' He muttered.

He walked back the way he had come for about a hundred yards and then began the shallow climb up the rocky hills surrounding the village.

Staying low, he made his way back again, creeping to the edge of the rise he was climbing and peering over. The extra height gave him a much better view of the village layout now.

From where he was, Finn could see that the village ran back into a gully of rock, and chiselled from the rock itself was a huge cave. The glow of light-bulbs inside cast a sickly, orange light across the grey, chipped rock-face.

He looked through his binoculars again, adjusting the lenses to keep the shadows brighter without flaring the light-sources.

Instantly, a dozen or so men became visible through the greenish tint of the binoculars.

They were working along a long bench filled with tubes and bottles, glass pipes and alembics, and spread across the whole table top were hundreds of tiny, white packets with mounds of grey-white powder being carefully sifted into each by the men.

All of them were naked from the waist up and they were all wearing an expensive, breathing device over their mouths and noses. And more importantly - to Finn's mind at least - they were all big and all were armed with small, sub-machine guns.

Not a simple, local, gangs hideout this; this place was established and well maintained and run by someone with an ordered mind.

'Heroin smugglers.'

*Yes.*

'Heroin smugglers with muscles and machine-guns.'

*Yes.*

'There's twelve of them down there, we can easily double that number and say that the rest are inside somewhere.'

*Probably even more given the size of the cave.*

Finn's lips tightened and an eyebrow raised. 'You're not helping.' He said, quietly.

*It really makes no difference what I do, whether I am helping or not; you're still going in there and bringing her out.* She responded icily.

Finn could feel the sudden warming of her anger. 'But there's too many!'

A sharp crack across his mental jaw sent Finn stumbling sideways.

*Cuchulain killed a host with nothing more than a rowan branch and a loincloth!*

Finn rubbed his jaw and then frowned hard. 'Well bloody Cuchulain can make me *his* hound if he can show me how to kill a host armed with machine-guns!'

He felt her breath close to his cheek.

*Fair point, but pointless nonetheless; she's there and you are going to find her. If there were seven hosts of Formorians and their spell-weavers lying in that cave, you, Finn of the Seven-Spears and Nine Northern-Stars, you will still be going in there.*

'But I'll die! And then-!'

She had him by the throat then, her clawed hand holding him by the hair while her jaws clamped down around his neck just enough to stop his words and his breath. Like a deadly lover's embrace.

*I don't want you to die, my love, but if you* are *going to die then it will be when I release you and not before,* she almost purred.

He could feel her tongue tasting the flesh of his throat, kissing him almost.

*You will go and find her, or I will hold you're geis forfeit and you will never come home. Green isles or bloodied rock, Finn?*

He dropped to his knees, gasping as she released her hold on him.

*Quickly! Look to the setting sun!* She suddenly ordered.

Finn looked, the dusty sandscape seemed to have no ending. 'I see nothing.' He said, still rubbing his throat.

*Use the glasses, hurry!*

Finn looked through the binoculars, setting them at their highest zoom and slowly scanned the horizon.

The distance still seemed to be endless, the edge of the horizon itself shimmered under the glare of the low sun.

A sudden white flash caught his eye. He focused on it. It wasn't anything distinguishable, but seeing as the binoculars were telling him that the white dot was ninety-six miles away he wasn't surprised.

'What is it?' He asked.

*The cavalry,* was all she said. *Go there and show them the way.*

Finn lowered the binoculars and stared, eyebrows raised, impressed. He wouldn't argue, she knew something, had scried something out, he would know soon enough.

After returning to the motorbike and filling the fuel tank, Finn set off in the direction of the white pinprick in the distance. Pink, floral goggles firmly back in place.

It took almost three hours of careful riding across the broken, sometimes sandy, sometimes rocky desert, but once he was within half-a-mile of the dot, which now showed as a carefully constructed barracks of some kind, Finn stopped the bike and dismounted.

The sun wouldn't last for more than another fifteen minutes, he would have to act fast.

As soon as he had seen the armoured truck entering the tall gates and he had realised that the buildings were military, Finn had formulated a quick plan.

He knew he couldn't just march in there and tell them about the cave and the smugglers; once in amongst an armed platoon - which is what he was hoping to gather - there would be no chance of getting away from them again. His only option would be to make them follow him.

Walking slowly as though he were worn out, Finn pushed the bike the last eight hundred yards toward the garrison, keeping himself in perfect view of the watch-tower.

The guard had seen him and was stood watching, looking through his own binoculars.

Finn kept his head down and eyes raised, the guard didn't seem alarmed and just waited patiently for him to get closer.

Over to Finn's left stood a gnarly, leafless tree. He pushed the motorcycle over to its broken and scant shade and propped it up.

Huffing and puffing, he walked out and on to the entrance, stooping like an old man. He raised his arm to the guard in the tower and called out a wheezy *Salâm* without looking up.

The guard responded and then enquired as to why an old man had such a large motorbike.

Finn laughed and wheezed and pointed to the large gate set into the stone archway.

The young man in the tower scoffed and shook his head and turned away from the window to make his way down to the gate.

As soon as the he had disappeared, Finn, quick as a flash, pulled the grenades from his tunic and tugged their pins free.

He counted to three and then rolled them at the gates and then quickly turned around and dashed out of the grenades' range.

They exploded with a quick double-bang and the gates shattered inward, leaving a hole smashed in the middle the size of a shed.

Finn legged it back to the motorcycle while the guard in the tower had obliviously trotted down the steps to talk to the foolish old man about his bike.

He was halfway down when the grenades went off and so was the first through the gaping hole in the large, wooden gates.

He sprinted to the corner and raised his machine gun at Finn, who by now was kneeling to the left of his motorbike and the tree with his pistol held out in front of him, waiting.

The soldier pulled his trigger and a ragged, sharp burst of fire cut the air, filling it with a half-dozen bullets which flew harmlessly over the tree Finn was kneeling beside.

Finn slowly released the breath he had been holding and then squeezed his own trigger once.

The guard jerked as his right shoulder was pierced by the hot lead. He screamed and dropped the semi-automatic rifle as he took a staggering step backward and then fell in a dead-faint to the sandy ground.

'Time to go.' Finn said, to himself. So far so good.

While he pulled down his pink goggles and started the bike's engine, the diesel roar of a war-machine engine accompanied the crashing sound of the breaking gates as the twenty-ton, armoured vehicle he had seen entering the garrison came hurtling out.

The man on the turret-gun spotted the fallen tower-guard and shouted something down to the men inside. When he looked up again he saw the dusty trail and red taillight of Finn's motorbike receding into the night. The chase was on.

Speeding away, weaving a path between small rocks and pebbles and boulders and sometimes rusted-out vehicles, Finn was wondering if he had actually bitten off more than he could chew.

He hadn't counted on a monster, armoured truck picking up the chase. He'd guessed they would have sent out a truck full of soldiers and maybe a jeep or something, but a fully-armed and complimented piece of war-kit was something else.

The roar of the engine drowned all sounds of his own bike's engine out; a deep, menacing growl, roaring along behind on chunky tires and semi-halftracks.

If Finn had wanted, he could have used his binoculars as night-vision goggles and simply turned his lights off, but the trick was to not lose them until they were right in the cave.

At the rate they were going, he didn't think they would be long in reaching it; they were travelling much faster than Finn had been on his journey here.

It was all he could do to hold his concentration together and avoid hitting any of the bigger, rocky obstacles which were scattered everywhere and all around.

More than an hour-and-a-half passed of this cat and mouse chase between motorcycle and armoured truck.

Twice Finn had found himself cringing as he heard the mounted machine-gun fire out a few rounds in the vain hope of hitting him.

His eyes narrowed when a tracer-bullet zoomed high over his head like a tiny, red comet, arcing over and dropping back to the earth before the red glow died out.

He began to wonder if he had strayed from his path and had missed the village in the cleft, but no sooner had that thought entered his head the small, wooden gates which marked the entrance appeared in the beam of his lights.

The wooden struts of the herders-gate were no match for a sixteen-stone Finn on a motorbike.

With a single, loud crack the wood exploded outward and was hurled around in all directions, Finn had to cover his face with his arms to stop the deadly flurry of needle-sharp splinters from tearing his face and neck apart.

He smiled to himself as he felt the tiny, wooden shards breaking on his protective clothing.

He turned the bike and steered straight for the cave. He could see a group of men standing at the ready, peering out into the night and wondering at the lights and the din.

Pulling the brakes hard, he dropped himself and the bike to the ground, sending it into a sideways slide which came to a halt surrounded by dust and exhaust smoke, a few feet from the cave and the men.

Turning away, he pointed to the gates behind him, shouting; 'The army! The army is here!' In almost-perfect Farsi.

The men quickly showed the extent of their training by immediately forming into three groups of four.

Finn wished he had saved one of the grenades now.

The armoured truck came crunching to a halt fifteen yards from where Finn lay, spraying dust and stones in the air as the pneumatic brakes squealed.

Finn took the chance to jump to his feet and run straight into the cave.

The men ignored him and concentrated on the vehicle in front of them instead.

Inside, the cave didn't go much further back before it ended at a wall with a normal, door-sized hole in it.

Drawing his pistols, Finn darted through the carven doorway just as the mounted gun on the truck erupted, roaring out its deathly presence with it's uniquely, terrifying voice.

The air was suddenly alive as hundreds and hundreds of firefly tracer-bullets ricocheted around the cave, while the hundreds more bullets without the burning trace-material could only be heard and not seen.

The table and its contents were ripped to pieces in a second. White, chalky puffs and plumes of the forbidden powder, rose like miniature eruptions.

The twelve, armed men ran to the covering edges of the cave entrance, one man from each group automatically covering their retreating comrades with quick bursts of their sub-machine guns.

Either the man on the mounted gun was unlucky, or the men inside the cave, including Finn, were very lucky; so far none of the bullets had found a living target.

Finn ran along a short passageway which exited to another, larger cave. Inside, structures and living quarters had been erected along the walls, leaving a wide natural courtyard in the middle.

Finn darted behind one of the wooden buildings and crouched down on his haunches.

The fire-fight outside had dropped to a moderate exchange now as both sides dug-in and formulated their plans of attack.

He waited and listened.

A door was thrown open and then another and another as the men inside the buildings were woken from their rest and came running out to help with the fight.

Finn counted another seventeen, armed men run past his hiding place next to the doorway they were all running through.

Once he was satisfied that no one else was going to run past, he stepped out and looked around at the buildings which had their doors opened. There were two buildings at the back of the cave which had closed and barred doors.

*There!*

Finn loped down the steps and then sprinted to the two, wooden shacks at the end of a row of other shacks which some of the soldiers had been occupying.

The windows were barred and the doors had a wooden plank dropped through steel hoops across their fronts, preventing them from being opened from the inside.

He quickly pulled the planks away and then threw the doors open one at a time.

There came a chorus of gasps and low moans and whimpers.

Finn stared as bodies beneath covers stirred and sat up, shielding their eyes from the light.

Both buildings were nothing more than an open room with basin and toilet in one corner and a row of eight, single beds along both flanking walls.

There were seven young women in the first, the youngest being fifteen, and the second building had six females inside, the youngest here was only twelve.

Finn walked amongst them, peering at them solemnly and stroking their tearstained and afraid faces. 'You are safe now.' He told them all. 'You are going home.'

The last bed he came to had the youngest child sitting upright beneath her cotton sheet.

He stood at the foot of her bed and looked down at her, smiling. 'I found you. I've been looking for you.' He said.

He lifted the child from the bed and held her closely to him. 'We're going home.'

Carrying the shaking girl, he walked out, gathering the rest behind him and leading them back to the opening. Once there, he released the girl he was carrying and then huddled everyone away from the hole in the wall.

'Wait here. You will know when it is safe to go out.'

The eldest of the group, a young women in her early twenties, approached Finn.

She had lines of experience on her drawn, grey face where lines such as those had no right to be present for at least another twenty years.

Her dark eyes looked up into Finn's own. She could see the sky there, and let her tears flow like the rains which she imagined would fall from it.

'The sky.' She whispered.

Finn looked at her, reached for her face and stroked her tears away. 'The sky is yours, child, live freely beneath it.'

He looked at them all again then, both frowning and smiling at the same time, before he turned away and drew his pistols once more.

There was still a lot of sporadic gunfire coming from the cave outside, but it wouldn't be long now before the army used its superior firepower to push the heroin smugglers back into this area.

Finn raised both barrels and knelt inside the small passageway. He didn't have to wait long.

Two of the smugglers suddenly appeared in his sights. They both dropped in forward lurches, one on top of the other, as each bullet found its mark in their foreheads.

Finn leaped up and sprinted to the other end of the short, man-made corridor of rock; another smuggler who had been running behind the first two had seen his comrades drop like boned fish and had quickly darted away to Finn's left.

Skidding to a halt, Finn kept himself concealed from the man he knew was around the corner waiting for him to run out.

He quickly lay down on his stomach and then rolled onto his side. After taking one deep breath he extended his arms and pushed his pistols out through the doorway, pumping the triggers four times each.

The beginnings of a yell came to Finn's ears which was then abruptly silenced, followed by the distinctive crumpling and thudding sound of a body hitting the floor.

He pushed his head out to see what had happened. A man lay on his front, a pool of dark blood gathering around his torso and head.

One of the shots had hit him in the chest while another had torn through his throat, cutting off his cry and then killing him instantly as the bullet shredded the back of his skull.

At the front of the building Finn counted nine more, dead smugglers and outside lay a dead soldier.

Behind the fallen soldier a four-man group of soldiers crouched, covering the entrance with their rifles.

To either side of the entrance, inside the cave, stood two, full squads of four smugglers on the left, while a three-man group on the right stood with another squad of four.

All were taking cover behind the stacked crates and boxes of heroin which were waiting to be shipped out.

Twenty-seven of the twenty-nine men were accounted for; that left two which Finn couldn't see any signs of. Leaders most likely, or at least one leader and his right-hand man. That meant there was another way out; fat-cats always had a means of escape.

The air was thick with the powdered narcotic and every surface inside the cave had a thin layer of the stuff covering it, including the men.

Finn couldn't see much through the thick haze, but far over to his right, well away from the entrance and almost hidden completely in the shadows, he could just make out a steel ladder running up the wall. It didn't seem to go anywhere but he knew that there was another way out up there somewhere.

The shooting had all but stopped now. Finn waited for the inevitable surrender to get underway.

He kept himself on his stomach and well inside the small corridor, watching as the commander of the platoon of Iranian soldiers came marching down to stand behind his four riflemen, eight more soldiers fanned out behind him.

A small, thin man with a serious face and equally serious, thick moustache, the commander stood with his hands on his hips, legs apart; dramatically superior.

Finn studied him; he was serious and well trained; good signs that the released women and children would be cared for and returned to their homes. But he wouldn't leave just yet, he wanted to measure the man by his next actions, watch him as he dealt with the roundup of the rest of the smugglers.

'What in the name of God, are you men doing here!?' The small, commander barked. 'Ten wasted lives are laying right there! Why?' He shouted, angrily pointing. 'That young soldier had a family! Those dead comrades of yours had families, *you* have families, so I ask you again,' his voice lowered, 'what are you men doing here? Are you dying or are you living?'

Finn smirked. Nice piece of diplomacy.

The air was still and quiet as the hiding men thought about the commander's words.

One of them, standing on the right, looked down at one of his dead partners lying at his feet still clutching his bloodied chest. He shook his head and then stood upright, steeling his jaw. 'We're coming out!' He shouted, and then threw his weapon out onto the ground in full view of the soldiers outside.

He took a wary step into view and faced the commander.

'Good.' The small man said, and nodded his head in approval. 'Sergeant?'

A big man standing next to the commander stepped forward, drew his pistol and pointed it at the man who had stepped out.

'Over there! Move!' He ordered, flicking the gun to indicate he should stand in front of the bodies.

'Order the rest of your men out.' Said the commander.

The man sighed and walked to the spot he had been told to stand, looking both left and right at the men still hiding behind the crates. 'Do it.' He said.

One by one, the men threw out their weapons and walked out to stand with him, he seemed to have some command over them but didn't look to be a leader.

The four soldiers kneeling outside jumped up and moved forward, stopping with rifles cocked and raised, aimed at the fifteen men standing in front of them.

The commander walked up to the first man who had thrown his gun away.

'A sensible choice.' He said.

He looked around at the dead. 'Did you know these men personally?' He asked, turning back to face him.

'No. Not really.'

'I see. Well, I know all of my men, I make a point of knowing them, getting close to them. They are like my own sons some of them.' He said sincerely. 'Hamed, over there,' he said, indicating the fallen soldier, 'he was our youngest, our baby brother.'

He stepped closer to the man and stared at him hard and cold. 'Why is our baby brother lying dead on your doorstep?'

The smuggler didn't respond, he could sense the menace and the pent up rage. He could also sense the very same thing which Finn had divined; the commander was well trained and took his job seriously.

He wouldn't help him lose his cool by saying something stupid, especially something like *sorry*. Better to be silent and let training win out.

'By rights I should line you all up now and shoot you; you are heroin peddlers and the sentence is death, you know this.'

Again, the smuggler didn't respond in any way, he merely blinked and waited.

Finn, now crouching in the shadows behind a wall of boxes, held his breath, also waiting. Waiting for that defining moment when the actions of the small commander would tell him whether he could leave the young women in his custody or not.

The commander looked each man hard in the eye before returning his gaze to the first smuggler.

He sighed. 'But I won't.' He eventually said. 'If I shoot you I defy the two things which should be at the very fore of every man's soul; God and law.'

Finn breathed out. It was safe to leave. Well almost; he still had to actually get himself over to the ladder. All eyes facing this way would easily see him if he darted out now, he would have to stay put and wait.

The commander questioned the smuggler for a few more minutes, asking about the operation and who was running it and if there were anymore of the gang hiding inside.

The smuggler answered the questions, telling him that all of the men were either standing in front of him or they were dead. He said nothing about the missing two men or the girls.

Finn's mind saw the commander's next move before he himself had even thought of it.

He quickly turned and ran back down the passage and back to the waiting huddle of young women. Stopping in front of them, he whispered to the oldest of them again. 'It's safe, you can leave now, but if I am seen I will have to fight and kill your rescuers. Do you understand?'

The young woman nodded.

'I need you to lead them all out now, before the army comes down here.'

He stared at her and then smiled a little. 'You can do it.' He said.

She nodded again and then turned to the rest of them, telling them to stay together and hold hands.

They walked past Finn, looking up as they each came near, marvelling at his scarred face and bright, blue eyes.

Moving noiselessly in a huddle, the girls walked out into the cave beyond, Finn creeping up on his haunches behind them.

As soon as they were clear of the doorway the huddle made its way to the left, making a beeline for the waiting soldiers.

Finn remained at the corner in the shadows and watched.

Each soldier turned and looked at the thirteen young women and children, the commander's face became a scowl; he knew what they were and why they were here. He gave the men standing in front of him a withering look of disdain.

'My laws and my faith are being sorely tested today.' Was all he said.

He turned away and gestured to one of the soldiers standing behind him. 'See if they are in need of medical attention, Cali, and then get them into the truck.'

The medic responded by trotting over to meet the huddle of girls. He removed his medical-kit from his shoulder as he dropped to one knee in front of them, turning his attention to the youngest first.

Still watching from the corner of the doorway, Finn waited until the medic began leading the girls outside, while the soldiers marched the smugglers out to the buildings to wait to be transported.

It was now or never.

Twenty feet in front of him stood a stack of crates, miraculously still standing upright. Heroin spilled to the floor from the myriad bullet-holes peppering the fragile, wooden boxes.

Finn darted behind the stack and crouched down again. He peered around the edge.

Nothing was amiss, the girls were still walking out with the medic and the soldiers all had their focus on the backs of the smugglers walking out on the other side of the cave-mouth.

Staying low, Finn sprinted to the next stack of boxes, a forklift-truck standing with its forks raised was parked behind the stack.

He crept around the vehicle to the other side and then checked the progress at the front again.

The smuggler who had surrendered his weapon first was looking him right in the eye.

Finn's heart lurched as he readied himself to attack, but the big smuggler merely held his gaze for a second more before shaking his head slightly and turning away.

Like the dog in the cave back over the border, Finn felt something had passed between them, an understanding; the last act of honour from a doomed man maybe.

He watched him as he walked away, noted his pulled back shoulders and high-held head. Whatever had just happened, the man at least thought he had done the right thing.

After a final look at the retreating huddle of girls, Finn dropped back into the shadows and crept to the ladder.

Looking at it he couldn't see it leading anywhere that looked like an escape route, but two men had escaped somehow and there didn't seem to be any other way out.

What if he was wrong though? He would be caught quickly if there was no way out down at this end of the cavern.

*Climb.*

He took a deep breath and did as he was told.

Almost at the very top he felt a breath of cold air caress his cheek.

A patch of grainy rock caught his eye and he pressed his hand up against it. It pushed inward; not rock, but a canvas patch crudely coloured to resemble the rock-face. From below the camouflage couldn't be seen at all.

He raised the flap back a little to reveal a small crawlspace leading off into blackness.

Quietly, he pulled himself inside and crawled on all-fours until he met more rock in front of him. He could feel cool air coming from his right, the tunnel continued this way, rising gradually.

His big frame pressed into the rock as he moved slowly along; palms and knees beneath him and back and shoulders above and to the sides.

Any normal man would have felt the weight of the rock pressing him down and the claustrophobic space would have gagged him with rising panic, but Finn was anything but normal.

He pushed himself into the space ahead claiming it as his own, pressed the rock back and kept it firmly in its place.

A few minutes later and he could just make out the dim, purplish glow of the night-sky coming from the small exit leading out onto the cliff-side.

He pulled himself through the hole and then remained crouched on his haunches, surveying the slopes and the ground below. There was no sign of the two men who had escaped.

'We've lost the bike.' He muttered.

*Maybe not.* She whispered back. *Move further up and make camp. Who knows what tomorrow will bring?*

## Chapter Thirteen

Bollinger hated wearing her firearm, hated the whole procedure of signing the damn thing in and out of the armoury, dreaded the day she would return it with a bullet or two missing.

If there was ever an indicator to the state of the world, being issued a gun to go out and do a job was at the very top of the list.

It wasn't about guns killing people, or even people *using* guns to kill people; it was the fact that there was the *need* to use guns and kill people in the first place.

Guns: the overused, overcompensated response to difficult, social problems; Bollinger looked forward to the day when education became the weapon of choice.

'Everything okay, Soph?' Shelby asked.

'Gun.' She replied, without looking at him.

He said nothing and looked back to the house, Harrison's house.

He knew how Bollinger felt about carrying her gun, he could remember holding the very same feeling himself for years until one day he had to shoot and kill someone.

After that? He still didn't like guns and what they represented, but until *everyone* felt the same way he did he would not allow pacifistic morality to get in the way of putting someone down who threatened life with *their* guns. Like it or not, there was only one way to fight that kind of fire.

They walked down the gravel path along the side of the big house and made straight for the guest house overlooking the channel. Neither the main house nor the guest house had any signs of life showing.

'It looks like that alarm of Harrisons didn't include calling the local police.' Shelby muttered.

He stopped. 'Drawn weapons from here I'm afraid, Soph.'

Bollinger nodded, agreeing, and drew her pistol from its holster beneath her jacket.

They made their way to the double patio-door and looked through into the room beyond.

The fridge-cum-door leading down into Harrison's tech-lab was standing fully open. Then simultaneously, both Shelby and Bollinger gasped as they looked through the rear patio-doors and saw the charred remains of Harrison.

There was no mistaking the man by his dress.

'Shit!' Bollinger hissed. 'What the hell happened to him?'

'It looks like he was electrocuted,' Shelby replied, 'and I don't believe for an instant that it is merely a coincidental accident.'

'Me neither.'

She pulled the patio-door closest to her and it slid open a fraction. She looked at her partner and then waited.

After Shelby nodded she pulled it open all the way, stepping quickly inside and making for the top of the stairs to the lab.

Shelby covered her from the door while she peered over the top.

'Clear.' She said, and remained standing with her gun aimed down the stairwell.

Shelby crossed the open room and made straight down the stairs, stopping at the bottom with his weapon aimed into the lab beyond.

'Clear.'

They continued like this for another, five minutes before they were satisfied there was no one else in the building.

After re-holstering their weapons they went back up to examine the body.

'It's definitely electrocution.' Shelby said, as he knelt by Harrison's side.

He stood up and pointed to the railing. 'He was holding onto the handrail when it happened.'

'Lightning?' Bollinger offered, scanning her gaze over the length of the railing, looking for any tell-tale signs that lightning had touched down here.

'Possible,' Shelby shrugged, 'but I don't think so. We haven't had any storms for months and I can't see any strike marks on the railings. Unless it struck him directly, which is a possibility I suppose.'

'But you still don't think so?'

'No, I don't.'

Shelby traced his fingers over the metal rail all the way from one side to the other. He stopped beneath the wall-mounted lamp attached directly above the rail. The bulb was blackened.

Without a word he marched off back down to the lab, Bollinger hot on his heels.

At the far end, screwed to the centre support-post, was the fuse-box and circuit-breakers. Shelby opened it and pointed to the blackened fuse socket.

'This is where the power came from, the fuse is clearly marked as the upstairs lighting ring, but for that to happen to Harrison would mean the power would have had to been going through him for minutes; the fuse would have blown almost instantly.'

Bollinger stooped down and picked up the six-inch nail which the murderer had used to foil the fuse-box. 'And I would be willing to bet it was this that was used to replace the fuse.' She said, handing the nail to Shelby.

He examined it and sure enough there were signs that the metal had been super-heated at two, specific points.

He held the nail up to the fuse slot and the marks on the nail matched the contact-points perfectly.

'I think our powerful man who tried to get rid of the phone in Turkey has extended his reach.' He said, turning back to Bollinger.

He looked at her sympathetically; she had liked Harrison, and even though she wouldn't say it, she would feel some responsibility for his death.

They stood in silence for a moment before Bollinger nodded and said; 'If he has, and it is the same man, then he is more powerful than we are giving him credit for; Harrison was almost untouchable, some of the smartest people in the government agencies, world-wide, have been looking for him and getting nowhere.'

'Well, we can't rule out that this is someone else's doing but it's murder nonetheless so I suggest you go back to base and report it to the local police when you get there. That will give me some time here to look through the lab and see if I can find anything-.'

He stopped mid-sentence and whirled around, striding over to Harrison's main computer console.

'Damn it! The phone's gone.'

He was mentally kicking himself for not noticing it earlier. 'I think we can almost say for a certainty that our powerful man has indeed extended his reach.'

He sighed and dropped his head, leaning over the consol-top with his knuckles pressed firmly into the Formica surface. 'We should have stayed with Harrison, one of us at least.'

Bollinger placed a hand on his shoulder. 'I was thinking the same thing, but being on home-soil led us into a false sense of security, Gray.'

Shelby stood up, nodding slowly. 'You're right of course, we underestimated the situation, but no more. From now on we must include no one else while we follow whatever trail it is we are following.'

He stood up straight and faced Bollinger. 'You go back to base and call the police, I'm going to see if I can find backups of any data which Harrison may have been working on.'

His eyes widened. 'Oh! God!' He moaned. 'Kevin!'

He pulled his mobile phone out and pressed the quick-dial button for Kevin Keys. The phone rang for a few seconds before being answered.

'*Hello, Graham.*' Keys' faraway voice piped up.

'Kevin, hi. Listen, are you at home?'

'*Yes, why?*'

'Good, stay there. Have you any security with you?'

'*Sean's with me. Is everything alright, Gray?*' The note of anxiety in Keys' voice couldn't be missed.

'Yes and no, Kev: Yes because you're okay and you have a man with you, and no because one of our men has been murdered and the phone stolen.'

'*Oh! God! No. What happened?*'

'I can't go into details, you understand? But let's just say that the breadcrumbs which have been thus far leading us to Finn have now opened up a completely different can of worms.'

'*Right. And you think whoever murdered your man may try and come for me? But that's insane! I don't know anything!*' Keys was clearly worried now, panic edged his words.

'You'll be okay as long as you keep a man with you until all of this is sorted out, but to be honest, Kevin, I think the very fact that you don't know anything will keep you well out of harm's way.'

There was a pause and then a deep, wavering sigh. '*If you're sure, Gray.*'

'I am. Don't worry. I'm certain your man O'Keel can handle anything anyway, just keep him with you, eh?' Shelby said.

'*Okay, I will.*'

'Call me if anything's amiss. I'll speak to you later, Kev.'

'*Will do, Gray, and thanks for the heads-up. See you later.*'

The two men hung up.

Shelby put his phone away and turned back to Bollinger. 'I'll see you back at base in a couple of hours, Soph. Do us both a favour and don't sign your firearm back in just yet.'

Bollinger nodded. 'Okay. I'll call you every thirty minutes until you're back.'

She left while Shelby settled himself into Harrison's cockpit of a seat. He had no idea where to begin other than starting with the 'On' switch. Where *was* the 'On' switch?

The whole consol in front of him was almost featureless; except for the socket on the retractable cable which was drawn out, the panelling and desktop were devoid of anything resembling a switch.

He pulled the socket and the cable drew back into its housing, the socket flicking up and sitting perfectly in its place. It was almost invisible now, and if Shelby hadn't known it was there he would have missed it until he inspected it more closely.

He sat forward and began peering along the ridges and edges of the sleek, white consol, looking for any sign of other hidden panels.

He ran his fingers along everything, inspected the huge monitor, dropped to his knees and looked underneath the consol, the chair, even the carpet, but there was no 'On' switch to be found.

The chair protested quietly as Shelby's big frame slumped back down into it.

Harrison's magnifying goggles rattled from their resting place on the backrest of the chair. He picked them up and examined them, still looking for the damn 'On' switch, but at the same time being childishly inquisitive.

He put the frames over his head and brought the lenses down. Everything became suddenly enormous and well detailed.

He raised his hand and marvelled at the clarity and detail of every single pore and hair and the leather-like creases of his knuckles.

He dropped his hand and scanned the consol again through the magnified view now.

A myriad of tiny blemishes and scratches were scattered like tiny road-networks all across the top, especially in front of the seat.

A flash of movement pulled his eye to the right

He swivelled his head just in time to see a large shadow detach itself from the ceiling above the wall of old video games.

Through the magnifiers, Shelby thought he was looking at a living shadow, an enormous, dark thing which cast no reflection or shadow of its own.

He scrambled to his feet, dragging the goggles up at the same time, his heart leaping in his chest.

The enormous shadow he had been looking at, now appeared as a tiny, black-clad figure which came hurtling toward him, landing a firm kick to his jaw once it arrived.

Shelby's head snapped to the left and he dropped to the floor in a daze.

His assailant dropped onto his chest while he was still trying to figure out what was happening.

He immediately snapped into focus when he felt a thumb pressing dangerously hard beneath his right eye.

'I know who you are, and I know you didn't kill Harrison, neither did I,' a female voice with a German accent said. 'But someone did and it was because of something Harrison was doing for you, Mr Interpol.'

Shelby blinked. 'Oh crap! You're *Nova-bug* aren't you?'

The head behind the black mask cocked to one side. 'Very good, I'm impressed that you knew that.' She replied.

'I know it's probably a stupid question, but what are you doing here?'

Shelby blinked again, his right eye was beginning to water and ache from the pressure of the little woman's thumb.

'You're right, it is a stupid question. If you know who I am then you surely know what it is that I do.' She wasn't asking a question.

'All I really know about you is that you are Harrison's second-in-command, you deal with the *physical* side of things,' he gulped when he said physical, 'and it feels like you have a thumb made of steel-encased lead.'

Although he couldn't see it, Shelby felt her smirk. The pressure beneath his eye relaxed a little.

'I'm going to leave now, I have what I came for and you will not try to follow me.'

Shelby nodded his head a little. 'What did you come for, if I might ask?'

The pressure returned as the little woman leaned forward, bringing her cloth-covered nose right up to his. 'The very thing you were looking for, Mr Interpol; the backup drives.'

'But we need those to find Harrison's killer, not to mention the case he was working on for us. Somehow they're tied together.' Shelby almost pleaded.

He didn't think she would do him any harm, but he instinctively knew he was no match for her; her reputation as a fighter preceded her like a legend.

'Even if I *did* let you have these drives,' she said, sweetly, 'you wouldn't get anything from them without the correct decryption. If you made one mistake with one, wrong password and key you would end up with a runny pile of melting alloy and plastic.'

Shelby felt her smug smile. Were they all so bloody arrogant?

With an uncanny grace and speed, the woman calling herself *Nova-bug*, suddenly stood up and leaped to the stairwell.

She stood poised on the bottom step, bathed in the fast-dimming rays of the sinking sun filtering down from the open room above.

'I will be in touch, Mr Interpol, I promise. Until then you will find the switch to turn on Harrisons computers underneath the battery-panel on the goggles.'

Shelby just stared, round-eyed - one of them watery - and slack-jawed.

'Thanks.' He manage to mumble, stupidly before she flitted silently up the stairs.

He stayed put and listened, waiting for the doors to slide open or to hear footsteps running across to the back patio, anything, any sound at all to tell him he hadn't just imagined his encounter with yet another legend.

All he could hear was the silence of the room and the distant hush of the waves outside.

He almost had a heart-attack then when his phone buzzed loudly from his pocket. He snatched it up, it was Bollinger.

'Soph.'

*'Just checking in.'* Her voice said. *'I've pulled into a services to get a sandwich. How's it going, have you found anything?'*

'No, but I now know there is definitely a backup system which has more than one drive to hold the data; I've just had a run-in with *Nova-bug*.'

*'Who?'* She asked.

'She's Harrison's second and his security, proper security, as in the physical stuff. She's bloody good at it too, Soph; she had me pinned with just her thumb!'

*'Right. Shit! Are you okay?'*

'I'm fine, a little shaken from the crack across the jaw, but I'll be okay.'

*'So have we lost our only lead or is she on our side?'*

'She's only loyal to *Code-8* and Harrison,' he said, 'but I'm almost certain that if and when she finds what it was he was working on for us, she'll get in touch as she promised me she would before she disappeared.'

*'Okay, as long as you're sure you're alright, Gray. We might as well call the police now then; the quicker they arrive the quicker you can be back at base.'*

'I'll call them from here, I'll probably only be an hour behind you.'

*'See you in an hour then, I'll call again in thirty minutes anyway, but let me know when you're on your way.'*

'Will do, see you shortly.'

He closed his mobile and slumped back to the floor, staring at the ceiling. The mischievous frown and smirk of 'The Cowboy' as played by Clint Eastwood, looked down at him from the cinema poster of *A Fistful of Dollars*.

'"I don't think it's nice, you laughin'."' Shelby quoted. '"You see, my mule don't like people laughin'. He gets the crazy idea that you're laughin' at him."'

The Cowboy's eyes were hard and unflinching. Shelby held the gaze and stared back.

'Who's laughing at us?' He muttered.

Someone had their tack on them but who and more importantly, how?

There was still the distinct but remote possibility that Harrison had been killed by someone completely unconnected to the Finn case and the phone.

Shelby didn't think so, but until he received word from *Nova-bug*, he wouldn't second guess either. He had to be certain, now more than ever.

He sat up and retrieved the goggles by his side before standing up and flicking the switch at the back. Just as Nova-bug had said, the computer whirred into life, the large monitor crackling with static as it switched itself on.

After a few seconds of watching the psychedelic, boot-up sequence, Shelby was presented with a flashing, red cursor sitting at the edge of the screen, obviously waiting for a password or command to be put in to get it going.

He sat down and waited.

Harrison was a very clever man, so much so that Shelby suspected he would have a destruct sequence in place once the alarm had gone off. A wrong password could be devastating, but waiting could do no harm other than wasting a little time.

Exactly three hundred and sixty-five seconds after the cursor had appeared, the computer clicked as the hard-drive started up and the screen went black, taking the cursor with it.

A heavy-metal riff began to play, fading in from silence, a mournful serenade to a dead man played on the wailing strings of an electric guitar.

The screen flickered again and a video appeared, the strings cried themselves back into silence and Harrison sat back in his chair, legs crossed and hands casually on his knee.

'*I like that,*' he said. '*One of my dear friends wrote that for me.*' His eyes wandered to look up in thought. '*Wonderful, Peter, a brilliant piece of digital-wizardry, my friend.*'

He turned his attention back to the camera. '*It would seem that the alarm has been triggered and that can only mean something dire has happened to me unfortunately.*'

He sighed and smiled resignedly. '*No matter,* Code-8 *will carry on with or without me. The backups will have been recovered, so whoever you are watching this, be it police or the manufacturer of my disappearance, or just someone who wandered in off the street, there is nothing left to be found.*'

He grinned then. '*Even as we speak and this video is playing, the hard drives and most of the memory modules are being melted by acid.*'

The smell of chlorine and bitter-lemon suddenly came to Shelby's nose as Harrison finished his sentence.

'*If I were you I wouldn't stand too close, the vapours will sear your throat and lungs if you breathe them in for long enough.*'

Harrison sniggered and made a gesture toward Shelby's left, indicating the stairs. '*The air would be fresher over there.*' He said, grinning.

Shelby jumped to his feet and stood in the stairwell. Harrison seemed to be looking right at him.

'*Much better over there don't you agree?*' He said. '*And since you are on the first step back to the top, I will say farewell now. But before I go,*' he leaned closer to the camera. '*If you are someone who knew me, knew me well enough to care, then I would ask you to do everything you can to bring the perpetrator of my disappearance to justice.*' He said, and his face had no hint of a smile now as he stared seriously into the eyes of Shelby through the camera.

'I will try.' He said quietly. 'I promise, I will try.'

And the video blinked out.

## Chapter Fourteen

Paran; a modern village with a population of less than a hundred people in twenty families.

Finn studied it through his binoculars as he stood behind the line of trees surrounding his camp. It was still some thirty miles away, but the Japanese military lenses brought everything into crisp detail.

The houses all had bright, red roofs and walls of either white or bright yellow. The Mosque was all yellow and stood almost at the centre, the tallest building.

Since leaving the cavern of smugglers, Finn had travelled along the lower slopes of the mountain range spanning northern Iran, effectively keeping himself out of the way of most of the populated areas.

Once or twice he had, had to stop and walk, pushing the miraculously recovered motorbike past small settlements and villages scattered in the wilder lands, but on the whole he had made good progress.

He was on the last tank of fuel now and needed a village just like Paran to refill the cans which Davar had given him.

He hadn't expected to be needing more fuel; he didn't think he would be using the bike to travel, but while he was still navigating the mountain slope after exiting the escape-tunnel, he'd heard the diesel hum of a truck and then the very distinctive growl of the armoured-vehicle start up. Both vehicles then drove away into the night, headlights bouncing over the pitch-black landscape.

Once he had found his way back to the outer wall and the houses, it became apparent that the commander had decided enough was enough and had left everything until they could come back when it was light Finn had presumed.

And there, lying exactly where he had left it, was Davar's motorcycle, completely overlooked, or at least its significance not being immediately apparent.

Only once the commander had interrogated the smugglers would he realise that the man who had shot one of his guards and blown up his gates was still at large.

Finn wasn't about to disappoint and set off as soon as he had checked that the bike was undamaged.

He lowered the binoculars and stood leaning against the tree.

There was plenty of fuel in there and it was pretty accessible but unfortunately situated right in the middle of the main square which was brightly lit.

'Great.' He muttered to himself.

His journey still had at least another thousand miles to go before he reached the southern border leading to Afghanistan. He wasn't overly bothered by the distance and how he would cover it, but the bike was a luxury he couldn't easily give up

Even though he had given himself three weeks to cross Iran unnoticed, he was pretty sure he could make it in ten days with the bike. That would give him plenty of time to reconnoitre his target once he crossed over.

Just a few gallons of fuel would see it happen.

Turning away, he made his way back to camp, mulling the puzzle over in his mind.

At most other out-of-the-way settlements this far north, there would be no wired connection to the outside world, a radio probably, but no telephones.

Paran was surrounded by telegraph poles, their wires streaming off to attach themselves to the buildings inside the ring, connecting the small village to the country's main infrastructure.

*You must not go in there, my love.*

The she-wolf's velvet words caressed Finn's mind. When she was this gentle he knew she was genuinely afraid for him and he always took notice.

'I know. I won't, but it's a sore trial to leave the bike.'

*Rest the day and see what the night brings. There are many vehicles down there, perhaps there will be one left unattended and within reach?*

'Perhaps.' Finn mumbled.

He knew why she didn't want him to enter Paran, could feel her thoughts flicking to the very same memories he himself was remembering and the old wounds which itched beneath his shirt.

Nevada.

He felt her shudder.

*Never will we be caught like that again.*

Nevada. The first time he had nearly died and his quest ended, simply because he had failed to stick to his rigid code of staying unnoticed.

\* \* \*

"So what brings you to our little town, honey?" The redhead waitress asked, smiling as she refilled Finn's empty coffee-cup. "Panaca aint exactly 'on the map' now is it?" She added dryly, casting a tired look out onto the empty street.

"Just passing through." Finn replied, and smiled back.

"If I saved a dime for every time I heard that I'd be livin' on the streets." She said, and laughed. "A town as small as Panaca doesn't usually attract many tourists and passers-by." Her eyes twinkled.

*Finn could sense the woman's eagerness for information, an inquisitiveness born of small-town boredom.*

*Fifty-two year-old Glennys Hanagan, knew the lives of everyone here.*

*Everything was so predictable. The days played out like a well-oiled clockwork-machine, populated with well-oiled clockwork people. So a stranger in town and sitting in her small diner was a little more than just a different face. And what a face! And those eyes! Eyes which had seen the whole world by the looks of them.*

*She stood and lingered by the table, coffee-pot held loosely by her side.*

*Finn felt uncomfortable under her gaze and looked away out of the window and across the empty street.*

Speak to her! She's already suspicious, speak to her!

*Finn flinched inwardly at the command and then turned back to the waitress.* "I've just returned from overseas," *he said, a small look of uncomfortable pain in his eyes.* "A small town is the best place to find a little peace." *He finished, and looked away again, embarrassed this time. Embarrassed because of the lie he had just told.*

*As intended, the waitress instantly mistook his embarrassment for a returning vet's humility and painful memories.* "Bless ya' honey, I hear ya'!" *She said, and leaned in and squeezed his hand tightly.* "Now, you drink your coffee in peace and I'll go and fetch you a slice of the best thing you will ever taste this side of the state line!"

*She stood back up and grinned.* "In fact, for a big fella like yourself I'll bring two slices." *She said, and wrinkled her nose as she turned away to scuttle off behind the counter.*

*Finn's embarrassment was furiously apparent in his cheeks. He hated to lie to good, honest people, and he could see that the woman called, Glennys, was high on the list of noble and honest spirits in this world.*

Don't dwell upon it, Finn, leave it be.

*He shrugged his big shoulders and huffed, slowly shaking his shaggy, blond head.*

*Behind him the door opened and the clear, polished note from the brass bell hanging on the frame announced the arrival of another customer.*

"Afternoon, Glennys." *A deep voice said, as the door closed*

*Heavy boots walked passed Finn sitting at his table.* "Am I too late for the special?"

"The special is always on for you, my darlin'." *The woman's voice piped up.*

*Finn looked up from his coffee-cup and watched the tall, heavy-set man stroll up to the counter and perch himself on one of the stools. By his dress, Finn thought he was a construction worker.*

*The man turned his way and nodded.* "Howdy, fella." *He said.*

*Finn nodded back and politely returned the greeting.*

"I don't think I've seen you round these parts, you new in town?" *The big man asked.*

"Just passing through." Finn said.

He drained his cup and stood up, strolling to the counter as he drew a bundle of creased-up money from his pocket. The same question asked twice was too much, he had to leave and get back on the road.

"On the house, honey." Glennys said, and then handed him a white, paper bag. "Two slices as promised." She smiled.

He took the bag without looking up, guiltily unable to meet the honest woman's eyes. "Thank you." Was all he said, before turning to the door and making his way outside.

All the way, he could feel the eyes of the big man on the back of his neck.

Main Street was almost empty as Finn made his way to the border of town. Rattlesnake Point was where he was heading and then from there he would make his way through the wild lands and onto the next task, the next town, the next killing-ground.

The day wore on. Rattlesnake Point came and went. Finn made his way along a lumber trail through the mountains, following the stumps as they paved the way northward.

As the light began to fade and he made mental plans to make camp for the night, the hum of an engine coming up the track behind caught his ear.

He stopped and looked back. A Black, four-wheel-drive truck was making good progress across the land, using the same track as Finn.

Get off the road.

He didn't need telling twice. Quickly scrambling up the slope to the tree-line, he stepped inside the deepening gloom of the forest still-standing and watched from behind a tall tree as the truck came quickly up the slope and then passed by in front. He couldn't see the occupants through the tinted glass.

As the tail-lights disappeared around the bend, the she-wolf stirred.

I don't like it. There is discord in the air, in the trees, in the very ground; something's not in its place.

"I feel it too." He answered quietly. "A confusion of wrongs, aye."

She isn't here, Finn of the Seven-Spears, but something is, something is waiting for us.

When she referred to him by his title, Finn knew he had to be at his sharpest.

"Aye." He whispered again. "There's death on this road, that's for sure; even the trees are afraid and too quiet."

He dropped to his haunches and stayed tightly pressed to the tree he was hiding behind, watching the road and the bend where the truck had gone.

He could still hear it, very faint now and getting quieter by the second. He hadn't heard it stop so it was highly unlikely that anyone had left the vehicle and was waiting in the shadows ahead. Unless someone had got out behind before he had heard it approaching.

At that very thought three things happened at once; his hackles suddenly rose, the she-wolf bristled in his mind and a hiss followed by a searing pain in his thigh sent the already darkening sky quickly through the remaining gray palette to the pitch of night. No time even to pull out the dart in his leg, the last thing he saw.

Time had passed, he could feel it, but didn't know how long. His head throbbed a little as his mind began to awaken. He kept his eyes closed and his body still, focusing instead on clearing away the smog which seeped in and around his thoughts.

He was sitting on a chair, there was a stench in the air; a smell of unclean bodies and blood in a dirty hay-barn was Finn's first thought.

He moved his fingers then his hands, they were bound at the wrist by something which felt like steel wire, the ends of the wire itself were twisted around the back of the chair.

He tried his feet, they were also tied tightly to the legs of the chair.

Next he became aware that he wasn't alone; he could hear the sleeping breath of someone on his right. He opened his eyes then and slowly raised his head.

He was in a dimly-lit room, there were no windows, the walls were bare bricks and mortar and the front wall was made entirely of iron bars, a little like the old-style, western jail-houses.

He looked to his right and saw the sleeper; a tall man, Afro-American by the looks, who was in the same predicament as Finn; drugged and tied to a chair in a makeshift cell.

The man's clothes told the story of a homeless soul; those people destined to wander under the stars, those people who had the greatest understanding of the universe than most and yet were rewarded by watching those who knew very little take everything for themselves.

Finn's attention was suddenly snapped away as a door opened in the corridor outside the cell and a fat, wheezing man appeared carrying a steel bucket in his hand.

He walked straight past the cell and made to go through another door at the opposite end of the corridor. He stopped in his tracks when he saw Finn was looking right at him.

"Holy sh- Cal! Cal! Get down here." He shouted over his shoulder.

Heavy steps quickly came down wooden stairs and then the man from the diner appeared through the doorway. "What the hell are you yelling about?" He said, as he approached the fat man.

When he saw he was staring into the cell, the man called Cal, turned to see what he was looking at.

Lightning-eyes sent a sliver of cold through his chest as Finn calmly gazed at him.

"He's supposed to be out for another six hours!" The fat man said, his eyes wide with fright.

"I know that!" The man called Cal, said, irritated. "Maybe he didn't get the full dose or sumthin'."

He studied Finn, looking for signs that the drug was still in his system, but it seemed by the way he was looking at them both - calm and aware - that he was in complete control of himself.

"How's that head, fella'?" Cal asked, smirking.

Finn said nothing and just continued to gaze passively at them both.

"What's the matter? Cat got your tongue?" He laughed then and nudged the fat man playfully.

The fat man just stared. "I don't like it, Cal, not one bit. Something aint right with thisun." He said, the fear in his eyes never wavering.

Cal scoffed. "You always were a fuckin' pussy, Gregory, my old friend." He responded, slapping the fat man on the shoulder. "Go on, get Chops watered, I'll deal with our Limey friend here."

Gregory took one last look at Finn. There was definitely something wrong with 'thisun', something just behind the man's eyes seemed to be making dangerous, silent promises.

He shuddered and then turned and almost fled down the remaining corridor and out through the door at the end.

Once he had gone and the door had slammed shut, Cal turned back to Finn, a look of derision on his face.

"I fucking hate Limey's," he almost growled. "Hate 'em almost as much as I hate fucking niggers. Niggers in white-man's skin, that's what you fuckers are." He said, pointing.

Finn didn't flinch, didn't move, didn't blink.

"Oh, yea! I know you're a Limey; no one says "just passin' through" like that. Not in my God-given country they don't."

He drew a packet of cigarettes from his breast pocket and took one, lighting it with a brass, petrol-lighter. He held the lighter up for Finn to see.

"This is my platoon's badge," he said, pointing to the shield and crossed rifles, "now, I know that you Limeys was in my war, but why would you pretend to be an American vet, is what I would really like to know?"

Finn remained unresponsive; until the man told him something useful - like why he was here - he wouldn't say a word.

"Glennys is a good woman, got a heart made of solid gold, so it irked me some when I realised you played her like that. Is that your game then, fella'? Taking advantage of good and decent folks?" Cal stared hard at Finn and waited.

Finn didn't waiver and remained completely unfazed.

When no reply came, Cal said; "Well this is the last stop for you, you Limey prick. You see, you've entered my world now, Cal's Pit. There's only two ways to leave this place; by the front door which you would have had to walk through as a-," he paused while he searched for the right word. "A patron." He finished, a grin spread across his face. "Or, like you and brown boy there, through-," he paused again, staring menacingly into Finn's passive eyes. "Well, I think I'll leave that surprise for later."

He tapped the brass lighter on the bars of the cell before turning away and leaving by the door he had come through. "Seeya later, Limey." He called, before closing the door behind him.

Finn listened to Cal's, heavy steps clumping up the stairs and then the sound of another door being closed.

Once it was silent again he dropped his head to his chest and closed his eyes; whatever was coming would need to be met with a clear and sharp mind.

Hours passed, Finn could feel the sun rise and travel overhead and then fall again.

The man next to him was awake now. Finn looked over to him; the man looked terrified.

"Peace, brother." Finn said. "I am Finn."

The man flinched at the sound of Finn's voice and flicked his head round quickly like a frightened deer, Finn thought.

"What? Wh-what's happening, man? What the fuck is happening? Oh Jesus, God help me!" His voice trembled and began to rise in panic.

Finn noticed the dried blood on the back of his hands and on the floor beneath where he had been struggling with his bonds.

"Peace!" Finn said again, harshly.

The man instantly snapped his mouth tightly shut and jerked his head back as though slapped.

"Be still now, brother, and tell me your name." Finn asked, soothingly this time.

"L-Lucas." The man said.

"Steady now, Lucas."

Finn peered at him, locked his eyes with his steely-blue gaze. "Breathe and think of the sky, the sky which is always there; always has been long before us, and always will be long after. Breathe."

Lucas breathed in deeply, jaggedly and broken at first, but after a minute he was sitting upright and breathing normally. His eyes were still frightened though.

Finn nodded his head and loosened his gaze a little. "Good. Now listen to me; it may be that we are going to die today, or tomorrow, or next year, that's what death is; the angel around the corner. Do not fear her, she brings an end to all miseries in the end, so to fear her is foolish."

Lucas blinked.

"The precursor to death is life," Finn continued. "And the precursor to life is death; one always leads on to the other, my friend."

Lucas blinked again, twice this time, quickly. His mouth twitched and opened and closed as he tried to understand what this white giant was telling him.

"I-I-I don't- what? What are you talking about, man? Oh, Shit! Are you on crack or sumthin? What?"

Finn raised an eyebrow at that.

"Fuck! Man, I knew it, I knew it. Get caught by a nigger-hater or end up in a crazy cell; I got both! Oh! Shit! Man! God, damn it!"

Finn frowned at him now. If there was a chance to escape from whatever fate Cal had in store for them it would take both of them to do it. Lucas needed an incentive to trust him.

"Okay." Was all he said before standing up.

The wooden chair groaned for a single second before splintering and exploding backward into the wall.

Lucas' eyes widened and he visibly jumped. "Fuck! What the fuck was that? Oh! Shit! You're on PCP aintcha? Been dancin' with the dusty angel. Oh! God! I'm gonna fuckin' die!"

"Will you shut up?!" Finn commanded. "I don't take drugs. Not by choice anyway." He said, casting a distasteful glance at his thigh.

"Well how the hell did you do that!?" Lucas asked, and then immediately began to strain to stand.

"Don't." Finn said, quietly. "You will hurt yourself, Lucas."

As soon as he heard his name spoken aloud, Lucas stopped his struggling and just looked at Finn, frowning.

The way the man had used his name, like a friend, was something he hadn't heard for a long time. "Who are you?" He asked.

"I am Finn of the Seven-Spears and Nine Northern Stars." Finn said, seriously. "And if you listen to me, it just may well be that we get out of here alive. Both of us."

Lucas continued to stare into those blue eyes, his own brown eyes now spilling his tears down his cheeks.

Here was a real force of honest love and power, a real hope for a world which had lost its way.

"Thirty-two years I've been on the road, thirty-two years of nothing but hate and abuse and darkness everywhere." He said, sobbing unashamedly. "Thirty-two years I've been looking for the light that was lost in people's souls." His sobbing increased. "And I've found it at last. Before I die, I've found it." His body shook as he cried. "Dear, sweet, Jesus! Forgive me for forgettin'!"

## Chapter Fifteen

As he wept, Lucas told Finn of his life on the road and how it had come about.

A lay-minister for a small town outside Memphis, he and his new wife had set up home and were happy. Happy for four years until one night, while they were out on the streets dispensing blankets and food parcels to the homeless, the Devil himself had ridden into town.

While Lucas had been retrieving more blankets from the back of their truck, his wife Crystal, had been down under the bridge sharing her smile and comfort with the inhabitants of this makeshift, cardboard town.

The growl of an engine had made him look up to the freeway ramp; a white van had exited and was careering down the smooth, concrete slope.

Instead of slowing down, the van had accelerated and Lucas had watched on in horror as it had ploughed through the people in its path.

Time slowed and the last thing Lucas had looked at was his wife's, beautiful face smiling sadly, and then she was gone, dragged under the wheels to be crushed and broken and killed.

The van carried on at speed until it made its way back onto the freeway at the other side. The driver was never caught.

Thirteen people had died that day, while eight more had been seriously injured. And one had lost his soul.

"I lost my faith that day,' Lucas said, quietly, 'my best friend and love, and my faith." He continued, his tears coming to an end.

He dropped his head and remembered the world as it had been, like waking from a nightmare to find that the sun was still shining.

He sat up straight, held his head high, reborn, and then turned to face Finn.

Finn nodded his head subtly; the man who had first used the name Lucas was now gone, while the man who was Lucas had returned.

"Thank you, Finn, thank you for finding me and bringing me out of the dark."

Even his voice was changed; the fear had gone and a sureness which had long been buried was back in its place.

"Welcome back, my friend." Finn replied. "Now, let me tell you where I think we are and what we may be able to do about it." He then said.

A mischievous twinkle in his laughing eyes made him suddenly take on the *appearance of the hunter instead of the hunted, and Lucas felt himself flush with a sudden pity for their kidnappers.*

Several more hours passed, the sun had set, when the hum of engines came to Finn's ears; the "patrons" arriving, no doubt. Twelve vehicles he counted altogether, so at least twelve, more men.

"Probably more." The she-wolf purred in his mind.

"Aye. Probably more." Finn replied.

"What was that?" Lucas asked, assuming Finn had been speaking to him.

"Nothing. Thinking aloud. Ready yourself Lucas, they will be coming for us soon."

Fifteen minutes later and the heavy steps of Cal came down the stairs. The door opened and he walked up to the bars to face his prisoners.

He had been smiling when he walked in, but the smile dropped the second he saw the Limey bastard standing on his feet.

A brief instance of alarm crossed his knitted brow, his friends warning echoed in his mind; "something not right about thisun". But Cal Halverstone was one 'tough son-of-a-bitch' as he often liked to think of himself, it would take more than a broken chair and a fucking Limey to faze him.

"Making firewood there were you, boy?" He said, nodding at the broken wood behind Finn. "You won't be needing fire where you're going; hot as hell it is." He leered. "What am I saying? It's not as hot as hell, it is hell!" He laughed loudly then and slapped his thigh.

Finn spoke. "You're making a mistake."

The sound of Finn's sure voice, unexpectedly calm and confident, brought Cal's laughing almost to an abrupt stop.

He stared malevolently into Finn's eyes. "Oh yea? And why might that be?"

Finn's eyes gleamed. "I can sense that you were once a true warrior, but now you have tempered your heart with hate. It has distorted your view and you cannot see danger anymore through your veil of arrogance."

Cal continued to stare. He had heard it all from everyone he had ever captured and brought here; pleadings, threats, remorse, prayers, cold acceptance. Everything. But never advice and never given with such alarming clarity and confidence.

"If you do not release us and end this madness for good, you and everyone out there," Finn nodded, indicating the waiting people above, "will die."

For a brief moment it looked as though the Cal Halverstone of old, the husband, father and all round good citizen of the United States, was actually taking notice and thinking about Finn's words seriously. But only for the briefest of moments.

His grin returned and he laughed, wagging his finger at Finn. "Nice try Limey, nice try," he said, "but I'm too good for you, boy."

He stood back and folded his arms. "Anything else?"

Finn lowered his head and nodded sadly and slowly. "That is regrettable." He muttered to himself. "Then I ask one boon only; that we walk freely as men into your 'pit'." He looked up. "Whether it be to life or our deaths, we walk freely to it."

Cal's brow furrowed. What was he up to? Why so eager to get on with it, and more importantly, why no pleading for his life.

He looked at Lucas. "How about you, boy? What do you say?"

Lucas smiled warmly at him.

Cal frowned again; what the hell had happened to the fucking hobo!?

"God loves you, child, you owe me nothing, but I would like to walk freely alongside my friend, Finn, if I may?"

Cal stood and studied them both for a moment, weighing up his options. Eventually he just shook his head and cleared his mind.

"Fucking crazy, the both o' ya." He laughed.

He drew a colt pistol from his jacket and then unlocked the door.

Levelling the gun and aiming it at Finn's head, he walked into the cell and around the back of Lucas.

He took a pair of wire-cutters from his pocket and snipped the wire around Lucas' wrists and then handed the tool to him.

"Free yourself first and then him. Slowly." He said, as he backed out into the corridor.

Once Finn and Lucas were both unbound and standing side by side, Cal pulled the door to the cell all the way open, its design allowing it to lock into place across the corridor, effectively keeping his prisoners away from him.

"I think you'll both be screaming like frightened girls once you meet my Chops." He said, nastily.

"You mean the bear you have also kidnapped and tortured and starved?" Finn replied, casually.

Cal was really shaken by that, even if he didn't show it, Finn had hit a chord of fear and uncertainty in him now. How the hell did he know Chops was a bear? And even more worrying; why weren't either of them afraid?

Even if Lucas didn't catch Cal's wavering, Finn did.

"End this way of life now and release us, all three of us, and everyone will go home tonight." He said.

Cal looked unemotional, his face stern and blank, but inside he was feeling the fear of old; the fear of what lies in the building, what death awaits him around the corner, which enemy bullet fired across the desert had his name on it?

I'm already dead. I'm already dead. I'm already dead; *his soldier's mantra automatically rising to the surface.*

"Fuck you." He said, quietly.

No turning back, the pair of 'em were full of shit, and Chops was hungry and pissed off. What were they going to do? Appeal to his better nature and ask him to be nice? No, the fucking, Limey bastard had got into his head was all.

He holstered his gun and then pointed to the door at the other end of the short passageway. "Through there." He said, flatly.

He had hardened his heart now, solid and resolute; *"an immovable object had met an unstoppable force"* as his daddy used to say, *"when minds collide, worlds divide. Remember that, Calvin."*

The tone of voice was all the indication Finn had needed to tell him that Cal had now gone well beyond the point of no return.

He gave his kidnapper a pitying smile and then walked through the cell door, Lucas following behind.

The end door opened into another passageway, similarly blocked off at the opposite side by steel bars. Immediately to their left though, through the first door, another, smaller door opened inward into a brightly lit, circular pit.

The hum of voices quietly talking from somewhere above came down to both men as they entered.

"Be ready, my friend," Finn said, quietly, "and do not be afraid."

"I fear nothing but God's wrath." Lucas replied. "A bear holds no fear for me."

"Do not be afraid of me, I meant." Finn's eyes were startlingly alive as he spoke; lightning-eyes, the storm smouldering.

As the automatic door closed and locked behind them, the spectators above moved closer to the wooden rails, the wooden boards beneath their feet creaked under their weighty steps.

No drunken, boxing-crowd this; the made-to-measure leather shoes which only the affluent could afford, were unmistakable to Finn's ear as they stepped closer.

The high gantry was kept in deep shadow, the lights illuminating the pit hung only a few inches above the ankles of the spectators.

The walls were thick panel-boards nailed to the posts which held the gantry aloft, set at eight or so foot intervals until they fully encircled the small arena.

Wood. Wood everywhere. Fools!

*Finn smiled to himself at the she-wolfs retort.*

Wood; a man's best-friend. *"Understand the trees, Finn, and listen to them. They each have their own voice."* His mistress had taught him. *"Understand the trees and you will always have a friend in a wooden house."*

Chattering voices from above made him cock his ear; they were betting, laying wagers on who would die first and how long they would last. It seemed they were betting per minute lasted.

So, this was the viewing, like racehorses paraded past the punters right before the race.

Finn's shame for his fellow man was hot in his heart.

His mind suddenly flared, a comet of white-hot urgency coming from the she-wolf.

*An One Mór tagann! The Great One comes!*

Above them, a voice called out.

"Thirty seconds gents," it was Cal's voice, "last bets, get 'em on the board."

Finn turned to Lucas, who was now looking a little shaken; the reality and finality of what was about to come through the door at the other side of the pit had thudded his heart and closed his throat into silenced dread at the 'thirty second' call.

"I will see you in this life or look for you in the next, Lucas." Finn said. "Be ready to fight and flee."

Lucas nodded and tried to smile bravely. He didn't feel brave, he felt shit-scared. Only three hours ago he had been a hobo; hobos were naturally scared of the world.

He forgave himself but remained shit-scared all the same.

The sudden hush of the crowd announced the arrival of Chops; a cage door somewhere beyond the pit clanged open and the bellow of the enraged animal came echoing down the corridors.

Feet shuffled closer to the edge to get a better view of the door where the legendry Chops made his entrance. It grated open, sliding to the side to reveal a dark tunnel ahead.

A smell of something wild and old came to Finn's nostrils. Blood filled his heart and the she-wolf came bursting to the fore to meet an old foe.

Lucas recoiled, startled at the sudden change and by the ferocity on the man's face, and by the love of Jesus, Mary and all of the Saints in heaven the man's eyes were no longer human.

He couldn't have said exactly how they had changed, but they were now flecked with feral, red violence.

So that's what Finn had meant by 'do not be afraid of me.'

Above in the gantry, only one other person had seen the same thing which Lucas had seen. Poor, scared Gregory.

While everyone else had their eyes on Chops' entrance, he had his eyes on Finn. As soon as he had walked into the pit, Gregory had been watching Finn.

His skin crawled when he saw the sudden change in his features, his posture, his eyes. Damn! God! His eyes.

'I knew it! I fuckin' knew! I said. Didn't I say?'

His brow dripped sweat and his chest ached while his stomach churned. He had to sit down.

He dropped heavily onto his seat beside the betting board, mopped his brow once and then WHAM! A six ton mallet of pain slammed him in the chest.

His jaw clamped down impossibly hard, the molars on the left of his mouth shattered and the splinters were driven deep into their bleeding sockets.

He flung his arms around his midriff as the muscles constricted tightly in his chest and shoulders, his tortured heart squeezing the last of the breath from his body.

Alone he had been born, alone he had travelled through his life, and alone he had died; no one had noticed, no one had cared, all of their attention fixed firmly on the drama about to unfold below.

Cowardly Gregory was the lucky one.

In the pit, Finn stared through red-tinted eyes as the blackness of the tunnel was suddenly pierced by duel pinpricks of reflected light; the eyes of the Great One.

Slowly his dark, shaggy bulk pressed itself out of the shadows, revealing a large and grizzled black-bear.

He padded down the remaining corridor, his mind full of rage and of death; death for those who tormented him.

He had done this countless times before; released to kill, captured again to be tormented. His old mind was on the verge of breaking for good, his true nature almost driven out entirely. But not quite.

The last step into the pit he charged and then abruptly stopped and roared, the charge a mere gesture to test his enemies will, get them to turn and flee and then he would have them.

The one directly in front of him didn't turn, so he stood upright and made himself as big as possible and roared again.

Finn flung his left arm up and out, palm facing the bear.

"Shealbhú go tapa!" His voice boomed, unnaturally loud. "Hold fast!"

"Féach dom agus cuimhnigh, namhaid d'aois! Ár naimhde ár timpeall orainn!" "See me and remember, old foe! Our enemies are around us!"

The bear shook his massive head and dropped back onto all fours, swaying slightly as he appraised Finn. This thing didn't torment it, this thing was bigger than itself.

The bear's mind was puzzled but no less angry. He struggled with something which he understood from his days roaming the hills and forests, this thing in front of him reminded him of that.

Finn spoke again. "Let me bring our enemies down to you and we will fight them together." He said, in English this time.

He looked the bear right in the eye and together they growled.

High in the gantry, the crowd were mesmerised by this fantastically-unusual display between man and beast. Usually by now at least one of the victims had been torn apart and killed, but here was a man who had not made the mistake of running away, something they had never seen before.

Finn could feel their astonished anticipation. It was time to let them have a better view.

Uttering the word of yielding under his breath, he suddenly turned and sped off to the left.

When he reached the wall he slammed both fists into the panelling where they were riveted to the post behind and sent a wave of force straight through the beam.

It exploded loudly and yielded as intended, splintering and then caving inward as the weight of the floor above pressed over the edge.

Within seconds the whole gantry was collapsing as each post twisted under the immense pressure of the whole floor moving.

The first of the 'Patrons' came sliding down, yelling and screaming and scrabbling in their tailor-made suits, trying to claw their way back up the boards.

But Chops could smell his real enemies now, his tormentors, and they were down here with him. His rage was perfectly complete.

Finn sprang backward in one incredible leap as the bear swung one massive, clawed paw at the black suit which had appeared right where Finn had been standing.

The man in the suit screamed as the claws gouged deeply into his face and chest, flinging him sideways and leaving a trail of spraying crimson hanging stupidly in the air behind.

Utter chaos ensued as the men from above suddenly found themselves on the wrong side of the betting.

A tall, slender man produced a small, black pistol from his pocket and levelled it at the raging bear.

Finn charged at the man, head held low, and crashed into him just as he pulled the trigger.

The gun sounded but the bullet flew high and struck the wall behind the betting-board, while the man was lifted clean over Finn's head and thrown like a ragdoll into the splintered and broken gantry.

He crashed straight through the floorboards and struck the post behind, his back breaking at the same instance the post gave way.

Standing almost at the very centre of the pit, Lucas stared at the carnage being wrought by Finn and the bear; no one was paying him any attention, all of the focus was either on the fight or escaping.

Every detail of what was happening etched themselves firmly in his eye and mind. He felt the passing of the moments go by slowly, even his own fear felt slow.

The gunshot had broken through the panic-barrier and the men who had suddenly found themselves down amongst the action instead of watching it from the safety of above, began to turn their attention to the counter-attack.

Lucas watched two men rush up behind Finn as he leaped up the fallen boards and grabbed the ankles of a man who had almost climbed out.

While Finn pummelled the man he had pulled down, the other two leaped on his back and began raining blows down on his head.

Lucas flinched to make a move to help Finn, but there was no need; he had the measure of all three of them.

Feeling the weight on his back, Finn tumbled himself head-over-heels, grabbing both men by the head as he did so and flinging them over his heaving shoulders.

The pair of them hit the wall with a ghastly crack.

Finn leaped back to his feet, and Lucas could see the black handle of the blade which one of the men had managed to stab into Finn's chest.

His big, blonde friend pulled the knife from himself without so much as a gasp and then went to work with it on his enemies.

Lucas wept to see such ferocity. Wept for the state of the poor man's mind which was driving his hellish rage.

Another shot rang out and the bear roared in pain as the bullet embedded itself into his flank.

He flung his massive head around to face his attacker just as the terrified man fired again.

The bullet tore through the bear's shoulder this time, missing his throat by inches as it passed under his chin.

He careered forward, meeting his enemy with his jaws and teeth, slamming him back into the wall which then split and cracked and finally gave way as the pair of them were driven through into the darkened corridor beyond.

Finn, covered in the blood of the three men he had just killed, turned his attention back on to the main fray.

His shirt was slashed and bloodied where one of the men had used his knife on him.

Lucas noticed several puncture wounds on his bare flesh as well as the opened slashes across his chest and abdomen, but Finn showed no signs of slowing his attack and in his hands he now held two blades.

Two more suits were about to fire into the back of the bear when they caught the blurred motion of Finn charging in from the left.

They both turned and fired as Finn lunged upward with his blades, piercing them both in the chest and lifting them clean off the floor.

He smashed them back into the wall and then quickly withdrew the blades and stepped back.

Two, dead men dropped to the ground, two, new holes in Finn's body; it was a fair trade-off he thought.

He began to laugh, turning his attention to the remaining six men in the pit.

Four of them held knives and for the first time, Finn noticed that all of them were the same; eight inch blades, black, leather grips, polished silver hilts and an ivory five-pointed star embedded at the base of the handles.

He had no idea what the symbol stood for, but he knew an elitist group when he saw one.

His eyes lit up and he grinned a terrible grin.

All motion is preceded by anticipation, but in Finn's mind his weight was already three feet in front of him, all he had to do now was make the simple gesture and allow his body to catch up with it.

He moved supernaturally fast, the snap of the air was the only warning the six men had before he was in amongst them, laughing like a gleeful madman, stabbing, slashing and hacking.

Blades rang out as steel struck steel, men grunted and groaned as they were pierced, but Finn was unwavering.

Lucas watched him being stabbed multiple times, only to turn one of his blades in the direction of the attack and slash and stab back.

The two men without blades picked up broken planks and waded in, cracking Finn from behind across his back and legs.

He dropped briefly to one knee and a blade found his shoulder as it was stabbed downward, aimed for his head, but he leaped straight back up and lunged out at the men behind.

He missed one as he jumped backward, but the other moved too slowly and that man felt the sting of the sharpened blade-edge slash his cheek open and then slide across the bridge of his nose.

The man screamed out and listed backward, clutching at his sliced face.

Finn was surrounded now, a false sense of security fell over the men; they had him trapped and he wouldn't be in any great rush to attack them while his back was vulnerable.

All six were bleeding from stabs and slashes, but none of them were as badly injured as Finn; it was hard to make out any colour other than red on the man.

He gave them a moment to fully relax their hold, let them find that false security in his injuries, and then he uncoiled both of his hands at the same time, flicking both of his captured blades out to the sides.

Before anyone could even register the movement, the two men holding knives who were at either side of the circle clutched their throats as they dropped to the ground.

Finn visibly sagged a little then.

You are not done, Finn of the Seven-Spears. Get up! I command it! Get up!

To Lucas' eyes it seemed something had entered Finn's body and had given him a renewed strength. How could he still be standing? How could he still fight? How could he?

The four men facing Finn were thinking the same thing. They looked at each other with a fear-edged wonder now, gripping their knives murderously and readying themselves.

Finn's eyes suddenly narrowed and he grinned again; he could smell death creeping up behind him.

"Did I not warn you?" He said, casting his glance over his shoulder.

"We aint all dead yet, Limey." Cal's voice.

He stepped out from the shadows of the broken gantry and boards, blood running down his face from a deep gash on his temple.

As the gantry had fell, so Cal had, had the presence of mind to leap over the back edge. Unfortunately for him, as he dropped to the ground the struts holding the walk-boards together splintered and were catapulted downward, one of them cracking him across the side of the head and knocking him out cold.

"Aye, not yet." Finn replied, and his grin widened as he heard the distinctive double-click of the hammer on Cal's colt.

"Tá tú ag gearradh sé fíneáil beag, foe d'aois." Finn said, glancing now to his right and through the broken door where the bear had crashed through. "You are cutting it a little fine, old foe."

Watching from the darkness, the bear heard and understood; the leader of his tormentors was there, he could smell him, smell the wrongness in his mind and soul.

His instincts had returned now, the veil of fear and constant anguish were gone, he was free again and this wrongness had no place in his world.

Cal's finger squeezed the trigger slowly as the bear burst from the shadows in a blur of broken wood and black fur, his muzzle wide and red and his claws still wet with the blood of his last kill.

The sudden rush and noise made Cal turn his aim toward the bear instead of shooting Finn in the back of the head.

The colt roared, hastily aimed, but the bullet found no target and Cal Halverstone disappeared with a scream into the deadly embrace of the Great One.

At the appearance of the bear, the four men in front of Finn had leaped away, effectively closing the distance a little between themselves and the blonde madman; better him than it.

Finn struck without hesitation.

Streaking forward to meet the first man, he uncoiled his right arm and sent his thumb smashing into the man's throat, driving the larynx inward and upward where it snapped.

The man dropped without a sound, blood foaming from his mouth and nose, left and ignored while he thrashed away the last of his life on the floor.

The second man managed to recoil as Finn then spun around on his heel and sent his fist tearing towards his head.

The blow glanced but stunned the man, causing him to stagger back a step which gave Finn an opening to attack the other two. They were both ready and met him with their blades.

A wild slash cut through Finn's palm as he deflected the strike which had been intended to open his throat, sending the blade and the wielders arm up, exposing the man's head.

Finn lunged and butted him squarely in the face, just as his comrade slashed and stabbed at Finn's exposed, right flank, opening up his side almost to the rib.

Grabbing the knife-arm of the man he had just head-butted, Finn sent the blade whipping back and into the chest of the man he had stunned with his punch.

The man collapsed, gasping as though he had been suddenly submerged in icy waters and then fell back against the wall, dying as he sat clutching at the bleeding hole in his chest.

Once again, Lucas took a step forward to help his friend, the terror in his heart no less now than it had been when they had first entered the pit.

And once again, he was cut short. By the reappearance of the bear this time.

Finn had dropped to his knee again, the last attack on his ribs had seen the blade pierce his lung and he had found himself suddenly gasping for breath, stars popping in front of his eyes.

The last two men approached, confidant this time that Finn was down for good.

The man who Finn had butted, stepped eagerly forward again, snarling through the blood and snot and broken teeth, and raised his knife, readying to stab Finn in the back of the neck; the killing blow.

Be still, my love. *She said in his mind. He could feel her smiling, resignedly.*

"I have failed." *Finn's voice was wheezy and quiet.*

Yes. *She replied, without a trace of anger or disappointment, only sadness.*

He closed his eyes and waited for the blade to drop and bring an end to his geis. He waited but it didn't come.

He opened his eyes again and watched the feet standing in front of him first tremble a little and then suddenly become expensive, leather islands surrounded by a spreading puddle of urine.

The bear had no mind to taste the leader of the tormentors; his wrongness was foul, his blood stank of filth. He had killed him quickly, crushing his skull with the immense pressure of his terrifying jaws and then had turned his attention to the last two, completely ignoring the statue of Lucas as he padded past him.

Like a story from the bible, Lucas felt the enormous presence of the bear even before it had walked by, brushing his shoulder firmly as it did so.

"Lions and the lambs, and all that shit." He mumbled to himself, his eyes wider than the 'O' shape of his mouth. And then quickly he added; "If you'll pardon my language, Lord."

His eyes flickered heaven-ward. He wasn't sure who he was more afraid of; the Lord, the bear or the man who had just destroyed a fighting-pit with his bare-hands.

The last two 'Patrons' on the other hand, were well aware of who they were afraid of.

While the one standing in front of Finn was pissing himself, his comrade was backing away, tugging at the others shirt and encouraging him to step back as well. It made sense that the approaching Chops would attack the weakest first; Finn.

The bear saw everything, watched his enemy hide behind the thing which was bigger than it was, saw their fear, saw them.

If the two men had turned and fled, escaping up the broken gantry, the bear would have left them be, but they still had it in their hearts to see this man in front of them die, be killed by Chops, and then escape, taking an unbelievable tale of heroics out into the world with them.

They stood in the shadows as Chops came alongside the man on his knees.

"Síochána, Ceann Mór." Finn said, touching his hand to his breast and keeping his eyes lowered. "Peace, Great One."

The bear paused, a brief moment to smell the one bigger than itself; it was dying, he thought.

Slowly the massive, shaggy head turned back to stare at the two men waiting. The stare was unemotional; the last of a thing to be done was standing *right there, waiting for it to be done.*

*The bear's mind made the simple connection and turned the power back on.*

With his jaw gaping, Chops ran at the two men; they didn't stand a chance backed up to the boards as they were. There was no escaping the flailing, great paws and claws of him and both of them went down to be finished off in less than ten seconds.

He huffed and postured over them before backing away, the bloodlust leaving him almost instantly once he knew no enemies remained.

Lucas' mouth was dry, his eyes were dry and mercifully his bladder was dry, because when the bear had finished with the two men it had backed away and turned around to face him.

Its face was red and dripping and grizzled, claws with shredded cloth and skin alike still attached, and it was looking right at him.

And yet, behind the blood and death and fear, Lucas could see eyes which were puzzled but at peace.

He smiled. "He found us both, didn't he?" He whispered, and lowered his own eyes respectfully.

## Chapter Sixteen

Few and far between were the people Finn could say he trusted, but Lucas was one of them. And not a trust born simply because of the preachers ministrations and sixteen week vigil and care of him. No, Lucas was transparent to Finn and all Finn could see was goodness and life and a driven need to make things right.

Without Lucas, neither Finn nor the Great One would have made it out of the pit alive.

*He was a good man, I wonder what became of his wanderings?*

Finn smiled as he remembered his days in convalescence, with Lucas as his nurse, maid and *"your general get-it-together-man"* as Lucas himself put it.

'He was a *great* man!' Finn chuckled. He had not been the best of patients.

*"Get your head back down on that pillow, boy. If you bust them damn stitches again I swear by all the Saints above, I will strike you! Damn it! You've got me talkin' like you now! Get-get back-! Right! That. Is. It."* And Lucas had actually removed his belt.

Finn felt the warmth of affection grow in his mind; she had really taken to Lucas when he had done that.

Friendly people were always around the corner, some genuine and others not, but there was one other who Finn trusted and this man he hadn't even met. Well, not properly at any rate. Graham Shelby, Interpol inspector.

Finn had watched Shelby in Dusseldorf, had stood shoulder-to-shoulder with the man – while wearing a 'borrowed' Police uniform - and listened to him as he discussed the murders which Finn had just committed.

As he had hoped, Shelby had talked extensively about the four, missing children which had been rescued.

By his words and the tone of his voice, Finn had assessed correctly that Graham Shelby was one of the good souls in the universe, someone he could trust to get the children back to their homes and families.

And now someone he was trusting with even far more than that; his very quest.

'I wonder which paths *your* wanderings are leading you to tread.' He muttered as he turned his gaze to the west.

\* \* \*

The gate was open when Shelby arrived at number 43, Sealcrest Road, a sign from Bollinger to let him know she wasn't alone.

He parked his vehicle out of sight and then drew his pistol.

Creeping along behind the high, front hedgerow, he peered through the tiny gaps between the foliage.

There was a single light on in the front-room, but other than that he could see nothing else.

After steadily following protocol and training, moving slowly and silently, he reached the open gate.

He checked the way with a quick look through to the front door and then slipped quickly up the path and darted under the eaves of the small, wooden porch. All drama, done to the letter; his old instructors would be proud.

Peering through the green-stained frosted-glass produced nothing more than the same glow coming from the room beyond.

He reached out, feeling for the door-handle while keeping his eye on the hallway.

Slowly he pressed it down, tightening his jaw reflexively as the spring groaned and clicked. The door opened, the hinges were un-oiled, more jaw-clenching and a little grimacing now.

Not a sound came from within, but the air was filled with an aromatic and well-flavoured wine.

He frowned as he stepped across the small hallway and made straight for the front-room.

Creeping forward, he held the gun out in front of himself and peered around the edge of the door.

The first thing he saw was Bollinger sitting on a chair with a glass of wine in one hand and an open book on her lap.

At almost the same instance he saw his partner a thumb appeared from behind the door.

'Hello, Mr Interpol.' The thumb said, with a female, German voice.

'Oh, crap!' Shelby muttered.

From behind the door stepped a small, grinning woman with short-cropped ginger hair.

'That is the second time you have greeted me with that expression, Mr Interpol,' she said, 'is it an English thing?'

Her sarcasm wasn't lost on Shelby as she folded her arms and raised an eyebrow at him.

He turned to Bollinger and gave her a questioning stare? She simply replied by tipping her glass and smiling.

'Want one?'

He turned back again to the small, German woman with thumbs of steel. His jaw worked but no actual words came out.

'You could start by being polite and putting your pistol back in your trousers.' She said. 'Or are you really *that* excited to see me?' Her eyes twinkled.

Shelby caught the blush before it began and didn't flinch, but he did put his pistol away. 'Would someone mind telling me what the hell is going on?' He sounded genuinely miffed.

Without waiting for an answer, he raised his own eyebrow at Bollinger. 'And you! You left the gate open.'

'I did. Sorry.' She answered. 'I forgot to go out and close it once I became aware of who Anna was.'

'"Anna?"' He felt a little jealous that Bollinger had learned the name of the legendry *Nova-Bug* before he had. '"Once you became aware?" You mean you saw there was someone already here and you went in by yourself anyway?'

'Oh. No. I didn't know there was anyone else here until I was at the front door. I was led inside at thumb-point, you understand?' She replied.

At the word *thumb-point*, Shelby broke out into a raucous laugh. He couldn't believe they had both been bushwhacked by someone so tiny and with just her equally tiny thumbs at that!

'I think I will have that glass of wine now, thank you, Sophie.' He said, between fits.

'Ah! The ice has broken.' Anna said. 'You Englishmen can be so *stiff* sometimes, you know?'

Shelby laughed just a little harder at that; the tiniest *German* he had ever seen was calling *him* stiff!

She walked to stand by Bollinger and picked up her own glass of wine from the dining table.

Shelby followed and took the waiting glass from Sophie and then the three of them took a seat around the Deere's table. Shelby noted Sophie had brought the book she'd had on her lap.

Once they were all seated Anna spoke first, her tone becoming serious and businesslike. 'We retrieved all of the data from the backup drives,' she began, 'and the video from the cell phone you had entrusted to Harrison.' Her eyes were hard when she spoke of the video.

'By the look on your face I would say you saw something very disturbing.' Sophie said.

Anna paused and frowned. 'Yes.' She answered. 'Yes, *disturbing* is one way of putting it, I suppose. But the murder itself and the killer are only a small part of that; what is worse is the man and the children; a man whom you know, who your country knows.'

Shelby looked shocked, but deep inside he had known it was going to be something like this. 'Who?'

'A man called, Bradley Hinds.' Anna replied.

Sophie frowned and asked the question this time. 'Who?'

Shelby recited the name over and over until he had it. 'Oh. God, yes, Hinds; he's one of a few minor Euro-MP's. I can't remember exactly where his constituency is but I know it's in one of the smaller hamlets around New Forest somewhere.'

'So one of our MP's has been murdered and we are only just hearing about it now?' Sophie asked, sternly. 'Surely someone must have noticed he hasn't been into work for almost three-weeks!' It wasn't a question.

The three sat in silence for a few moments, Shelby's mind working the bread-crumbs beneath his frown.

His face suddenly blanched and he sat up straight. 'Hinds worked for the department which Kevin Keys is the head of!'

'It was Keys who gave us the phone in the first place.' Sophie said, to Anna when she noticed the questioning look.

'Ockham's razor?' Anna replied, shrugging her shoulders.

'I damn well hope not!' Shelby said.

He sat back and sighed, running his hands over his face. 'It can't be Kevin, it's too obvious. Why would the man set us up with the very thing which could bring him down?'

'Perhaps he is a puppet on a string?' Anna said.

Shelby looked at her puzzled.

'You know? Someone is blackmailing him and making him cover things up, but at the same time he is trying to tell you something.'

Shelby dropped his gaze to the tabletop and mulled over what the small, German hacker had just suggested. It was not out of the question; blackmail was a very effective weapon in the higher cliques of society. But if that was the case, what was Kevin's sin?

He turned to Sophie. 'We have to ride it out, Soph.'

'What do you mean?'

'Hinds' disappearance hasn't been reported; whatever happened in Turkey is still going on. We have to ride it out, we can't be the ones to break the news about his death.'

Sophie stared hard into Shelby's eyes. 'You're certain that you know all of the consequences if it all goes wrong don't you?'

Shelby lowered his gaze again.

'Treason being top of the list.' Sophie added.

'I know.' He replied, without looking up. 'I know.' He repeated and nodded his head.

He sat up straight and sighed then. 'My loyalty lies with Finn and his quest; Hinds was on the wrong side of his diplomatic status; he used it to commit acts of indecency which are illegal in the country which he represents.' He said, stiffly. 'His crimes are laid on the path which Finn is following and by extension, the path we are foll-.' He stopped and looked at Anna; she was scribbling notes in a small, black book.

'What are you doing?' He asked.

Sophie looked questioningly to Anna as well.

She flicked an innocent gaze between the pair. 'I'm writing down everything you say.' She said. 'I've also made recordings.'

When neither of them spoke further, she added; 'If this international turd hits your British fan then I can almost guarantee that someone will be made to take the blame; this way I can assure you both that it will not be you; I am *Code-8*, the truth will always come out.' She said, seriously. 'Please continue.'

The unintentional arrogance in her voice wasn't lost on the pair. *Bloody hackers*!

Shelby looked to Sophie. She nodded; it did make sense to have some kind of backup plan.

'As I was saying;' Shelby began again. 'We are following Finn, he has led us to an international scandal, but in doing so we now have a higher power than us 'tidying up' behind him so to speak. Whoever is responsible for *that* will almost certainly escape the justice he deserves if we allow everything we know to become public right now.'

He paused and took a sip of his wine. 'I can't tell you how much I hate the hypocrisy of it all; it damn well rubs me up the wrong way, but I know that if we don't follow through with Finn we will never bring this kind of thing to an end. We have to catch the masterminds and make sure it closes down for good and doesn't just get discreetly passed over to *new owners*.'

'Just what kind of "thing" do you mean?' Anna asked.

'I really have no idea, but it is something very big and Finn is trying to lead us to it.'

He turned to Sophie. 'I think we have it all wrong about him wanting our help, Soph; I think he needs us to expose the truth and the path to that truth has begun with Bradley Hinds' murder.'

Sophie nodded. 'I think you're right; we've seen for ourselves what Finn is capable of, it makes more sense than him asking for help.'

The three of them sat quietly and sipped at their wine, Anna looking furtively over the rim of her glass at the Interpol officers sitting opposite her.

Eventually she spoke. 'So, err, does this mean you are both now working *outside* of your country's law?' She asked, taking another sip of wine and keeping her eyes on them both.

'I'd prefer to think of it as pushing our country's laws to their limits.' Shelby replied. 'But I suppose there is a distinctive *rebel* note attached.'

Anna put her glass on the table and reached into her pocket.

Shelby and Sophie heard the tiny click of a button as Anna pressed it.

'I've switched off the recording now. I have to tell you something about your man, Finn.' She said, quite abruptly. 'I warn you; if you try to arrest me after you hear what I say I will be forced to retaliate.'

'You mean you'll take on two, armed officers with your thumb?' Shelby scoffed, not too harshly.

'No. I mean I will take on two, armed officers with *both* of my thumbs.' She said, holding the aforementioned digits out for them to see.

She grinned. 'I mean it; just listen to everything I say before you do or say anything.'

Shelby sighed. He had no intention of getting into a fray with *Nova-bug*, she'd probably kick the hell out of both of them and leave the embarrassment to finish them off.

'Okay, out with it. I promise I won't say a word until you have finished.'

Anna looked at Sophie.

'You brought the wine,' Sophie said, 'I would never be so rude to such a gracious host.' She raised her glass and smiled.

Her eyes, however, said; *bring crap to my table and I will show you what twelve years of kick-boxing can do for your looks.*

'Good.' Anna said, and re-holstered her thumbs.

*Her* look for Sophie said; *you have just gone very high up in my book, let me take you to dinner.*

She turned her attention back to the matter in hand and sat up straight, preparing herself. 'Right. Finn has eluded you for so long because *Code-8* provided him with the software to navigate the *Dark-Web* unnoticed.'

'You WHA-.' Shelby began.

'Ah! Ah! Ah!' Anna wagged her finger at him. 'Let me finish.'

When Shelby sat back in a huff, snatching up his wine and taking a hateful gulp, Anna continued.

'*Code-8* has developed software to combat the Onion Browser, a *Dark-Web* browser which I'm sure you have heard about.'

Shelby and Sophie both nodded.

'As you know, the Onion Browser accesses a part of the internet which provides direct links to certain, shall we say, *unsavoury* websites; arms and ammunition dealers, drugs of all descriptions, pornography to cater for every, single desire, fetish and taste. In short; anything can be found and bought on the *Dark-Web*, *anything* at all.'

She picked up her glass and swirled the red liquid around, watching it sadly. 'All I ever wanted to do was bring down the *Dark-Web*.' She said, quietly.

She raised her head and looked at them both seriously. 'I coded the sequences into our software which dealt with the selling and acquisition of weapons and ammunition; it is directly because of me that your Finn has acquired the weapons and equipment that he has.'

Neither of them said anything, but then again neither of them thought that what they had heard so far, was any worse than sitting round a table and sharing wine with a member of an internationally-wanted hacker-group. They were still waiting for the sting.

Anna sighed. 'And if that isn't bad enough; the memory-stick containing our software came directly from my hand to his. That was more than six years ago now'

And there it was and it stung like hell for so many reasons. For one; *Nova-Bug* had actually been face-to-face with Finn.

It was Sophie who spoke first. 'All I want to know, Anna, is; did you know that the man whom you gave the software to was a murderer? A serial-murderer at that.'

The little woman shook her head. 'It was supposed to be *Allegro* who I passed it off to, but I had never met him so I didn't know what he looked like. The time and the meeting place were so far out in the Mexican desert that the only person who should have been there was *Allegro*.'

'I take it *Allegro* is another member?'

Anna nodded. 'Yes. He had an assignment in Mexico City. I was to get the new software to him so he could complete it.'

'What happened to him?' Shelby asked.

'Nothing, he was fine.' She replied. 'He didn't receive the instructions for the meet. We have no idea how, but the coded messages for him were somehow intercepted and deciphered by someone else.' She said. 'Finn, as I have very recently found out. The only clue we had was *Allegro* told us about his new neighbour moving in only a few days prior to the meeting being arranged. When we checked out the neighbouring flat, it was empty.' She shrugged her shoulders.

'It's stupid, I know, but we thought that we ourselves had been cleverly hacked. We spent months sending out messages to all the hackers and crackers in the world, congratulating them and asking for a meet. Nothing ever came of it though.'

A big piece of the puzzle fell neatly into place; with the aid of *Code-8's* superior software, Finn had not only been able to kit himself out with weaponry which could only be found in the military world, he had also used it to track down his targets.

The *Dark-Web* was notorious for its continued distribution of evilly-sick pornography and *"snuff"* movies, it would be easy for Finn to sit at any computer in the world, plug in the memory-stick, run the software and pick his targets at leisure, completely anonymous and untraceable.

'We don't hold you responsible, Anna.' Shelby said. 'You, in my eyes, are completely blameless. I have stumbled around the Finn case for more than seven years, I am just glad to know that it wasn't because I wasn't doing my job.' He said.

Anna visibly relaxed. 'I take it back, Mr Interpol; you Englishmen aren't as stiff as I supposed.' She raised her glass to them both. 'Thank you. *Down the hatch*, as you say.'

All three tipped their glasses to the new understanding between them and drank their wine.

Sophie finished her wine first and placed her glass at her side. She pulled the book she had brought to the table up in front of her. 'I think I can give us a little more insight into Finn.' She said, as she opened the book. 'Courtesy of *Code-8*.' She nodded at Anna.

She flipped through the pages until she found what she was looking for. 'Here is our Finn, and he's in uniform.' She passed the book to Shelby.

'Well I'll be damned.' He muttered.

'He was a field-medic. A tour of Afghanistan, two tours of Iraq, decorated twice for bravery. Finished his nine years and retired from the military with a full pension.' Sophie added.

Another piece fell into place. Even though both Shelby and Bollinger had guessed at it, it wasn't until now that they knew they had been right; he was highly-trained and had been in the military, it didn't surprise them at all that he had seen combat and had been decorated.

Shelby looked up suddenly. 'Could your software have allowed him to have removed himself from electronic records?'

'Oh. Yes. Quite easily; he could travel the world and never be noticed. Electronically that is.' Anna replied.

Shelby sat back and ran his hands over his face. 'I think I know the answer to this question but I'm going to ask all the same; can the software be traced? Does it leave anything behind which we could use to pinpoint its location when it boots up?'

Anna's silence was answer enough, but she gave him that dry look of disdain which all hackers seemed to have anyway.

'Great.' He said. 'Just great.'

He sighed and sat heavily back in his chair. 'I don't know how the two of us are going to handle all of this now, Soph.'

'*Three* of us, and a small army of hackers.' Anna put in, seriously.

Shelby remained silent and just looked at her.

When he didn't say anything, she said; 'With or without you *Code-8* is going to find the person or persons responsible for Harrison's death; it makes much more sense for us to work together.'

Shelby lowered his eyes, thinking about the little woman's proposition.

He looked up and met Sophie's gaze. She gave him a slight shrug which said, *it's up to you, but she's right*.

He nodded and sighed heavily again. 'We are in so much trouble on so many levels now.'

He pushed his chair back and stood up, his frame clearly sagging under the weight of his responsibilities.

His face was drawn and tight his partner thought; she had never seen him look so set and serious.

The two women watched as he paced from one side of the room to the other, slowly and with his head down. His mind worked the pieces and began formulating a plan, weighing up the danger which seemed to be all around them now.

He stopped his pacing and stood with his hands on the back of the chair he had been sitting on, it groaned under his tightening grip. 'There's only one thing we can do now; we have to break away from our daily routines.' He said. 'The office is now out of bounds to us, Harrison's place is also off the map to us, that leaves this place. I think we should set up base here; Finn has made sure he has remained anonymous, we may as well use that to our advantage.'

He turned to Anna. 'Would it be possible for you to set us up with internet-access and secure lines of communication?'

'Give me twelve hours and I will have this room looking like Harrison's tech-lab.' She replied.

'Good.'

He turned to Sophie then. 'Tie-up anything you need to and then lock up your house and stay away. I'll do the same.' He looked pained. 'I'll have to get Rachel out as well; she'll hate it. I'll call her-.' He was interrupted by Anna.

'No! No mobile-phones. Give them to me. I have replacements for you both. I will have to destroy yours I'm afraid.'

Sophie smirked. 'You have replacements? Really?'

'Of course.'

Sophie leaned closer, the smirk turning to a frowning smile. 'But that implies that you knew you would be joining us.' She said. 'You *planned* to be staying here and joining us, didn't you?'

Anna's face remained serious. 'Of course.' She repeated, a note of annoyance in her voice at being asked a question so stupid. 'Why else would I have met you here?'

'Just like Harrison.' Sophie said, and scoffed as she sat back, folding her arms across her chest.

'Thank you.' Anna replied, her annoyance turning to a proud smile.

'It wasn't a bloody compliment!'

'Oh. It was. It definitely was.' Anna said.

## Chapter Seventeen

The rabbit was almost cooked, spitting and sizzling over the small fire. Salya poked at the embers which had rolled out onto the sandy, cave floor, rolling them back into the fire with her fire-stick.

She picked up one of the wild carrots she had collected earlier and sat munching it while the rabbit finished.

A small pile of chewed chukri-ends lay at her side, wild rhubarb as it was known in the west. She had promised herself she wouldn't eat all of it before she had eaten some of the rabbit, but it was too sweet and juicy and delicious to resist.

Salya had been in the mountains for almost three weeks; she had survived on the skills she had learned throughout her young life living on the mountain slopes with her family.

She was clean and well fed; there was plenty of water and food on the mountains if you knew where to look.

Because she didn't know her exact location, Salya had carried on moving away from the compound she had escaped, but after a week of travelling as fast as she could, she began to slow down; it didn't seem anyone had picked up her trail and was following.

The days trickled by, she walked for a few hours each day before searching out the smallest cave for shelter and her fire.

She had to keep a fire going at night; there were often large packs of wild dogs roaming and hunting the mountains. Mostly they hunted during the cool of dusk, but even though she hadn't seen them, she had heard them at night, calling to one another high up on the slopes.

Her heart sank remembering a bedtime-tale her father used to tell them about the *"Watchers on the Mountains"*, the dogs who lived on the high slopes.

The story went; *an old, blind beggar walked into a lavishly rich town, looking for a charitable crust of bread and cup of water, nothing more, and then he would be on his way.*

*The people of the town saw him coming and quietly laughed at him; for he couldn't see the place he had entere the splendour of the unblemished buildings, the shining, clean streets, the tall and proud and wicked-of-heart people. They had everything and delighted in the knowledge that there were* many who had nothing, delighted that their smiles were built upon the misery of other human-beings.

As the beggar walked down the street, doors and windows opened, people came outside to stare and sneer, laughing behind their hands, and soon the whole town were enjoying themselves at the expense of the old, blind beggar.

A youth of quite exquisite beauty stepped up to the man and asked him if he would like some water. The old man replied that he would.

"We are a poor village, on the edge of starvation and bitter times ourselves," the youth had said, sniggering slyly to all the people around, "and our water isn't the freshest, but you can share it with us."

He picked up a dirty bowl from the watering trough used for the horses and goats. He filled it and then handed it to the old man.

The beggar thanked the youth for his kindness and drank the muddied water from the dirty bowl.

When he had finished, he handed the bowl back. The youth then asked him if he would like a little bread for his journey.

Once again, the old beggar thanked the youth for his kindness and sympathy.

"Our bread isn't the best or the freshest, but you can share it with us." The youth said, and handed the old man a dirty, piece of stone with a mouldering and maggoty crust of bread upon it.

The beggar took the bread and placed it in his pouch. "Thank you for generous and kind hospitality," he said. "I will pray for good fortune for you and your town."

The old beggar then waved his goodbyes to the people who he had thought were treating him kindly, praising and blessing them while they sniggered and laughed at him behind his back.

The youth walked by his side until they came to the other end of the town. To move on to the next town the old beggar would have to follow the road which ran off to the right, but the youth thought they would have one, last laugh, one last act of wickedness.

"If you follow the road straight and up," he said, turning the old man to face the left path, the mountain path, "you will come to a fabulously rich town, where the water is cooler and the bread softer."

So with the people of the town still laughing and enjoying the wicked joke they had played on the old, blind beggar, he began his journey up the mountain.

For three days and nights he walked, breaking off small pieces of the mouldy bread to eat, but every time he put the food near his mouth a gust of wind would blow it out of his hands.

On the fourth night he sat down exhausted and cold and hungry, he could go no further without food.

He took the remaining bread from his pouch and broke a piece off when a voice suddenly spoke.

"Do not eat that, old man," the deep voice said. "It will poison you. I have watched you try to eat it for three days now and have blown the bread from your hands. Here, eat this instead."

The old man felt a hairy hand take the crust away from him and replace it with something round and soft, a sweet smell of freshly-cooked bread came to his hungry nostrils. He devoured the bread in one go and then said his gracious thanks to the voice.

"How did you come here and why are you eating poisonous bread, old man?" It asked.

The old man told the voice his tale of the poor town and the kindly people who lived there.

"The town is not poor and the people are not kindly; they have tricked you and in doing so, old man, they have earned my wrath!"

"Who are you?" The old man asked the voice.

The hairy hand took the old man's and clasped it gently. "I am the mountain," the voice said. "I am the grass at its feet and the snow on its shoulders, I am its roots to the core and its tip to the clouds. I am older than old, the first am I."

The old man felt a deep, shuddering rumble like the breath of a giant sighing deep beneath the earth.

"When the world was new I was old even then. I watched over the birth of humans, watched them as they grew and grew. I gave them the power of the earth, taught them how to use it and care for it. Like my brothers of the sea and the air who gave them fish and birds, so I gave humans the mountain beasts and the sweetest pastures of the valleys.

"Then a great fracture split the earth into four parts, and over the ages I have seen humans change from loving brothers and sisters into warring enemies. I have seen false gods change men's hearts so that they have forgotten where they have truly come from.

"The people in that town are people who have forgotten that which is true and right. Come, there is a lesson to be taught."

The old beggar felt himself raised up by unseen hands and placed on the hairy back of the mountain-god. In one, mighty leap he carried them both over the edge of the mountain and through the air, dropping like a stone into the centre of the rich town.

Even though the sound of the god landing in the square was terrific, he left no marks upon the earth. But every building, every window, every ornament, picture, or piece of furniture rattled and jumped and vibrated until eventually the lights in the houses began to come on and the people ran to their doors.

As soon as the people had taken one step over the threshold they began to change.

Faces and bodies grew hairs, whether they were male or not, ears grew long and noses were pushed out. Necks grew sleek, hands were replaced with paws, and as the last of their garments fell to the ground and they fell onto all-fours, a *long, shaggy tail sprang out from between their back-legs.*

*A hundred dogs marched forward and sat at the feet of the mountain-god, whining and crying. He put the old man on the ground and told him what had happened to the people.*

*"You will never want for food or water or shelter ever again," the god told him. "And neither will you suffer torment and ridicule at the hands of any man. This town is yours now, my only command is that you welcome the people who come here as you would welcome your own brothers and sisters, and you provide for them the hospitality and respect which all living things have a right to."*

*He turned to the dogs and commanded them to listen to the old man, to serve him during the day and to watch over him from their mountain dens at night.*

*Years and years went by and more and more people came and the town grew and prospered.*

*The old man had done everything he had been told to do and had welcomed everyone with open heart and open arms, and in turn, the people who stayed had taken up his way and always welcomed strangers just the way the mountain-god had wanted them to.*

*But the dogs never forgot and became resentful and once the town was grown again, they turned their backs on it for good, heading for the mountains where they looked down from their dens and watched it enviously from above.*

Salya wiped her damp eyes and took the rabbit from the spit.

She wished she could hear her father's voice again, telling the story while they sat around the kitchen table eating supper before bed.

She wished she could hear her little brother's, stupid questions about how the dogs served the blind beggar; *did they carry trays on their heads*?

A small laugh found its way to the surface, startling the girl and then suddenly she felt ashamed and guilty as the image of Rafiq being carried out of the truck came to her minds-eye. She wished he was still alive.

As usual, after thinking of her murdered brother, Salya's thoughts turned to revenge and the small fat-man who was responsible for his death.

In her young imagination she manages to find her way home to her village and family and then they all march down with the local police, descending upon the fat-man and his *child-prison*, bringing all of the men there to justice and releasing the women and children and bringing them home.

She wiped her sniffling nose. She knew it was just fantasy; no one would listen to her except her father, but no one would follow him, no police would come, no army of rescuers would march alongside her.

They would be sympathetic for her father's loss, but the tale would simply be added to the tales already told to their children about staying away from strange men, especially in uniform and especially Russian. "Remember Rafiq," they would say. "*He didn't listen to his parents and the bad men got him!*

*Remember Rafiq!"*

Salya remembered her little brother, she would never forget him.

'I'll do it myself,' she whispered to the shadows of Rafiq. 'I promise, little brother, I will do it myself or die trying.'

Salya had been making this promise each night for the three weeks she had been travelling through the mountains, but her mind had never managed to find that last handhold to pull herself right over the top of the fantasy and make it a reality.

Usually she fell asleep by the fire and woke in the middle-night from her nightmares.

But not tonight; something had stirred inside the young girl this time, a spirit of justice rather than of vengeance, and for once she slept soundly until dawn.

* * *

While Salya curled up in front of her campfire and slept a dreamless sleep, a killer who had once called himself Detective Brown boarded his flight to Iran.

He loved to fly. There was nothing better than being surrounded by hundreds of mere mortals, all of them filled with the tiny primal-fear of being so high off the ground.

But not him. He loved to fly. He loved to fly almost as much as he loved to kill.

*There are only a handful of ways in which to fly, but there are infinite ways in which a man can die.* He chuckled to himself as he sat down in his first-class seat. *But only the best death I provide.* He laughed loudly then.

The other passengers glanced up at him from the corners of their eyes, wondering what was funny and privately hoping they hadn't been confined with a drunk or a *nutter*. They needn't have worried about him being drunk.

He ignored their furtive looks and frowns and laughed all the same. It was going to be a good flight, the most exciting flight he had taken for a long time.

Oh. The flight itself was just the same as it had always been, but this flight was taking him to the *Grail* of his career, the pinnacle of his deathly-skills; *Finn*.

'Only a god can kill a god.' He murmured, becoming abruptly serious, his fingers steepled in front of his face and his chin resting on the thumbs.

If he hadn't spoken he would have looked like he was praying.

'What was that?' A female voice asked.

He looked round and met the smiling gaze of the woman sitting over to his left.

He leaned closer and looked her seriously in the eye, frowning ponderously as he said; 'I said; *"only a god can kill a god"*.' His tone was flat and cold.

His eyes darkened and the pupils grew round and black and showed far too much of his soul.

'Deep.' Was all the woman said, before turning away a little too quickly and returning to her open laptop. *Holy fuck! What was* he *on?*

The killer returned to his musings, the 'laughing-man' gone and the 'thinker' in his place now.

*Only a god can kill a god.* Did he *want* to kill him, though? That was the question.

His masters had always thought that they were in control - truly as a lord holds sway over his serfs - but they weren't. *He* knew they weren't, but they must never know that it was *they* who were *his* subjects, *he* watched over them silently. He did their bidding because it was their wish, their prayers to their god; *him.*

But Finn was different; they were sending him to kill another one like himself and they didn't know that either; to them, Finn was just another obstacle in the road they had sent him to remove.

*Only a god can kill a god. Only a god can kill a god.*

*Only a god...*

He raised his eyes and looked out across the tarmac to the horizon and beyond, through the veil of sky and out into the universe.

*Only a god can* save *a god?*

Why would he do that? Why would he ignore the prayers to have him removed? Why?

*Because I am alone, because the plural of god sounds better than the singular, because he is like me, like a brother.*

Cain killed *his* brother.

*And so will I if it comes to that but first let us see what my brother is like in the flesh, let us meet and see one another, see each others power.*

He sat back in his seat, a satisfied smile across his face.

*And if I don't like him I can always just kill him anyway.*

He laughed again loudly.

Everyone gave him another quick glance without seeming to be rude - or confrontational. Everyone, that is, except the woman sitting on his left.

She kept her head down, buried in her laptop, and wished to God that she could change her flight.

* * *

Shelby walked up the driveway to his front-door; he'd sent a 'messenger' ahead to let Rachel know she should get packing, he could see her flitting to and fro through the bedroom window doing just that.

He opened the door and was met by the muzzle of the semi-automatic weapon belonging to his 'messenger'.

'Maurice! Good to see you.' Shelby said. He shook the armed-officer's hand.

'You too, sir, it's been a couple of years.' The grinning Maurice replied, pumping Shelby's hand enthusiastically.

'I really appreciate the trouble you must have gone through to get here,

Mo. How the hell did you manage to sign that out?' Shelby asked, nodding at the firearm hanging on the guard's shoulder.

'I'm on the firing-range for the next two hours.' Maurice said, still grinning.

'Oh. I really don't want to know how you managed to pull that off, Mo, my old friend, but I'm really glad you did.'

Shelby gave Maurice a friendly slap on the shoulder.

He stepped to the foot of the stairs and listened; he could hear his wife moving around in their bedroom, opening drawers and cupboards.

'As soon as Rachel's ready you can get back to it.' He said, turning back to Maurice. 'The quicker the better really, but keep your phone with you; at this very point in time you are one of only four people I trust at the moment, and one of *those* is a bloody serial-killer!'

Maurice frowned and smiled at the same time; *say what*?

'I kid you not, Mo.' Shelby said, reading the puzzled look on Maurice's face. 'I've been chasing this fella for more than seven years and now he's led me to something far bigger and far more dangerous than himself.' He shrugged. 'That's why I need all of this; *your* help and Rachel's disappearance.'

Maurice nodded his head. He knew Shelby well, owed the man his life; if he said he needed *extra*-covert protection then Maurice would provide it.

He trusted Shelby implicitly, if aiding him and breaking protocol - breaking even the laws he was supposed to be upholding - meant his friend and one-time commander could gain the upper-hand in a case and stay safe, then Maurice wouldn't bat an eyelid at breaking all of the rules from here to kingdom-come.

Footsteps running across the upstairs landing made both men turn to see Rachel come hurrying down the stairs carrying her enormous suitcase.

Dragging it noisily, bumping and thumping it down behind her to the bottom of the steps would be a better way to describe her descent.

'I'm ready.' She said, breathlessly.

She blew her fringe out of her eyes and looked at her husband. 'I bloody hate this, Gray.'

'I know, love, so do I, but hey; it's only the second time in fifteen years, so,' he shrugged his shoulders, 'you know? My record's not *that* bad.'

Rachel grabbed his lapels and pulled his head toward hers, planting her lips on his and kissing him loudly. 'Your record's impeccable, my love,' she said, and kissed him again. 'But I still hate it all the same.' She ended with a bite for his lip and gentle-but-firm slap for his cheek.

Shelby held her close. 'It'll be okay, love. A few days hopefully' He said, as he released her. 'I know you know the protocol but I'm going to recite it anyway just as you know I will.'

'Maurice will provide you with a secure mobile-phone and then will drop you off at a random location. From there you'll get a cab and have it take you to one of the smaller train-stations outside town.

'Next; you'll take yourself to wherever you have planned to stay, but not for more than seven days; if you have to move you will do the exact same thing; call a cab, get dropped off somewhere random and then call another cab to take you to a station.

'You'll do this until someone calls you and addresses you by your mother's maiden-name. Don't forget to split your luggage' He looked at her silly-sized case.

Rachel saluted. 'Permission to kiss you one, last time before I leave. Sir!'

She lapelled him again, kissing him firmly first before wrapping her arms tightly around him and hugging him close. 'Be safe Gray, I'll be thinking of you.' She whispered.

'I will, I promise.' He replied. 'I love you, don't worry and be safe yourself.'

Rachel squeezed him even harder, breathing him in deeply. 'I love you too.'

She stood back and wiped her eyes. 'I mean it; stay safe.'

'Yes sir; stay safe.' Maurice echoed.

Shelby punched Maurice gently on the arm. 'I have the very best around me, Maurice, safety is for the other side to worry about.' He said, more for the benefit of Rachel than Maurice.

'Good luck, sir, I'll be hearing from you in a few days then.' Maurice replied, also for the benefit of Rachel.

He picked up her suitcase. 'I'm ready when you are, Mrs S.'

Rachel gave Shelby a final kiss and hug goodbye and then left the house they had shared for so many, happy years.

As the door closed, Shelby's heart bumped in his chest; the Deere's house had been like this once; a final door closing and a silent, empty doom settling into the spaces which once had held dear, precious, loving life.

He stood for minutes which he didn't notice, just thinking of James Deere and his dead family and empty, lifeless home.

Suddenly he blinked, springing into motion, and turned on the lights in the hallway. Then quickly, almost running, he strode through to the living room and turned on those lights and the TV as well.

Into the kitchen, the overhead tube-lights clicked and crackled and then flickered into, bright, glowing life.

Shelby stopped and stood by the sink, gripping the ceramic edge tightly, his head bowed low, breathing heavily. His chest heaved; the pain of grief he suddenly felt for James Deere threatened to overwhelm him, drag him to his knees.

The poor, tortured man; *what weight you must have carried; how heavy the ghosts of your past must be.* How very heavy.

Shelby shuddered and then sighed, resolute. He *would* be safe. Life would not leave this place. It would not.

---
*

# Two

# Paradise Ends

## Chapter Eighteen

Brown sugar. A delight.
*I'll fucking kill that little bitch when she's brought back.*
Nazari dipped a crude-cut piece of amber-coloured sugar into his thick, black coffee, allowing it to fill up and turn dark before putting the stuff in his mouth.
*Fucking kill her! The smiling, little slut!*
He sat and ate his sugar, calm and placid on the outside while he sat in his office, his own, little domain.

His authority had been stung, stabbed deeply. It almost shamed him he felt, to have been fooled.

He bit down hard and crunched the sugar into spiteful oblivion.

*By a fucking girl!* He would rather have a dog outsmart him. *Fucking, little bitch!*

His flabby cheeks wobbled as he ate, while the nostrils of his hooked nose flared as he breathed heavily.

And if that wasn't enough, he had just been informed he would be getting a visitor, one of the bosses. Completely unconnected to the slave's escape but the timing couldn't have been worse.

Salya had been gone for almost three weeks now, Nazari's men had found no trace of her during their searches back along the roads they had arrived by. It had been more than a week later before they had discovered the toilet which had been moved.

The two nurses in charge of getting the children cleaned up that day, both denied any knowledge of how Salya had escaped and both of them knew nothing about the toilet. She must have slipped away somehow they said.

Both of them *had* known, however, that whether they had told Nazari straight away or not they were going to be punished anyway.

Silently they had agreed to give the spirited girl as much running time as possible before they had to report her disappearance. They held small hope that she would somehow bring help. Slim hope, a slave's hope but still hope nonetheless.

Nazari shuffled the papers he had in front of him, squaring the edges; the books were ready for inspection when his boss arrived in the morning.

All squared-up and accurate apart from the bitch who had escaped.

He had to alter the transit record to show *three* children had died on their way here instead of two. He would be damned if he would admit that one of them had actually escaped.

Hack, Nazari's number-one, had made sure that all of the soldiers and the other *staff* were well aware of what would happen to them if they ever spoke of the escape to anyone other than the 'Chief' as he referred to his boss.

Hack was mean and cold to the core and everyone took notice when he made his threats; they had seen with their own eyes the way in which he dealt with trouble-causers.

The two nurses were testament to that fact; both wore scars on their faces now where Hack had slashed them with his cutthroat razor. If the nurses hadn't been skilled and necessary to the running of the compound they would have both been ashes in an oil-drum by now.

The fat commander sipped at his coffee and chewed more sugar.

He stared coldly at the large couch at the back of the room.

The small, unmoving shape beneath the hastily-thrown sheet annoyed him. *She* had made him do that, lose himself in his anger. *She* was to blame, the *fucking bitch*, escaping like that.

Well God help her if he ever managed to get his hands on her. God help her.

A knock came at the door and then it opened. Hack walked in; a thickset man, brawny and chiselled with a full-face beard and a perpetual scowl.

He had an honest face, honest enough for it to tell you that if you ended up on his wrong side he would remove your head with his bare hands.

'Chief?' He said.

'Get rid of *that*.' Nazari said, distastefully, without looking up as he waved his hand in the direction of the couch. 'And then see that the Penthouse suite in the villa is made ready for our guest's arrival tomorrow.' He ordered.

The big soldier did as he was told and without a word left the room, carrying the small bundle in his left hand as though it were just a pile of dirty washing.

Nazari waited for the door to close and then picked up his mobile-phone, checking for messages from Azziz. There was one. *Found third camp. Heading west.* Was all it said.

The fat, little commander sighed and dropped the phone onto his desktop.

If anyone had a chance at finding the girl it was Azziz. As much as Nazari disliked the man, he was the best tracker they had; he knew the mountains better than any of the other soldiers at his command.

Eighty miles away, Nazari's tracker almost walked along the same path which Salya had used. He had just left the remains of her third camp behind.

Once the toilet had been discovered, Azziz had spent another week searching for the girl's trail before he eventually found her first campsite.

More than two weeks head-start she had.

Azziz didn't mind; once he had her trail he would follow her to the ends of the earth if need be, she couldn't stay hidden forever.

He crouched down on his haunches, chewing a piece of *khat* as he studied the way ahead.

From this view, Azziz could see the track which the girl had left; broken grass-stems, rocks which had been rolled out of their resting places leaving fresh patches of earth.

And dogs. There were at least a half-a-dozen, different dog-tracks following the girl through the mountains.

He raised his eyes and looked far ahead. If the dogs got to her first...

He let the thought trail off; he had been ordered to bring her back alive at all cost.

He knew his commander would blame him if she died, simply because Nazari liked to point his fat, important finger at people and have them tremble. He couldn't stand the man, but they both had a job to do and he knew the feeling was mutual.

Spitting out his *khat* and replacing it with a fresh piece, Aziz the tracker stood up and began walking into the west again.

* * *

Fire. The thing which it knew but couldn't understand, could only fear.

The huge dog stood at the top of a small, rocky knoll and peered into the greying twilight at the fire and the young, female *growler* sitting behind it.

*Growlers* were not prey because usually there were many of them.

The big dog's mind was confused. He and the five other dogs in this small pack had been following Salya through the mountains, picking up the scraps of the rabbits she left behind, nothing more. But as the days went by she became more and more the focus of their attention.

The *growler* was small and alone.

Salya flicked at the fire with her stick, sending firefly-comets rising to meet the dusk.

She smiled inwardly when she saw the dog sniff at the air; that's right, *fire*.

She had spotted them four days ago, slowly becoming more detailed as they drew closer. Finally they had stopped and didn't come any nearer than fifty yards.

She wasn't particularly bothered by the dogs, she knew exactly what they were up to; her life on the mountains had shaped her to the land, she wasn't afraid.

The dogs sensed the very same thing; the *growler* was small and alone but it wasn't weak, it smelled strong and dangerous.

The young girl stoked up her fire some more and ignored the dogs, turning her attention instead to her plan for exacting justice on the fat-man.

Weapons were the problem, or *a* weapon. She had made herself a crude knife the way her father had taught her, but what she really wanted was a gun. The rifle her father owned would be perfect; not too small, not too big, and she had been taught how to shoot it.

Salya was now on the lookout for a village or herders hut; she thought she might be able to find a gun she could steal - or borrow, as she preferred to think of it. She hated the thought of stealing but had little or no choice if she was going to have any chance of killing the fat-man.

She also thought of the weapons which were in the compound; could she get her hands on one of those? A pistol would be ideal if she found herself inside.

Her plan, however, was to hide high in the mountains and wait until the fat-man came outside. She could shoot him and escape that way.

She felt guilty about leaving the other children but what could she do? She couldn't kill everyone in the compound, but killing the fat-man would at least keep him from harming any of them further.

But someone else will harm them, someone else will come along and take over. They will always be in harm's way. How had the world changed so much in so little time? How?

She gave the fire a final, harsh prod, sending the flames blazing higher, and sighed unhappily. 'How?' She murmured.

Staring into the fire gave her no answers, it only reminded her of home and supper and of her family. Her family minus one.

She didn't know, even now, if she would ever see them again, but she thought if she died trying she would at least see her little brother again. There was comfort in that, a convincing comfort; either way she would be going home.

She lay down on her nest of grass and twig with that thought in her mind and fell asleep behind the safety of her fire.

Fire. The thing they didn't understand. The dogs lay down as well and waited.

* * *

Sand and dust-devils chased the two vehicles as they drove southwest following Afghanistan's western border.

The black, four-wheel-drive Chryslers were unmistakably for the affluent, but beneath the wealthy façade lay a vehicle which was more akin to a fighter-plane-cum-tank than a car.

They were fitted with enough armour-plate to withstand landmine and rocket attack, were armed with two, well hidden, front-mounted machine-guns and a single gun at the rear, and had an array of defence systems which would put many fighter-planes to shame. The only thing they couldn't do was actually fly.

Of the fifteen men riding inside the vehicles, only one of them was wishing that they *could* fly.

*What's wrong with using a damn helicopter?*

Jimenenko *'Jimi'* Ladislav had made this trip twice-a-year for the last eight years and it annoyed him more than any other, single thing in his life that he couldn't have a helicopter take him out to check the fat, little Nazari's books.

He hated these trips as it was, but this one was going to be the icing on the cake he thought.

His orders were to take command and set up his own, fourteen soldiers. They were expecting trouble; an "unknown force" was apparently on its way to Nazari's *Paradise Begins* and this force was *not* to be trifled with.

His brow furrowed and his dark eyes narrowed.

A single man he had been told. One man and they were going to set up enough firepower to start a small war.

When he had asked who and why, his handler had given him a file, inside it contained a single image of a snarling man.

The look on the man's face and in his eyes gave Ladislav the shivers, but he still thought they were going over the top with the excessive arms and soldiers for this one, insane man.

But what did he know, eh? He'd only been doing this job for twenty years.

He looked out of the tinted window across a dry and arid landscape, hemmed in by the mountains on the right and grazing off into the haze of the horizon on the left. They would be reaching the compound in little over an hour.

Even though the car was air-conditioned and luxurious, Ladislav could still feel the prickle of the heat under his white shirt and the aches in his back and legs from sitting in the leather seats for so long.

He itched to be free of the confines of the vehicle and looked forward to getting to his rooms. He would have a bath and then a massage he thought, maybe even a woman before he sat down with Commander Nazari.

The only perk of this trip was the women. He had no mind for children, or any woman under the age of thirty for that matter; Ladislav liked his woman to be older and experienced.

He caught himself thinking of the last time he had been here and the nurse who had been sent to *look after* him, hoping she would be available again. Then he kicked himself mentally for allowing even the smallest of attachments to a slave.

They were just things, objects, tools and toys to be taken and used as he pleased.

She may not even be there anymore, either dead or shipped out. But once again unbidden came the hope that he would see her.

He pulled his focus back from the landscape and focused instead on his reflection in the window. *You're getting softer the older you get*, his reflection said.

He was only forty. His dark-brown - almost black - hair had only the slightest hint of gray and his features were ruggedly handsome with a crescent-shaped scar framing the outer edge of his right eye, eyebrow to cheek.

*Soft*, he thought again, *soft and handsome*. He hoped she was there.

He thought back to the night she had entered his room with her eyes downcast and her hands held tightly in front of herself.

He wouldn't admit it then and he wouldn't admit it now but he had fallen hopelessly in love with her in that moment.

Flowing, black hair, eyes of deep ochre and the voluptuous figure of a mature woman. Nim she was called, and he had shown her a night of unfettered passion that had left her both exhausted and satisfied, something she had never received from a man before.

On the return flight after that particular visit, Ladislav had caught himself numerous times wishing he had brought her with him. Maybe he would this time, maybe he would.

His reflection seemed to be sneering at him. *What the hell would you do? How would you live? You're a fucking lieutenant in the Russian underground for God's sake.*

But why shouldn't I be happy? Why is it so, damn hard and complicated?

He ignored his reflection and returned his gaze to the passing landscape.

Maybe it was a mistake coming here, maybe they should have sent someone else this time.

He tightened his jaw. No. Maybe *this* time he *would* take the chance, risk everything and just disappear into the night.

His skin prickled again, with anger and frustration this time. They would find him. As free as he was, in reality it was just an illusion; he was no less a slave than the woman he loved.

A slave with power, how very *Kappo*-esque.

Every life on this small, blue planet has a defining moment, sometimes apparent and other times subtle.

Ladislav flushed while his heart raced as he realised that the disgusting label fit. Well, not anymore.

He didn't know how he would do it or how long it would take, but he would free both himself and Nim if it was the last thing he ever did.

## Chapter Nineteen

*I can hear the bluebells, daddy.*

The last words Finn had heard before he was clawed awake.

He had been dreaming the same dream for the past four nights; a voice beyond the veil of water, a female child.

As the place in the mountains where Finn planned to cross over into Afghanistan drew nearer, so the dream had began, always ending with the child's voice before the *she-wolf* attacked him and drew his attention away from it.

He knew better than to question her about it. He could feel her waiting, readying herself to stop his queries with her teeth and claws, like a subtle pressure waiting to be released.

But it frustrated him that he didn't know who she was, the child, or why he was dreaming of her. He felt he should know.

He stood up and kicked dust onto his small fire, smothering it before he began his climb up the mountain and then over into Afghanistan.

'Why haven't you ever questioned me about where I am going?' He said.

In his mind he felt her huff.

*Is that a real question, you straw-headed dolt?* She replied.

He could feel her mocking smirk.

Finn smiled. For some reason he smiled. Then his smile turned to a frown and he wondered at that. Why did he smile when she called him that?

'I thought you would have been angry.' Was all he said.

He turned his attention away from thoughts of the child and his dreams and looked high up the cliff face which he was about to climb instead.

*I'll be angry if you don't make it to the top in one piece.*

That was strange, Finn thought; she changed the subject when she could easily have just slapped him and made him get on with the climb.

Tying the small pouch of salted goat-meat around his waist which he had traded for the bike a few miles back, he secured his own pack to his back and then took the first handhold on the cliff.

The almost sheer wall of rock ran upward for three hundred feet, probably more.

He felt the man who was always at the back of his mind, usually sitting silently somewhere in the shadows, cringe when looking up at the place they were trying to reach.

*Shit.* The man rasped.

'I wondered where you had been hiding.' Finn said, as he lifted himself from the ground and pulled with his fingertips until his foot met a step and hold.

*I hate heights!*

*Be still!* The she-wolf commanded.

*You be still, you sadistic bitch!* The man retorted, his courage being buoyed by the fearful heights he could see.

*I will flay your salty skin straight from your bones!*

*Or you could just fuck off and die!*

*How dare you! I will not be spoken to thus by a coward!*

*Rather a coward than a mangy, flea-bitten hag!*

'Will you shut up!?' Finn's voice echoed and bounced around the rocks. 'In case you haven't noticed; I'm trying to climb a damn mountain!'

He felt a sudden release of the pressure in his head as both the man and the she-wolf blinked in surprise.

*Coward.* She hissed.

*Hag.* He spat.

And then they were gone, taking their argument with them.

Finn paused, holding himself effortlessly with just the fingertips of his right hand and the toes of his left foot while he stared at the rock.

That had never happened before; usually she scared the man into running away; this time it felt almost as though they had reached some strange understanding.

He shook his head; better together than apart he supposed.

The rock was grey and sharp, there were plenty of hand and footholds, and Finn climbed with all the ease of someone climbing a ladder. He soon reached the shelf he was aiming for.

A shallow incline led away up and left next, creating a zigzag path between boulders and through sharp clefts in the mountain-face. Soon though, he came to a place where he had to climb again.

He continued like this, climbing and then zigzagging on to the next face, until he came to the last climb before he would reach the summit.

The morning had passed into noon, this last stage was at least another eight hundred feet to the top.

Un-slinging his pack, he took his water-skin, drinking from it until it was almost empty, and then ate some of his goat-meat and grapes.

The grapes he had picked himself, found growing wild in the rolling, verdant, Iranian valleys at the very toes of the mountain he was climbing. They were large and green and sweet.

He sat back against the rock for awhile and looked out at the world lying before him; an endless carpet of greens and russet rolled out ahead, browns of earth and silvers of water, all covered by the infinite, blue sky.

It was good to be alive. For some it was good to be alive.

Behind him, over the mountain's border into Afghanistan, Finn could almost feel the misery emanating from the place he was heading for.

Like a river of poison with vaporous, tributary fingers leading out into an unsuspecting world but all leading back to its source if you knew where to look and how to follow.

He felt he had been following this road for an eternity, every stop and task completed moved him one step forward to this end but never in sight, always eluding him.

And now he suddenly found himself so very close, the road coming to an abrupt halt with a final goal ahead. His *geis* was coming to an end, he would be going home soon.

A small smile played across his scarred features and his lightning-eyes were full of life and happiness and a rare, excited fluttering in his chest bore his spirits up higher than he had felt for a long, long time.

He stood up and turned to face the east. 'I am Finn of the Seven-Spears and Nine Northern Stars, and I am coming.' He said, as he laughed. 'I am coming.'

He took the first hold on the rock and then began climbing, grinning, sometimes chuckling, sometimes laughing loudly, as he scaled the last leg of the mountain.

Anyone seeing him would have thought they were looking at a spider-man; no one should be able to climb the way he climbed; he gave no thought and no pause as he reached ever upward, finding holds and slivers which even the most experienced of climbers would have not been able to use.

Finn had no fear of rock or mountains or heights; he only had the indefatigable belief in his own body and spirit, his unfaltering respect for himself and the space he occupied in the universe.

When he trod the forest paths, the forests welcomed him, when he swam the rivers, the rivers flowed with him, and when he climbed the mountains, the mountains embraced him. His respect for everything rewarded him with every respect.

Soon he reached the top, taking the edge under his palms and then lifting himself over onto the craggy, dusty ledge.

He stood up and surveyed the landscape flowing off into the east; a patchwork of rolling hills and small forests, broken here and there by the settlements which had been built up and around them.

South of him, a few hundred miles away, lay the border to Pakistan. While three hundred miles or so away to the North lay the place he was making for.

He had made it in good time, plenty of time to spy out the way and plan his moves.

A pathway, narrow and cracked, led down to a massive outcrop of rock topped with hardy mountain-grass. He could see hare-droppings scattered all around.

Further down, a leap of ten feet, and a huge, slab of rock broke away from the mountain, leaning obliquely into the east.

Between mountain and rock a crack ran on into blackness; a good place to make camp.

He set a wire snare in the grass and then jumped down to the leaning rock and the crack.

Two days he planned to stay here; he needed a wash and so did his clothes, he suspected that he smelled like a gutter. Or worse.

After checking the narrow cave for any other occupants - not least of all snakes and wild dogs - he left his gear inside and then went wood collecting.

There was plenty of old, fallen branches and twigs, dried grass and good, springy moss to be had and after recovering two, large arms full he went in search of water.

He could smell it on the air; there was a rush and tumble of it somewhere nearby, he could just make out the almost inaudible hiss of water falling.

After half-an-hour of searching and following his nose, Finn came to the small spill of water he was looking for.

A thin line cascaded down from its source higher up the slopes, falling and then landing into a small pool below.

He smiled; he could shower under the fall and wash his clothes in the pool.

He stripped down, laying his peasant's whites and the black shirt and trousers on a boulder by the side of the water.

After gathering up a few small stones and rocks, he made a small bowl shape at the edge of the pool and then began dropping dirt into it, allowing it to absorb the water which he had trapped. He soon had a pile of thick, soft, silky, grey mud.

He soaked his garments and began washing them with the mud, working it into the clothes and scrubbing them gently together, trapping the dirt and grime and odours and drawing them out of the fabric.

Once they were all sufficiently covered and scrubbed he began rinsing them in the water.

The mud flowed away, a cloudy stream heading over the edge of the pool and spilling down into the next one below.

The trick was to not allow the mud to dry; it would stain if it hardened onto the cloth.

He spent more than an hour washing his clothes before laying them out on the grass to dry under the sun. The grass would absorb much of the water and replace it with a fresh, natural smell.

Using the remaining mud, Finn covered much of his body in the stuff, once again working it in and gently scrubbing his skin with it.

He paid particular attention to his feet, using a handful of straw-grass to scrub away at the callused skin of his heels and big-toes.

If anything could bring a quest to an abrupt end it was trench-foot; the soldiers bane.

He worked the mud into his hair and neck, behind his ears and lastly he covered his face. He stood up, a tall, grey, living statue he seemed to be.

Unlike his clothes, he left the mud to dry and tighten, pulling the dirt from his pores, before he stepped into the fall of water and began rinsing himself off.

The water was mountain-cool and he felt the thrill and invigoration take his breath away, making him laugh happily to be alive and now clean.

The sun, high and behind him, warmed his naked skin as he revelled under the strokes and caresses of the silky water.

He began to hum a tune and then quietly at first, he began to sing.

'Deer, the fleet-footed, runs along by my side,
Whether running from wolves,
Or driven by faery kings,
Never will he catch me, even in his pride.

'Hare, the highest leaper, leaps me to and fro,
From playful joy of free air,
Or escaping tightening snare,
Never will he catch me, from dawn until home.

'Fox, the cunning thinker, pads softly on my flow,
Whether hiding hunted scent,
Or quenching hunters thirst,
Never will he catch me, however far he roam.

'Man, tall and awake, dams me and shapes me,
But sailing for home or victory,
Or catching the fish in my bower,
Never will he catch me, he knows always I am free.

'But to all of you living things, of land, sea or air,
I give and give you breath of life,
Wash away your stains of day,
But never will you catch me, and never must you dare.'

'Oh! I do love that song, Cait, I could sing it all d-.'

Finn's whole body suddenly stiffened as the she-wolf attacked him in his mind.

He toppled backward, hitting the wet rocks heavily before sliding down into the pool. An inky stream of dark-red trickled from the back of his head, flowing out and away over the edge.

The sun was at least three hours older when he opened his eyes. His head ached and there was a throbbing lump at the back.

He touched it softly and drew his fingers away, examining them. There was a little blood but not much.

He could still hear the small waterfall he had been showering beneath musically tumbling somewhere in front of him.

He was laid under a tree, a small fire burning at his right hand. He was still naked, he felt, but there was a large, white towel laid across his legs and torso.

His mind reeled as he realised someone had moved him and covered him up.

He sat up and looked around, wincing as hot hammers pounded the top of his head.

There was no one in sight. But he could feel someone. Someone watching him.

Rubbing his head, he lay back down and relaxed, the tension at the top of his skull released almost instantly.

'Whoever you are, I thank you for your assistance.' He said. 'You will forgive me for not remembering what it was that happened to me.'

Everything remained silent for a moment more then came small, light footfalls from behind a tree on his left, over on the other side of the fire. A young girl stood there.

'You fell into the pool and hit your head.' Salya said, quietly. 'You were going to drown.'

Finn's blue eyes caught the girls own frightened brown eyes, holding them. 'What is your name?' He asked.

'Salya.' She replied.

'I am Finn of the Seven-Spears and Nine Northern Stars. I am in your debt, Salya.' He said, solemnly

Only once before had he spoken those words to someone; Lucas, many years ago now it seemed.

Salya remained where she was, fearful of the giant warrior; for warrior was exactly how she saw him, his scars were all the proof she had needed.

But his eyes, as serious as they seemed to be, were gentle when they looked at her.

'You need not fear me, child. You will endure no harm while in my company, neither from myself or anyone who might happen by.'

And Salya believed him.

She stepped forward and produced a large, snared hare she held in her hands. It was almost as tall as she was.

Finn recognised the snare as his own. He smiled at her then; she had obviously found his camp and yet here she was. She could easily have just relieved him of his things and left him under the tree.

'That is a good catch.' Was all he said.

Salya stepped up to the fire and laid the hare on the ground. She removed the snare and coiled it back up, holding it out for Finn to take.

'You keep hold of it for now.' He said.

She took it back and slipped it beneath her belt and then produced two knives from her waistband. One of them was a wooden knife; a small, pointed stiletto thing.

Her father had shown her how to make these survival knives, telling her that if she was ever lost and hungry a knife like this would see her through if she used her wits and stayed strong.

The other knife was one of the daggers which Finn kept beneath his shirt, she must have found them when she had picked up his snare and discovered his camp.

'I would like to use this knife, sir,' she said, holding the steel dagger up in front of her, 'because it will be quicker than using my own, wooden knife. But only with your permission.' She said, lowering her eyes.

Finn raised his eyebrow at that; hadn't the girl heard him when he had said he was in her debt? 'Look at me, child.' He said.

Salya looked up and met his gaze.

'While we are in each other's company we are friends; you saved my life and I will not forget that. So please, call me Finn, and use whatever things of mine you may need.'

He could see she was having trouble digesting his words, it was apparent that she hadn't heard anything like that before.

'If you will trust me as I trust you,' he added, 'then I'm sure things will be easier for the both of us.'

She nodded subtly, still unsure of the correct etiquette, but she did feel much better and a little safer. Not least of all because of the weapons and equipment she had also found in Finn's bag. *Use whatever things of mine you may need* he had said.

She frowned a little and then picked up the hare. 'I'll go and prepare this while you dress.' She said, before she turned away and walked back to the shallow pool.

Finn watched her go, he could see there was something troubling the young girl and he was pretty sure it wasn't just him she was troubled about; she looked to be carrying a burden as heavy as his.

At the pool, Salya was busy skinning and cleaning the hare, putting all of the useless stuff into a pile on the rocks beside her.

Once she had the head, tail and feet removed she washed the innards and then picked the lot up and waded to the other side.

She continued to walk into the shade of the trees overhanging the rocky ledge and looked down. Although she couldn't see them, Salya knew the dogs were down there somewhere.

She dropped her offering over the edge and watched it sail ten feet until it met the ground with a wet thud.

As she turned away, the bushes and scrub below rustled as the dogs moved in for their daily, free meal.

She washed the carcass before returning back to the fire and Finn.

He was dressed and sitting up against the tree now, staring into the flames.

Salya was familiar with that look and the feelings which accompanied it.

Finn blinked and brought his attention back to the present, taking a good look at the meat in Salya's hands.

'We could feed a small army with that.' He nodded. 'I hope you're hungry, Salya, because Old Maeve knows I'm famished.' He grinned at her, genuinely happy.

Salya felt her face flush and then she returned his smile and nodded. 'I have some chukri and carrots.' She said.

'And I have grapes and a little goat's cheese.' Finn added. 'We will have a feast in honour of our new friendship.'

He stood up. 'I will go and fetch them and a pot to cook it all in.'

He walked away to his camp.

Salya watched him go, holding a quiet yet unsure respect for the tall man.

By the time Finn had returned, Salya had spitted the hare and was slowly turning it over the fire.

The flames sizzled and popped as the juices dripped.

Finn collected the water in his cooking-pot and then chopped up the carrots and a little of the chukri, dropping it all into the water. He placed the pot onto the edge of the fire and then sat and stirred with his knife.

Both of them sat in comfortable silence whilst each attended to their cooking.

Once the meal was cooked and ready, they sat now as they ate at the edge of the fire facing one another.

'Did you mean it when you said you were in my debt?' Salya asked, her voice small and wavering.

Finn stopped his eating and placed his leg of hare on the lid of the cooking pot.

He sat up straight and met Salya's eyes. 'Yes I did.' He replied. 'I mean every word that I say; to lie, to say the thing which is not, is a ridiculousness which should be beyond the measure of even the most foolish.'

Salya thought about that and then smiled weakly. 'My father always taught us; that if you always told the truth then you would never have to remember anything.' She said.

Finn nodded. 'Someone else once said that, an American bard, long dead now, but he was right was he not?'

Salya nodded her head in agreement.

'So tell me, my new friend,' Finn said, reassuringly, 'what it is that is troubling you and what I may do to help; I can sense you have something to ask of me but is too afraid to say the words.'

Salya didn't know what to say. How do you ask someone or tell someone that you want a man dead? Where do you begin a conversation like that?

Finn was right; she was afraid to say the words. She had never spoken out loud what she had been through and the things she had witnessed, like saying the words made them real, made her nightmares and fears more real.

'A man killed my little brother.' She suddenly blurted out.

Finn nodded slowly. 'Tell me about him, your brother, what was he like?'

He sat and listened as Salya spoke of Rafiq, his infectious, mischievous laughter and cheeky grin, the way he always asked questions and never stopped talking.

She told him of her whole family and what they did on the mountain slopes, how they lived and were happy.

She didn't cry as she spoke, Finn noticed; resolute.

Eventually, Salya came to the parts of the story where she and Rafiq had been kidnapped.

She told Finn of her rape and of Rafiq's small, dead body being carried from the truck, of the fat-man and the slaves, the burning oil-drums, and finally she finished by telling him of her escape through the sewer-pipe.

Finn listened with all of the grace and understanding afforded a best friend, and when Salya had finished, he sat deep in thought for a moment.

The place she had described was no doubt the very place he was heading for, a twist of fate had led their paths together.

Eventually he looked up at the young girl and spoke. 'It would seem that your god and mine have conspired to bring us together, Salya, my friend.'

He raised his eyes to the skies and scoffed.

Salya followed his gaze, furrowing her brow, puzzled. What did he mean?

When the sky gave her no answers, she dropped her gaze again. 'You know of the place?' She asked.

Finn dropped his own eyes then. 'Aye, I know of it.' He nodded. 'I'm on my way there now.'

The alarm in Salya showed on her face and the sudden tensing of her body, but she tried to remain as calm as she could.

It didn't work; Finn could see her fear rising as though he were watching a goblet fill with mead.

'Why are you going there?' She asked him.

He cocked his head as though listening to something on the breeze and then looked straight at her again. 'I'm going to kill the men that are there.' He answered solemnly. 'And release the children and the slaves. Then I am going to burn it all down to the ground.'

Salya sat in silence, her face still afraid. Only now afraid because she could see that the man with the lightning-eyes was telling the truth and could feel by the conviction in his voice that he was powerful enough to do what he said he was going to do.

Her lips began to tremble and her voice quivered. 'I will help you.' And her tears ran down her cheeks.

'I know you will. You already have.' Finn replied. 'You have given me the perfect way to enter the place unnoticed for one thing.'

He stood up and came and sat by Salya's side. He draped his huge arm over her and drew her close to him.

'We will see justice is delivered for Rafiq and all of the others who have suffered.' He said, as he wiped her tears away. 'And then you will go home, Salya. We will all go home.'

## Chapter Twenty

The living room at the Deere's, bay-side cottage had been transformed from quaint abode to hi-tech lab almost overnight.

Most of the furniture had been relegated to the hallway, stacked, piled, taped and tied. While an assorted array of computer desks and consoles, not to mention a few miles of cable and half a dozen monitors, were moved in.

Anna had been very busy, and exactly as she had promised she had the tech-lab up and running within twelve hours.

A single, inconspicuous, drop-gate truck had turned up after a quick phone call. Three men had jumped out who immediately began moving the equipment in and setting it up straight away.

One hour later - almost to the minute, Shelby had noted - the three men had said a hasty farewell to Anna and then had driven away.

Shelby and Bollinger had stayed in the dining room, watching fascinated as the living room slowly changed its appearance.

Anna sat now, at her personal station, and finished the security coding which would see the network stay hidden and off the grid. 'I am almost done.' She said. 'Two, more minutes.'

Her petit fingers were a blur as she typed in the final lines of code. She ended with the usual flourish and then stood up, making her way to stand in front of the master consol at the centre of the room.

The display wasn't quite as big as the one in Harrison's lab but it was impressive enough.

The small, German hacker pulled the white keyboard out on its sliding tray and began punching in a series of commands.

The large monitor flickered into life, rolling code streamed upward rapidly. The code suddenly disappeared and was replaced by a blue background image split into six boxes; three above and three below.

'And we are up and running.' Anna said.

She turned to face Shelby and Bollinger. 'From here,' she nodded, indicating the monitor behind her. 'I can access all of the hardware which will be doing our searches and communications.'

She pointed to the machines on the other side of the room. 'I can work them individually or as a tethered group.'

Sophie scoffed. 'Now you're just being smarmy for the hell of it.'

'Of course.' Anna replied, and winked.

She turned to Shelby. 'Where would you like to begin, Mr Interpol?'

'Do you really have to call me that? I don't go around calling you Mrs Nova-Bug, now do I?'

'I thought it was quite catchy.' Sophie said, innocently.

Shelby gave her a wry look and then turned back to Anna. 'Gray will do fine.' He said. 'And to answer your question; I don't know, I'm not sure what your setup is capable of yet.'

It was Anna's turn to dish out the wry looks. 'Let us just say that my setup is capable of *everything*. If you give me something to do and I can't do it - and I will take that very personally if you do, you understand?' She said, in a lowered voice. 'Then I will simply tell you. And more than likely tear mine, yours and anyone else's hair out while I try to find a solution to the problem.' She ended with a sweet smile.

Shelby and Bollinger just looked at her; they knew she was serious.

'Well, I'm sure you and your setup will be able to do pretty much anything, so-,' Shelby shrugged and left the sentence unfinished, unsure what to say anyway.

'Why don't we start with something close to home?' Sophie suggested. 'Let's see if we can find anything connecting Kevin Keys to Bradley Hinds, other than the fact that Keys was Hinds' boss?'

'Good idea. Can you get on with that, Soph?' Shelby answered. 'I've been thinking about Afghanistan.'

He turned back to Anna while Sophie sat down behind one of the linked-up consoles. 'Can we get a map of Afghanistan up there?' He asked, pointing to the big screen.

Anna sat down at the console and tapped in a few command lines. A satellite view appeared in one of the six windows. She tapped another key and the image filled the entire screen.

Shelby was impressed. 'Is that a live image?' He asked.

'Yes, of course.' Anna replied.

'Can you get a map image instead, one that will show borders?'

Anna stared hard at Shelby. 'What colour would you like the borders to be?' She said, a little tightly.

'Um. Red would be fine.' He answered, wondering what he had said to deserve *that* withering look.

The satellite image remained in place, but thin, red lines suddenly appeared, marking out all of the borders and giving the names of all the countries in the view, not to mention major city-names too. All in real-time.

'Oh. Right.' Shelby said, impressed and suddenly understanding the look she had given him. 'I didn't know you could do that.'

He leaned over and raised his hand to point at the border of Afghanistan but Anna pulled him back and handed him a slim, metal tube.

'Point at the screen and move the red dot around, hold the red button if you wish to write something, or the blue button to remove something.' She said.

Shelby took the tube and pointed it at the screen. Only then did the small dot appear. 'This is a great bit of kit.' He marvelled.

He practised for a minute, pressing the button and writing and then erasing. 'Got to get one of these back at headquarters.' He mumbled.

He shook the marvel from his head and carried on. 'Right. Afghanistan.'

He pulled up a chair and sat down next to Anna. 'Finn's message to me saw his journey from Turkey start here.'

He marked the place where he was almost certain Finn had been seen using an old, mountain track.

'His message mentioned the months April and May, so I think - if Finn really is as meticulous as we think he is - I think he means to be doing something in the last few days of April and during the first few days of May.'

He flicked the marker to draw a crude line over the top of the Iranian and Afghanistan border, highlighting it. 'Given that we are now at the end of the second week of April we can correlate his rough place of entry into Afghanistan from the Iranian side.' He said, then added, 'and I am almost certain he *has* crossed over now.' He looked at Anna.

'What makes you so sure?' She asked.

'Whatever it is Finn is going to do ties up with a politician or politicians, someone very high up who can manipulate the authorities and someone who can order men to kill.'

Shelby waited until his words had sunk in. 'Now, I may be climbing in the wrong forest entirely, but I would say that anyone big and high up must be hiding something big and high up; something like a slave outpost, or a smuggling depot, or more probable; both.'

Anna nodded her head, agreeing. 'And something that big would have to be in a prime, anonymous location to be able to operate.'

'Exactly!' Shelby said. 'Not only that; if they hear of Finn coming their way - which I am almost certain they have - then they will have to send in backup and get to reinforcing the place. Finn will surely try to get there as fast as he can to avoid having to tackle more men than he has to.'

He studied the map. 'We're looking for somewhere highly secret and well out of the way.' He said, distracted.

Before he could elaborate further, Sophie spoke. 'Somewhere like in the desert, maybe?'

They both turned to face her.

'I've just pinged about a million emails,' she glanced at Anna. 'Your software is amazing, girl, simply amazing.'

'In the ten-minutes since you started?' Shelby laughed. 'Really?'

'Okay, maybe not exactly a million but near enough. Anyway, the software does a strange spider-trace thingy and looks at emails from outside Hinds' contact circle.' Sophia said, clearly impressed.

'What do you mean?' Shelby asked her.

'She means; the trace goes down the networks of anyone who sent Hinds an email or vice versa.' Anna put in casually. 'It will trace their emails to any depth which you set; I think it is currently set to ten. In short; it bypasses all of the cyclic-redundancy-checks between sender and recipient and catches the communication-matrix before it can encode the messages.'

'Yes; what she said.' Sophie said, pointing to Anna. 'Well, it came back with a couple of emails sent to a mobile phone.

'I noticed something strange when I saw that the first two were received in Russia, but the next one was suddenly received in Afghanistan.'

She leaned forward and took the tube from Shelby's hand. 'Somewhere here.' She finished, and drew a circle around an empty zone of desert in the south-west of Afghanistan.

'Bloody great work, you two!' Shelby grinned. 'Why in God's vagina didn't we get a set up like this in the earlier days of searching for Finn?'

Anna sniggered.

Sophie smirked and then sniggered herself because Anna had.

'What can we do with what we know, Anna?' Shelby asked, ignoring her snickering. 'Can we zoom in at all? To that area for example?' He pointed to the circle on the map.

'We can,' she replied, 'but it will only go so far; this is an old Korean satellite we are using to view through, but I will do my best. I think at the very least we will be able to make out structures, they won't be highly detailed but they will break the landscape enough to show themselves.'

'That's good enough for me.'

Shelby turned to Sophie then. 'Were any of the emails directly from Hinds to the Russian recipient?' He asked her.

'Yes, one. It was an invitation to a party, a charity event held earlier in the year.'

'Who was the Russian recipient?'

'Someone called Mary Popplegrade.' Sophie's look said it all, but before Shelby could say anything, Anna laughed.

'Ha! Sugar-mail.' She said. 'Harrison invented that, you know?'

'Did he now? And what exactly *is* sugar-mail?' Shelby asked, a little icily.

'"*A sweet way to mail and be mailed and not be seen.*" Harrison's words, not mine.' She replied, looking innocent. 'It is a way to send an email from a domain which the software creates - a bogus, non-existent domain - before it sends each email.'

'Clever.' Shelby said. 'Very clever, the mails would only be able to be traced so far back if at all.'

'Yes exactly.' Anna nodded. 'It really is a wonder that they came to light at all, but having said that; *Code-8* are very clever people; the software we are running is looking in places which you wouldn't believe existed.'

'Well, we have taken a huge leap forward in our task,' Shelby said, impressed. 'And that email has confirmed my suspicions; I thought it would be more probable for Finn to have another country in mind to escape to, or a place where he can release any victims he recovers to the authorities at least. I'm pretty sure he is well aware that he couldn't hand them over to any Afghani authority, not with any sure conviction of their continued safety at any rate.'

He took the tube back from Sophie and then pointed it at the monitor. The red dot hovered over the south-western border leading to Pakistan. 'I believe that he will try to come back this way. It's what I would do; I wouldn't backtrack over the mountains, not with children to look after, I'd go down to the flatter plains and then head for a country which held European consulates and embassies.'

He looked between the two women. 'And of course, we'll be there somewhere.'

He turned back to the map. 'What do we know about this area.' He asked, pointing to the north-west of Pakistan.

Anna tapped keys and a rectangle with amber lettering appeared over the location.

'Mining mainly, copper and gold; the Saindak Copper and Gold Project lies fifty kilometres south of the border.' Anna read aloud. 'There are a few small mining settlements but nothing more significant than Saindak.'

'It's a good place to head;' Shelby said, 'they will have a good policing system around a town like that, not to mention good communications such as the internet. I would be willing to bet that Finn knows of it.' He finished.

He lean back in his seat.

The whole game had opened up now, the Finn side of things at least. There was still the mastermind behind it all, but Shelby refused to believe it was Kevin Keys, there was some connection somewhere which involved his friend, but it wasn't Keys who was at the top. It couldn't be. Could it?

He swivelled around in his seat. 'Right, I think I need to pay Kevin a visit.' He said. 'While I do that; Anna, could you make a comprehensive scan of our target area, make notes of everything relevant?'

He turned to his partner. 'And you, Sophie, could you work those email and communication searches, try and find a common link?'

'Okay, Gray, but if the people we are looking for *are* using this *sugar-mail* system then we're not going to get very much.' She replied.

'I know, but every little bit helps. You had a great hit with the random desert trace.' He said, nodding his head, indicating the big screen. 'You never know.'

\* \* \*

The four-hour drive back to London felt slow and tedious but it gave Shelby time to think things over.

Kevin was at the centre of something - or very near to at least - but did he know that he was? He had the obvious connection of Finn; he had been following the case as closely as was possible, he'd admitted that. He also had connections to Hinds, who had crossed paths with Finn.

Now that didn't make sense; surely Kevin would have been on the lookout for Finn if he was truly in cahoots with slavers and underground sex rings? But if he was, why would he set Hinds up to meet Finn? Why hadn't he made his business more secure and doubled the guard so to speak? It just didn't make any kind of sense.

Then there was the message to Shelby from Finn. It was without a doubt now that someone else had accessed the information and knew about Finn's plan to do something in Afghanistan.

That was one piece of this sordid puzzle which made Shelby angry, because it pointed the finger directly at Interpol, maybe not the mastermind himself but someone definitely in his grasp. And to make matters worse, he couldn't begin an investigation from that angle because he would have to reveal Hinds' murder.

The Russian connection was interesting; the Russian underground had a notoriety at Interpol which superseded that of even the public's knowledge and opinion.

They were extremely intelligent and very well organised, they had fingers in pies and people in their pockets from all around the globe, and their 'business ethics' were amongst the most ruthless and brutal.

Is this where the trail was leading? Was the man at the top the top-man in the Russian underground?

Shelby had frowned deeply and angrily at that idea. If that was the case then that man would surely escape, somehow withdrawing his reach and covering his tracks well before he or anyone else could approach him.

As London came into sight, Shelby turned his thoughts to Rachel. Her having to hide made him angriest of all.

He knew she would be frightened and worried for him and he couldn't imagine what she would go through if anything happened to him, but at least he knew she was safe and hopefully untraceable.

It played on his mind that the very technology he was using himself to track Finn could be used against him by the people who were clearly keeping tabs on the case.

By the time Shelby arrived at Keys' door he was in a black mood.

He rang the doorbell and waited.

A few seconds later and it was opened by a man Shelby had never met before. Tall, mid-thirties, dark, short-cropped hair, dressed in a suit and tie and wearing all the demeanour of a highly-trained security-guard.

'Yes?' The tall man said.

Shelby could just make out the small bulge of the man's gun-holster beneath his jacket.

His left hand was hidden from view behind the door as though he were holding the handle.

Shelby knew that he was holding his gun in that hand.

He pulled his wallet from his own jacket and flashed his Interpol identification. 'Inspector Shelby,' he said, 'I'm here to see Mister Keys.'

He put his wallet away and gave the man the chance to appraise him properly.

In Shelby's mind he saw the man as extra security; Kevin must really be taking him seriously which led him to believe even further that Kevin Keys wasn't intentionally involved with whatever was going on. His mood lightened a little.

The man stood back and re-holstered his pistol. 'Sorry about that, sir; I'm on security duty you understand? Please come in, Mister Keys is in the sitting room.'

Shelby walked through into the hallway and then turned left into the living room.

Keys was sitting in his favourite chair, watching the business channel. He leaped up when he saw Shelby walk in. 'Graham!' His voice sounded anxious. 'What brings you here unannounced? Is everything alright? Has something happened?'

Shelby noted the genuine fear and alarm in his friend's voice and by the look on his face.

He relaxed further; if Kevin was involved and knew what he was doing then he was doing a damn fine job of hiding it.

'Nothing to worry about, Kev, I was just checking in and following up on a lead.'

He nodded to the doorway. 'I see you've got some extra security in.'

'Not extra; a replacement. Sean's on leave for three weeks, gone home to Ireland to catch up on his fishing.' Keys said. 'George out there is the usual chap who comes in when Sean takes his leave. He's a good man.'

He gestured to the chair opposite the one he had been sitting in. 'Whiskey with a touch of dry-ginger?' He asked.

Shelby sat down. 'That would really hit the spot, Kev, thanks.'

'So what's this lead you are following?' Keys asked while he poured the drinks.

Shelby relaxed and put on an air of casual enquiry. 'What do you know about Bradley Hinds?'

Keys turned around and carried the two whiskies back to the seats. 'Hinds? He's one of mine, Enterprise Liaison.' He said, handing Shelby his glass. 'He's a few steps down from me, you realise? I don't have much to do with the man personally. But his records are neat and he is prompt with his reports and doing his duties. Why?'

He sat down and waited for Shelby to speak.

'Could you give him a call?' Was all Shelby said.

'Of course.' Keys frowned but picked up his mobile and pressed the buttons.

fter a few seconds he spoke. 'Hello, Melanie? It's Kevin.' He paused as he listened to the woman called Melanie on the other end. 'Yes, I know what I said and I promise you I am taking it as easy as can be.'

He covered the mouthpiece and spoke to Shelby. 'Melanie's my PA and constantly worries. As if I don't have enough of that with Margret!' He rolled his eyes.

He returned his attention to the woman on the other end of his phone. 'I'm calling for a friend, could you give me Bradley Hinds' number please?' He said, when she had finished.

He paused as his PA retrieved the number. He then began scribbling on the pad he had in front of him on the coffee table. 'That's great, Melanie, thank you.' He paused again. 'Yes, yes I will, I'll tell her you send your best. Thanks again, Melanie, see you in a couple of weeks.'

He disconnected the call and then sighed loudly. 'I'm sure those two are in it thick-as-thieves; one always feeds me up and the other always makes me rest; it's a damn conspiracy to get me fat, I tell you!'

Shelby chuckled. 'You must have that kind of personality which just brings out the mother in all women, Kev. I would take that as blessing if I were you.' He tipped his glass.

Keys just grinned and raised his own glass. 'Can't argue with that.' He said. 'Right, let's give Hinds a call.'

He tapped in the number he had been given and waited as it rang. 'Oh. It's gone straight to his message box. Let me try it again.'

He redialled and waited, but again the connection went straight to Hinds' answering service. 'Hello Bradley, it's Kevin Keys. Could you give me a call as soon as you get this message. Thank you.' He hung up again.

'Well I'm sorry about that, Graham, it seems Hinds is unavailable at this point. He may be on annual leave somewhere, I can easily find out if you like?'

'That won't be necessary, I can wait, but thanks for trying anyway.'

Shelby sipped at his drink. 'Can you remember the last time you saw Hinds?'

Keys thought for a moment. 'Hm. About three or four weeks ago at a charity party in Bulgaria.'

Shelby sat in thought. What were the chances of Keys' house being under surveillance? He wasn't about to test the theory and kept what he knew about Hinds to himself.

'Well Bulgaria has never cropped up.' He said, manoeuvring the subject a little.

'What do you mean.'

'Well, I have a theory,' Shelby began his lie, 'that Finn may be finding his targets whereabouts by using the internet to hack and trace emails. I have a hunch now that Bulgaria may be next on his list.'

Keys wasn't stupid, he knew something wasn't being said. 'So how does Hinds fit into all this?' He queried.

'He doesn't really. I was simply curious where Hinds had been located in the world when he sent out the invitations to that charity party.'

'Well why does *that* have any bearing?'

Shelby sighed, he would have to reveal a clue if he was going to get away with the whole lie. 'One of the recipients to that invite was completely anonymous.' He said, not liking even that small piece to be possibly heard by prying ears. 'We think it may have been Finn intercepting it.' And hoped that, that part of the lie would sufficiently cover the truth.

He finished his drink and placed his glass on the table. 'To be truthful, Kev, I think that avenue is going to prove useless anyway; it was really a stab in the dark. I'll still have to make enquiries into Bulgaria to be sure, but I'm not hopeful.'

Keys studied Shelby; his friend was lying. He wasn't lying directly to him, but he was definitely lying.

His brow furrowed as he came to the conclusion that he was lying to someone else, someone who maybe listening. He was lying to protect him.

He sat back and gulped down his own drink ready to join in with the misdirection. He hoped Shelby would notice he was going along with him.

'Well if I can help you with that let me know; I have a few friends in the consulate over there.' He smiled.

Shelby saw through it right away; Kevin knew he was lying about something and was playing along. Good; it meant Kevin knew that he was trying to protect him by not giving him any knowledge of where the Finn case was really heading.

The two men sat and talked for an hour more, keeping the subject well away from Hinds, talking mainly about the rugby or their university days or business and the world in general.

Shelby left Keys' house feeling a little lighter; knowing his friend wasn't involved with enslaved children and smugglers was a relief beyond measure, but he still had the feeling that Kevin was still involved and still in danger to some degree and that weighed heavily on his mind as he drove back north to the Deere's house.

## Chapter Twenty-One

Beauty without was merely a gilded lie if there was no beauty within.

Nim looked at herself in the mirror. Where is my beauty within? She couldn't remember what that was like, the feeling. She had the memory, but memories were only shadows of things, things she couldn't have anymore.

All of the feelings of anger and fear and anxiety which she had held in the early days, years ago now, were relegated to the same memories. Nim didn't feel much, she just moved through space and time, a speck waiting for itself to be eventually blown along to the end of its existence.

The mirror was neither cruel nor kind, only showing her the truth; she was just a human mote of dust, moved along a path which others had carved.

Years ago she would have cried at that, but now? No tears would come, even if she tried; she was empty.

She ran her finger along the lines of the scars on both of her cheeks; Hack's punishment.

What would *he* say about that, the Russian who insisted on being so nice to her, what would *he* say about Hack's work on her face?

She flushed when she thought of the Russian. She still couldn't bring herself to think of him by his name, Jimi, as he had asked her to call him. But the flush in her cheeks meant something, a feeling she was afraid of.

The flush travelled down into her chest where it heaved, sending butterflies skipping around in her stomach and a swell of warmth into her groin.

She hated him for that, hated herself for allowing that. How had it happened?

She knew the answer and dropped her gaze, her own soul looked back at her and she couldn't face it down.

It had happened because the Russian hadn't just been fucking her, using her as she was meant to be used; he had made love to her, and his passion had seemed limitless, pure and unrestrained the way a lover should be. He had even held her in her arms and stroked her and kissed her until she had fallen asleep. And always, always he called her by her name.

She raised her head again and looked at herself. 'You are not a stupid girl' She said aloud. 'You are not a stupid girl.'

Then why did she feel like one when she had been summoned to the village again? Only he would have asked for her, only... Jimi.

She blushed even harder, clutching her arms to her chest as the unfamiliar warm feelings set the butterflies off again.

A cold knot of fear wormed its way through the warmth. What if he didn't want her once he saw what had happened to her face?

Why do I care? Wouldn't it be better as it was? Just left alone to be a nurse to slaves and wander to the end of days until it all ended?

She studied her face again. *How is that better than hope?* Her soul was telling her.

But if there was one thing which Nim understood it was that hope was merely a carrot on a stick; always there in full view, but like tomorrow it never actually came. Not for her, not for many.

Hope was the greatest weapon of all, wielded with sly expertise by the rulers of the world.

She took a deep breath and released it slowly. Whatever will be, will be. If the next step on her path led to rejection then it could be no worse than the rejection she had already endured by the male half of humanity, for no other reason than being a woman.

She opened the makeup bag in front of her - the best makeup and perfumes were always readily available in the compound - and took out her eye-shadow and lipstick.

Women? Why would God create such a slave?

Nim had spent the better part of fifteen years at *Paradise Begins*, but before that she had been a ward nurse at a hospital in Iran, educated to degree level.

She had seen some of the world and knew of its ways, saw the difference between east and west, saw how cultures clashed and clanged against one another ceaselessly, ignorantly. But everywhere she travelled, Nim always saw the same women.

The difference in cultural background was academic; women, every place she had ever been, were always second to men; whether in the *modern* world, or in the strictest countries of the far-east, a woman was still considered the weaker of the sexes and by logical extension - to the minds of men at least - there to be dominated.

Even Jimi?

She leaned closer to the mirror and applied her subtle, emerald eye-shadow, staring her reflection straight in the eyes.

Of course even Jimi; she had been summoned not asked. Did he even realise that? And did he understand that he would still be controlling her even if he did use love? Did he see her as having any other choices before her?

If they had met in her old life, Nim couldn't find any outcome other than rejecting his advances. But here and now?

She turned her attention to her other eye, gently brushing the powder makeup onto her eyelid.

Here and now were a million miles away from her nursing life, here and now, as much as she hated to admit it, was where she wanted to be.

Leaning back and studying her dusted eyelids, she spoke to her reflection. 'Perhaps you *are* a stupid girl.'

Warm, evening air breezed through the open French-window in Jimi's apartment, clearing the remaining odour of his steak dinner from the room.

He sat in one of the chairs by the open window, his legs crossed and a large brandy swilling around in the glass in his hand. He looked out at the vista of the purpling mountains and green hills.

Nazari had made a good show of welcoming him when his entourage had arrived.

There was always something about the man which made Jimi think of eels, no matter how gracious and welcoming his smile was, and so it was with a little satisfaction that Jimi had told Nazari his command had been relinquished for the time being and that Jimi's own men would be adding their presence to Nazari's.

The fat, little man had not liked that at all, even after Jimi had explained the reasons, but he hadn't shown it on his face which remained smiling and gracious. Only the man's eyes were full of the angry indignation which he was feeling Jimi had noted.

An angry man could soon be placated, but a man who felt his honour had been stained could turn out to be a very dangerous adversary if not treated carefully. And he *would* have to treat him carefully if he was to free Nim and himself.

He sipped at his brandy and watched the gossamer clouds stretching thinly over the mountains and out of sight. His plan felt as thin as the clouds, but it was the only one he had and it had to work.

There would be casualties, deaths at his own hands, but when hadn't there been? His work always had an element of death and violence attached so why should his own liberation be any different?

It weighed heavy on his heart though; he would have liked nothing more than to leave behind the death and start a new life which wasn't founded upon it.

But he could see no other way around it; people would have to die for him to break away and be assumed to be one of the dead. No other way.

His Rolex itched on his wrist. It was engraved with his name, a gift from a friend in the organisation and now an intended gift of death to someone he would give it to before murdering him. All part of the plan, but who would he give it to? It was a shame, he thought, that the fat, commander Nazari didn't fit the bill.

Heavy footsteps came to Jimi's ears as they climbed the stairs up to the landing outside his door. His heart thumped and skipped; she was here.

He stood and banished all thoughts of his plan to the back of his mind, facing the door and trying not to seem too excited.

The footsteps stopped and a knock came.

'Come in.'

The door opened and one of his men appeared, a young foot-soldier named Dominic.

'I've brought the woman, sir.' He said stiffly.

He stood to attention and held the door open and then turned to stand with his back to it.

Nim, dressed in a deep scarlet, silk sari edged with magenta satin so deep as to be almost black, stepped passed her escort and into the room, her head and eyes lowered.

Jimi stood frozen, mesmerised, and just stared.

Here was his Goddess, his heart, his soul. And oh. How he had missed her. How could he deny her to be anything else? How could he question the feelings he had tried to shy from when here she stood and all he could see was light?

A moment passed, the soldier, still standing with his back to the open door, stared ahead of himself trying his damnedest not to look at his commander, or feel the discomfort of being a third wheel.

Nim raised her head, puzzled, and stood to face Jimi.

The look he held in his eyes almost made her faint with giddiness. All of her doubts and childish musings, self reproaches and admonishments flew away out of the window in that moment, to be carried away on the dusky breeze and out of mind.

Here was a man, a man! And he loved her, she could feel it from where she stood, it brushed up and down her naked flesh beneath her clothing, surrounded her like a warm mist, took the very breath from her body and then replaced it with a breath of icy-fire of its own.

She could feel herself trembling as that breath worked its subtle way into her heart and mind.

Jimi blinked. She sees me, he thought, she sees me properly.

He flicked his attention briefly to the soldier on the door. 'Thank you, Dominic, that will be all.' He said, lamely and then turned his eyes back to Nim.

The soldier left with a curt nod, closing the door behind him before he hurried back down the stairs.

Jimi took a step closer to the woman he had fallen so deeply in love with.

She clutched at her chest and gasped.

'Nim' He said, and took another small step.

Nim breathed hard and fast. 'J-Jimi.' She replied, and without another word rushed forward to meet him, to be caught up in his embrace and kissed passionately.

He pulled his lips from hers and said; 'I've missed you.' And then kissed her again, harder, holding her body in his strong arms.

She replied by grabbing him by the back of the head and holding him as tightly as she could, pressing her body firmly back into his.

She whimpered as tears she thought she would never cry again began to roll down her cheeks, to be gathered up between their lips and fused with their kisses.

Jimi's fingers found Nim's face and wiped at the tears. He pulled back when he felt the scarring beneath the makeup on her cheeks. His faced burned angrily as he looked at them. 'Who did this to you?'

Nim's heart suddenly felt like lead and she relaxed her grip, readying herself to be pushed out of the room. But it didn't come.

Jimi pulled her closely to him and stared at her, nothing but the pain of a loved one in his dark eyes. 'Who did this to you, my love?' He asked again, kissing her tenderly.

At the words *my love*, Nim knew then for certain that this man truly loved her and wanted to be with her. 'It was Hack.' She said, and wept freely. 'I'm sorry.'

He drew her close again, nuzzling her neck. 'You have nothing to be sorry for, my Nim, my beautiful Nim.' He whispered to her. 'Nothing. It is I who am sorry. Sorry for allowing this to happen to you.'

He pulled back and looked at her again.

She wouldn't meet his eyes.

He lifted her chin with his gentle finger until her eyes met his. 'I love you, Nim. Nothing bad will ever happen to you again.' He said, sincerely. 'For as long as I live and breathe, I promise you.'

Taking her cheeks in his palms, he stroked them and then leaned in to kiss her again, gently this time.

Nim responded by stroking his face with her own palms and then opened her eyes as they kissed. He was watching her.

Their lips parted an inch, their breath mingling.

'I love you, Jimi.' She whispered, allowing her lips to briefly meet his. 'I don't understand how that can be, but I do, I love you.'

Her eyes were bright as a golden dawn and her tears were like the falling stars of the leaving night and her words were like the heralds of any perfect, new day.

Jimenenko Ladislav was reborn under the sky once more, free this time, free to love and be loved.

Nim took a tentative step backward and held her head high, serious if not a little righteous.

She pulled at the shoulder of her sari, drawing the silk forward which was thrown over and down her back, pulling it over and across her chest to expose her naked breast.

She let the heavy silk slip from her fingers and fall to the floor and Nim's beauty was gradually revealed as the layers of crimson slowly fell away, languidly unravelling and exposing the perfect skin beneath.

As the last of her sari fell to the floor in a quiet hush, Nim's beauty within spoke.

'I stand before you as I was the day I was born.' She said, holding her palms face up for him to see. 'And only like this can I tell you; you are my first and only love.

'Before-before,' she faltered, trying to find the right words. 'Before I was brought here, I had never known another man's touch, I had never had a sweetheart or a lover, or someone I was deeply in love with.'

Her eyes filled with tears and she cried then. 'I stand naked only to tell you this truth, to show you I give myself freely. And if you accept that - accept me - then I will be Nim the slave no longer.' Her sobbing increased. 'I will be just Nim. Your Nim.'

Jimi knew that her oath was probably one of the hardest things Nim had ever had to say or do given the circumstances of how and where she lived. It both hurt him and succoured him at the same time.

'I don't know if there are any correct words, Nim,' he said, gently, 'but you will always have my undying love. You are no more a slave to me as I am to you.'

He walked toward her. 'You *are* my Nim and I am yours.' He said, gathering her up and holding her. 'We will be together and neither of us will be a slave again.'

Nim believed his words, hammered home by the pounding of his heart which she could feel beating strongly in his chest.

Yesterday she had been a slave, today she was Nim. And tomorrow? Well, tomorrow never came did it? There was only the perfect now.

The reborn lovers lay in each other's arms, cocooning their love between them and breathing it in peacefully now.

Nazari ate while he watched them on the soundless monitor in front of him.

They had been at it for hours, what was the damn Russian up to? You didn't fuck a slave like that and for that length of time. Not unless you felt something for it.

Nazari leaned forward and switched the monitor off and then sat back, his fingers steepled in front of his face.

The stupid, Russian bastard! He's fallen in love!

Nazari smiled a spiteful smile. Fucking idiot; brought down by a foolish word.

Love. A stupid four-letter word which was only used to build bridges from a man's cock to a woman's cunt. An unnecessary word here at *Paradise Begins*; here you showed your love by opening your wallet and then by taking anything you pleased.

Love! Nazari scoffed. Idiot! He had only been with the woman twice for God's sake! How could he think that he loved her?

Nazari's small-minded and callous nature simply could not entertain the idea of two people, two strangers, falling in love together and in equal measures, two hearts becoming one at the first experience of each other.

He shook his head at the unbelievable, romantic connection he had just witnessed, frowning as he tried to understand why *he* had never come across it, no matter how vague or distant. Why hadn't he?

'Fucking idiot.' He muttered under his breath. Who needed that when he could just take what he wanted?

But at the back of his mind the thought that he had never been loved and needed for himself, as a man, as a person simply fed his sneering hatred for those who had. Those like the Russian and the slave.

He couldn't do anything about it now, not while the Russian was here and in command. But when all was returned to normal and he had gone? Then he could do something about it, do something to hurt and destroy this stupid idea of love.

Watching them fuck had done nothing for him; a mere window into another man's lust. But the thought of hurting them and their love, dragging their souls apart and destroying them, sent a deviant pulse of erotic shame straight to his groin.

He sat for a few minutes, revelling in the feeling and sensation, smiling as he thought of the ways he could lay waste to their love. It was delicious, he thought, delicious and sweet.

A final shudder ran through the fat commander's body and then he stood up and left the secret room of cameras and monitors.

He turned and closed the doorway by pulling a tall, wooden cabinet on a hidden hinge back into its place.

Standing behind his desk in his office now, he stared at the pile of unfinished paperwork still laying where he had left it on its polished surface.

Nazari sighed and brought himself back to the present; there was the task of securing the compound still to be done. A damn nuisance.

He would need to get Hack and the other sergeants in and tell them about the Russian and why he was here and more importantly, tell them about the impending attack coming their way. By one man!

He took his seat. Twenty-five men at my command, but still another fourteen were seen fit to be drafted in, all the way from Russia at that. Thirty-nine men to take on one.

Had the world turned upside down? Was there a real *superman* at large? What the hell needed thirty-four men to stop it!?

He took the brown folder from the top of the pile of papers, the folder the Russian had given him when he had relieved him of his command. Inside were only two sheets of paper.

The first sheet had half of its page taken up by a grainy photograph of a snarling, scar-faced man holding knives.

The picture didn't present much in the way of the scale of the man, but Nazari could see that he was big. Big and very pissed off, he had never witnessed such a look of engorged rage on a man before.

'You would do well to come and work for me, my angry, western friend.' He muttered as he studied Finn's contorted face.

He turned to the second page, a sparse list of details which had been gleaned.

The man called himself Finn, he was able to travel the world unnoticed, he had visited eighteen countries and had killed more than thirty-nine of their population single-handedly and incredibly brutally.

He targeted his hits and then simply got on with it, usually using surprise as his main tactic.

Nazari flicked the page and looked for more on the back. It was blank.

He returned to the picture and studied it some more. Thirty-four hardened and armed men await you, my friend; are you really that good? Or are you really just very lucky because you take your victims unawares?

He scoffed and shook his head. Well, we are expecting you and I think you will find our welcome to be a little more than you can handle or are used to.

Nazari understood legends, he knew that a man whose legend preceded him may inspire extra caution and vigilance in his enemy's minds, but once caught he always begged and pleaded, cried and bled and died just the way any ordinary man did.

He returned the papers to the folder and then closed it, flipping it back onto the desk.

The paper sitting next on the pile showed the month's stock-taking.

Nazari frowned at it, annoyed. A tiny smudge of liquid paper could just be seen at the end of one of the columns, the original entry being covered up and the false entry written in. The missing girl.

Nazari's tracker had sent a text earlier that morning telling him that he was close now and it shouldn't be more than a few more days before he had her in his grasp.

A few more days? The thought made Nazari's skin prickle with hot fury. A few more fucking days! He wanted the bitch back now and his usually meticulous bookkeeping putting back to rights!

The smudge and false number glared at the fat, little commander, teasing his mind with its implications; you got it wrong, you made a mistake, your error is plain for everyone to see, *especially* you.

Especially me.

He slammed his fist down hard onto the sheet. 'Damn you!' He hissed, and slammed his fist down again. 'Damn you! Damn you! Damn you!'

His fingers and knuckles buzzed and throbbed painfully. The smudge never changed, completely unaffected by his attempts to smash it into oblivion and wipe it from sight.

He rubbed at his hand, the pain replacing much of the anger and frustration which had caused the outburst in the first place.

The impending attack and the girl - especially the girl - not to mention the loss of his command status, temporary though that may be, and now the stupid love between his own commander and one of the slaves were all chipping away at the hold he had over this life of his.

He could feel the control being drawn away gradually, slowly, like string being pulled through the palm until eventually the end snaps free and you catch the empty air.

Nazari narrowed his eyes and continued to rub at his aching hand.

He would not let the string be pulled free from his grasp. He would tighten his hold if need be and be damned with the Russians; this was *his* place, his own designs, his own paradise, he would *not* let it be so easily taken from him.

If the Russians thought he was without friends of his own then they were wrong. His days in the military had seen him make friends and allies throughout the middle-east, not to mention his very useful British contact.

Nazari relaxed and smiled a little then, taking comfort in that thought. No, he wouldn't let go of paradise that easily.

## Chapter Twenty-Two

The Wrekin, one of Shropshire's most prominent and famous hills, surrounded by 20,000 hectares of land known as the green-network, with forests of oak and birch and of holly and rowan. A ramblers paradise. If you were a rambler.

Rachel was not a rambler; she loved nature, loved being in nature, but a nature which had pathways and fences to follow to take you from one place to another, not the nature she was dragging herself through wishing she had a machete.

One hand was scratched and bleeding a little, while the other itched and stung after a brush with nettles. 'Where's the bloody dock-leaf then?' She muttered to herself, while she scoured the ground.

Telford lay behind her while Wellington lay ahead, the place she was trying to get to.

She stood and rubbed her hand with the dock she had found, looking at the way ahead; a green and dark-olive expanse of trees and bushes carpeted the ground as it rose gradually upward.

The sunlight streamed through the gaps in the canopy, casting searchlight beams of emerald and gold across the leaf-littered floor.

She was still heading in the right direction she thought. She only hoped that she would make it before dark; she didn't fancy the idea of *sleeping rough* and wanted to catch the last train heading into Wales.

She wistfully thought of the quilted bed and soft sheets back in her room at the hotel in Telford.

Rachel had been spooked. By a woman who she saw three times in the four days she had been at the hotel.

Twice she had seen her walking past the foyer entrance and once she had spotted her sitting in the cafe across the road. Maybe nothing more than a local who used this road regularly, but if Graham had taught her anything, it was that a good dose of paranoia and over-caution was much better than someone creeping up on you and catching you unawares.

Well if she *is* following me then I hope she gets a face-full of nettles!

Rachel tried to keep her spirits high but it was difficult, not least because she feared for her husband. If *she* could find herself well off the beaten track, hacking her way through a forest to escape the attention of-of of whoever, then Graham could be up to his neck in quicksand and surrounded by the bad-guys by now.

Don't be such a drama queen, Rachel, it's more than likely that no one's following you.

But Graham? She hated the thought of him being in danger, surrounded by life-threatening situations like the last time.

She'd had to stay incognito for almost two weeks that time, two weeks of hiding and having no word from him; all she could do was worry and hope until someone finally called the mobile-phone he had given her and asked to speak to Miss Langley - her mother's maiden-name.

She would never forget that day and the sudden, incredible relief she had felt; the weight of her ordeal and the fear she held for her husband surrounded her like an ever-tightening cage, squeezing all other senses and reasoning into the tightest knot and banishing them from her mind. All she had to focus on was the fear that something terrible was happening to her love.

After the caller had told her Shelby was okay but injured, Rachel had travelled immediately back to London and to the hospital where he was being treated to find he had been shot. Twice.

It wasn't until after they had been reunited that Shelby could tell her anything about the case he had been working on; arms traders.

He and the team he was a part of had been tracking a particularly big transport of weapons as it crossed Europe, heading for Britain.

They had only been married for four years and up until that point, Rachel, even knowing that Shelby's job demanded a little secrecy and couldn't discuss his cases in any depth, assumed he spent most of his time gathering information - which he did - and then someone else with the guns and whatnot would take up the reigns and bring the bad-guys to heel.

Seeing him lying in his hospital bed with two bullet holes in his body and an array of tubes attached had brought home just how serious Shelby's job really was.

She remembered the day he came home after spending nineteen days in the very hospital which she now worked for.

They had, had nine, glorious weeks of peace and quiet, Shelby making a quick and full recovery and both of them falling in love all over again.

But all too soon the day came when he told her he would be going back to work.

Rachel's anxiety had returned almost instantly and although she'd tried hard to keep it locked up and away from Graham, he'd noticed nonetheless, how couldn't he?

She felt guilty and ashamed that her emotions were bearing down on him so heavily after his own trauma must have been heavy enough as it was.

And so it was, with just four days to go before Shelby returned to his Sergeant's position at Interpol, the telephone rang and a man called George

Appleby asked to speak to him.

Rachel would never forget the look on his face when she told him the name.

"*George Appleby?!* Deputy Commissioner, *George Appleby?!*" He'd sounded - and looked - like he was having a minor seizure.

After spending fifteen minutes talking to the Deputy Commissioner, with many a "yes sir, thank you sir." Shelby had hung up and turned his grinning and still a little astonished face to his wife.

"*I've been promoted to Inspector.*" He'd sounded like a child receiving a gold star.

Rachel had been initially as thrilled as Shelby, but then she came to the quiet conclusion that higher rank meant more danger, but Shelby had been quick to see the look in her eyes and he grinned even harder.

"*It means I can sit behind a desk more, in my own office and with a partner and men at my disposal.*"

It had taken her a minute or two to fully digest what he was telling her, but she did in the end and that feeling of relief which was fast becoming her best-friend flushed around her body and soul all over again.

Back in the forest, Rachel checked the compass hanging from her backpack and double-checked she was still going the right way.

'And yet here we are once again, my dear love, hiding and running from the baddies.' She muttered as she lined the needle up, still trying to stay aloof and above the anxiety which threatened to scatter her thoughts.

She returned the compass to its side-pouch and then carried on.

Ahead she could see a thick line of wild blackberry blocking the way. She picked the berries and ate them as she walked around the large, scrubby bush.

The sun was still high, she thought she would definitely make it before dark and so lingered while she collected more berries; eating some and stashing some for the rest of the walk ahead.

Everything was quiet and still, she suddenly noticed.

The birds had been piping since she had first entered the tree-line, but now there was no sound other than the very distant roar of a jet somewhere high in the skies above her.

She stood still and turned around on the spot, looking as deeply into the dense trees as she could. There was nothing to be seen or heard; not a twig snapping or a bird calling.

Caution. Caution and paranoia. It was most likely some reasoning of nature to have a quiet moment in the day, a kind of siesta, but Rachel thought it better if she got moving on straight away and quickly.

She followed the impenetrable line of thorny blackberry until she came to a place where a small stream cut through the hedge, shaping it into a small arch, like a natural bridge of blackberry.

Sliding down the shallow embankment, Rachel plopped into the water, her walking boots holding most of the water at bay.

She ducked beneath the bush and squatted down almost, shuffle-walking all the way to the other side.

On any other day, she would have had her camera out in a flash and taken a dozen photographs of the strange and magical bridge and stream. But today she had to turn her back on it without even giving it a second glance and jog up and over the ridge and away.

More trees met her, more bushes, more nettle traps, but she had set her mind to caution and carried on the best she could, as quickly as she could.

She waded through the nettles with her hands held safely above their furry, stinging tops.

It made sense that if she couldn't see the ground then the next best thing was to wade through the scattered ponds of stinging-nettles which filled almost all of the gaps between the trees and bushes in this particular part of the forest.

She wondered briefly if she should have stayed on the other side and gone all the way around the blackberry line instead. That could have added hours onto her journey though, making her follow a line away from her goal for God knows how long. Better to stay straight, but heaven forbid if she should trip and fall.

She pulled the zip of her jacket right up to her chin and then put her hood up, lastly pulling her hands into the sleeves and gripping the ends to seal them off.

Better to be safe than sorry, she thought, secretly wishing she had at least picked a few pounds of dock to carry with her.

An hour or more went by before Rachel came to the end of the trees and nettles. Her arms ached from holding them out for so long, she rubbed them and revelled in the relief she felt in her shoulders and neck.

She stood at the edge of the trees and looked out.

The land before her was open now and she could see the clear-cut paths for hikers and ramblers snaking down into the valley and away to the furthest hills and trees. Her destination lay at the other side of that open land.

As she stood and ate a few berries, staring out and formulating the best plan of action, the hum and distinctive whipping sound of helicopter blades came down to Rachel's ears.

She froze and turned her gaze upward; the noise was coming from behind and growing quickly louder.

A minute later and a large blue and white helicopter appeared, zooming overhead a few hundred feet from the ground. It flew straight ahead and a few minutes later was miles away and getting quieter by the second.

Rachel breathed out.

Couldn't have been anything to do with her, who would want to send out a helicopter just for her for God's sake? She was jittery that's all. First the woman, then the running away through the forest, then the sudden quietness... it had all added up and now the damned helicopter was trying to muscle in on her thoughts as well.

Just relax woman, she told herself.

But Shelby's insistent, tiny voice continually urged her to remember the rules and stay cautious.

The quickest route she could see from up here led an almost straight path which cut diagonally across the valley before it reached the trees at the other side.

It twisted and turned to avoid larger hills and outcrops of rock here and there, but on the whole it was pretty much the fastest choice. She quietly noted that she would be almost completely exposed to prying eyes from all around though. And above, she amended dryly.

The other choice was to stay firmly in the tree-line and walk the long way around, but that would take her well into the night and the more she thought about it, the more she knew she didn't want to be out here after dark.

No other choice then; the path it is.

She scrambled down the small ridge and then made a beeline for the path some three miles ahead, wading through thigh-high ferns of all varieties, tall, scrubby grasses and a little gorse, but no nettles.

She reached the path in little under an hour and began following it immediately.

There were signposts pointing to the different paths and the landmarks they led to. The one Rachel followed simply stated *Wellington*.

After an hour more of walking, Rachel listened as the helicopter returned, coming back this time.

She assumed that whatever rich bugger who could *fly* to wherever he needed to be, had done his business and was now on his way back. Simple.

Another two hours passed as Rachel plodded forward.

She ached and wished she had done more to exercise. She swam regularly, but drove to and from the pool. Maybe she would take up jogging there and back when she returned to normal life.

She hadn't seen any other hikers, but she had spotted a hare or two darting through the grass, and a kestrel had been flying around for half-an-hour before dropping into a dive and capturing whatever unfortunate, little rodent was hiding in the grass and flying it back to its nest. Other than that, Rachel felt completely alone out here.

And then the helicopter flew over again.

She jolted as the sound came suddenly clear, causing her to dart off the path to her left and sit behind a gorse bush, peering up through the gaps between its spiky branches. There was no doubt about it, it was the same helicopter.

She didn't really know what to make of it, but she thought hiding couldn't do any harm. It really was probable that the helicopter was simply going about its daily business, and flying over the Wrekin and surrounding lands may be part of that business.

Or it could be someone trying to kill her.

She gave herself a mental kick in the arse, driving the paranoia back to a healthy level. But it was still there, the tiny seed had grown and she could feel it growing still; something bad was going on right now and she and Graham were right in the middle of it.

The helicopter had gone, reduced to a faint buzz somewhere ahead.

Rachel wasted no time and made straight back to the path and began walking briskly along the final leg.

The sun was going down, she had another three hours to go she thought, before she would reach the forest and then the outer skirts of Wellington itself.

She force-marched herself. Sometimes running along the well-worn track when it dipped downward, and sometimes almost crawling when it went back up.

Climbing up even the smallest inclines was a nightmare torture on her legs. By the time she had reached the trees almost four hours later, she was exhausted and simply threw herself down on the grass underneath the shade of the first of the trees.

'Fucking Nora!' She groaned breathlessly, while her arms and legs throbbed in aching agreement as they splayed themselves out at her sides. 'Oh! God! I think I'm going to be sick.' She squeaked. 'Oh! God! Please! I don't want to be sick.'

The thought of the berries coming back up did little to stop her bile from rising and the nightmare view of her dark, red vomit made Rachel weep.

'Oh! Shit.' She muttered, spitting foam and snot alike out onto the ground. Which then made her sick up again. 'Oh! God! No more!'

Her stomach's heaving eventually subsided and she sat back against the bole of a large rowan, weeping pitifully. She wiped her face and running nose on her sleeves. 'I hate being sick.'

She forced herself to stand up, knowing that if she settled down too much her body would want to go into full rest-mode and would take some serious, mental effort to get going again.

After cleaning herself up with her travel-wipes and drinking her water-bottle dry, she checked her compass and then set off in the direction the needle had pointed out.

She'd taken no more than a few dozen steps when the familiar sound of her hounding helicopter came to her ears again.

She tried to ignore it and carried on the way she was going, following now the path as it ran through the forest. If anyone in that helicopter was really looking for her then they wouldn't be able to find her under the trees now would they?

Rachel walked along the path for another twenty minutes before she came to a place where she could see through the trees down into the car-park where the path ended. There were only two cars parked down there; other walkers perhaps?

Taking herself off the path, she slowly approached the car park using the trees for cover as she carefully moved closer. She wanted to make sure there was no one around and to get a better look at the cars.

She stopped and hid herself behind a large, thick oak, some two hundred yards away from the first of the cars.

Peering from behind her hiding place, Rachel could see both vehicles clearly now; one a black Mercedes and the other a dark-blue, four-wheeled drive BMW.

The driver-side door opened on the Mercedes and someone got out.

Rachel gasped and sucked her breath in wildly. It was the woman from the hotel! What the hell was she doing here? It could only mean one thing; all of the paranoia was real; the woman, the eerily quiet forest, the bloody helicopter, it was all real and happening right now.

How? How had they found her? How could they trace her that easily?

Rachel's mind worked frenziedly at the pieces, trying to find the link which tied everything together and would tell her the answer?

Tracking? Had they got an actual tracker out into the woods? Someone who was following her and relaying information to the helicopter and the woman? Surely someone trained like that would have caught her up by now.

She looked frantically around, searching even the smallest shadows for signs that there was someone coming up behind her. She couldn't see anything.

What else then? How can they know where I am with such pinpoint accuracy?

The phone! The only item she was carrying which didn't really belong to her; it had been given to her by Maurice as part of her disappearing act.

The bloody phone. But what could she do about that? If she dumped it she would lose all contact with Graham, how would he get in touch with her and tell her it was safe to come home again? She could be running and hiding for years!

On the other hand; how could she keep it with her knowing it could lead to her being captured by the very people Graham was attempting to catch?

Once again she found she had only those two choices but only one of them was the right thing to do; she had to dump the phone.

She took it out of her pocket and placed it in the crook of a tree-branch and then backed away slowly, keeping her eyes on the women and the cars.

She noticed the woman was scanning the trees, left to right, as though she were looking for something, or someone, coming out.

Rachel made her way up a steep incline and then dug herself in amongst the bushes and grass, her back firmly planted against a large, grey rock. No one would see her here unless they practically stepped right on top of her. She sat and waited and watched.

In the car-park, the woman was looking more and more agitated and kept staring down at something in her hands, her own phone possibly, but the way she tracked from side to side made Rachel think of Star-Trek and handheld scanners.

The woman tapped on the door of the BMW and four men got out.

After a brief word and an indication that she wanted them to go into the trees, the men strode off to the path and fanned out, slowing down as they began searching the bushes and undergrowth while they moved along.

One of the men came toward the place where Rachel had been hiding behind the oak watching the car-park. He couldn't fail to miss the phone sitting in its lower branches.

'Over here.' He called out.

The woman and the other three men ran through the small gate and made their way straight to the man with the phone. He handed it to the woman.

She snatched it from his hand and made an inaudible retort, then raised her head and looked around her. 'She was right here. Damn it! She must have been watching us before she realised the fucking phone was tagged.'

The woman thought for a minute before speaking. 'Right. Pack it up. We're not going to find her with just the five of us.'

She looked at the first man. 'Get the chopper called in; if she knows we're looking for her and she's gone back in there,' she said, and pointed to the forest and almost right at Rachel as she crouched in her hiding place, 'then the chopper won't be any use anyway.'

All of the men looked a little astonished at the command Rachel thought. Something was going on between them, they didn't like to be called off so easily. Why?

Because they wouldn't normally be called off with their quarry so close at hand? Had to be. This meant that the woman was up to something, some plan which she thought cunning enough for Rachel to step right into a trap.

Well they had no chance of that; she might not have wanted to spend the night in the dark forest alone, but she now thought that her best chance of getting them off her trail would be to stay right where she was. Especially since she had now seen through the woman's subterfuge.

The last place they would think to look after realising she wasn't coming out this way would be right here where she had been in the first place.

Rachel smiled a little to herself then.

What the hell are you smiling for? You're in danger, Graham's in danger, there's danger all around and you're smiling?

She smiled again. She might be in danger, but for some strange reason she felt quite exhilarated to be outwitting the bad-guys - or women as the case may be.

Knowing a thing and being able to see it and deal with it was much better than being anxious as you waited for it to arrive. She'd heard things like that said about soldiers on the battlefield.

The men lingered for only a moment more before a simple raised eyebrow from the woman made them all fall-in and make their way back to the vehicles.

She stood alone for a moment, staring off into the fading light between the trees.

She was quite a handsome woman, Rachel thought, tough and well trained. But trained by whom, who the hell are you people?

The woman turned away and walked back to her own car, both vehicles then backed out onto the tarmac road and drove away.

Rachel sighed with relief as the backs of the vehicles disappeared around the bend.

Her heart hammered away giddily, sending hot waves flashing through her face. The mix of emotions was overwhelming and Rachel soon found herself sobbing through her smiles and then weeping wholeheartedly.

'Oh! Graham.' She whispered. 'What am I going to do, love?'

As the night drew on and the sun finally sank from view, Rachel tucked her legs up to her chin and folded her arms around her waist, settling in for the long, dark night ahead.

## Chapter Twenty-Three

Anna stood in the doorway which led from the large dining-room through to the kitchen. She blew on her morning coffee as she watched Shelby pacing back and forth in front of the big screen. His own coffee sat on the desktop.

Sophie was used to her partner's penchant for walking holes in carpets and left him to it while she looked through the bookcase.

It was filled with books which were mainly Celtic and Gaelic histories, myths and legends, but a few of them were books on wildlife and herb-lore, forestry and husbandry as well as a collection of tomes relating to flowers.

There were two books which were outsized; the first was a winemaking encyclopaedia; a thick, hard-covered bookwhich went into great, scientific detail about the art of making wine, while the second book was similarly big and went into an equally great depth about fly-fishing.

She squatted down onto her haunches and studied the lower shelves.

These seemed to be all fiction of some kind. Everything from the complete works of Tolkien and Gemmell, Jorden and Pratchett and a few other fantasy writers, to a handful of Azimov, Clarke and Hamilton amongst others, filling in for the science-fiction section. The complete *Dark Tower* series of books stood out proudly in the remainder of the collection, which seemed to be horror and supernatural.

A book had been left lying across the top of the others instead of in the space beside them. Sophie pulled it out, there was a bookmark in it.

'What have you got there.' Anna said, sidling up to her.

'*The Wolfen*.' She replied, showing Anna the cover. 'Someone had been reading it I think.'

She paused and looked down at the book. 'Probably the last thing that was ever read from this shelf.' She said, quietly.

She opened it at the marked page, there was a small hand-written message on the bookmark.

'*My beautiful Cait, I read this at work, you'll love it. She reminds me of you. Love James.*' Sophie read aloud.

'What's it about?' Anna asked, taking the book from Sophie and turning it over to read the back.

'Hm.' She huffed. 'Wolves in New York; sounds a bit cheesy.'

'I've seen the movie.' Shelby said, briefly looking up while he paced. 'Way back in the eighties. I enjoyed it I seem to remember. Something about a big, female wolf trying to protect her urban pack from land developers, or something like that anyway.'

Anna handed the book back. 'Still sounds a bit cheesy to me.'

Sophie closed it and left the bookmark at the same page before returning it to its proper place.

She stood then and looked at the two photographs which took up places on top of the bookcase.

The first was of James and Caitlin holding each other and smiling into the camera which framed them from the waist up. Behind them was a running valley of wild-land, a fen or moor, which ran all the way out of sight into the distance. The sun had been low and behind them that day and its white-hot intensity created a subtle lens-flare which seemed to halo the couple, celebrating, or revering almost, their obvious love for one another.

The second photograph looked to have been taken here, in the back-garden.

James sat on the stone wall while Caitlin stood next to him. He had his arms wrapped around her swollen waist as she draped her own arm over his shoulders. The look of peace in their eyes and on their faces was enough to stir something in the most hardened of spirits.

Sophie's heart ached when she looked at them; probably the only photograph with all three of the Deeres in it, albeit that Samantha couldn't actually be seen.

'They are a beautiful couple, no?' Anna said.

Sophie just nodded but didn't say anything.

'When you look at that picture,' Anna continued, pointing to the photograph of James and a pregnant Caitlin. 'I mean *really* see it for what it is, you can see something of the man beneath, the man called Finn, and you can understand a little better the intensity of his actions.'

'Yes.' Sophie replied. 'You can see it in both their eyes; they would die protecting each other.'

Anna agreed. 'A love as intense as that must leave the worst scarring when it is broken.'

'And Finn *is* that scarring.' Sophie added.

'So it would seem.'

Anna turned and faced Sophie. 'Doesn't it strike you as strange that the James Deere in these photographs is clean and unscarred? Whereas Finn has always been described as being scarred.'

'It's a point to be taken, yes, but given that he's actually attacking people at close-quarters it's hardly surprising is it?' Sophie answered. 'Someone out of his thirty-nine-'

'Forty-two.' Corrected Shelby; the brothers from the steel shack and the pimp had come to light that very morning.

'Forty-two,' Sophie continued, with a nod for her partner. 'One of them would have had a go back. I mean some of the places had ten or twelve bodies with his signature on it. And a lot of those were armed with weapons of their own, including guns which had been fired.'

'My point exactly.' Anna said. 'The state of his mind, or should I say the power of it, would have to be nothing short of super-human to be able to remove bullets and stitch up holes in himself.'

'Welcome to Finn's world.' Shelby said.

Sophie just looked at Anna and raised an eyebrow, agreeing with Shelby.

'So he really *is* capable of taking that on?' Anna said incredulously, pointing at the image of the map.

While Shelby had been visiting Keys in London, Anna had scoured the map around the location Sophie had circled. When she found nothing she widened her search until eventually, after hours of eye-watering staring, she came across a cluster of unusual shapes out in the middle of nowhere.

She had marked it up and made highlights of the shapes; there was no doubt about it, it was a cluster of buildings where there should have been just rocks and sand.

'Capable? I'm not sure. The only thing I am sure about is; he is going to try.' Shelby answered, stopping his walk and looking now at them both. 'The thing that I can't grasp is: how telling us is going to help him. I mean he will know that we can't just go marching into Afghanistan waving our flag, so that only leaves his complete and utterly unshakable belief that he is going to be coming back out and meeting us in Pakistan.'

He picked up his coffee and sipped it, staring at the red dot on the Iranian side of the border.

Sophie had added it and had given him some interesting information when he had returned last night. It had been too late to do or think about much right then, but he had his mind on it now.

The dot in Iran represented a communication received, while the sender came up on the map as being somewhere in the west half of London, the half Keys resided in, but it was the time it was sent which interested Shelby the most.

He had arrived at Keys' house at a little past six-thirty. It had been no more than ten minutes later that Keys had called his PA and asked for Hinds' number; Shelby had clearly heard the woman's small, tinny voice on the other end of the line as she spoke to Keys.

Less than a minute later and keys was calling Hinds' mobile, twice, only to reach the message service instead. Again, Shelby could hear the automated female voice as it spoke the options to leave a message.

The communication to Iran had been sent at six fifty-one, just a few minutes after Keys had made his calls and while he was still sitting with Shelby in the lounge.

Shelby looked at the map of London and sighed.

There was a lot of land within the radius of the circle which represented the area where the communication had come from. It could be just pure coincidence that Keys lived within it. There were numerous politician residences within the circle, not to mention prominent buildings including Interpol.

And who was to say that the users were actually at their own residences? They could be in the pub, visiting from miles away for all he knew. But something just smelled a little off.

He turned to face Sophie and Anna again. 'I don't think that's a coincidence.' He said, gesturing to the red dot in Iran. 'I think it's our powerful man extending his reach again; I think it's someone going after Finn.'

'Then that could only mean - if the communication *did* come from Keys' house while you were there, that is - that his security guard, the man you called George, sent it, or there was someone else there that you didn't know about.' Sophie said, stepping down into the living room and up to the monitor.

Anna followed.

'If it did come from there,' Sophie continued. 'Then you can't alert Keys; it will put him in direct danger simply for knowing about it.'

'I know.' Shelby said.

He wasn't happy about it, but he couldn't get back in touch with Keys anytime soon, not without running the risk of alerting the wrong people. IF they were the wrong people. He hated the guessing game, but sometimes his hunches and intuition were just too strong to ignore, sometimes coincidences *did* happen for the right reasons.

While they stood contemplating what they should do next, the mail-monitoring computer which Sophie had been using pinged shrilly.

Anna sat at the main console and brought the screen up from the external computer to sit at the edge of the map screen.

She tapped a few keys and a red dot appeared on the map, again on the Iranian side of the Afghan border, but further south now and well within the radius to be just over the border itself.

That was where the message had been sent from; it had been received in Russia, somewhere around Moscow.

Although the software couldn't identify each individual mobile device used and therefore couldn't match communications to any one device, it was probable that any communications within their target area were one and the same.

'I'm even more convinced that someone is coming up behind Finn now.' Shelby said, pointing to the map with the laser-tube. 'Look how close that is to the place we thought Finn may have crossed. Whoever that is, they are definitely on his trail and it looks like they have been travelling fast, in a vehicle, which means they have the proper paperwork to be there in Iran and can travel openly, day or night.'

'He'll be on foot by now though.' Anna said. 'I'll be willing to wager that he has just had to lose the vehicle and is now going to climb over into Afghanistan. Maybe even on the exact same path Finn used.'

She turned and smiled smugly. 'He's just called his masters to let them know that he is in the wild now.'

Shelby nodded. 'You're probably right, Anna.' He said. 'If that *is* the case then Finn will be adding another victim to his list; one man would have to be extremely skilled and lucky-'

'Or as mental.' Sophie said.

'Or as mental to be able to bring Finn down, I'm sure of it.'

'I'm beginning to believe it myself.' The little hacker replied. 'But what if it isn't just one man? What if it is a platoon of men or something?'

It was Sophie who replied. 'A platoon of men would look highly suspicious climbing a mountain for a start and would be seen from miles away should Finn look behind, but really, if they were going to send an army after him they would have had it waiting on the other side somewhere.'

'Ah! "If you have a journey of a thousand miles to meet a foe, what should you always ensure? That the journey is his."' Anna quoted.

'Exactly.' Sophie said, smiling at the well-known rhetoric. 'So it makes more sense to have the whole army waiting for him at the site and have one man creeping up behind while Finn's focus is set on the ones ahead.'

'He'll still have to be very good though,' Shelby added. 'Finn's not stupid, he'll be watching his back.'

'You say that with a certain amount of admiration.' Anna said, turning on the swivel seat to face Shelby.

He and Sophie gave each other a small, guilty glance; Anna had hit a sore point.

The little German hacker noticed. 'You *both* really admire him, don't you?' She said. 'Don't be so uptight about it; the man's doing an amazing job which you are not permitted to do.'

That stung. Shelby more than Sophie. 'Don't get us wrong Anna; we do not condone the things which Finn does; his brutality is frightening to behold in the aftermath, God knows what it is like while he is doing it.'

He stared hard at her. 'If you think that we would like to bring down these horrendous places and organisations then you would be right, and you would also be right to say that we are not permitted to track them down using the means which Finn uses, but we would not do it with gun and blade, Anna, pain and death. We are not judges or executioners.'

Anna looked a little guilty and smiled softly. 'I'm sorry. I wasn't implying that you were murderers and executioners, but you have to admit that you hold the man in a higher regard than most of your other criminals don't you? He does a great job of getting into these awful places.'

'You're beginning to sound like her.' Shelby muttered, indicating Sophie. 'She thinks we should give him a medal and get him to teach *us* a lesson or two.'

Anna turned to Sophie. 'I would have to agree.' She said, smiling at Sophie

'Well, he *would* be a major asset if handled well.' Sophie said, a little defensively.

Anna winked at her. 'There are a few members of the um, 'criminal element' who could do with being handled well.'

Sophie blushed furiously.

Shelby just stood silent for a moment and stared straight ahead. And then pulled the innuendo from the words and blushed as well, for Sophie's sake.

'Ah. You English,' Anna laughed, 'so easy to tease.'

The computer pinged again, thankfully changing the subject both Shelby and Sophie thought at the same time and with some relief.

'The master replying the hit-man no doubt.' Anna said cheerfully.

She twirled the chair back around and tapped more keys. Sure enough a communication from the same place in Russia was received by someone at the same Iranian location.

*'Be careful, look out for snakes and madmen, see you back for dinner. Love Ivan.'* Anna said, grinning again.

'It's a shame we can't get the contents of these communications.' Shelby sighed. 'Isn't there some way we can boost the signal?' He asked Anna.

She looked at him and rolled her eyes. 'You've been watching too much *Star-Trek*.' She said. 'But there maybe something I *can* do, or rather something which *Code-8* can do.'

She turned back to the console and began typing in commands. A small, white window popped up and Anna began typing a message into it.

*Good morning, Charles*, it began.

Shelby leaned down to get Anna's attention. 'Hang on, what are you doing?' He asked, rather sharply.

'I'm "boosting the signal".' She replied innocently and without stopping her typing fingers.

*Physics lessons at 19:30, your place. Today's lesson is about how sound and light travel.*

'Just hang on a minute! Who's Charles?' He said, sounding irritated and a little worried now.

'Charles is the codename for a *Code-8* member; *Snooker-boy*.' Anna replied casually, as though that should explain everything.

Her fingers continued to type. *There will be one moon-phase and we will be examining it remotely.*

'But what is it exactly, that this Charles - or *Snooker-boy* - is going to be doing?'

The fingers never stilled... *Your esteemed teacher, Prof. Violet.*

'Don't you send that!'

...And finished by hitting the send button.

Shelby huffed. 'We really need to talk about your communication skills, young lady.' He said, prodding her in the arm. 'Now, tell me what is going on. Who is Snooker-boy and what is he going to be doing to boost the signal?'

Anna smiled. 'Don't be so serious.' She answered. *'Mr Interpol'* She added, prodding him back with her thumb. *'Snooker-boy* is our youngest member and newest protégé.'

'How will he be able to help us?' It was Sophie who asked this time.

Anna turned around in the chair and then stood up. 'We have a device which can remotely hook itself into almost all communication devices, including PC's and touch-pads.'

She gave them the smug-look they were both expecting and then continued. 'Unfortunately it has its limits; it can't access landline devices, not without alerting the telecommunication hosts, and it needs to be in fairly close proximity to the place which is being monitored.'

'When you say "it hooks itself in", do you mean it takes control of the device?' Shelby asked. His fondness for the hacking world and the gizmos and techniques it employed were a constant wonder to him.

'Yes, apart from being unable to switch any devices that are switched off, on, we can do pretty much anything. And by switched off, I mean powerless and unplugged. If the device has power.' She snapped her fingers. 'Then I will have it.'

Shelby thought about the implications, but it was Sophie who was quick on the uptake. 'You mean we can access cameras and microphones in someone's house don't you?' She sounded astonished.

'Yes, absolutely that.' Anna said, wrinkling her nose up at Sophie.

'I'm not going to like the place you have in mind to plant your spying-device am I?' Shelby said, as he ran his hands over his face.

'Well you did say you wanted to *boost the signal.'* Anna shrugged her shoulders. 'At least this way we can be sure that any communications we are monitoring are coming from your friend, Keys' house or not.'

'And if they are, we will have a better chance of learning what the communications are about.' Sophie said.

She was clearly impressed and gave Anna a friendly nudge. 'Did you have anything to do with its development? The device, I mean?'

'Of course.' Anna replied in her usual *what-a-stupid-question* manner. But she smiled nonetheless.

'Of course.' Sophie echoed.

Shelby stood in thought, seriously contemplating what it was that was actually being proposed. 'I don't like the idea, but I have to admit that it would set my mind at ease one way or the other to know if those communications are coming from there or not.'

He ran his fingers through his hair this time. 'I'll go with it, but you have to tell me everything; how is the device going to get there and is this *Snooker-boy* capable of doing it?'

'Oh. He's the perfect candidate, I assure you, and to answer your other question; *he* will be delivering and setting it up himself.'

'Yes, I gathered that, but how *exactly* will he be doing it? I want to know the plan.' Shelby persisted.

Anna looked like she was withholding something, Sophie thought. Not lying but definitely not revealing everything.

'Well, he'll probably be attaching it to one of the outside walls. It's a very quick setup, wouldn't take him more than a few seconds really.' Anna answered, her face remaining unusually blank. Or was she wishing she was behind her mask?

'Well that presents all sorts of security problems; alarms, cameras, a guard.' Shelby said. 'How would he get past all of that?'

'Oh. That's easy; he would just walk up to the front door during the day, there would be no need for hiding.'

'And let the front-entrance cameras pick him up? I hope you don't mind me saying so Anna, but that's a crap plan.' Shelby sat back and folded his arms.

Sophie smiled to herself as Anna continued to squirm away from something.

'Well he would be disguised, wouldn't he?' The little hacker said, and sat back herself, mimicking Shelby and folding her arms.

'You're avoiding me, Anna.' Shelby accused. 'What will he be disguised as?'

'I don't know, maybe a paperboy or something.' She shrugged and stiffened her upper-lip.

'A paper-' Shelby almost guffawed, then his face suddenly went quite pale; *our youngest member.*

He clearly sagged in his seat. 'Oh. God!' He said lamely. 'He's a child isn't he?'

'Well, *technically* yes, I suppose you could say that; he will be fifteen in November.'

Anna nodded and shrugged as if to say; *you know?*

Sophie scoffed. 'I knew it! I knew there was something you were trying very hard not to say.'

Shelby leaned closer again. 'Anna? Look; as much as I think it's a good idea to get your device in place at Keys' house, we can't have a child doing it for us.'

'And how would you go about doing it then?' She asked, but didn't wait for an answer. 'You? Will you go down to London again and do it? No, you can't because you will endanger your friend. For the same reason, Sophie can't do it because she too will be recognised and endanger your friend. I can't do it because I am needed here.' She gave them both a hard look then, like a matron. 'Not least because I have to look after both of *you*.'

Sophie and Shelby both raised a questioning eyebrow at that but remained silent for the moment.

'So I suppose I could get one of the other members to be a window-cleaner or something is that it?' Anna continued sarcastically. 'It's not as though I have all the personnel in the world at my disposal you know. But I do believe in and respect the capabilities of the members of *Code-8* that I do have, all of them, and I'm telling you *Snooker-boy* could do this in his sleep.'

She glared seriously at them both, challenging them to doubt the skill and ingenuity and loyalty of the members of her elite group.

'*And* he only lives twenty minutes from the location.' She finished and folded her arms.

Shelby sighed. 'But he's still a child doing our dirty-work, Anna; it's not that different from what terrorist cells get up to; brainwashing children and whatnot.'

'It is *nothing* like what they do!' The little German almost spat angrily. 'If your case is all about the liberation of child-slaves then why should a child - a very capable child at that - not play his part and help in the liberation?'

Shelby didn't know what to say to that, he felt there was something twisting his morals when he heard her put it like that.

She could see him wavering and pounced. 'It will take mere seconds for him to attach the small device to a wall while he posts a newspaper through the letterbox. He won't be recognised because he will disguise himself.' She said, stepping closer to Shelby. 'Which he is also very good at.'

She looked up at him. Her face had softened and she had a genuinely sympathetic look in her eye. 'Trust me, Graham, and trust my judgement; I wouldn't send a child into unnecessary danger.'

Shelby believed her.

He looked to his partner. 'What are your thoughts, Soph?'

'I'm with you on this, Gray, but I can hear Anna, I can see the twisted sense to it, but it's your call.'

After a minute of further contemplation, which entailed a slow, four-lap pace of the rug, Shelby sighed and stopped again. 'Very well then,' he said, nodding slowly. 'Get your man - boy - to set the device in place, but I insist that he isn't alone.'

'But-.' Anna began to protest.

'Don't worry, I didn't mean a shoulder-to-shoulder bodyguard, but I want someone out there with his eyes on him. You shouldn't tell *Snooker-boy*, though.'

Anna seemed to be struggling to accept the terms.

'Like you said yourself,' Shelby added, '"trust me".'

The little woman eventually nodded. 'Funnily, Mr Interpol, I do.' She raised her smile again.

Shelby nodded and winked at her. 'Good.' And then turned to Sophie. 'Get Maurice on the phone will you? We have need of a babysitter.'

## Chapter Twenty-Four

He hadn't tried to touch her. Three days they had been travelling together and he hadn't so much as looked at her 'that' way. Why hadn't he? That was what men usually did wasn't it? Sniffed you out and tried to touch you? Not that she actually wanted him to touch her, she just wanted to understand why he hadn't that was all. Wasn't it?

Salya sat beside Finn in front of the fire as they took their supper. The sun had completely gone but the moon was full and bright.

She marvelled at the silvered lines which criss-crossed his hands and face, the way the firelight edged his bright-blue eyes with a corona of molten gold.

Maybe she did want him to touch her; she felt funny when she sat near him, both relaxed and alert at the same time, hot and cold, asleep and awake all at the same time.

She wondered if he had ever been married, a flash of childish, angry envy accompanied the thought.

She looked away guiltily; she had no right to wonder about such things, no right to feel anger or jealousy when she had seen the life he had led by witnessing the scars on his body.

She suddenly flushed inside when she thought of him laying in the pool unconscious and then dragging his naked body out of the water and drying it before covering him up with her towel.

Was this what love felt like, she wondered, all hot and afraid and jealous? Why did they call it love then if it was? Wasn't love supposed to be pleasant?

Her mother had told her all about sex and men, that was easy to understand, but she hadn't really told her what love was. Salya had asked her, but her mother couldn't put it into the right words and had simply ended by saying; *you see how me and your father are? Well that is love, Salya. Not a thing which is easy to come by for us women and sometimes scary when you do come by it.*

What did she mean it was scary when you found love? Why would a thing which was supposed to be so good be so scary?

It made a sort of sense, a bit like having a great treasure and being afraid that you will lose it or it will be stolen.

Maybe that was it; love was a great treasure, so great that it carried with it its own price of fear and anxiety.

Well that didn't feel right, it was close, but fear and anxiety were not ruling her parents, she would have known. So what was it?

She turned her head to look at Finn again. He was watching her, his gaze soft and understanding.

Salya gasped involuntarily as her heart skipped a beat. How long had he been looking at her?

Finn smiled a little. 'Sorry, I didn't mean to startle you, Salya, you were so lost in your thoughts that I thought you had fallen asleep.'

'I was just thinking of home.' Was all she said, holding his gaze.

'Tell me.' Finn said.

Salya looked away then, she could feel her sudden blush prickling in her cheeks. She couldn't tell him what she had been really thinking, her face would melt right off her skull with embarrassment! 'I-I was just thinking how much I missed them.' She managed to say.

Finn took her hand and held it. 'That is understandable, but be comforted knowing that you will be seeing them again.' He gave her hand a comforting squeeze. 'I promise you.'

Salya felt the hairs on the back of her arms and neck suddenly stand up as her skin prickled with goose-bumps at Finn's touch. He squeezed her hand gently once more and then released her.

Her heart was in her mouth. Stupid Salya, what's wrong with you? He was being genuine and caring and his promise was sincere, and all you can think about is being touched by him.

She turned her head away and continued to blush as she stared back into the fire.

Finn could see the girl's turmoil and felt for her; he understood how her attachment to him was growing and completely respected the feelings which this young, teenage body was torturing her mind with.

He turned away and poked at the fire, smiling as the dance of the fire-nymphs began all over again, rising frenziedly up into the starry sky.

Salya watched him, smiled when he did, at the childish wonder in his eyes as he followed the sparks.

He was big on the outside, but on the inside he was huge she thought. A body filled to the brim with life, but on the outside his body told the opposite tale of death. How could he be both, she wondered?

'How are you alive?' She suddenly asked.

Finn pulled back from his musings over the fire and turned to her. 'I don't understand.' He said.

Salya fidgeted a little and glanced away shyly. 'Your scars,' she said, unable to stop herself from seeing the memory of his naked body as she dried him. 'You've been shot and stabbed hundreds of times, how are you alive?'

Finn just stared at her, unable to find the answer which would satisfy her; he couldn't tell her that it was his she-wolf who had kept him alive all these years with her never-ending, vicious love, she would think he was mad.

'I don't know.' He finally said. 'I must be very lucky.'

He smiled weakly and looked at his hands, peering at his palms as though the answer lay hidden there. 'I have never expected to live or die doing the things I have done, I have only expected to do them until they are finished.'

He looked back up at her. 'There is still much to be done so I don't think I am allowed to die just yet.'

He grinned cheekily then, hoping to deflect some of her inquisitiveness a little.

Salya wasn't fooled, she could see the pain etched behind his eyes.

'I'm sorry that you have had so much pain.' She said. 'I wish I wish I could take it away.' She looked down, shyly.

'You are my friend, Salya, I owe you my life; you have already taken much of my pain away.' Finn replied.

He leaned over and placed his hand under Salya's chin, gently turning her head toward him and looking her in the eyes. 'Do not feel sad for me, I have delivered judgment and justice on evil men and women in this world, my own pain is a small price to pay.'

He stroked her cheek with the back of his hand. 'It is your pain which we must ease, my dear friend.' He said, and sat back.

Salya dropped her gaze. He was referring to her ordeal at the compound, when really the pain she felt was an ache in her young heart for him.

'Do you see me as a girl? A child?' She suddenly blurted, trying hard to look at him like an adult, a woman.

Finn frowned a little, he had to be careful not to hurt her feelings or sting her with rejection. 'But you are a child, Salya-.'

'Even after- after-,' she struggled with the words she needed to say. 'After I was used as a woman?'

'Sex does not define us that way.' Finn answered gently. 'The time you have been alive and the experience you have gained, the knowledge and the wisdom, these are the things which define us, define the stages of our lives.'

He looked at her sympathetically then. 'But our bodies like to play tricks on us sometimes.'

She stared, a subtle frown on her face.

'Let me show you.' Finn said.

He placed his palm on her chest just below her chin, supporting her with his other hand on her back at the nape of her neck. Gentle but unyielding.

Salya suddenly thrummed with a flush of unreal excitement. She felt herself swell at Finn's touch, surrounded by a halo of vibrating sound which only she could hear and feel.

She breathed heavily and looked at him with moony eyes. What was happening?

'The feeling you are experiencing, rushing around your body like a wildfire, is one of those trickeries, Salya.' Finn said. 'You love me, as I love you; we have a strong bond of life between us,' he continued, 'and that love comes from a place inside of us, right here beneath my palm, but unseen and not a part of our bodies, but a part of our spirits, our energy, the very thing which we really are. Do you feel it?'

Salya nodded a little, her eyes wide. She did feel it, a hot place which seemed to be disconnected from the rest of her body.

Finn nodded approvingly. 'That is the love we all have for one another, a power beyond any measure.' He said.

'The love then, which courses through our bodies and makes us feel a certain *way*,' he cocked his head a little then and raised his eyebrow, 'does not come from there.'

He smiled and leaned forward, kissing her on the forehead before releasing her and sitting back again.

'That love comes from here.' He said, patting his abdomen. 'It is a powerful energy centre which sometimes tries to completely take over. It is only by understanding that *you yourself* are in control,' he patted his chest then. '*You*, in here are the master of your mind and body and not the other way around, that we bring harmony between the three. Do you see?'

Salya nodded again, her beating heart and wandering mind still making it difficult for the words to sink in however.

'The love of the body pales in comparison to the brightest love of our whole being.' Finn said. 'And it is a sad failing of man to forget this.'

His voice dropped as he thought about those failings, the horrors he had witnessed, one of the reasons he was on this path in the first place.

Like a strange puzzle, Salya suddenly understood something about herself, about people. She couldn't have said what exactly, but Finn's words had made a kind of sense even if she didn't understand all of them; people were more than just their bodies and its whims.

She thought she understood now, how Finn could be bigger on the inside; he was in control of all of himself and the whole was much, much larger than the sum of its parts.

She gazed at him again. She did love him and she did understand her feelings now, a little better at least, but they were still there all the same, fighting for attention, making her heart swell and her skin tingle.

Finn continued to stare into the fire, his mind still wandering the past, when he was suddenly startled by Salya laying her head on his lap and curling up.

He looked down at her and then draped his long arm over her shoulders, stroking her hair gently. He smiled as her lids first began to droop and then finally close as she fell asleep.

'Walk peacefully in your dreams, my dear friend.' He whispered.

*I love you daddy, I'm tired*. The sudden voice of a child from a memory he couldn't place made his heart start.

He frowned as he looked at the sleeping face of Salya, her innocence moved him like the memory of the child's voice, somehow they were connected and the same and yet not the same.

*She loves you.* The she-wolf purred. It felt as though she had just awoken; Finn could feel her mentally flexing and stretching herself in his mind. That had never happened before.

He shook his head slightly, bewildered; he hadn't felt or missed her presence for the whole time Salya had been with him. What did that mean?

*Did you hear me? The girl loves you.*

'I know.' Finn kept his voice low. 'I have talked to her.'

*I hope you didn't hurt the poor thing?* She sounded genuinely concerned that Finn may have been overly harsh, but more concerning to Finn was the fact that she didn't already know.

'You didn't hear? Where were you? Where have you been for the past, three days?'

He could feel the she-wolfs confusion at his question and then felt it grow ten-fold when she couldn't find an answer.

*I've been right here, my love, have I not?* She was trying to sound sure.

'No, you have not. I have not felt you for three days.' Finn's honesty was cutting. 'And strangely I had not realised that until you spoke just now.'

*I remember resting by the waterfall last, I was weary beyond anything I have felt for a long time.*

Finn felt her shudder as she remembered something, the thing which had made her weary most likely.

He didn't know it, but she was remembering her punishing attack on him while he had been singing under the waterfall. She had been unnaturally exhausted afterward she thought.

Finn remembered none of it, not even the song he had been singing.

'Well, no matter, you are here now.'

He felt her shake herself, clearing her thoughts, and then she pressed herself into him, warming him with her deep fur and hot breath.

*Tell me about the girl.* She said, soothing his temples.

As Finn related how he had slipped and hit his head and told the she-wolf what he knew of Salya, seven pairs of eyes watched them sitting in the fire-glow; six pairs belonged to the dogs which were now still for the night, and one pair belonged to Azziz the tracker.

He sat on his haunches at the top of a small hill a half-a-mile away peering through his powerful binoculars. The slave had just laid her head on the man's lap and he sat and stroked her hair now.

At one point Azziz had seen him lean over and place his hands on the girl's chest and back; he thought the big man was going to push her onto her back and mount her but he hadn't; he seemed to be telling her something instead, trying to get her to understand something which had needed that demonstration.

Who was he and why was he treating the girl that way?

Azziz had no notion of the situation back at the compound and so had no idea he was looking at the man who his commanders were waiting to kill. If he had, he would have taken his rifle out straight away and just shot him and worried about the girl afterward.

The man intrigued him though; he and the slave were heading back toward the compound, so what business did he have there? And why was the slave going back with him?

It was clear that the man hadn't captured her, she was travelling freely with him, so what had he done? Talked her into doing the right thing by handing herself in?

Azziz didn't think so, it was more probable that she had told him about the place she had escaped from and he was going there to have a look for himself. If that was the case then he must be equipped and able, trained even.

Maybe it was much simpler than that; maybe they were only going that way because the slave had told the man where she came from, her village? He might be just seeing her safely back home; he was bound to have a map if he was travelling all the way out here.

If he *was* taking her home then Azziz would know in a few days; the man would have to bear off the northern path and travel into the north-east.

Whatever the reasons, his naturally inquisitive, tracker's mind compelled him to find out. Which was very unfortunate for him.

He rose to his feet and turned his back on his quarry, making his way back down the other side of the hill and to his own concealed campfire. He would keep his distance for now, he thought, wait and see if they turned away from the north and the compound.

He could see the pallid glow of his fire waiting for him twenty yards away.

Perhaps it was the dark pushing at his back while his fire called him on, or perhaps it was just his own weariness and fatigue, whatever it was, Azziz the tracker caught his foot in the gnarly root of a long-dead tree and the first of his misfortunes began right there.

His heart lurched as he tumbled forward, the root holding firm and causing his foot to twist before he fell sprawling to land heavily on his shoulder and hip.

There was a loud crack and Azziz cried out in pain and fright at the thought of his ankle snapping.

He cursed and winced as he untangled his foot, sitting beside the offending root and gingerly pulling his trouser-leg up.

He tried to move his toes first and then his whole foot. It wasn't broken, thank God, but it was sore and sprained, he would have to get it strapped up as quickly as possible.

He managed to stand and tested his weight on the ankle; it wasn't good enough to run around anywhere but he could walk and that was the main thing.

Limping and cursing and hissing between his teeth, Azziz made it to his camp and flopped heavily down onto the ground.

How could he have been so careless?

*Foolish! Clumsy!* He berated himself as he carefully removed his boot and then his sock. The ankle was swollen and bruised, throbbing painfully.

'Bastard!' He said, aloud.

He would have to let Nazari know. It stung him that he would have to report his failure to that fat, little bastard. He could almost see his sneering face waiting for him when he finally arrived back.

'Bastard, sister-fucker!' He spat.

He flexed his ankle and drank from his wineskin, trying to calm himself before he messaged his commander.

With a final mouthful of wine and a huff of derision he pulled his phone from his pocket along with several bits of broken plastic.

He looked down silently at the smashed phone lying in his palm; the cracking noise he had heard when he had tripped.

Azziz had never considered himself lucky or unlucky, but as he stared at the broken phone he felt that all the bad luck he had ever avoided in his life had just fallen on his head in the past, ten minutes.

He threw the broken bits to the ground in a temper. He would have to continue as he had planned now, but it would be painful and tiring.

Like Salya, Azziz had been brought up on the mountains; he wasn't worried about his survival, he knew he would make it back safely. It was all the pain which was going to be involved which made him grimace.

He hated pain, didn't particularly like inflicting it either, he liked things to be quick and clean and precise like a good tracker should.

'Foolish.' He hissed angrily, slowly turning his foot.

He had never really taken any interest in any of the slaves, emotionally or otherwise, but he was beginning to hate that little bitch and the trouble she was causing him. He would definitely catch her now, after all he had gone through and was going to go through, he would catch her, even if it was the last thing he ever did.

He unloaded the small, medical field-kit he had in his pack and took out the bandages.

As each turn of the supporting bandage caused flashes of pain to shoot up his calf, Azziz hissed and swore under his breath, aiming it all at the slave. He *would* catch her, as God was his witness, he would.

More than a hundred miles away to the south, a tiny, one-man tent rustled quietly under the strokes of the mountain's night-breeze, its occupant sipping coffee laced with Russian brandy.

The killer smiled with his eyes closed, happily savouring the taste of the dark coffee, his second cup since he had pitched up for the night.

A simple pleasure and joy to end a perfect day of climbing.

It had been a few years since he had done any serious mountaineering, he found he had the old aches return once he had reached the top, marvelling at the view as he stretched and limbered the muscles which had been underused for so long.

As soon as he had stepped off the plane in Iran he had been travelling south-east, making for the borderlands between Iran and Afghanistan.

A vehicle and a driver had been provided for him and it had only taken two days to reach the site where he would be crossing.

Before returning back to the place which he had set out from, the young, Russian driver had furnished the killer with all the necessary equipment and weapons he would be needing, including the military micro-tent which he was now sitting in.

His eyes remained closed as he swayed along to the music he could hear through the earpieces he was wearing. They were connected to a piece of equipment which he had brought along himself; his iPod.

His smile broadened as the cheeky pace of Mozart played wildly into his ears, a sound which seemed to be actually *rocking it* at times; wild and semi-chaotic, full of questioning chords and answering riffs.

He wondered whether his brother liked music. He hoped he did, he would know soon enough, however; he wasn't that far ahead now.

He could feel him in his fingertips when he pointed them out in that direction, he could feel them tingle, pulling him on. A connection that only brothers had, gods who were brothers.

The killer felt genuinely happy, a very rare feeling for him. He had felt happiness before, but this was the *final* happiness, the *meaning* of happiness itself, he felt he would burst with it.

For so long he had been and felt very unique, a uniqueness which carried with it its own brand of loneliness.

But now he didn't feel alone, for the very first time he felt part of something else which was the same as him and that resulted in the most profound happiness. Only a god could feel as happy as this and bear it so.

He laughed as he rocked to Mozart. 'Oh! Brother, I do hope you take to Mozart.'

He spoke too loudly over the music, laughing as it carried him away on a sudden, violent almost, crescendo of piano chords and wailing violin strings.

He continued to laugh joyfully and swayed with the music, laying back on its cushioning mad-vibrancy and submitting to the universe's chaotic-call which the music was hurling him toward.

A laughing comet of sound and joy speeding on and on through a cosmos unexplored is how he saw himself.

The track continued until it reached its final crescendo and then abruptly ended.

There were tears streaming down the killers cheeks from eyes which were still closed, and he sat with his head tipped back and his arms opened and pushed out, palms face up. Like a man revealing his soul and receiving his blessing.

Suddenly his eyes flashed open and he sat forward, gathering himself up until he was just the killer once more.

He pulled the earphones out and rolled them up, then sat back and sipped more coffee, his face now blank.

He sat like that for minutes, just staring into nothing and thinking about nothing, his arm automatically rising and falling as he lifted his cup to his lips to sip at his drink.

His mind at that very moment was a vast, black canvas, empty of everything; no thoughts, no needs, no emotions, just a black emptiness.

It was a place where his mind would go when it had thought everything it had needed to think, no good going over things over and over again only to come to the same decisions; think it through thoroughly once and leave it at that.

Minutes later and the black canvas was replaced by the normal, mundane thoughts which all people had, the killer never really realising that he had been there in the first place.

He sat there now, thinking about the message he had received in the car on his way here; the Interpol inspector Graham Shelby, had been snooping again.

All very well that they had needed him to get to Finn, but George had told him that Shelby had specifically asked about Hinds. That was worrying, it could only mean that the hacker Harrison, had somehow made copies of the video from the phone. That meant he, the killer, had made a mistake and that was his biggest worry.

Of course, as soon as he had worked out what the danger was he had got back to his masters, informing them that Shelby knew more than he was letting on and it was probable that he knew Hinds had been killed by Finn.

They should be, even as he sat in his tent on this mountaintop, tracking down Shelby's wife; capturing their enemy's family for use as bargaining chips was always their first tactic.

The killer lay back and flicked the battery-powered light off. He stared into the darkness and wondered how he had failed to find all the copies of that video.

Hinds deserved everything he got, he thought, but how stupid was the man really? Who in their right mind would take part in the illegal things which he did and also film themselves doing it? The man must have thought that his powerful position made him untouchable.

In the dark, the killer smiled to himself, thinking once again of his brother-in-waiting. 'Thank you for proving him wrong on that point, brother.' He said, before closing his eyes and falling into a dreamless sleep.

## Chapter Twenty-Five

The tall, blonde woman snatched the buzzing phone from her pocket and answered it. 'Dilger.' She said, annoyed.

She waited patiently as the voice on the other end spoke. 'Yes sir, I understand.' She finally said, before hanging up.

Her chest heaved as she sighed deeply, her annoyance turning to frustration.

She dropped her phone back into her coat-pocket and turned her attention back to the tree-line at the back of the car-park.

They had waited all night for the stupid woman to come out. Placing themselves off the road a quarter of a mile away and then creeping back to watch from the shadows. She hadn't bloody shown up!

The woman called Dilger could have kicked herself for not sending Robinson and his men straight in to meet her instead of waiting for her to come out. She hadn't counted on her being so well informed in the ways of stealth.

It was clear that she had been spooked early on, possibly at the hotel. Making a quiet run for it was the sensible thing to do, but to work out that she was being somehow tracked and then realising it was the phone which was her tag, not to mention dumping it and escaping, was very clever Dilger thought.

She scoffed at her admiration for the woman; she wouldn't have expected anything like that from a civilian nurse, even if she *was* married to an Interpol inspector.

Back in the edge of the forest, Dilger's men were fanned out, slowly walking through the undergrowth in the area where they had found the phone.

Dilger was just about to call them back as she had been ordered, when the voice of her second shouted her name.

She could see him waving his arm, beckoning for her to come and have a look at something.

She strode off through the gate and then veered straight off the forest path and made a beeline for the man called Robinson.

He and two other men were standing around a large boulder fronted by tall bushes and shrubbery, they were looking down at something on the ground between rock and bush.

Dilger approached the group and sidled up to Robinson, turning her gaze to look at what they were frowning at. 'God fucking damn it!' She hissed under her breath.

Pressed into the soft, mossy ground, the instantly recognisable imprint of a sleeping body slapped Dilger around her stupid, mental face.

'She was right fucking here!' She growled. 'What kind of stupid, moronic, half-witted idiot stays around the very place they are in danger?'

'The kind that escapes?' The man called Robinson said.

Dilger turned to him and gave him an icy stare.

He shrugged apologetically, making it worse.

'If we weren't *friends* I'd shoot you and leave *you* in the undergrowth!' She said seriously.

Robinson smiled shyly and pursed his lips. 'I know' He replied, nodding slowly.

Dilger just huffed and then looked away, turning her attention back to the ground and studying the implications which the woman-shaped indent now presented.

'If she spent the whole night here,' she began, 'then she can't have been on the move for more than an hour.'

She turned her head and looked at the car-park. 'She didn't come through there and I'd be willing to bet that she didn't go all the way back through there either.' She said, turning to face the forest and nodding.

Dilger thought for a moment, weighing up the only two options she now felt she had; do as she had been ordered and return to base, or have one final sweep of the only two ways which the woman could have gone.

'Split into two groups.' She eventually said. 'Search along this line in both directions; she must have come out somewhere along here.' She then said to Robinson. 'I'm going into Wellington to make a recce of the train-station.'

Robinson nodded and then turned to the men. 'You heard the boss; Devlin and Melford with me, McKenzie? You and Simmons take the north stretch.' He said.

He turned back to Dilger. 'When we find her trail I'll send the lads back to the train-station. I'll stay on her until I either find her or find out where she went.'

Dilger nodded. An hour, maybe a little more or less, but she wasn't that far in front of them. If and when they picked up her trail she knew Robinson would stay on it.

'Get to it then boys,' she said, 'and I'll see you back in town in a couple of hours.'

The drive back to Wellington was pleasant, the roads were open and almost empty of other traffic, and the low, stone walls offered a breathtaking view of the surrounding countryside. Well, it was if you were paying any attention to it all.

Dilger drove on auto-pilot, the countryside and the clear skies and empty roads all lost on her.

How could she have been so lax and stupid? She had, had the woman right there within her reach, a mere hundred yards away, and yet she had missed her. It felt like she had been standing right next to the bulls-eye, aiming straight for it but missing the board entirely.

The woman was wily alright, Dilger thought to herself, she had underestimated her, but she wouldn't make that mistake again.

They *would* pick up her trail and she *would* report back that all was still on the go, hopefully redeeming herself in the process; she couldn't abide failure as it was, but a failure borne of stupidity made her face blaze.

To hell with what her bosses thought, it was what *she* thought which counted the most.

It wasn't long before she was heading into the train-station, the twenty minute journey a complete blank to her.

Her mind was still buzzing with the thoughts of coming so close and missing. She needed to wake up. Coffee was what she needed now.

The station café was open and welcomed all travellers passing through the doors and onto the platforms with its aromas of toasting sandwiches and bubbling-in-the-pot coffee.

As she passed from the normal world outside into the subtly changed world of track and diesel engines, Dilger noted the four, closed-circuit cameras fitted in the high corners of the short arcade which led onto the platforms. They effectively watched every square-inch of the station entrance, including the ticket windows and the café and news shop.

She shook her head, coffee first she decided.

After buying the biggest, blackest cup of coffee she could, Dilger sipped it through the silly plastic top which these take-out cups always had.

The trouble was, without the lid the cup might as well have been made of tissue, usually crumpling up and spilling its contents without the sturdy, plastic lid - with stupid mouthpiece like a fucking baby's feeder-cup - to support it and keep it in shape.

She slurped unintentionally as she drank, walking across the arcade and toward the only ticket window which had a clerk sitting behind.

The young, bespectacled man looked up as she approached and smiled congenially, readying himself for a transaction, and one with a gorgeous woman at that he thought.

His timid chest puffed up.

'I'd like to speak to your supervisor.' Dilger said, abruptly, poker-faced and serious. The coffee was working.

The young man visibly shrank, blushed furiously and then began to stammer, completely flummoxed. 'I-I-I-I-,' his head twitched a little with each vowel, then he went on with; 'Am-am-am-am-,'

Dilger held her hand up. 'Stop.'

She sighed and put her hand into her pocket and pulled out a pair of earphones attached to her personal phone.

She slid them both through the payment gap at the bottom of the window.

The clerk just stared and then opened his mouth to speak again, but Dilger stopped him with her hand a second time.

'Don't speak. Put the earphones in.'

He did as he was told. She could see he was perspiring. Stupid boy.

'Now. I would like to speak to your supervisor.' She said, and then pointed to the buttons on her phone. 'Press the green one and then answer.'

Again the clerk did as he was told and pressed the green button. Loud rock music suddenly erupted in his ears and he cringed.

'Now speak.' Dilger said, also gesturing her request.

'I am the supervisor.' Was all he said. A look of total astonishment painted his face at being able to say the words so precisely and without stuttering.

'*You're* the supervisor? How?'

Dilger's face looked as astonished as the clerk's. 'You look about twelve!'

'I'm the only one here so I'm the supervisor.' He replied. 'And I'm twenty-nine thank you.'

Dilger just looked at him, looked for the sign that he was lying about his age, but he wasn't.

'Well,' she leaned closer to the glass and peered at his name-badge. 'Supervisor Brian, I would like to take a look at the security-footage for the past three hours.'

'And under whose authority would that be.' The clerk replied, loving every word which came perfectly out of his mouth. 'I can't let just any old, Tom, Dick or Harriet come into the security room I'm afraid, madam.'

It would usually take him three weeks to say all of that to a beautiful woman. He beamed proudly through the screeching strains of *Metallica*.

Dilger sensed his pride at his newfound verbal skills. 'I'll be wanting that back,' she said, pointing to her phone, 'so get your own.'

She took her identification from her pocket as she spoke. 'Now, about that footage.' She said, and pressed the wallet up to the glass for him to read. 'I think you will find that this is all the authority I need, Brian.'

The clerk leaned closer to read it, pushing his glasses up his nose as he did so.

*Special Detective, Caroline Dilger,* the card read. *Interpol Security*.

\* \* \*

The scenery wasn't streaming past fast enough Rachel thought, she still felt eyes were at her back.

She had been right to stay where she was, but she'd paid for it when she woke up; the aches were only a distant memory now, but once her eyes had opened and the dew had dripped from her nose and lashes, she had tried to move and found she was made of cold, hard, living clay.

It had taken the better part of fifteen minutes before she managed to even sit up, groaning like a geriatric. Her fingers and toes were numb.

She'd given the car-park a wide berth and travelled down across its boundary instead and then stayed on until she cleared the trees and hit the main road.

From there it was a simple walk through fields and walled farmland until she came to the skirts of Wellington.

She shivered remembering the twenty minute walk through the empty, morning streets.

She was aware of every, single footfall she made, cringing as she loped along as quickly as she could, wondering at every corner whether someone was going to step out and grab her.

Strangely, once she had reached the town centre which had a decent crowd of morning people crossing it, she felt a little easier. She thought that being under the scrutiny of strangers would have made her feel even more paranoid, but it didn't. She came to the conclusion that it was because she knew that *everyone* couldn't be out to get her now, could they?

She looked at her reflection in the double-glazed glass as the outside world ambled past.

Her hair was a little dishevelled and her eyes were puffy, but she thought she didn't look too bad.

She had cleaned and groomed herself as much as she possibly could in the hand-sinks in the toilets, but as far as *pits and bits* were concerned she would have to wait until she arrived at her final destination.

The train she was on was heading for Shrewsbury, from there she would catch a train into Bangor.

Waiting for the train to pull out of Wellington had been the longest forty-five minute wait she had ever had to endure.

Sitting in her corner seat, hiding almost behind her backpack while the train sat silently until the driver arrived, Rachel had found her eyes were amazingly good at looking everywhere at once.

She had imagined to see a parade of armed men come marching down the platform, flinging the carriage doors open and searching the aisles. All drama and very *Von Ryan's Express* she thought afterward, once the train had actually pulled out.

She planned to stay one day in Bangor to rest and recoup in a bed-and-breakfast before catching a bus into the Snowdonia parks.

It would be easy to find another bed-and-breakfast around there and the countryside was also easily accessible should she need to escape again. God, she hoped she wouldn't need to.

'Tickets please!'

The conductor's, loud voice startled Rachel and she jumped an inch off her seat and almost squealed. She sat an clutched her backpack to her chest and breathed deeply.

'Tickets please!' The voice called again.

She fumbled with the pockets on the bag, hurriedly unzipping and re-zipping them, looking for her ticket before realising she had put it in her coat pocket.

She pulled it out and handed to the ticket-collector.

A middle-aged, robust man in a uniform which seemed two-sizes too small - peaked cap and all - looked over the rims of his round glasses at Rachel. 'Everything alright, miss?' He asked, after noting her sudden panic.

'Um. Yes.' Rachel replied sheepishly. 'Sorry, I was half asleep when you called out.'

The conductor checked Rachel's ticket and then clipped it with his punch before handing it back to her. 'Sorry to have disturbed you, miss.' He said, touching the plastic peak of his cap.

He carried on down the aisle calling for tickets, leaving Rachel still clutching her backpack.

*Come on woman! Get it together.*

She breathed in and out slowly, bringing her heartbeat down a notch.

She looked at herself again in the window. Her features hardened when she noted the genuine fright she had in her eyes; how dare that bitch and her cronies make her feel like this! How fucking dare they!

Her heart hammered again, with anger this time. Well fuck them! She wasn't afraid of them.

Her anger rose to the surface and actually felt liberating she found, pushing the fear well away and then choking it into non-existence, releasing much of the tension and anxiety she had been running on for the past twenty-four hours.

She continued to breath slowly and surely, staring at herself and watching satisfied as her eyes slowly changed from round and afraid to narrow and confident.

She would play that bitch's game and keep on running and hiding if necessary, but she wouldn't let fear rule her every waking moment, or have it influencing her decisions and plans.

No, she would be as confident as the woman who was looking for her was. Confident and fearless.

Rachel raised her chin stoically.

They're bound to have guns.

Her chin drooped a little.

That's just fear trying to get a word in; what does it matter that they have guns? They still have to find you to be able to use the bloody things don't they?

She suddenly felt she wanted to cry.

How have I got here, thinking thoughts like that? About guns and killers and bitches who are trying to catch me? How did that happen? And oh! God how am I going to find Graham?

She turned away from her reflection and looked down at her feet, unable to meet her own eyes in case she did start to cry.

Her heart ached sorely when she thought of Graham and what might or might not be happening to him, but her real worry lay in how he would now get in touch with her when it was safe again.

The only option she had would be to get in touch with someone at Interpol, but she couldn't do that yet, it was too early; whatever Graham was working on he had hinted that it would be at least a couple of weeks before it was seen through.

So, at least two weeks of running. She could handle that, but if and when she did make contact with Interpol, who would she be able to trust?

Graham had taken her and himself off the grid; for all she knew that meant he didn't trust even his own colleagues.

God, she hated this game, this game of goodies and baddies, spies and agents, hunters and prey. Bloody children, the lot of them, Rachel had often thought.

She looked back up and out of the window, the scenery was moving past much faster now. The clear, blue skies promised it was going to be a beautiful day.

Whether you were a goodie or a baddie, the sky was impartial and would keep its promise, Rachel thought, bad things still happened under beautiful skies.

She tutted quietly and shook her head. Stop being so bloody morose, miss half-empty; good things happen under dismal skies as well, it's not the bloody sky that dictates it is it?

A field slid by, filled with a dozen or more cows. They were all standing and chewing on the grass, all except one; that one was laying with its legs tucked beneath it, waiting for a rainy sky.

Rachel felt like that cow, laying down and waiting for the bad weather while everyone else around her could see it was going to be a beautiful, sunny day.

Get up you silly cow, it's not going to rain.

The cows disappeared from view, the train was idling along now she noticed, coasting and slowly reducing its speed. They must be close to Shrewsbury.

She still felt that they were still too close, Shrewsbury was only a fifteen-minute train journey from Wellington, probably half-an-hour by road, she wouldn't feel safe until she was on the train to Bangor.

A few minutes later and Rachel was standing on the busy platform at Shrewsbury train-station, milling commuters bustling on and off their trains in a strangely synchronised dance.

The people all moved to a soundless score, no one jostling anyone else and everyone flowing around everyone they met, an unconsciously practised piece of synchronised avoidance.

But not for Rachel, who wasn't supposed to be here in the first place.

She bumped and prodded her way through to the ticket windows, producing glares and frowns from the *professional* commuters who saw her as some kind of *newbie* to commuter-travel.

After buying her one-way ticket, she ran the gauntlet a second time as she headed over the footbridge and onto another platform.

Her train was sitting with its engine switched off and its doors closed. The platform was lined with passengers waiting to get on.

Rachel took a place to wait and stood with her back to the waiting-room wall, trying to make herself as small and inconspicuous as possible.

From where she was standing she could just make out the station entrance through the waiting train's windows.

She stood upright and squinted through the glass when she caught a flash of something moving fast like a running person or persons.

A man and a woman suddenly burst out into the daylight, huffing and puffing as they pulled their enormous trolley-cases behind them.

Rachel slumped back and breathed out. Relax Rachel, it's just Mister and Mrs *Late-for-their-train*.

She scoffed at herself as she watched the couple dragging their cases to the foot of the stairs leading up to the bridge. And then she almost lost her eyeballs as they popped in her head because her heart had just missed several beats.

Walking confidently and surely behind the couple with the bags was the blonde woman from the car-park, she was sure of it.

The windows of the train were distorting the image a tad, but Rachel could clearly see it was a tall, blonde woman at the least.

'Shit!' She squeaked.

Following the woman were two men and once again, even though she couldn't make out the details of their faces, just the fact that three people who fit the description of her pursuers had casually walked into the same train-station as she herself was in, made her feel certain that they had found her.

She cringed back against the wall, trying her hardest to be a part of it, and watched as the woman pointed to one of the men who then walked away in the opposite direction, making his way to the other platforms.

The other man backed himself up against the wall next to the entrance and stood leaning against it, swivelling his head as he scanned the passengers.

The woman climbed the stairs to the bridge, held up behind the huffing and puffing couple.

Rachel was suddenly jolted into action as a whistle blew loudly and the doors to the train hissed open.

Oh! God, yes! She thought and surged forward.

She didn't give a damn if the other passengers were in her way or not, or what they thought of her; all she wanted to do was get into the lavatory and lock the door.

'Sorry, excuse me.' She said without waiting to be let through and pushing past anyway.

She made the doors, the toilet was to her left, she sprinted the remaining ten feet and then barged in, slamming the door behind her and locking it.

She flopped heavily onto the seat and sat holding her chest, panting as though she had just run a mile.

How the hell had they found her? She was certain they hadn't got anymore tracking devices on her, or else they would have walked right up to the spot where she had been sleeping and nabbed her.

No, it was detective work was that, people with badges which they could flash at ticket-sellers.

Rachel's instincts told her it was something closer to home than was comfortable now. Authoritative figures, sporting badges were no stranger to her life.

As her mind struggled with the implications, the diesel engine roared into life and she lurched gently as it pulled the carriages away.

With any luck, the woman and her men would spend some time in Shrewsbury looking for her; she could only hope that they wouldn't reckon on her catching another train.

All she needed to do was stay ahead of them until Bangor.

Her plans had changed now that she had seen them so close on her trail.

Instead of staying the night at a bed and breakfast in the city, she decided she would now make her way straight to the bus-station and change her mode of transport.

Once she was in the Snowdonia region she could easily lose herself again in the wild.

'But what I wouldn't give for a hot bath and brandy before bed.' She muttered to herself, her eyes brimming.

Rachel kept herself locked in the toilet for ten, more minutes after the train had pulled out.

She gingerly opened the door and peered through the gap, trying to get the best view up and down the aisles.

Once she felt it was safe she opened it and made for an empty seat near the automatic door but still within leaping distance of the lavatory.

She noted with some embarrassment that some of the passengers were looking at her with sly smirks on their faces; *night out on the curry was it?* They seemed to be saying. If only they knew.

It was like being in a bad, horror film, where the heroine was surrounded by the good people, but for some uniquely strange reason couldn't tell them anything or ask for help. Why was that?

No time for psychology 101, dear; at its basic, it's simply because we're afraid we'll look silly and people will think we're mad.

Rachel felt like she *was* going mad, she was a nurse for God's sake, not a bloody ninja!

She sat back in her seat and stretched her legs out in front of her, rubbing the muscles at the bottom of her spine.

Hot bath and brandy and a warm bed and movie. And maybe some more brandy. The thought warmed her inside.

The trundle and clack of the wheels began to lull Rachel with their metronomic precision, and her lids soon began to droop until eventually she was drifting away on her thoughts of bubbling baths and strong, dark brandy.

## Chapter Twenty-Six

The red dots, which signified the communications being monitored on the big-screen map, had been pinging up with a clockwork regularity for the past four days. The newest location setting off a string of communications between London, Afghanistan, Russia and now Wales.

Shelby, Sophie and Anna, all sat in front of the screen, each of them looking a little rough around the edges from their constant vigil of the communications.

A pattern was emerging; London to Wales and back again, two or three times, then London to Russia once, Russia to Keys house once, and intermittently from Keys house to Afghanistan.

Hours would pass and then the same or very similar, pattern of communications started up again. It was almost as if someone was reporting regularly and the report was travelling through a loose chain of command.

Anna's protégé, Adam Henley - aka *Snooker-boy* - had done an amazing job of getting the *Code-8* listening device into place.

The hardware made it possible for them to correlate all of the encrypted communications they were monitoring and then cross-reference them with the information which the device was sending back.

It turned out that four of the communications came directly from the Keys residence while a further fifteen were still coming from an unknown location somewhere in the West London area.

The three of them soon realised that Keys himself was not responsible for the communications when he made two calls using his own phone.

The first was to his PA and the second was to a friend to arrange a game of squash. Both conversations had been crystal clear to hear and the numbers were unmasked and traceable, including Keys' own phone.

So that only left Margret the housekeeper or George the stand-in security guard.

If it was Margret, then Shelby vowed he would quit his job and become a circus clown, because that is how he would feel, he said, if he found out it was she who was the culprit.

The sudden Welsh connection was interesting; altogether, over the past four days, nine communications had been sent and received between the Welsh border and the London suspect.

The red dots over the Welsh area had seemed to be moving from east to west, England to Wales.

None of them had actually said it, but it seemed as though those dots were following something. Or someone.

Shelby sat up straight and stretched his back and arms and then sighed heavily as he relaxed back into his seat.

His mind was very good at solving puzzles and breaking patterns and codes; he had a theory, but he didn't like it.

Sophie took his hand and gave it a reassuring squeeze, knowing exactly what was going through Shelby's mind. She wouldn't insult him by telling him everything was going to be alright, or not to worry, all he needed from her was to know she was there.

He sighed again and nodded slowly. 'Right, this is what I think is going on.' He said, casually pointing to the map. 'We'll start with Keys; I went there after we had effectively gone off the grid and straight away we had a flurry of communications from our three, main locations; Keys, Afghanistan and Russia. It's interesting to note that the final communication in that chain, the fourth one, came last from the anonymous London suspect.'

He pointed to the Welsh communications. 'They didn't start to come in until after my visit to Keys had been reported and what's more, they only go as far as London; the Welsh dots have never joined up with the Russian, Afghanistan, or the Keys dots.'

He turned to face them both again, holding Sophie's hand tightly. 'I think the Welsh communications are coming from someone who has been sent to find Rachel.' He finally said.

The two women looked at him sympathetically and were about to voice their support when the communications computer pinged loudly.

Anna typed in the commands and two red dots appeared linked by a thin red line.

The communication had been sent from Russia and received near the Welsh border, but not in the same location as the first Welsh contact.

'There's two of them.' Shelby muttered.

What did that mean? Two assassins - he mentally kicked himself for his poor choice of words - two *pursuers*, both looking for the same thing? Why? God damn it, what did it mean?

Anna stood up, catching the look on Shelby's face; he was flustered and knotted up inside, who wouldn't be? But she wasn't, she came to a strange but feasible conclusion.

'We have a friend in London!' She suddenly said.

When Shelby and Sophie just looked at her, wondering which elite member she was about to produce now from her little clique, she pointed stiffly at the map without looking at it.

'You went to Keys, someone eavesdropped and informed their master in Afghanistan, who in turn informed *their* masters in Russia. It was the Russian connection which contacted the anonymous London contact.' She raised her eyebrows. 'Don't you see? The London contact has sent someone to find your wife because he or she knows that the Russians will be sending someone to do the same.'

She lowered her arm and looked at the map now. 'And that new red dot looks like they have just arrived.'

Shelby just stared, first at Anna and then at the map.

The piece fell nicely into place, but it wasn't a certainty; for all they knew, there was just another team being added to the search for Rachel. But he did like the little hacker's thoughts on it, they offered a hope at least.

He turned back and relaxed. 'I think you may be onto something there, Anna.' He smiled at her. 'Well spotted, and quickly.'

'Oh. You would have got there eventually.' She replied and smiled back.

'Bloody hell!' Sophie looked astonished. 'Was that modesty!?' She said, looking straight at Anna.

Anna shrugged. 'Of course.'

'And she's back.' Sophie said, rolling her eyes.

Shelby rose from his seat and walked over to the table at the back of the room where he poured coffee for them all from the percolator. 'If Anna is right, then that means Rachel is definitely in danger now, if not before - if we are correct in assuming that the Welsh contact is indeed looking for her, that is.' He said. 'But we can't dismiss the possibility that the new recipient at the Welsh location isn't just another addition to the first group.'

He came back to his seat carrying three mugs of coffee. 'Or isn't connected with them at all.' He said, handing Rachel and Anna their cups.

He took his own seat again and continued. 'I hate to think of Rachel being in danger, but if that *is* someone trying to capture her,' he pointed to the screen, 'then by the looks of things, she is doing a good job of staying ahead of them.'

He stared at the trail of dots leading from England to Wales. As much as he tried, he couldn't make it impossible for those dots to not be connected to his wife somehow and the more he stared and thought about it, the more he knew they actually were.

'I still say we should give her a call.' Sophie said, for the fifth time that afternoon.

'Risky.' Anna said, also for the fifth time.

'But at least we would know for certain if the Welsh communications have something to do with Rachel.' Sophie, insisted.

'Yes and we may find out that they have nothing to do with her, but end up alerting someone else to her whereabouts.' Anna argued casually.

She knew where Sophie was coming from, but felt that the pros and cons were weighted too heavily on the side of the cons.

'I think we should wait, see if the communications can tell us anything else.' Shelby muttered. 'I can't take the risk just yet; if they are following Rachel, then we have just got to hope that she can avoid them for long enough.'

It hurt him to say those words, angered him to think that his wife was in danger because of him. No, because of bloody Finn. *If we ever meet, my psychotic friend, I'm going to punch you on the fucking nose for that.*

He shoved the childish sentiment away; it wasn't Finn's fault, if anyone was to blame it was the people who were doing the atrocious things which had led them to this situation.

That subtle itch under his collar and in his feet at standing around waiting for too long began to nag at his thoughts. He was frustrated and felt stagnant just waiting and watching, analyzing and theorising, he needed to move the action along somehow, but he had no idea how to do that at the minute.

Anna leaned across Sophie and chinked her cup loudly against Shelby's.

He flinched at the noise. 'What?'

'Nothing.' Anna answered.

'What was that for?' Shelby frowned.

'You looked like you were about to put your coat on and go for a walk. To Wales maybe.' She said.

Shelby's eye's narrowed a little, frowning at himself more than Anna; she was right, the itch was heading for the door and the only place feasible for it to lead him would be to Wales, adding a third person in the hunt for his wife. *If it was his wife they were hunting.*

'You're right,' he eventually said, relaxing again. 'The thought wasn't right there just then, but I'm sure it would have arrived. It's a bloody trial though, is all this waiting and watching and figuring it out, I don't know how you two can take it so easily.'

'Well I don't know about Anna, but I'm not taking it that easily, Gray, but I can't see any sure step forward just yet, not until we are closer to the date Finn has in mind. Might as well stay focused, eh?' Sophie said.

'I'm with Sophie,' Anna nodded, 'but I am also a programmer; I have endless patience to see a thing done and number-crunching comes naturally to me. We should wait a little longer.'

She shrugged her shoulders. 'If what I gather from you two about your wife Rachel, is right,' she shrugged again, acquiescing to the point. 'Then she seems more than capable of staying out of harm's way.'

It probably wasn't too apparent, but Shelby found a lot of comfort in what Anna had just said; coming from someone like her, so self-assured and very well-trained and capable, went a long way to help keeping his fears in check.

'Yes, you're right, both of you, we should wait a few more days at least.' He said. 'Which brings me on to a new question then; how we are going to get into Pakistan when the time comes?'

'We'll alert all the known authorities as soon as we raise our heads at any airport,' Sophie began, 'but if we time it-.'

She was cut short by Anna clearing her throat rather loudly. 'I think I may be able to help with that.' She said.

'Don't tell me you've got a jet stashed away somewhere?' Sophie's question was genuine.

'Sort of.' Anna replied innocently. 'We have access to practically any choice of vehicle, if you know where and how to acquire them, or rather *hire* them. For free that is. So borrow them would be a better way of describing it.'

'And by that you mean steal them?' Sophie folded her arms beneath her breast and sat looking sternly at Anna with raised eyebrows.

'Sort of.' Anna said again and laughed lamely. 'We don't keep them, just sort of *commandeer* them for the duration of our need if you know what I mean?'

Shelby scoffed and then threw his arms up in the air. 'I give up. I didn't think it possible for us to fall any further into the *dark-side* and then that's exactly what we go and do.'

He laughed, the women couldn't tell if it was genuine or not.

'We're now going to steal British aircraft and fly through God knows whose airspace! I've lost count of how many bloody laws we're breaking anyway, never mind the pile which comes with just doing that!'

Anna leaned closer to Sophie. 'Is he getting hysterical?'

'Oh no, he's well past hysterical.'

'*Well* past.' Shelby emphasised, running his hands over his tired face.

'Well it's not as bad as all that, you know?' Anna said. 'The plane and the flight-plan are all recorded and booked correctly. It would be as if that actual flight existed at both ends.'

'So you hack a bogus flight-plan into,' Shelby paused, he didn't know how the international flight system worked. 'Into what?' He finally said.

'Simple; we source a plane at our airport of choice, then plan the journey and hack into any country's aerospace program to add the flight until we reach our destination.'

It did sound simple.

'And that's it? We get on a plane to Pakistan and no one will know?' Sophie asked.

'Yes.'

'And you've done this before?'

The little hacker just huffed. 'How do you think I got here?'

Shelby just sat and stared, didn't know what to do or think, the world had just turned a new flavour of crazy. He didn't even know *this* level of crazy existed until he had met Harrison; secret lairs and labs, running from pursuers, hacking and encrypted messages and now secret flights to equally secret locations and their missions.

He'd never been much of a James Bond fan and after this he thought he never would be.

'I don't suppose you could arrange the travel to that mining town and get us into a hotel as well could you?' He asked, lamely.

Anna scoffed and then chuckled. 'Of course, road or helicopter?' She asked grinning.

Sophie just shook her head.

'You are rather brilliant in your own, dark way, Anna.' Shelby said, and he meant it.

'Oh don't bloody encourage her.' Sophie growled, nudging him hard with her elbow and then turning on Anna. 'Don't you dare say *of course!*' She mimicked sarcastically.

Before anyone could say *of course* or anything else, the computer pinged again causing everyone's face to suddenly take on the same, serious appearance as they immediately turned their attention onto the big screen.

Anna typed. The second red dot which had appeared near Wales lit up and connected to the dot in Moscow.

'Someone's reporting in.' Anna spoke aloud what they were all thinking.

The computer pinged again a minute later, the Moscow dot lit up first this time and then the one in Wales; the reply.

The three of them sat and waited in silence. Several more minutes went by before the computer piped up again. This time it was Moscow to London.

'If we are on the right track,' Shelby said, quietly, 'then the next communication should go from London to the original Welsh recipient.'

They waited. Five minutes went by and then sure enough, London contacted Wales.

There was a small chorus of released breaths from the trio; it was reassuring to think that someone just might be trying to get to Rachel first and *that* someone could even be a friend.

But to even the balance of the scale, particularly for Shelby, was the Russian dot now represented in Wales. It had moved quite some distance and was much closer to the first dot.

That last communication had shown that the original dot had only moved a few miles to the south, close to the Snowdonia park area.

'I don't know if we *have* a few more days.' Shelby said despondently. 'They're getting closer to whatever it is they're looking for by the looks of it.'

'Or maybe they've lost the trail.' Sophie added. 'They could be wandering around in circles looking for it and that's why they're not moving much.'

'Maybe.'

Shelby wasn't totally convinced, but he supposed it was a possibility. 'It's no use worrying,' he said, 'we just have to keep watching, especially for anything going into or out of Afghanistan; Finn will be getting close to his target by now.'

'We'll know as soon as whoever it is that's following him lets his masters back in Russia know that he has spotted him.' Sophie said.

The waiting game. Shelby's head ached from waiting. He needed to get out for a while, run across the beach for an hour maybe and clear his mind. The sea air would do his head wonders he thought. 'Well I can't sit here any longer.' He stretched and stood up. 'I'm going for a run on the beach, if either of you want to join me?'

Both women shook their heads and declined.

'We should probably only go out in pairs anyway.' Sophie said.

'Or stay in, in pairs.' Anna added, smiling coyly at Sophie who tried to ignore her, but found that she really couldn't.

Shelby just looked at the pair of them like an innocent schoolboy who had no idea what innuendo meant let alone what it was that the smirking, redheaded German was talking about.

'I'll err, be back in an hour then.' He said eventually, smiling weakly before walking out to change into his running pants.

The water and the sand rushing between his toes and splashing up his ankles felt good Shelby thought, cool and relaxing.

The salty breeze of the air revived him as he jogged, giving his mind the space it needed to breath and reorder the pieces of the puzzle.

Something was coming, for many people at once it seemed.

They'd been expecting it of course, but now it was right on the doorstep and about to ring the doorbell he felt he couldn't do enough to be ready. If ever they could truly be ready, that is.

He could feel the pace of the thing, slowly but surely speeding up now, the thing which Finn was planning was only days away, the starting gun to the beginning of the end. End of what though? And more importantly, to what end?

While the seagulls called out from overhead the last remnant of a ship's foghorn came floating across the bay making Shelby think ominously of the horn of Hades for some reason, calling from across the foggy chasm leading to the land of the dead.

He looked across the water into the hazy white of the distance, the unseen, and wondered what fate had in store for them all out there.

Not just himself and Rachel, or Sophie and Anna, but Finn too. Finn and all of the people he was about to touch.

They were now moving in Finn's time, at his pace, it was all down to that one thing now; when his presence showed up on the map at the site they were sure he was making for.

That would only happen once he began his attack and they were sure there would be a flood of frantic communications going to and fro between the site and Moscow.

Shelby's breathing was steady and his mind now clear and focused again.

He was still glad to have Sophie and Anna there to set him straight if it came to that though, and Anna had been right; he had seriously taken a step toward flitting off to Wales to look for his wife, calling her if necessary.

But the pace had been set and he must stick to it if he wanted everyone to come out unscathed at the other end, there was no speeding things up, so all he could do was relax and watch and wait, be ready.

While Shelby jogged through the foamy edge of the sea, accepting the fact that he could do nothing to speed things up and they would have to wait until they knew Finn had made his move, two men standing at the very top of the cliff, living proof that Shelby had got it wrong and things *could* actually be speeded up, were watching him through their binoculars.

Behind them, two big, black ford transits were parked side by side, twenty armed men clad in black, protective gear sat in the back of the vans, waiting professionally.

'That is one of them.' One of the men said in Russian, lowering his binoculars.

'Agreed.' Replied the other, joining him. 'Take Yanov and Boski, and follow him back when he returns, the other one will not be far away.'

'Yes sir.' The first replied.

'And don't engage until we are all back together, is that understood?'

'Yes sir.' The first Russian repeated.

He turned away and loped off back to the waiting vans.

The boss returned to his binoculars, watching Shelby as he carried on barefoot through the water.

Maybe they wouldn't need to capture the woman after all, he was thinking.

## Chapter Twenty-Seven

Haltering rain had quickly led onto a thick wall of bruising cloud creeping overhead with the drizzle.

Slowly at first, but soon it had turned cold and then very quickly the whole mountain range had darkened as the sky had disappeared behind an enormous, stormy, weather system fronted by thick, billowing banks of black thunder-clouds.

The rain was lashing down in blinding sheets, Finn had Salya walking almost attached to his side as he held her closely, shielding her from the worst of the battering wind and rain.

Overhead the thunder rolled bumpily along, quietly rumbling and then bursting into a deep trundle before rumbling out again; *The forge of Wayland the smith being stoked*, as Finn's mistress used to say. *Just wait until his hammers* really *start to pound and the sparks begin to fly and the falling tears of the heroes slain by his weapons fill all the seas.*

'Up there.' Finn shouted over the wind and rain, pointing to a dark crack in the rock.

He pushed Salya in front of him, helping her to climb the rock and grab onto the shelf below the crack. She pulled herself up and scrabbled across the slippery, wet mountainside and ducked inside the shallow cave.

Finn strode in behind her.

The sudden calming of the air made the cold, clamminess of her wet clothes more apparent and Salya shivered, hugging her arms to her chest.

'You need to get out of those wet clothes.' Finn said, moving toward her.

He produced the white towel she had taken with her from *Paradise Begins*, pulling it from his bag. He draped it across her sodden head and shoulders and began drying her hair. 'Strip and wrap yourself in the towel.' He said. 'I'll build a fire up.'

Salya moved as far back into the shallow cave as she could and began undressing.

She kept her back to Finn, but knew he wouldn't look at her anyway and if he did, he wouldn't see anything other than Salya, his friend.

She stirred inside again, but after mulling over Finn's words a few days ago, she at least understood what the stirring was and accepted it as just a small part of her whole being.

She didn't think she would ever stop loving him though, or thinking about him.

She glanced over her shoulder, he was stripped of his whites which he had laid out on the boulders behind, but he was still wearing his black clothes which looked to be only a little damp here and there.

He had a small pile of twigs and dry, wind-blown grass piled up in front of himself which he was just lighting.

The grass and twigs crackled and popped crisply and soon there was a decent flame going.

Finn fed the small fire with more twigs and wood, slowly building it up until it was a fair-sized blaze.

Salya just stood drying her hair thoughtlessly, watching him and the fire. He seemed to grow as the fire grew, the flames making his shadow seem to add to his already huge presence.

He looked like he was glowing Salya thought, surrounded by a dark, throbbing light as he sat there on his haunches, snapping wood with his large, scarred hands and feeding it into the fire.

Whatever weight he carried in his soul he carried it well, especially now in this light, Salya thought; he looked like he could carry the whole world and not show the strain.

But on the inside, Salya knew he was in torment because of his burdens; she had heard him speak to someone who wasn't there on more than one occasion and he had talked in his sleep, speaking sometimes in English and sometimes in another tongue which she couldn't understand.

In all of his dreams she had heard him call the same name, Samantha, but when she had asked him who Samantha was he said he didn't know and Salya could see that he was telling the truth, or at least thought he was.

The fire was high now, Salya wrapped the towel around herself and picked up her clothes, laying them next to Finn's on the boulder.

Finn patted the ground on his left, away from the crack leading back to the storm outside. 'Come, sit here, get warm.' He said.

She sat down and he draped his large arm over her, pulling her into his own body.

She noted that his clothes were dry and he was warm.

She wrapped her arms around him and squeezed herself into his chest, her cold cheeks instantly warming up. 'How come you are dry?' She asked, smiling as she warmed herself against her human pillow.

'My clothes are, err, a little different.' Was all he could think to say.

'Different?'

Finn thought. 'They were made for the military I think,' he eventually said. 'I don't know exactly who, but I acquired these in Russia a long time ago.'

'Russia?' Salya shivered. 'Why would you go to Russia? They are evil there.'

Finn leaned down and kissed the top of her head. 'Yes, the people I visited there were evil, but Salya, my dear, Salya,' he kissed her again. 'The whole of Russia isn't evil, it is a beautiful country with its fair-share of beautiful people.'

Salya let the words sink in, but it was hard for her young mind, a mind which had been filled with nothing but bad stories of Russian soldiers since she had been old enough to understand. 'I've never heard any good stories about the Russians.' She said quietly.

Finn stroked her head, easing her painful memories a little. 'I know, little one, but believe me there are more good stories than there are bad. Throughout the whole universe.'

'It was a Russian that-that-,' Salya struggled with the memory of waking to find she had been raped.

'I know, Salya, and what he did was evil, but as a wise man once said to me; *"Evil may leave its mark on our bodies, but it cannot taint our spirits unless we let it."* That evil cannot get inside unless we allow it to do so. Don't let it, Salya.' He squeezed her reassuringly.

'Believe it or not,' he continued, 'there are countries in this world which think the same of you and your country as you think of Russia.'

Salya was shocked to hear that and pulled away to look up at Finn. 'Really? Why? We are a good people I think. Well most of us.' She looked puzzled for a moment; what Finn had said about all Russians not being evil suddenly made complete sense.

'You are.' Finn smiled warmly; she understood. 'Especially you.' He laughed and pulled her in to squeeze her again. 'You see the illusion a little better now, the illusion or disillusion that we should all be afraid of one another when really we shouldn't.'

He laughed as though it were so simple and obvious, hugging her tightly.

Salya gasped. 'I can- beav!' Her tiny, muffled voice came up from beneath the folds of Finn's massive arms and chest.

He continued laughing and released her. 'Sorry.' He said, through his laughter. 'It makes me happy beyond comprehension when another person grasps things as they really are; there is no feeling like the one when watching an awakening.'

His laughter was loud enough to drive out the sounds of the storm still raging outside.

Salya smiled at first then giggled softly, but eventually caught the virus of Finn's mirth and laughed almost as loudly as he did

The lightning flashed while Finn and Salya laughed, its stormy wind howled while they howled and the rains pelted the mountainside as their own tears streamed down their creased up faces.

The evil on the outside world was no match for the happiness in the cave.

But no more than two hundred yards from where the pair sat and laughed themselves into oblivion, crouched an evil that had its aim set upon them both. Especially now that he could hear them laughing.

Azziz crouched on his haunches under a small, bushy tree, his waterproof sheet thrown over his head and wrapped around his body.

His ankle throbbed annoyingly, constantly reminding him that he had fucked up and what's more, while he sat in the cold and damp with an ankle which felt like a melon in his boot, those two bastards were sitting in front of a fire and they were laughing!

What the hell was there to laugh about out here? What the fuck was so funny about a thunderstorm?

He spat angrily on the ground and cursed under his breath.

Maybe he should just walk in there right now and shoot the fuckers. Him in the head and her in the leg so she couldn't run away again.

As much as he would have liked to have done just that, Azziz knew that the advantage was against him; it was wet and dark and they had the high ground. Damn the skies for changing while he was so close.

The heavens flashed, lighting up the massive cloudbank rolling in from the south.

The tree which Azziz was crouching beneath groaned in the wind while its roots made sucking and slurping noises under the thick, wet mud. He would have to move up to higher, firmer ground; the mud would slide away soon, bringing down any trees which were not anchored deeply enough.

He looked longingly at the cave and the fiery glow coming from within. What he wouldn't give to be able to remove his damn boot and warm his throbbing ankle in front of a fire.

Well tomorrow he would, and what's more, he would have the little bitch tethered and tending for him.

He raised himself up, grimacing as his ankle flared and ached hotly, and began limping onward, heading for the firmer ground away from the trees and the mud.

His rifle made a good support; holding the barrel with two hands and digging the butt into the ground, Azziz managed to pull himself forward one limping step at a time.

It was no good though, he wasn't resting his injury for long enough for it to even begin healing, but if he missed his chance in the morning he knew he probably wouldn't get another one.

The sneering face of Nazari came to his minds-eye making him flush with annoyance and then anger. The fat, little sister-fucker would love every minute of his misfortune and failure, would take great pleasure in embarrassing him with some form of degrading punishment or other.

By the time Azziz had reached a safe ledge of rock and a small cave of his own to hide away in, he was thoroughly burning with frustrated anger, his ankle all but forgotten.

'That bastard,' he muttered, 'bastard sister-fucker! I'll show him.' He continued cursing while he pulled himself over the last edge and into the small cave. 'I'll show you, you fat bag of shit.'

He sat down heavily, breathing hard, his ankle now suddenly demanding his full attention by sending searing shots of pain up his calf and into his knee.

It brought his mind into sharper focus and he wondered seriously now whether Nazari would send anyone out to look for him. It had been four days since he had lost the phone.

He didn't think his commander would send anyone else out just yet; he knew Azziz was skilled and could look after himself. More than likely Nazari would be thinking one of two things; his tracker had lost the use of his phone, or he was dead at the hands of a girl.

The anger suddenly rose back to the surface, burning Azziz's cheeks. He would love that wouldn't he? To think that Azziz had been bested by a girl? Well fuck him; it wasn't Azziz who had lost the girl in the first place was it?

'Fuck you.' He said aloud, turning his head to look out into the night.

Lightning seared angrily across the mountainside as if taking his insult personally and then slow thunder rolled in behind as if to insult him back.

* * *

Nazari stood at his window overlooking the compound, the rain making everything look darker than usual.

He liked it when it rained, that feeling of that immense weight of water floating over your head, enough to crush the life out of you or drown you if it all came down at once.

He hoped it was all coming down at once on Azziz's head.

Idiot! What the hell was he doing? Four-days without calling in. That could only mean that he had somehow lost his phone or he was injured or even dead.

As much as Nazari hated the man he held his skills in the highest regard and would hate to lose them.

He fidgeted with his thumbs behind his back, contemplating whether it was worth sending someone else out to look for his tracker.

His chest heaved as he sighed, coming to the conclusion that no one would be able to leave the base until the lunatic had arrived and had been dealt with. Strictest orders.

His fists clenched involuntarily when he thought of the Russian's cool insistence, the way he had casually brushed aside his own experience and command-knowledge, the simple arrogance of the man.

Still, once the lunatic *had* been dealt with, the Russian would have to leave at some point or other, handing command back to Nazari.

His mouth curled up at the edges, a sly smile playing on his lips. He would start with the nurse, the one Hack had punished and the one which was still in the villa with the Russian even now.

Yes, he would wait until the Russian bastard had gone and then he would let his men have the woman on a nightly basis, not enough to damage her too much - she was a needed asset after all - but used as much and in any way which his men pleased.

243

He had plans to film her fucking like a bitch in heat and then somehow get the Russian to watch it.

He didn't know how he would get the Russian to watch the film just yet, but he would and if he could be present when he did, well that would be the best of all wouldn't it?

The pouring rain and the darkened skies embellished Nazari's deviance and his hateful thoughts with a sense of perfection, a feeling that the day was exactly as it should be when thinking of such wonderful things.

He watched as the storm moved languidly toward the camp from the south, creeping like a slow, smoky beast.

Oh yes, what a perfect day.

While Nazari entertained himself with his miscreant fantasies, the object of his lurid plans stood holding one another in the living room of Ladislav's luxurious apartments.

They swayed to the soft strains of orchestral music coming from the designer media-station.

Nim had never felt so alive. The past four days had been a beautiful reminder that she was still a human-being and she was free. Free to love and be loved as passionately as she had been, free to laugh sincerely and cry unashamedly, free to simply be.

Every colour seemed brighter, every sound more vibrant and noticeable, everything she touched had a new feeling and meaning. And when she was touched, touched by Jimi, she almost felt the whole meaning of love and life flowing through his fingertips, through his lips, a lesson she had been made to wait for, but a lesson well worth the wait.

She looked up at him now, he had been telling her something, something about the music but she had been lost in him and hadn't heard a word.

She raised herself up onto her toes and kissed him lightly on the lips. 'I'm sorry, my love,' she said. 'I was in another world just then; what were you telling me?'

Jimi grinned, he knew how Nim was feeling, he was feeling it himself; that sudden realisation that there was a world still going about its business all around you.

'I said; I found this little gem of an artist by accident. He's a British composer, largely unknown, *Micronasia* he calls himself.'

'I like it, I don't think I've heard anything quite like it before.' Nim replied, cocking an ear and listening. 'It feels good to move to it.' She said, grinning.

Jimi just grinned back.

'We can listen to it all day and night when we get out of here.' He said. He leaned down and kissed her on the lips. 'We can do anything we like once we are away.'

Nim believed him, but she still didn't know how he would make it happen, he was reluctant to talk to her about his plans in any depth and now she had heard whispers that an army was coming to attack the place.

She lowered her eyes as her smile dropped a little. 'There has been talk of an army coming to attack us.' She said quietly.

They stopped swaying to the musi.

Jimi raised Nim's head and looked into her eyes. 'There isn't an army coming, Nim, just one man, and once he has been dealt with you and I can leave.'

She held his gaze. 'One man? Then why have you brought extra men to help?' She asked.

Her heart was beating unnaturally fast; she had never had the courage to question anyone before, let alone a man.

But Jimi wasn't just any man, he held her as his equal and had made it clear to her that if she had something on her mind, anything at all, then she shouldn't hesitate to say it.

'Apparently this one man is very skilled and dangerous, we are just making sure we have all areas covered that's all.' He smiled again. 'Don't worry, you'll be safe here.'

Nim placed her palm gently on his face, caressing his cheek, and looked up at him, there was a twinkle in her eye. 'I know I'll be safe,' she said, 'it's you I'm worried about, you fool of a man.' And then slapped him quite firmly to emphasise her words.

Jimi held her hand to his cheek and then after a moment turned his head and kissed the palm.

He stood and faced her again then. 'I won't tell you not to worry, Nim; if you love me the way I love you then worry we will, eh?' He winked at her. 'I promise you I will stay as safe as can be, though. I can't lose this precious thing which we have only just found. I won't.' He said.

'Then let me help you.' She said. She'd already asked him twice.

He sighed. 'You are already helping me, my love, truly. You are all the strength I need to see this through, but to do it I must know that you are safe and out of harm's way.'

'I'd rather die by your side than not have you come back to me.' She looked deadly serious. 'I too, have found something which I will not give up easily you know?' She actually looked a little angry.

'I know, I know you have. I'm sorry, I didn't mean to sound as though it was all about me.' He took her hand.

She sighed and relaxed. 'You didn't and I know you don't.' She said. 'I was being childish. I just can't stand the thought of being so close to happiness and then finding it is snatched away.'

She suddenly pulled him toward herself, wrapping her arms around him and holding him as tightly as she could while she rested her head on his shoulder. 'You must be careful of Nazari,' she spoke quietly, 'he hates you, hates us.'

'You leave the fat-man to me.' Jimi's voice was hard and confident, he had plans for the repellent, little commander.

'But he won't go anywhere without Hack by his side.' Nim argued.

'You don't have to worry about him either, trust me, I've dealt with much, much worse.'

The crescent scar on his face itched at the memory of one of those things which had been much, much worse.

Nim could feel Jimi's heartbeat, it was calm, steady and confident and if she couldn't believe in just his words she could believe in his heart; *he* believed in what he was doing.

Wasn't one of those *un*-conditions of love the simple, unfaltering faith and belief in ones lover?

Nim didn't know for certain, her experience being limited to the past fifteen years living as a slave, but it did feel right to abandon herself completely into Jimi's care, trusting him without question when he asked.

'I just wish I could help you, be there with you when the danger comes for you, help you to fight it off.'

She squeezed him hard again, closing her eyes and breathing him in.

Jimi returned her squeeze, kissing her head. 'I bet you would too wouldn't you?' He replied. 'Fight it off, I mean. You would look good with a pistol in one hand and a knife in the other I think. Like an Amazon.'

Nim giggled. 'Fool man.'

'Maybe a couple of grenades tucked away in your bra too? The place where you hide your *big* guns.'

Even though Nim couldn't see his face she knew he was grinning.

She laughed and pulled herself away to face him. 'Big guns, eh?'

The dark mood evaporated almost instantly and the heady, loving mood returned in the blink of an eye.

Nim took a step back, smiling slyly.

She pushed her thumbs through the straps of her dress and then pulled them over her shoulders, allowing the silky material to roll slowly down her chest.

With a small tug she pulled the top of the dress over her breasts, allowing herself the pleasure of the sensation running through her hardening nipples.

She leaned forward, her breasts spilling gently out of the remainder of her dress, and pointed them at him. 'Freeze!' She purred. 'Or I will shoot you with my big guns.'

Her eyes wandered from his wide-eyed, smirking face to his bulging crotch. 'I think we shall have to disarm you of *your* weapon.'

She stood up straight and walked back to Jimi, unclasping his belt as she peered into his eyes.

'Let me help you with that holster.'

## Chapter Twenty-Eight

Everything had that fresh, new smell about it when Salya came out of the cave. The rocks and trees and even patches of the grass were steaming under the mid-morning sun.

The storm had broken sometime in the night, leaving behind a slow drizzle of cleansing rain.

Finn had gone to get water he said, leaving Salya to her usual task of checking the snares.

Neither of them were certain that they would catch anything after such a stormy downpour, but Salya took the remaining water with her anyway, just in case they had and she needed to clean the food.

She made her slow way down the mountainside, passing through small patches of tall trees and bush.

She smiled happily when she disturbed a family of buttonquails, giggling as they streamed from beneath their bushy hiding place, their tiny legs a blur as they darted and zigzagged out of harm's way.

Further down she caught the flashing tail of a fox as it sprang out from beneath the branches of a low-hanging tree, darting into the undergrowth and sprinting out of sight.

All around her Salya noticed the subtle bustling of life; small creatures stirring and returning to their proper dens and burrows and nests after being caught outside by the storm and hiding themselves away wherever they stood to wait it out.

'Good morning!' She called, cheerfully cheeky.

She walked on through the trees for another five minutes until she came to the site of the first snare. It was empty. She gathered it up and carried on until she came to the second snare, it too was empty.

'Goats cheese and lemon grass for breakfast then.' She muttered to herself.

She moved herself back up the slope and made for the edge of the trees; the last snare was set over there on a clear patch of grass.

As she passed from beneath the boughs of the trees and into the bright sunlight, Salya caught the sliding shadows on the ground of hawks in the sky.

She stood and watched them, her hand held to her brow as she looked up and squiunted into the sunshine.

There was a pair of them circling high in the air while they watched the open ground below. They called to one another, a high, piercing sound, sending each other instructions and information.

Salya loved the hawks, loved their power and freedom, they made her feel safe when she watched them. Safe and at peace.

The hawks continued to circle and call, slowly moving north and away from Salya.

She turned back to the rocky path ahead, scrabbling down onto the grass below. She smiled when she saw that there was a large, grey hare caught in the third snare.

She raised her hand to the retreating pair of hawks and called out to them. 'Thank you.' She said, grinning and waving.

The hare was as big - if not bigger - than the first one she had found, days back at the waterfall now.

She dropped to her knees beside the carcass and removed it from the wire snare, immediately setting about cleaning and preparing it.

The knife which Finn had allowed her to use on that first day of their meeting was still on her belt; as often as she had tried to return it, he had simply said she should keep it there for him until he had need of it.

The Japanese steel made light work of skinning and gutting the carcass and as usual she piled up all of the useless stuff to one side; her offering to the dogs which were still following her.

Although Salya didn't perceive it as such, she and the dogs had a bond now, a silent pact of mutual trust and gain; she had protection in the night and they had breakfast in the morning.

It wasn't often that she actually saw them now, usually just a glimpse of a tail, or the flicker of trees and leaves as they walked through them, but they very rarely came closer than fifty yards.

She washed the skinned and emptied carcass using the bottled water she had brought, finally rinsing off her own hands before packing everything away.

She stooped down and began to roll up the plastic bag with the head, feet and giblets inside, when she heard the almost imperceptible clack of a small stone rolling down the slope behind her.

Her hand automatically gripped the handle of Finn's dagger as she spun around on her heels, her survival instincts being fuelled by the hammering-engine of her heart pounding in her chest.

She could feel herself trembling and suddenly felt very large, filled up almost.

Remaining on her haunches, poised to spring away if necessary, Salya scanned the rocky ridge and the trees standing behind, looking for some sign which would tell her where the sound had come from.

Minutes passed, her eyes never wavered from their tree-line vigil, her brow knitted and furrowed in concentration; she would never be taken unawares again.

A needle of rage sprang up inside her, knotting her stomach when she thought of how she had been crept up on and then kidnapped, how her brother had been kidnapped and murdered.

Since her escape, Salya had been constantly looking over her shoulder, expecting to see a dark, sinister dot in the distance, her pursuer, but she had never spotted anyone or anything until she had bumped into Finn.

So the reality of her situation now and how it had come about was suddenly uniquely real and vivid in her mind again.

I will be strong she thought, I will be stronger than I was last time!

The dagger-grip felt wet and slippery she realised, she was gripping it furiously, she needed to relax her body and keep her mind alert. Easier said than done.

Finn had told her that by keeping your body relaxed and your mind always alert and ready, you would be prepared to meet any situation which came your way, whether it be love or war, you will be able to meet it with clarity and zest.

He had fist-pumped the air to emphasise *zest*, she remembered.

Her eyes ached from staring. It's okay to blink she could almost hear Finn telling her.

She blinked and refocused. The tree-line and the slope were both still and quiet as they should be. She relaxed her shoulders and lessened her grip on the dagger, standing to her feet to catch her breath.

She stood with her hands on her hips, looking still at the trees and then scoffed and shook her head; fool. A pebble probably, knocked over by some tiny insect-creature.

After both admonishing and praising herself for her reaction to the noise, Salya picked up her things from the grass behind her, picking up the bag of dogs-breakfast lastly.

She turned back to the slope and trees but stopped in her tracks, her skin prickling with an aura of shock which seemed to throb out from her whole body.

An Afghani man stood there, glaring down his hooked nose at her from the edge of the slope, his rifle raised and aimed at her chest.

He looked like he had something wrong with one of his legs and had been walking for hours, sweat dripped down his brow and from his nose and chin.

'Thought you could run away, did you girl?' Azziz spat, shaking his head vigorously, flinging droplets of sweat out to the sides.

Salya remained emotionless, the initial shock quickly dissipating and being replaced by a strange sense of calm and control. Her control.

She looked at the sweating man and recognised him; he had been with the men when she and the others had been unloaded from the truck. She knew nothing more than that, but it was definitely one of the men from the compound.

Her eyes narrowed venomously; she would kill him if he tried to touch her, she would stab him in the neck and kill him.

'Don't you look at me like that, you fucking little slut.' Azziz was genuinely enraged by Salya's impertinence and defiance.

'Why? Are you going to shoot me, you stupid sister-fucker.' Salya's mouth almost burned when she said the words, she had never used such profanity before, but added with a smirk she knew that the sweating man would almost burst a blood vessel with anger.

She was right.

'You cunt-bastard! I'll fucking kill you! Get up here you fucking cunt-pig! GET UP HERE.' Azziz screamed, stabbing a finger at the ground, pointing at his side with his free hand.

His face wobbled and the sweat dripped, he wasn't a man to be trifled with he always said.

Salya continued to smirk and remained where she was.

If she was going to die then she was going to die here and now, she wouldn't be taken back there again, but she didn't think she would be dying today, not at his hands anyway.

If he had been sent to kill her he would have done it by now, so just the fact that he had been sent in the first place could only mean that he was under orders to bring her back alive.

He could just kill her and say he couldn't find he, of course, but Salya pretty much didn't care, she spoke again anyway.

'Why don't you go fuck your mother on your father's grave, you son of a pig-bastard.' She laughed.

Azziz roared. 'I'LL FUCKING KILL YOU!'

He began the shallow scramble to the bottom, placing more weight on his injured ankle than he should have. He screamed in pain as his boot found a loose rock and slipped from under him, bending his ankle awkwardly.

'Fucking KILL YOU!' There were tears in his eyes now, tears of frustration and pain.

He dropped onto his backside, sliding the rest of the way down the slope and using his good leg to stop himself at the bottom while he kept his injured ankle well up and away from the ground. His rifle remained pointed at Salya, even if it was waving around unsteadily.

As he came to a halt, Azziz tried to raise himself to his feet again using just his good leg, but he was too exhausted.

'Help me! Help me to my feet!' He barked at Salya, his authority as a male, automatically, foolishly, leading him to believe that the world had returned to normal and all women must do as they were told. 'Are you fucking deaf you stupid cunt!? I said help me to my feet!'

Salya's smirk dropped, replaced by a dangerous look in her eye, a mad look.

'Help yourself, you sister-fucker.' She said quietly. 'Sister-fucker.' She said again, still quiet, still unemotional, still staring madly. 'Sister-fucker! You sister-fucker.' She said over and over again, her expression never changing. 'Help yourself, sister-fucker!'

Azziz was actually stunned by what he was witnessing. Never had he seen a woman, let alone a little girl, look so dangerously defiant, had never heard words which he was hearing now, come from a woman's mouth.

He glared at her. 'Oh. They are going to enjoy hurting you back at base and I'm going to enjoy watching.' His voice was low. 'The men will be lining up to put their cocks into a disobedient, little cunt like you, I promise you.'

Salya stopped talking, snapping her mouth closed.

'I thought that might shut you up.' The sneering Azziz said.

He remained where he was, sitting on the ground, he felt the control had been returned to him now.

He gripped his crotch, taunting her. 'All of them with cocks as big as mine, and then they will let Hack have you.' He watched, but the girl remained closed-mouthed now and simply stared, neither afraid or otherwise.

Azziz continued. 'You won't know about Hack yet, but you will, even if it is only for a short time.' He leered. 'He has a way with blades you know? He likes to cut young sluts like you while he fucks does Hack. One of the worst of men I would say.'

Still Salya remained unresponsive and showed nothing on her face other than a blank contempt in her eyes.

The tracker made himself more comfortable and leaned back a little, propping himself up on his pack. He kept the rifle pointed in Salya's general direction, but left it lowered and resting on his boot.

'Well, I'm glad you realise just how serious your situation is, girl.' He frowned and smiled at the same time. 'I suppose I could forgive your madness; you've been alone for too long in the mountains, no place for women and children.'

His voice was commanding and sure. 'I'll tell you what I will do; if you take care of me until we get back to base, I will make sure that nothing harmful happens to you. You will be punished for escaping, of course, but it won't be severe.'

He winked at her. 'So why don't you start taking care of me now.' He said, rubbing his crotch again. 'You've put me through a lot of trouble, I think I need to relax a little before we go and take care of your friend back there.'

He opened his fly and let her see what he wanted her to do for him. 'Don't worry, I don't normally go for children, but you are much older than you look, aren't you? But I promise I won't fuck you, just come here and sit by my side, eh?'

Salya's face remained impassive and blank, watching uncaring as the man touched himself in front of her.

He was nothing, she hadn't even heard half the disgusting words he had said, most of them just ending up as meaningless grunting and noises.

Watching him now was just the same; a meaningless animal and base gesture which had no emotional value whatsoever.

No, what *did* matter to her at that moment and indeed had mattered since the moment he had began his promises of her certain torment, were the six, huge dogs standing at the top of the slope, silently watching.

Unafraid, Salya had kept her eyes away from the dogs, firmly keeping them locked on the injured man's own eyes, something which the dogs understood.

Azziz carried on touching himself and beckoned to Salya, holding his hand out to her. 'Come and sit, come.'

Salya remained where she was but spoke now, while at the same time she opened the bag of bloody hare-parts. 'You are an animal, you just make noises which don't mean anything.' She said. 'The animals of the forest and the mountains are better than you.'

She took the head from the bag and threw it so it landed on the ground between Azziz's knees. 'Eat.' She said, pointing at Azziz.

He looked startled. 'What? What are you doing? I thought we understood-.'

Salya lobbed a handful of the giblets to join the head. 'Eat.' She said again, still pointing. 'Eat! Eat! EAT!' She shouted the last word, her anger unable to be held back anymore, this man was going to die, needed to die.

Azziz didn't know what was going on, had the little slut gone mad again? What did she want him to eat the fucking head of a hare for?

He opened his mouth ready to shout at her, admonish her, tell her to calm down and come and sit by his side, but before a single syllable passed his lips he heard the soft footfalls of padded feet coming from directly behind him.

He turned around quickly, automatically reaching for his rifle and ended up staring straight into the puzzled face of a mastiff mountain-dog. It had a quizzical look in its eyes.

Azziz scrambled back away from the dog, whose jaw dropped as it panted, almost smiling he thought.

He almost shat in his pants when he saw the other five hounds slowly approaching from behind and flanking their leader.

'Allah, preserve us.' He whispered, backing away slowly on all fours.

Salya held her breath the same way she always held it when she watched the hawks diving and capturing their prey.

Her eyes were wide with a mix of wonder, awe and terror; the dogs were *so* big when they were this close.

Azziz couldn't get his rifle up and into firing position without spooking the dogs which would almost certainly lead to them attacking him.

His best chance would be to get closer to the girl; together they would be a bigger target, but at the same time he would be able to get up onto his knees to shoot.

He continued moving backward, never taking his eyes off the dog. It followed step for step, tongue lolling, eyes vacant, unemotional.

'When I get to you stay by my side so I can take a shot, okay?' He whispered, as he closed in to where he thought Salya was standing.

When she didn't reply he repeated his instructions, louder this time.

She still remained silent, but before he could look, his foot suddenly caught on something and he glanced around anyway, it was Salya's foot, she was looking down at him with the same look in her eyes as the dogs.

'Help me.' He said, holding his hand out to her.

Salya looked down at it impassively and then back up to his face.

She took a step away from him and moved to stand next to the leader of the dogs, keeping a respectful distance between herself and this enormous animal.

'For Allah's sake, what are you doing you stupid child?'

Azziz felt a terror grow in his chest that he had never felt before. The look on her face told him that he had made the last mistake he was ever going to make. 'Allah help me.' He pleaded.

Salya nodded. 'He will.' She said, quietly and then pointed. 'Eat.'

As the dogs took a step forward, Salya took a step back and then again and again, and she kept on moving backward until she was at the top of the slope, never taking her eyes from the man and the dogs.

She could hear him now, even though he was almost lost beneath the rippling carpet of fur, pleading with Allah and commanding the dogs to leave him alone, but they paid him no heed and moved in to eat, the little *growler* had given them their breakfast.

Salya wept as the screams began and turned her back on the ripping and crunching and the crying and choking, walking back to the forest, back to the camp and to breakfast, back to Finn.

She needed Finn right now, she needed him to tell her that what she had done was the right thing to have done, because right now she felt as evil as the man she had just killed.

While the dogs ate the unfortunate Azziz, and while Salya wept alone as she walked back to the camp, the lower branches of a large, dark oak parted and a figure dropped to the ground.

'Well that was interesting.' The killer mused to himself as he watched Salya's back disappearing into the forest. 'Can't say I've ever seen anything quite like that.'

He felt immensely privileged.

He walked over to where the dogs were feeding and stood watching them from the top of the embankment. 'Oh! That is just grim.' He muttered, frowning seriously.

One of the dogs turned its bloodied muzzle to look at him.

He tipped *his* cap. '*Bon appetite*.' He grinned. 'Don't mind me.' He said amiably, but then added; 'but if you do then be ready to be shot.'

The dog lingered for a moment and then turned back to its Azziz-breakfast.

The killer turned away and made back to his own camp, wondering what the girl had been doing and where she had come from and more importantly, who was she travelling with.

He had an intuitive itch at the back of his skull which rang alarm bells concerning Finn. She knows him, somehow that girl knows Finn, I would bet my life on it.

He couldn't put his finger on what it was, but something by the way she acted made the killer think of Finn, for no reason other than intuition. A god's intuition though, he thought and smiled.

It was unfortunate he felt, that he hadn't arrived a little earlier so that he could have heard everything the man had been saying to the girl; he had only caught the parts where he was trying to get her to play with his cock.

His intuition, however, told him the man had something more to do than just harass young girls in the wild, and as they weren't that many miles away from Finn's next target, the killer wondered if the man was actually a scout or a collector, kidnapper, or whatever they termed these fellows. It was a provocative thought.

But why do you think the girl has some connection to Finn, man? Because of the way she did what she did? So what?

'I don't fucking know, *so what*.' He said aloud, swiping angrily at the tops of the grass.

But the way she had killed the man, or had set it up, was a calculating mind which the killer only felt that another killer could have; a young girl like that shouldn't be thinking like that surely? Unless she had been in contact with another killer. Finn.

Well, it would do no harm to pack up his things and make his way along the forest edge and head the way the girl had gone. If he was right he would be able to at least spend a few nights with his brother before deciding whether to kill him or not.

Watching the girl and seeing the results had put a definite tick in the *not kill* box.

He felt quite excited and rubbed his hands together gleefully, speeding up his march back to his camp. He was eager to get underway.

To think that in just a few hours he just might be meeting the man he had secretly wished to meet for years, a man who may very well be a brother no less.

He whistled as he folded away his bedding and micro-tent, packing it into his backpack.

Five minutes later and he was off, walking as merrily as any tourist one might find hiking in the countryside, walking-staff and all.

## Chapter Twenty-Nine

If broken bones felt like burning needles dipped in hot lead then Rachel thought she must have broken her hand.

Oh God! What was she thinking?

The doorways streamed past her as she ran while clutching her hand to her chest.

You punched her straight in the face! God! You're a nurse for Christ's sake!

The evening crowd of people stared at her as she fled past them, she didn't care, all she wanted to do was put as much space between herself and the woman as possible.

She dodged in and out between the pedestrians, some of them moving by intuition while others were simply jostled out of the way.

Rachel ignored them and concentrated on moving forward. Her hand was throbbing like *blue-murder* as her auntie Lynn used to say.

She began to sweat when she saw the image of the woman collapsing to the floor in a dead faint.

Don't feel sorry for her.

What if she's dead?

One punch and down! Oh! My God! Graham would be so proud.

Yes, but what if she's dead? What if she haemorrhages or something? Maybe she smashed her skull on the tiles and brain matter came out?

Oh. My hand hurts.

But what if she's dead? What if?

Round and round Rachel went, she couldn't get away from the fact that she just might have killed someone.

It was no consolation that the person may have been trying to kill *her*; she still might have stopped a life from continuing on its journey. There was no thought which sickened Rachel more.

Well other than her maybe-broken hand that was.

Doorways, some lit, others darkened, some shops, some flats, but none of them which passed were what Rachel was looking for.

And then she suddenly saw it, a round, white neon sign with a green cross in the centre; a pharmacy.

She slowed to a brisk walk, trying to compose herself as best she could before going inside.

She put her bruised and swollen hand in her coat pocket for support and then pushed the glass door open and walked through the single, glass door. The air was heavy with the smell of chemical disinfectant and throat sweets.

Rachel walked up and down the aisles, searching for bandages. She found some and picked up two crepe bandages and an elastic wrist support.

The next stop was the drug aisle, eventually stopping at the cough medicines.

She picked out two brown bottles of cough syrup with a dark - almost black - thick liquid inside. Two packets of codeine finished off her shop at the chemist and she took it all to the till.

The young cashier looked at what she had bought and then glanced straight at Rachel's eyes and face, looking for any signs she might be a junky Rachel thought.

How dare the little bitch. But looking at what she was purchasing she understood she supposed. The cough medicine was a strong one and had a tendency to be a junkies preferred shoplift item when out of the real deal.

Rachel also knew that when mixed with alcohol and codeine it knocked your bloody block off.

The things you picked up in a hospital, I bet you didn't know *that* did you love, Rachel thought to herself as she paid for the items.

Outside and she now scanned the street for somewhere she could buy some gin or vodka.

She couldn't remember seeing an off-license or mini-market as she ran up to here, but then again she couldn't even remember running up to here in the first place, not clearly anyway.

She turned right and carried on the way she had been running, walking briskly now and hoping she wasn't being followed.

It was getting dark quickly. All the better for her.

A few streets along her route and she came to a shop which sold alcohol and then a few minutes later she was back out on the street, two small bottles of gin secreted in her pockets.

Now all she needed to do was find somewhere quiet to fix herself up. Where though?

She didn't feel confident that any of the nearby hotels or bed and breakfasts were secure or far enough away from her encounter with the woman.

That bloody woman. Where *had* she sprung from? How could she possibly have known that Rachel was in that particular lavatory? Or did she not know really? Was that *even* the woman who had been following her?

The thought had crossed her mind that the woman she had floored may well have been someone who just looked a bit like her and Rachel had spooked enough to lash out. Brilliantly, she might add.

No, it was her, the look she gave Rachel as the door closed behind her, a look of recognition and then of sudden alarm as a fist smashed into her nose.

Rachel had leaped over the still-crumpling body, yanked the door to get out which she accidentally cracked the woman's head with - oh God! - as she shot off through the coffee-shop she had just been using to plan her next move.

I hope she isn't dead. But if she is, I hope she was going to kill me and I just got to her first.

She saw a pub sign ahead and had a flash of inspiration; she could lock herself in one of the women's cubicles until closing time. That way she could bandage her hand and take a dose of her *medicine*, staying out of sight for a few hours.

It felt like the forest all over again only this time she would have a toilet to sit on. Great. Another toilet.

*The Laughing Fox* had a few patrons inside its wooden panelled lounge, some seated and others standing at the small bar.

The barman glanced up and nodded at Rachel who smiled weakly and then scanned the room as though looking for someone.

He returned to his conversation, allowing Rachel to quietly slink off to the lavatories.

Once inside she checked there was no one else using any of the four toilets and then locked herself in the last stall. She was thankful that the toilets were well maintained and cleaned regularly by the looks of them.

She perched herself on the edge of the seat and unpacked her medicines onto her lap.

Her hand was bruising across the back and up her wrist. She flexed her fingers and found that she could move them somewhat, the pain flaring hotly if she tried too hard to make a fist.

Well at least it wasn't broken, or if it was it wasn't too badly damaged. The pain kept on trying to tell her otherwise though.

She opened the bottle of cough medicine and swigged half of it straight from the bottle, grimacing as the thick, dark liquid fired its way down her throat.

Next she took two codeine tablets and washed them down with a mouthful of gin, shaking her head and grimacing some more.

Finally, she began wrapping her injured hand with the crepe-bandage, covering all with the elastic wrist-strap once she had finished.

She sat back and smiled moonily through the haze of her unorthodox medicine, her hand's throbbing reduced to a dull reminder. Oh that's better.

Rachel's ordeal was pushed to the furthest reaches of her mind as the mix of drugs took control; nothing mattered now that the pain was going away and her head was warm and fuzzy. The woman and her cronies can just bugger off.

She sat herself back, leaning against the cistern, her eyelids heavy and her head beginning to nod. Her body felt like it was made from cotton-wool; soft and malleable, everything dull and far away.

She must have nodded off completely because the next thing she was aware of was a hammering coming from the cubicle door. A voice, too far away in her sleep to make out what it was saying, called out as the door rattled.

The door hammered again and Rachel's level of awareness shot up as her heart giddied up too quickly. She could hear the voice now.

'Hello? Everything alright in there.' It was a man's voice, the barman's presumably.

'Yesh, shorry, I'm not fee-hing too well.' Rachel managed to slur out.

Her mouth felt like it was an uncontrollable cavern with a disobedient, swollen slug of a tongue inside.

'You've been in there for over an hour.' The voice replied. 'Open the door, you can't stay locked up in there.'

His voice was firm, he meant business.

Rachel leaned herself forward and wiped the phantom spittle from the corner of her too loose mouth, surprising herself when her hand came away dry.

She stood up and wobbled, supporting herself with the toilet-roll dispenser.

The man knocked again, but remained silent.

With fumbling, spongy fingers, Rachel pulled the lock all the way open and the door swung back on its hinge.

The barman stood there, looking at her with something akin to disgust on his face. 'Not in my pub.' He said, and caught Rachel by the collar of her jacket and dragged her out of the cubicle.

Rachel's eyes widened with surprise and a little fright, what was he doing? Who did he think she was? 'I- I'm shorry, I was jush-,' Rachel began.

'I know what you were *just*.' He said. 'Well you can *just* piss off and do it somewhere else.'

He pulled her to the door and opened it, pushing Rachel through before him.

'But you don' un-ershand,' she tried again. 'I've hur' my han' an-.'

'Well maybe you should try using your *other* hand when you're making your drug money, eh?' The man said, prodding her along toward the main door.

She looked around at him, the meaning of his words slowly dawning on her through the medicine's filter. He didn't really mean what she thought he meant, did he?

He was leering at her.

He did! She felt her anger rising right behind her embarrassed indignation.

'Don't look at me like that, you little tart, I don't allow your sort in here so bugger off and don't come back. It'll be the law for you next time.'

He had her by the arm now, squeezing it hard as he pushed her out onto the street.

She stumbled a little, staggering to the kerbside and bracing herself against a lamppost. She was too far gone to argue with the idiot man.

She raised her foggy head and looked at him. 'Oh, jush fug off.' Was all she managed to say.

The barman just shook his head and turned away and went back inside.

Rachel sagged, she wished she had found somewhere proper to hide out for awhile; she was now on the night streets of Caernarfon and as high as the proverbial kite.

She had her wits about her. Well, enough to know what she was doing and what needed to be done, but communicating her thoughts and getting her body to receive and understand was a different matter entirely.

That bloody woman. This was her fault, it was all her fault, the damn hag.

The night sounds and bright colours coming from the street-lights and neon signs swelled to and fro slowly, sometimes becoming sharp and clear and then slowly fading to soft and dim.

The sounds were the worst, hitting her with minute detail as something loud like a bus drove past, or a raised voice shouted out, rising above all of the other sounds.

Her ears latched onto the multitude of differing cacophonies while her eyes darted involuntarily from one interesting, bright flash to another.

She felt giddy and sick, but closing her eyes made it even worse.

She needed to lie down somewhere quiet and sleep now, a cardboard box in an alley would do, she didn't care as long as she could close her eyes.

She suddenly felt the pattering of cool raindrops splashing down onto her upturned face, refreshing her a little and invigorating her mind enough to get her moving.

Only there was no rain, the skies were cloudless and black, full of spring stars and a waxing moon.

Rachel marvelled at the experience for a moment, using it to raise her mind out of the fog as much as she could.

She didn't care that it was an illusion, that her mind was hallucinating, creating the feeling of rain on her skin; it gave her a strange kind of clarity and she wasn't about to waste the opportunity.

Pushing herself away from the post, Rachel took one slow step after another, making her way down the street and toward the only hotel she could see a few hundred yards away.

The phantom rain was dripping down her face now, rolling icily down her neck and spine, flowing down the backs of her legs and then dripping from her ankles and toes.

She smiled to herself; she would have to do this with Graham sometime. Her smile rose to a grin; wicked Rachel, you'll go to hell.

She floated along the path, the sounds and the bright lights were behaving themselves at the moment, but the feeling that her body was dripping with water seemed to be growing until she could feel herself being stroked by sheets of warm liquid or silky invisible hands.

Up and down her whole body, beginning at her thighs, the sensation of having something soft and large rolling up and caressing her to the top of her head and then beginning again at her thighs, began to make Rachel sway as she moved.

Pulse after glorious pulse; it was almost like being massaged as she walked.

The hotel drew closer, Rachel found herself walking right up against the buildings lining this street now, supporting herself with the walls and windows as she struggled to stay upright.

The pulses coursing through her body were continuing their sensual assault, increasing in frequency with each step that she took.

She stopped walking and propped herself up in an unlit doorway, gasping for breath. The pulsing immediately slowed down to a more manageable level as her heart-rate dropped.

Holy crap! What the hell was that?

Rachel felt like she had been in the throes of an orgasm only there was no lust or sex attached, it was simply pure pleasure, through and through her body. Everything which felt good seemed to be happening at once under that strange, pulsating caress.

Her chest's heaving slowed down and after a few minutes of trying to relax, she was almost back to herself again. Still dulled and foggy-headed - and no pain, thankfully - but she could at least focus again.

After a final deep breath, Rachel stepped back out onto the pavement and turned to walk up to the hotel, fifty yards away now.

She stopped in her tracks. 'Oh! For God's sake!' She said angrily.

The woman was standing in front of the entrance.

Rachel stepped back to the doorway and slipped into the shadows again, she peered out and up the road to where the woman stood. 'Why? How?'

Rachel was pretty astounded that she was being hounded so closely and cleverly. 'Bitch.' She muttered. Well at least she wasn't dead.

The woman raised her hand to her head, talking on a phone. She seemed to listen for a few seconds and then turned her head to look down the street, almost right where Rachel was hiding.

Her lips moved as she replied to whoever it was she was talking to and then she hung up and put the phone back in her pocket. She hadn't taken her eyes off Rachel's hiding place at all.

'Oh shit.' Rachel hissed under her breath.

The woman continued to watch for a minute more and then began walking toward the doorway.

Rachel could have cried. She was too drugged to run and there was no way she would be able to get very far anyway if the caresses started up again. She knew she couldn't even fight really. So what could she do?

Well I'm not going to cry she thought to herself, stiffening her lower lip and raising her chin stoically.

The woman was less than thirty yards away now and seemed in no hurry to get to where Rachel stood, in fact she looked as though she were casually walking to meet an old friend.

Rachel flushed with guilt as she drew closer; both her eyes were darkened and swollen and her nose had a large band-aid across its ridge. Well she would be damned if she would say she was sorry.

Twenty yards now and a blue car pulled casually up to the kerb, the window rolled down electronically and a man spoke from inside. 'Mrs Shelby? Get in.' He said urgently. 'Quickly, she is almost here.'

Rachel's foggy mind stalled her for only a second before she was running quickly for the rear door. She dragged it open and leaped inside at the same time she heard the woman call out.

'STOP! Miss Langley!'

But too late. The car door slammed behind her as the driver screeched away, speeding down the road and out of sight.

Rachel sat up and brushed her hair out of her eyes and looked at her saviours.

She was in a car with three men, all of them were looking at her, the driver through his rear-view mirror. Why did she feel like she was in the wolf's den?

'Are you hurt, Mrs Shelby?' The man who had told her to get in asked.

Rachel shook her head. 'Who are you?' She asked back.

'We are associates of your husband.' The same man replied.

'Associates? Is he alright? Do you know where he is?' Rachel asked anxiously.

'Yes.' The man replied, taking a mobile phone from his pocket. 'We know where he is.'

Rachel heard the click of his call and then the ring-tone. He just smiled at her as he waited to be connected.

Rachel looked at the man sitting on the back seat with her.

He wasn't smiling, he was just looking at her. A little menacingly she thought.

The man on the phone spoke, a short message in Russian which Rachel didn't understand, and then he hung up.

He smiled again. 'Why did that woman call you *Miss Langley*?' He asked.

Rachel's mouth went suddenly dry, her chest tight and frightened.

She had called her Miss Langley because that was her mother's maiden-name, the name Graham's contacts would use when trying to find her, the name which told her she was safe.

Rachel sat frozen to her seat, she couldn't speak, she could only look at the man and cry like she said she wouldn't.

## Chapter Thirty

Standing under the trees, some way behind the Deere's residence, the Russian who had watched Shelby jogging along the bay peered through his binoculars at the cottage.

The lights were on downstairs, but other than that there was no indication of how many people were actually inside. It left him frustrated, especially as he had been ordered to stay back and observe until further notice.

He could feel the unease of his men and their own frustrated impatience; why were they sleeping in the vans instead of just getting the job done? Did it matter how many people were in the house? How many people could a house of that size hold?

Orders were orders though and no matter how frustrated they felt, they all knew that to break orders was to invite severe punishment.

He pulled a packet of cigarettes from his pocket and was in the middle of lighting one up when his phone buzzed.

He answered it and listened, sucking hard on his cigarette as the voice spoke, and then blowing out the smoke as he acknowledged the command he had just been given.

'Understood.' He said. 'I'll get onto it right away.'

He hung up and took another long drag on his smoke.

The woman had been found, he had been given the go ahead to eliminate the Interpol agents anyway.

He stared for long seconds at the house, taking a third and final drag on his cigarette before flicking it away into the undergrowth.

However many people were in that house it made no difference to the surprise they were about to receive.

He turned away and walked back to his men, the last of his smoke still trailing from his nostrils leaving a thin, blue wisp lingering behind him.

In the cottage, Shelby and Sophie were staring at the big screen; a new dot from the second Welsh suspect had appeared a few minutes ago, making contact with the one in Moscow again.

Anna sat poised at the console; they were waiting to see if there was going to be a reply, new instructions maybe, anything to tell them that the second dot still hadn't found Rachel and needed to be told how to proceed.

The familiar ping came and they buzzed.

'Here we go.' Shelby muttered.

Anna brought the locations up, the dot over Moscow was flashing but there was no dot over Wales, it was over Hartlepool this time, a completely new recipient.

'They're here!' Anna said, and scowled, suddenly standing up.

'How the hell have they found us?' Sophie asked, glancing around the room looking for the obvious bug or camera.

Anna typed a command into one of the computers they were using as a slave, a small oblong plate slid out from the front of the main console. It looked like an archaic coin-slot Shelby thought.

Anna walked back to it and produced a silver, coin-sized disc from her pocket and dropped it into the slot, pushing the slot back in.

Almost immediately the front panel to the console hissed and dropped forward revealing a hidden space filled with a large, metal box.

The little woman dragged it out and then placed her thumb on the small, blue pad on the front. There was a chorus of clicks and springing noises and then the lid popped open while the front fell forward.

'Fucking HELL!' Sophie said, her eyes were as round as saucers. 'Why-what-, I mean, where did you get all that?' She finally blurted out, pointing a shaking finger at the massive collection of heavy weaponry inside the steel box.

Anna just glared at her, she was in combat mode now and had no time for niceties and civilities.

'Stupid question.' She said, and pulled a large semi-automatic weapon from the box, slamming an ammunition cartridge into the gun's slot.

She threw the gun to Sophie. 'There's a time to talk and a time to die, they are both the same time.' She said, still scowling. 'This time, *now*,' she pointed to the ground to emphasise the now, 'is killing time.'

Sophie looked at the little German with a newfound awe and respect, and if she was to be completely truthful she found her commanding posture quite attractive. 'Sorry.' She said, and nodded her head.

Anna took another semi-automatic and loaded that one as well, throwing the gun to Shelby.

'This is *my* job now,' she looked at them both seriously. 'I am trained for this, but be warned; I am my own trainer and you may find the things I do a little unorthodox.'

She reached back into the box and pulled out three pairs of what looked like ski-masks, except you couldn't see through them and each pair had a black disc attached to the straps on either side.

'Put these on.' She said, and handed them a pair each. 'Pull the discs over your ears.'

They both did as they were told and gasped when the view changed from gray plastic to a blue, false-light view of everything in front of them.

'Wow!' Shelby and Sophie chorused.

'The discs will muffle out eighty percent of most sonic weaponry, while the lenses are designed to keep the light ratio to a medium which stays constant, so flash-bangs, for example, will not blind you.'

Shelby whistled. 'An impressive bit of kit.'

'Can we stay focused and do the admiration and ego-rubbing later, please.' Anna said, cutting Shelby off.

Without waiting for any acknowledgment to her admonishments she picked up the front of the cabinet which had been concealing the gun box.

She pressed the edges and a sliver of metal fell out allowing the single front to break in two. She handed them a piece each.

'Bullet-proof.' Was all she said. 'Stay behind me and keep your attention on the back entrance and the dining-room windows.'

She turned away and marched up to the console standing next to her own computer.

'Um. What about you?' Sophie asked.

Anna looked over her shoulder. 'What about me?'

Sophie tapped the shield. 'Where's your bullet–proof, computer, thingamajig?' She raised her eyebrow as though she were challenging. 'Hm?'

Anna turned back to the keyboard she had pulled out and typed in another command. 'I don't do bullets I'm afraid.' She said tartly. 'Not unless I'm handing them out,' she continued as she hit the final return to set off whatever it was she had been doing. '*Then* I do bullets very well.' She finished with a curt nod.

The console hissed just as the other one had and then fell apart. There was a tripod-mounted machine-gun inside, its bullet-belt dripped down through a slit in the box it was secreted in.

Anna looked at them both and grinned her widest grin now. 'I call him Albert,' she said, 'we're very old friends.'

Shelby couldn't help himself, he started to laugh; the gun was almost as big as the woman wielding it, it was just too absurd.

Sophie turned her wide-eyed head in his direction and then elbowed him in the ribs. 'It's a fucking machine-gun Gray!'

Shelby tried hard to stop his laughing, but craziness had left the building now, this was just inter-galactic lunacy and it forced its way into this world through his mouth. 'I know.' He managed to sputter. 'Look how big it is!' He almost gagged then.

While he choked, he saw lights above the window suddenly appear, tiny red lights.

'What's that?' He said, pointing, his laughter rapidly coming down.

Anna huffed. 'They are here, right outside.'

She watched the lights flicker on in three different locations and then flash as though they were being triggered repeatedly, which they were. As every fourth trigger occurred the light altered its hue slightly.

'There are at least twelve people now approaching us from the gate, the far hedge and from our left flank. More than likely there will be a few more than that.'

She smiled warmly at both of them. 'Watch that dining room, I expect them to come through there... any... minute...'

She pulled Albert's trigger.

The heavy-weaponry roared, Albert was a very angry-sounding machine-gun.

His destroying expletives ripped effortlessly through the curtains and bay-window, glass, wood and brick alike, sending splinters of everything ricocheting around the whole of the front area of the room.

Anna's face was contorted in a wild grin as she pointed her old friend in the direction she wanted him to administer her pain.

Most of the bay-window was gone after only a few seconds and the roof of the thing sagged and collapsed down, first creaking and then cracking as the wooden supports burst, and then finally crashing inward and almost sealing the hole in the wall which had once held glass and frames.

But Anna didn't release Albert's trigger just yet.

Spinning the handles quickly to her right, she swivelled the muzzle to the left, aiming through the doorway and into the hall and beyond, sending a blaze of bullets to rip up everything from the living room doorway onward.

All the way through the hallway to the front door which shredded and flayed like balsawood, out to the porch where the birdfeeder took enough of a hammering to leave just the roof hanging on its chain, and even past the hedges lying further ahead still.

Shelby and Sophie both had that stupid look on their faces, the one that said they were in shock, but just as Anna had said, the furthest windows away, leading into the dining-room, burst inward as two figures came careering through them.

Almost at the same time heavy gunfire from outside started up. The living room was suddenly alive with the zinging and cracking of bullets.

'They've got their own Albert!' Anna shouted.

Shelby and Sophie both fired their weapons at the same time that the gun outside started to rip the living room up.

The two men who had crashed through the window, probably trying to escape the bullets which Anna had just began to pour their way, grunted as they both received bullets to the chest and legs and crumpled back to the carpeted floor.

Sophie sagged and then dropped, sitting heavily on her behind. She had just killed a man, a human-being.

Her mind felt numb and slow. The room around her was being ripped apart by slow gunfire, the sounds were dull in her ears and all she could think about was the man she had just shot in the chest. The way he had groaned and fell, his wide eyes full of fear and surprise.

Gray was shouting at her but she couldn't hear him.

She watched Anna jump away from her machine-gun, taking painfully slow strides to get out of the living room and away from the hail of flying lead.

Sophie could see, actually *see*, the blurry lines of the bullets as they passed through the wall of the living room and bounced around, shredding anything which they came into contact with.

She dully felt Shelby tugging her sleeve and shouting again, trying to get her up.

And then she saw Anna jerk to the side as a bullet hit her square in the chest.

The little woman was knocked off her feet and slowly sank spinning to the boards while Sophie's world angrily sped back up again.

She whipped her gun up and stood behind Shelby and his shield, keeping the muzzle of her weapon pointed at the doorway while Shelby pointed his own at the windows at the back of the dining-room.

The gun outside went quiet, dust and floating debris hung comically in the air.

Sophie took a step to the door, glancing down at the body of Anna as she passed.

She was laid on her front with her eyes closed and didn't look to be breathing.

'Bastards!' Sophie muttered angrily, holding back her tears for later.

Shelby nodded for her to take a look into the hallway while he himself gingerly stepped right up to the back windows.

He caught a flicker of movement coming from the right, someone dashing back round to the kitchen windows he thought.

Cautiously, step by step, he moved forward, creeping up to the archway leading to the kitchen.

Peering through, he saw the same flash go past the last window; someone making for the porch.

He looked back over his shoulder to the back door in the corner, intuition told him not to leave it unattended, but the kitchen windows, even as small and narrow as they were, were still an access point which needed to be guarded.

He looked at Anna, but there would be no support coming from there, she hadn't moved since she had dropped. Someone was going to pay for that.

Shelby's anger fuelled his resolve to be more careful, making sure that the people who had done this would either die or be brought to justice. He didn't care which; Anna was an unlikely ally and friend, but a friend she was and she had proved more than once that she was on the right side.

Sophie had made it into the hallway, the front door was shredded but still standing. She crouched down with her back to the wall and waited, peering through the broken panels of the door.

The man Shelby had just seen twice running from the back of the building to the front, suddenly appeared in Sophie's sights.

She squeezed her trigger without hesitation, spraying half a dozen bullets through the broken door.

The man took three of them, yelling and then groaning as he fell to the ground.

For Anna, she thought to herself.

She crept to the stairs, slowly backing up them as she continued to face the door.

Training dictated that she change her last shooting-position as soon as she was able, ensuring that any remaining enemy could not exploit her position based upon her firing trajectory.

Or to put it plainly, as one of her old instructors used to say; *shoot and then run away*.

The stairs creaked as she moved, but she saw no one else as she reached the top. She backed into the shadows and then waited.

After all of the noise of the two, roaring machine-guns battling it out to see who could be the loudest and most destructive, the air seemed eerily quiet for a few, stupidly-long minutes

And then suddenly Shelby had almost jumped out of his skin when Sophie's gun erupted from the hallway.

He had heard her on the stairs and knew where she would have gone after firing her weapon. He wondered if she had hit her target though.

He calmed his twitching nerves and flicked his head to peer round the corner into the kitchen. A muzzle-flash and crack met him coming from the left, corner window.

He pulled his head back as the bullets smashed through the doorframe and embedded themselves in the brickwork.

He stood panting with his back to the wall. After three, deep breaths he dropped to his knee and smoothly leaned out, his gun raised and ready.

He squeezed the trigger and the smooth eruption sent a stream of lead straight to the window where the gunfire had come from.

Glass and wood exploded as the gunman squeezed his own trigger, sending another volley straight at the place where he anticipated Shelby's head and chest would be.

A nasty *thuk-thuk-thuk-thuk*, told Shelby that his bullets had found their mark while the gunman's own bullets had simply shattered more wood and plaster above Shelby's head.

The man died silently; Shelby only heard him dropping to the ground outside the window, but there had been no choking gasp or moan.

He leaned back out quickly to have another look just in time to catch an arm releasing a slender, black tube.

'Grenade!' He shouted, ducking back and cringing.

He heard another grenade rattle into the hallway and at the same time a hand appeared in a gap between the missing bay-window and its fallen roof and threw a third into the living room.

So, at least three more men Shelby casually deduced as the grenades went off in almost perfect synchronicity.

The explosions weren't as damaging as Shelby had first thought they were going to be and he quickly realised that they were actually stun-grenades. The goggles he was wearing had worked perfectly.

He smiled to himself deviously and leaned around the corner again, two men were clambering through the windows.

'Hello.' He said, and pulled the trigger on his semi-automatic.

It rattled out twice in quick succession and the men slid from the worktop to the floor and remained silent and still.

In the hallway, three men came bursting through the wreckage of the front door, making straight for the living room while another three were busy clambering in through the smashed bay-window.

And straight in front of Shelby, the back, patio-door was just being kicked open and a black-clad body came rolling in while his partner crouched in the opening and held the door back.

Everything happened at once.

Sophie shot at the men running into the living room, killing one and bringing another to his knees with a leg shot.

He turned and fired up at his attacker, sending a spray of bullets to shred the stairs and wall, pushing Sophie back around the corner and on to the landing.

The third man made it into the living room just as Shelby fired at the crouching man in the doorway, but the man who had rolled in was up and on his knees now, levelling his Vityaz SMG at Shelby.

The man in the doorway fell back screaming and clutching at his bloodied chest and arms.

The three men who had entered by the broken bay-window were lined up and also aiming at Shelby now.

Five, highly-trained men had the drop on him and he didn't think they were playing to capture him. Well he would go down fighting to the last at least, he thought grimly.

His chest heaved and his heartbeat slowed, the moment became clear.

His gun began to turn, the trigger finger poised and tightening ready to fire and be fired upon.

To hell with them. He closed his eyes, I love you Rachel.

And then five, silenced shots suddenly hissed out in startlingly quick succession;

*thu-thu-thu-thu-thup*! And as Shelby opened his eyes, five bodies crumpled to the ground.

Anna knelt on the spot where she had fallen, two pistols held expertly in her hands while she steadily surveyed her work.

She quickly aimed both pistols through the doorway and fired again just as the soldier who had fired at Sophie raised his semi-automatic and fired it in the hope of spraying the little woman.

He died almost instantly, his own bullets finding nothing more than the ceiling of the living room.

Sophie came running down the stairs, skidding to a halt when she saw the little German standing on her feet.

'You're alive, but-what? How? I saw you shot.'

She stepped closer to her and examined the spot in the middle of Anna's chest where the bullet had struck her.

'I told you, I don't do bullets.' She said, and lifted her shirt up to reveal a very slender body-armour.

Sophie smiled and then grinned and then cried, throwing her arms around Anna and kissing her full on the mouth and ending with a loud MWAH!

It was Anna's turn to look shocked and it was genuine. She was the very best when it came to teasing and flirting, but when she was taken by surprise like this, she was right out of her comfort zone and felt like a flustering teenager.

Sophie didn't care and kissed her again. 'I am so glad you're not dead, Anna.' She said and then hugged her.

Anna blushed and turned almost the same colour as her hair. 'Well so am I.' Was all her embarrassment would allow her to say.

'Modesty and now embarrassment, Anna?'

It was Shelby's turn to tease and he relished it, just a little. 'You'll be joining us mere mortals before you know it.' He said and winked at her.

Anna continued to blush, but managed to regain her voice at least. 'Well if we've had enough fun at my expense, I suggest we finish off the rest of them.'

She nodded behind her.

Shelby and Sophie both snapped their laughing mouths shut and stared.

'What do you mean? Isn't that all of them?' Sophie asked her.

'Of course not, the leader is still out there, he wouldn't come in here would he?' She answered, as though it were the most obvious thing in the world. 'And it's likely that he has someone with him.'

Shelby frowned.

'You know; the boss always has a lackey by his side, doesn't he?' Anna continued.

Shelby just nodded stupidly. 'Of course he does.'

The little woman gave him a dry look and then carried on. 'You two go out that way,' she said, pointing to the back door, 'I'll go through the front, meet me at the gate when you are certain the area around the house is secure.'

Shelby and Sophie both nodded and looked at her.

'Well go on then.' Anna said, rolling her eyes.

The pair of them jumped and turned for the back door.

'And make sure you shoot the ones you find alive in the head.' She called after them.

They stopped in their tracks and turned back, the beginnings of very angry looks breaking out on their faces.

Anna grinned.

Sophie shook her head. 'I *knew* you didn't mean it really,' she said quickly, and then turned to Shelby, 'I *knew* she didn't mean it.'

Shelby just looked around the room at the bodies. 'I didn't.'

'I think I prefer you when you were shot.' Sophie said, haughtily and sniffed before turning round and walking out of the back door.

While Shelby and Sophie walked the perimeter of the house, Anna made her way straight to the front gate, passing nine unfortunates who had been caught by Albert when she had let him loose.

She peered through the open gate into the darkness.

Looking through her goggles now she saw the boss in his big, four-wheel drive Mercedes. He was parked between the two vans which had carried the soldiers. All three vehicles were riddled with Albert's vomited destruction.

She walked up to the boss' car, he was sitting upright at the wheel, the back of his head completely disintegrated

It seemed that he had sat and waited as the soldiers were sent in to do their work, but had himself ended up dying in the first exchange of fire.

'Unlucky.' Anna muttered, as she leaned into the vehicle and checked the passenger side and the back seats. They were empty, the boss had been sitting alone. 'Very unlucky.'

She turned away and went back to the house just as Shelby and Sophie appeared at the gate.

'Everyone's dead.' Shelby reported. 'Did you find the boss?'

'Yes, he's back there,' she replied, indicating the vehicles with a flick of her hand, 'with part of his head sitting on the seat beside him.'

'Oh.' Shelby said, not surprised really. 'So, now that the fighting has stopped does that mean command comes back to me now?'

Anna nodded. 'Yes, Mr Interpol, command goes back to you.' She gave him a warm smile when she said it though, not a hint to say that she was teasing him.

'I've already said it, but I'll say it again,' Shelby began, 'you are an amazing woman, Anna, if not a little strange, dark and,' he turned and looked at the demolition work on the front of the house. 'A little unorthodox as you put it, but I would have you on my team any day.'

He reached out and pulled her toward him and hugged her. 'You saved all of our lives tonight, I know I speak for Sophie as well when I say; we will never forget it.'

He released her and stood back.

Anna blushed only a little and smiled a crooked smile as her eyes welled up.
She nodded her head and then sniffed, looking up into the night-sky. 'I like being on this team.' She quietly said.

## Chapter Thirty-One

The killer sat high on the mountainside, looking down at Finn and Salya through his binoculars as they walked.

He had been elated to find that the girl had indeed been travelling with Finn, his heart had swelled full of pride when he had lain eyes on his brother-to-be; he was so much *more* than what he had imagined.

For two days he had watched them, keeping to a safe distance and just observing, but he had a mind to introduce himself now.

The pair of them were only two or three days away from *Paradise Begins*, whatever was going to happen there needed to come *after* he and Finn had met.

He lowered the binoculars and looked down at the track below him; they would be passing by in around twenty minutes. Better get to it then he thought and scrambled back down the slope.

Over a mile away, Finn and Salya were walking easily along, Finn telling Salya the story of *Finn MacCool and the Giant Cuchulain*.

'So, as I have already said, the giant, Cuchulain, was mighty put out that there was another giant living so close by and who was supposed to be a champion amongst champions, and so he put on his war-gear and picked up his club and crossed the sea in nine, giant strides.'

Salya gazed up at Finn as he spoke, completely mesmerised by the tale.

'Now, Finn, as big and as strong as he was, was definitely no match for the giant Cuchulain, and when he heard that he was on his way to fight him, he turned to his wife and told her the state of affairs and asked for her help.

'His wife, being a strong and clever woman, said to Finn; "Husband? I have an idea!"'

Finn put on his best female voice and for some reason that included making his eyes round and wide.

Salya giggled behind her hand.

'"What is the idea?" Said he.' Finn continued. '"Take off your clothes and get into the firewood basket." Said she. And so Finn did as he was told. Then his wife covered him up in a swaddling fleece blanket, just like a baby. "Now you stay put and quiet, and I will talk to the giant when he comes."

'Well, not long after, there came a thudding up the pathway and then a pounding at the door. "It is I, Cuchulain, I have come to fight the giant Finn MacCool."'

Finn pushed his lower jaw out when he spoke, revealing his bottom teeth like an ogre would, and spoke in a deep, deep voice.

Salya's face was a picture; her eyes were round with wonder and her jaw loose as she listened, occasionally laughing at his voices.

'Finn's wife opened the door. "We have been expecting you, but you have arrived a little earlier than we thought. Won't you come in and wait until Finn comes home?"

'Cuchulain dropped his club and other weapons on the ground and then went inside. He sat at the table, noticing the huge baby sitting in the basket. "Who is that?" He asked.

'"That is our son, only one-month old." Said she.

'Cuchulain wondered at that; if this baby was Finn MacCool's son, then how big must the father be? But he said nothing and remained at his seat.

'"I'll pour you some tea while we wait." The wife said. She took two mugs and filled one with water straight from the boiling pan and the other she filled from the pan of cold water next to it. She made the tea and then handed the boiling cup to Cuchulain, while Finn the baby, received the cold cup.

'Well, Finn drank his cup down in one go and dropped the cup to the floor, as a baby would. Cuchulain put his own cup to his lips and poured the boiling tea straight into his mouth, sorely burning his tongue. He coughed and spluttered the burning liquid straight back into his cup. He couldn't finish his tea while it was so hot.

'He looked at the baby again, astonished, wondering to himself again, if the baby could drink boiling tea, then his father must be able to drink molten lead! But he still said nothing and remained in his seat.'

A spill of fallen rocks and boulders blocked their path ahead, but without even taking a break from his story-telling, Finn picked Salya up and shuffled her around to sit on his back, her arms draped over his shoulders, and then climbed as though he were simply strolling casually up a hill.

'Finn's wife smiled cleverly to herself.' He continued. '"I've just baked a batch of rock-cakes." Said she. "I'll put some out." And so she turned back to the stove and on one plate she piled up four rocks from the hearth itself and on another plate she put four, soft buns which she had just baked.

'She gave the soft cakes to baby Finn, who immediately wolfed them down. She then handed the plate of rocks to Cuchulain. He put one in his mouth and bit down hard, two of his teeth cracked, but no matter how he tried, he couldn't crack the rock and eat it.

'Now he looked at the baby and thought to himself; if the baby can eat four of these without even having any teeth, then surely his father must be able to bite steel and iron without hurting himself.

'Without a single word, the giant Cuchulain leaped to his feet, throwing the rock-cakes back to the table, and fled out of the cottage and ran all the way back to Ireland.'

Salya giggled again. 'Finn had a clever wife.' She said.

'He did, he did and he loved her so much for helping him, that-.'

Finn's words abruptly ended as he stopped in his tracks; there was a naked man standing in the path ahead.

Once he knew he had been seen, the killer raised both his arms and slowly turned around, letting them both see he was unarmed. Once he was facing them again he pointed to all of his equipment which he had laid out on the rocks at the side.

Although he couldn't see everything that the man was pointing to, Finn could still see a light machine-gun, small and compact, and at least two pistols.

'I mean you no harm.' The man said.

'Who are you?' Finn asked.

The man stooped down to his clothes piled at his feet and pulled on his briefs. 'There, that's better,' he said, smiling amiably, 'I couldn't introduce myself completely naked.'

He chuckled as he walked toward them, holding his hand out to Finn once he was standing in front of him. 'My name's Sean,' he said, 'Sean O'Keel.'

*There is something wrong with this man.* The she-wolf growled; she didn't like the smell of him at all.

*He's insane and dangerous.* It was the other man who spoke this time, startling Finn a little.

'I am Finn,' he replied, and took the proffered hand. 'This is Salya, my friend.'

O'Keel peered over Finn's shoulder. 'Hello Salya, it is a pleasure to meet you.' He said.

Salya remained impassive and quiet, but she did nod her head slightly. She too could sense something wrong about this man.

Finn nodded to the laid out equipment. 'You have gone to a lot of trouble to let us see your weapons,' he said, turning back to face O'Keel. 'That can only mean that you expected to bump into us; any stranger passing by wouldn't have been met with such curious courtesy I don't think.' He ended with a small frown.

'Very astute,' O'Keel replied, shrugging, 'but not "us", you, I expected to bump into you.'

Finn studied the man for a moment; he wasn't posing any immediate danger and looked friendly and honest enough, but there was something underneath, something attached directly to the man's madness which made Finn's skin crawl.

'Why?' He asked.

'Simple; because I had been sent to kill you.'

O'Keel carried on smiling, friendly and completely relaxed.

'I see,' Finn replied.

He let Salya drop to the ground and made sure she stayed behind him.

'Well that is very honest and noble of you to say, but you say "had"? Does that mean you have changed your mind?'

O'Keel simply nodded. '"Honest and noble",' he echoed, seeming to think about something. 'Yes, that may well be, but to answer your question; yes, I have changed my mind. In fact; I never really intended to kill you anyway.' O'Keel said, still smiling. 'Not until after we had met at least.' He added and then laughed jovially.

*Kill him! Kill him and be done with it! His madness stinks foul in my nostrils!* The she-wolf's hackles rose.

*She's right, get rid of him and quickly, he's dangerous.* The man was agreeing with the she-wolf! What next?

But Finn refused the command; he needed to know more about why this man was here and how he had found him. This was new territory for Finn, being tracked and discovered.

'Well if that is so, we should build up a fire and drink and talk; it's not every day I meet a man who has been sent to kill me.'

Finn raised his own mirth, aligning it with that of O'Keel's, being the man that O'Keel wanted him to be.

It worked, O'Keel looked ecstatic to being asked to join him. 'Wonderful!' He almost shouted. 'I will go and dress and meet you here in three minutes.'

He laughed all the way back to the rest of his clothes and laid out equipment.

'I don't like him, he scares me. There is something not right with his head.' Salya said, as she sidled up to him and took his hand.

'I know,' Finn replied, squeezing her hand reassuringly. 'But I know this sort of madness; he is no danger to us as long as he feels that we accept him and are like him.' He looked down into her young, fearful face. 'We can play that game, Salya, easily.'

She nodded slowly, she could play along, but she wouldn't let go of the handle of her blade until the man was either dead or far, far away.

'Okay.' She said.

'Come, let us make a fire and prepare some food and drink.'

Together they got a fire going and placed a pan of water over it to boil.

O'Keel rejoined them and then gave a hand with the preparation. 'I have something which I think you will find fitting for such a meeting of new friends.' He said.

He opened his bag and produced a sealed, silver-foil bag. 'Italian coffee.' He said, beaming and then after dipping back into his bag, he brought out his flask of brandy. 'And Russian brandy.'

'Drinks fit for gods and kings!' Finn replied.

His enthusiasm wasn't lost on O'Keel, whose spirits rose further still. 'Exactly! Gods and kings. We are the gods, you and I, and the kings furnish us with the very best of their gifts and prayers.'

Finn had absolutely no idea what that was supposed to mean but slapped his new *friend* on the shoulder. 'I couldn't have put it any better myself, my friend.' He said.

Minutes later and they all had a plate of food on their laps and a steel cup in their hands.

'So, tell me, Sean, who is it who wants me dead.' Finn asked, chuckling and taking a hearty swig of his brandy-laced coffee.

'Mm.' O'Keel began speaking through a mouthful of rabbit-meat.

He nodded behind himself, indicating the way they were heading. 'The people who own that.' He said. 'The place you're heading.'

Finn lowered his cup and his smile at the same time. 'They know we are coming?'

'Uh, mm.' O'Keel mumbled, still eating enthusiastically. 'Just you, there was no mention of young Salya here.' He raised his fork with food on the end and wrinkled his nose up cutely as he pointed to Salya.

He pushed the food into his mouth and ate noisily. 'That's one of the main reasons I introduced myself now while you are still a couple of days away from it; because they are prepared for you.'

He shovelled more food in. 'This is superb rabbit,' he said, pointing at his plate. 'I mean, I've prepared a few rabbit-stews in my time, but this.' His eyes widened, dramatising. 'This is simply divine. I'll never cook rabbit any other way, ever again.'

While O'Keel ate, Finn's mind was running in overdrive.

So they knew he was coming, which meant his entry-point most likely had been compromised; they would be watching all entrances

His plan had hinged on stealth, getting inside the compound to run around and cause mayhem from the shadows, now he had to formulate something completely different.

He noticed O'Keel watching him, slowly chewing now.

'I know what you are thinking.' O'Keel said. 'You're thinking *how the hell am I going to get in now that they know I am coming?*'

Finn nodded. 'It seems that I shall have to devise another way. Maybe I will drop in from the sky.' Finn said and laughed, slapping his thigh.

O'Keel joined him, truly enjoying this bonding time.

'Well, I think I may be able to help you with that.' He said. 'Getting in that is, not dropping from the sky.'

Finn's laugh sounded genuine, even Salya grinned when he laughed loudly at O'Keel's joke. But it was far from genuine; Finn now realised he needed O'Keel.

It was logical that if the man had been sent by them to kill him and now had changed his mind, the only thing he could do was to help them. Even before O'Keel had offered, Finn had led him onto the right path.

'How would you do that?' He asked, his laughter dropping now.

'Quite simple really.' O'Keel replied. 'They know I am out here somewhere, looking for you as far as they are concerned. I could just call them, tell them I am coming in because I have finished the job.' He smiled, slyly. 'They don't know what I look like, I have never been there before.'

Exactly the words Finn wanted to hear. His mind instantly began formulating a new plan, one which included O'Keel as well.

Finn leaned closer to O'Keel, giving him a good look at his face. 'So I go in and say I am you. I bet you're glad we don't share the same face though, aren't you brother?'

He winked and grinned and then laughed like a warrior, knowing full well that, that was exactly what O'Keel wanted to hear too.

He was right; O'Keel's chest swelled with pride; he had called him *brother*. Brother! He knew he hadn't been wrong about Finn, he knew it and now they were going to bask the world in their glorious, cleansing light. Together as brothers.

He laughed at his brother's joke. 'Well it could be worse you know? We could look like her.' He said, and pointed at Salya, laughing raucously and bringing her into the clique.

Finn almost panicked; Salya must do the right thing *now*, this was the defining moment of this strange alliance and if she played it wrong, if she ended up alienating herself from him, she would be in constant danger.

All he could do was laugh along and give her a playful nudge and wait and see how she reacted.

Finn needn't have worried so much, Salya had already agreed to play along and she was clever and astute enough to see the vast change in Finn's behaviour when interacting with the man called, O'Keel.

Just now he had laughed at his joke which she was the brunt of, she understood that he was keeping on O'Keel's good side and the nudge had been a warning more than anything else, to do as he did.

She sat up straight and placed her hands on her hips, glaring at them both. 'You would be very lucky to look like me!' She admonished, wagging her finger. 'I'll have you know that I have emptied rooms with this face.'

She stuck her chin out, stretched her lips thin, bloated her cheeks and squinted her eyes at them.

Exactly the right thing to do.

O'Keel choked and spluttered and changed colour from peachy-pink to scarlet in about three seconds.

His mouth opened wide and he fell over sideways, making a noise which was supposed to be laughing but actually sounded like someone letting the air out of a balloon very slowly.

Finn's laughter covered his thoughts as he planned their next moves.

It was back on now and couldn't have worked out any better; O'Keel was clearly a trained killer, he would be invaluable in the assault. The only worry was what would happen afterward? Would he still be a willing player and see the slaves returned to safety? And after that even?

Finn couldn't see any further ahead than doing the job he had set out to do, everything after that was a dark fog; he had no plans for himself let alone anyone else.

But he wouldn't let his guard down with this man, he would kill him the moment he thought he was a danger to Salya or himself.

The trio sat for an hour more, just chatting and strengthening the bond between them, making plans for the coming attack and making a count of their weapons.

Finn told O'Keel of his plan, O'Keel adding titbits here and there until they had a well polished and workable strategy.

O'Keel would make his call in the next hour and tell the commanders at the compound that he had dispatched Finn and that he would be arriving there in a day or two, probably arriving late night.

They would naturally stand the men down and return to normal alert level. That would enable Finn to enter by the front gates while Salya showed O'Keel to the sewage-pipe.

Once inside, Finn would sweep through the barracks, killing anyone he came across while O'Keel would cover the grounds of the compound with his silenced pair of Walthers.

Salya would be in the slaves sleeping quarters, rousing the women and children and getting them out back through the pipe.

The young girl had been furnished with a small pistol to add to her belt with the knife.

The camp was dropped. While Finn and O'Keel repacked the bags, Salya took the remains of their food to the edge of a drop as she usually did, where she knew the dogs had gathered, and threw the remains down to them.

The three of them set off again then, steadily walking under the high, midday sun, an unlikely trio of liberators bringing their own brand of justice to the unlucky occupants of *Paradise Begins*.

## Chapter Thirty-Two

He hated this damn country. Not particularly Wales, just Britain. Why the fuck couldn't he have a job out in the states for a change, or the Bahamas, or anywhere the sun shone and the women didn't wear much.

Ilia Guryev, special command assassin for the Russian underground, sat in the old, well-worn armchair with a glass of whiskey in his hand, resting on the chair arm. He was staring into the space directly in front of him, lost in the depths of his thoughts.

He had just received a very disturbing call; the Interpol agents had escaped and Yezhov and his men had been massacred. How the fuck had that happened?

He sipped at his whiskey absent-mindedly.

Yezhov had twenty men at his command, how did twenty men get themselves killed by two Interpol agents?

Unless there wasn't two.

Allies then? Who could possibly be strong enough and have enough skill and weaponry to take out Yezhov and his men? Someone who had strong connections with this man Shelby, but who?

No matter how he played it over in his mind, he couldn't see how his esteemed comrade, someone he had known and respected for years, had been so easily wiped out at what should have been a simple execution.

He carried on with his whiskey, thinking about the woman upstairs. He had originally been ordered to kill her, but all that had changed when Yezhov had been taken out. So for now he was left babysitting their bargaining chip.

He had actually felt sorry for her when she had realised she had just escaped her saviours and jumped right into the arms of her enemies. The poor woman simply cried and didn't even try to resist when Kazakov had rolled up her sleeve and injected her with a heavy tranquiliser, putting her to sleep almost instantly.

She was tied-up on the bed now and had still been asleep when he had last looked in on her over an hour ago.

Guryev raised himself out of the chair and stepped over to the small tray of drinks. He opened the bottle of whiskey and poured a double into his glass, adding two cubes of ice from the bucket sitting next to the tray.

He turned and then raised his glass. 'Yezhov, my old friend.' He said. 'Wherever it is you are, take your vodka cold and your women hot.'

He took half the whiskey and chugged it back, closing his eyes and respectfully relishing both the passing of his friend and the hot, amber liquor as it warmed his throat and chest.

He gasped appreciatively. 'You finished the race before me, old man.' He muttered and then sat back in his seat.

While Guryev numbed his senses with the whiskey downstairs, upstairs, Rachel was just waking up.

She felt warm and hollow, her head felt too large for the person residing inside, while her eyelids were made of lead blankets and wouldn't open properly.

She took deep breaths while her head swam, trying to get the purifying oxygen around her body and into her mushy brain.

It was difficult to breathe deeply, she found her mouth was covered by something, something she couldn't push away with her tongue; some kind of tape.

Her panic rose; what if she was sick? She would choke.

Stay calm woman, you're not dead yet, breath and stay calm.

The cocktail of drugs which she had in her system, not discounting the ones she had put in there herself, were oozing around her body, licking at her muscles she could feel, causing them to ache as though they had been unused for days.

She suddenly felt exhausted again and released herself to the slumber, falling deeply asleep in the blink of an eye.

Ten minutes later and she was awake again and again fighting with the drugs.

This continued for at least an hour; Rachel fighting to wake herself and then suddenly falling asleep again as the tranquiliser passed round her body.

Eventually though, she opened her eyes and kept them open, the drug's effect lessening now that her body's own defences were disposing of it.

Her mouth was dry. She looked around at the room she was in.

She was laid on her side on a double bed, her hands tied in front of her and connected by a tether to the knots which were tied around her feet and ankles.

She could only move a little, just enough to stay reasonably comfortable, but she couldn't raise her hands to her mouth to remove the tape without raising her knees, but then she found that the clever knot went all the way up her back and was tied around her neck; when she tried too hard to get her hands up to the tape she only managed to choke herself.

The room itself was small and compact, a neat and tidy room in a house she thought. A rented house or a b&b maybe. Somehow she didn't think it was a bed and breakfast establishment.

There was a bedside table with a small, lit lamp sitting on its top and next to it stood a decanter of water and a glass.

At the front of the room stood a large, white wardrobe with a full-length mirror attached to one of its doors.

Over to her left was a window, the curtains were drawn, but Rachel could just make out the dim, orange glow of streetlights outside.

She looked back to the water and her tongue suddenly felt too large and made of rock-wool.

She turned herself onto her right side and shuffled over to the edge of the bed, bringing the small, nightstand up to her face. She began rubbing her cheek along its edge where she thought the tape which covered her mouth began.

It worked. After five minutes of rolling the edge back, tediously slowly, she managed to get a corner of the tape pressed firmly onto the corner of the stand.

She rolled her head and pulled it backward at the same time, peeling the tape from her mouth and leaving it stuck to the corner of the small table.

Lying back, her chest heaved as she breathed in deeply, that had been much harder than she'd expected.

The water rippled at her side, teasing her.

She rolled back onto her side and raised her head, looking at the empty glass and the full decanter. How the hell would she get the water into her mouth?

She knew she could probably sit up, as long as she kept her legs straightened out so that they didn't pull on her neck, but then she still wouldn't be able to lean over and get the bloody water for the same reason; the tether from legs to neck would choke her.

Her eyes fell on the empty glass; why couldn't they have been thoughtful and left it filled? She could have leaned over and at least taken a sip.

And then she had it.

Rolling back onto her side once more, Rachel slowly *caterpillared* her head and shoulder up onto the small end-table, bringing her face right up to the glass tumbler.

She picked it up with her lips and then carefully drew it in between her teeth, rolling herself away and back onto the bed.

Flipping the glass down onto her stomach, she then allowed it to roll off onto the bed.

After using a fold of the bed's blanket to cover the glass over, she rolled on top of it and pressed down hard with her hip. The tumbler broke with a sudden crack.

Carefully she rolled away and then uncovered the broken glass, picking out a long, slender shard.

Immediately she began working on the rope which connected her tied hands to her ankles. It took less than a minute to cut it all the way through.

She sat up, dropping the shard back to the covers, and then raised her hands to her mouth and began biting at the knots, pulling them with her teeth.

Untying her hands was much more difficult than obtaining the shard and cutting the rope. The nylon climbing-rope had been tied expertly and the knots were tight and binding.

Rachel cringed as her teeth squeaked on the rope and grated together when they slipped off, but through her tears of frustration, she finally managed to loosen the bite of the rope and draw the first loop through the knot.

She made quick work of the remaining loops and soon she was sitting on the edge of the bed, rope free and her mouth plastered over the rim of the water decanter, drinking deeply.

Lowering the now well depleted decanter, Rachel sighed. 'Best water I've ever had.' She mumbled, and smiled, satisfied.

Her smile soon dropped though, when she looked around and realised where she was and how she had got here.

What was she going to do now that she was watered and free? She found she was actually afraid to move in case she made enough noise to attract the attention of her captors.

Just remembering the big thug who had injected her was enough to make her realise just how powerless she had been, powerless and afraid.

Rachel shook her head and closed her eyes. Come on, come on! Get your fucking head in gear woman! Being afraid is exactly how they would want you to be, so don't be.

She sipped more water and then rose to her feet unsteadily, coaxing her lethargic muscles to perform.

The bed creaked and she flinched, freezing on the spot with her ears sharpened, listening for the sounds of running feet and raised voices.

Nothing happened, the silence remained.

She took a trembling step toward the foot of the bed, gingerly placing her foot down and releasing her weight onto it slowly, expecting the floorboards to click and creak.

Again nothing happened.

Another tentative step and then another, she reached the foot of the bed and then turned to the window, creeping along on tiptoes.

She pulled the curtain back an inch and peered through. She was upstairs in a house, her window overlooked a long street lined with houses, cars parked outside their fronts.

Her still-tingling fingers fumbled with the catch and tried to raise the window-sash but it was painted firmly shut. 'Shit!' She hissed.

She turned to face the door. She was afraid of opening it, afraid even of touching the handle; it was a direct connection to the outside, the place her captors were, the thought of touching it made her feel like she was tempting her luck by stroking the lion.

But what other choice did she have?

She breathed in deeply and then held it, mentally counting to ten before slowly releasing it.

Fuck it she thought, and walked confidently straight to the door, pressing the handle as soon as she touched it. It was locked.

Rachel's galloping heart thudded away in her chest; she had been ready to walk straight out into the unknown then, but finding the door locked had actually made her feel a strange sense of relief that she couldn't go out into the domain of her kidnappers.

She felt guilty for her cowardice and then a sudden, rising anger at her predicament.

Her head snapped up straight. Bastards! How dare they? How dare they drug her and tie her up and then lock her in a room!?

Rachel's anger fuelled her resolve to escape, she would *not* accept her lot and give in.

The broken glass was back in her hands in a flash and she walked to the sealed window with it.

Using the sharpened tip, she began scratching away at the offending paint. It was old and shattered like thin plastic, splintering along quite quickly.

Rachel dug her makeshift tool into the revealed gaps between window-sash and frame, pulling out as much paint as she possibly could.

After around twenty minutes of scratching and scraping and sucking her sliver-cut fingers, Rachel dropped the glass to the sill and pushed the sash upward with her palms.

It still wouldn't budge, it needed a firm crack to finish off the final hold which the paint was exerting.

Not to be deterred, she padded softly to the wardrobe and opened it.

Just as she had hoped, there was a row of empty, steel coat-hangers hanging from the rail. She took one and closed the door again.

Taking the hanger back to the window, she uncurled one end of it and then began rubbing it on the wall, pushing it down through the wallpaper and plaster until she met the brick underneath.

She rubbed the steel against the brick until she had the end sharpened and flat.

Now she worked the small blade into the cracks again and slowly but surely she drew it down and around the sash, repeating the procedure at the other side.

It was a painstakingly long process, but after a further forty-five minutes, Rachel had the window slipping open with the stupidest of ease.

It rose an inch at a time, jerkily and with a scraping noise. She didn't care, she had been at it for so long she just wanted it over and done with now.

Once it was fully raised she stood back and listened; the same silence came back to her, only now she could hear the noise of a sleeping, outside world coming in through the window.

Once she was satisfied that she hadn't been heard, she leaned out of the window and looked down. She would probably hurt herself if she jumped she thought, there was nothing but concrete for her to land on down there.

She pulled herself back inside and looked around. The rope on the bed, tied to a sheet, would give her enough distance to drop down.

'I'm in a bloody movie.' She muttered to herself.

It took her ten, more minutes to make a long enough rope and then she turned to tying it to the leg of the bed. She looked long and hard at the steel-framed bed and then looked down at herself. 'Bloody hell.'

The bed would move as soon as she put her weight on the rope.

She looked at the bed-leg, it was quite large and round. She knelt down beside it and began cutting away at the carpet around it. Once she had the carpet cut all the way through, she silently lifted the leg and pulled out the useless bit.

Now when the leg dropped back down it sat neatly in a hole. Rachel pulled as much of the carpet up and around the leg as she could and then stood back, pulling hard on her rope. The bed stayed where it was, tethered by the carpet.

'You're a genius, darling.' She said, and then instantly grimaced as her knuckles suddenly flared hotly, reminding her that she had cracked someone across the nose with them.

The pain-killers had decided to give up.

She looked around the room for her bag, but it was nowhere in sight. 'Gin and bloody codeine. You're a *junkie*-genius!' She muttered, flexing her hand a little.

She threw the other end of her rope out of the window and then looked down again to see how far she had to drop. It was no more than six or seven feet from the end of the rope to the ground now.

And then with one foot on the sill, Rachel had turned, startled by the noise of the door being unlocked.

She froze; her options were two; jump and then be caught injured, or stay put and be caught uninjured.

As much as she wanted to escape, she really didn't want to break a leg or two in the attempt.

The door opened and a big man took a step inside, stopping in the doorway as he settled his eyes on Rachel.

She noticed him standing there, a posture of un-assumed casualness but at the same time she could see he was looking for five different things in ten different places.

She knew that look, that look which only the people who had a profession in violence had, she had seen Graham do it.

He looked from broken glass to twisted coat-hanger, scratched and damaged wall and window to makeshift rope and finally the sliced carpet around the bed-leg. 'I hope you realise we have a non-returnable deposit on this place.' He said casually.

Rachel frowned. 'What?'

He pointed to the damage she had wrought in her escape attempt. 'We have a deposit.' He said, again.

Rachel just continued to frown and then blinked. 'Oh. Right. Sorry.'

Guryev scoffed. 'No need for apologies, Mrs Shelby, I have after all kidnapped you.'

He raised his half empty whisky glass and then took a sip. 'You can take your foot down if you like.' He continued, nodding at her foot still perched on the sill. 'Or jump. I'll see you at the bottom anyway and we can continue our conversation down there.'

Rachel took her foot from the sill and stood back. 'What do you want with me?'

He cocked his head. 'I don't want anything with you so please don't take it personally, but the people who I work for,' he paused, 'well, they want you as their bargaining chip.'

'You mean against Graham?'

He sipped his drink again and looked at her over the rim of his glass, studying her face, her emotions; she loved her husband, he could see it.

He nodded his head slowly. 'Yes, against your husband, Graham.'

'But why? What is wrong with you people? Going around shooting and kidnapping people. There is much more to life you know.' Rachel said angrily, folding her arms and taking another step back.

Guryev noticed; she thought he had come up here to attack her. 'Like I said; it's nothing personal, just business that is all.'

He finished his drink. 'And if you must know, I agree with what you said, there *is* much more to life, but for you and I? Well, this is what life is serving us at the moment.'

Rachel relaxed a little when he said that. He wasn't up here to hurt her or torment her that was clear, but she felt that if he was ordered to kill her he would do so without even thinking twice about it. Just business.

'So what do we do now?' She asked.

'I think to start with you should bring *that* back in,' he pointed to the rope, 'close the window and draw the curtains again and then after that I would think that you would do pretty much anything to have a hot bath and some food and drink, hm?'

He raised his empty glass. 'I am going to be having another so you need not worry about drinking alone.'

Rachel was lost for words. What the hell was he playing at? Being so nice and civil, giving her hot baths and food? It was like a weird kind of reversed Stockholm-syndrome.

He noticed her apprehension. 'You needn't worry about myself or my men, we are all happily married.' He smiled at her. 'We could just go back to being tied up on the bed if you like? There is a decent-sized cellar beneath us as well?' He raised his eyebrow.

'Why are you being so nice to me? Kidnappers aren't nice, they're mean and evil and hurt people.'

'I see. So you have been kidnapped on numerous occasions and have been treated horribly, I take it?'

Rachel blushed, more with embarrassment than the anger she suddenly felt. 'Well of course not, but you know? I hear the news of things like that.'

Guryev chuckled. 'Yes, we are all the same aren't we?' He said sarcastically, continuing to tease her. 'Look, we are not terrorists, Mrs Shelby, we are a business organisation, and business - in my experience at least - is always conducted best when things are civil and comfortable for all parties involved.'

Rachel thought long and hard about what he was saying. Stupidly she found it made a kind of sense. Whatever the outcome of this particular *business* venture was going to be she may as well face it after a bath and some food. Beats being tied to a bed, gasping with thirst.

She relaxed and nodded her head. 'Okay,' she said, 'what's for dinner?'

## Chapter Thirty-Three

A distant call of a lone nightjar broke the silence as the three of them sat on top of a hill overlooking, *Paradise Begins* a quarter of a mile away.

Finn and O'Keel were watching the complex through their binoculars while Salya sat huddled into Finn's side for warmth.

They would be setting off in thirty minutes.

'The guards have changed on the wall.' O'Keel said, keeping his binoculars raised. 'The night shift is settling in.'

'Aye.' Finn responded. 'The guards at the front of the villa have gone inside as well.'

The Malas brothers had been very helpful when providing him with the layout details of the place, but they had said that the village outside was mostly unoccupied, only being used for special dignitaries and VIP visitors.

It was just bad luck he thought, that someone was using it right now. That someone would almost certainly have their own security.

Or was it bad luck after all? If there really was a person of some importance in there then he or she would be found in there dead and with his mark left on them.

Still, it stretched his skills to have such a potentially big threat at his back.

'Are you sure you don't want to take the villa out first?' O'Keel asked.

'No, we would find ourselves on the outside of the barracks and weapons store when the alarm went off.' Finn replied casually. 'Besides; I want to use some of those weapons in that store to level the villa and the whole village to the ground.'

His eyes flashed in the low moonlight as he spoke and his grin was easy to see.

O'Keel grinned back. 'Marvellous, brother, simply marvellous.' He said.

The minutes ticked by and then it was time to go. They set off down the hill. Once at the bottom Finn pulled Salya toward him and hugged her. 'I will see you when we come back out over there.' He said, pointing to the hill at the other side of the drainage culvert.

They had arranged for everybody to meet behind the hill, but Salya had been given the extra responsibility of getting the rescued people to safety if Finn didn't return.

She looked up at him and then hugged him back, kissing him on the cheek. 'I love you, my friend.' She said, and then released him, stepping back. 'Come back to me.' She murmured the silent prayer under her breath.

Finn turned to O'Keel, he had to show some kind of display of warm kinship to the man now. As much as he loathed to do so he held his arm out for O'Keel to clasp. 'You too brother, be safe and we will meet again shortly, you and I, inside the compound.' Finn said, and pulled the smaller man in to hug him firmly once.

O'Keel stood back, his bottom lip stiff and proud. 'Be safe... brother.' He answered.

He turned to Salya and held out his hand. 'Come, dear Salya, let us go and begin this fight for freedom.'

Salya only paused for a second to look at Finn who nodded almost imperceptibly and then took O'Keel's hand and walked away with him to the drainage culvert.

Finn watched them go for a minute, making oaths and promises of death and retribution at O'Keel's back should he fail in his promise to keep Salya safe.

And then he was off himself, marching the last leg to the entrance of his final goal.

His smile returned, grinning with teeth that shone like starlight in the night.

Jimi sipped his brandy while Nim lay dozing on the couch. He stood looking out at the compound through the large, front window. She would be going back in there soon.

He felt sick at the thought, but what could he do now? The stupid, fucking assassin had been killed and wasn't going to be coming here after all; his plans had revolved around that one, single thing and it had gone fucking wrong at the root.

He hadn't had the heart to tell Nim yet, the guilt was just piling up behind each brandy he drank to build the wall he was hiding behind. It wasn't going away, just festering.

What if they just left now, in the middle of the night? Took a car and drove to the Pakistani border and then crossed over and disappeared? Disappeared for how long though?

Jimi knew he would be hunted for the rest of his days, that was the way of the organisation he worked for, not a day would go by when he wasn't looking over his shoulder, or worrying about coming home to find Nim had been murdered, men waiting for him.

He turned away to pour more brandy when the dark figure of a man appeared, walking around the corner of the compound and heading for the gate. A tall man.

Jimi almost dropped the glass he was holding in his hand; it was him, the madman, and he was standing right there talking to the gate-guard!

His first instincts were to shout wolf, but he knew those were only his misplaced, instilled loyalties barking at him to do the thing which he was *supposed* to do and not the thing which was *right*.

He steadied his arm and then raised his glass. 'Good luck, my insane friend, may our paths never meet.' He said quietly, and took a sip of his brandy.

His plan was back in action.

The guard on the gate was having apparent trouble with the paperwork on his clipboard, licking his finger and flicking the sheets.

He had been informed and knew full well that a boss would be coming through the gate tonight, but the guard had remembered the scratchy printout of a picture of the man they had been told was coming to attack them. For some reason the man in front of him made him think of that picture.

Finn was wise to him and knew that he was stalling for some reason.

He scanned the open yard ahead. There were two men sitting at a table at the back of the compound just inside the huge doorways of a large warehouse, and sitting in the guard station on his immediate left, just behind the guard who was stalling, sat the other gate-guard.

*It seems that it begins now*. The she-wolf said casually.

Finn took a deep breath.

*Bring it on!* The man's voice piped up. He was standing next to the she-wolf and the pair of them were actually allied in their bristling.

*The three is stronger than the one*. His mistress' voice.

Finn's heart swelled and his time slowed down almost to a standstill.

The guard blinked slowly, Finn's hand shot out and grabbed him by the larynx, squeezing hard until it cracked.

The guard dropped his clipboard, clutching at his attackers hand as he was raised from the ground.

Finn watched emotionlessly as the clipboard tumbled slowly through the air, heading for the concrete where it would clatter and arouse the attention of the guard in the box.

He casually snaked his foot out and caught the board before it could give him away and as he let it slip quietly off his boot to the ground, the guard in his hand lost consciousness.

Keeping the unconscious guard upright and at arm's length, his boot-tips only just touching the floor, Finn drew his dagger with his free hand and then swivelled around, bringing his arm up and through the doorway, straight into the neck of the second guard.

He held him in place until his thrashing had stopped and then pulled his blade free, allowing the body to fall back in its seat.

Next he walked back around the corner to the outside and laid the body of the guard he had choked behind the guard-box, calmly walking back to the entrance when he had done so.

He stood there and surveyed the yard again. The men at the table were oblivious to what had just taken place in the last eight seconds.

Concealing his daggers in his hands, Finn marched up to the men, taking note of the lit up windows in the main building next to the warehouse; the fat commanders office.

The two men looked up as Finn approached, puzzled looks on their faces at the sight of this stranger in the compound.

Even though they also were expecting an arrival, they were still wary, especially since this stranger was so big and looked like he had just walked out of a warzone.

Finn nodded his head and smiled. 'Salâm.' He said.

The men relaxed and returned his greeting, one of them raising his cup. It exploded in his hand as Finn's dagger passed through it and embedded itself in the startled man's throat.

Finn's other blade protruded obliquely from the left-eye of the man's table-partner.

He arranged them both so that they sat slumped at the table as though they were still talking.

After retrieving his blades he then carried on walking into the warehouse.

To one side stood a truck, a pair of legs sticking out from beneath it; a mechanic working on the vehicle.

Finn walked up to him and pulled him out by the legs.

The man began to complain but was soon cut short as both of Finn's blades dropped in unison, piercing his chest and lungs.

His hands scrabbled at Finn for a few seconds, thrashing at the arms pinning him beneath the blades, but he soon quietened and slowed down and eventually his arms fell back to the floor and his eyes closed.

Finn pushed the man back under the truck and then raised himself and scanned the warehouse; it was exactly as Salya had described.

The unlit office where she had been examined stood at the back of the warehouse and next to it was the door which led to the armoury and barracks.

In the corner at the opposite side to the door leading to the armoury stood another door, this one presumably leading up to the offices and the commander's suite.

Finn loped to that door and pulled out a grenade, jamming the device behind a water-pipe running up the wall and then pulling the ring out on a steel wire and wrapping it around the door-handle.

He would be dealing with the soldiers in the barracks first, anyone coming through this door to attack from behind would lose an arm and a leg doing so.

He ran back to the armoury-door, sheathing his blades and replacing them with his silenced pistols. He tried the handle, it was locked, but he hadn't expected anything less.

He took a tiny aerosol canister from one of his pockets and then held it up to the keyhole, angling the equally tiny nozzle downward. He pressed a release on the side and there was an almost imperceptible hiss.

A wisp of acrid smoke rose laboriously out of the keyhole as the tumblers and springs were melted.

Finn rattled the handle again and the door clicked open this time, swinging inward.

He stepped inside and closed it behind him, flicking the light switch on at the side.

*Now that's what I'm talkin' about!* It was the man.

Rows and rows of arms and ammunition rolled out before Finn, filling the small room almost entirely.

'Are you sure you are feeling alright?' Finn said, puzzled that the man was actually embracing this mission.

*He's feeling fine, aren't you love?* The she-wolf replied for him.

*Strangely, yes, I feel great.*

Finn frowned; what were they up to? Why the sudden camaraderie between them?

*The three is stronger than the one.*

He remembered his mistress' words again, but still couldn't understand why they had chosen here and now to be allied with him together.

*Because we know that the three is stronger than the one.* They both said in unison, their voices strangely harmonious.

Finn continued to frown and think, but even though he had at first been stunned at their reconciliation, it was without doubt that he felt more whole now than he had felt for a long time. He could feel the seven spears which he was meant to wield.

'Aye,' he nodded, 'we are strong.'

He turned to face the left wall, his gaze settling on one of the three RPG-7's hanging there. His eyes twinkled. 'We'll be needing one of those, then.' He said.

While Finn helped himself to arms and ammunition from the store, Salya and O'Keel were just stepping out of the door of the lavatories in the shower-block.

It had taken them longer than they had anticipated to get through the sewage-pipe and up through the toilet.

The front of the pipe entrance had been covered over with a steel mesh while the toilets themselves had been bolted to the ground.

O'Keel had cut the mesh and then had to spend fifteen minutes unbolting the toilet which they were going to move. Luckily the bolts had been driven all the way through the rock and then locked tight with steel nuts.

The killer stepped out into the corridor first and made straight for the door leading to the outside. There was a guard sat at a table by the door, his head on his chest and his snores loud.

O'Keel dispatched him with a quick thrust of his knife to the back of the sleeping guard's head.

He opened the door and peered outside. There were two men sat at a table over the other side of the open compound.

He narrowed his eyes to look closely at them, they weren't moving. 'Well done brother.' He muttered and chuckled.

He slipped out of the doorway and sped across the yard to the corner of the central building where the commander resided, taking his place amongst the shadows and waiting for the fighting to start.

He had never felt so thrilled, so maverick, so rogue, so... so... so needed. That was the main thing; he was needed.

He had been all over the world on assignments, had fought in wars both his own and sometimes others, but that wasn't because he was *needed*, that was because he was *wanted*.

Here and now he was needed; he had found his family and they needed him as much as he needed them.

He crouched down on his haunches, watching and smiling from his hiding place.

Salya slipped quietly along the corridor, opening doors as she went and peering inside, looking for the children.

An office, a storeroom, a cleaning room, washing room and then eventually a room which had someone inside.

The man looked up from his girly magazine and leered. She had entered a small guard-room.

'Well, hello little girl.' His greasy voice said. 'Don't be shy, come in and sit.'

He pat his lap with a dirty, coarse hand.

Salya stepped forward, she felt like ice on the inside, nothing moving, emotionless and insensitive.

The man reached out as she approached, placing his hand on her bottom and pinching it lightly.

If he'd had any presence of mind the man would have noticed how the young girl was dressed and wondered why she was wandering around at night like that.

But like most of the other soldiers here he was complacent when it came to women and children; they were living stock that was all.

'Good girl.' He said.

He raised his hand to grope at her small breasts. 'Come and s-.'

And Salya drove her stiletto blade which Finn had given her hard into the man's ear.

His eyes widened and he flinched only slightly as the cold steel sliced through his eardrum, shredding its way straight through the skull and into both lobes of his brain, right to left.

She pulled the knife free and stood back as the body fell from the chair onto the floor.

Finn had shown her how to do that, telling her that all she needed to do was drive the blade as though she were trying to actually stab something at the other side of the skull.

After all of the practising on hare and rabbit skulls she had done she was both disturbed a little and pleased that it had worked for real; it had felt like she had been pushing her knife through soft bark rather than a hard, bone skull.

She relieved the body of its weapon and ammunition, cleaning her blade on the man's shirt before leaving the room and closing the door behind her. She now had two pistols.

Salya continued down the long corridor, the next door opened into a dark room with two beds inside, only one of them occupied.

The sleeping woman stirred as the light from the corridor spilled into the room and fell across her closed eyes.

She moaned and then sat up sleepily, her long, black hair stuck to the side of her face.

Salya walked into the room and switched the light on.

The young nurse screwed her face up, fighting off the glare, and then slowly blinked until her eyes adjusted.

She looked straight up at Salya then and gasped. 'You came back.' She said, quietly, raising her trembling hand to the scars on her cheeks. 'You came back.' She repeated, as tears spilled down her face.

Salya took another step forward, holding out the pistol she had taken from the guard. 'Take this and get dressed. We are leaving. All of us.' She said.

She stood up as tall and proud as she could. 'I am Salya.'

She sounded just like Finn.

The nurse just stared, she had never seen a woman - a girl - carrying such a look of ferocious freedom.

Freedom? She had found freedom and returned with it.

She tentatively reached out and took the pistol from Salya's hand, looking at it and then clasping it to her chest tightly. 'I am Suki.' She said.

A pained look suddenly crossed the nurse's brow and she shook her head. 'No,' she stammered, 'I *was* Suki, but when I first came here I was Kurshid.' Her eyes hardened. 'I *am* Kurshid.'

She slipped out of bed and removed her nightgown and then opened a drawer and produced a pair of jeans and a thick, dark sweater.

She dressed and then turned back to Salya. 'I'm ready. What do you want me to do?' She asked.

She was breathless and understandably excited, Salya could see she was trembling.

She stepped closer and put her hand on the woman's chest, just as Finn had once done to her. 'Firstly you need to relax, you are free now.' The young girl said. 'Breathe deeply and focus your mind, we need to be calm and focused if we want to get out of here.'

She looked up into the nurse's eyes, serious and unblinking.

Kurshid's own eyes widened and her breath caught in her chest. She drew a long, deep breath in and held it then let it out slowly, her eyes locked with

Salya's.

'Good.' Salya said, smiling reassuringly. 'That is better.'

She could feel the nurse's heartbeat slowing down a little, dropping from a mad gallop to more of a florid trot now. It would have to do, they needed to get moving.

She stood back and made for the door. 'Come, let us wake the children.'

They left the room and Salya followed Kurshid to the next door down. Inside the room were eight girls aged between ten and fifteen, all sleeping.

Kurshid pointed to a door on the other side of the corridor.

The youngest are in there; three boys and five girls.' She looked down at the ground. 'There is a girl missing from in there.' She said, and then looked back up. 'She is with Nazari I think.'

Salya's eyes hardened, but remained focused and with the plan. 'You deal with those, they will know your face, I will get these up and dressed.'

Kurshid nodded and went straight into the other room, while Salya flicked the light-switch on in this room and began gently encouraging the sleepers to wake up.

The children grumbled in their sleep, questioning mumbles and gasps as they were coaxed out of their dreams.

Salya walked amongst them, making sure all were fully awake, before standing by the side of the two eldest girls, the fifteen year-old and a girl the same age as herself.

All eyes were on her.

'I am Salya.' She said, firmly, and looked around at them all. 'We are going home.'

The children all opened their mouths at the same time, ready to do the thing which children did the best; sound their emotions.

Salya's hand shot up in the air, everyone's first syllable died on their lips. 'And we are going to be doing it very, very *quietly*.' She put her finger to her lips and hushed them.

Once she was satisfied that they were not going to start running around shouting and giggling, she said; 'Now, get dressed as quickly as you can, not a sound.' She wagged her finger.

Everyone slipped quickly out of their beds and began throwing night-clothes off and putting trousers, skirts, sweaters and shirts on.

Salya turned to the eldest girls. 'Make sure they are dressed warmly and stay quiet.' She said to the girl her own age. 'What is your name?' She then asked.

'Rana.' The girl replied shyly.

'Wait for us here, Rana, we will be back soon.' Salya smiled confidently at the frightened girl.

She turned to the older girl now. 'What is your name?'

'Parisa.' She answered, still pulling her under-trousers on.

'You come with me then; we need to find a few supplies to take with us when we leave.' Salya said.

The girl finished dressing and then followed Salya out of the room.

They turned right and went back down the way Salya had come, stopping outside one of the doors she had left open, a store room.

'We need torches.' Salya said, stepping inside. 'And soap and matches.'

They rummaged through the shelves, pulling off the things they needed and piling them up in their arms.

Parisa found some toothpaste, sensibly adding it to her pile of torches; she had found three. While Salya had found a sturdy, canvas linen-bag to put it all in, she herself had another three torches and an armful of matches.

The two girls left the storeroom and went back to the children.

The nurse was inside now, the children from the other room gathered around her.

Salya's heart dropped when she saw the woman was holding a baby, no more than a year old.

She moved forward and held her finger out to stroke the baby's cheek.

There was a fury in her fuelled by the touch of this innocence beneath her finger; a baby! How could a baby be of any use here? How?

The nurse watched her, reading her expression. 'She was born here.' The nurse said, stooping and kissing the baby's head. She looked up and smiled at Salya. 'She is called Delara.'

Salya frowned, not fully understanding at first then her eyes widened as it dawned on her. 'She is yours.' She muttered, thinking aloud.

If Salya could have enumerated her reasons for doing what she was doing, she could have easily said now that the number had just been multiplied by a million; this woman and the young life she held in her arms had to escape and be protected.

Salya moved her finger from the baby's face and raised her hand to the woman's, saying nothing but meaning everything as she stroked her cheek.

The nurse frowned a little; had this girl just made some silent promise to her and her baby? She was still a child herself.

But she was a child who had escaped and then come back.

She peered deeply into Salya's eyes, acknowledging the silent oath she had just received. She noticed now that the child hadn't come back after all; this was a woman standing in front of her, a strong woman.

## Chapter Thirty-Four

Finn stooped to his haunches by the door leading into the soldiers sleeping quarters.

He would be damned if he was about to start killing men as they slept in their beds, but he wouldn't have them coming out through here without paying for it.

He tied off his grenade booby-trap and then backed away through the canteen area.

He set two more traps using the legs of the dining tables to pin the grenade's wire hoops to, the trip-wire spanning the gangway leading to the outer door, the door to the armoury.

He closed that door behind him as he left and set his final grenade-trap on the handle.

Now for the two wall guards, the final phase in this part of the plan before the fireworks began.

So far so good then.

If everything was going to plan, Salya would be on her way back out of the shower block by now and O'Keel would be waiting at the back of the compound yard, somewhere in the shadow of the main building.

He crossed the warehouse and returned to the dead men sitting at their table, picking up the RPG-7 he had stashed there after he had found it.

He slipped the weapon over his head and shoulders, resting it on his back, and walked past the table and men and turned left out of the building.

Ahead of him a long ladder ran up the stone wall leading to the walkway ending at a metal handrail set into the brickwork.

He stayed close to the shadows and watched. A minute went by before one of the two guards came into view.

If they were following the same pattern as he had observed from the hill through his binoculars, they would be walking from corner to corner and then back again, meeting somewhere behind the main building, the area of the rampart he couldn't see.

The guard who had walked into view was walking that way now. Finn readied himself, waiting for him to pass the spot where the ladder ended.

The guard took three steps past the handrail and then Finn suddenly blurred down the shadows of the wall, streaking supernaturally silent almost, to the foot of the ladder.

With three steps still to take before he actually could reach out and touch the rungs, Finn leaped high into the air and landed with his hand gripping the very top of the steel handrail.

He lifted his head around and saw the guards standing exactly where he expected them to be.

They chatted and exchanged cigarettes, stalling for just enough time to allow Finn to pull himself up and onto the rampart without a sound.

Landing with his head down and his legs fully loaded, he then sprinted off like a hunting cat, keeping his weight well in front of himself and his head low chasing it.

The guards didn't know what hit them. Literally. They had no notion of what had suddenly befallen them. One second they were talking, breathing, smoking and then the next...

With a silent snarl on his feral face, Finn slammed into the men with the full force of his sixteen-stone assault. His arms encompassed them and their lights went quickly out.

The head of one of the men snapped viciously to the side breaking his neck as he took the last puff of his final cigarette, while the other was lifted off his feet with a sucking gasp, ribs and pelvis cracking noisily.

*His* cigarette remained stupidly where it was as the hand which had been holding it was whipped violently away.

Before the tumbling cigarette had settled on the ground, the guard was thrown over the edge, landing on the concrete below with a ghastly, life-ending crack.

O'Keel stared wide-eyed at the body and then looked up.

'Brother.' Finn peered down, grinning.

'Brother.' He returned.

Finn's shadowy form disappeared from view as he pulled back.

O'Keel simply chuckled as he was wont to do and then carried on with his wait. Which would be coming to an end very, very, shortly he thought.

Above, Finn ran all the way around the rampart and came to a halt at the far corner, opposite where O'Keel crouched and almost directly above the gate where he had started.

He crouched down onto one knee and removed the RPG-7 from his back, bringing it up onto his shoulder and flicking the safety off.

*Good morning campers!* The man's voice rang out.

Finn furrowed his brow. 'I don't know what that means,' he muttered as he lined up his sights. 'But it will do.'

He pressed the trigger and sent his herald straight at the oil containers which fed the complex; compound and village both.

The whoosh of the rocket was loud and startlingly clear and all who heard it looked in its direction, but none had time to move further before the night lit up with a furious, orange glow and the terrific boom and explosion rattled their teeth.

Flames and oil and fumes were vomited two hundred feet into the air, black smoke suddenly filled the night sky, quickly spreading its oily stench over everything.

Finn dropped the RPG and took out his silenced pistols, crouching at the corner and watching both the yard and the village at the same time.

Salya and her rescued group all flinched when the oil-tanks had gone up.

She turned to the others. 'Don't be afraid, that is my friend,' she said, 'he is fighting for us.'

She hesitated. Fighting for us?

She turned to the nurse called Kurshid, a sudden change in her expression. 'There has been a change of plan; you lead the others out to the place I told you about. Wait for us there.'

The nurse reached out as Salya began turning away. 'What are you doing, child? This is not for you, fighting men like men.' She looked at Salya with pity in her eyes.

Salya merely patted her hand. 'Yes, but this fight is for freedom; all should be given their chance to fight it.'

The older woman merely stared; such hardened wisdom coming from someone so young.

She released Salya's arm and nodded her head. 'I should have known really.' She said. 'You came back after all, why wouldn't you fight?'

She continued smiling sadly. 'Please be as safe as can be and don't take unnecessary risks, hm?' She stroked Salya's cheek like her own mother used to do.

Salya nodded and then turned away, leaving the others to clamber down into the sewer-pipe and escape on their own. She could feel the nurses concerned eyes on her back.

The guard who had been dispatched by O'Keel still sat at his station, now relieved of his sidearm which the fifteen year-old Parisa, had tucked in her waistband.

Salya ignored him as she stepped past, focusing instead on opening the door and taking a look outside.

She had just spotted Finn crouched at the end of the rampart when the first grenade-trap went off inside the barracks.

Jimi and Nim stood holding each other looking out at the compound as the oil tanks blazed somewhere over to their right, away from the buildings and out of their sight.

They could clearly see the man who Jimi had been sent to wait for and deal with crouching low on the rampart, a pistol in each hand.

A grenade went off somewhere in the buildings attached to the compound warehouse, and at the same time Nim sucked in her breath and pointed. 'She came back.'

Jimi looked to where Nim's finger pointed, a young girl stood in the doorway of the shower building. 'You know her?'

Nim shook her head. 'Not really, she was only here for a few hours before she escaped.' She looked seriously into Jimi's eyes. 'We must help her.'

'What? Why?' Jimi sounded startled.

He turned to face Nim. 'You said you didn't know her for more than a few hours.'

Nim looked as embarrassed as she used to as a slave for a second then composed herself. 'She's the reason I have these.' She said, not too harshly, stroking her scarred cheeks. 'Myself and Kurshid, the other nurse, we saw how she had escaped and didn't say anything for hours.'

She stepped closer to Jimi and took his hands. 'We hoped she would come back and she has, and she has brought help. We must help her.'

Jimi stood and looked back at the girl, he understood why Nim wanted to help her; she was here rescuing everybody after she had already escaped, when she could have easily just found her way home and forgot all about her adventure.

Little did he know about the death of her brother and the drive it inspired in her heart.

Before he could say anything they both heard the booted, running steps of men on the landing and coming from downstairs; Jimi's own men.

The boots stampeded down the stairs and through the front doors of the expansive villa as fourteen, armed men ran to the compound's aid.

Another grenade went off, coming from the barracks again, and then a few seconds later another, somewhere further inside the warehouse this time.

Smoke and flames began to fill the yard with orange and gray swatches.

Jimi turned back to Nim and sighed. 'I don't know if I can help her, Nim, but I will try. Stay here and stay ready.'

He held her and looked at her seriously. 'Promise me.'

Nim just looked back and remained silent.

Jimi smiled; she wouldn't make a promise that she might have to break if she thought he was in serious danger. 'I knew it was right to love you.' He said, and kissed her.

Nazari's drink left his hand and clattered to the floor when the tanks had exploded.

He'd hurriedly rolled out of his bed and dressed himself, ignoring the young girl sitting up terrified, huddled with the sheets pulled up to her chin.

He dashed to the window and looked through the blinds. 'Fuck!' He yelled.

He ran as fast as his fat, little heart would allow from his private rooms into his office.

The outside door burst open moments later and Hack came striding in.

'Chief?' He said.

Just then the unmistakable blast of a grenade went off.

'That came from the barracks!' Nazari almost choked. 'Take those two outside and go and see what the fuck is happening.' Nazari ordered.

Hack turned away and barked an order down the corridor, aiming it into the room where his own, two men were housed. They came running out and waited for him to speak.

'You two take the stairs, meet me at the front of the warehouse. I'm going out through the roof and down the wall.'

The men nodded and ran for the stairwell while Hack sprinted off down to the other end of the corridor, past Nazari's office and through an unmarked door. It opened into a storeroom with a steel door at the back leading out onto the rampart itself.

No sooner had he put his hand on the handle, the sound of another grenade blast made him look up, and before he had turned the lock and pulled the door open, another closer, much closer, blast rattled through the soles of his feet and into his ankles.

He stopped at the door and turned around, scowling.

Grenades going off and no shooting? Traps! Could only be traps. And traps were usually set by the few to tackle the many.

He went back the way he had come and ran down the stairs.

His men were laid next to each other, thrown ten yards away from the doorway, their bodies and faces shredded by being so close to the blast and receiving more than ninety percent of the fragments.

The other ten percent had left the door in tatters but still hanging.

The scowl on the big man's face deepened and he flexed his muscles, brutish and evil, pulling out his ugly, long blade and stalking to the warehouse front.

He was halfway across the floor when the fourth of Finn's traps went off.

Hack just scowled even deeper still, if that was possible, and carried on marching to the open doors.

Through them he could see the Russians running from the villa, crossing the open ground and heading straight for the gate-arch.

Of the twenty-five men that Nazari had at his command, four of them were now dead and another two were seriously injured and dying at the hands of Finn's traps. But the remaining fourteen were making their exits from other doorways now, gingerly checking every corner, nook and cranny for more hidden grenades.

O'Keel, from his place in the shadows, watched the door open where he had come from. There was only one person who could be there.

'Salya?' He hissed.

Before she could answer, four men came running from a doorway further down the shower block, a door which O'Keel couldn't see.

He raised his pistols and fired.

One of the men screeched and keeled over, the others fanned away, sporadically returning fire in the general direction of the back of the compound, unsure where the shots had come from.

O'Keel fired again at the man who was trying to run to the door where Salya was standing, the bullet grazed his arm and he flinched but it didn't stop his running.

The pistol which Finn had given Salya suddenly went off as she pulled the trigger.

The man heading for the door took the bullet straight in the middle of his chest. His legs took a single, faltering step and then he fell face-first to the ground.

The remaining two men immediately turned their automatic weapons in the direction of the gunshot and opened fire, letting loose a deadly volley of metal.

Salya ducked and made herself as small as she could. She quickly let go of the door and whipped herself back inside.

The door thudded as the bullets passed through it and then the wall behind cracked as they came to a stop there.

Finn, from his hiding place, watched on in fearful horror as three things happened at once then.

While the two men who had just shot at the door where Salya had stood ran headlong toward the back of the compound, crossing away from the shower-block and making for the warehouse, a big mean-looking man walked out of the warehouse front and stalked toward the main-gate, stopping in his tracks to look at the second horrifying thing which happened.

Salya pushed the door back open and peered out again, catching a glimpse of the running backs of the men who had fired at her.

She pulled the door open fully and slipped out, running away to the right and into the shadows, only then noticing the large man watching her.

She could see O'Keel on her right looking at her, shrugging his shoulders at her; *what are you doing?*

And if that wasn't enough, fourteen armed Russians came running in through the gate, nine of the group heading toward Hack and the warehouse, while the other five ran off to the right and made for the shower-block and the guard-house which Finn and the others hadn't known about.

Finn's mind let loose a flurry of drugs in that instant as his adrenaline levels rocketed beyond any normal endurance.

His eyes flickered rapidly as he took in the information he was being fed. All motion slowed to a snail-pace as his eye scoped and assessed each individual target.

He raised himself slowly in his time, casually as his body filled and swelled with the three which had become one.

He could feel the muscles in his back and neck, arms and legs swell and tighten, a throbbing drumbeat forced his veins open, driving fire and harmonious violence through his body.

His eyes flashed as the storm was unleashed and Finn became the Seven-Spears he was meant to be.

He ran three steps along the rampart and then veered off to the edge, springing over the low wall, pistols suddenly hissing as he fired into the backs of two of the Russians.

They stumbled forward, their body-armour protecting them from the bullets but not from the elbows of a plummeting Finn.

He slammed them both in the back of the head, driving their faces into the ground, either killing them or fatally wounding them.

The rest of the men turned and raised their own weapons, but they were moving almost four-times slower than Finn in his own time now.

He dipped and darted, pirouetted and sloped, and wherever his dance took him a man fell at his feet.

The soldiers couldn't keep track of him as he zipped about, far too quickly for any normal man; dropping to his knees and raising one pistol while levelling his other in the opposite direction, firing up into the chin of one soldier whilst simultaneously firing into the throat of another.

Then a leap and spin, his arms flinging out briefly to fire again, two more men drop with bullets in their foreheads, then turn and fire behind and in front at the same time, two more men drop.

Finally, the last of this group of nine soldiers managed to get a shot off. The burst being aimed at Finn's head and chest.

With a simple flick of his head, Finn dodged the bullet meant for his brain and by dropping his shoulder as he turned, the remaining bullets flashed across his chest, bouncing harmlessly off his specialist combat-shirt.

Allowing his momentum to carry him down to the ground where he rolled quickly over onto his shoulder, Finn lunged upward with his pistol as he came to his knees again, ramming the barrel into the windpipe of the soldier and pulling the trigger.

The startled soldier dropped to the ground, his eyes round and unseeing.

The five soldiers who had run off to the right had looked back when the gun of the last soldier had fired. They wore a unanimous look of awe and wonder as they saw the big man stand up amongst the bodies.

Their looks of disbelief at seeing their comrades dead without getting any more than those four shots off soon turned to horrified respect.

Finn smiled at them and holstered his pistols.

His smile was the grin of a wolf, his eyes, lightning-blue and wide pupils sitting on a blood-red background, were the eyes of a demon, and his vivid scars the last brushstroke of this glimpse into a world where darkness and death reigned supreme.

And then their looks changed again, from horrified respect to respectful fear, as Finn drew his blades and began to laugh.

They smirked and glanced at one another uneasily; was he fucking crazy or what?

And that was all the pause which Finn of the Seven-Spears had needed.

Once again he pushed his weight and enormous presence out in front of himself, suddenly blurring into motion as his body constantly strived to catch it up.

The men were twenty feet away, relaxed with their guns lowered. By the time they had reacted and began to raise their weapons, Finn was less than six foot away, moving so quickly that they could hear the snap of the air as his first blade slashed out.

O'Keel watched, mesmerised as his brother brought his singularly unique brand of justice to the soldiers spilling into the courtyard.

He had almost wept when he had seen Finn flying through the air to land amongst the nine soldiers, spinning, dropping, leaping around until all that was left were nine bodies and Finn standing amongst them.

As Finn took off again, pelting toward the remaining five soldiers, Salya blurred past his vision, running toward the warehouse.

O'Keel rolled around the corner, watching the sprinting girl's back as she ran.

What spirit! What guts! What a family to be a part of!

His own grin rose just as the last, six men under Nazari's command came hurtling out of the door Salya was heading for.

O'Keel leaped to his feet and levelled his pistols as he ran toward the men. He saw Salya do the same and they both opened fire at the same time.

Two men dropped to the ground.

Salya and O'Keel fired again. Another one dropped.

Salya was almost on top of the remaining three soldiers now, who all had their eye on her and were raising their own weapons readying themselves to mow her down.

She saw the first three men drop to the ground clutching at their respective bullet-wounds and moaning and wailing.

She could feel O'Keel coming up behind her.

Homing in on the other three men she focused entirely on their eyes, waiting for the moment when she could see they were about to pull their triggers and fire at her.

The three sub-machine guns barked into life at exactly the same time Salya dropped to the ground and rolled over and over, staying well under the line of fire.

She heard the double hiss of O'Keel's pistols go off behind her and when she rolled back up onto her knees, two of men were falling backward, blood spraying from their chests and necks while their trigger fingers squeezed out a final roar from their weapons, sending the bullets uselessly up into the air.

The last man standing in front of her seemed to be looking at three places all at once, a look of complete disbelief and confusion on his panic-stricken face.

Finally he settled on Salya again and turned his weapon to face her, but he had been too slow on the pickup and Salya's own gun fired first, the bullet ripping through his shoulder. She fired again as his gun arm sagged and hit him in the chest this time.

He fell to the ground screaming and groaning and then thrashed noiselessly for a moment as he died.

Salya ignored him, no room for pity or guilt, there was only her goal; Nazari.

She leaped over the fallen bodies and ran straight into the warehouse, running to the blackened door at the back.

O'Keel watched her go and made to run in after he, but a large shadow moved in from the side and he felt a massive, iron-grip hand grab him by the scruff of the neck, lift him from the ground and then hurl him headfirst into the wall.

O'Keel felt the wind knocked from his body as the unyielding, concrete wall halted his motion.

He slid to the ground and came face to face with the large boots of Hack.

Nazari's guard stood over the smaller O'Keel, looming and menacing, the large blade in his hand polished and sharpened to a murderous edge.

The blood he could taste in his mouth infuriated O'Keel; how dare you? I am a god!

He lashed out with his boot and caught the unsuspecting Hack across the ankles, sweeping the big man's legs out from underneath him.

Hack reacted and twisted as he fell, breaking his fall with one, massive arm.

O'Keel snatched at the opportunity and rolled away from the big man, coming to his feet and pulling his own blade free.

Hack grunted as he pushed himself up, first onto one knee and then up onto his feet.

He faced O'Keel now, looking at the little man as though he were nothing more than an insect, a bug, an annoyance which needed to be squashed.

From the corner of his eye, O'Keel could see Finn attacking the five Russian soldiers in the yard. One of them had already gone down and the others were desperately trying to defend themselves against his whirlwind onslaught.

O'Keel grinned just as Finn had done and then moved in toward the staring Hack.

He whirled as Finn was whirling, sending his slashing blade to cut across Hack's thighs, first one way and then quickly spinning madly back in the opposite direction and slashing at the big man's stomach.

Hack parried with his own, large knife and the steel rang out as it clashed, but O'Keel had found his mark more than once and Hack grimaced in pain as his chest was slashed for the second time.

But most of the damage was superficial and he could see that the smaller man was in some kind of madness, not paying attention to the results of his actions as the other man was.

Hack waited, biding his time and suffering slash after slash until eventually he saw his opening and thrust his blade-arm out.

O'Keel, dizzy with the power and the spin, suddenly gasped as he came to a thudding halt straight into the long blade of Hack's knife.

He pulled back, the blade sliding free of his chest. 'Oh.' He muttered, and scoffed.

He looked up at Hack. 'There must be some kind of mistake.' He said, and chuckled. 'You don't understand, you see? I'm a god.'

He looked at the blood on his hands, his eyes still disbelieving even as his knees buckled and his legs crumpled, dropping him to the ground. 'I'm a go-.' He gurgled and fell forward onto his face.

Hack stared for a second more and then turned his attention back to the warehouse; the girl had run in there, the girl who had escaped.

He stalked back the way he had come, ignoring the grunting and fighting still going on around Finn. He would kill the girl first and then deal with him.

## Chapter Thirty-Five

Nine guards had fallen just like that, a flowing form descending on them from the night-black sky and bringing them low under its deathly shadow.

Jimi had watched in silenced awe as the man he had been sent to stop, dropped to the ground and dispatched nine of his own men in almost complete silence.

He realised now why they had needed more men to tackle him, thinking that his bosses had made the mistake of not sending enough!

All around the man there seemed to be an invisible cloak of darkness blurring him and concealing him almost, like a smoke which he billowed as he moved, making it difficult for anyone to train on him.

How could he move like that? How could *anyone* move like that?

Jimi waited until Finn had turned his attention on to the remainder of his men and then slipped unseen into the guard hut. There was a door at the side which led into the main complex.

Through the barracks he would have to go, but it was the only way he could see that would get him into the commander's office, the place he knew the girl had run to, without having to cross the courtyard and the attention of Hack and Finn.

He opened the door and walked into a cloakroom, another door lay at the back. He walked straight through into the sleeping quarters.

The lights were on but the dormitory was empty, all of the beds had their covers thrown back and a few of the doors to the lockers were standing wide open; the mess left behind in the frenzied-wake of the men as they rushed out to take up their posts.

He sprinted to the other door which exited into the canteen.

The doors were blasted and blackened and a dead soldier lay over to the right, flung against the tables as the booby-trapped handle exploded.

Further in lay another two men, flung to either side of the blackened patches on the ground.

Jimi slowed his pace now, checking the way for more traps, but it became evident when he reached the armoury and found the door open, that the men had triggered the last of Finn's grenades.

It was ironic that they then fled straight into the waiting bullets of Salya and her accomplice.

As Jimi crossed the warehouse he thought about the man he had seen covering the girl's sprint toward the doors with his pistols; he recognised him, he thought, but if he did know the man from somewhere, it was from a long time ago.

The stairs to the commander's suite and offices were empty. Jimi leaped up them two at a time and stopped at the top, turning slowly around the corner and listening. He could hear voices.

'You fucking little cunt!' Nazari was shouting. 'I'll rip your fucking eyes out!' He screeched.

The sounds of tumbling furniture and scrabbling feet sent Jimi flying down the corridor and bursting into Nazari's office.

The little commander stood behind his desk, sweating and trembling, a bloody patch spreading across his shoulder where the fucking bitch had stabbed him.

Salya stood at the other side of the desk, breathing heavily but not out of breath.

The knife she had used on Nazari was red from its tip to two inches down the blade.

He had been lucky; she had slipped on a pile of paper which had been knocked to the ground, sending her thrust to his heart wide and into his shoulder.

The three of them stood for stupidly-long seconds, flicking their gazes between each other.

'Well don't just fucking stand there!' Nazari eventually screeched. 'Kill the fucking bitch!' He pointed, snarling venomously at Salya.

Jimi blinked and stepped into the room.

Salya turned her knife toward him and readied herself, the look on her face told him she wouldn't go down without taking something of his with her at least.

He held his hands up, showing her the pistol and his finger which was clearly away from the trigger.

'What are you doing?' Nazari said incredulously. 'Fucking shoot her!'

'Shut up!' Jimi barked, casting his own, poisonous look at Nazari.

He looked back to Salya. 'I'm not going to hurt you, I'm a friend.' He said.

'I don't know you.' Was all Salya replied.

'I know, but the woman I love, the woman I am here to take away-.'

'That slut!?' Nazari scoffed nastily. 'You're not taking any of my staff away from here, she's mine!'

Jimi lowered his gun and aimed it Nazari. 'Then you are going to have to die and I can't say that I'm sorry to have to do it because I'm not; I'm glad.'

Nazari's eyes widened in frightened shock as he watched Jimi's finger tighten on the trigger.

But before he could get a shot off, Salya raised her arm and pointed urgebtly to something behind him.

Hack came careering into the room, bringing his knife down onto Jimi's gun-arm.

The steel bit deeply into his flesh and muscle, coming to a halt as it nicked his bone, while Jimi dropped his arm to lessen the blow which could easily have taken his arm off if it hadn't been for the girl's warning.

The big guard pulled the blade free as the gun fell from Jimi's hand, swinging it viciously at his face and throat.

Jimi ducked and rolled, coming up behind the flailing Hack's huge arm.

He brought his fist straight up into his bearded chin and smiled inside satisfactorily as he heard teeth crack and break.

Hack cried out and staggered back a foot, spitting out blood and bits of broken enamel. He wiped his mouth and glared at Jimi through watery eyes. 'I'll fucking kill you for that.' He growled.

Jimi scoffed. 'Oh. And you weren't trying to kill me already?' He asked sarcastically. 'You are an idiot, my friend, and you are going to die an idiot.'

Hack snarled and rushed forward in his rage, his bulk usually being enough to snuff out anyone's attempts to fight him. But not this time.

Jimi was much faster than he looked and he dodged and boxed his way around the big, stumbling Hack, landing punch after punch on the big, hairy idiot's face.

While Jimi and Hack were fighting, Salya turned her attention back onto Nazari, her eyes narrowing and her lips pursing.

She pointed at him with her long knife. 'You killed my brother.' She spat, taking a step forward.

'And I'll kill you too, you stupid, little cunt!' Nazari spat back.

All Nazari's small, bigoted and spiteful mind could see before him was a girl, a stupid, disobedient animal which needed to be taught a lesson.

They feared us did women, feared all men, we are superior and they all know it, it's in their very blood to be commanded by us.

He leaped around his desk, a serious look of *you're in trouble now* on his face, blindly and obtusely expecting his authority to be immediately obeyed.

Salya didn't even flinch, not even to ready herself to stab at the fat man.

Nazari's resolve suddenly fainted to a halt, bringing his feet to a standstill when he saw the look in the bitch's eye. 'Drop that fucking knife girl! I swear to God, I will take it from you and ram it so far up your arse that-.'

Salya lunged and slashed, a backhand cut across the fat, little man's face.

Nazari screamed, blood gushed down his slashed nose and cheek. 'You fucking bitch! You're just a bitch! A bitch! A bit-.'

And then her rage followed up the slash with a killer lunge from below, sending the knife up behind Nazari's ribs and into his corruption-soaked, evil heart.

She raised herself, the blade still deeply embedded, throbbing slightly with each beat of the dying fat-man's ending life.

'Yo- Fuc- bi- ch!' His words were full of blood and vomit and his continued, stubborn disbelief.

After a few seconds his eyes gradually darkened as the blade throbbed less and less until it finally stopped altogether; *killed by a fucking girl!*

'That was for my brother,' Salya whispered, her face close to Nazari's, staring into his dying eyes. 'He was called Rafiq.'

She pulled her knife free and let the body slip to the ground, spitting at it before turning around and facing the fight still going on in front of her.

The two fighters were both bloodied, but Hack more so than Jimi, who had been dancing around him and avoiding him, landing his blows like a professional boxer. He was getting tired now though, and the bigger man's ability to take more punishment was becoming apparent.

Hack had fought small, fast men before. Admittedly this one was from a better trained and more able clique, the bruises and cuts on his face were a testament to that, but he could see that he was tiring now, it was only a matter of time before he had him and crushed his skull.

And then the sudden sting of the wasp behind him made him groan as her knife stabbed twice in quick succession into his thigh.

He flicked an enormous open hand at her and sent her spinning across the room with a loud slap.

Salya crashed into the wall-cabinet, smashing through the wood and the glass alike, hitting her head hard on the back and then sliding to the floor in a boneless heap.

After a glance at his dead boss, Hack turned back to Jimi, pulling Salya's knife from his thigh and throwing it to one side.

He advanced on the Russian again, a growling, dark shadow.

Jimi sighed; it was Brazil all over again, he thought, the scar on his face tingled.

As hack drew closer, Jimi spun around and landed a roundhouse kick on his knife-hand, causing the blade to fly from his grip and go clattering through the doorway, coming to a standstill on the boards outside.

He followed his kick with a punch to the big man's head, landing it square on his temple.

Hack grunted and then swung wildly out with his big fist.

Jimi ducked and landed a pile-driver blow to the man's kidneys, raising himself and leaning back as Hack grunted again and grabbed for him, missing.

Now on his back foot, Jimi rolled out a flurry of blows to Hack's exposed face, opening up cuts on his nose-bridge and left eyebrow, ending with a slamming hook to the jaw.

Hack's hands flailed in front of himself as he tried in vain to bat the attacking fists away. Each blow that landed made him open his eyes in astonishment, stars popping in front of them.

Jimi stepped around him and back into the open space, his back to the door.

Hack just shook his head, blood and sweat and not more than a few tears sprayed off in all directions

He narrowed his eyes and raised his arms up in a boxer's guard, advancing once more.

Jimi continued to dodge and weave, throwing punches, but Hack didn't let more than a few of them through now, managing to block the worst of them with his guarding arms.

Jimi felt himself weakening, he had to end this soon, but it was impossible to bring the man down, he was like an ox.

The big man lunged at him again and this time caught Jimi a glancing blow across his face.

Hack smiled slyly as Jimi shook his head and rubbed his jaw.

He rushed in then, moving far more quickly than his size - not to mention his current condition - indicated he could, and grabbed Jimi around the torso, trapping his arms and then squeezing hard.

Jimi groaned as his breathing came to a sudden halt, his bones creaking and cracking beneath his skin. The pressure was immense and relentless.

He looked down into the straining features of Hack and then butted him hard on the nose. And then again and again until Hack had no choice but to open his arms and pick him up over his head.

He roared as he threw Jimi across the room, straight over the top of Nazari's big, wooden desk.

He slammed into the cabinet which doubled as the door to Nazari's secret room of cameras and monitors.

Just like the cabinet which Salya had crashed through, this one also disintegrated as Jimi smashed through the glass and wood.

He fell to the floor, crashing through the wooden desk-chair as he did so, and landed on his stomach, gasping for breath and wincing at his complaining body.

Definitely Brazil all over again.

He watched beneath the desk as Hack's big boots stomped toward him, coming around the side.

He closed his eyes tightly and grimaced, readying himself to be picked up and thrown again; they always threw you around for a while, the big ones, something which always reminded Jimi of gorillas for some reason.

He kept his eyes closed until he had sailed back over the table, landing heavily on the floor next to Salya. And there, bless her little heart, there was her pistol peeping out from beneath her ruffled shirt.

As Hack came back and grabbed Jimi by the scruff of the neck and the seat of his pants, Jimi's hand curled around the grip of the pistol just as he was lifted from the ground a second time, ready for another throwing.

Hack stood up and coiled his arms, ready to throw Jimi through the door, after which he intended to then throw him down the corridor and finally the stairs.

Funnily, Jimi sensed that, that was the case. Typical.

'STOP!' Jimi shouted, dangling above the ground. 'Just wait a minute.'

Hack paused, frowning. 'Well?' He said, gruffly, waiting to hear what the stupid Russian was about to say. Not that it mattered anyway, he was going to throw him down the stairs regardless.

'Nothing, sorry,' Jimi replied casually, 'I couldn't find the safety that's all.' He finished, and shot Hack first in the feet and then twice in the stomach.

Hack's hands opened automatically and then clutched at his flame-filled guts.

Jimi fell back to the boards as the big Iraqi crumpled backward, landing heavily on his behind and groaning and moaning as he rocked to and fro like a big baby.

Jimi sat up and levelled the pistol at Hack's face. 'You hurt my Nim.' He said coldly, and pulled the trigger.

The bullet hit Hack square in the nose, tearing through it, leaving a nasty, gaping mess.

The big Afghani's eyes rolled up into his head, a strange noise coming from his throat like a long-sounding *oh!*

The noise continued as his body began to vibrate spastically, gradually slowing down to a horrible pulsing twitch as it finally gave up trying to receive messages from its mangled brain.

Jimi leaned over and prodded him in the chest, causing him to fall backward onto the floor. 'You shouldn't hurt my Nim.'

The bloodied Russian shook himself off and groggily got to his feet, his bones ached.

He was tired of having his bones ache and looked forward to when he could just ache because he had been working hard or playing hard or loving hard instead of fighting hard and being thrown around even harder.

The girl still wasn't moving. Jimi crossed to her and turned her over.

There was blood in her eyes and running down her cheek from a nasty cut on her forehead just below the hairline, but she was breathing steadily and her heartbeat was strong.

He stooped to pick her up.

In the compound yard, while Jimi had been fighting Hack, Finn had been dealing with the last, four Russians.

They were definitely having a hard time of it, but were managing to defend themselves adequately enough to keep the major attacks at bay.

But every time they had managed to get a shot or two off, the bastard had somehow just not been in the place where they had fired at him, magically almost materialising in a swirl or roll a few feet away from them.

*Stop showing off and finish them.* The she-wolf said.

He could still feel her prideful smile though, as he danced around with his blades.

He stopped his movements and stood up straight, facing the men, no more than six feet between them and himself.

They were startled into a pause by his sudden stop, but only for a second. They quickly raised their weapons in unison and pulled the triggers exactly as Finn knew they would do.

He had only waited for the moment when they would have their focus suddenly snapped back into action, causing them to overdo their next moves a little which they did.

All of the bullets went too high while Finn dived forward underneath them in a low arc, releasing his daggers at the same time with a flick of his wrists.

The man at the furthest left clutched at his face as the dagger penetrated his skull through his eye, while the one furthest right choked and gasped as Finn's dagger ripped through his mouth and into the back of his head.

As the two soldiers flopped down, Finn's dive ended as his hands dropped to the ground like a puma, or some other big cat, and he propelled himself head over heels, bringing both of his boots up to crack the two men standing in the middle, square in the chest with the back of his feet. They took off with a chorused *oof*.

Finn broke his back-fall with his splayed hands and arms, flicking himself back up onto his feet before either of the soldiers had even landed on the ground.

From where he was standing a few feet away, he then sprang into the air, launching himself over the top of the two men with his arcing arms curved out to his sides and legs tucked up beneath him, bringing his weight and momentum over the top of the arc of his jump and then dropping down with both knees planted firmly in the chest of one of the men.

The soldier squealed as the impact broke his ribs and punctured his lungs and mercifully he was unconscious by the time Finn had stood back up.

The last guard raised his pistol from his position on the ground, but still wasn't fast enough as Finn closed in with a single, snapping chop to the bridge of his nose.

He froze as all of his muscles went into rigid spasm and then relaxed and flopped back as they all closed down again.

Finn looked around for the next opponent but was met by a yard full of the dead. His eyes settled on the still form of O'Keel lying at the back.

He loped over to him and crouched down at his side, rolling him over. His eyes were open, a look of astonished realisation on his features.

*I am glad he is dead, even if he did aid us.* The she-wolf looked down her nose at the dead psychopath.

*Me too.* The man also said, agreeing again.

*There was something wrong in his mind.* She continued. *His meat smelled wrong.*

*You know that sounds absolutely revolting don't you?* The man asked.

*Why? His meat* did *smell revolting, it smells much better now that it is dead.*

Finn could feel the man frowning for a moment, thinking, then saying; *Does my meat smell revolting?*

*No, my love, your meat smells delicious.* And she purred throatily.

The man laughed, he actually laughed. *Do I take that as a compliment?*

Finn stayed crouched by the side of O'Keel, completely motionless, lost in this strange conversation which only he could perceive.

They were actually getting on really well. He could understand the need for working in harmony and being civil, but just now they were joking like old friends.

He forced himself away, leaving them to do whatever it was they were doing and stood up. He had to find Salya and leave.

The big soldier who had been fighting with O'Keel had also gone and the only place he would have bothered to go to would be up to his commander's offices.

Finn sprinted all the way through the warehouse and leaped up the stairs, the fear of what he would find laying painfully in his heart.

He rounded the corner to the office and was confronted by a man stooping over Salya's prone body, reaching down for her.

He ran at the man and grabbed him by the collar, yanking him backward and then throwing him through the doorway.

Jimi crossed the corridor several feet from the ground, sailing over the tiled space and whacking into the soft plasterboard of the stud-wall at the far side. It cracked with a dull, resounding thud and left a stylised, Jimi-shaped dent in it.

He groaned loudly. 'Always with the damned throwing.' He muttered, as he pushed himself up from the boards to sit with his back to the wall.

He held his palm out. 'I submit, you can have her, I don't want to clean her wounds and help her to wake up, for God's sake.' He said, gesturing to Salya. '*You* can fucking do it, but if you are going to kill me, then can we do it quickly and without any unnecessary throwing me around and bashing me into things?'

Jimi smiled through his bloodied and bruised face, shrugging and dipping into his pocket to produce a packet of cigarettes.

Finn stood poised, but he saw this man wasn't like the others, it could well be he had been helping Salya. But it could also well be that he had been about to kill her and was just a good actor. 'I don't trust you.' He said, flatly.

'Wise.' Jimi winked. 'I don't trust me either.' He replied, lighting his smoke and then offering the pack to Finn.

Finn just frowned.

Jimi shrugged. 'I don't blame you, I don't know why I started again in the first place; gave up for eight years.' Jimi said, taking a long drag.

'When did you start again?' Finn asked, not really knowing why.

Jimi held the cigarette up for him to see. 'Just now.' He replied.

Finn couldn't help himself and grinned and then laughed.

Running footsteps coming up the stairs made him quickly duck back into the room and wait hidden round the corner.

The footsteps reached the top and took a few paces down the corridor before stopping.

A woman gasped. 'Oh! God! Jimi! What happened?' Nim said.

Finn stepped back out casually and just looked at her.

'The madman.' Nim breathed, unable to contain her thoughts or the look of fear on her face.

It was Jimi's turn to laugh then, slapping his thigh.

Finn turned his look Jimi's way, scowling. 'Why did she call me a madman?'

'Well, aren't you?' Nim asked, and took a step closer.

'No!' Finn replied, indignantly. 'I am Finn of the Seven-Spears and Nine Northern Stars.' He said, proudly.

Jimi laughed again. 'It's not every day that one gets to hear a *sane* man say words like that is it?'

Finn just stiffened his bottom lip and shrugged haughtily.

Nim crouched down by Jimi's side and cradled his face in her hands, checking his wounds. 'Oh. My poor darling.' She said, and then slapped him. 'You promised you wouldn't get hurt!' She fired angrily.

Jimi rubbed his cheek and looked at her like a lost child. 'Well you can blame him for that.' He said, pointing accusingly at Finn.

Nim turned her head and looked at him.

'Don't look at me! He was pretty messed up before I threw him out of the room, I've hardly touched the man!'

But Nim ignored them both and seemed to be staring through Finn.

She suddenly jumped up and ran into the office, mumbling something about stupid men and how much she would like to slap *all* their silly faces.

She stopped by the side of Salya, dropping down and feeling the girls face. She picked up her hand and kissed it and then kissed her again on the forehead. 'Thank God you're alive.' She said, holding her in her arms and cradling her.

Finn stooped down by her side. 'You know Salya?'

Nim shook her head. 'No, and I didn't even know her name until now, but...' She trailed off and looked down at the unconscious girl. 'She came back, she came back with help, with you.' She continued, looking back up at Finn. 'I will always love her for that, I will always be in her debt for that.'

Finn nodded and placed his hand on Nim's shoulder. 'Then we both owe the same debt to the same person.' He replied.

The pair of them started when they heard the whimpering of a child coming from Nazari's bedroom.

Finn jumped up and rushed to the bedside and pulled back the covers. The young girl who had been forgotten in the fight lay huddled with a pillow.

'Do not be afraid child.' Finn said, leaning down and picking her up.

She was trembling with terror.

'Do not be afraid.' He said again. 'You are safe now.' He squeezed her reassuringly and stroked her hair as he carried her back out to Nim.

She rushed forward and took the weeping child from Finn's arms.

'You are safe now, my poor child.' Nim repeated Finn's words. 'We are all safe.'

\* \* \*

The five of them left the office and went back into the warehouse, Finn carrying Salya in his arms.

Nim led them to the small office at the back, there were medical supplies inside.

While Nim attended to Salya and the girl, Finn and Jimi raided the armoury for all the explosives they could find.

Finn was adamant that the whole complex needed to be razed to the ground and wiped from the map for good.

They spread the explosives equally in all of the buildings and then Finn brought the fuel truck in and doused the village as he drove past, circling the buildings and vehicles and spraying them with petrol until the tanker was empty.

Jimi found one of Nazari's soldiers who fit his build and swapped watches with him.

He carried the man to the barracks which were soaked in petrol and laid him down on the sodden floor.

Back at the small office, Salya was sitting up on the edge of the examining bed, a swathe of white bandaging around her head. The young girl sat by her side holding her hand.

Finn strode up to her and embraced her tightly. 'It's good to see you awake.' He said.

Salya looked up at him. 'Aren't you angry with me for disobeying you?' She asked tearfully.

'No, Salya, I am not angry at all; I didn't expect anything less from someone like you.'

He smiled at her and then his smile turned to a chuckle before he kissed her on the forehead.

They left the office and warehouse, Finn and Jimi now carrying an RPG-7 each on their backs and a carry-case with two extra rockets in their hands.

The five of them marched away into the night, heading for the hill and the rest of the escapees.

The site where they were all huddled was silent and unlit, but Finn and Jimi, through the tinted low-light view of their NV goggles, could see one of the young girls standing apart from the main group, a little higher up and crouched down. She held a pistol in her hands and seemed to be the one protecting them.

Finn halted the group. 'Call ahead to them Salya, tell them we are coming in and they are to switch on their torches.'

Salya stood forward and did as she was told, waiting until the first torch came on and then switching on her own.

One by one, everyone who was holding a torch switched it on.

The nurse called Kurshid, with her baby Delara, came rushing forward to meet them, embracing Salya first and kissing her face. 'You beautiful, brave girl.' She said and hugged her tightly.

She raised her head and saw Nim standing there. She held her arm out to the woman, weeping and laughing at the same time. 'Nim? Oh Nim! I thought they had killed you.' She cried.

Nim ran forward and joined her in her embrace. 'I missed you Kurshid, dear, I couldn't get a message to you.' Nim said, her own tears now running down her laughing face.

The group huddled together, Finn, Salya and Jimi standing in front of them. The youngest were yawning and moaning.

'We will have to move away from here,' Finn began, addressing them all, 'and keep walking until the sun rises, then and only then can we stop and rest. But before we do that, there is one, last thing which needs to be done. Gather yourselves and follow me.'

He led the way and walked up the hill overlooking *Paradise Begins*, facing the scorched and smoking compound and watching the oil-tanks burning brightly on the left.

Jimi came and stood by his side, waiting for him to begin.

Finn turned to the women and children. 'Bear witness all you who have been recovered from this evil place, bear witness for those who didn't manage to escape its vile grip.' He said, sadly.

He pulled the RPG from his back and aimed it at the place where the armoury was situated, while Jimi raised his RPG and sighted it on the villa.

Both areas were stacked with explosives and sodden with petrol.

*Solas os cionn an dorchadais*, the she-wolf said, quietly, light over darkness.

*Solas os cionn an dorchadais*, the man repeated solemnly.

'Light over darkness.' Finn said, aloud and pulled his trigger.

Jimi was one second behind him.

Finn's rocket exploded first, a smaller boom of the warhead followed instantly by the massive blast of the stacked up explosives in the armoury.

The entire right-hand section of the warehouse building and the rampart wall it was built into erupted behind a wall of glaring fire and smoke.

The petrol caught fire all along the inside and outside of the perimeter buildings, most of which had more explosives sloshed in petrol thrown around inside.

Jimi's rocket went off next, exploding through the main window in the villa penthouse where he and Nim had been standing earlier and then exploding again as his laid out grenades and C4 went up.

The entire penthouse suite and the roof above it exploded up and outward, searing brightly white and then yellow and then angry orange and red.

The fire quickly spread, following the trail of petrol which Finn had trailed around the whole village.

He dropped his RPG to the ground; they wouldn't be needing another rocket after all.

He felt a hand clasping his and looked around. Salya stood at his side, watching the fires and the explosions as they ripped through both the compound and the village.

He squeezed her hand and she looked up at him. 'I am glad you are here, my dear friend.' He said.

She studied him for a moment, seeing him beneath his scars and formidable size, looking deeply into his shining eyes.

She fell into their warm depths and threw her arms around him, holding him tightly. He was everything good in this world, beneath the evil which had beset his body he was everything which was good.

A bright, full moon hung low behind the burning *Paradise begins*, like the eye of some great, dark god watching as some great works of evil came to its justified, conflagrant end.

The people on the hill watched it burn, each of them remembering their time there, long or short, and each of them wishing private curses upon their tormentors, the ones who had actually used and abused them, cursing them with eternal hell which the compound was now beginning to resemble.

Eventually after the last of the explosives had gone off and every building was aflame, Finn turned away pulling Salya around with him. 'It's time to go home.' He said, and led her back down the hill.

The orange, fire-shady silhouettes of Jimi, Nim and the crowd of young women and children, followed steadily behind.

*Paradise Begins* was no more.

# Three

# Going Home

## Chapter Thirty-Six

Shelby, Sophie and Anna sat around another screen; they were on the plane to Pakistan now, but Anna had set up their monitoring system onboard.

The satellite image displaying the area and buildings which Anna had marked out as the probable site for Finn's attack, took up the entire window. The image now showed those buildings to be burning.

She and the others had spent thirty minutes - *"not a second more!"* Anna had insisted - gathering up the things they would need to take with them before leaving the Deere's cottage, making sure they were gone before the local law-enforcement turned up.

They loaded one of the vans the Russians had been using.

*"You're not taking that!?"* Sophie had said, alarmed as Anna came puffing out of the house carrying her mounted machine-gun called Albert.

*"If my mother and Albert were in there,"* she had replied, indicating the house with her head, *"then my mother would have to wait."* She puffed on past Sophie.

Sophie had scoffed. *"Great! What if I were in the house?"*

Anna had puffed her way back, still holding Albert, and brought her nose right up to Sophie's. *"Then I would make you carry Albert while I carried you."* She said, very seriously.

Sophie had blushed madly and looked down shyly, grinning.

She sat on the plane next to Anna now. 'I still can't believe that we were attacked at the same time that, that kicked off.' She muttered, indicating the smoking buildings.

'I still can't believe we were attacked in the first place! Full-stop!' Shelby replied. 'How could they have found us so quickly?'

'I've been thinking about that.' Anna said.

She dipped her hand into her pocket and produced her phone, dumping it on the table and then nodding at it.

'But I thought you said your phones were secure?' Shelby asked.

'They are and I am going to kick myself for saying this, but I think I made a mistake with *your* phones.' The hacker replied. 'Not the ones I gave you, but your personal phones which I destroyed.'

'A mistake?' Sophie scoffed. 'You?'

Anna shrugged. 'Maybe. I'm not certain, but it could be that the very last place your phones were transmitting to their satellites from was logged and held for awhile.' She shrugged again. 'It's not impossible. But if that is the case then they are more capable than we are giving them credit for.'

'How do you mean?' Shelby asked.

'It is very difficult and time-consuming to search for mobile-phone numbers amongst the thousands and thousands of servers which make up the mobile, communication network.' She said. 'And even when the numbers come to light it is still a daunting task to trace the places they have been.'

She sat back and folded her arms. 'I mean, *I* could do it, I have both the software and the hardware to do things like that.' She sniffed. 'It can only mean that the Russians also have clever hackers and their software working for them.' She sounded quite disgruntled when she said that.

It smarted to think that there was someone out there who could do the things that she could do, the things *Code-8* could do, and was using those skills for the worst, possible reasons. But that was just her ego's silly excuse wasn't it?

Anna admonished herself, she had never felt so embarrassed; she had let her ego get in the way of sense.

Destroying the phones and dumping their parts in the bay they were holing up next to was stupid and arrogant and could easily have led to them all being killed.

She should have given the damn things to *Diago* and *Pacman* when they came with the equipment. They could have driven them to the other side of the world and dumped them if they needed to.

Sophie read Anna's face and understood. 'So you think by dumping them so close we left ourselves wide open? That still doesn't explain how they found us there, I mean at that *exact* location?' She said.

Anna thought about it. 'You're right,' she said, 'but if they had access to your findings at Interpol-,'

Shelby cut her short. 'If they had access to our findings at Interpol then they would have the exact location anyway.' He said, giving her a reassuring look.

'It may or may not be that dumping the phones so close played a part in our being discovered,' he went on, 'but it wasn't a fault Anna, it was an underestimation and God knows we have been found guilty of that ourselves.'

He wagged his finger at her. 'Don't you take on that blame; you saved our lives, *you* Anna, that comes before everything as far as I am concerned. Besides, I now know what you meant when you said you had to look after us.' He finished, patting her hand.

Anna relaxed. 'Well I won't underestimate them again.' She said defiantly.

'Exactly what we said.' Shelby returned.

He sat back and looked at the image again. The red dots which once had littered the screen were now gone; Anna couldn't set up that same network of slave computers again, not until they had arrived at their rooms in Saindak.

*Code-8* had already made the arrangements and would have been and gone by the time they arrived.

He thought of Rachel and the red dots which had been looking for her, that sinister last communication they had seen come up from the Russian in Wales to his masters back in Moscow.

The communication which had been received in Hartlepool, right before they were attacked, had come only a few minutes after that first communication from Wales, they had seen it with their own eyes.

All three of them reached the same conclusion; the Russian in Wales had either found Rachel or had given up.

Unfortunately it was more likely that she had been found and was taken hostage to ensure that the Russians still had a bargaining chip should the execution fail, which it did.

He jumped when he felt a hand placed on his arm, bringing him out of his miserable thoughts.

'They won't harm her, Gray.' It was Sophie. 'As long as they don't know where you are they will have to keep her,' she paused, just a tiny misstep as she caught herself from ending her sentence with *alive*. 'Safe.' She finished.

Anna leaned over then. 'She's right; they won't harm Rachel; they need to contact you first. And before you say you should be there looking for her yourself; no you shouldn't, there is someone already looking for her.' She said, meaning the first of the dots in Wales which they had at first presumed were the bad-guys looking for Rachel.

'You are exactly where you are supposed to be Gray.' She added softly. 'Finn and God knows how many rescued slaves need you to be right where you are.'

Rhetorical wisdom. Shelby hated it because it was right. 'Bloody Finn.' He said, lamely. 'If we get him back after this I'm sending *him* to fucking Wales! *He* can explain to Rachel why she's been running around, hiding from Russians.' He finished, forcing his anxiety back into its corner.

The girls chuckled, Sophie leaned over and hugged him and then kissed his face.

'She'll be alright Gray, she's probably doing that matron thing on them and giving them a right old, hard time.'

\* \* \*

Rachel sneezed, the damp was irritating her nose. She had been relegated to the cellar for trying to escape again.

Well, at least she wasn't tied up; the door to the stairs leading back up was made of iron and secured with bolts, locks, probably chains and padlocks as well thought Rachel, there was no way she was getting out through there unless someone let her out.

She could have kicked herself for being so stupid. Of course he had let her go, he was bloody testing her wasn't he? Seeing if she was going to be a good captive and stay put or not. How dare he not trust her!

The door at the top of the stairs thumped open and feet came clicking sharply down the old, stone steps.

The steel door unlocked and Guryev walked in, a tray of food and drink in his hands. 'Ah. It is good to see you are still here.' He said, sarcastically jovial.

'Funny!' Rachel huffed, rolled over to sit up on the edge of the wooden camp-bed.

Guryev placed the tray down on the little table sitting beneath the single, uncovered light-bulb.

The food smelled delicious and Rachel came eagerly to the table. There were two of everything; two plates, two glasses, two napkins. 'You're joining me down here for dinner?' She said, shaking her head and folding her arms. 'Wouldn't we be better eating upstairs?'

Guryev laughed. 'Yes, it would be much better, but seeing as you are hell-bent on leaving our company.' He shrugged and clicked his tongue as if to say *you know?*

He poured two glasses of wine and gestured for Rachel to sit. 'It's not much fun eating by oneself, somehow the food is only able to be half appreciated, don't you think?' He asked, raising his eyes as he poured.

Rachel sat down. 'You mean like watching an epic movie by yourself; it's great and you enjoy the movie, but afterward there is something missing; there's no one there to talk about it with?'

'Yes! Exactly!' Guryev answered, pleased that she understood. 'Besides; Kazakov only talks about football and John Wayne.' He finished, as he sat down. He took a sip of his wine.

'And what do you talk about?' Rachel asked, sipping her own wine.

Guryev cut at his steak. 'I like art and music, philosophy, psychology.'

He put the meat in his mouth and chewed as he shrugged. 'Anything intelligent really.'

Rachel was actually a little impressed. 'But you have such an evil background.' She said casually, as though the word *evil* should be attached to his organisation. 'Isn't there anything in your philosophical mind which tells you that what you are doing is wrong on so many levels, not just law?'

'Evil? It is interesting that you would say I am evil, I am certain my wife Natasha, would disagree.' He smiled genuinely.

'Ah, but does Natasha know what it is you do for a living? I mean everything?' Rachel sipped at her wine some more, it was a good red for this steak dinner.

'If you mean does she know that people die sometimes, by mine or my men's hands, then yes she does. I am a lieutenant, that is a soldier's rank and she knows that soldiers sometimes have to kill.'

Rachel dropped her knife and fork to her plate noisily and sat back looking at her kidnapper. 'Oh. No. No, no, no, you're not getting away with pulling the soldier card; soldiers don't kidnap people, terrorists kidnap people.' She said, angrily. 'I think your excuse is pathetic and only designed to make you and Natasha feel better.'

Guryev looked stung, which he was.

Rachel dug in further. 'If your boss called now,' she said coldly, 'and told you to kill me, you'd do it. Would you tell Natasha you did it?'

The big Russian wiped his mouth on his napkin and then sat back, just staring at Rachel and frowning.

Eventually he spoke softly. 'Twelve years ago, back in Russia, I was sent to assassinate a man, a private investigator who had opened a door in his case which would have been best left closed.' He said.

He picked up his wine and sipped. 'I found his home, his wife, his daughter. I let myself in and surprised the woman and the girl, tied and gagged them in their living room and waited. And I waited. He didn't show for four days.'

He sipped more wine and carried on. 'During that time I became familiar with the woman and the daughter; the private dick really was a dick it turned out. He frequently beat his wife and beloved girl and was generally a very bad man to live with.

'The day before he came back to his home, my boss had called, worried that the PI was avoiding us purposely, *"give him a message"* I was told, *"send an eye to his offices in the city."*

'"Whose eye?" I asked. *"Your choice,"* they said, *"just see that it is done."'*

He paused while he topped his glass up. Rachel sat silently, listening.

'So, I had been ordered to blind either a ten year-old child or her mother. Business cards was all it was, business cards.'

Rachel still said nothing, but it was plain to see that her captor was not happy about his encounter or the order he had been given, even now, twelve years later. 'So what did you do?'

Guryev nodded his head sideways and shrugged? 'I sent an eye to the man's office.' He said, as though it were obvious.

Rachel almost gagged at the thought; no matter which way you looked at it, imagined it - God! Stop Imagining it - whether he had held the woman down and stabbed her eye out, or held the tiny child's head and scooped one of hers out with his finger, he'd still done it. Rachel did gag a little then.

'Whose?' She asked, swallowing hard.

'I don't know the name,' he replied, looking up at her. He was smiling.

Rachel wanted to hit him for that smile, that dirty, evil smirk which probably had been there when he had pulled whichever poor victim's eye out.

The bastard. The dirty, stinking, ev-

'But he or she was a handsome thing, hanging there in the window of the butchers.' Guryev finished.

Rachel's thoughts snapped to a halt as fast as her mouth snapped closed. 'What? In the butch-.' Her eyes widened. 'You sent a pig's eye!'

Guryev chuckled. 'It made no difference as far as I could see, an eye was an eye, he would never be able to tell it wasn't human unless he knew his pig's eyes.'

Rachel grinned then. She picked up her wine and toasted the man sitting opposite. 'Clever.' She said, and took a sip. 'So what happened when he came home?'

'Oh. I shot him.' Guryev replied casually.

Rachel threw her hand up in exasperation. 'I'm sorry I bloody asked!' She said. 'And the woman and her daughter?'

Guryev laughed then. 'Don't look like that; I had a job to do and I did it.'

'Okay, fine, but what about the woman and child?'

'I let them go.' He said, turning his palms face up and shrugging. 'Honest. I gave them some money and moved them to a new town and they were forgotten.'

He leaned closer. 'I could not have killed them,' he said seriously, 'they had already lived such miserable, fearful lives. They deserved better and I did what I could for them.' He finished, and leaned back in his seat.

Rachel nodded. 'I understand.' She said. 'I think.'

She took up her knife and fork again and carried on eating, trying to hide her shame at thinking the worst of the man.

And then mentally slapped herself; he'd kidnapped her for God's sake! Had her locked up in a cellar! Don't you feel compassion for him, don't you dare.

In her mind though, Rachel was struggling with the concept of evil and how she had applied it; it was clear that her kidnapper wasn't an evil person.

'What would you say evil is then?' She asked, looking up.

Guryev raised his eyebrows, thinking. 'It is a good question,' he replied, 'for anyone to be asked and difficult.'

'Why is it difficult?'

Guryev shrugged again. 'Because good and evil are not black and white and there is no mystical balance which needs to be preserved in order for everything to work; people act according to their environments and situations, sometimes their acts are good and sometimes they are evil, it depends on the perspectives of the recipients of their acts.'

'So you don't believe in a cosmic balance, a *yin* and *yang* so to speak?' Rachel asked.

Guryev scoffed. 'Of course not! Are you telling me that if everything were good and there was no evil or badness that the universe would stop working?' He scoffed again. 'Pah! That is just an excuse for man to commit evil when he deems it necessary.'

Rachel thought about that, she and Graham had, had these sorts of conversations before and had come to similar conclusions, but coming from a different angle. 'I agree; we are not born evil-,'

'Or good.' Guryev put in.

'Or good.' She echoed. 'We are born almost as a blank sheet. That's the main point which tells me that good and evil don't exist initially, they have to be added afterward.'

'Exactly.' Guryev said. 'Good or evil has to be nurtured and there is nothing stopping humanity from nurturing just the good is there?'

Rachel was actually a little impressed.

She sat and talked with her captor for almost two, more hours, mainly philosophy and life, but eventually Guryev cleared the empty plates and glasses away and went back upstairs, leaving Rachel with her thoughts.

She actually did feel a little safer, she thought at least she wouldn't be killed, not by Guryev at any rate, but she did wonder about Graham.

So far they didn't know where he was, but how long would it be before they did and *he* received a pig's eye?

## Chapter Thirty-Seven

*Cascading water still covered the entrance. Rolling, verdant hills and valleys and a blue, cloudless sky invited me to pass through the watery curtain and join the child I can see standing there.*

*She has her head bowed down, looking at something in her hands. I don't feel afraid of looking, I'm not afraid of my she-wolf. I am afraid of something far worse.*

*'Who is she?' I ask.*

*'She is our secret.'*

*I turn to see who has spoken and the man is standing there. It is like looking into a mirror except where there should have been scars criss-crossing his features there was only unblemished skin.*

*His eyes bore into me. 'Take our secret back.' He says.*

Finn sat up with a heavy grunt, his eyes wide and round and his brow covered in sweat.

Salya and Parisa, the fifteen year-old girl Salya had furnished with the pistol back in the compound, sat at the other side of the fire watching him. It was their turn to watch through the night.

Parisa had taken to Salya as Salya had taken to Finn, and while they travelled she was always at her side, just as Salya walked at Finn's side.

The children were all huddled between Nim and Kurshid and Jimi on the ground. No one but Finn stirred.

He pushed himself up and sat with his head bowed, clearing the troubling dream away.

Salya came over to him and crouched down, drying his face with her towel. When she had done she stood up and hugged him, kissing the top of his head and then sat back down next to Parisa without a word.

Parisa then stood up and picked up her water-bottle. She stepped around the fire and then she too crouched down in front of Finn.

The same as Salya, without a word, she unscrewed the cap and handed the bottle to him.

He took it with a grateful look for the girl and then drank deeply. Once he had taken his fill and handed the bottle back, Parisa returned to her seat and the three of them sat and watched the fire in silence for awhile.

It was quiet under the trees on the mountainside, only the occasional call of the abundant nightjar or two broke the slumbering peace.

'You two get your heads down and sleep for a few hours.' Finn said, to the girls. 'I can't sleep now, I may as well keep watch.'

The girls nodded, Parisa was particularly tired.

Salya was used to it and knew to snatch her sleep when she could, but would have stayed up until the following night's camp with no problem.

She curled up by the fire where she sat, Parisa already slumbering by her side.

Finn watched over them as their breathing changed from quick and awake to shallow and asleep.

His gaze settled on Salya. Dear Salya. He loved her, as close as she was his own flesh and blood he loved her.

Her courage was limitless and her silent understanding of things was an inspiration he thought. No wonder the young girl Parisa had taken so keenly to her. She was a fine example for anyone to take after.

*But Salya is taking after you, love, doesn't that reflect kindly on you also?* The she-wolf murmured.

Finn's love for Salya was so great that it hurt him to think she was becoming like him. 'But is that a good thing? That she forfeit her innocence for the hard life of a warrior?'

*I think you are being a little too hard on yourself, my love.* She purred, stroking his temples. *The girl - nor you for that matter - would be on these evil paths if the world had already been turning as it should be. She is merely learning how to cope better because she is strong enough to learn and to cope. Do you see?* She asked.

'I think so.' He replied, closing his eyes and tilting his head back a little.

*Her innocence wasn't lost when she killed the tracker, the first time she had killed, nor was it when she had been raped; her innocence was stolen from her by the very forces she now feels compelled to oppose when they killed her brother.* She said vehemently. *It was they, Finn, who set her on this path, but I say to you; who better than, Finn of the Seven-Spears to learn from? Who better can keep her safe with his knowledge passed on?*

When he heard her talk so passionately like this, Finn's heart swelled with love and pride for her; she was right; it was naught but a shame that Salya had reached this way of life, but as the she-wolf had said; only the strongest of the good could ever make it this far.

'You are right,' Finn said. 'I think I have a father's anxiety.'

'What did you say?'

It was Jimi. He had rolled over and had been watching fascinated as Finn held the conversation with someone in his head.

*The joker has awakened.* The she-wolf said wryly. She still hadn't made her mind up about Jimi yet; his smell seemed to be okay, but there was something cunning and foxy about him which threw her.

Finn merely glanced at the man and then looked back at the fire, shutting his thoughts away in his head.

Jimi sat up and then groaned as his bruises and aching muscles complained while he ambled over to sit by the big man.

Finn could feel the man's inquisitive eyes on him, but resisted the urge to look at him.

Jimi sat and stared at his giant - he hesitated to think friend, but it was close - acquaintance.

His scarring was astonishing, it was a wonder that the man had a face at all. Even more remarkable was the complete lack of stitch marks; whatever he had done to heal himself he had done it without the use of needle and thread.

His hands were the same, criss-crossed with huge scars, knuckles thick and well used. Enormous they were and he had seen how Finn could use them; his strength was immense, so focused.

And he had also seen him being as gentle as a lamb when handling Salya after she was hurt, the way he was with the children who all seemed to love him once they saw that he wasn't what he looked to be.

But Jimi's mind always came back to that picture of him killing his men at the gate. He had felt a strange urge to look away, blanch away would be a better way to say it. He had wanted to cower his eyes from this demon which had just leaped eighteen feet from the roof, silently dropping down to kill two men outright.

And then he had begun to move. Jimi had actually felt a feeling then which he hadn't felt since he had been a child; terror.

The enormous, black figure of Finn had swirled around like a blurry smoke, freezing for half a split-second to kill and then was off again.

From roof to ground, nine men had died in little under four, eternal seconds.

Finn's cheek itched. He sighed and then frowned. 'Do I have something on my face, friend?' He asked.

'Oh yes.' Jimi replied, nodding his head.

Finn turned his frown, now a scowl, to face Jimi. 'And what might that be?'

'Right now?' He paused and looked as though pondering. 'I'd say thunder.' He eventually answered with a grin.

Finn narrowed his eyes at the man. 'If you are itching for a bar-room fight I suggest you take it that way and go and find yourself a pack of wild dogs.' He said, pointing down the slope to the bottom of the hill where Salya's dogs were sleeping.

She was still feeding them and now they had swelled their ranks to nine, big hounds.

Jimi snickered. 'Oh. You're just fucking evil, man. Beneath all that,' he waved his hand to indicate Finn's scars, 'all that other evil you're just a grumpy, old *dedushkah*, no?' He teased.

Jimi had to see if the beast would reveal itself at a mere prod. He didn't care what the others thought of Finn, Jimi had to be certain they weren't suddenly going to become his next victims because someone inadvertently enraged him.

Finn's eyes narrowed further still. 'Why do you prick me so, *man*?' He asked coolly.

Jimi made a face which said he was hurt. 'Me? I'm just playing with you, man.' He gave Finn a friendly slap on his steel shoulder. 'Just playing.' He repeated.

He pointed to Salya on the other side of the fire. Prodding Finn with personal things had done nothing at all to the man, he would widen the scope a little then.

'You're lucky to have her,' he began, 'I bet she *plays* good.' He leered, just a tad. 'I saw what she did to the fat-man; I'd have her on my side any time.' He said, his leer increasing now as he looked at her.

He could feel Finn's anger rising, but the man still only scowled and stared.

'So, did you err,' he paused, shrugged one shoulder and clicked his tongue, 'you know, have a *play* while you were out in the wilds alone?'

Finn bubbled with anger, what was he doing?

Time to play an ace, Jimi thought. 'I know I would,' he said, lying, and reached out as though he were going to pat the sleeping young girl on the rump.

And there it was.

Finn was one second sat by the fire a good three feet away and then the next second he was hoisting Jimi to his feet, silently by the throat.

Jimi stared down into a nightmare of bloodshot lightning-eyes blazing behind a snarling snout above bared teeth. Here was the demon from the courtyard.

He pressed his gun into Finn's temple and just stared at him as his windpipe was clamped closed.

He had been ready for when Finn would strike, even if he *had* been taken completely by surprise when it had actually happened.

Finn lowered him back to the ground and released him, stepping back and sitting down again.

He stared long and hard at Jimi, his brow knitted as he thought about the Russian's stupid, provocative behaviour.

He had no intention of killing him and Finn thought Jimi knew that, so what was he playing at? 'You were testing me, weren't you.' He asked, not angrily.

Jimi lowered his gaze and nodded. 'Apologies. I had to be sure.'

'Sure of what?'

Jimi shrugged. 'Sure that it takes more than a little insult to get you to turn into *terminator-franken-monster*.'

Finn laughed quietly. 'You could have just asked.'

'Oh. I see. You can just get angry and do those things without thinking about it eh?' Jimi asked, scoffing.

Finn flinched a little and a blade suddenly appeared in front of Jimi's boot, sticking up from the ground.

'Yes.' Finn said, and grinned.

Jimi's eyes were round and impressed. 'The world is a crazy place, my friend, and I have seen more than my fair-share of crazy, but you,' he paused while he looked at Finn's still grinning face, 'you are a whole different pot of crazy. How do you do that?' He finished, plucking Finn's blade from the ground and handing it back to him.

Finn shrugged. 'Focus, concentrate.' He simply said. 'Bring all parts of yourself together and join them in one force.'

Jimi sat and thought about it but Finn could see he was having trouble understanding.

'Imagine that there are three of you, but two of you are always asleep. Only sometimes,' Finn pointed to Jimi's scar, 'do we find ourselves in a situation where we are in extreme danger; that scar looks like it has a dangerous tale behind it.' He continued, raising his eyebrow in question.

Jimi nodded, but didn't elaborate.

'Whatever that danger was,' Finn carried on, 'you met it with all three parts of your being and because you are sitting here, talking to me, it shows that you overcame that evil.'

Jimi nodded again, interested.

Finn leaned closer. 'But I would be willing to bet that if you think about what you did to survive you would whistle to yourself and wonder how the hell you managed it. Am I right?'

'Yes, but isn't that something which everyone has said at some point or other in their lives?' Jimi asked.

'Yes, it is, but it should *never* be said; everyone is capable *all of the time* of being whole.' He leaned back again and waited for his words to sink in.

'You're talking about the trinity, aren't you?' Jimi asked.

'Yes,' Finn replied, 'but not the trinity as it is being extolled in the world today.'

He frowned deeply as a wash of anger flashed across his eyes when he said those words.

'So you are not religious then?' Jimi said.

'I am not.'

'I can see I have touched a nerve?'

'You have.'

Jimi poured himself some water and thought. 'Let me guess; you feel let down by your god, disillusioned at the way the world is heading?'

'No, I have never believed in god.'

'I see. Well that is the only known reason to me I can think of. It's a bit clichéd I know.' Jimi said. 'So why does it sting you, my friend?'

Finn looked into the fire. 'The trinity has been dissected and detached, pulled away from each other part, and it has happened because of religion, mysticism, foolish stupidity and pride.'

'So you're saying people should be denied their faith, their right to worship?' Jimi asked, frowning.

Finn looked up exasperated. 'No, man, listen; people are worshipping the thing which is already inside them and doesn't need worshipping, it needs to be understood and then correctly used.' He said.

'Take a child and teach it from its earliest understanding the correct way to see and harmonise with its world and there would be no worshipping of gods, there would be only understanding.' He finished.

Jimi scoffed. 'People would become soft. God help us if we should ever be visited by an alien force or something; we wouldn't be able to fight them, we would be too busy trying to *harmonise* with them.' He laughed.

Another dagger suddenly arrived at Jimi's feet and he visibly jumped.

Finn smirked. 'I said harmony not pacifism. Everyone would be stronger than they are now, the whole planet would be stronger.'

'I don't think I'll ever get used to that.' Jimi said, plucking the dagger from the ground and handing it back again.

'So, is that what happened to you? You were taught from being a child?' He asked then.

Finn looked at him blankly; a child? Finn?

Jimi could see he was having extreme trouble with that. 'You don't have to answer that, my friend,' he said warmly, 'I was just being nosey, I just want to know who you are.'

'I am Finn of the Seven-.'

'Yes, yes, I know all of that - and if I might say; if there is anything which makes you sound like a madman, it is that.' He pointed to Finn with raised eyebrows to emphasise.

He lowered his finger. 'But *who* are you? Where do you come from? That's what I mean.'

Finn just looked and then slowly turned his gaze back to the fire, his frown back in place. 'I am Finn.' He said quietly, because he didn't know what else *to* say.

Jimi didn't push it and sat back, joining Finn in his night vigil of the camp.

When the dawn came Jimi's head snapped up as Finn's boot nudged him awake.

'It is time to rise.' He muttered and then turned away to rouse the others.

Jimi stood up and un-cricked his neck as he watched the big man stooping down and waking Nim and Kurshid.

Salya suddenly appeared at his side, startling him, causing him to flick his head around too quickly and prang the crick in his shoulders and neck painfully.

'Good morning.' He said wincing.

Salya remained silent, also watching Finn's back. She turned to Jimi. 'I heard you talking to him last night.' She said, a stern expression on her young face. 'It would do you well to not torment him anymore.'

Jimi frowned and looked at her. 'Oh. I think he and I understand each other, he won't harm me I'm sure.'

'I wasn't talking about him, I was talking about me.' She said, quietly.

The big Russian, towering over the little girl, looked down at her with a respectful stare. He could see she was deadly serious. 'I will say to you what I said to him, Salya, and apologise. You must understand that I had to know what the limits of his temper were that is all. But I hear you and I respect your wishes.' He smiled and held out his hand. 'Peace.' He said.

Salya looked at the proffered hand and suddenly her resolve dropped in her confusion; she had never had a man - or a woman for that matter - hold out their hand for her to shake. It was so adult.

She took his hand and he gently clasped hers.

'I will just have to tease you instead, I think.' He said cheekily.

Salya couldn't help but suddenly grin like the child she was.

From the background Finn saw the exchange and it made him happy to see her smile like that. She had been so serious for the past few days. He hoped she would always remember how to smile.

Once the camp was awake and had finished with its stretching and urinating, grumbling, yawning and more stretching, the five eldest children went about their morning tasks of bringing in the water and any catches from the snares.

Jimi and Finn had the task of scouting the landscape both ahead and behind, while Nim and Kurshid prepared the youngest children for the day's march ahead.

It was a good system which worked surprisingly well Jimi had thought, Finn had some very extensive and far-out survival skills. He still yearned for the comfort of travelling by vehicle though - they could have had any number of trucks or cars from *Paradise Begins* - but Finn had been adamant that they stay well away from known roads and tracks; they had to stay as deep in the wild as possible.

The big man had argued that it may take much more time, but they would have much more chance of staying out of the reach of any pursuers - which Jimi had insisted would definitely be sent out as soon as it was known what had befallen the compound and its commanders.

So far they had seen no sign of anyone coming up behind, but it made sense that if and when the pursuers set off they would be going along the road networks first anyway, just as Finn presumed.

There was still more than four hundred miles to go and still plenty of time for anyone to catch up with their trail though. Only time would tell.

## Chapter Thirty-Eight

Ten chimes from the church clock-tower. Dilger looked up from her seat in the park at the clock and then down again at her watch, the tower was half-a-minute fast.

She watched the gates to the church as the Sunday congregation moved slowly through, chatting to one another as they left.

The vicar stood on the step talking to a young couple who were beaming as brightly as their crisp, Sunday suits.

Planning a marriage? She thought.

She envied them, their normal, nine-to-five lives, wandering around their mundane paths, completely oblivious to what was happening in the world outside the comfort of their ordinary walls.

The plain, cheese sandwich she held suddenly felt heavy in her hand.

The lives of the couple talking to the vicar were just like her cheese sandwich, she thought; a safe option for getting something nutritional but completely lacking anything which resembled an adventurous spice.

She rolled the sandwich back up in its wrapper and lobbed the lot into the bin at her side.

Her envy turned to pity, who was she kidding? She couldn't live a life without spice.

And then Robinson sat down on the bench next to her and her envy was back in place.

Dilger loved Robinson and she was sure he loved her, but they wouldn't say it, the danger of the job wouldn't allow them to say it, but if she ever did get married then she thought it would be to Robinson.

'I'd have had that.' The Interpol sergeant said, nodding to the binned sandwich. 'Can't turn your nose up to food when you're in the field, never knowing when your next stop and meal might be.' He said, sniffing like a well-worn veteran.

'We're in bloody Wales!' Dilger said.

'Hard battlefield is Wales.' He replied, seriously.

Dilger chortled and nudged him in the ribs. 'Divvy. So what did you find? Are we going back to London or not?'

Robinson handed Dilger a slip of paper.

'I found them, we're staying.' He said and smiled.

He knew just how badly Dilger took mistakes and failures, particularly her own, so it made him happy, especially after all the slipups and mishaps which had followed on their heels, to finally tell her that he had found the woman.

Dilger read the address on the paper. 'Oh! You're a star, Andy, a bloody star!'

She darted a look around to make sure they weren't being observed and then leaned in quickly and kissed Robinson on the mouth. 'Excellent work, you sexy soldier.' She said,

She sat back. 'What's the place like and how many are inside do you know?'

'It's a tall, old house on a fairly busy street. I would guess that there could be as many as six guards inside, but I've only seen two. I saw the woman as well.'

Dilger looked stunned. 'You did? Was she alright?'

'She seemed to be, she was leaning out of a window upstairs, then she threw a sheet-rope out, then she went back inside and a few minutes later the sheet was pulled in and the window closed.'

Dilger frowned and thought. 'She was trying to escape. Good girl. Someone came in and caught her and made her close the window. Well at least we know where she is being kept.'

'They won't have left that window to be opened again, they will have nailed it shut, or even moved her to another part of the house where there are no windows; the houses all have a cellar.' Robinson added.

Dilger nodded and then turned her thoughts to how they would rescue the woman called Langley. 'What do you think, Andy? Can we do it or do we need to call in for backup?'

'I think we can do it.' He said, without even having to think about it. 'Six of us and maybe six of them, we have the element of surprise.' He shrugged his big shoulders. 'We might not be sure on the numbers, but we can be certain that we have the experience.' He finished.

'Okay, good.' Dilger replied. 'I'll get one of the houses acquired opposite our target.'

'There's a few b&b's down that road, we won't have any problem holing up somewhere.'

More good news. Dilger wondered if she was missing something. 'Well, it looks like it's turning around for us. Feels a bit *too-good-to-be-trueish*.'

Robinson just laughed. 'I'm not surprised you're feeling like that after the run-around she's given us. You have to hand it to her though; she did well.'

He made a point of looking at her blackened eyes and swollen nose.

'Oh. *Ha! Ha!*' Dilger said, sarcastically. 'I'm laughing so hard I could shit comedians!'

It still stung that she had been floored by a woman a good inch and half smaller than she was. 'She took me by surprise.' She said in a huff, and folded her arms, frowning at the flowerbeds in front of her.

Robinson nudged her and she looked up into his silly, grinning face, giving him a sullen, icy stare. 'Well, she did!'

'I know, I'm just teasing.' He paused and smiled. 'Just like I promised I would if it ever happened to you.' He said, emphasising the word *you* by pointing at her.

Dilger couldn't help herself then and laughed. 'Oh God! I'd forgotten all about Harrogate, thanks for the reminder.'

Almost three years ago they had been on exercise in a field on the outskirts of Harrogate. Robinson had been fooling around, teasing the goats which belonged to the farmer whose land they were using.

Thinking he was safe standing behind the wire fence, Robinson had been bleating at them and making jokes about their weird, staring eyes and asking them stupid questions like; *where are your dunce caps?*

The finer arts of animal husbandry being completely lost on Robinson, he had no idea that the females which he was teasing were in that enclosure for a very good reason; to keep them away from the ram, or more accurately; to keep the ram away from them.

At exactly the same moment that Dilger shouted *"look out!"*, Dante - the ram so named by Mrs Evans, the farmer's wife - came belting across the grass and butted Robinson in the arse, sending his feet flying out from under him to flip right over his head and then fail to meet the ground again at the other side.

He landed flat on his face in the muck and dry goat-droppings. And if that hadn't been enough, when Robinson had got back to his feet, wobbling groggily around like a drunk on the town, Dante had turned and charged again.

The terrified soldier had spent almost fifteen minutes running around the field, Benny Hill style, with a very pissed off Dante on his heels.

'Bloody Dante.' He said, chuckling. 'I should have shot the little bastard.'

They laughed together.

'As much as I enjoy your company, Sergeant Robinson,' Dilger said, once they had finished laughing. 'I think we should part ways and get on with rescuing our damsel in distress.' She said, and leaned in to kiss him one, last time.

'As you wish, ma'am, special detective Dilger, sir.' He replied, and stood up.

He noticed the church and the last of the people still congregating on the path outside the gates.

'You know?' He said, thoughtfully. 'We really should think about getting ourselves into desk jobs after this.'

Dilger stood up by his side and first looked at the church, then back to Robinson, then back to the church - just to make sure - and finally settled her round eyes back on Robinson.

He turned to face her. 'What? What's wrong with that?'

Dilger continued to stare and blink before saying; 'Are you on about what I think you're on about?'

'Maybe. Why not?' He replied. 'I don't know; I just think we sometimes push our luck with the job we do. I don't mean we take stupid risks, I mean we are always in the line of fire; the odds get better for something bad happening the more we do it.'

He could see she was puzzled, pleased and a little alarmed all at the same time.

He couldn't say he blamed her; they had been together for six years now and hadn't even told one another that they loved each other. God, they had shown it, but the words never came. Maybe it was time for the words to take over.

He took a deep breath. 'I think, um, what I'm trying to say - not very well - is, erm,'

'I love you too.' Dilger said, astonishing herself even more than she astonished Robinson.

He grinned, his breath thoroughly taken away. 'That's it; I love you, is what I'm trying to say.' And they both laughed again.

'You do realise we have just endangered the mission, don't you?' Dilger said.

'No we haven't, if anything we have just strengthened our team.' Robinson replied, winking at her.

She hugged him and laughed. 'How very Celtic of you.'

*　*　*

Less than twenty four hours later and the bbed and breakfast named *Castle View*, had been taken over by Dilger and her five men. The owners, an elderly couple called Mister and Mrs Howe, had been spirited away to a seaside cottage courtesy of the Interpol treasury.

'You can only see the castle if you stand on your tiptoes in the back garden!' It was Devlin, the youngest member of Dilger's team at thirty. Youngest and smallest and the fastest on his feet.

'Well, it's just as well that they're not keeping her in the castle then isn't it?' McKenzie said, cleaning his weapon and not looking up.

McKenzie towered over the younger man, McKenzie being the oldest of the team at forty-two, and compared to Devlin's clean-shaven, boyish good-looks, the veteran looked like a grizzled, old lumberjack, shaggy, dark hair and beard to boot.

'I know, I was just sayin' like, cos the place is called *Castle View*, innit?' Devlin replied.

'It'd sound stupid if it was called *Castle View from the backyard* though, wouldn't it?' McKenzie said, still cleaning and still not looking up.

Devlin stood at the sink, tapping his fingers on the edge in his fidgety way, and looked out of the window into the back garden. 'I don't know,' he said, faraway, 'maybe just call it something else.'

'Like what?' The bigger man enquired.

Devlin thought. 'Maybe something like; *Castle View - Not.*' He said seriously, railing the invisible words in the air with his hand.

McKenzie's laugh boomed throughout the kitchen.

In the living-cum-dining room, Dilger stood at the window and looked at the house across the road.

Robinson was at her side while Simmons was sitting at the monitor which showed the view of the house opposite from the camera they had installed upstairs.

The image on Simmons' monitor flickered and changed to a view of the street from the junction up the road. A few seconds later and the image changed again, now showing a view from the other end of the road.

All exits were covered by camera; unless the Russians could move about invisibly they wouldn't be coming out of the house without them knowing about it.

Dilger nudged Robinson. 'Someone's coming out.' She said, and nodded through the widow.

The door to the house they were watching opened and a tall, young man walked down the steps, turning right to walk down the street.

'He's a new face.' Robinson said. 'That's definitely three then.'

'He looks a bit young to be messed up in this sort of thing doesn't he?' Dilger remarked.

'Hm. He was probably born into it,' Robinson said. 'Don't let his youth deceive you though; they wouldn't have sent someone to do something like this if he wasn't capable.'

'Oh. I know, I know,' she answered, 'it just feels like the face of the job is getting younger by the mission.'

Robinson chuckled then. 'I never thought I'd hear you say something like that. You're not getting old on us now are you, boss?'

From behind them they heard Simmons laugh. 'The boss doesn't get old, mate, she gets even.' He said, swivelling himself around on his chair to face them.

He pointed casually out of the window. 'Our lad's just gone into the shop on the corner; breath mints and Clearasil I bet.' He said.

'Damn shame we are on standby.' Robinson sighed. 'We could have had a go while they were a man down.'

The whole team felt that - the frustration of idleness - but there was a good reason to wait, even if Dilger didn't know what the reason was exactly, she knew enough to wait for her orders before they went in.

'I know,' she said, empathising, 'but orders are orders and we can't endanger the field-agent who is involved in all of this somehow. If they attempt to move her though?' She looked at both men and shrugged, leaving her thoughts unsaid but the message clear.

'I hate being right at the centre of a mission and not knowing what the *actual* mission is. Are you sure you don't know anyone named Langley?'

Robinson asked.

'Doesn't ring any bells. Besides,' Dilger answered, 'they would fit her up with an assumed name when she went on the run.'

'It smacks of something international.' Simmons put in. 'The secrecy is usually to stop ourselves being embarrassed in front of the neighbours.' He said, tapping his nose.

'You're probably right.' Dilger answered. 'All the more reason to do it right then.' She replied, meaning the rescue.

Just then they heard the front door open and close. Melford walked through the dining room carrying bags of shopping.

'Boss.' He said, nodding at Dilger. 'Lads.' He then said to Robinson and Simmons. 'Tuna-pasta bake for dinner followed by chocolate-dripped sponge-cake and custard.'

'Nice one, Melly.' Simmons said, and stood up to give Melford a hand with the bags.

Melford was the team's cook and medic when they were in the field, and commanded a quiet respect from the others; if Melly said sleep, you slept, if Melly said eat, you ate. Didn't matter what your rank was, you listened to Melford and did as you were told, a fact that Dilger had learned first-hand.

*You will rest for eight fucking hours before taking command of this squad again, or so help me God, I will shoot you in the leg and send you home!*

She would never forget those words or attempt to blindside her medic ever again.

'I think I saw one of them in the shop.' Melford said to Dilger.

'Young, tall?'

'Yea, that's him. He was talking in Russian on his mobile while he wandered around the aisles.'

'Did you manage to catch what he was saying?' She asked.

'Something about no brown bread only white, and then something about showing his ID for buying booze.' He paused. 'My Russian's not brilliant,' he said shrugging, 'but I'm sure he didn't mention the woman.'

'Sounds like they're settling in just fine.' Robinson said, dryly.

'Well, if they're digging in it can only mean they are waiting for the same thing we are; orders.' Dilger said.

'He's on his way back.' Melford pointed to the monitor.

'Did he manage to get any booze?' Simmons asked, leaning down to have a look.

The young man on the screen was carrying two loaves of bread and nothing else.

'Looks like he was asked for his ID then.' Dilger said, and chuckled.

Melford and Simmons carried the shopping through into the kitchen, still chatting about the unsuccessful booze-buy.

Dilger and Robinson moved back to the window and watched as the young Russian walked past and entered the house.

A sudden, dark silence grew between them; they were both thinking the same thing about the young man; there was a very good chance he was going to die.

Although the couple were professional to the letter, Dilger still reached her hand out and brushed Robinson's fingers with hers; she needed the warm contact right then.

'What's the point, Andy?' She said, quietly, keeping her eyes on the closing door across the street. 'What's the point to that young man's life?' She asked, turning to look at Robinson then. 'To come here and die? To get this far in his life and then simply be snuffed out and wiped away?' She shook her head in frustration. 'Fucking stupid.'

'Life can be pretty fucking stupid sometimes, but the point of life? Our lives?' Robinson cocked his head. 'I think it is to make sure when you cross paths with another life or lives,' he pointed to the house across the street, 'that it is you who walks away unscathed.'

He stole a quick glance through the doorway leading down the short passage to the kitchen and then dipped his head and stole a kiss from Dilger once he saw it was clear. 'I'll tell you this, Caroline; if it came to a bullet for him or a bullet for you, he would win that prize anytime and it would be no blame on him.' He said, and stood back again. 'But I hear you; I don't like it anymore than you do and I'm certain those lads in there,' he continued, pointing down the passageway, 'know and feel exactly the same thing.'

'I know, still stinks though, especially for someone as young as him.' Dilger replied.

They turned back to the window and looked out at the world through the netted-curtains, standing side-by-side in silence again.

It was a pretty day and the sun was smiling down like everything was going to be just fine.

## Chapter Thirty-nine

The big leader of the dogs, quickly becoming known as *"Salya's pack"* by the rest of the group, stood and sniffed the air; food was coming. His pack was now twelve strong; the *growlers* they were following were leaving plenty for them to eat.

As nomadic as the wild dogs of the mountains were, this was the furthest south they had ever strayed in their constant quest to find food. They were content to stay well out of sight and just keep following from a distance.

He nodded his big head and snuffled; the food was here. He waited until he heard the footsteps of the *growler* who left the food turn away and then moved in to breakfast, the pack rushing up behind once they saw him begin to eat.

Salya stood by the small trickle of water coming from the rocks and washed her sticky hands.

She had grown quite fond of feeding the dogs and in a strange sort of way, ever since she had set them on the tracker, she had thought of them as her silent guardians, her unseen watchers.

Parisa stepped up to her side and silently held out a plate of food for her.

Parisa; her other silent guardian.

Salya didn't really know what to make of Parisa or the affectionate fealty the older girl seemed to hold for her.

She liked Parisa, but felt a bit strange to be waited on by someone older than she was. She had tried to tell her that it wasn't necessary, she could look after herself, but Parisa had only nodded and then carried on anyway.

Salya took the plate. 'Thank you.' She said. 'Come, wash your hands and we'll sit and share breakfast.'

Parisa's mouth curled up at the corners just a little and then she began to wash her hands.

She had rarely spoken or smiled, sometimes she had gone a whole week without uttering more than a sentence or two. Over the few days she had been with Salya and the group, however, she had smiled at least once a day and even though she wasn't exactly chatty, she did speak more.

Nim and Kurshid had known the young girl since she had been brought in, so it made them both happy to see that the eleven years of slavery in which she had been raised was being driven away so quickly.

They were also secretly pleased that she had attached herself to Salya, whom they loved as their own sister; what better strength was there to guide a young mind back onto a happier path?

In Parisa's mind, Salya was everything to her which Finn was to Salya; she had seen her strength back in the compound, watched her bravery show itself in her eyes. She wanted to be like that; to be brave and to be able to help the weak.

She had no family of her own, all lost during a bombing raid on her village. She had been four when that had happened and it had been nothing short of a miracle that she had been found alive under the rubble.

Unfortunately for her, she had been found by one of the roundup teams for Nazari's *Paradise Begins* and had been taken there, where she had been deemed good enough to be reared for the use of the paying clientele which visited.

The girls sat by the trickle of water and ate.

'Who is Finn?' Parisa suddenly asked.

Salya cast a look in the direction of the main camp, Finn and Jimi weren't back from their scouting trips yet.

She turned back to Parisa. 'He is a warrior.' She said. 'He is a champion of good, he is everything which we should all try to be. He is Finn of the Seven-Spears.'

Parisa remained silent, the answer wasn't the one she was expecting or looking for and she only understood a little of it. 'But who is he,' she then said, 'where does he come from?'

Salya didn't know what to say because she herself had been asking the very same questions only to find that Finn didn't seem to know either.

'I don't know, Parisa,' she eventually replied, sighing and glancing back at the main camp. He still hadn't returned. 'Maybe he has been sent from heaven, who knows?' She continued, and turned back to face the young girl. 'But I do know this; he is much bigger on the inside than the outside, there is a whole universe inside him, a universe of truth and light.' She finished.

It was the best she could do to translate her own understanding of Finn.

Parisa frowned as she digested Salya's words, they made a slim connection to her own thoughts on Finn; seemingly a giant monster on the outside, but once taken and held by his lightning gaze, she had found that there had been an endless well of gentleness and understanding in his eyes.

Salya watched as Parisa frowned into empty space and though about Finn, and then she checked the watch he had given her again; he was now fifteen minutes late in returning.

She suddenly stood up, startling Parisa and allowing her food to fall to the ground from her lap. She stared off into the east, her eyes blazing.

Parisa jumped up and followed her gaze. 'What is it?'

Salya, suddenly sprang into action. 'Quickly!' She said, and darted off back to the camp.

The others stopped their eating and stood up when they saw Salya hurtling towards them.

'Gather up the children and get into the cave! GO!' The young girl shouted to them.

Nim and Kurshid didn't need to be told twice; they didn't know what the urgency was but they trusted Salya.

'Come! Up, up! We have to hide for a while.' They were saying. 'Don't be frightened, everything is going to be okay, but we have to get into the cave now.'

As the children stood themselves up, all fearfully looking at Nim and Kurshid, the two women heard the distinct *Whup! Whup! Whup!* Of the helicopter's blades which Salya had heard first, coming from somewhere far away to the east.

Salya smothered the small cooking-fire and then called for Parisa. 'Go with them,' she said, indicating the retreating backs of the women and children. 'Stay at the entrance and shoot anyone you don't know who tries to get in.'

Parisa looked terrified.

Salya placed a hand on her shoulder just the way Finn had done to her, locking the frightened eyes of the girl with her own. 'If we stay calm and do everything right,' she squeezed Parisa's shoulder, 'then nothing will go wrong.'

The girl nodded, her eyes still round and frightened, but Salya could see that she would master it.

'Go and look after the others, I'll be back soon.'

Parisa turned away and trotted up the slope, catching up with the group as they were entering the small cave in the mountainside.

Salya turned the other way and headed toward the helicopter still *whupping* in the distance but which was definitely getting closer.

She scrambled down the incline, weaving her way between the boles of the large trees until she came to a place which had a massive boulder pushing its way through the foliage causing the trees to shy away from its edge.

She climbed up to the top and lay down on her stomach and watched the skies to the east.

After a few seconds of squinting and searching, her eyes fell on the dark silhouette of the chopper still some miles away.

There was no reason to believe that the helicopter had anything remotely to do with Salya, Finn, or the escaped slaves, but as she watched it growing larger and louder, Salya knew, she just knew that it had come from *Paradise Begins*.

Finn had said that it would be more than likely that any search parties would begin looking along the roads and tracks first. From where she lay it looked to Salya as if that was exactly what they were doing.

The chopper seemed to be moving side-to-side in the air, sweeping from left to right and then back again, all the while making its way slowly west and toward the escapees.

Salya's eyes hardened; damn them.

There was nothing she could do now except return back to camp and let the others know what she had seen.

Well, at least she knew now why Finn was late returning; he would have been down the slope and watching the helicopter long before anyone else had heard it.

As she stepped into the area where the campfire had been, Finn appeared from the trees over to her right.

He smiled at her. 'You saw then?' He asked, meaning the helicopter.

Salya nodded. 'Everyone is in the cave.'

They walked together to the entrance, Parisa and Jimi stepped out from the shadows at either side, both holding their pistols.

'Was that who I think it was?' Jimi asked Finn.

Finn nodded. 'A scout, they're sweeping the roads.'

Jimi grit his teeth and clenched his jaw. 'Damn. They'll be relaying orders to a ground team somewhere behind them.'

Finn just looked at him.

'What?' Jimi asked.

'They have set up a small outpost in the forest on these slopes not more than ten miles ahead. We cannot go around them either way.'

Jimi shook his head. 'God damn it.' He muttered. 'Did you see how many?'

'At least eight men.' Finn answered casually. 'There is another cave about five miles away, we need to get to there and then I can go and deal with the outpost.'

Jimi scoffed. 'Just like that, eh?' He clicked his fingers and sucked his teeth. 'Eight men dead.'

He thought he would never get to grips with the way Finn had dealt with his own men back at the compound.

He turned away, muttering to himself about crazy people and supermen as he walked inside the cave to bring the others back out.

Finn turned to the girls. 'It is going to be difficult from here on out.' He said. 'Once I have taken care of the outpost they will know we have travelled through there.'

He didn't have to say it, they both knew what he was getting at; once their pursuers discovered that the outpost had been taken out they would use the helicopter to drop men off further ahead who could lie in wait for them in the mountains.

A sly smile crossed Finn's eyes as he saw the looks on their faces they both noted; he knew something they didn't.

Whatever it was, he didn't have time to say before the children appeared, walking in a huddle with Nim and Kurshid at their sides while Jimi took up the rear.

They all had the same blank look of quiet fear on their upturned faces as they stood at the entrance, looking up at Finn.

He peered down at them and smiled warmly through his scars and fearsome presence. 'The bad men have come, they need me to teach them a lesson.' He said, to them all as though he were simply addressing a class of children on an outing.

A young boy of six spoke. 'Will the bad men come here?' He asked, his words breathless and afraid.

'No.' Finn replied and stooped down to meet the child's eyes. 'The bad men will not be able to get past me.'

The boy reached out his small hand and touched Finn's, giant's face, looking at his scars.

'Bad men can't get past you.' He said, and smiled. 'Bad men can't get past him.' He said, again for the others, and then laughed.

The laughter rippled along the ranks of children and even reached the smiles of the adults as they stood around this giant, scarred warrior with eyes of lightning-blue.

'The bad men can't get past you.' The children chorused.

Finn raised himself back up and looked down at them all, grinning happily back at them. That was better, much better, a child's face *always* looked better when it was smiling.

He allowed them their moment of happiness and the feeling of sure safety which they took from being close to him, but they had to get moving.

He held his hands out and hushed them. 'We have to go now, so can we all do our little bit and pick up our camp?'

They quietened down and nodded.

'And can we do it as quiet as a mouse would do it?'

They nodded again.

'Good. Off you go then, Samantha.' He finished, moving to one side to allow them to march silently past.

Salya and Parisa followed the children so they could supervise the quick clearing away of the camp, but both girls were glancing back at Finn and frowning. Salya looked worried.

Nim, Kurshid and Jimi stayed at the cave entrance just watching Finn with very strange looks on their faces.

'What?' He asked.

What had he done now to deserve whatever that look was? He noticed Salya was hanging back a little too, watching him.

He turned back to the others. 'What's wrong?' He asked, puzzled.

Nim put her hand on his arm, he looked down at it, his puzzlement only rising.

'You called the children, *Samantha*?' Nim said, gently. 'Who is she?'

He raised his eyes again. 'Samantha?' And frowned deeply. 'She's my-!'

*N-O-O-O-OO!*

The she-wolf screamed in his mind, filling it with silver-hot fury and blinding his eyes with agonising molten-white light.

Finn's body went suddenly rigid, his eyes rolled back under their lids and he trembled as though a thousand volts were being passed through him.

Nim had hold of him first as he crumpled to the ground, cushioning his fall and making sure he didn't hit his head.

Kurshid and Jimi were by her side in a second and all three of them looked down at him.

'What the hell was that!?' Jimi blurted out. 'Did you see his fucking eyes?'

Nim elbowed him.

'Sorry,' he said, sheepishly, rubbing his side, 'but how did his eyes do that?

They had all seen it, Finn's eyes had suddenly gone from his normal steely-blue to a sudden amber and red, blood-flecked and feral.

'I don't know,' Nim replied, 'but I have heard of things, things to do with the mind, while I was a nurse. Sometimes a mind can be broken into different parts without breaking the body. The parts all hide something which the whole doesn't want to know, but function normally as individuals.'

'You mean like a *schizo*?' Jimi said.

'That's a misnomer, Jimi, schizophrenia doesn't really mean multiple-personalities.' Nim said. 'No, I think Finn is the product of a broken mind and it has something to do with a girl called Samantha. And this,' she pointed at Finn, 'I think is the product of another part of that broken mind.'

Salya coughed, she had been watching them, standing quietly in the shadows. They turned to look at her.

'He dreams of her, Samantha, he calls out sometimes. I think she was his daughter.' She said. 'He has also called out to someone called Kate, or maybe Kaylin.'

'Who are they, do you know?' Nim asked.

Salya shook her head. 'And neither does Finn.'

'You've asked him?' It was Jimi this time.

'Yes. He doesn't know.'

'And does *this* happen when you ask him?' He carried on, and pointed at the prone Finn.

'Once,' she replied, nodding, 'while he was singing under a waterfall. He said *Kate* and then did that.' She said, and pointed at Finn herself now. 'He'll wake up in an hour or two and won't remember anything.'

She looked at them all then, individually, hard and serious. 'You will not tell him.' She said, firmly.

The three of them nodded slowly.

'If *this* is what happens then we can't tell him, can we?' Jimi said. 'We'll be caught before we can get another twenty miles if we have to keep stopping.'

He caught Salya's look. 'Don't worry,' he said to her, 'I'm not suggesting we should leave him; apart from liking the fellow I don't think any of us have a chance of taking on our pursuers without him.'

He stood up and ran his fingers through his hair, sighing heavily. 'I think we should carry on and do as he said; get to the other cave. You should stay here with him.' He said, looking at Salya. 'By the time we reach the cave, he should be awake, it wouldn't take you both very long to catch up.'

Salya agreed.

'What will you tell him?' Kurshid said.

'I will tell him he has been sleeping.' She answered, and shrugged.

'Sounds a bit weak, will he believe that?' Jimi asked, not convinced.

'Yes. It's strange, but after this happens to him he sort of just carries on like the whole thing is just a blank, but he doesn't know there is a gap.' She shook her head, that wasn't right. 'It's hard to explain.'

'It is the other parts at work.' Nim said. 'They are protecting him from something, something bad which has happened to him a long time ago.'

She looked down at Finn, his eyes were rolling under the lids as he walked the planes of whatever dreams he had been dragged to.

Nim crouched back down by his side and placed her hand on his cold, pale brow and said a silent prayer for his tortured spirit: *You are not alone, Finn, or whoever you are. You are not alone.*

\* \* \*

*"Ho! Listen and hear me, I've a story to tell,*
*Tra-la-la-la-laa, tra-la-la-la-laa, it's long is my tale."*

The she-wolf danced as she sang. Tall, two-legged, her silver mane flowed around her like heavy swaths of shimmering silk dragged through still water.

*"Now, sit down beside me, your head 'pon my lap,*
*Laa-la-la-la-laa, laa-la-la-la-laa, oh, sweet is my harp."*

*"So now I will tell you of my lover called Dermot,*
*Fearless and brave and the bearer of the love spot,*
*Fair of face and large of heart, he stole my kiss,*
*Tra-la-la-la-laa, laa-la-la-la-laa, and now my heart!"*

Round and round she swept, swaying to some silent music which only she could hear.

She stopped and looked down, still singing, still swaying, watching the twitching, red body of Finn at her feet.

He tried to smile through his smashed teeth and lips, tried to say he loved her, but the only sound which came was a pitiful mewling.

She continued to dance and sing, radiantly happy, her clear feminine form shimmering under her silver fur.

*"A hundred young maidens, Dermot had loved,*
*But none had ever held him, and none ever would.*

*And until he met me, his love was free,
Then a kiss by the lakeside and he went down on one knee!"*

She sang and Finn smiled as her beautiful voice washed over him, soothing his ripped flesh, knitting his sinews together with her music.

On and on until he was healed.

## Chapter Forty

What the hell was happening!?

Keys paced the small space of his custom-built panic-room, glancing every now and then at the small, black and white image on the door-side monitor.

His bodyguard was going to kill him! What the hell had happened?

Keys had been standing at the top of the stairs, heading down, when he heard George talking to someone on his mobile. He'd stopped in his tracks when he heard George say "*dead?*" as though he were repeating the word just spoken to him.

Keys had listened right up to the point where George had said; "*Yes, sir. I'll deal with Keys immediately*", before dashing off to his study and pushing the panic-room button.

So that's how you say you are going to kill someone; you say you are going to *deal* with them. But who had been *dealt* with and had died already? Graham? Oh! God! But why would they want to now kill him?

The screen flickered with movement as the bodyguard called George came into the study, still talking on his phone.

He paced around the room, looking for something, a hidey-hole Keys thought.

'*He's not here, I have no idea where he went.*' George's tinny voice said.

He paused as the voice on the other end replied. '*Well if he did, he didn't come in through the front door.*' He said, and paused again.

'*Yes sir, I understand, but I'm almost certain that no one, including Shelby, has been to the house for the past two days.*'

Graham wasn't dead! Whoever George was talking to they thought Graham may have been to the house Keys thought, and whisked him away before anyone could get to him. I wish you had, Gray, God knows I wish you had.

George carried on with his search for a few more minutes and then left the study, closing the door behind him.

Keys sighed and slumped down in the chair at the small table, what the hell was he going to do now?

The button which held the lifeline out into the world beyond the safety of his panic-room, glared annoyingly at him; big, red and unlit.

He couldn't push it and let the agency know that he needed help; George came from the very same agency.

'Well, that's a stupid f'king oversight.' He muttered to himself, meaning how the panic-room system was so tight that it allowed that singularly, glaringly-obvious loophole of the agency itself being the bad-guys.

There was enough food and water for a single person to live on for a month - six-weeks if you really stretched the resources out.

*Whatever it is that you are doing Graham, hurry up will you, old man? I'm not excited by the prospect of living in* here *for a bloody month!*

\* \* \*

Cricket and machine-guns. Somehow the two just didn't seem to go together, but here he was, standing outside the Saindak cricket pavilion, while two, armed guards held the doors open for him.

Cricket and machine-guns. Shelby had been dryly amused at the simple weirdness of it.

After landing at the airport in Turbat, just south of Saindak, and passing unhindered through customs, a small, white van had taken Shelby, Sophie and Anna the three miles down the airfield where a helicopter sat waiting with its rotor's idling.

Both Shelby and Sophie had been extremely impressed with the planning and execution of it all.

"*You know? In all my years in the job - and I've had a few,*' Shelby had said, as they trundled along in the van. "*I've never done anything so bloody outrageous and with such perfect planning - without me I mean.*"

"What do you mean, "without you"? We wouldn't be here if it wasn't for you." Anna had remarked. "I may have made it happen physically, but it was you who set us on the path; I am merely a tool."

Sophie and Shelby had both snickered.

Anna had looked between them both, trying to understand what they were being so childish about.

Sophie draped her arm over Anna's shoulder like she was comforting her and had looked into her eyes with something akin to resignation. "*You* are *a tool, Anna.*" She had said, nodding solemnly.

It wasn't much cooler inside the pavilion, the overhead fans swirled around slowly and the only breeze they seemed to be making was a warm one.

Shelby mopped his brow. 'Whoever heard of a town without a hotel?'

There were one or two guest-houses in the small mining-town, but nothing big enough to cater for all three of them *and* the equipment they were carrying.

An almost identical setup of computers to the one back at the Deere's house, was already up and running at the back of the large room.

Sophie stood by the big monitor, but instead of looking up at it she tapped the console with her foot which lay beneath.

'Is Albert in there?' She asked, turning to Anna.

The small German nodded to another console sitting beside her own computer. 'He's in that one.' She said.

'Oh. Yes. Silly me; this one has all the *other* illegal weaponry in it doesn't it?' Sophie said, dryly.

Anna just shrugged and returned her attention back to unpacking her small kit-bag out onto the bunk she had chosen for her bed.

'So, we're miners now are we?' Shelby said.

'Seismic surveyors.' Corrected Anna. 'Commissioned by the Chinese.'

'Right, the Chinese. Always a good nation to get on the wrong side of.'

Shelby's sarcasm was unmistakable.

'You worry too much.' Was all she said.

She walked past him and gave him a reassuring pat on the shoulder as she made her way to the opposite side of the long room.

'I'm going for a shower if anyone would care to join me?' She said, without turning around or addressing anyone in particular called Sophie.

Her back disappeared through the door leaving Sophie blushing and Shelby smirking, one eyebrow raised.

'Insufferable bloody woman.' Sophie muttered, dragging her clothes out of her own bag and throwing them down onto her bunk.

She caught Shelby's silly smile. 'You can shut up as well.'

Shelby just chuckled and held his palms up in surrender. 'I wasn't going to say anything, but you know she's only teasing you? She teases me all the time.'

Sophie stopped her unpacking and turned to face him.

'I know,' she said, and then looked around the room, 'but this isn't the time or the place for this sort of conversation, Gray.'

Shelby nodded. 'You really like her too, don't you?'

'Of course I do, the stupid little witch makes me blush doesn't she?'

She sounded exasperated as though it were obvious.

She sighed then. 'Sorry. Look, Gray, she wouldn't be my first girlfriend.' She waited for him to react.

'Okay.' He said, waiting for her to elaborate.

She had obviously expected him to be shocked, but as his partner, Shelby honoured and respected her without judgment and as his friend he loved her, again without judgment.

When he didn't say anything else, she continued. 'It's just that I've had my fill of the attached stigma to words such as *dyke* and *lesbian*, God knows there are some very narrow-minded people in this bloody world and I've met a few of them.'

'Yes, I can understand that.' He replied. 'All I can say is,' he paused and took hold of her by the shoulders, holding her at arm's-length. 'I don't care; you're my partner and friend before anything else, Sophie.'

He released her and his eyes suddenly twinkled. 'Let's have some fun at someone else's expense for a change.' He said, and indicted the showers.

He held his finger to his lips to tell her to be quiet and then tiptoed through the changing rooms and stood outside the door to the shower. 'I think I will take you up on that shower after all, Anna.' He said, loudly.

The noise of plastic shampoo bottles being dropped or kicked or both came to the pairs ears.

'Eh!? What?' Anna shouted through a mouthful of water and suds.

Two days had passed since their arrival at Saindak, it had taken almost a whole day for the Korean satellite which Anna had used to watch the area over Afghanistan, to come back around the earth and be hacked and controlled by Anna's system again.

They had gathered round and watched the still smouldering compound.

'Finn did that.' Shelby had said.

It had felt incredible to be witnessing the actions of the very man he had been chasing for more than seven years, almost live.

For all of that time, there had been a flurry of communications between three, different users in Afghanistan and Moscow. The Afghanistan users seemed to be steadily moving south toward the Pakistan border.

The red dots glared at Shelby as he tried to piece them together into a picture which would give him a clue as to Finn's whereabouts.

All he could come up with though, was they were still moving slowly south, which could only mean Finn also was moving southward.

The closest of the dots to the border still lay two hundred miles to its north, while the other two were around four or five hundred miles further north still. Finn and his rescued children must be somewhere in between.

His heart sank, the territory was just too vast to make any valid guess, all he could do was wait it out a little more and think.

The red dot closest to the border lit up again. It didn't seem to be moving south anymore and had been pinging every hour on the hour since it had stopped.

An outpost most likely, a trap for Finn.

Shelby noted the time; it had come in twelve minutes early. A few minutes later and Moscow pinged up on the map, this time contacting both of the other recipients in Afghanistan at the same time.

Shelby sat forward, something was going on.

The girls were sleeping, it was his turn to watch through the night.

The pitch-black landscape, now only outlined by Anna's graphics, dragged Shelby's gaze into its vast well of the unknown; *what are you up to*?

The first one pinged again, he could almost feel the urgency in it. Something was definitely happening out there.

The chopper was ready and available for them for when they moved over the border to meet Finn, but Shelby had been secretly wondering if they should go in early and meet him well inside Afghanistan.

When he had voiced his ideas Anna hadn't argued, but had warned them that the chopper wasn't equipped with any weaponry.

Sophie had been pretty adamant though; they shouldn't go marching into another country until they were absolutely, one hundred percent certain that they would be at least doing their job and apprehending a known criminal. Anything else would seem like an act of war.

He'd had to agree with that.

The other dots Shelby had been unconsciously willing to reappear, the dots over Wales, had been silent for most of the time. He didn't know what to make of that, good or bad.

There had been two communications yesterday from Wales to London and back again, but the Wales to Moscow line had been constantly silent.

A hand on his shoulder made him start and turn around. It was Sophie.

She wiped her bleary eyes and yawned. 'I heard the pinging.' She said, indicating the monitor. 'Everything okay?'

'Something is really not okay for someone out there.' Shelby said, turning back to face the screen.

He used the silver tube to point at it, circling the dot closest to the border. As he finished, it pinged again.

'That's the third time it's called home in the last ten minutes.'

Sophie took a seat next to Shelby's and picked up the half-mug of cold coffee from the desk. She swigged it down with a grimace, not caring whose cup she had just drunk from.

She smacked her lips and then wiped her mouth and shuddered. 'Right, I'm back on the clock.' She said, and forced her eyes wide.

She studied the map of dots and noted their times. 'Bloody hell! Do you think that's Finn?' She said, pointing at the circled dot.

'I'm almost convinced. I think they set an outpost there while they searched the roadways and whatnot.'

'Poor bastards.' Sophie replied. 'Well, I'm sure we'll know soon enough.'

'What do you mean?'

'If that *is* Finn going about his business, then those communications will stop very soon.'

Shelby just blinked, why hadn't he thought of that?

Sophie saw his face and knew what he was thinking. 'You're tired, it would have come to you once they had stopped.'

She was right. 'More coffee then.' He said and stood up.

'As if you need the excuse.'

She was right about that too; the coffee here was exceptionally good, Shelby had developed a habit of coffee, work, loo and then more coffee.

He stood by the percolator and heaped generous amounts of the brown powder into its filtration chamber when the monitor pinged again. It was from the same place.

'The last communication from a dying man, I bet.' Sophie said.

Shelby returned and placed both of their fresh coffees on the tabletop. 'You think that was the last one?' He asked her.

She nodded.

'Why?'

'Because those communications have a feeling of urgency about them.

The first one was the report that something was amiss or that they had spotted something.

The second was the contact report, the third an update on what was happening to them and finally the fourth, *I'm dying, send help.*'

Shelby was impressed. He was always impressed by Sophie's way of thinking around the box. 'Well, like you said, time will tell.'

He raised his mug to her. 'I hope you're right and if you are, great piece of puzzle-solving.'

It was now a case of simply waiting for at least another hour just to make sure that the communication was really closed down.

The coffee in their mugs slowly disappeared and after almost an hour Shelby stood up, tall and serious, his eyes boring into the last communication from that doomed outpost.

'He's coming.' He said quietly, and nodded slowly. 'He's coming.'

## Chapter Forty-One

'What the fuck are we doing out here, Ehsan? I didn't take this job so I could sit hiding in the fucking dark!' The young soldier almost whispered.

The soldier called Ehsan pulled hard on his cigarette, his pimply, teenage face flaring up in the orange glow. 'Who cares? As long as the sister-fuckers pay me I'd sit in shit all day.'

The leader of this three-man squad, an older man in his thirties, chuckled behind them. 'I've had to do that and *didn't* get paid.' He said.

He swivelled his head around and looked at the two young soldiers crouching below him, glowing eerily green through his night-vision goggles. He knew they couldn't see him properly as they had no goggles of their own.

Leaning down, he plucked the cigarette from between Ehsan's fingers and took a drag.

He handed it back as he blew the smoke out. 'Didn't even have any smokes either.' He said.

He sat back up and looked back out through the trees. It was still quiet, the night animals knew they were there.

He and his two soldiers were highest on the slopes, while below him another two, three-man squads were waiting spread out, just as they were.

Their commander, the sweating Russian, was sat in his tent back on the main road.

His watch told him he would have to call in, in fifteen minutes.

Suddenly Bahram, the soldier who didn't like the dark, stood up, startling the older man.

'Someone's singing!' The young soldier whispered.

The three of them cocked their heads and listened. There it was again, the soft voice of a woman singing somewhere in the forest.

'Stay here and keep your hands on the flares.' The older man said, and stood up.

They listened as he moved away into the dark and then sat back, each clutching their weapons and a flare in their hands.

'Who would be out at this time? And singing!?' Bahram asked, his voice shaky.

Ehsan didn't reply, he just continued to listen to the ghostly voice of the woman. He found it strangely beautiful and frightening at the same time.

'What if it's a ghost?' Bahram continued. 'I've heard stories about the lost souls in the mountains.'

Ehsan still didn't reply, he was still listening, the singing had stopped.

They swivelled their heads around, trying to look at and listen to everything from everywhere at the same time.

'If it's a ghost,' Ehsan then said, 'then Haashim won't be able to fight it.'

He fumbled around with his radio, he didn't give a fuck if they were calling in early or not, something was going on out there.

'Capture-1 to Hill-base. Do you read me?' The radio clicked and Ehsan waited.

*'Hill-base to Capture-1. I read you. Everything alright, you're calling in early?'* The Russian voice on the other radio asked.

'There's something in the woods Hill-base, Haashim has gone to investigate.'

There was a pause and then the radio clicked and the Russian spoke. *'Okay, keep me posted, Capture-1, but I'll tell you now; if it's nothing more than a mountain-dog, you three will be dining on dog-meat for the rest of the month. Hill-base out!'*

Ehsan spat, and threw his radio down. 'Fuck you!'

He reached into his pocket for another cigarette and stopped and flicked his head around to his right, peering and listening. The woman was singing again.

'Oh fuck, Ehsan! What is that?'

Bahram was terrified; flesh-rending ghosts and slaver-jawed demons and restless spirits were running around them, flitting through the trees, reaching out in the dark to touch him.

He rubbed at his neck, batted away the phantom fingers which reached out to tug at his hair.

'Stop acting like a fucking pussy!' Ehsan said, kicking out at Bahram. 'Just listen and be ready with your flares.'

Bahram whimpered. 'It's ghosts, Ehsan, I'm telling you, it's fucking ghosts.'

'Fucking shut up! There's no such thing as ghosts.'

But Ehsan wasn't convinced by his own words, he was more convinced by that mesmeric voice.

It seemed to be moving from left to right and back again, somewhere in the deeper gloom of the shades, the deeply resonant echo of a beautiful, if strangely accented, voice.

And then it went silent again.

The only thing the two young men could hear now was their own deep breaths and the hammering of their hearts in their own ears.

Nothing stirred, nothing moved.

'It's coming.' Bahram whimpered, he sounded like he was crying.

'I told you; there's no such thing as ghosts, for God's sake.'

'Isn't there?' A deep, female voice purred, right next to them.

Ehsan struck his flare as fast as he could blink, darting down to Bahram 's side. He gripped his radio murderously, but before he could shout for help the flare settled.

A black-clad giant sat on the lip of the tiny dell they were hiding in, its misshapen and scarred face drawn into a snarl and its eyes, oh! God, in heaven protect us! Its eyes were wild and aflame.

It held out its long arm and the head of Haashim stared at them unseeing.

The boys began to scream.

\* \* \*

Four miles away, the commander of the outpost stared in wide-eyed horror at his screaming radio.

He sat for a minute after the screaming had stopped, just staring stupidly at the offending piece of metal and plastic before shaking himself into action.

He picked up his mobile phone and made his second report; contact had definitely been made.

He jumped when the radio crackled into life a moment later. *'Capture-2 to Hill-base. Come in?'*

And then again. *'Capture-3 reporting in. Do you copy Hill-base?'*

He grabbed the radio and pushed the button. 'Hill-base to Capture-2 and Capture-3. Report.' He said.

*'Capture-2 to Hill-base. We heard screaming coming from further in the forest, I think it was coming from Capture-1. Over.'*

*'Capture-3 to Hill-base. Same here; we heard screaming, but so far nothing has come through here. Over.'*

The commander sagged in his seat. 'Hill-base to Capture-2 and 3. Capture-1 has been compromised, stay alert and don't separate. I want reports every five minutes. Hill-base out.'

He dropped the radio back onto the fold-away table and reached for his half-empty glass of beer.

God damn it! That shouldn't have happened. With the equipment the men had nothing should be able to sneak up on them let alone attack and kill them.

He sipped at his beer, it had still warmed up quickly even though it was now night-cold outside.

If fucking Ladislav had done his job right this would never have happened.

He raised his glass to a dead comrade. 'Happy hunting, Jimenenko, you handsome bastard.' He said, throwing the last of his beer down his throat.

The radio suddenly clicked twice and then was silent again. It sounded like someone had pressed the talk button without speaking.

A few seconds later and he then heard the distinctive sounds of small-arms fire coming from the forest.

The radio burst into life.

*'Capture-2 to Hill-base. We've been engaged!'* Came the hard voice of the

fighting man at the other end.

The gunfire the commander could hear coming from the forest echoed through the radio as the man spoke.

He snatched the handset up. 'Hill-base to Capture-2. Can you see who it is you are engaging?'

'Negative Hill-base. Something is running through the trees, I've got one man down. Over.'

The gunfire continued, sometimes sporadic and sometimes concentrated.

'I see him, Hill-base. Allah prot-!'

The voice on the other end of the radio was snapped off at almost at the same moment the guns went quiet.

'Hill-base to Capture-2. Come in.'

There was no reply.

'Hill-base to Capture-2. Report please.'

Nothing.

He slumped back in his seat. What the hell was happening?

The radio crackled in his hand, a woman began to sing.

'The moon is my lover, the night is our bower,
Stars watching over us,
Stars watching over us.

'Stay through the night, and hold my heart,
Love washes over us,
Peace lies around us.

'But come the morn, you'll leave at dawn,
Our love will sunder and drag me under,
A blanket of sorrow,
Until tomorrow,'

The voice held the note of the last word perfectly before finishing by saying; 'When you are reborn.'

It paused for just a second before venomously adding; 'But not you.'

The radio clicked once and then went dead, the commander sat motionless; had he just dreamt that? Was there really a woman in the woods singing songs and killing his men?

The radio crackled again. 'Capture-3 to Hill-base. Over.'

The commander sighed and pressed the talk-button. 'Hill-base here. Go ahead.'

'Capture-3 to Hill-base. What the fuck was that!?'

'That was our enemy, Capture-3, that was our enemy.' He replied, resigned. 'Get yourselves together and get back here. Hill-base out.'

During the fifteen years he had been doing this job, he had never felt as alone and out of his depth as he did now. And if being stalked by a singing murderess wasn't enough, the icing on the cake was he now had to report in and make his excuses for losing six, good men.

He sent the message and report and then threw his phone down on the table in disgust. No sooner had it settled the gunfire started up again, much closer this time.

He snatched up his radio again. 'Capture-3. What's happening?'

*'She's fucking behind us!'* The soldier shouted. *'She's still fucking singing!'*

The gunfire continued to rail out, quick bursts as the men retreated down the slope.

*'It's not-! Fuck! Haaqim!'*

The commander listened as the soldier shouted out orders to his two men.

*'Hold this position!'*

Then spoke directly into the radio. *'It's not a woman, Hill-base, it's a big man, I think!'*

What? What does he mean he *thinks* it's a man. It's a fucking woman isn't it? 'What do you mean capture-3?'

*'It's a fucking big man, or at least something on two legs. It moves fast and it doesn't have a gun and it's singing like a woman!'*

Did he know how crazy he sounded? 'Well whatever it is, Capture-3, I want it dead, do you understand?'

*'What do you think we've been trying to do for the past fifteen minutes!?'* Came the angry, frightened reply.

The gunfire lessened but didn't stop.

*'Haaqim's gone! Oh! fuck! He pulled his head off! Fuck! I think he's carrying blades or something!'*

One man with a knife, singing like a woman and killing fully-armed and well-trained men in the dark of night? It was a nightmare straight from the annals of Victorian horror!

'Get back here!' The commander shouted down the radio.

*'We're almost out of the trees! Oh! fuck, it's there!'*

The two remaining machine guns fired simultaneously, burst after burst as the two men attempted to cover each other as they ran for the tree-line. One of the guns suddenly went silent.

*'Oh! fuck! I'm the last man! I can't see him.'*

The commander listened, slack-jawed, as the soldier gasped as he spoke, his frantic footsteps clear to be heard as he crashed through the undergrowth in his panic.

*'Oh! God! Oh! God! I see the road. I'm almost there!'*

The Russian commander stood frozen to the spot, willing his man to put on an extra burst and break through into the clear, open ground.

*'I-I think I've lost it.'* He almost whispered. *'Oh! God help me! I'm out, I can see th-.'* The soldier's words died on his lips.

The tent! He was going to say he could see the tent.

The commander fumbled with his pack, looking for his pistol, cursing and sweating when his fingers couldn't find it, then dragging it out viciously when he did, causing it to snag and then finally he dropped the damn thing once it popped free.

He quickly stooped down and picked it up, holding it out in front of himself in one trembling fist, aiming at the door-zipper.

Silence was everything, everywhere. He hated it, it carried his breath away, his heartbeat, gave him away and marked him out.

His sweating face wobbled as he swung his head around, hearing imaginary noises coming from first the left then the right and now behind.

He jumped and skittered around, aiming the pistol at the blank canvas of the tent as he sturned.

Nothing. Nothing there. Keep it together.

He fought hard to bring his breathing down, but he wasn't a soldier, he was a commander, a lieutenant born into the business.

Keep cool, keep cool, she's probably gone. She can't see him in here and why would she look?

His mind played the argument over and over, reinforcing the belief that because he offered no threat and couldn't be seen, the singing woman would just leave him alone.

Minutes passed, his heart-rate and breathing both dropped to normal levels, but he still stood rooted to the spot, swivelling his head from side to side while he listened.

He could hear only the night, the deep, heavy, silent night.

'The moon is my lover, the night is our bower,'

The song began again, right outside the tent.

Terror coursed through the Russian's veins and his hand pumped frantically at the trigger, firing off all twelve shots of his pistol in the direction of the singing voice.

'Stay through the night, and hold my heart,'

He dropped to his knees and rooted through his pack again, looking for his extra clip of ammunition.

He didn't take his eyes from the holes in the tent, the direction the singing was coming from.

Where's the fucking clip!? Come on, come on, come on.

His sweating fingers found the cold, steel cartridge right at the bottom of his bag. He dragged it out, freed the empty and slipped the fresh one in place.

An eye suddenly appeared at one of the holes, staring madly right at him.

His heart almost burst. 'No!' He screamed, as he pumped the trigger furiously again. 'Not me! Not Me! *Nooo!*'

The eye disappeared before he fired off the first round.

And the gun clicked empty five times after the last before he stopped pulling the trigger.

He dropped to the ground and delved into his pack again.

He knew he had no clips left, he had never even used one full clip before, let alone reload and use up another. The shooting and killing - and dying - was done by the fucking grunts.

He carried on searching, vainly hoping that some god somewhere would provide him with one. His eyes fell on his phone as he rummaged and prayed.

Pulling his hand out of the pack, he stopped and listened; it was silent again outside, perhaps he had killed the bitch this time and she was lying dead right outside the tent-flaps.

The quiet hurt his ears and chest as he tried to stay as silent and invisible as possible, forcing his lungs to take in as little air as they could so his breathing couldn't be detected.

*Please God, please God, please let her be dead!*

He prayed with all the hypocrisy of any sinner who had never set foot in a church in their lives; heartfelt pleas made with biblically sincere and over-pious promises.

He glanced at his phone again, finding the courage to actually lean out and reach for it, moving ridiculously uncomfortable in order to maintain the perfect silence necessary to keep monsters at bay.

His hand came down gently on top of it and he lifted it an inch.

With a ripping ping and a swish the tent suddenly disappeared upward as it was uprooted from the earth, leaving the base of the thing still squarely pegged and chair, table and Russian still in exactly the same places.

The terrified man screamed briefly, snatching the phone back and sitting huddled on the ground at the side of the chair.

His shaking body and hands made it almost impossible to press the buttons and type the message. 'Come on! Come on! Come on you bastard!'

His jaw ached as he clenched his teeth in frustration at every spelling mistake he made. Eventually he just sent; *Send everyone here.*

As soon as the communication had been sent quiet footfalls came to the Russian's ears.

He sat up startled as a tall, blond-haired man walked into the weakened glow of the lamp on the table.

His eyes were piercing blue and locked the Russians in a passive stare.

'Who-?' The Russian began.

Twin, silenced pistols darted up quickly and shot the startled Russian in the forehead.

'I am Finn.'

## Chapter Forty-Two

The children were tired, their feet dragging through the undergrowth as they marched along behind Finn.

He had roused the camp as soon as he had returned and only gave them five minutes to pack and prepare for the march.

*"We'll break our necks trying to travel in the pitch-black!"* Jimi had argued.

But Finn had produced five, more, night-vision headsets which he had recovered from the outpost soldiers to add to their own two pairs.

He handed them out to Salya, Parisa, Nim and Kurshid, giving the final one to the oldest of the boys in the group, a fourteen year-old called Simeon.

Without a word, Finn had picked up the smallest of the toddlers and placed her on Salya's back, he did the same for another small child, putting him on Parisa's back, while the last of the smallest children was carried by Simeon.

He paired off the adults with the next smallest children to carry, he himself picking up two.

Kurshid carried her own baby, Delara.

Eight children still had to be led, however, huddled between the adults, clutching their garments or hands tightly in their small fists and following blindly through the dark.

Without Finn's strength of will, the children would soon have floundered in the ocean of darkness and been swallowed up by its abject terror of the things which lived in the night.

The adults too would have been lost without him, but he held them together with his own, undeniable and limitless self-belief, cloaking them all in an unseen cover of protection and safety.

It was late morning now and Finn showed no signs yet that they would be stopping.

Once the sun had fully risen, the goggles had come off and all but the smallest of the children were put down to walk.

Finn now carried the two children which Salya and Parisa had carried, while Jimi carried the child who had hitched her ride with Simeon.

Nim manoeuvred herself up to Finn's side and looked up at him as they walked. He didn't seem to notice her.

'The children are tired.' She said quietly.

Finn's head twitched and then he looked around at Nim.

'You haven't slept either,' she said, 'and you were out doing God knows what all night.' She then added.

But looking at the man she couldn't see any signs of the fatigue that she would have expected to see in any normal person.

'I have rested.' Finn replied. 'I was resting just then.' He smiled faintly.

Nim scoffed. 'Only a fool man would say something like that. You can't rest while you are walking.'

There was a hint of pitying wisdom in his eyes as he looked at her, that look which the old gave the young when they knew something that they didn't. 'No; *you* can't rest while you are walking.'

He peered into her face, scanning it as though looking for signs of something just below the surface.

He settled his eyes on hers then. 'But you could.' He finished with a grin.

Nim just frowned. She should just laugh at that, but he was serious; he *had* been resting and he *did* think that anyone could do it like that.

Finn could see that she believed him, but that still left the question of the children and he could also see that, that was still on her mind.

'The children are fine, they are far more resilient than the adults.' He said. 'But we will be stopping for a break and some food when the sun reaches its highest point.' He looked up through the tree canopy. 'Which should be about two hours from now.'

Nim lowered her gaze and just nodded. He was right and she felt a little ashamed that she had projected her own concerns onto the children like that.

She of all people should know that children are made of the toughest stuff, it is the adults which break easily.

Finn nudged her and she looked back up at him. 'Shame doesn't suit that face, Nim,' he said, seriously, 'that is the old face of a slave.'

She blinked as though stung; how dare he? How dare he be... right?

He simply shrugged and smiled and carried on walking.

'You may not be a *normal* man,' Nim said, 'but you still have all the qualities of men who make women want to slap their silly, smiling faces.'

Finn laughed. 'Yes, I've heard that before.'

Nim's question died on her lips, she had been about to ask him who used to say that to him, but knew in her heart that it was the woman from his sad past who had said it.

'If we reach the border,' she began, changing the subject.

'When.' Finn said, interrupting her.

'What?'

'*When* we reach the border.' He answered.

The man's confidence was astounding, it oozed about him like a sure fog and occasionally whipped out and thumped you, like it had done just now.

'Yes, *when* we reach the border.' She repeated.

It was almost as if there was nothing dangerous standing between him and his goal; he would achieve what he set out to do and everything else in the middle were just necessary diversions.

'Yes?' He had to prompt.

'Err, sorry, I lost my train of thought.'

'Really? I didn't notice.' Finn replied. He looked down to her. 'Why don't you tell me what's on your mind, Nim?'

Nim took a deep breath. 'Alright.' She began. 'I've recently escaped from slavery with seventeen children to care for, we're being chased through the wild by armed killers, we have children carrying weapons and military equipment and I'm following a madman,' she held her finger up, 'a madman who turns out not to be so mad after all, but is capable of the most astonishing and frightening things. It is like you are some kind of mortal god, Finn, I don't know whether to be afraid of you or to worship you.'

Finn frowned, pondering her words. 'You should do neither.' He said. 'Fear is for the weak and worship is for the sheep.'

'Is that how you see us, as weak sheep?' Nim asked, not unkindly.

Finn looked around at the marching people and nodded. 'Yes. But do you see that girl there?'

He indicated Salya walking behind. 'She also was a weak sheep when we first met and look at her now.'

Nim followed his gaze over to the young girl. 'Yes.' She said, agreeing with Finn's unsaid point. 'I understand. She isn't the same child who came to us on the back of a truck, raped and afraid, not at all.'

'What do you see in its place.' Finn asked.

Nim looked at Salya again, watching her as she talked and smiled to the two children marching by her side. 'I see a beauty, a furious beauty coming from her, a shining confidence and a strength in her heart. Not like you though, Finn.' She said, and turned back to face him. 'She is more human with it, rather than *super*-human.'

'We are all super-human, Nim, all of us. You have heard the stories of mothers who have lifted vehicles off their children in accidents, or people falling incredible heights and surviving? Well, that super-humanness is what we all carry around with us, but unfortunately we are not educated from birth in its ways.'

'Instead we fear and go to temples.' Nim said slowly, understanding.

'Yes, exactly.' Finn laughed.

He turned his head to the two children on either side of his massive shoulders. 'Did you hear that, my little friends? She got it!' He said, in wide-eyed mock astonishment.

He laughed loudly then and the children giggled.

'She got it!' The pair echoed.

Nim walked with her sniggers hiding behind her hand, but then she too laughed and the four of them walked along chuckling together.

The group made fairly good progress considering the slow pace they had to make for the smaller strides of the children, but noon soon came and they eventually stopped on the slopes, making a small fire under the shadow of the rocks and trees.

Finn had held a line as high up the slopes as was possible, making any attempts to follow as difficult as he could for their pursuers.

It didn't stop anything approaching from the air, however.

Finn looked up first, casting a frowning gaze to the east and through the canopy of trees.

Salya turned her head to follow Finn's next and then a minute later everyone looked up; they could hear the chopper coming over again.

'Everyone up! Quickly! You know what to do.' Nim said, taking charge of the youngsters.

Salya and Parisa took care of the small fire and then everyone slipped into a hiding place.

Finn stood with Jimi in the shadow beneath a hanging rock. The chopper whirred closer.

'It's a pity we didn't keep one of the RPG's.' Jimi said, wistfully.

'We don't need an RPG for that, but we don't want to take it down anyway.' Finn replied.

'Why not?'

'Because if we do they will only send another with even more men, but if we don't they will have to search in all of the places which we *aren't* as well as the place where we actually are.'

Jimi's mouth twitched, that made some kind of sense even if he didn't know what exactly.

In his experience though, you destroyed the enemy when you saw him, not let him fly all over the place to come back another day.

Finn understood what it was Jimi was thinking. 'Don't worry, there will be time to deal with the chopper. For now though, it is helping us.' He said, turning his head toward the direction it was flying in from.

'How's that?' Jimi asked.

'Every time it passes near us it will report back that there is no sign of us, the men will be staying out of the forest for now, especially after what happened to them last night, and won't be any closer than thirty or forty miles.'

He looked back to Jimi. 'As long as we hear it and it doesn't see us, no one will be coming too close to us and we will always have a good idea where they are.'

Once again, Jimi's mind found the twisted logic to what Finn was saying; if they carried on killing the soldiers as they tracked them it went without saying that they would send more, a small army if necessary.

He nodded and raised his eyebrows. 'So when do you think we will have to deal with the chopper then?' He asked.

'When we no longer have the forest for cover.'

Jimi suddenly looked a bit worried; he had expected to be out of the forest once they were over the border. Not that he knew the land or had ever seen any maps of it, he had just assumed.

'No longer have the forest?' He said lamely.

'Yes. About a hundred miles or so to the south the forest ends and the land is flat and open for at least another forty miles. It is the most dangerous part of the journey.'

'Most dangerous part?' Jimi repeated. As if there hadn't been enough danger already; what could be more dangerous than a gang of slavers and smugglers, giant henchmen and Russian mafia soldiers?

'Yes.' Finn said, frowning. 'You do know that repeating what someone says is not a conversation, don't you?' He added dryly.

Jimi sagged inside, his plan to escape had gone horribly wrong from the very start and now he just couldn't find the light at the end of this nightmarish tunnel.

How the hell were they supposed to safely escort seventeen children across an open expanse of forty miles without being noticed?

He knew the type of men who were following, they weren't stupid, they may be a little predictable to Finn, but there was no way they would miss the chance of having the open area covered and watched.

'You seem troubled.' Finn asked.

'Do I?' Replied Jimi sarcastically.

He dropped to his haunches, sighing heavily as he pulled out a pack of cigars. He offered one to Finn.

'Are they Cuban?' Finn asked.

'No. Would you have had one if they were?'

'No.'

'Then why did you ask?' Jimi asked, scoffing.

Finn shrugged. 'I just wondered if you were a clichéd mafia-boss.'

'I'm not a boss, or rather I was never a boss, just a lieutenant.' He said, lighting his cigar.

Finn squat down by his side, peering at him, into him. 'You are a puzzle to me.' He said, to Jimi.

Jimi looked stunned. 'What!?' He blew his smoke out and gave Finn a puzzled look of his own. 'Are you serious?'

'Yes, of course.'

'Go on then, why do I puzzle you?' He asked, flicking his ash onto the ground.

'Because you aren't dead.' Finn replied, seriously.

Jimi's dark eyes narrowed. 'What do you mean?'

'I mean you are alive instead of being killed by me.' Finn's reply was casual and without a hint of any emotion. 'Somehow you managed to end up on the right side in the nick of time. It makes me wonder why, what have you been saved for?'

Saved for? What *have* I been saved for? Jimi had asked himself the very same question as he had witnessed Finn during his killing dance.

'It is intriguing don't you think?' Finn then asked. 'Why was it you decided to leave your old life? It was surely that which truly saved you.'

Jimi glanced over to where Nim and the others were huddled. 'It was because of her,' he said, 'the love I have for her.'

Finn's smile widened. 'Yes. Yes, very good, the very best reason to unshackle yourself from evil; love.'

Jimi chuckled and shook his head slowly. 'You know you sound like something from *The Lord of the Rings* when you talk like that don't you?'

'Is that a bad thing?' Finn asked.

'Oh. No, that's fine,' Jimi replied sincerely, 'just a little weird and about three hundred years old that's all.' He finished with a wink.

The helicopter had turned back before it had actually made it over the top of them, and its *whupping* was moving away again now.

'If Nim had not returned your love would you be here now?'

That was an unfair question. Finn's delivery was perfectly innocent and lacking any form of judgment, but it still struck a little below the belt.

He evaded a little. 'How do you know Nim *has* returned my love?'

'Because I am not blind. She looks at you with her whole self, aims all of it at you through that gaze. But that wasn't what I asked.'

Jimi shrugged resignedly. 'I'd be sat in the penthouse suite with a hole in the head.'

'I didn't go into the penthouse suite.'

'I was speaking rhetorically.' Jimi said, stiffly.

He raised himself, butting the cigar and putting it back in his pocket. 'But if you must know,' he said, and looked up as Finn also stood, 'I agree with you, it is intriguing, divinely so maybe.'

Finn rolled his eyes. 'It would have been better to catch the bullet, my friend, instead of catching religion.' He said, pityingly.

'I haven't *caught* religion, pah!' Jimi said, seriously. 'But it does make one wonder if there is someone pulling our strings somewhere doesn't it?'

Finn shook his head slowly. 'No, not really. Things happen because people and circumstance make things happen. That's it. No gods, no devils, no-.'

'Intelligent design!' Jimi held his finger up and smiled with something akin to triumph on his face.

A dagger appeared in the ground with a thud at his feet.

'Exactly!' Finn said, happily. 'If anything, it is that, but not a bearded man in a chair, sitting in the clouds.'

Jimi looked at the dagger, he hadn't even seen Finn move, not a blur or a flinch. 'You know? Sometimes I wonder if you are just bullshitting all of us and you're really taking drugs!' He said, and stooped down to pick the blade up from the ground.

He handed it back. 'You've got to show me how to do that.'

'I have. Three times now.' Finn replied sincerely.

'So, you do believe in intelligent design then?' Jimi persisted.

'No.'

The exhaserbated Russian threw his arms up in the air, *I give up!*

And without a word, he turned away back up the slope and to the waiting group, shaking his head and muttering in Russian under his breath.

Finn watched him go, he liked the Russian, there was an honour in what he had done so far with his life, whether the man had been on the side of right or wrong, he had always tried to carry out his orders honourably. Maybe that was why he had been saved.

He followed him back to the group and then took his place at the head with Salya.

Sari and Khalid, the two youngest children, were waiting for him with their open smiles and held out arms.

He picked them up one at a time and placed them one on each shoulder. 'Hello, my little friends.' He said, and smiled to them both. 'Are you ready for some more walking today?'

They both giggled and nodded in unison and then wrapped their tiny arms tightly round Finn's neck as he strode onward.

The chopper landed on the highway - if highway was what you could call it; it was more like a long, straight, dusty track which cut its way through the landscape.

A large tanker started up and drove the fifty yards to where the helicopter sat idling, coming to a halt behind it.

The driver and the passenger both got out of the truck and began the refuel.

The pilot sat and cleaned his sunglasses while his passenger stared into the empty space in front of himself.

His eyes were black and cold, empty of all but one thing; the kill. Like a shark.

Colonel, Igor Votsky, quite simply put; the man whom you *didn't* want to be sent to clear up your messes. His reputation as a ruthless commander was known throughout the organisation.

His legend told that he killed his first man at nine years-old, a fishmonger who had caught him stealing. It was said that he took the man's own knife and slashed his throat with it before escaping.

If his legend had been true it paled in comparison to the vicious truth.

Igor Votsky had been six when he had killed his first living thing, a cat, and on his eleventh birthday he had killed his first person, the fishmonger. But he hadn't been caught stealing.

He had made himself a birthday promise to kill a man, the fishmonger was someone he knew who lived alone and was old and weak.

He had lain in wait on the evening of his birthday and when the old man had arrived home, Igor had charmed his way into the unsuspecting man's house and had murdered him at the dinner table.

Sitting opposite the old man, Igor had eaten and laughed with him and then had calmly climbed up onto the table top, still laughing, and had reached out with his stolen scalpel, neatly slashing the old man's windpipe gleefully.

He was fifty-four now and the sight of that hole suddenly appearing in the old man's skin like that, the hollow space beneath, the trachea; amazing. Still one of the very best memories he held.

The old man had died, thrashing in his seat while his breathing rasped to a gagging halt as his lungs filled with blood.

Igor had lost all interest then. The kill was all that mattered. He had calmly finished his food and then had left.

To this day no one really knew who had killed the fishmonger.

A man appeared in front of the chopper and indicated that it was refuelled and all set for flight.

'Take me to the south this time, show me where the forest ends.' Votsky said, his voice as unemotional as his eyes. 'And get the men on the march heading that way. Leave two men here.'

So far the escaped slaves had eluded them.

But Igor Votsky hadn't been looking for them for all of that time now had he?

He cleared his mind of everything but the scent of his prey, narrowing his dark, murderer's eyes.

## Chapter Forty-Three

It was coming. Somehow it had sneaked up on them without him realising it; a doom which he had always looked for, but would never have expected to meet on such a simple mission. It was definitely coming, why else would they have ordered him to kill the woman?

Guryev stared out of the window at the small house across the street, the bed and breakfast called *Castle View*. They must be very good indeed to have found them so quickly.

He sipped at his whiskey.

Kill the woman and leave. Fucking pointless.

He hated this part of the job, the pointless murdering. How does killing the woman help their cause? It didn't, it was an order which came from a cold mind, a mind completely detached from the reality of the job in the field.

He folded his arm across his chest, resting his hand on his gun in its holster under his armpit. Kill the woman and leave.

It would be dark soon. The men were packed, armed and ready.

He sipped more whiskey and thought about the occupants of the house across the road.

It was strange that he had been informed just in the nick of time to the whereabouts of the Shelby woman, but then escaping only to be found again so quickly? Something felt a little oily about that.

He and his men were definitely not being tracked and the woman had not been carrying anything concealed like a tracking device when they had scanned her down.

And yet here they all were, neighbours. If he didn't know any better, Guryev would have said that someone was coordinating both teams.

He didn't like that, being a pawn. Oh. He had been a pawn all his life, but he was a pawn that had known which side of the board he was on; now he felt like he was on someone else's board entirely and didn't know which rules to play by.

A small, white van drove slowly down the road, turned into a parking spot by the curb and stopped. *Ajax Cleaners*, the stencilled panel read.

Guryev smiled to himself; and so it begins.

The driver-side door opened and a tall woman got out, dressed in cleaners blues with a black pinafore tied around her waist. She was carrying a small, plastic basket with an assortment of cleaning equipment inside in one hand and in the other she held a piece of paper which she was reading from.

She scanned the doors looking for the numbers and then finally settled on Guryev's front door.

He chuckled to himself as he watched her climb the steps and ring the doorbell.

Anatoly would answer, she would try to gain entry, he would stop her, but her goal was really only to get a glimpse through the main entrance, anything else like actually being invited in to clean would be simply a bonus.

Everything Guryev had thought would happen did happen and the woman walked back to her van and drove away.

'That wasn't a cleaner, Ilia.' The man called Anatoly said, stopping in the doorway as he passed it on his way back to the rear.

'I know, Anatoly, I know. Did you give her a good look through the door?'

'Yes.' He replied, nodding once.

'Good. Then I think we are all set don't you?' Guryev then said, and turned to Anatoly.

The soldier nodded, his expression serious and as ready as his commander expected him to be.

Guryev returned to his vigil of the house across the street. 'Let us eat before the show begins.' He said. 'I think I will take my dinner with our guest again this evening.'

Anatoly nodded his head again slowly, then dropped his gaze to the floor and ambled away quietly.

Downstairs in the cellar, Rachel sat at the small table and read one of the books Ilia had left her. She sipped tea as she read *Who Killed Marilyn Monroe?* And not the movie icon but a beach-donkey of the same name.

During the six days she had been here, Rachel had read everything greedily, sometimes twice when new material wasn't immediately available. There was nothing to do at all and without the books she thought she might have just curled up and gone mad.

Her captors were treating her well and Ilia had dined with her twice more since that first time, but she hadn't seen him for the past two days.

She was allowed to use the bathroom whenever she asked, which she did by banging on the metal door, and she was brought food three-times a day, but other than that tiny exposure to other people or the outside world, Rachel had been completely alone.

The waiting and the boredom were the worst; strangely she didn't feel the expected fear, mainly because she didn't know what it was that she should fear anymore.

Ilia had been overly kind and accommodating, even providing her with a kettle and supply of tea and milk.

She suspected it was all part of a bigger plan to keep her compliant and behaving like a good little captive. They were right if it was, she was behaving just nicely.

Not that she really had any choice to do otherwise. On the contrary, they were so rigid when she moved around to use the bathroom that she could see no opportunity for any kind of escape; the bathroom windows were nailed shut and the larger of the two had been boarded over completely.

If there was a way to incapacitate any of them who guarded her she couldn't see a way to do that either, she would have to be some kind of super-nurse with kung-fu powers or something, they were all just so bloody big and tough.

Not least of all Ilia, who moved around like a jungle-cat, his eyes on everything at once.

Just like Graham. Another reason she needed to keep her mind well occupied; it stopped her from worrying about her husband.

He was alive, she was sure of it, and what's more he had caused the *other side* some major trouble, or so Ilia had hinted. But what she wouldn't give to just hear his voice.

Footsteps moved across the floor in the room above. Rachel raised her eyes to the ceiling and listened. It sounded like it was the older, bigger set man, the one they called Anatoly.

The room directly above was the kitchen she thought, it was usually Anatoly who she heard moving around up there and so guessed that the excellent food she was receiving was being cooked by him.

He was also usually the one who brought the food down. Although on one occasion she had been served by a tall boy.

She had been silently stunned at how young he seemed to be. He was tall and athletic, but his face said he couldn't have been more than nineteen years-old.

He was very shy and had kept his eyes lowered as he placed the food on the table.

Hagen he had said his name was when she had asked, but had quickly left the room before she could coax anymore out of him.

Those were the only three of her kidnappers that she had seen, but she knew there was at least another one up there somewhere.

She dropped her gaze and her book and stood up and stretched her back.

She took a step to the kettle, flicking the switch to on and then stood in the middle of the room, stretching her arms upward, standing on her toes.

Then she slowly lowered herself and reached down to the ground, easing her aching back into giving her the room and reach to touch the dusty floor.

After five minutes of this, the kettle plinked off and Rachel had managed to get both palms flat to the ground.

She stood back up, breathing deeply, satisfied that her body held no more knots.

Footsteps came to the door at the top of the stairs.

Rachel poured the water into her mug and listened. The door clicked open and she heard Ilia coming down.

She turned back to the tea, smiling, and selected another mug. She dropped a teabag inside and then filled it up.

The metal door clicked and rattled as it was unlocked and then opened as Ilia walked in carrying a tray with two plates of food on it.

'Oh. You're dining with me again? Kazakov's football and John Wayne too much for you?' Rachel asked, innocently.

Guryev closed the door and turned back around, smiling casually.

Rachel's breath caught in her tight throat as she noticed he was carrying his gun in his usually empty holster.

She quickly turned back to the tea and stirred it.

Guryev had seen her look but said nothing, instead he placed the food on the table and then threw the empty tray on the bed.

'I-I made tea.' Rachel said, weakly.

Guryev took his seat and watched the woman's nervous stirring. 'Well that is fortunate.' He said, jovially. 'Because tonight we are having fish and chips the Russian way.'

Rachel turned around and carried the two steaming mugs back to the table.

'You British seem to have a penchant for fish and chips and a mug of steaming tea don't you?' He asked, as he took his mug from Rachel. 'Thank you.'

Rachel sat down and tried to regain her composure. So what if he was carrying his gun? She had seen guns before, Graham had to wear one occasionally. Ilia had just forgotten to remove it that's all.

'Well, I can't say the clichéd view doesn't fit,' she began, 'but just like Hobbits, there is much more to the British than just tea, rain and fish and chips.'

Guryev chuckled at the rain reference. 'It isn't *us* who say it always rains in Britain, that is the Americans. They say similar things about us; we have enough weather of our own.' He said, and laughed.

Yes, he had just forgotten to remove it that was all.

Rachel laughed back and raised her cup. 'To the wet and cold.' She said.

'I'll drink to that.' Guryev replied, and raised his own cup.

They sat and ate, chatting happily, Rachel enjoying the superb food and Ilia's excellent company.

At the top of the stairs, Anatoly stood with his back to the door, looking down the hallway to the front entrance.

It was almost dark, the enemy across the street would be making their move soon. Well they were ready. As ready as they could be.

The others were in their positions covering the rear exit for when they made a run for it.

*If* they made a run for it; it was still touch and go whether they could actually get out and escape or not. But they couldn't have the enemy on their tail if they did, they had to do something about the immediate threat before they left and the best place to do that was as they came through the front door. The aim was only to disable them for as long as possible.

Then there was always the chance that they had been *made* and were surrounded, in which case they would have to fight their way out, literally, onto the streets. That was never a good scenario, running through enemy streets at night.

Anatoly shuddered as Kosovo flashed painfully across his mind. He had never known fear as he had known it for those few days he had been trying to get back out of the war-torn and murderous city.

The people had been the worse, more terrifying than the chemical mortars, or the bombings; the people were animals, taking delight - *delight!* - In torturing their captives. Publicly torturing them, encouraging whole neighbourhoods to take part in the most barbaric murders.

To this day Anatoly had always said that if he hadn't managed to find a way out he would have shot himself in the head rather than being caught by the mob.

You are in Wales, Anatoly, they don't do mobs in Wales.

He still wouldn't be caught though; to be caught on the job only meant death would be served later.

Back on home soil that wouldn't happen. Get caught on home soil and you served your time, sometimes luxuriously, and then returned to the fold.

It was a different kettle of fish entirely when being caught by another country's law enforcement.

Why are you thinking about being caught? You're not going to get caught.

But something nagged and nibbled at his senses, had been doing so since he had closed the door on the cleaning woman. There was just something he couldn't quite pin down with their exchange as she insisted that she had the correct address.

She had made no noticeable attempt to have a good look down the hallway, even though he had held the door open wide enough, but he knew she was noting and remembering everything; he knew that look, that stance, that composure, he was trained to notice it.

She knew, the nagging nibble itched. She knew you were letting her have a look inside, that's why she didn't.

He imagined himself as a cleaner, a real, bona-fide cleaner who had been sent to a job only to find he had the wrong house, what would he do?

He would call his boss and insist that the owner speak to him. He would ask if there was someone else in the house who may have made the order for the cleaning service. He would ask if the road name could have been mixed up and then ask for directions.

Anything but a shrug and a *"are you sure?"*

She fucking knew. That meant they probably wouldn't be going out of the back after all, but it didn't change the plan much, at least not the beginning anyway. He would have to get Jaco and Levin to fit the back gate and fence up with a few surprises.

Maybe it was for the better; sneaking out of the rear could easily have led into a trap, at least this way they knew what they were up against.

It felt a little safer for some twisted reason to know where the people who were shooting at you were.

It was a shame it had come to shooting. It had almost been a foregone conclusion that once the woman had been captured the rest would be plain-sailing, but no, somehow they had been found. Either someone on the other team was very good at tracking, or someone, somewhere wasn't playing fair.

He sighed heavily, the reasons didn't matter, what mattered was that it had happened and they were cornered, all they could do was play for as long as possible and hope that they could escape to find out another day.

God help the poor bastard if they should find out who the dirty-player was.

The streetlights were bright and orange. Anatoly looked at his watch; just after nine-thirty. They should be *pulling the hammers back* on their weapons over the street by now he thought. This was it then.

'Jaco?' He called through to the side-room.

'Yea?' The man called back as he peered round the doorframe.

'Take Levin and go rig a welcome for any guests who might come through the back.' He said, and nodded down the hallway to Levin and the backdoor.

Both men looked at him curiously. 'Why? We're leaving now aren't we?' Jaco asked, stopping in front of his superior.

Anatoly's mouth dropped at the corners a little and his eyebrows raised. 'Maybe not straight away.' He said, with a small shrug.

It was all he would give in explanation to a subordinate and both Jaco and Levin knew not to question him, it was a generous gesture as it was.

Jaco nodded once and turned to Levin. 'Open the packs.' He said, and walked back into the kitchen.

They were good men, Anatoly liked having them on the team, they never crossed boundaries, but were always quick and inquisitive enough to get to the place where the boundaries edge lay.

Being a soldier was one thing, being a thinking soldier was another.

He pulled his hip-flask from his pocket and unscrewed the silver top, a present from his sister before she had died.

He took a mouthful of the darkened rum inside and smacked it back with a hot gasp.

This was the only part he hated more than the actual battle; the waiting on the very knife edge of it, never knowing when it will actually start, but knowing that it is going to be soon. How the hell long *soon* actually was could only be measured in the swigs of rum he took.

It would start soon though.

He chuckled to himself. Someone would start shooting soon, they always did.

His heart whammed in his chest as the two gunshots muffled with a pillow or blanket came up from the basement.

Anatoly looked down at his shoes, suddenly feeling very old and very out of place.

The shooting had already begun.

## Chapter Forty-Four

*Fucking rumbled! How stupid? Stupid, stupid, stupid.*

Dilger stood by the monitor, severely kicking herself for being *made* so easily.

She had got everything she had needed from her glance down the hallway, but had resisted the urge to push it further once she realised she had been sussed. He had made it more than obvious he was letting her see inside.

But how the fuck had they known about her in the first place? There was no way they had spotted her; none of the team had used the front entrance, always using the handy back alley system on this side of the road.

The whole operation had to be altered now, they couldn't storm the front, that had relied on their targets being unawares. Now the Russians would have the hallway and the back entrance sealed tight with traps, most likely flash and stun grenades.

She and Robinson studied the blueprint sat next to the monitor, it showed the layout of the building they were going to hit.

'I think these two double-bay windows are the best option.' Robinson said, pointing to the dining-room area on the right. 'The stairs are here and the cellar door is here.' He looked up at his commander. 'If she's in the cellar we've got our work cut out for us is all I can say. The back will be well covered, we can't go in there before the front is assaulted.'

'It's not much easier if she is being held upstairs.' Dilger mumbled.

So much for keeping the noise to a minimum. 'We're going to have to blow both those windows and the front door *and* the main front window on the left.' She said, and sighed loudly.

Robinson whistled. 'That's a lot of noise, we will have to pick our covers just right so we don't expose ourselves to it.'

He flicked a switch on the monitor control and the view changed to a shot of the street running away downhill, the house on the corner clearly in view.

'We could try these two trees at the front, but for the side bays we are going to have to be very close. Here.' He said, pointing to the base of the house-wall itself, right beneath the windows in question.

'Shit.' Dilger breathed. 'How the hell can we get there without them noticing?'

Devlin looked over their shoulders.

'I can run that.' He said, and nodded.

'What do you mean, lad?' Robinson asked.

'I can crack a shot off from here where they can't see me,' he said and pointed to the corner at the opposite side of the road, 'and still get across and through the window right after it's gone off.'

He looked between them both, his eyes wide and serious. 'Honest. I can make that, easy.'

Dilger gave him an appraising look and then smiled, turning to Robinson. 'What do you think, Robbo?'

'I think Speedy Gonzales here could do that in his sleep.' He replied without hesitation.

He turned to the younger man. 'Nice one, son.' He said, to the beaming Devlin.

Then turned back to Dilger. 'One window down, one to go. We have to have all of them taken out.' He said.

Both men then stood and looked at her.

'What? Me? You can't be serious?' She said, stunned.

'If I had to say who was always second fastest on their feet it would be you. We know your *mile* times.'

'That was ten years ago!'

'Aye, but like Simmons has already pointed out; the boss doesn't get old, she gets even.' Robinson winked.

'He's right, boss, you're the quickest on their feet next to me.' Said the smaller man, Devlin.

'Great!' She said, shaking her head. 'Okay. That's the entry covered, but you,' she pointed to Devlin, 'time your run to coincide with mine; you do *not* go through that window before anyone else. Is that clear?'

'Yes, sir.' He said.

'Good.' Dilger acknowledged. 'Then it looks like we have a plan, I think we should begin as soon as everyone is briefed.' She continued. 'Let's get everyone in the kitchen for *equip-check* and then we're off. Ten O'clock start, lads.'

Ten O'clock came and the six, Interpol agents stood now in the back alley behind their temporary base of operations.

'Right, I'm off.' Robinson said. 'I'll see you inside.' He gave them all a short nod and then disappeared into the dark.

Robinson's position was at the rear of the house.

He was their best tracker for a very good reason; he could spot a broken blade of grass from yards away.

So it went without saying that he would be the one to run the gauntlet of traps set up around the back; with his night-vision goggles firmly in place, he would scout his way to the backdoor and then wait until the fireworks began before breaking the door down and entering the kitchen.

If everything worked according to plan, anyone in the hallway or kitchen would be momentarily stunned by the sound and light of the blasts, and if the soldiers had decided to go upstairs and avoid the blasts altogether, then they would have the ground floor to themselves to set up on.

Somehow he didn't expect them all to be upstairs though.

'Right, you two,' Dilger pointed to Melford and Simmons, 'take up your positions behind the trees and wait for my signal.'

The two men lowered their goggles and trotted off.

'Come on then Speedy, let's get in position.'

She and Devlin jogged up and away from their target, taking themselves in a wide semi-circle around the back's of the houses and then back onto the main road.

They slipped across and made a path for the corner, kneeling down in the shadows, pressing themselves tightly up against the brick wall of the corner house opposite the Russian's house.

Across the road and almost directly in front of the target-house, Dilger could see Melford and Simmons crouching down behind the boles of two of the fat, oak trees which lined this side of the road.

McKenzie was hidden in the tiny front garden of *Castle View*, lying down behind the low, stone wall.

His experience gave him the job of entering anywhere he saw fit, he would assess as he ran across the road. That way, any of the team taking fire and in need of backup would almost certainly get it and quickly.

The neighbourhood was very quiet at this time of night, a solitary car or two drove along back streets somewhere but nothing stirred much in this part of town, all the action being miles away in the centre.

Dilger lifted her one-shot stun-gun and smiled devilishly; the neighbours were in for a surprise, early sunrise and thunder storm tonight, all rolled into one.

It was a fine, quiet night, it hadn't rained for weeks.

She raised her hand for all to see, ticking off a count of three with her fingers before pulling her trigger.

The stun-guns popped in unison and four whooshes filled the night-silence, suddenly.

But only for a moment.

The four grenades were designed to explode at first impact, not once they had gone through the glass but actually as they hit the glass. *First-contact* grenades Devlin had nicknamed them.

The street and houses and trees and parked-cars all flared white-hot under a monstrous glare while the silence was shattered by a terrific, sonic boom.

The wood and glass exploded and disintegrated as the grenades were designed to do, leaving a gaping hole of brick which was untouched.

Devlin had leaped up, dropped his empty stun-gun and sped off to the window he had aimed for even before the grenades had reached their targets.

He leaped straight up onto the smashed window ledge and then squatted there with his sub-machine gun raised, scanning the room ahead.

Dilger sprinted after him. I'll fucking kill him, she was thinking.

He hadn't gone through the window she noticed, but the little bastard was playing the fine-line game.

She reached her own window and then jumped straight through the gap, landing in a devastated dining-room just as Devlin landed on the floor at the other side of her.

Gunfire suddenly erupted from the room opposite, the unmistakable sound of a semi-automatic rifle coming from the room Melford and Simmons were assaulting.

Dilger and Devlin ran to the doorway and stood at either side.

The gunfire was being replied now by the quick bursts of Melford and Simmons' subs.

A movement, a shadow on the stairs, caught Dilger's eye.

She leaned out quickly just in time to catch a tall man throwing a grenade down at them from the landing.

She had seen him pull the pin and then throw it straight away, a bad rookie mistake she thought, and then it hit her; it was the tall boy.

The grenade landed just inside the doorway.

Devlin pounced on it and picked it up in a flash, streaked out into the hallway and lobbed it back up the stairs before zipping back into the room again.

He jumped when it went off, as though he hadn't been expecting it.

'Fucking hell. That just happened.' He said, weakly.

He shook himself off and then stepped back into the hall to check the damage.

'No!' Dilger shouted, reaching out to grab him, but too late.

A handgun fired somewhere from the left, the end of the hallway where the front door was.

Devlin's head flicked over slightly to the right as the bullet tore through his cheek, travelled across his tongue, searing it, and then exited through the other cheek in a spray of blood and teeth.

He crumpled to the ground and mercifully fell backward, back into the dining-room.

Dilger grabbed his lapels and dragged him all the way inside.

All she could do was turn him onto his face to try and keep his airways clear of blood. She had to leave him until he could be looked at properly once the fighting had stopped.

She backed herself up to the wall and listened for sounds of the shooter down by the front door. How the fuck did they get down there? We covered that with grenades.

The fire-fight was still raging in the other room, but the handgun had just fired again as well.

Melford screamed.

Dilger's eyes flashed angrily; fuck! They had waited upstairs and were dropping down behind them from the windows. Clever fucking Ivan.

'WATCH YOUR SIXES!' She screamed loudly over the noise.

If the gunman was firing on Melford and Simmons then he wasn't in the hallway. She threw her head out and back in quickly, checking the front door.

A machine-gun fired a burst as she ducked back inside, but it had come from the stairs.

'Shit!' She hissed.

Robinson's gun suddenly roared out down the hallway to the right. He was firing from the kitchen to the front door.

Dilger dropped to her knees and rolled up to the doorway in one, swift movement, rising back onto one knee as she fired her sub-machine gun up the stairwell.

Her bullets ripped a line up the wall, *clack, clack, clack, thud, thud.*

A man screamed and then fell headlong down the stairs, tumbling head over heels until he crashed to a halt at the bottom.

Anatoly lay on his back, his breathing almost impossible with his torn up chest and lungs.

He stared up at the ceiling with wide, terrified eyes. *Where am I going?* And died with a single tear rolling down his cheek. *Where?*

Melford came staggering out of the room, blood covering his left leg and arm. He made eye-contact with Dilger just as an acknowledgment, but then stooped to the ground and lay in the hallway, aiming at the front door. 'Fucking shot me! Twice!' She heard him mutter angrily.

Simmons was still shooting at someone, but it seemed he was firing out of the building now, and then Melford opened up with a burst through the front door.

Someone had just darted past, running from Simmons' fire.

Dilger ducked back into the room just in time to see a big man in white shirt and - oddly - a tie, raise his Desert Eagle through the gaping hole of the bay and pump off three rounds straight at her.

All three slugs slammed into her bullet-proof vest, sending her careering backward into the hallway.

She crashed through the banister and landed in a crumpled heap on the bottom three steps.

Melford was up and heading for the front door, trailing his blood and grimaces behind him.

He turned left just in time to see the bastard Russian's legs disappearing through the bay window.

'He's back in the dining room, Stu!' Melford shouted to Simmons.

He limped slowly to the window and stood flat against the side-wall. After two deep breaths he darted a look and peered in quickly and then pulled out again. The room looked empty.

What? And then quietly; 'Shit!'

The thought that the gunman was hiding behind the very brickwork he himself was on the other side of came to him at the same moment the Desert Eagle appeared from out of the room and shot him in the face.

Melford fell to the ground and lay with his legs twitching and kicking out unnaturally as they still tried to run away.

Guryev stood against the wall and reloaded.

They were a good team, the entry was unexpected. But he was better.

He slammed the new cartridge in the slot and stepped over the unconscious body of Devlin, taking up a position where Dilger had been standing.

He looked out without sticking his head out. His chest hurt when he saw the open-eyed body of his friend lying on its back.

*Good hunting, Anatoly.*

The woman he had shot was laid on her side, she was still breathing.

He looked into the room opposite, the room where he had dropped down to from the window above.

It looked empty. Where was the one he had heard being called *Stu*? And who was left of his own men?

He thought Jaco and Levin were still going, at least one of them was firing from the backroom into the kitchen. Hagen should still be upstairs. That left Kazakov, he had been in the room opposite.

Guryev sighed; it looked like it was fifty-fifty, they each had at least three men down.

Bracing himself, he lunged out of the doorway and sped down the hall to the kitchen.

A gun opened up behind him, the one called Stu, no doubt, and he felt the air whip and stir as bullets passed him by.

He reached the doorway and dived headfirst over the dining table, smashing into the two wooden chairs behind and crushing them to splinters as they all crashed into the sink and cupboards together.

The machine-gun carried on firing into the upturned table, sending it spinning and splintering all over the kitchen.

Levin appeared in the small doorway leading to the other backroom, he was covered in blood. It didn't seem to be impeding his movements whatever wounds he had.

Guryev rolled out of the way of the gunfire and toward Levin, looking at him with pity in his eyes.

'It's not my blood, it's Jaco's.' He said, looking both shocked and pained. 'He fought well.' He said. His face was pale and drawn.

'Where did the other one go? The one who fired down there.' Guryev asked, and nodded in the direction of the hallway entrance.

'He ran back out, he's climbed up.' Levin replied, and looked up at the ceiling.

Robinson crossed the carpeted floor as quickly as he could and listened at the door. He should be at the end of a landing hallway, opposite the bathroom and with the stairs lying dead right. All he could hear was the sporadic exchanges of gunfire coming from downstairs.

It had to be now; the room next to the bathroom was where he had seen the woman when he had first found them. He wasn't convinced that she was being kept in there, especially after being caught trying to escape.

No, if it were him he would keep her underground and the cellars here were perfect for such a thing; deep and soundproof. But he had to see for himself now that he was up here.

He pulled the door open a fraction and looked through the gap, the landing seemed to be empty, but he knew from the blueprints that there was a corner ahead which led straight down to the stairs, and further ahead still was another corner leading to the master bedrooms at the front of the building.

He pulled the door all the way open and stepped out into the small corridor. The floorboards creaked, he could feel them, but the sound of the noises coming from downstairs drowned out the tell-tale clicks and groans.

With his gun held up and ready, he gingerly crossed the space to the door and without a pause, turned the handle and pushed it open.

Just the fact that it was unlocked told him that she wasn't in here but he had to have a look anyway. Just in case.

The room was dark and the curtains were drawn but there was enough light spilling in from the landing to show him that the bed held no dead woman and was just an empty bed.

His relief was thrown to one side as a gun sounded from the top of the stairs.

As he himself moved to the corner, whoever was up here ran down the stairs straight after shooting. So he had someone on the retreat then but who?

He made it to the top of the stairs and looked down, there was a Russian laid out on his back, dead, but no one else.

The door on the right had a shadow moving across it.

Robinson stepped down carefully, glancing occasionally down the hallway to the left and toward the kitchen.

He made the bottom step when the gunfire started up again, coming from the kitchen now.

A man suddenly appeared, running out of the kitchen and down the hallway and looked with all intent and purposes to be running into the room on the right.

Trying to blindside somebody already in there maybe Robinson thought.

The Russian didn't see Robinson immediately, but when his eyes met the Interpol officer's he had looked surprised and then suddenly his face had dropped to relaxed shocked as a hail of bullets coming from the front door mowed him down.

McKenzie stood there.

'Where's the boss, Sarg?' He asked Robinson, a grave look on his face. 'She was laying right there.' He said, indicating the steps Robinson was standing on.

The shadow in the room, the Russian running to blindside someone, it had to be Dilger in there.

He nodded toward the doorway. 'I think she's in there,' he mouthed, 'go look through the front window, watch your back.' He said, using sign-language to get his orders across.

McKenzie nodded and then ducked back out of sight.

Robinson turned down the hallway and approached the kitchen.

If Dilger was coming up through the back room then anyone remaining would have to come through the kitchen or stand their ground and fight it out with her. Either way, the cavalry was here.

Guryev hugged his bleeding side.

Fucking stupid boy! Why had Hagen come down the fucking stairs? Idiot! Not only had he lost the upper ground and a strong advantage, they had now been bottlenecked and trapped.

Levin had tried to break the grip before it could take hold, but had been seconds too late.

'You're a stupid, fucking bastard, Hagen.' Guryev said, quietly, wincing as his stomach complained.

The man called Stu lay sprawled at his feet, dead, but not without shooting Guryev first as he followed him into the backroom from the kitchen.

The boy looked over, scowling.

'Don't look at me like that you fucking little shit. You fucked up and now we are fucking cornered like rats.' Guryev said, angrily. 'Stupid fucking boy.' He added quietly.

He couldn't blame Hagen entirely, he was naive in the field, this mission was supposed to have been pretty low-key and not too dangerous for a first-time mission.

That had all gone to shit the moment they had holed up.

He still should have known to hold the high-ground though, fucking amateur.

Well, there was only one thing for it now; unless he was mistaken, there would be two coming through the front, one of them the woman who had taken three in the chest. That left one in the kitchen. The kitchen it was then.

'Follow my lead, the only thing through there is killable,' he pointed through into the kitchen, 'so don't hesitate. Understand?' He said, to the still scowling Hagen.

Hagen nodded and then shifted his gaze to the doorway like a petulant child Guryev thought.

If they got out of this he was going to kick so much shit from the bastard he would need surgery to close the gaping wound of his ass!

He took a deep breath. God, this was going to hurt either way. He might even be shot again. Damn the stupid boy.

He darted forward and charged through the door, leaping head-first toward the pile of broken furniture in the middle.

He landed heavily on the pile just as the gun he was expecting to hear, fired a quick burst.

There was pain all around, he still couldn't tell if he had been hit or not.

Hagen grabbed the barrel of the gun and yanked it from Robinson's hands, quickly thrusting the butt back into his face, knocking him to the ground.

The young Russian flipped the weapon over and was about to fire it at Robinson when his attention was alerted to the room he had just come from. He turned that way instead and opened fire.

Guryev and Robinson both rolled to their knees and then up onto their feet, Guryev holding his wounded side and Robinson his broken nose.

Guryev raised his Desert Eagle a split second later than Robinson had picked up the flour bin and lobbed it at him.

The gun went off and the bin exploded, flour and bits of plastic sprayed the room.

Before the dust had even settled, Robinson was charging in, head lowered.

He connected with Guryev's midriff and brought him down with a flying rugby-tackle, the gun in the Russian's hand whipped free and was left behind as both men smashed into the ground.

Robinson rolled to the right as the Russian lashed out with his fist, glancing him across the chin.

Both men rose and both of them held a jagged sliver of wood from the broken furniture in their hands now.

They were soldiers and faced each other as soldiers, may the best training win out.

Guryev lashed out first, a depth-testing slash to see how far he could reach out before he entered his opponent's strike-zone.

Robinson was a master knife-fighter however. He rolled around Guryev's slash, spinning on his heel anti-clockwise.

The movement allowed him to quickly close the gap by at least six inches and at the same time he stayed out of the way of his opponent's weapon.

His own wooden blade flashed out and struck Guryev in the shoulder, snapping off at the tip and staying embedded in his skin.

Guryev yelled and pulled away while Robinson danced back again the other way, releasing his free hand this time to crack across the retreating man's jaw.

The Russian staggered but only for a second. His mind quickly adapted to the methods which his enemy was employing.

He dropped the sliver of wood and grabbed two pans from the draining-board instead.

Banishing the pain from his bleeding side and shoulder to the back of his mind, Guryev waded in, lashing out with the two metal pans and deflecting Robinson's attempts to stick him again.

The Interpol man stepped back and then again, each attack he made being thwarted, he had to change tactics.

As Guryev swiped at his head, Robinson ducked and dropped his piece of wood, and grabbed one of the table-legs instead.

He rose up and cracked the pan which had almost reached his head.

It clanged loudly as it was deflected heavily back, exposing Guryev's stomach.

Robinson drove the butt of the leg hard into his ribs and the Russian cried out in pain as his bullet wound flared agonisingly.

He lashed out wildly with both pans, catching Robinson a cracking blow across the back of his hand, sending the leg scattering to the ground as Robinson yelled out. Two of his fingers throbbed hotly, broken.

The Russian stepped back and cursed his pain, taking the lapse in Robinson's concentration to gather his own thoughts and nurse his side.

In the front room, Dilger was exchanging fire with someone, she couldn't see who as she couldn't get far enough inside the back room to have a look.

She knew she was holding back a little, getting shot had something to do with that she suspected. Her chest hurt like hell where the three rounds had cracked into her vest.

She could hear the sounds of fighting coming from the kitchen, so that could only mean that these were the last two.

Flicking her gun through the doorway she released a quick burst into the room and then pulled back again.

Whoever was in there fired back at her, sending wood and plaster spraying across the room as the doorframe and wall took the impacts.

McKenzie reappeared at the front window, he was carrying his one-shot stun-grenade.

'On three.' He said. 'One. Two. Three.'

The grenade launched into the room leaving a trail of smoke behind it.

Hagen leaned out to look into the room beyond, just catching a quick view of the man in the window aiming a large barrelled gun into the room he was standing at the back of.

The young soldier leaped over the debris on the floor and sprang through the doorway and into the kitchen just as the grenade exploded on the back wall.

The whole kitchen lit up brightly for a second and-a-half and the windows rattled under the extraordinary booming sound which reverberated throughout the whole house.

Robinson and Guryev both turned their backs on the light and covered their ears from the terrific sound, but Robinson had been facing the doorway when the grenade had gone off.

He was half-blind and knew he was in trouble now if they should start fighting again.

His combat-trained mind and his specialist, master blades-man training gave Robinson an edge right at that moment, he would never know how he had done it, but he had, had a flash of memory come to his minds-eye, just an after-image of the scene immediately around him: Guryev was in front of him by the back door and turning away from the noise of the grenade.

The boy had come rushing in only a moment before the grenade had exploded.

And down by his left boot, not more than three feet from where he was cowering from the stunning blast, lay the Russian's Desert Eagle.

A saving move was available to him, even in this half-blinded state, and he took it while Guryev only just began to turn his attention back onto him.

Following the dizzy path his head wanted to throw him anyway, Robinson dropped straight to the ground and then rolled over once.

His hand came up against the cold steel of the gun and he gripped it, rolling back to face the memory-image of Guryev standing in front of him.

He pulled the trigger twice and that was all he could do, the clip was empty.

Guryev groaned and then fell heavily to the floor, leaning back against the counter.

That was a smart move he thought to himself and coughed.

His chest wheezed and the blood spilled down his clean, white shirt, darkening behind his red tie and matching its hue almost perfectly.

Hagen watched in horror as his boss fell back against the kitchen counter, blood pouring from the two holes in his chest.

The grenade had almost knocked him out with its awesome sound and he had staggered and then briefly fallen to his knees.

He was back up now and Robinson was kneeling in front of him with an empty gun in his hands, ready to die.

He raised Robinson's own UMP which he still clutched after yanking out of his hands just as Dilger ran through into the room behind him.

Oh! God, not the boy.

She shot him in the back at the same time McKenzie shot him in the chest from the backdoor.

He spun around and then dropped to the floor in silence, having no chance to fire Robinson's weapon before he fell.

He lay there gasping for a few seconds and then was still.

Dilger and McKenzie rushed inside, McKenzie making a beeline for the hallway where he took up position by the cellar door, watching the stairs, the front door and both side-rooms at the same time.

Dilger knelt by Robinson's side and held his head up so she could look into his eyes. 'How do you feel?' She asked, noting the slight dilation of his pupils.

'Like the inside of my head is having a loud party while my body is trying to sleep.' He replied groggily. 'The woman wasn't upstairs.' He then said.

'Right.' Dilger replied quietly. Sighing heavily she stood up again. 'I'll go check the cellar. The local authorities will be on their way I would think. Sit tight and wait for a medic.'

Robinson grasped her hand. 'How many have we lost, Caroline.' He asked.

'Two.' She replied, the pain clear to hear in her voice. 'Melford and

Simmons. Devlin's wounded but he'll live.'

Robinson nodded his head. 'They were good lads.' Was all he managed to say.

His eyes fell on her vest and then the three, crushed bullets embedded in its surface, and he frowned, his pain growing tenfold in his chest.

Before he could say anything, Dilger spoke. 'Desk-jobs wasn't it?'

He reached out and touched her face. She was alive, she had three bullets in her chest and she was still alive. There was only one way to take a message like that and that was seriously. 'Desk-jobs.' He repeated.

Dilger stood up and went to the cellar door. 'I think we got 'em all, Mac.' She said to McKenzie. 'Go out and wait for the police, get the medics into Devlin and Sarg when they get here.'

McKenzie un-cocked his weapon and set the safety to on, nodded and after one last look at Robinson went out of the front door.

Dilger pressed her ear up to the cellar door and listened. It was silent. They were pretty sure that all of the kidnappers were accounted for, but it was stupid and thoughtless to presume.

She opened the door and peered down the steps. There was a large metal door at the bottom, closed but with its bolts drawn back.

She climbed the stone steps to the bottom and then listened again at the door. It was still silent.

She tried the handle, it wasn't locked so she pushed it open and walked in.

'Miss Langley?' She said, to the tearstained woman sitting on the camp-bed. Rachel nodded.

'I'm Caroline Dilger,' Dilger said, holstering her weapon. 'I'm with Interpol, you punched me in the face.' She carried on, not unkindly.

Rachel laughed and wiped her eyes. And then stood up and wept some more. 'Oh! God!' She said, and ran for the door.

Dilger frowned but let her go and ran up the stairs behind her. 'You're safe now, Miss Langley, I can assure you.' She said, mistaking Rachel's flight for panic fleeing.

At the top of the stairs, Rachel scanned from left to right, pausing for a second when her eyes fell upon the motionless body of Anatoly.

She had just eaten his food she thought, and now he was dead. He wouldn't cook his delicious meals for anyone ever again.

To her left her eyes found what they were looking for; Ilia sat with his back against the counter, blood covering his chest.

She ran over to him and dropped down by his side. 'Oh you bloody man!' She said, weeping freely and picking up his hand.

His eyes opened and he looked at her. 'Ah! Mrs Shelby. I am glad to see you.' He said, weakly, coughing shallowly.

'Why did you do that, Ilia? You could have lived, we could have helped you.'

Rachel's words were scattered with her sobs and her chest ached from the pain she was feeling for this brave man. 'Why did you do that Ilia?' She asked again, lifting his hand and kissing the back of it.

'Because the end of the story had to be told.' He said.

'What story?'

He coughed and gagged, pain etching his features. 'You remember I told you of the private-eye who really was a dick?'

His voice was wracked with the trapped air-bubbles coming from his open chest.

'Yes.' Rachel replied, sniffing, frowning through her tears. 'But don't talk, the ambulance will be here soon, save your energy.'

He shook his head slowly and merely smiled through bloodied teeth.

His hand squeezed hers gently. 'I told you that I had moved the woman and her daughter to another town, kept them safe.'

Rachel nodded.

'The young girl went on to become a first-class doctor of medicine, Annalisa is her name, she will be twenty-three this year. All the boys want to be with Annalisa, but she is too good for them.' He said, chuckling and then wincing in pain.

He gasped and then carried on. 'Her mother is finally happy, truly content as a heart as good and as shining as hers deserves to be. She is called Natasha, *my* Natasha; I married her not long after I relocated them both.'

Rachel sobbed loudly.

'So do you see, Mrs Shelby, how the tale needed to be told to the end?'

'Y-yes.' She replied, gripping his dying hand and holding it to her chest.

'I know she will miss me and will wait for me as I will wait for her, but I-,' he coughed and wheezed. 'I would love to-,' blood trickled from his nose and mouth and the colour visibly drained from his face. 'Love to see her. One,' he blinked slowly, 'las-,' and then his eyes closed. 'Ti-.'

Rachel wailed. *Why did you do that, Ilia?*

She gripped his hand and rocked back and forth, her face screwed up as she cried.

In the cellar, after dinner, Ilia had suddenly stood up without a word, walked over to her bed and fired his gun into the pillow, twice.

He had turned around to her then with his finger on his lips and a mischievous look playing around the corners of his eyes and mouth. 'Sit and be quiet.' He had whispered.

'But-.'

'No time for *buts*, I've already fired my gun.' He winked at her, his cheek right on the surface.

He had done that on purpose, he was planning something and not giving her the chance to talk him out of it.

'Don't move or make a sound no matter what you hear. Don't come out at all until someone calls you by the other name, Langley wasn't it?'

Rachel had nodded, round-eyed and afraid, but had sat on the edge of the bed obediently, folding her hands across her lap.

'I have enjoyed your company, Mrs Shelby, until the next time.'

He had tipped an imaginary hat and then had walked out of the room, closing the door behind him but not locking it.

And not long after that someone had let a bomb or six off in the rooms upstairs.

A hand on her shoulder made Rachel start.

'Miss Langley?'

It was the woman.

Rachel looked around at her. 'He saved me.' She said. 'He pretended to kill me and then saved me.'

Her face contorted with grief.

Dilger looked down at the assassin she had been trailing.

Two of hers were dead because of him. Maybe only by circumstance of the job, but he was still responsible for pulling the trigger.

She couldn't find any pity for the man, but after hearing what the woman had just said she did wonder if everyone didn't deserve a fucking desk-job.

## Chapter Forty-Five

The flashing dots had been pinging up all through the night and early morning, to and from all locations on their satellite map.

The Wales to Moscow connection had stopped pinging up at around two in the morning, but the Moscow end had continued to send communications to Wales long after they had stopped replying.

During the same time-period, the Wales to London connection had been pretty silent, but once the Wales to Moscow line had stopped they had continued to ping up for another hour or more afterward.

It may at first seem like a very positive thing; the action going on in that part of the world had come to an end, *thank God*, one might have said.

Shelby sat alone at the monitor, staring holes through it and through the walls and the countryside beyond.

It was definitely an end to the crew, or whoever they were, in Wales, and it seemed that their *friend* in London had prevailed, but what was the outcome?

A conclusion could be drawn on either side of the scale; an end was an end, but it was to *what* end that mattered.

He heard Sophie coming up behind him.

'You okay, Gray?' She asked, taking the seat next his.

He nodded. 'I'm fine. It just feels worse now somehow.' He said.

She knew what he meant; while the communications had been firing there was hope that Rachel remained unharmed, but once they had stopped the silence didn't give any clues to anything one way or the other. They were left standing in a horrible kind of limbo.

'I know exactly what you mean.' She said, and sighed.

They both sat and watched the quiet screen, trying not to think of the outcome of Rachel's adventure and focusing instead on the trail of communications which were leading an almost straight line down the satellite image, moving southward toward the Pakistani border.

The dots were following a major road.

'You know; Finn can't be travelling along that road, surely?' Sophie said, after a few minutes. 'If he was then he would be moving much faster I would have thought.'

'Agreed; I doubt he would use a vehicle unless it was something which could fly, but the roads?' Shelby shrugged. 'Just not Finn's style is it?'

He picked up the marking-tube and pointed to the screen. 'I think he has used the inaccessibility of the mountains and the cover of the deep forest. Here.' He said, running the red marker along the edge of the mountains. 'But he's going to have a time of it if he has when he gets to here.' He continued, pointing the marker at an open expanse of land now which lay further south.

'That isn't very far from the border is it?' Sophie remarked.

'Can't be more than a hundred miles.' Shelby muttered.

He peered at the screen. 'What's that?' He pointed at a small, discoloured patch on the land about five miles from the other edge of the open plain, almost at the edge of the trees where the forest began again. They hadn't noticed it before.

Sophie leaned closer. 'I don't know, it just looks like a sort of broken rectangle. It's tiny though, it could be anything; it could be a mark on the lens or something.'

Shelby frowned, he didn't think so. 'We need to get a map up; where's Anna?'

'She's going over the equipment in the chopper.'

'Again!? What have we got on-board that needs-.' He snapped his mouth shut and cut off his question before he could finish it. 'Don't bother answering that if you know and if you don't, don't bother to find out.' He said, dryly.

As soon as he had begun to ask what equipment could possibly need so much attention, his mind had given him a kick in the arse as it reminded him of the sudden and noisy entrance of Albert, Anna's dear friend, the mounted machine-gun.

'She'll do whatever she's going to do, so?' He just shrugged.

Sophie just shook her head. 'I'll go find her.' She then said, and walked out to the cricket-pitch.

As the door closed behind her she stopped on the step and smiled.

Anna was having a hard time keeping her focus on her equipment check.

Surrounding her was a small gaggle of young children. She was letting them wear the pilot helmets and talk to each other through the in-built radios.

'You go right over there.' She was saying to a small girl wearing the enormous helmet. 'And when you get to the benches press this button.'

The little girl giggled and then ran off down the field, her tiny legs whizzing round like cartoon-legs and the overly-big helmet wobbling left and right, causing her steps to zigzag and sway from side-to-side.

Sophie laughed and walked down the pavilion and onto the field. 'A little young to be training, isn't she?' She called.

Anna turned around, a childish grin on her face. 'Oh! God! She is just so cute!' She called back.

Sophie was taken by surprise by the girly-voice Anna had just used and by the way she was wringing her hands and clutching at her chest, almost as if she were having a heart-attack brought on by acute adorableness.

She stopped in front of her, her own grin underlined with her puzzlement. 'You really are full of surprises.' She said.

Anna just laughed, the children standing around them laughed and then the tiny voice of an angel blasted through the radio-speaker.

'I'm *here! I'm here! Can you hear me*!?'

The little girl was standing on her tiptoes, waving frantically with one hand while her other tried in vain to hold the helmet in place.

It slipped down over her eyes over and over again as she called out and waved. *'Can you see me? I'm here!'*

Her laughter was so pure that it pulled on the heartstrings, she could have broken a storm and made the sun shine with that voice.

Anna flicked the switch on the receiver. 'We can hear you, my sweet princess.'

'We can hear you, Dizi.' The other children shouted and waved.

The little girl called Dizi, jumped up and down in the air and then began sprinting all the way back down the field again.

'When playtime is over,' Sophie said, and tugged Anna round to look at her. 'You're needed inside; there's something on the satellite we'd like enhancing.'

'Okay.' Anna replied, still grinning. 'Give me five minutes and I'll be in.'

Sophie gave the sprinting Dizi one, last look, her own heartstrings tugging gently as she laughed at the comedy, sprinting legs with huge, wobbling head before she turned away and walked back up to the pavilion.

When she got back inside, Shelby was standing by the coffee-pot, stirring his cup and staring off into space. He hadn't notice Sophie come back inside.

'She said she'll be in, in a minute.' Sophie called ahead.

Shelby flinched and then blinked. 'What? Oh. Okay. Sorry, I was miles away.'

He returned to the monitor. 'It's a fresh pot.' He said, meaning the coffee and trying to sound casual.

Sophie poured two more mugs and then took them back to the table. She sat down next to Shelby again.

What they needed right now was a movement, something to get the wheels turning again; so far they had simply been voyeurs, watching red dots and trying to work out their meanings.

Anna returned, making her way straight to Shelby and Sophie.

'So, what do you need enhancing?' She asked. 'Is that for me?' She said, pointing at the third cup of coffee.

And just like that, Shelby the Interpol Inspector was back; something needed puzzling out. 'What do you make of that?' He asked her, ignoring her question about the coffee and pointing to the small smudge on the satellite image.

She peered closely and then sat at her keyboard. After typing a few commands three, green words appeared over the site: *Al'fezid. Abandoned. Minor.*

'What does that mean?' He asked.

'It's an '*old world*' overlay, it shows settlements that no longer exist. I don't know what the *Minor* means, but *Al'fezid* is a name and abandoned,' she subtly shrugged her head, 'well that goes without saying.'

She picked up the coffee which she assumed to be hers and drank.

Shelby looked back to the satellite image. 'So it's an abandoned village?'

'Looks that way.' Anna replied and tapped more keys.

A green number popped up this time: 1965.

'That's the date it was abandoned, or at least when it was noticed.'

Shelby sat back and frowned, narrowing his eyes in thought. What were the chances that Finn knew of that old village? What were the chances that the red dot looking for him knew of the village?

'What is it, Gray?' Sophie asked, joining him in his frown.

'I don't know, Soph.' He muttered, but didn't take his eyes off the screen. 'But there's something about that old village that gets my hackles up.'

Anna joined them in the vigil and all three of them seemed to be trying to outstare the unblinking screen.

The little German suddenly sucked her breath in. 'Shit! Why didn't I see it before?' She said angrily.

'See what?' Sophie asked her.

'Those dots moving up the road; they sometimes made a communication further back instead of further on and we assumed they were scouring the area, but looking now at the times and the distances between the communications.' She slapped the table. 'How stupid am I!?' She shouted.

Shelby and Sophie sat and waited for her to tell them.

'They are flying around the area in a chopper!' She finally said, folding her arms and angrily sitting back in her seat.

Shelby and Sophie's faces both widened in dawning surprise.

They had assumed four-wheeled drive trucks and jeeps to be looking for Finn and the escaped slaves, especially since they seemed to be always using the road networks.

'Well why the hell are they staying by the road then?' Sophie asked, throwing her arms up in the air. 'For God's sake! I'm really beginning to hate our man F-!'

She stopped mid-sentence. And then she and Shelby suddenly realised why Anna had been so angry.

'He's been hurting them?' Shelby said, for the both of them. 'He's been making forays into their safety-zones and hitting them, I'll bet anything on it.'

'Yes, exactly.' Anna said, a little petulantly. 'And that means that, that village is his goal; he has been frightening them into staying far away from him.'

There was only one way Finn could hide, travel, attack and not be seen and that was staying on the high slopes of the mountain and under the safety of the forest, effectively keeping his pursuers confused and afraid enough to stay out of the trees.

Once the forest ended though, he had a march of at least forty miles across open ground before he would reach the abandoned settlement. He had been trying to keep them as far away as possible to allow him as much time as he could get to get across the open space.

'That's not just Finn's goal.' Shelby eventually said, heavily. 'That's the place he meant for us to meet him all along.'

'But that's inside the Afghanistan border.' Sophie said, the alarm clear in her voice.

'Borders? Finn doesn't give a damn about borders, does he?' Shelby answered.

He stood up and looked down at them both. 'This is it; Finn will be making for that village in the next two days. He could even be almost there now! I can't believe I'm saying this after so many years, but; let's go get our man.'

'What? Now!?' Sophie jumped up as though she had to be in Afghanistan, yesterday.

Anna was next up on her feet. 'I'll call my contacts to come and clear up behind us.'

She left them with her customary, curt nod when things became serious and walked over to her bunk to make the call.

'Fucking hell, Gray! Are we really doing this?' Sophie asked lamely.

'It looks like it. We can't break any more laws than we already have can we?' He shrugged his shoulders.

'I suppose not.' She replied.

She could remember a time when her partner wouldn't even drop litter let alone abscond his country and break into another.

'I'll be ready in fifteen minutes.' She said.

She walked away. They were really going for Finn now. It didn't feel like they were going to arrest a fugitive serial-killer though, it felt more like they were going to rescue an old friend from mutual foes.

Behind her, Shelby watched her go, he could see the lightness in her step even if she herself couldn't feel it yet; she was free of all burdens now, just like he was, just as they all were. An abandonment of the pressures of daily-life.

It was like a liberation of the mind and spirit, allowing oneself to go on and fulfil the tasks ahead without the worry of reprimand or judgement.

The final stage. They had made it here relatively unscathed. Had they just been lucky? He thought not; they had skills between the three of them which some organisations had whole departments for.

No, they were no luckier than the average person; they had arrived here because they had been careful and professional. And they must remain careful and professional; there would be no stumbling at the finish-line.

Once they were all packed and Anna had switched off and packed away their equipment, she disappeared for twenty minutes.

Shelby and Sophie waited for her in their seats in the chopper.

When Anna returned she climbed into the pilot's seat while Shelby and

Sophie sat in the rear, staring horrified at the back of her head.

'Um. Where's Jit?' Sophie's concerned voice asked Anna through the helmet's earphones.

Jit was the chopper pilot who had picked them up from the airport and brought them here. He had left them to themselves and made his own bed in the officer's compound in the north of town.

'He's getting a lift home in the morning. He's made some new friends with the army.' Anna replied.

She flicked a few switches above her head and a panel lit up.

'No, Anna? What I meant was; *where's our fucking pilot!?*' Sophie actually sounded afraid more than she did angry.

Anna turned around in her seat and peered at her through the tinted visor of her pilot's helmet. She looked at her as if to say; can you see the helmet I'm wearing and the seat I am sitting in?

'You can fly a helicopter as well!?' Shelby grinned, truly impressed. 'That's ace, Anna.'

'Don't fucking encourage her!' Sophie elbowed Shelby hard.

She was really afraid; she didn't like flying at the best of times, but a helicopter with a pilot whom she didn't know could fly one somehow seemed like a death-crash in waiting.

Anna saw her concerns and pounced.

Keeping her eye on Sophie's, she fired up the engines and throttled the rotors into slow-moving life. 'I'm sure it's really easy,' she said, 'I've spent a few hours on a flight-simulator that I wrote myself, don't worry, it can't be that much different.' She shouted over the engine's roar.

Her wink was very well pronounced, almost as pronounced as her widening grin which then turned into a squeal of laughter when Sophie's face went perfectly chalk-white.

The engine roared and the blades *whupped* and Anna gave them a beautiful, emergency take-off, ascending like an elevator from hell to heaven and spinning around in a dramatic curve to face the way they needed to head.

The nose dipped dramatically as the engines roared even louder and then they zoomed over the township and officer's compound, leaving Saindak behind in just a few seconds.

'Everyone okay in the back?' Anna asked.

Shelby had just had the ride of his life! His tears of straining to hold on and sit still were still running down his grinning face.

'Bloody brilliant!' He shouted.

He turned to Sophie, strapped in at his side. 'Sophie's fainted though.' He said, and then just laughed because if he didn't he thought he would probably just faint himself.

## Chapter Forty-Six

Salya's dogs were restless tonight. It was Finn who noticed, no one else could perceive their low mutterings and nervous twitching.

*They sense the same thing which you do, my love; death. Death on the horizon, death before dawn.*

The she-wolf snickered seductively in his mind. *Come. Let me sooth you awhile*. She said.

The firelight heat warmed his hands and face, while at his back *she* curled her body around his and embraced him, the heat of her silver fur pressing hard into his back and shoulders while her hot breath and soft kisses warmed his neck and throat.

She ran her fingers across his temples and through his shaggy hair, whispering in his ears. *Do you love me, Finn?* She purred, the question mere whimsical rhetoric.

'Yes.'

*Do you hate me?* She then asked. It sounded like a kind of pout.

'Sometimes.'

She laughed teasingly, giggling seductively, and then licked his ear. *Oh. I don't blame you; I can get so very angry sometimes, can't I?*

'You can.'

She ran her claws through his hair at the back of his head and then grabbed a handful, pulling his head back slowly and taking his throat between her powerful jaws.

She moaned and purred deeply. *But you know I love you, I only hurt you because I love you?*

'I know.'

*But did you know that even without your* geis *I love you? I have always loved you.*

Her hot breath pushed his own back as she brushed her wolf-lips past his and then kissed him.

*We promised*. She said, embracing him and holding him tightly.

Finn fell into her, allowing her to cover him, almost smother him, inside her powerful hold, but he frowned and wondered.

What did she mean? He had always loved her and she had always loved him. Wasn't that how it always had been?

Always? When did *always* begin? He couldn't bring the memory of their beginnings to mind; they had just always *been* he thought.

She continued to hold him and stroke him and then she began to sing.

*"It's time! It's time!" Cried the king of the fair-folk,*
*"Bring me my blade of light!" Said he.*
*"Bring me my shield of justice!"*
*"And bring me my seven-spears!"*
*"Bring me my seven-spears!"*

Sitting across from Finn, at the other side of the fire, Salya watched stern-faced and silent.

Someone was with them, with Finn right now. And she didn't mean the others; all were sleeping except Salya, Finn and the unseen thing he was speaking and reacting to.

She watched in fascinated horror as he swayed as though he were actually being caressed and then his throat had looked as if it had constricted, closing slightly as if something were strangling him.

Salya had almost leaped up then and struck out at whatever it was that was trying to choke him, but she quickly noticed that his breathing hadn't changed and he didn't seem to be in any distress.

*A sickness of the brain which splits the mind.*

Nim had said something like that. How could she help her friend? How could anyone help him with a sickness like that?

She hurt as she watched him, even if he did seem to be enjoying whatever was happening to him. She hurt for his mind, for the person he once had been. But without him a great evil would still be at large in the world.

'Why does great good always have to be born because of great sadness?' She muttered silently.

She would have thought it would have been the other way around and great evil would be born because of some great sadness or other evil.

Maybe it was both; maybe it was all down to who the person had been in the first place?

She continued to watch Finn and he continued to sway and occasionally mutter replies to questions only he could hear, but after five more minutes his head dropped back forward and his eyes snapped open. He saw Salya watching him.

He held her gaze silently.

She looked back.

His expression was placid and calm, he knew she had seen him with the she-wolf, but he wouldn't offer any explanation.

As if hearing him, she came to the front of his mind and examined Salya herself. She loved the girl, she was strong and faithful.

'You are a strong, young thing.' She said.

Salya's eyes widened in fright, but she managed to stop herself from panicking and running away as her body was trying to get her to do.

In the blink of an eye, Finn's face had changed, only subtly, but it was definitely changed, and then he, her, it! What? Had spoken in a deep, female voice.

She just looked back as his scarred face smiled. Like a woman.

'Do not be afraid, child.'

'Who-who are you?'

He leaned forward and placed a finger on his smiling lips. 'I am a secret.' The woman's voice said, and then he leaned back again.

'What?' Finn's voice then asked. 'Sorry, I missed that; what was it you said, Salya?'

Salya stumbled a little. 'Err. Um, nothing, I was just saying that we are getting close.' She answered, turning her attention to the fire and prodding it uselessly.

'Aye, that we are.' Finn replied, completely oblivious to the last ten minutes.

He stood up and picked up his backpack and NV goggles.

Salya looked startled. 'What? Where are you going?' She whispered, standing up herself and readying her own pack.

'I won't be long. And no, you can't come, you are going to be needed here.' He said.

He hugged her and then lifted her arm with the watch on it. 'Exactly four hours from now, get everyone up and start moving as fast as possible across the open land, make a straight line to the village I told you about.'

'But what about you?' She protested.

'I will meet you before you reach the village. Trust me, my brave, young friend; an opportunity has arisen and I think I will take it. Stick to the plan, make for the village, I promise you I will meet you.' He stooped down and kissed her forehead.

She reached up and flung her arms around his neck. 'Be safe, Finn. If you do not return I swear by all of the gods, yours and mine, that I will search for you until I find you.'

She dropped back to the ground. Someone stirred in their sleep.

'I have to go.' Finn said. 'I will meet you in around eight hours. Fast as you can, Salya, four hours from now.'

She nodded her head and Finn turned away, lowering his goggles and trotting off into the dark.

Just like that, Salya thought, mentally clicking her fingers.

She couldn't understand why, but she had the feeling that the woman who had spoken to her through Finn was more dangerous than Finn himself was. Strangely, there was a small comfort accompanying that thought.

Night-eyes of the small creatures hiding in the undergrowth, flared white through Finn's goggles, tiny, hot pinpoints of light before darting away from him as he sloped past.

Forty miles away he estimated the chopper would be laid up for the night.

If his understanding of soldiers was correct, that's what he would do, keep a nice even number of miles away, forty miles was well within striking distance of most helicopters and well away from the danger of the forest.

But that was still a run of ten miles an hour for those forty miles and then another four hour run back again. If it all went well though, they would have an edge, just a small one. Would it be enough? Enough to get the children to the buildings?

Shelby. He was the key now. Was he smart enough to know where Finn would be heading?

Of all his calculations and plans, Shelby was the flimsiest link; he could fail to make the connection, he could even be dead for all Finn knew.

But the thought didn't stop him from running through the forest; he would continue until he had finished it now. And by Maeve's honour, he *would* finish it.

The ground suddenly eased up its grabbing attempts at tripping him as Finn broke through the tree-line and hit the open grass and dirt ahead.

His pace picked up and before long he was loping along at the ten miles an hour he needed to be at.

His feet peddled the earth beneath and past him as he pushed it behind and dragged the next few yards forward and underneath.

Half-waxed moonlight threw his shadow out in front of him as he ran, a pale stencil-cut shape of a stretched-out running man. They both moved through the night silently.

"And bring me my Seven-Spears." She smiled as she sang the verse again.

*It is a pity we don't have Davar's motorbike.* It was the man who spoke.

'I was thinking exactly the same thing.' Finn answered.

*We know.* The she-wolf purred.

*I had a bike like that once.* The man continued. *A Honda mine was, but a two-fifty four-stroke like that one.*

'What happened to it?'

*I crashed it into a wall.* He said, and both he and the she-wolf laughed. *The missus banned me after that, wouldn't let me buy another bike, said if I wanted to end up in hospital then she could easily oblige.*

The three of them laughed at that, Finn out loud.

*And then she hit me with the helmet while I lay in my hospital bed with my leg up in traction!*

The hours and miles dribbled by, the three of them loped along and kept each other company, regaling one another with stories of things they knew, things they had done and things they had seen.

The boundaries of each personality in Finn's mind were clearly wrought; no sensitive questions were asked and certain parts of their stories were automatically circumnavigated to avoid the dangerous reality of the memories.

With only a few miles left to go they all suddenly hushed to silenced awe and Finn slowed his strides and then almost stopped.

From behind a large copse of trees stepped a huge, male deer.

*Is that real?* The man asked, his jaw sounding like it was on the ground.

'Aye, it is real.' Finn replied.

*Well what the hell is it doing here? Everything's been wiped out by all the years of war here, Deer went extinct in the 70's, didn't they?*

*It is Bactrian.* The she-wolf said, as though that should answer their questions.

The deer stood and looked in their direction, his own night-senses telling him that there was a predator abroad. But a strange predator it was; the deer sensed no danger to itself.

His antlers tossed gently as he sniffed the air, puzzled but wary.

'We go that way.' Finn said, quietly, and indicated his immediate left.

With one, last amazed look for the resurrected Bactrian, Finn took up his run again, making a wide birth around the animal.

*If there was ever a sign of hope, I think we have just witnessed it.* The man said, quietly.

The she-wolf sighed happily and rubbed herself against them both.

There was a warm feeling accompanying the man's words, shrouding them all in a shielding cover of truth and right; the tenacity of good to overcome evil was embodied by that deer, that species of life which had been thought to have been wiped out.

Good could always be found in even the smallest of recesses of an evil domain - and wherever war erupted, evil *did* make that place its home.

It mattered not that you were the defender or the aggressor, war always carried with it, its own cowl of fear, fear being the tool to extract the evil in man.

But every evil place always had its own *Bactrian stag*, a pearl of bright goodness just waiting to be found.

And sometimes, like Finn, that pearl carried itself to those dark places, fighting dark-fire with their own fire of light.

Dead-ahead a swell of that darkness faded slowly into view through Finn's night-vision goggles; the outpost where the chopper was laid up for the night.

The camp had been settled on an open expanse and there were no hiding places to approach from, but Finn hadn't expected anything less.

He looked at his watch; four hours was just coming up, Salya would be rousing the others by now.

Dropping to his haunches he moved quickly and silently forward and slightly to the right, giving himself a better view of the camp and chopper.

He stopped and dropped to his knee. Something was wrong. Where were the men? Where were all the tents?

Two, small field-tents stood side-by-side, the chopper standing ten yards away. Who pitches a tent so close to a chopper?

His heart sank. This was the very reason he had made Salya wait instead of getting them on their way before he had left; the main body of soldiers were not here, there was only one place they would be heading; the village.

If he had made them leave straight away they would have run into the soldiers before he could get back to them, they wouldn't stand a chance.

He shook his head in disbelief. It felt like he had made a mistake even though he knew he hadn't, or else he wouldn't have planned for this eventuality. Nevertheless, he now had to run *plan B*.

He couldn't destroy the helicopter now and he couldn't start killing whoever was in the tents; the soldiers camped out on the road toward the village somewhere would be alerted and made to get to their target as fast as possible.

He waited.

There would be at least one guard in there somewhere, watching the night and the camp while the commander and the pilot slept. It was probable that there was another soldier in there somewhere too, sleeping.

That left at least fifteen more men heading Salya's way. Probably more.

The perimeter guard suddenly walked out from behind the helicopter. He was wearing NV goggles of his own and had been out walking in the blackness.

They were still very jittery after his treatment of them in the woods Finn thought.

*Then if that were the case, why aren't there more guards?* The man asked.

It was a good question and one which prompted Finn to frown deeply.

Without a word or a sound he flopped to his stomach and crawled across the ground, heading for the back of the tent nearest him.

He pulled out a blade and silently sliced the silken sheeting, opening the gap and looking inside. It was empty, not even a camp-bed.

*What does that mean?* The man asked.

*It means it is a trap, but a trap not set for us, a trap set to distract us.* The she-wolf answered, echoing Finn's conclusion perfectly. The real trap was for Salya and the children.

'I underestimated them.' Finn whispered, dropping his head.

*Regrets don't make new plans.* She said a little scornfully. *Do either of you have the skill to fly the machine?*

It felt as though she were standing with her hands on her hips, lecturing them both. *No, of course you don't, so let's skip the regrets and go straight to plan C and get running, Finn of the Seven-Spears.*

The man took his normal place in the shadows at the back of Finn's mind, cringing almost at the she-wolf's commands.

Finn stayed low, turning away, and sprinted off silently back out into the night, leaving his regret behind and aiming his wrath ahead instead.

Torch lights bounced along the ground, illuminating the running legs of the children. They had been going for twenty minutes now and the forest had been left behind.

There had been a little tension when Salya had roused them all, but it hadn't taken her long to explain and get them going. Only Jimi still complained about being left in the dark and being treated like a child.

Parisa had her usual place a hundred yards in front of them, wearing her goggles and scouting ahead while Salya led the column of children.

She had a plan to stop and let them walk for fifteen minutes at a time and then pick up the pace again and jog for fifteen minutes if they could manage it.

She had promised them she wouldn't push them too hard, but she had also promised herself that they wouldn't be stopping until they had Finn back with them.

The group trundled across the landscape through the night beneath a star-filled canopy and dim, crescent moon.

Silent and determined, adults and children alike, they all sensed the need to get back with Finn.

## Chapter Forty-Seven

Abandoned village? The words brought to mind a settlement like a ghost-town; windblown and empty, creaking gates and clinking chains, empty, dark houses.

Votsky was very disappointed.

The place he had arrived at earlier that evening was more like a child's maze of broken, straight walls and roofless, crooked-brick rectangles. It was a good thing that he had all twenty of his men with him.

They had begun the labour of securing three of the largest and most intact of the buildings as soon as they had arrived, fitting metal-sheet roofs, blocking any windows and securing doorways with anything they could find.

The largest of these buildings was to be a temporary prison and holding place for the slaves when they were recaptured. While one of the remaining two was Votsky's command centre and the other the place they would be holding the man who had been causing them so much trouble.

Votsky smoked and sat in his chair, staring at the clock on the wall. It was after midnight now, the man would be making his foray to the chopper anytime soon - if Votsky had his mind understood - but if he didn't, then he would still be heading for this place and Votsky's soldiers anyway.

The man was a fool, Votsky thought, he should have stayed close to the cover of the mountains; the terrain and high-ground would have given them a big advantage.

Instead the idiot had chosen the most obvious place to head for before he made the final leg of the journey over the border and into Pakistan.

As soon as the man saw that the camp where the chopper was sited was empty he would probably try and make his way back to the slaves as quickly as he could.

Votsky had another half-dozen soldiers laying in wait to ambush him on his way back.

If they actually managed to capture or kill him, then that would be perfect, but if they didn't and he killed them, then their silence wouldn't go unnoticed.

Votsky didn't care either way, the lives of his men were nothing to him.

His black eyes flicked to the ground by the doorway.

A large, yellow scorpion crawled in from the outside, squeezing itself beneath the gap below the door. It stopped as it detected the light, pausing to take in its new surroundings.

Votsky didn't take his eyes off it, watching unemotionally as it began crawling across the sandy floor toward him.

It reached the tip of his boot and stopped for a second before climbing up the front and onto the laces.

Votsky still didn't move.

Death crawled up his bootlaces and onto his fatigues, the creatures black-dot eyes sparkling under the glare of the Tilley-lamp.

A predator watching a predator.

It reached his knee and then paused again as the angle it was climbing changed from vertical to almost horizontal.

Votsky's expression and shark-eyes remained impassive as the scorpion pulled itself over the edge and took a step up onto his thigh.

It paused for the fourth time, facing him, sensing the sudden danger in front of it now.

Its stinging tail flexed, the onyx-black chitin tip swaying over its own head as it poised itself ready to fight.

With a single graceful gesture, Votsky stabbed down with his own stinger, his stiletto blade, piercing the scorpion through its carapace.

The blade-tip just subtly pricked the fabric of his combat-fatigues beneath.

He lifted the scorpion up on the end of his knife and watched while its legs thrashed and its stinging tail lashed out uselessly.

Cocking his head from side-to-side, Votsky studied every movement of the dying creature, reading its death-throes until finally it stopped moving and just lay with its legs splayed out limply and its tail dangling.

He carried on watching for a minute more, making sure he wasn't going to miss anything, and then flicked the carcass across the room where it hit the wall at the other side and fell to the floor, forgotten.

A single tear of blood ran down the tip of the knife. Votsky wiped the blade on his calf and then sheathed it again, sitting back and resuming his vigil of the slow-moving hands of the clock.

Outside, the ten men remaining at the camp were in their positions, secreting themselves around the perimeter of the village and hiding in the abandoned buildings.

The other ten had been sent out to meet the slaves who Votsky was sure would be making the journey without the man until he returned.

Of course, he could be wrong entirely and the man and the slaves had escaped over the mountains or were still hiding in the forest.

But Votsky didn't think so, the man felt like a predator not prey; predators didn't easily run away.

Ten miles to the east, Votsky's six men sat crouched in the dugout they had hastily made. All six were scanning the open, unlit landscape all around them through the lenses of their night-vision goggles.

Finn lowered the binoculars and then dropped his own lenses down again.

*They are being much more intelligent than before.* The she-wolf murmured.

'Aye. I'm in two minds whether to just leave them and disappoint them or not.'

Oh. She purred. *You know you can't do that now, my love.*

Finn sighed. 'I know, but it would have given them something to think about.'

She laughed lightly.

He rolled over onto his back and pulled his blades free and then took a flare from his belt.

Rolling back over onto his stomach, he took one last look at the dugout laying a mile up ahead.

*Let us bring the Seven-Spears to them.* She whispered.

Finn leaped to his feet and began sprinting across the ground, head down, powering forward. He would get maybe a minute of running before they saw him.

The dust flew up from his speeding heels as he ran, leaving a billowing streak hovering a few feet from the ground. It was this which the first of the soldiers had been alerted to.

He nudged the man crouched next to him and pointed. 'What's that?'

The other soldier looked. What *was* that? It looked like a creeping fog snaking away into the night. Or was it snaking toward them?

Both men followed the trail to its source and suddenly jumped when they made out the sprinting form of Finn.

'Stalin's merciful balls!' One of them breathed. 'How can he move like that?'

The other soldiers had gathered around now and were all staring at the incredible sprinting man.

'Who fucking cares?' Another soldier said, and opened fire.

Within seconds the whole front of the men was ablaze with the fire from their automatic weapons.

The silence was smothered under the hail of rattling gunfire, the sporadic *crack-crack-crack!* Coming from the blazing barrels of six guns.

And on Finn came.

Darting supernaturally from left to right, rolling over and coming back up to his feet, but ever streaking closer.

Bullets flew past him, over him, but never near enough to be any danger to him.

The soldiers were frantically trying to pin him down, training their weapons on the next place they thought he was going to be.

'Don't all shoot straight at him!' One of the soldiers shouted. 'You two on the end shoot at his flanks!'

It was the right thing to do and if they had done it a few seconds earlier they would have probably managed to at least wing their target.

With less than thirty yards to go, Finn pulled the tape on the flare and lobbed it hard, straight at the firing soldiers.

As it sailed overhead he pulled his goggles off and dropped them to the ground, readying his knives now.

The flare exploded and for a brief moment the soldiers were blinded by the sudden eye-watering blooms coming from their own night-vision goggles.

They all released their triggers and threw their hands to their heads, pulling the headpieces off and rubbing their star-popped eyes.

A moment later, Finn dropped in amongst them and the gunfire started up again. This time though, it was accompanied by a terrible screaming.

Three hundred feet above, a large eagle owl circled, it had been hunting the ground below, spotting the unfamiliar heat-signatures of the men sitting in the hole.

It watched now as noise and light spilled from the place, scattering a dozen, or more small animals away in all directions.

The owl chose its target and homed in, moving its circular flight to match the unsuspecting rabbit's getaway path and as the last of the gunfire and screaming came to an abrupt end, it dived and caught its prey, neatly breaking its back and then flying away into the night.

Finn stood up, panting hard, his eyes tracking the noise of the retreating night-bird's wings.

Unlike the prey in the clutching death-grip of the bloodied talons of the bird, Finn's prey lay dead at his feet while his own *talons* dripped blood to the earth.

He turned to the embankment of dirt which the men had piled up in front of the dugout and stabbed his blades deep into it, cleaning the blood away.

Turning to the south-west, he bore his gaze into the night and the direction of the village. They would know he was coming now, so that would be the place he *wouldn't* be going.

If they were expecting him there then he could be certain that someone would be sent out to wait for Salya, a smaller group probably. He had to get them before Salya and the others did.

After retrieving his night-goggles, he drank water from the dead men's canteens and then set off again, sprinting in the direction where he thought it most likely Salya would be in another three hours.

For the first time since he could remember, Finn felt a dark spot of anxiety lying in the depths of his stomach.

What if Salya had made better time than he expected them to? He had already underestimated once, what was to say he wasn't wrong about that as well?

Damn it. So close now.

He could feel the she-wolf right at the front of his mind, lending her will and her strength. Then the man crept forward and joined them, the three became one.

He gradually increased his speed, steadily lowering his head forward and streamlining himself as he sped along at a casual twelve miles an hour and then fourteen, fifteen until over the space of around ten minutes, Finn had his sprint up to a comfortable nineteen miles an hour.

He would be damned if he couldn't make the rest of the run in two hours. He just prayed Salya wasn't moving too quickly.

'My legs are hurting!' It was Faria, she was only seven and a petit thing with a strong heart but frail body.

Salya stopped them. 'We'll walk for awhile, you have done well and I think we have moved very quickly.'

She approached the small girl and held her arms out to her. 'Come, I will carry you while we walk and you can rest a little.' She said, smiling encouragingly at Faria.

The small girl held her hands up for Salya and allowed herself to be picked up and rested on the crook of Salya's arm.

Jimi, Nim and Simeon lowered the children they had been carrying to the floor and then all three wiped their brows and stretched their aching backs.

'You're a hard master, Salya.' Jimi said, as he sidled up to her.

She noticed him checking her out, looking for signs of her own fatigue and weariness. 'I'm fine before you ask.' She said. She sounded a little icy.

'You don't seem it, what's on your mind?' He asked her.

Salya looked ahead into the night, watching Parisa's softly glowing shape moving in front of her through her night-vision goggles. She raised them and looked over to Jimi walking by her side.

'I don't know. Something feels wrong, something waiting for us in the dark.'

Jimi nodded his head slowly, looking around him. 'A disturbance in the force, you mean?' He muttered.

'What?'

'Nothing, I was just being smart.' He replied, looking back at her. 'What do you think it might be?'

If there was something Jimi had learned from being with this group, particularly Finn, it was that parts of the big man rubbed off on you.

Salya had spent more time with him than any of them, if she said something wasn't right then it was sensible to take heed.

'Something that knows we are coming.' She answered.

Somehow it didn't surprise him, he had been a dog on his master's leash once and his masters had been relentless at times.

Once he had been sent out to kill a man who had betrayed them in the late thirties. They had found him after almost seventy years, which sent out the message that the organisation would never stop looking, the task would always be passed down the generations until it had been completed.

They carried on walking in silence, the children had their heads bowed, following the torchlight, silent and determined.

The dark, even through the night-vision, looked expansive and deep like the bottom of the ocean where darkness prevailed and creatures skittered about the edges of the light-shadows. Unseen things watching from just beyond the veil of visibility.

Even Jimi felt it now, a movement coming from the east, stirring the air and making his skin prickle.

He dropped back to where Nim walked at the side of the children.

He took her hand and spoke quietly into her ear. 'There is something approaching us.' He whispered. 'Be ready, Nim, to drop your equipment and gather the children around you.'

'But-!'

'No buts, trust me and do as I say when the time comes.' He said, and squeezed her hand.

She had a fearful look on her face and her eyes were brimming with tears, but she nodded her head.

He lifted his own goggles and leaned down, kissing Nim gently before he returned to Salya at the head of the column.

'We have to be ready if we are going to meet something in the dark out here.' He said, to the young girl.

'I have my pistol and you have-.' She began.

'No, Salya, we will not be able to fight them, not with children in our group.'

He could see she was thinking about that. They couldn't have bullets flying around.

'What should we do then?' She asked.

Before he could reply, Parisa came running back to them.

'There's a truck with men.' She said, breathlessly. 'Coming this way. It's moving slowly and they don't have the lights on.'

Jimi grabbed Salya by the shoulders and turned her to face him. 'Everybody must drop their weapons and equipment,' he said frantically, hushing her when she began to protest. 'Listen to me!' He hissed. 'They will kill everyone here if they sense there is going to be any kind of resistance. Do you understand? Everyone.'

Salya's face briefly took on the appearance of the child she was again, frightened at the sudden urgency in this man's voice, but she soon had it back under her control and nodded her head sternly.

He spoke sense, even if she didn't like what it was he was saying.

'You and the others give me your weapons then get together. They will only see two women and a group of children now. You have to be a child, Salya, if we have any hope of retrieving everybody.'

He looked at her and then softened his gaze a little. 'You are more useful on the inside than out. Finn and I can meet and then come for you all together. Once we arrive you will know what needs to be done.'

She hated it, the logic of it was infallible and she hated it even more because of that than because she couldn't fight; she had been backed into a corner of common-sense. 'You'd better come.' She said, balefully, and stared hard at him as she handed her weapons over.

She turned around and ordered Parisa and the others to do the same.

'Drop the goggles in a pile and cover them.' She said, once everyone was disarmed.

Nim and Jimi stood facing one another. 'Like Salya said; you'd better come back.' Nim said, with her eyes cast down to the ground.

Jimi's heart ached to see her in such pain, his own fears of losing her added to the anxiety which already sat heavily in the pit of his stomach.

'I'll come.' He said, trapping his tongue and stopping himself from saying something stupid like; *or I'll die trying*.

He wasn't going to die, neither was Nim, they couldn't, not now, it was so unfair. Please, God, not now!

With a last determined look for her, Jimi gathered up the weapons and sprinted away into the night, leaving Nim with her fears and her tears.

Salya watched his shadow disappear, promising herself she would hunt him down if he abandoned them, and then turned away and sat in the huddle of children, taking up the disguised mantel of frightened slave.

Parisa sat next to her, staring into the dark. 'I won't go back.' She said, quietly. 'I will make them kill me before I go back.'

Salya picked up her friend's hand and held it tightly. 'We won't be going back.' She said, defiantly. 'We won't.'

## Chapter Forty-Eight

Two hours had come and gone, Finn wondered if he had missed them in the dark, but soon shook the thought away; he would have to be miles and miles off track to not be able to spot their torches.

He bit into the dried meat he had been chewing as he ran, keeping his energy stores as full as possible.

*We are too late.*

Finn slowed to a trot and looked for whatever it was the she-wolf had spotted. Ahead he could just make out the double lines of tyre-tracks; a big vehicle had driven along here and very recently.

He stopped completely then and crouched down, following the tracks in either direction as far as his night-vision would allow him to see. He looked down at the marks directly in front of him, running his fingers lightly over the zigzag pattern of the tyre-tread. 'This is heading into the west, toward them.' He said.

He stood up and looked around.

*There*. The she-wolf said, turning his attention to a line of tracks about fifty-feet away.

Finn trotted over to them and crouched down again. The pattern was the same tread but this time they were heading back into the east.

*You must carry on, Finn, go to where you originally planned to meet them.* Her voice was hard but not unemotional.

Finn knew exactly what she was getting at; he had to go and see for himself what had happened while he had been parted from them. It wasn't much further he thought.

Steeling his resolve to finish his quest, Finn loped off again, following the tyre-tracks into the west.

He had been running for not more than ten minutes when he heard the noisy, thudding, running steps of someone to his far left.

He looked over and saw Jimi at the same time Jimi spotted him.

The Russian waved and changed his direction, making his way toward Finn. He was alone, Finn noted, his brow knitting with rising anger.

He changed his own direction and ran on to meet him.

As they approached one another, Jimi slowed down and bent himself over at the middle and stood gasping and panting hard.

'They-they've got them.' He managed to bluster, spitting out the cotton-wool froth in his mouth. He hated running. 'No one's-hurt.' He spat again. 'God! I think I'm having a heart-attack.'

Finn lifted him up by the shoulders and gave him his water canteen. 'I am glad to see you alive, Jimi,' he said, watching Jimi drink deeply, 'but you must tell me why you are alive here and not either dead back there,' he pointed into the night behind, 'or captured with the others.'

Reaching out, Finn carefully and slowly took Jimi by the lapels and lifted him off the ground, bringing his face close to his. 'Did you abandon them?' He asked, icily.

Jimi looked surprised but not afraid. 'Of course I abandoned them; how else can I be of use to getting them back?' He said.

Finn continued to scowl.

'Think man! Those people who took them are the same people I used to work for; I will be executed on the spot if caught and then what good would that be, eh?' He said. 'It wouldn't do *me* any good, *you* any good and most certainly wouldn't do any good for them.' His head flicked in the direction of the village and the children being taken there.

Finn's frown turned slowly to a smile and then he turned his lapel-grabbing hold into a bear-hugging embrace.

Jimi gasped as he was crushed.

'Apologies, my friend.' Finn said, and then dropped Jimi back to the ground. 'I forget sometimes.'

'What? That we all can't do the things which you do, you mean?' Jimi asked, as he straightened his lapels and then drank more water.

Finn nodded.

'Believe me, my large, dangerous friend, if I could do half of what you do I would have gladly died fighting them off.' He shrugged. 'But I can't, all I can do are the things which I know.'

Finn placed a friendly hand on his shoulder. 'And you do them well.' He said, looking down at Jimi.

The Russian just shrugged. 'Maybe.' He said. 'I can only try.'

He placed his hand on top of Finn's forearm then. 'So, what's the plan?'

'We rest for one hour and then we go that way.' Finn replied, indicating again, in the direction of the village this time.

'Okay. I think I will have a bath and a hot vodka before we set off.'

Jimi grinned and then flopped to the ground. 'Make that a sand-bath and water.' He finished and dropped onto his back, resting his head on the most comfortable rock he could find and closing his eyes. 'Damn! My ass hurts from running.' He muttered before falling asleep.

And then he opened his eyes again, just a blink-moment later.

'Come. It's time to go.' Finn said, shaking him again.

'Wha-! I've only just sat down!' He replied, and rubbed his eyes.

He looked at his watch; an hour exactly had passed. 'God I hate it when that happens!'

Finn stood back while Jimi roused himself.

Still sitting on the ground, he tipped the water canteen over his head and gasped as the cold water ran down his neck, back and chest. He then spent the next minute and a half coaxing his aching limbs to get him back up onto his feet.

'I'm ready.' He said, but groaned as his muscles clicked and his joints popped.

Finn cocked his head to one side. 'Then let us get moving.' He said, sympathetically.

Jimi set the pace, there was no real urgency to get there now, they were expected and so whatever it was they were going to be greeted by would wait for them.

The sun would be rising soon, they would meet it at the same time they arrived at the village, a couple of hours from now.

Salya and the children sat huddled in the room they had been ordered into once unloaded from the truck.

Nim and Kurshid had been in here with them until about twenty minutes ago when two Russians had ordered them to follow them out.

They had been left a single, sickly-glowing lamp, just enough to see the space around them.

None of the children were crying, but they were all frightened, pressed tightly close to Salya and Parisa.

The older girl stared at the door with murder in her eyes. She would die before going back she was thinking over and over, and if she got the chance to take someone with her she would do it. Just let the bastards try and take her back.

Salya reached out her hand and grasped Parisa's, startling the girl. 'Stay here.' Salya whispered. 'Don't think about them out there, think about us in here and be ready for when we get out.' She squeezed Parisa's hand firmly. 'He will come, Parisa, and we will be ready won't we?'

Parisa stared back, her eyes gradually softening. 'We will be ready.' She replied, and nodded, repeating Salya's words.

'Just stay strong, Parisa, stay strong.'

The girl nodded again.

'And remember; those out there think that we are just children.' Salya added. 'They think we are just frightened and incapable, but they will get a surprise when Finn gets here.'

The girls sat hand-in-hand, Salya wondering when Finn would arrive. It would be soon though she thought.

In Votsky's little room Nim and Kurshid stood side-by-side, their heads bowed and eyes lowered.

urshid had handed her baby off to Simeon when she had been called out.

Votsky sat in his chair and watched them.

The children held no fascination for him, they were too young, lives not yet lived. But it wasn't Votsky's morality which made the children uninteresting, it was the very fact that they hadn't lived yet, hadn't filled their minds with all the experience of years growing up; what was the point of taking a life which hadn't lived?

It was like sending a great hunter out onto the African plains and asking him to bag weasels. Pointless and completely unsatisfying.

In his life Votsky had actually only ever killed one child, completely unintentional and accidental.

He had been firing a shotgun through a partitioning wall, tracing the movements of one of the men he and his team had been sent to eliminate.

He had hit the man, peppering him with shotgun pellets, but the spread had been wide enough for some of the shot to miss, carrying on across the room and killing a toddler sitting on the bed at the other side.

Votsky had just looked at the small body without remorse or any feeling at all. The only tiny regret which ran briefly through his cold mind was the shame it was that this life hadn't developed; who knew? He may have met it when it was much older.

The women standing in front of him weren't much better. He despised women. It didn't push him to want to purposely hurt them, but he hated their weakness and vulnerability, their dependency on men. Their hold on men.

'Where is the man who was with you, the big man?' He suddenly asked them.

He had let them just stand there for the twenty minutes since they had entered, a guard stood by the door and all four remained silent.

His sudden question made both of the women jump visibly.

'I-, we don't know sir.' Nim replied.

Votsky raised his finger, barely perceptibly, and the guard delivered a winding punch into Nim's stomach.

She doubled over gasping and then crumpled to the floor, lying on her side with her knees drawn up to her chest.

'He left us, sir, he-he ran away into the night without telling us anything except to walk to here.' Kurshid then said.

Votsky nodded his head, again almost imperceptibly, and the soldier stepped forward again, this time lifting the still gasping Nim to her feet.

He released her and then stepped back to the doorway.

Votsky's dark gaze penetrated both of them, they could feel him probing beneath their very skin almost, looking for the lies in their answers. He would find none, they hadn't actually lied.

He left them standing while he thought about what these two women meant to the man, if anything. He wouldn't need to beat it out of them, they were telling the truth. So had he needed them because they could watch the children while he went out on his hunts?

'What is his name?' He then asked.

'He said we were to call him Finn, sir.' Nim answered, still clutching her aching stomach.

What was he looking for? He already knew that Finn would be on his way here, so why the obvious questions?

'Did he ever touch you?' Votsky carried on.

Nim stalled. 'Sir?' She said, knowing full well what he meant.

'Did he ever lay you down and fuck you?' He clarified, his voice academic and toneless.

Nim understood what he was probing for; he was looking for emotional attachment to them.

'He-he raped us both and beat us if that is what you mean, sir?'

Kurshid didn't know why Nim had told that lie, but went along with it and nodded her head, sniffling.

Neither of them would ever know it, but the lie had saved their lives. If they had been of any use to the man coming to rescue them, Votsky would have had them hung and torched on poles outside the village walls. A waiting greeting and a taste of things to come for him.

The shark-eyed Russian nodded his head again and the soldier opened the door. 'Out!' He ordered and then marched out behind them when they left, closing the door behind him.

Votsky didn't move, didn't bat an eyelid. Didn't see anything beyond the three inches in front of him. He just waited.

Eleven miles to the west, Finn and Jimi ran onward, Jimi tiring again but keeping a decent pace.

Finn suggested that they stop for another hour once they were five miles away and made sure the Russian ate some of the dried meat as he ran.

'I think we may be able to stop a little longer than an hour.' Finn said, talking as naturally as though he were walking in the park.

Jimi grunted.

'We have made good time and I think we will be needing the sun upon us when we enter the village anyway.' Finn carried on.

Jimi grunted again and then slowed down. 'Might- as well- walk now- then.' He said, gasping.

Finn slowed down and then walked by Jimi's side. 'Would you like me to carry you?' He asked. He was serious.

'I know you're- only trying to be- kind and help, but- you can fuck off, okay?' He flung a lame punch at Finn's arm. 'Sarcasm doesn't- suit you.' He said.

Finn smirked. 'I wasn't being sarcastic.'

Jimi scoffed. 'Then you're a bigger- dick than I am if you- think I'm going to let you carry me!' He was still gasping, but his breathing was much easier and the pain in his chest had at least gone.

'Why do you want the sun up so high?' He then asked.

Finn's grin spread across his face. 'Because I have a mind to die and have *you* carry me up to the walls.' He said, his eyes twinkling.

Jimi frowned for just a moment and then it dawned on him. 'Oh. Very clever.' He said, nodding and smiling back.

It would be impossible to approach the village, day or night, unnoticed; the soldiers waiting there were well equipped and on the lookout. But they wouldn't be on the lookout for one of their own returning with the prize now would they?

'You know I won't really be able to carry you though, don't you?' Jimi raised his eyebrows as he looked up at Finn. 'I'll have to more sort of drag you.'

It was Finn's turn to grunt now. 'Drag me?'

He turned his head and looked down at the dusty, rocky, rabbit-dropping covered ground.

Jimi shrugged innocently. 'It's your plan.' He said, and patted his big friend on the arm, walking past him away into the night.

## Chapter Forty-Nine

Deepening shadows stretched out from the buildings, the corona of the sunrise chasing the dark back, leaving only the cool memory of it in the shades.

The soldiers were awake and fidgeting, none of them sleeping through the night. They drank their water and chewed on their field rations as the sun came up behind them.

Votsky had moved from his chair only once, to make a walk around the perimeter, more to keep the guards on their toes than to look for approaching enemies.

Once he had done that he went back inside and sat back down again, resuming his vigil on the clock.

He had expected an appearance by now, before the sun had risen at least.

The six soldiers lying dead a few miles away may have injured their man and he was struggling to get here though. Maybe he was dead.

They hadn't had the time to make a call-in to let them know they had spotted him.

Votsky frowned slightly. That could only mean he had dispatched them very quickly. So why the delay?

The hunter can always feel the presence of another hunter; Votsky felt as though he were in someone else's game-plan, but couldn't pin down exactly what direction the play was going in just yet.

He didn't like that, he liked his plans to go from A to B in a straight and uninterrupted line.

A double knock came at the door and it opened, Votsky's guard stepped inside. 'There is a man coming toward us, sir. He says he is one of ours. He looks to be dragging a body behind him.'

Votsky abruptly stood. 'Show me.' He ordered.

The guard walked back out onto the dusty street, Votsky right behind him.

They quickly walked, almost trotted, along an avenue of broken walls and roofless buildings and then turned right and made for a row of similar buildings at the west side of the village.

The four, broken buildings at this end of the abandoned settlement had a line of soldiers secreted inside. Each man peered through the frameless windows at the man who was walking toward them.

He seemed to be struggling with a body which he was dragging behind him. He held the end of a rope, one end tied around the ankles of the body, thrown over his shoulder as he pulled it and himself along slowly.

Votsky followed the guard into the first of the buildings, the corner house. In its time this house would have served as the first house which any traveller coming this way would have arrived at.

The shark-eyes looked at the man, flicking from one detail to another as he grew more defined the closer he got. He was twenty feet away now.

'Jiminenko Ladislav?' He called out, in a cold, monotone voice.

Jimi raised his head and then slowed down. 'Oh! Shit!' He muttered under his breath for Finn's ears. 'We're in trouble.' And then for Votsky; 'Igor Votsky? Is that you?'

Votsky's eyes continued to dart from one detail to another, weighing, measuring, assessing. 'You're dead.' He said.

Jimi shrugged his shoulders and heaved onward. Fifteen feet now, the soldiers were tense, flicking gazes between their commander and Jimi.

'Clearly not.' Jimi said.

Votsky's head cocked. 'We found your body.' He said, flatly, his tone giving no indication to the whirring mind behind his obvious statement.

'Clearly not.' Jimi repeated.

He pointed down to Finn behind him, turning away so they couldn't see his face.

'I believe you have been looking for him.' He said loudly for them all to hear.

Under his breath he urgently said: 'He's going to open fire. Trust me, I know him, he's bad. Very bad. Be ready.'

Votskys flickering eyes fell upon Jimi's left hand and wrist; he was wearing a watch. His hunters mind found a pattern and ran with it and then reacted upon it.

Charred Body. Watch. Living. Watch. Swapped.

'KILL THEM!' He screamed, pointing.

The sub-machine guns roared simultaneously.

Jimi dropped Finn's legs and sprinted and then dived headfirst through the low widow of the building furthest away from them, twelve feet on his left.

The machine guns traced him as he ran, but the soldiers wielding them were concealed in buildings of their own and couldn't keep up with him.

Two soldiers leaned out of the window hoping to get a shot at him before he disappeared behind the broken wall of the building further up, and both were met by a bullet each in the head as Finn flicked himself to his feet and brought his pistols to bear.

His eyes met Votsky's briefly; a whip-crack moment as the cold, deathly void in front of him faced off with his own spearing, feral light.

The Russian brushed aside the man's appearance, his size, his ability even. But the look he had received in that brief stroke of their gazes had made him take note; there was a *very* dangerous predator in his territory.

Finn loosed his speed, leaving the shark-eyes behind, and leaped clean over the broken house-wall, landing behind Jimi who was watching the crumbling doorway.

Jimi looked over to him, about to greet him with a smart retort, but the face he found staring back at him wasn't the tall, blonde man he had come to call friend; this was a demon, *the* demon, the thing which swirled like smoke and killed without pause or effort.

He turned away again, muttering a prayer to his long dead mother, telling her if she could seek out his friend's mother here, he would appreciate it if she would ask her to tell him not to kill poor, old Jimi, eh?

Behind him Finn laughed, only the laugh was like there was more than just Finn's voice in the laughter. 'You don't need to tell my mother,' the strange, triple-voice said. 'I promise I won't kill you, Jimi.'

Jimi turned again just in time to see Finn stand up and then leap high into the air, gaining a view over the broken walls.

He raised his pistols and fired off a volley, men screamed and then Finn dropped to the ground again. 'That way.' He said, in his strange voice, pointing to the next building across the narrow gap of the street.

Jimi jumped up and ran across without question, skidding to a halt as he passed through the broken hole of a doorway.

Holy God and Moses! What am I teamed up with?

Finn, instead of following Jimi, hauled himself over the high wall and into the next building.

The soldiers who had been creeping up to enter it themselves, had been the soldiers who had screamed when Finn had jumped up and fired.

He landed and rolled straight up to the next wall ahead while Jimi did the same across the street; darting out and then back into the next house along.

Finn stood up and looked over the wall. He was met by a hail of gunfire coming from two houses further up and from two more soldiers in a house on the same side of the street which Jimi was going up.

Finn crouched down and signalled to Jimi that he had two ahead of him.

Jimi nodded and readied his stolen SMG, his pistols were stashed in his belt. He waited for Finn to give him the signal - whatever that might be.

Finn stayed low and took four steps away from the wall and then turned around on his heel.

Without a pause he sprang forward, jumping high and headfirst over the wall into the next building, his pistols blazing as he sailed over.

So that was the signal then.

Jimi rushed out of the doorway as all of the machine-gun fire turned on Finn while he was flying through the air.

He sprinted up to the two firing in the last building on this side. He could see their muzzle-flashes through the gaps in the broken walls.

As he approached he threw himself down onto his knees and skidded along sideways, flashing past the two, large gaps in the wall.

He fired up at the two men crouched there, both completely unaware of the danger almost right on top of them.

Before they had even stopped and dropped, Jimi had dived into the building and fallen onto his stomach, a blaze of gunfire following him in and spraying the walls behind him.

Across the street Finn ducked and rolled, landing back up on his feet and made straight for the last building. He could hear someone firing from the corner, pinning Jimi down across the road.

He raised his pistols and fired them through the powdery, brick wall until the gunfire stopped and the thudding of two bodies hitting the ground came to his ears. He grinned and turned to look at Jimi across the road.

Before either of them could say or do anything, a monster began ripping up the buildings and walls and the very earth itself as it fired from somewhere further inside the village.

Tracer-bullets pinged around like angry, red comets and the walls began to crumble quickly, resembling some kind of time-lapsed camera-view watching the ages pass as the decay settled in.

Finn dived across the room he was in, rolling along the ground and then springing away through the doorway as the building crumbled and cracked and slowly caved in, disappearing behind a cloud of yellow dust.

He came up to his feet and a dull thud rocked him sideways. He'd just been shot, he knew the feeling.

Rolling with the motion, he spun around and then ducked and rolled into the building nearest him, the building Jimi was crouching at the back of covering his ears against the din of the monster machine-gun.

He watched as Finn checked his wounded shoulder, probing the front first and then the back where the bullet had made its exit.

Jimi couldn't believe it when the maniac had smiled and then laughed, turning to him and showing him.

'One hole for us and about seven or eight dead for them! That's a good day in anyone's book.' He beamed.

Jimi was speechless; a good day? He couldn't reconcile getting shot with the words *good day* on *any* damned day!

'Er. Er. Okay.' His eyes said it all.

Finn just laughed louder, almost drowning out the roaring gun as it carried on disintegrating the walls and houses. 'This way.' The laughing Finn said, pointing to the wall and beyond where Jimi was crouched.

He picked Jimi up and heaved him over the wall just as the machine-gun turned its noise and bullets onto their position.

Finn jumped the wall while the room began to disappear beneath a hail of bullets and smoky dust. He landed on his feet and then collared Jimi again, dragging him along to the back of this broken house.

He hoisted him straight over the window ledge and then jumped over himself.

'Up there.' He pointed further up the street to a small building with a makeshift roof. 'Salya and the others will be in that one over there.' He continued, as they ran across the road, pointing to a larger building about thirty yards away to their right with the same style roof.

The machine gun was up there Jimi noted. Great.

They made the corner of the building Votsky had been using as his own, Finn crouched down and faced straight up the street to the south while Jimi crouched down at the other side of the corner facing the east.

The big gun went quiet, the soldiers were regrouping and on the move.

Finn rubbed at his shoulder wondering who had managed to get a bullet through him.

He suspected that if he hadn't been moving quite so quickly the bullet would have hit him square in the chest. A good shot then he thought. Had to be the shark-eyed man.

When they had looked at one another Finn had sensed a mind with only one purpose; to kill calculatingly and without remorse or second-thoughts, a mind trained for that one, single purpose.

Even though Finn hadn't seen or heard the man fire, he knew that he must have been further up the street across the road right at the end, hiding himself in one of the buildings up there.

A single shot.

Finn hadn't seen a rifle in the man's hands so he must be armed with a big handgun. A Colt or a Desert Eagle he thought most probable judging by the size of the hole in his shoulder.

Damn fine shot then from that distance. Damn fine.

Two soldiers ran across the gap at the end of the street at the top.

'Move down.' Finn ordered, in that strange tri-voice.

Jimi ran to the opposite corner, mirroring the run of the soldiers Finn had seen running across the top.

He opened fire as soon as he had dropped back to his knee, spotting the first soldier as he turned the corner and began his sprint down toward them.

The soldier flinched and feinted and then ran back the way he had come, a line of bullets chasing his heels.

Finn moved quickly up to the next broken house and ducked through the doorway.

The big handgun which had shot him boomed out again, the slug slamming into the wall by his face.

That was definitely a Colt he thought as he casually brushed the dust and bits of brick from his shoulder.

The mounted machine-gun remained silent, too many of the cracked buildings lay between it and its intended targets, but the soldiers were on the move again, Finn could hear their running feet somewhere ahead of him.

'They're moving away from where they first met us.' He said, and grinned.

Removing three of the six grenades he had in his kit, Finn pulled the pins of all of them at the same time and then lobbed them hard over the wall he was crouching behind.

The three grenades sailed high into the air, fanning out as they approached the last houses at the top of the road. They exploded simultaneously while they were still six feet from the ground.

The whole of the top end of that road suddenly disappeared behind a flash and a bang and fast-moving smoke.

Finn darted out and sprinted straight up and into it.

Jimi heard the grenades go off and saw the smoke.

He ran out and up to the next doorway just as he heard the SMG's of the soldiers begin to fire and then the soldiers began to howl as Finn passed through them with blade and pistol.

Two soldiers ran out ahead from Jimi's left, sprinting toward their screaming comrades ready to give support.

Jimi's sub-machine gun took the legs out from underneath them both and then he ran up and finished the job before the two men could recover themselves and fire back.

He quickly scanned around, looking for anyone else coming this way and then through the fast-disappearing grenade-smoke, his eyes settled on the still-smoking barrel of the monster machine-gun.

'Crap.' He whispered, just as the soldier behind it pulled the trigger.

Jimi threw himself through the window-space of the building he was crouched down beside, landing flat on his face and covering his head with his hands and arms, curling himself up into the smallest target possible and gritting his teeth tightly.

In only a few seconds the whole room was alive with the cracking and thudding of bullets and breaking brick, Jimi was covered in a slow-falling pile of settling, yellow dust, but the beast never let up its deadly outpouring and Jimi could feel the walls getting lower and lower until eventually they would expose him completely.

Finn, using the confusion of the grenade blasts, darted around in the smoke of it, using his hearing supernaturally to pinpoint his enemies and bring them down.

He stood with his blade firmly pinning the last of the four soldiers up here to the wall through the chest, holding him from the ground and looking to his right.

The beast had just started up again and it was concentrating its fire straight ahead of it.

'Jimi.' He growled.

He let the dead man fall to the ground and then picked up one of his comrades lying at his side. The smoke was clearing, he would have to be fast.

Laying one man on top of the other, Finn looped the straps of the backpack on the man beneath around the arms and shoulders of the man on top, effectively trapping them both together tightly.

Effortlessly he hoisted them up and held them in front of himself and then sprinted toward the roaring monster.

The smoke bulged forward and then burst altogether as Finn came hurtling out.

He heard the Colt boom out behind while the monster roared on in front.

His thigh flared, another bullet from the shark-eye, he was trying to bring him down.

He dismissed the pain before it could even register the wound and ignored the damage altogether.

The tone of the monsters voice subtly changed as it turned from the target in the building to this new prey running straight at it.

Finn heard the bullets cracking up the street as the gun turned his way, he braced himself as the first of the monsters death slammed into his body-shield.

His sprint was slowed somewhat as the bullets tore through the bodies, hammering away until some of them passed through and thumped hard into Finn's arms and chest.

Most of the bullets cracked against his protective shirt, slamming him like tiny ten ton mallets, but three of them made it through the specialist material and embedded themselves in his chest and arms.

He ignored them and laughed with a triple-voice; the fool soldier who was pulling the trigger was wasting his time and his bullets, he should have been trying to cut Finn's legs from under him.

As if that thought had somehow managed to be transmitted to the soldiers own mind, he lowered the muzzle slightly.

But Finn was only ten feet from him now and before any of the rounds could find their target, the soldier heard the unearthly roar of the demon as it threw its bloodied and tattered flesh-shield right at him.

As the bodies left his grip and smashed into the machine-gun and its operator, Finn drew his blades again and sailed over the top of the now prone and struggling gunner, landing behind him.

He turned quickly and dropped down, bringing his blade down swiftly into the chest of the soldier.

Just as he withdrew his blades he heard a girl cry out. It came from behind the doors and sounded like Salya.

Before he could get to the door the Colt roared out again, very close this time, and Finn's hip slewed to the right slightly as the bullet found its mark.

Jimi sat up and shook himself off, the piles of dust leaving him looking yellow and grimy.

He patted himself all over quickly and then laughed. 'I'm alive!'

He heard a big handgun go off then, jolting him back to the situation in hand. Finn had taken the machine-gun out but someone was still firing up there.

And then at least four more sub-machine guns began to fire somewhere from Jimi's left, just outside the walls of the village he thought. Backup in waiting, must be.

He crouched and leaned out past the now well diminished wall, raising his weapon and waiting.

Two men ran out, firing their weapons as they ran.

Jimi traced them and then fired. Both men spun around as the bullets ripped into their legs and torsos and then they dropped to the ground, crying out and holding their wounds.

Behind the fallen soldiers and through the smoke and fast settling dust, Jimi could just make out the building where the women and children were being held.

Finn stood there, firing the machine-gunners own sub at the corner of the street on Jimi's left.

Jimi could see the blood running down Finn's chest and legs and arms. 'How are you alive, my big friend?' He murmured. How?

Without thinking of his own safety, being driven only by the compassion he was suddenly feeling for his injured friend, Jimi sprang to his feet and ran straight up the road, staying close to the left-side buildings and watching the right for Votsky.

He knew it had been Votsky's gun he had heard.

And there he was, creeping along and trying to blindside Finn as he held off the attackers on his other flank.

Jimi fired at him, the bullets tracing up the dusty path and catching Votsky in the chest.

He just grunted as his bullet-proof vest caught them and raised his gun mechanically, firing straight at Jimi.

The bullet tore through his upper-arm and Jimi groaned, but still sent another burst up to the ice-cool killer.

Votsky darted backward, giving Jimi enough time to step up and run into the building on his left for cover.

He tore off his shirt sleeve and wrapped it tightly around the bleeding bullet-wound, clenching his teeth as the pain shot up his arm as his veins closed off.

He sat back and spat, breathing hard.

The shooting had died down, Jimi risked a look around the corner and up toward where Finn crouched, flicking his head out and back in quickly.

When no bullets came to tear his head off he looked out again. Votsky wasn't in sight.

Jimi jumped to his feet and ran to the very end building now, darting inside and then looking out at Finn and the street where Votsky had been. There was still no sign of him.

Finn signalled for him to hold that position.

Jimi nodded and then continued with his search for the bastard Votsky. Of all the fucking dead, why couldn't one of them have been him?

The two remaining soldiers who had fired at Finn from outside the village walls, had backtracked now and disappeared, leaving their two dead comrades in the street.

The shark-eye had also withdrawn. So that could only mean that they were now regrouping.

Staying low, Finn approached the door, keeping his eye on the empty streets behind him. He listened with his ear pressed up against the metal. It was silent.

He slid the bolt back and then pushed the door inward slightly, glancing down at the ground inside.

The first thing he saw was a naked foot, the leg it was attached to was covered with black trousers.

He recognised the trousers instantly; it was Salya's foot.

## Chapter Fifty

Salya had made everyone move to the far back and right-hand side of the big room they were in when the shooting had started, placing the adults and bigger children in front of the smaller ones. The tiny Faria sat at the back holding baby Delara in her frightened arms.

The two soldiers who had been posted inside with them, crouched by the door and waited. They were the *surprise* for anyone entering without shouting out the right word.

Votsky had told them to wait until the very last moment before turning their weapons onto the women and children should anything go wrong outside.

Salya and Parisa crouched side-by-side, closest to the soldiers, feigning fright and keeping their heads low.

Parisa had her head on Salya's shoulder, wrapping her arms around her and acting the frightened child she was supposed to be. All the while she listened to what Salya was whispering to her.

'I still have my wooden knife.' She said. 'I'll only get one strike with it, so we have to make it count.'

Parisa squeezed her to acknowledge.

Everyone including the two guards, jumped and flinched when the mounted machine-gun outside the door suddenly erupted.

Salya pulled her feet up underneath her and then began to unlace one of her boots, pulling it and her sock off and then leaving them behind her.

She reached back and retrieved the small, wooden knife she had hidden inside her leather, walking boot when they had been waiting for the truck in the dark.

Nim and Kurshid were watching the girls, both of them resisting the same mothering urges to tell them to stop what they were thinking, let the men do the killing and dying.

Both women welled up with tears when they realised that they couldn't - shouldn't - stop them; the guards were going to kill them before Finn could get through the door, why else were they secreted here with them?

Nim turned her head and teary eyes to Kurshid's, the silent message between them being clear; they would have to be ready to help the girls when they did whatever it was that they were going to do.

She raised her hand to Kurshid's scarred face and stroked her cheek, *we might die*, her eyes were saying.

Kurshid responded by stroking Nim's cheek in return, *but the children won't*, she smiled back.

The gun outside dropped to sudden silence, leaving behind faint, phantom, pealing bells ringing in everyone's ears.

Smaller bursts from the sub-machine guns still rattled out and then above that din came a single loud bang of a handgun.

Parisa squeezed Salya firmly.

'Not yet.' Salya whispered. 'But very soon. He's coming.'

As if to herald her words at the arrival of her friend, Finn's grenades exploded in the street outside, shaking the building and rattling their teeth.

The children whimpered and the youngest began to cry, looking fearfully around at the walls as the gunfire continued to rail out.

Salya was tense, she could feel he was getting closer by the sound of the sub-machine-guns which were shooting at him, and then she listened as men began crying out and screaming and dying. That was Finn right out there, it was Finn, she knew it.

More guns suddenly added their fire to the fray, soldiers shooting from somewhere further away Salya thought. And then the monster guarding the door suddenly erupted again, shouting down most of the noise from the smaller weapons.

The two door guards were looking anything but professional as they crouched down on one knee, eyes boring into the door as their trigger-fingers sweated and itched.

They flinched and whipped around in the direction of every sound which was coming to them from the street beyond the walls and bolted door, gasping and sometimes almost grunting with terror.

Salya looked with some satisfaction at the fear on their faces as they too, could also quite clearly hear their comrades dying.

Jittery was a good state to have your enemies in when you were about to spring your trap on them. Jittery worked just fine.

'*Now*, my dangerous friend.' Salya whispered to Parisa, pulling her away and then kissing her on each cheek.

They looked one another in the eye, the corner's of their mouths each turned slowly upward and a flickering light of menace twinkled in their deep, brown eyes.

Parisa, being slightly bigger, had the job of tackling the guard furthest away.

She kissed Salya back and then the pair of them leaped to their feet, startling Nim and Kurshid who had been watching them silently, expecting them to do something, but when it had come they had still jumped half out of their skins.

The older girl pelted toward the two guards and leaped over the first, aiming her dive to crash into the second.

Both men tried to whip around and shoot, but then the first guard saw Salya suddenly appear in front of him and aimed his weapon at her instead.

With wide, terrified and definitely jittery eyes, the guard squeezed his trigger as he watched Salya smile evilly at him, standing only three feet away.

A split second before he could fire, the second guard's weapon went off, just once, as Parisa dropped on top of him and at the same time Salya spun herself around to the left as this guard's finger finally fired the damn shot.

The bullet whizzed harmlessly passed Salya's spinning, blurred form and as she came around again she lunged out with a straight-armed stab, adding her weight onto an extended and bended knee to thrust her wooden knife straight and knuckle-deep into the guard's, left eye.

He juddered for a few seconds as she held his head up firmly, and then she pulled the wood free as he slipped backward onto the ground where he remained silent and still.

She turned to the other guard just in time to avoid Parisa as she was thrown past her, landing in a heap on the floor by the door.

Without a look to her friend, Salya dropped and rolled forward, coming up as the guard scrambled for his weapon which had been knocked to the ground by his side.

She delivered a terrific, bone-jarring kick to his chin when he leaned over to retrieve the weapon.

He grunted and rolled with the blow, trying to create some distance between him and the girl.

She was having none of it and rolled again, this time coming up fast and hard with the top of her head cracking into his chin and throat.

Stars popped in front of his eyes, he fell back on his rump and clutched with his left hand at his bruised windpipe while his right fumbled at his belt, searching for his sidearm.

Nim and Kurshid watched on in disbelief while the warrior-girl kicked the hell out of the big, armed soldier. What help they thought they might have been able to offer they had no idea.

Salya's movements were so precise and sure, slick and well rehearsed, but when or how she had found the time to practise they couldn't imagine.

She stood there now while the soldier tried to grasp his pistol, standing over him and imposing her will upon him through her eyes, just the way Finn did.

Salya looked down and waited for him to find the pistol which he did and then levelled at her.

She gave his hand a cracking roundhouse kick which ended with the wooden knife protruding from his neck as she brought it around in a right-handed, stabbing arc.

She stepped back and looked down at the soldier as he clutched at his wound just as the gun outside was silenced by something smashing into it.

Salya whirled at the door as it rattled under the heavy thud of the same something crashing into it and then her eyes fell on the prone Parisa at the same time Nim's and Kurshid's did.

Everyone gasped and Salya ran to her side, dropping down and bringing her head up, holding it close to her own.

'Parisa? Parisa?' She said, her voice trembling with the fear of what she knew in her heart had happened.

Parisa's eyes stared open and blank into the space in front of them, lifeless and empty. Blood trickled from the corner of her mouth and from her nose and a hole in her chest spread a wet, red blotch across her woollen shirt.

Salya ignored the continued, sporadic gunfire coming from behind the door, the pain in her young heart allowing nothing else to encroach.

'Oh! No!' She wailed and then dropped her head to meet the dead girl's.

She wept and spilled her tears into the open eyes of Parisa, sharing her tremendous love for her dead friend which had now borne her to such tremendous grief.

The children wept behind her, knowing that the girl who had always helped them had died.

'I will miss you, Parisa.' Salya whispered, and then clutched her to her chest, holding her in her arms and lying down on the floor with her, sobbing.

The gunfire had stopped now.

Nim and Kurshid slowly stood and made to go to the weeping Salya's side when the bolt on the door was drawn back. They both stopped and backed up, shielding the children, watching with terrified eyes as the door was pushed open a few inches.

A shadow loomed there and then with a gasp and a rush, Finn stepped in, dropping straight down and turning Salya to face him.

She looked up through the blur of her tears, not at first understanding who or what she was seeing. It looked like Finn, but not entirely.

The two women standing back made no attempt to rush up to greet him as he walked in. They stood instead and stared at the terrifying face he was wearing and the eyes of the demon he had become.

He caught their looks and threw them a glance. 'Do not fear me.' He said in that, strange triple-voice, calm and reassuring though it sounded.

Salya flinched and rubbed her eyes dry, but when she looked up it was just Finn again.

'It is good to see you again, my dear Salya.' He said, picking her up and embracing her tightly.

What had just happened? Nim and Kurshid looked at one another, they had just seen a miracle they were thinking. His face had changed ever so subtly and then Finn had returned.

Whether it was a sickness of the mind or not, Nim still felt that she really was in the presence of a god - little *g* though it was.

Salya pulled away and frowned, looking Finn up and down. 'Oh! No, you've been shot.' She said, her tears spilling down her face once more. 'Again!'

Finn stood and pulled her up. 'There is no time for being shot, we have to leave.'

He stooped again and took Parisa's lifeless hand. 'It was an honour to have known you, dear Parisa.' He said. 'I hope we will meet again in the next life, I owe you a debt, my friend.'

He kissed her fingertips and then gently lowered her hand back to the ground and closed her eyes softly with his big, gentle hand. 'Síochána.' He muttered. Peace.

Standing back up he turned to and addressed everyone. 'We have to leave.' He said.

Nim closed in on him. 'You need attending to, Finn, I can see at least four bullet wounds in you!'

He looked at her sympathetically. 'There is no time, Nim.' He said, gently. 'We must go south to the border and it is still a fair distance away.'

Before Nim could argue further Jimi rushed inside and closed the door.

'There's an armoured truck coming up the street.' He said, breathlessly.

He looked at Nim and smiled.

She looked back in horror at the bullet wound in his arm and the cuts on his face.

He didn't say anything, instead he turned to Finn. 'Let us tourniquet you where we can and then let's get the hell out of here.' He said, trying to find the middle ground regarding Finn's wounds.

Finn nodded. 'Quickly.' He said. 'We cannot leave by the door now anyway, it gives us a few extra seconds.'

While Nim, Kurshid and Jimi ripped up anything they could find to make ties for the tourniquets, Finn removed a grenade from his belt and unscrewed the top.

He fumbled around as they tied his wounds up and patched the holes as best as they could, trying to get the firing mechanism out and remove the wire coil he needed.

'That will do for now.' Nim said.

Finn looked at himself and then up at his nurses. 'Thank you. That will be most helpful I think.' He said, and smiled.

He dragged the bodies of the two, dead guards over to the entrance and then set about positioning one of their sub-machine guns between them, aiming it up at the door.

He ran the wire then, all the way through the trigger and pulled up the strain so it was sitting tightly back. He then lifted one of the dead men's arms and looped the wire once around the wrist before finally running the last end up to the door handle.

He gently lowered the dead guard's arm and smiled as it took up the strain perfectly. Anyone opening the door would drop the arm and pull the hair-pin trigger. It should fool them for a few minutes at least.

'Let's go.' He said, turning back to the others.

They all looked at him, then at the door and then back to him.

'Where?' Jimi said, voicing the question for all of them.

'This way.' Said Finn's, triple-voice before lunging off to the back of the room.

He delivered a powerful standing thrust-kick straight at the old bricks and a hole the size of a small child appeared as the bricks disintegrated and exploded outward.

He kicked again and then a third time and then pushed himself through the hole he had created, quickly flicking his pistols up to either side of himself. 'It is clear.' He said, over his shoulder.

Jimi shrugged lamely. 'Oh. *That* way.' He said.

He passed through and then stood by the impromptu doorway, helping the others through.

Once they were all out, Finn pointed. 'We go that way.' He said, indicating the forest a few miles away. 'We need to get back under the cover of the trees.'

He pointed then to Kurshid. 'You and the youngest at the front, run as fast as you can but stay together.'

She nodded her head quickly, obediently, her eyes wide and terrified, her thoughts almost echoing those of Nim's perfectly; what was this man? This-this god-man?

She pulled her gaze away from him, gathering the youngest around herself and then jogged slowly away through the dust and scrubby grass.

'The rest of you keep behind them and help where you can.' Finn said, next addressing the older children left. 'Go.'

He nodded in the direction he wanted them to run.

They set off without a word and caught Kurshid and the others up, taking a position at the rear and readying themselves to pick up the stragglers as they began to appear.

Finn handed the weapon from one of the dead guards to Nim.

'We will take up the rear as best as we can, I want Nim in front, Salya behind, you next Jimi, and then myself.'

He looked at them all to make sure they understood what he was telling them to do. 'Good, let's get to it then. We may still get the better of them yet.' His triple-voice said, through his widening grin.

Jimi and Nim both looked on in quiet awe, Nim wondering just how much longer Finn could last with the amount of blood he had already lost.

But the voice, the voice of the creature he had become? Could it be that more than just his appearance and voice had changed? Could it be that he really didn't feel the pain or lose the blood or die?

Die? Don't die, Finn, Nim thought as she turned away and began running after the children. Please don't die.

Salya turned next, but before she followed Nim she looked deeply into Finn's eyes, cocking her head to one side slightly, looking for something.

'I am still here, my dear Salya, fear not.' He said, reassuringly and then he was just Finn again.

Salya smiled, just a little, at least he knew who he was even if *they* didn't fully know sometimes. 'I know.' She said, and then ran on behind Nim.

'You are a scary bastard, my friend,' Jimi said, as he passed Finn, slapping him on the shoulder. 'I hope my dear mother remembers the message I asked her to pass on to yours.'

Finn just chuckled as he watched Jimi trot on and then turned briefly to look back through into the building.

He could hear the armoured truck which Jimi had said was coming up the road now. They wouldn't have long before they realised that the building was empty.

He turned quickly away and suddenly found himself staggering light-headedly as he tried to run.

He breathed in quickly and deeply, forcing the popping stars in front of his eyes to fade and disappear.

After shaking his shaggy head he began running, he had turned around too quickly that was all.

## Chapter Fifty-One

Votsky's backup slowly halted its approach, pulling up outside the building the slaves were being kept in.

Of the twenty men the Russian commander had with him in the village, only two remained, one of those his door-guard.

They stood with him now as the doors of the armoured truck were thrown open and eighteen more soldiers jumped out.

He had waited patiently out of sight as the vehicle had trundled up the road, watching coldly as the traitorous Ladislav had run across to the building once he had spotted the truck himself, quickly ducking inside and closing the door behind him.

Well they were all trapped together now, but Votsky had watched as the big man had smashed through his mounted machine-gun using bodies as shields.

The power of the man was inspiring, Votsky couldn't wait to kill him and watch him die. He would be one of the highlights of his murderous career he thought, if not *the* highlight.

But he had to be careful with this beast, it didn't die as easily as normal flesh and blooded men, bullets seemed to do nothing but enrage it.

The men from the truck lined up in front of Votsky.

'Fan out in front of this door.' He said, speaking quietly and pointing at the door behind him. 'You. Open the door when they are in position.' He said to the man directly in front of him.

The soldiers did as they were ordered and fanned out, silently making a line in front of the doors and kneeling down, muzzles raised.

The soldier who had been ordered to open the door stood at the side of it, one hand on the handle and the other in the air holding three fingers up. He counted them down silently and then pulled the door open.

Finn glanced back over his shoulder as his gun-trap went off, smiling satisfactorily.

Two men screamed.

Votsky's eyes narrowed as the door swung shut and the gunfire ceased, the two soldiers kneeling directly in front of it fell backward in a heap, their screams cutting off as the bullets snaked from their chests to their necks and faces.

'Open it again.' Votsky barked. 'Quickly!'

The soldier did as he was told and threw the door open again.

The weapon opened up once more and the bullets flew harmlessly this time through the space where the two dead soldiers had been kneeling.

The soldier by the door used his gun to hold the door open, keeping his body back and low out of the path of the fire until the gun ran out of ammunition a few seconds later.

'In!' Votsky roared.

The four soldiers nearest to him jumped to their feet and rushed the door, streaming inside and taking up defensive positions around the door and the hole in the back wall.

Votsky walked inside and looked down at the two guards who had supposed to have been guarding the prisoners.

A strange feeling wormed around inside his brain as he looked at them, their staggering failure being the source. Was that anger?

He raised his eyes to the hole in the wall, the worm moved to his chest and face making it swell and grow hot. Yes. That was anger, he was sure of it. A feeling he had never experienced before.

He looked back down at the bodies, their failings once again fuelling that horrible worm to move around inside him. How could he stop it? How could he make the worm be satisfied now that they were dead anyway?

It moved and slithered and his breathing increased with his beating heart. Sweat on his brow was the final sign of this new feeling.

With no indication of what he was about to do or the rage he was feeling, Votsky stamped hard on the head of the dead guard closest to him.

There was a crack and Votsky looked down unemotionally. Then he stamped again and again and again, on both of the heads, until he was breathless with the effort and the mess of pulp and bone and teeth were spattered all around.

His boots needed cleaning now he thought, as he looked down at the blood spattered leather boots. An eyeball looked up at him, stuck to the tip of the sole at the front of one of them, crushed into the tread by its stalk.

He stooped down and plucked it free, dropping it back onto the pile of mess that had once been the heads of two men.

The soldier by the door gagged and then wretched, leaning outside and throwing up.

Votsky watched him and then noticed for the first time that his heart was beating normally again and his breathing was shallow and easy. He did feel better after all. He must remember that if he ever felt angry again.

Turning his attention to the gaping hole in the wall, he caught sight of Finn's back a mile or so away, his head bobbing gently as he fled.

He wouldn't get much further with the wounds he was carrying though, Votsky thought. A hole made by a Colt was a nasty, nasty wound and didn't heal very easily. Especially when you were still moving around.

If only Votsky had know about Finn's protective clothing and more importantly, the state of his mind.

He raised his arm and pointed through the back. 'Kill them.' He ordered.

His door guard called the rest of the men still standing outside and ordered them through the hole which Finn and the others had left by.

They filed through and began running across the dusty ground, Votsky strode out last and jogged along slowly, never taking his eyes from the men at the front and Finn's back.

His guard ran with him, waiting for the order to open fire.

Finn could hear the feet running behind him now and stole another glance over his shoulder at his pursuers, looking for the shark-eyed man in particular.

His heart dropped when he saw how many they were, but on the other hand they had managed to put a great deal of distance between themselves and the Russians. More than he had anticipated or could have hoped for.

But their numbers were a worry now; when they started shooting - and they *would* start, there was no doubt - there was going to be a lot of flying metal in the air. He could only hope that the strays were wide of *all* marks, not just his own back.

His knees suddenly buckled and the world took on a gray, hueless aspect for a moment. His chest ached as he coughed and he could taste the familiar coppery tone of blood in his throat.

He staggered and dropped to a knee, breathing deeply and closing his eyes.

*Wake up, you big, blonde fool.* A woman's voice said, but not hers, not his she-wolf's voice. It giggled musically as it spoke. *Come on you sluggard*, she teased, *get your cute arse up there.*

Who was she? Who was encouraging him to run?

'I am trying Cait.' He said, aloud. 'I am coming.'

His eyes flickered back open and he raised himself back to his feet, unaware of what he had just said, but feeding from the emotions he could feel coming from the woman.

He began to run again toward the forest, watching Jimi's back running along ahead of him.

He'd taken no more than ten, more strides when the machine-guns behind began rattling out in their chattering voices full of murderous intent.

He could hear the bullets flying past and around him, two of them found his back and slammed him onward but didn't manage penetrate the shirt.

Ahead of him though, the sound he had been most dreading to hear came in the form of young Simeon's scream.

The boy fell and rolled, clutching at his leg and crying. He scrabbled in the dirt and managed to rise, hopping along as fast as he could.

Nim rushed to his side and draped his arm over her shoulder and then Salya did the same, taking his other arm. Between them they managed to keep the pace up.

'You'll be ok, Simeon.' Nim soothed. 'I know it hurts, but be brave, my boy. It will heal and you will live.'

Jimi saw Nim and Salya helping the boy, they had to buy them some more time.

He turned to Finn. 'Shuffling fire.' He ordered, and dropped to his knee, opening up on the soldiers now.

Finn ran past him and then dropped down and did the same; returned the fire while Jimi made his retreat.

Two soldiers went down and didn't rise again, but the rest continued to fire and advance as Finn and Jimi slowly covered the escaping children.

Jimi yelped as a bullet tore into his side, but he only flinched for a moment and then carried on sending burst after burst into the soldiers until Finn came up and crouched down, taking over.

Jimi staggered to his feet and turned to run, taking three, swaying steps while blood poured from his wounded side. Another bullet found his thigh and he cried out as it passed through him.

He dropped to his knees and turned around, lifting his gun and sending a volley back down using his weapon with one hand while his other clutched at his wounded side.

Finn turned and ran back, noting the blood covering Jimi's body and leg as he passed him. He took up his position behind his friend and opened fire.

Jimi didn't move this time, he stayed where he was and just continued to fire at the oncoming soldiers, gritting his teeth and waiting for the final bullet which would end his game and bring him down.

But before that happened the world turned red for Finn as he heard another child's voice scream out as she was shot from behind.

Little Faria's voice. But this time the scream ended abruptly and the small girl didn't stand back up.

Finn's rage accelerated through his veins as it swelled his body with its molten violence.

Leaping to his feet he ran past Jimi, snatching his weapon from his hands, and then sprinted off toward the soldiers, the pair of SMG's blazing in his fists and his triple-voiced bellow roaring out above all.

Jimi just watched, there was nothing he could do to help. Not Finn or the soldiers, all the doom in the world was running down that hill and it wouldn't stop until all lay dead and silent in its wake.

But he stood up groggily and pulled his pistols free anyway. What the hell, at least he had loved, truly loved, and been loved in return. It wasn't such a bad day to be shot after all.

He took an agonising step forward and Salya stepped in front of him, holding him back by the arm. She was carrying Nim's sub-machine gun.

'Go back to her.' She said.

Jimi couldn't meet her eyes and tried to move around her so he could carry on and help Finn.

She slapped his face. 'Go back to Nim.' She said, tears rolling down her defiant face as she spoke. She didn't sob though.

'But-.'

She slapped him again. 'Don't you dare leave her now!' Her voice was hard and firm, clashing with the tears running down her cheeks. 'You go back to her and you stay with her.' She finished.

Jimi rubbed his cheek, a stunned look on his face.

He suddenly reached for her, pulling her in with his uninjured arm. 'Be fast and careful, Salya, and make sure you kill as many as you can.'

He kissed the top of her head and then released her.

With nothing more to say, Salya turned away and sprinted after Finn, her sub-machine gun blasting out as she ran.

Jimi dropped his head sadly, hobbling his way back to Nim and the limping Simeon.

No sooner had he hooked his own arm around the boy's shoulder he felt his heart drop at the sound of an approaching chopper. Gods! They would never make it now and the fucking forest was right there, less than a mile away.

He stopped and urged Nim to carry on. 'I'll catch you up.' He said, weakly. 'They won't stand a chance now the chopper is back. You must get to the trees, my love, get everyone under the safety of the leaves and then keep on going.'

'Jimi, no! I-.'

But before Nim could say any more the roar and *whup* of the chopper passed straight overhead, making a beeline for the fight.

The three of them watched as Finn and Salya continued fighting their way down toward the oncoming soldiers while the chopper dipped dramatically nose forward and looked like it was about to smash into the ground.

At the last moment the nose lifted and the blades connected perfectly with the world, bringing the machine to a perfect standstill.

Three people leaped out and ran toward the fight, firing into the flank of the soldiers.

Jimi, Nim and Simeon just stared in smiling wonder. The cavalry had arrived, a cavalry consisting of two women and a man.

One of the women had a head of fiery, orange hair which was matched and complimented perfectly by the muzzle-flashes coming from her blazing SLR.

'Carve left.' Anna shouted as the chopper touched down.

Shelby and Sophie jumped down from their seats and ran around the chopper, following Anna as she ran left and down toward the flank of the soldiers firing at the children. She opened fire with her own semi-automatic rifle as she ran.

The two, Interpol officers couldn't take their eyes off the flying form of Finn. Everything they had imagined about the way he killed was thrown out of the window as they saw his supernaturally-fast gestures blur along in a kind of liquid movement.

But before they could take him in further, their attention was dragged away as the soldiers they were running for retuned Anna's fire.

Shelby and Sophie dropped to their stomachs, laying down covering fire as best as they could, concentrating on the soldiers immediately in front of the still running Anna.

Two men fell before her and then another on her left dropped in a spray of crimson as Sophie's bullet found its target.

Anna dropped to the ground then, covering the mad run of Finn as he careered down toward the remaining ten men.

She saw him fling his empty weapons down to the ground and bring out a pair of pistols from holsters beneath his armpits.

Finn ducked and rolled once the pistols were in his hands, ignoring the pain of the three new holes in his shirt and body.

Six more soldiers had died under the hail of his automatic weapons. The remaining men would feel the bite of his pistols next.

Bullets flew over his head as he rose up to one knee, levelling his pistols and snapping of four shots, two more soldiers fell to the ground.

He rolled again to his right and brought himself up onto his feet in one, slick motion and then darted forward, his movement a blur of explosive, kinetic power.

The shark-eye was standing down there, hiding behind the wall of his men. Well he could hide no longer, the *Seven-Spears* were heading his way.

The soldier dead-ahead fired at Finn's head and torso, but he suddenly found he was shooting into empty space and a pistol had been lodged firmly under his chin. Mama!

Finn pulled the triggers of both pistols, the man in front of him dropped with a gasp while the man to his right clutched at his chest and stomach and screamed as he fell.

Shark-eyes fired his gun and Finn stumbled back as the bullet found his right breast.

He staggered and dropped his pistols and then snarled, a snarl which then turned into a grin and finally a roar of laughter.

Finn pulled his blades free from their scabbards, revelling as the steel sang out as if to welcome the blood they were about to spill and the life they were going to end.

The man to his far right raised his gun and fired, but was hit by the hail of bullets coming from Salya's gun as she came screaming up behind Finn. The bullets missed Finn as he took the first step toward his target.

The look of rage he gave him as he blurred forward made Votsky wonder again at this new thrill he was suddenly feeling. The thrill of death. His own death.

He stood his ground as the predator raged toward him, raising his Colt and training it on the blurry form of Finn

The Colt boomed again, Finn's thigh erupted and sprayed blood but he didn't stop.

Three soldiers fired at him from his left, he ducked toward them and felt the bullets bounce from his shirt.

Rolling his shoulder while he ducked he brought his hands around and stabbed upwards quickly into the chest of two of the soldiers.

Flinging them to the sides he then jumped forward and butted the third soldier in the face before stabbing him in the back of the head as he turned to run away.

Finn carried on running and was only a few feet away now, Votsky and two soldiers were all that remained.

A hunter never ran, a hunter finished the job. Votsky continued to stand his ground and fired his weapon again as the predator reached him.

Finn's daggers thrust viciously upward and easily sliced between the shark-eye's ribs, piercing his lungs and heart with their cold-steel force.

Votsky's eyes were wider than they had ever been before in his life. He stared down into Finn's, snarling face as his gun dropped to the ground.

Three new feelings in one day, he thought to himself. Anger, fear and now surprise. What a day it had been.

'Goodbye.' He said, for no reason apparent and then closed his eyes with a final shudder.

Votsky slipped from Finn's blades as he lowered them and fell with a dull thud to the ground.

The two remaining soldiers fell to the dust as well, before they could open fire on Finn, joining their commander in his long sleep.

Anna had used her scope to take out the man on Finn's left while Salya sprinted at the man on his right, spraying him with a hail from her weapon.

Finn turned to face her and smiled broadly when he saw that she was uninjured. 'I am glad to see you alive, my friend.' He said, and it was Finn whom she loved that spoke.

Her hand dropped limply by her side when she saw the state of her beloved friend, the gun she held clattered to the ground as her hand lost all strength. 'Oh! My dear love.' She whispered as she began to weep.

His body was covered in blood, maybe not all of it his own, but she could see the holes in his shirt and trousers, see the blood seeping slowly out and dripping to the ground, see the life in his eyes growing quietly dimmer as his body emptied.

'My dear, dear love.' She said, again and walked toward him.

The world beneath his feet suddenly shifted and sent him dropping into a sitting position, landing with a heavy thud and a groaning gasp. Blood spilled from between his lips and ran down his chin.

*Oh. My love, we have done it*, the she wolf whispered. *Your geis is fulfilled, Finn of the Seven-Spears and the Nine Northern Stars.*

The earth groaned and shifted again, jolting Finn and causing him to fall backward.

Before his head could hit the ground, Salya was by his side, catching him and then cradling his head on her lap, looking down into his beautiful lightning-eyes.

'Salya.' He said, looking back up at her. 'My love and precious friend above all others. It seems my task is complete now, we can all go home. Including me.' He said, taking her hand and holding it to his breast.

She wept freely.

Footsteps approached and Shelby, Sophie and Anna all crouched down around Finn.

Finn's eyes found Shelby first. He smiled weakly, but held his gaze strong. 'Shelby. I am so glad you managed to make it. I must apologise for my lack of proper decorum.' He said, seriously. 'I am Finn of the Seven-Spears and Nine Northern Stars. It is an honour beyond anything you can imagine to meet you properly at last.'

Shelby and Sophie both looked stunned, their emotions rushing around all over the place beneath the surface.

Shelby took Finn's free hand and clasped it between both of his. 'The honour is all ours, Finn.' He replied. 'I can see you, *we* can see you; you aren't the madman we thought we were looking for after all; you were our hidden ally and I am glad to have met you.'

Finn squeezed Shelby's hand weakly. 'Take my backpack, there is a very interesting set of diaries inside. I took them from the commander's office in the slave compound. I think you will recognise many of the names inside.' Finn said, his speech slurring a little.

*Finn, my sweet love? It is time, we must go.*

She rubbed herself along his body, easing his pains as she licked at his wounds.

Anna caught his attention, bringing him back into sudden focus. 'Oh. I would recognise that hair anywhere. Have you come to teach me a lesson for stealing your memory stick?' His smile was laced with mischievous humour.

Anna smiled warmly back. 'I reserve a very special form of kicking for pirates such as you.' She said, and leaned down to kiss him lightly on the lips.

Finn actually blushed a little.

Anna sat back and peered down into his eyes, frowning beneath her small smile. 'You are a master warrior,' she began, 'it was my privilege to fight alongside you today.'

Finn just nodded solemnly, silently acknowledging her own expertise and the praise she had just given.

His eyes flicked skyward, caught by the sudden shifting hues of the clouds.

*It is time, my love, time to go home.*

The clouds swelled over, bright and pinkish, but then fading and throbbing down to bruised purple before passing through bluebell shades and then settling on deepest violet.

Finn smiled.

'Finn? Finn, my dear Finn?' It was Salya's, frightened voice.

'I am here Salya.' Finn replied, his eyes suddenly snapping back to life again. 'Do not be frightened.'

He reached out and took her hand again. 'I am glad to have met you in this life, my friend, I know we shall meet again in the next; our debts may be paid, but we still have a friendship which will not allow us to be kept apart now.'

Salya's tears streamed and she sobbed. Sobbed like a child. She gripped his hand to her chest and watched his eyes as they gradually grew dimmer and dimmer.

The sky throbbed again, *thump*, Finn felt his body throb with it, like a lifting and pulling of his soul. Peace was in his heart and his lips turned up into a serene smile.

He pulled Salya forward and kissed her brow, whispering in her ear as he pressed something into her palm.

He lay back then and smiled up at the sky.

*Thump*. Purple flashed across the clouds.

*Thump, thump*. The purple splashed over to deep blue.

*Thum-*. And then the deepest violet of all faded all the way down to black and a silent peace.

Salya threw her head back and wailed and then howled, screamed at the sky and the gods looking down on them, screamed out her grief into the universe, the only place big enough to hold it all.

Out in the far and wide world beyond, Lucas sat by a riverbank holding his rod over the water. The river flowed past gently, not a sound, not a whisper on the evening air.

He suddenly frowned, feeling uncomfortable in his seat. He glanced up to the sky, catching a glimpse of the first stars appearing, and for no reason he could think of he turned his thoughts to his big, scarred friend called, Finn.

Two hundred and eighty miles to the east of where Lucas sat fishing, a big, old, brown bear had just been roused from his sleep, his mind still holding the dream-scent of the thing he had once encountered, the thing which was bigger than itself.

The bear yawned and lay his huge head back down on the ground, his eyes remaining open as it thought of that day again.

In Mexico, a young teacher sat on the edge of her desk, standing by as her class walked passed and handed their assignments to her on their way out of the door at home-time.

Gabriella smiled happily at the children and then she frowned. She had suddenly thought of words once spoken to her by a tall man with lightning eyes; *go home child*.

She raised her head and looked out at the setting sun, the light was fading fast. Another light, she felt, had already dimmed.

All around the globe, men, women and children, any who had been touched by Finn all did the same kind of thing and felt the same sudden need to remember their personal moments when they had been rescued by him.

\* \* \*

The walls of the cave were dry now, whatever tears were keeping them slick and running had been cried to their conclusion.

Finn stood by the arch and looked through the veil of water, smiling at the view of the green valley and bluebell-strewn fields beyond. He felt his heart swell as he listened to the child singing somewhere from just out of view.

'She has a faery-voice, hasn't she?' The she-wolf stood next him on all fours, but as high as his shoulder.

Finn moved closer to her and nuzzled his head into her neck. 'She does that.' He replied.

'We have to go.' She said, and rubbed herself against him, coaxing him round to face the back of the cave and the place where she usually sat and watched him.

He stepped up onto a low shelf of grey rock covered in thrown pelts and turned around to face her.

She brushed her wolf-lips against his and he breathed in deeply, inhaling her breath.

'I love you.' He said.

'I love you, my Finn of the Seven-Spears.'

She turned her head and looked back to the arch and curtain of water.

Finn followed her gaze.

The man stood there, staring into the water, a fearful look in his face.

'All is well now, my love.' She said.

He turned and looked at them, his fear suddenly turning to a smile when he saw them both standing next to each other.

They were surrounded by a halo of sunshine, a bond of the strongest love could be seen clear as day between them.

'Thank you.' James said. 'Thank you and peace to you both.'

The light shone brightly around them as they smiled back at him, sparkling through them as they gradually dissolved to specks of emerald and silver dust which swirled for a moment on an unseen breeze and then gently floated to the ground and dissipated in a chorus of tiny, water-droplet tones.

'Thank you.' James whispered again, and then turned slowly around to face the watery arch once more.

He stepped closer to it and listened, cocking his head to one side.

A child laughed again from somewhere just out of sight.

He took another step and a deep breath this time and then ducked his head through the water, his eyes tightly shut.

He opened them again when he felt warm sunlight stroking his still-dry skin and the smell of heather and wildflower, rosemary and bluebell came to his nose.

The child laughed again and he whirled around.

'Sam?' He said, peering ahead. 'Is that you?'

He frowned for a moment and then suddenly beamed, his whole face lighting up as brightly as the sunshine

'Samantha!' He called. 'There you are, I've been looking for you, Puppy!'

---

\*

## Epilogue

*3 months later.*

Their footsteps clicked crisply across the polished floor of the Interpol reception foyer; Shelby and Rachel walked casually to the desk, arm in arm.

'Morning sir.' The young man sitting behind the large, oval desk said. 'Miss.' He finished, nodding at Rachel.

'Morning Peter,' Shelby replied, 'has Soph- Bollinger arrived?' He said, catching himself before he used his partner's first-name.

'Yes, sir, she went straight up.' Replied the smiling Peter.

He handed them a book and a pen. Shelby signed himself and Rachel into the building directly underneath Sophie's signature. He smiled when he saw Anna's name as her guest visitor.

He slid the book back over the reception-counter.

'Thank you, sir.' Peter said, and retrieved the register.

Shelby and Rachel took the lift to the top-floor, exiting onto an expansive lounge area with office-doors leading off on all sides and comfortable chairs and settees, coffee-tables and planters placed expertly all around the space.

Sophie and Anna were stood talking to someone, a man with his back turned to them.

'Kev?' Shelby said, as he and Rachel removed their coats and approached them.

Keys turned around, smiling at them both. 'Oh. Gray! It's great to see you.'

He held his arms out and they hugged. Then Keys turned to Rachel and hugged her too. 'It's been far too long, Rachel.' He said, squeezing her and then holding her at arms length and just peering at her.

She knew what he was looking for; the very same thing she could see etched on his face; subtle lines around the eyes and a look deep within them which hinted at the mortal-dangers they had both faced and survived.

She took his hands in hers. 'It's good to see you too, Kevin, and yes; it has been far too long.' She agreed.

Even though he hadn't seen much in the way of bullets and bombs, soldiers and Russian hit-men, Keys had still come face-to-face with George and his gun.

After spending four, sweaty days in his panic-room, Keys had decided he had to come out, even if it *was* just to shower.

He hadn't seen or heard anyone since George had left the room, still talking on his mobile to someone about killing him.

After spending an eternity creeping across the room and eventually finding the courage to open the blasted door, Keys found himself staring out onto a silent, dark landing.

It sounded as though the house were completely empty. Which was strange, because Margret should have been around somewhere. She always was.

And then Keys had realised that if George was going to *deal* with him, he would have to also *deal* with Margret.

He had wept as he tiptoed across the lushly, carpeted landing making for the bathroom at the end of the long corridor. Poor Margret, she deserved better than that.

And then Keys had almost had a heart-attack when the door to the bathroom opened and George stood there, holding a newspaper in his hand and the toilet still flushing behind him.

'I knew it! I knew you were still in the fucking house.' He'd said, scoffing.

'You bastard.' Keys spat back through his tears for Margret. 'You traitorous, murdering bastard!'

George had just laughed and taken his gun from its holster.

'Why?' Keys continued. 'Why did you have to kill Margret!? She was old for God's sake! How could she possibly have been a threat to you, eh? *You fucking coward!*' He spat.

The rogue bodyguard didn't stop his laughing as he screwed the silencer onto the tip of his gun. 'I have no idea what you're squeaking on about, but if you must know; I did it for that age-old reason that has been with us since the dawn of time; money. Lots of money.'

After raising his weapon he had paused; one, final insult. 'Don't take it too personally, it's just business you know?'

And then his eyebrows had raised, his eyes had gone suddenly round and he gasped in surprise.

And then BOOM! His shirt bloomed crimson and he dropped to the floor at the same time as a body crumpled to the carpet behind Keys.

The terrified MP had whirled around.

'I never did like him.' It was Margret. She sat there on her rump where she had been thrown when the gun had gone off. She held an enormous, silver revolver in her hands, struggling to keep the barrel level. 'I suppose you're going to retire me after this, aren't you?' She had said, sulkily.

'You must be joking!? You're the best bloody bodyguard I've ever had! And you can cook! You're not going anywhere!'

Keys stood back with a final nod of quiet acknowledgment for Rachel, for them both, and then gave Shelby a nudge. 'I've been getting acquainted with your new, red-headed friend over there.' He said, indicating the small woman as she stood talking to Sophie. 'She's a feisty one, isn't she?'

Shelby just scoffed and rolled his eyes. 'Tell me about it.'

Before he could elaborate, a woman spoke behind them.

'Coffee, black, one sugar.' She said, and a hand snaked through them to pass Keys a steaming, plastic cup. 'Vending-machine, I'm afraid.'

Rachel turned around to see who had spoken and was passing the coffee. She took a step back and closer to Shelby. 'That's the woman I punched in the face!' She said, loudly enough for everyone to hear, her thoughts not exactly realising that they had been spoken out loud.

Shelby and Keys both looked at tall, graceful and well trained Dilger, and then at smaller, rounder Rachel, and then finally settling back on Dilger again.

'What?' She said, and threw her hands up. 'It was a good punch.'

She ignored the men and held her hand out to Rachel. 'It's good to see you again, Miss Langley.' She shook her head. 'Sorry. I mean, Mrs Shelby.'

Rachel brushed the hand to one side gently and pointed at Dilger. 'No, *you* call me Rachel.' She said, seriously and embraced the woman.

'My friends call me Caroline.' Dilger replied, hugging Rachel in return.

'Caroline has just been approved as my new bodyguard.' Keys put in proudly.

Dilger's new "desk-job" had begun almost as soon as she had returned and Keys had been found to have lost both his usual bodyguard *and* the replacement.

She found she quite liked the quiet life as a shadow.

Sophie and Anna stepped into the circle of friends when they heard Rachel's voice rise and exclaim that the woman she had punched in the face was standing there.

They both did the same thing as the men and appraised Dilger and Sophie. It would have had to have been a good punch as well they were both thinking, the taller woman definitely could handle herself, they could see it in her movements.

Anna reached out and took Sophie's hand, squeezing it tightly. She had never felt as safe and as secure amongst a group of people as she did now. And Sophie, by herself, meant more to her than everyone else combined.

Sophie returned her private hand-hug and looked at Anna; I'm glad to have you by my side her look said, I'm glad our sides found each other.

The six of them stood and chatted for a while longer. Shelby voiced the question which they had all been thinking. 'Does anyone know why we are here?'

There was a chorus of no's and shaking heads.

'I feel like I'm waiting outside the principal's office or something.' Keys said.

'It's funny you should put it like that.' A man said, from the doorway across the room. 'I've been feeling exactly the same. Only in this case I *am* the principal.'

They all turned to see a tall, grey-haired man holding the door open.

'Deputy-Commissioner.' Shelby said, acknowledging his superior.

'You can all come in now.' Commissioner Appleby said, gesturing into the room.

Once they had all entered and taken their seats around a large, oval, glass-topped table, Appleby closed the door and took his own seat at the head. A plain, brown folder sat in front of him.

He looked at them all over the rims of his spectacles and then pointed to the folder. 'This is the report of the Finn case.' He said, blankly. 'Your report.' He continued, looking straight at Shelby.

'Yes sir?' Shelby said.

Appleby sat back and sighed, removing his glasses. 'Before I comment, before I say what the Deputy-Commissioner is supposed to say - *is* going to say, that is.'

He paused while pulled his wallet from his jacket pocket and removed his badge and Interpol ID.

He threw them onto the table. 'I have to fill you in on some of the missing points in your report and I can't bring myself to do it as anything but your equal.'

Shelby frowned and felt uncomfortable. 'Permission to speak freely if I may?' Shelby said.

'None of that Graham, we've known each other long enough to be friends; when I say I'm speaking as your equal I mean it. To all of you. We are just people sitting around a table.'

Shelby sighed himself then; what was going on? 'Okay. So what's on your mind, George?'

Appleby ran his hands over his face. 'Oh. God.' He mumbled. 'I cocked up Gray. Badly. I made a near-fatal mistake, an underestimation if you like.'

Anna chuckled. 'There is that word again; underestimate.' She said.

It still stung a little that she had almost got them all killed by not disposing of their old mobile-phones more efficiently.

Shelby nodded, agreeing with Anna.

'What did you do?' He then asked Appleby.

Appleby raised his shoulders and shook his head slightly. 'For want of a better way to put it; I fed the Russians the information which they were then using to trace you all. It was me, Gray, I was somehow turned into a bloody mole, right in the organisation I was looking for a mole in!'

He looked right at Rachel and Keys then. 'I am so sorry for everything you went through. I did my best to keep them from getting to you first, but I failed.'

Anna leaned forward, a grin on her face. 'So *you* were the London friend!'

Appleby looked startled.

'We knew it!' The little German laughed. 'Ha! You did well, we could almost feel the frantic responses in your messages.'

'What? What is she talking about?' Appleby asked Shelby.

'We were monitoring communications.' Shelby said. 'We watched yours as they travelled back and forth between London and Wales.'

'Impossible! The network I was using was untraceable.' He said, confidently. 'Sweet-mail or something it was called.'

'Sugar-mail.' Sophie said, a small smile on her face and her eyebrow raised.

'Yes, that's it, Sugar-ma-.' He stopped and thought. 'Oh. So that's how they did it.'

'Did what?' Shelby asked.

'Knew where I was sending Dilger and her team.' He answered.

'And how did *you* know where to send her?'

'Oh. Nothing fantastic, or any clever trickery; just a map, a few gallons of coffee and a good dose of detective work. Robinson did the rest.'

'Robinson?' Shelby said.

'He's my number one,' Dilger said, leaning round to face Shelby. 'And probably the best tracker this side of the Scottish border. It was him who found their trail to the house in Caernarfon. Commissioner Appleby pointed us to the right areas from here.'

Anna coughed. 'Pardon me for seeming stupid, but I'm still failing to see the *mole* part of this.'

Appleby shifted uncomfortably. 'Ah. Yes.' He said quietly. 'Well, that brings me to this first; I had suspected a leak here somewhere for years, I couldn't trust anyone you understand?' He looked at Shelby. 'Not even you I'm afraid to say, Graham.

'You see, I found a strange connection to the places which Finn was attacking, a connection I have only recently found out was a complete fluke on his part but a connection nonetheless.

'Some of the buildings which, let us say, entertained the kind of thing which Finn targeted, were owned by trading companies which had all been passed to hold European trading licenses.'

He flicked his gaze to Keys then. 'All stamped and signed from your office.'

Keys fidgeted. 'But you're not suggesting I knew what they were doing are you?'

'Oh. No, on the contrary, I know you had nothing to do with any of this sordid matter, not knowingly anyhow.

'No, once I spotted the connection though, I had to get a man inside, but I couldn't just have some clerk or office boy placed in there, I needed someone long-term.'

'O'Keel.' Keys said, quietly.

Appleby nodded. 'Yes, the damnable O'keel.' He sounded angry. 'That was my big mistake, he was running both sides of the field and I fell for it.'

'But so did the other side.' Shelby said, as though that should help.

'Oh. Yes, I have no doubt about that, O'Keel was his own master, but I still made the mistake of placing my entire trust in the man. Above you and Bollinger, my own superiors even.'

'And he duped you. He duped us all.' It was Keys who offered the reassuring words.

'Quite. But how? How could he pass every, single test - especially the psychological tests - with flying colours, almost faultless? How could that happen? Look where he ended up and what happened. And I, me,' he said, pointing to himself, 'placed him *your* house and nose-deep in *your* case.' He finished, and pointed at Keys and Shelby in turn.

He sat back and shook his head. 'And all the time he was letting the very people I was trying to catch know everything I was doing to catch them.'

He sat forward again, and again looked at Keys and Rachel, especially Rachel. 'I can't begin to tell you how sorry I am for what I helped to put you through.'

They both just nodded, both knew that the case had been anything but straightforward as it was. At the end of the day he had been as far down in the deep-end as the rest of them.

Shelby spoke. 'What put you in mind that there may be a mole in the first place?' He asked. 'And when was that?'

'It was right about the time of the *Cougar-cash* arrests, remember that?'

Shelby nodded. 'Yes, six years ago at least now. What happened?'

'We followed the moving dirty-money and went for the arrests. *Twice*.' He said, holding two fingers up to emphasise the point. 'If you read the case-file, we had a team waiting in Istanbul to intercept the trucks and the cash as it passed through on its way to the shipping ports.

'Well that all went south down the creek didn't it? The trucks were empty and the drivers were just hired men. Someone had snitched and let them know we were coming; there was no other reason three, empty trucks would drive over the border.

'But twenty-four hours later we received reliable intel that the money was actually running further south and heading for a tourist resort and the quays there. Fethiya. And there it was when we arrived and made the catch.'

Appleby sat back, his eyes wide. 'It was there that I was introduced to the charms and wiles of O'Keel. He was mission sergeant.'

He frowned angrily then. 'I can't believe I actually fell for it. He had orchestrated himself into a very unique position, both on our side and the Russians. The man must have had balls of bloody steel - pardon my language,' he said, and looked at the women, 'to think he could manipulate them, let alone *us* as well. But that is exactly what he did.'

Keys visibly shuddered. 'I never saw that in him, you know? Almost seven years he had been my guard and aid and I never saw anything like that in him.' He said, quietly, shocked.

Shelby, sitting by his side, elbowed his friend gently. 'Did you ever see Margret firing a Magnum 57?'

That worked and Keys smiled and then chuckled. 'She deserves a medal for that doesn't she?' He said, thinking about it. 'You're right, it's a façade which we hide behind, isn't it? He just played the game longer and better than anyone else.'

Anna leaned around Sophie. 'You own a Magnum 57?' She asked Keys, smiling as the bulky title of her second-favourite weapon rolled across her tongue. It was a good feeling to meet a mutual connoisseur.

'Yes, but God forbid, I've never fired the thing.' Keys answered, a look of distaste on his face.

Anna's face dropped a notch.

'I hate guns.' Keys continued. 'In fact I think Margret may have been the first to have ever fired it. I don't really know how she knew how to load the damn thing! I know *I* don't!' He finished, rolling his eyes upward.

Heathen, Anna thought, unappreciative, ignorant heathen. She folded her arms and sat back and scowled.

Appleby placed his hand on the file. 'Well, if you are all sure you don't want to punch me on the nose.' He smiled and looked at them all.

Shelby laughed. 'I've wanted to punch you on the nose ever since you said Finn was a psychopath serial-killer.'

Appleby joined him and laughed as well. 'Yes, well, I had to keep you on the right track and away from me, didn't I?'

He frowned seriously then and tapped at the folder. 'If everything you say in your report about the man is true, and I don't doubt for a second that it isn't, then,' he sighed unhappily, 'he was something bigger than us wasn't he? A force we may never understand. Which makes it all the more difficult for me to now say the Deputy-Commissioner's piece.'

He picked his badge and ID back up, placing them both back in his pocket and then sat up straight, businesslike.

'Firstly; you two came within inches of becoming traitors to your country, if it hadn't been for some slimy words to the man upstairs you would both be sitting in a cell in Pentonville by now.

'You took it upon yourselves to disappear from our radars and set up a secret base of maverick operations to solve a case in the name of her Majesty.

'Secondly; you allied yourselves and by extension to your case her Majesty, to internationally wanted criminals.'

He glared at Anna who squirmed. 'I can assure you that her Majesty does not take very kindly to having her good name associated with hackers with prices on their heads!'

Of the six people sitting in front of the Commissioner, three of them were flushing with embarrassed guilt. The other three were feeling it for them anyway.

'And if that isn't enough;' Appleby continued, 'you took her Majesty's good name with you and stole a British aircraft, flagrantly and wantonly flying it through all and sundries airspace!

'And the icing on this Guy Fawkesien tale of sordidity and miscreance is that you then drag her Majesty across a border into a country which is already a little cheesed off with us to begin with and you start shooting and killing people!' He paused to glare over his spectacles.

'I am surprised to see you all sitting here with your damn heads still attached to your shoulders! Be damned that we don't have the death-penalty anymore; her Majesty would bring it back just for you!'

The four of them sat stoney-faced and thouroughly told off. But all of them silently wondering why they *really* hadn't ended up in prison.

They had their answer a moment later.

Appleby picked the file up in front of him and dropped it into the bin by his side.

He returned his gaze to them and sat with his hands folded on the tabletop in front of him.

'What? I don't understand.' It was Rachel who spoke up.

She had been sat listening, terrified that her husband was going to be carted off to some jail somwhere in the world, who knew which one considering the countries they had apparently passed through.

Anna scoffed first, quickly followed by Shelby and Sophie.

Keys remained silent, but he knew what was going on; they were being swept under the carpet. Well he would be *damned* if he would let that happen.

Appleby turned his schoolteacher's gaze onto Keys then as though he had heard the man's thoughts.

He slid a sealed, white envelope over to him. It had the seal of the Royal house across the back.

It was Keys' turn to scoff now. He knew what that was too; he would be keeping quiet after all.

The commissioner didn't finish there, his eyes settled on Anna next.

Go ahead she thought, make your threats to keep me quiet, *Code-8* will never be silenced. Never.

'Their freedom will be revoked and they will begin two, twenty-five year sentences for treachury to the crown.' He said, to the wilting Anna while he pointed to Shelby and Sophie. 'Their sentences will be effective the minute they are captured - and believe me, Miss *Nova-bug*, we *will* find them. The mounties' motto is *"we always catch our man."* Well, I also have a motto; I always catch my women.'

He took a long glance at Sophie and then back to Anna. 'You will keep your silence if you value your friend's freedom.' He said, sternly.

'That goes for everyone.' He then said, addressing them all.

He produced a sheet of paper, it was blank apart from a crest at the top. 'Do any of you know what this is?' He asked them, letting them have a good look at the crest.

When none of them spoke, he said; 'This is the crest of one of the royal houses in the Far-East.' He waited until they had grasped what he was saying.

'A hand-written letter, on a sheet of paper just like this one, was delivered to our Prime-Minister last week.'

He raised his eyebrows. 'The following day, I had a similer letter with our

Prime-Minister's crest at the top, delivered to me here at Interpol. Everything I have just said to you and threatened you with came from that letter.'

He sat back and waited.

'I'm guessing the threat extended your way as well, Commissioner?' Sophie said, understanding.

Appleby remained silent.

They all then sat in silence for a few minutes more before Commissioner Appleby spoke again, quitely this time.

'I don't think there is anything left to be said now, do you?'

'What about the diaries,' Shelby asked, 'and the names inside?'

'The diaries will dissappear, but don't worry, the names inside are being scrutinized carefully even as we speak.' He winked, very, very subtly.

Sophie shook her head. 'So that's it then? We go back to our lives and carry on as though nothing happened and nothing matters?'

'What do you want me to say, Miss Bollinger?' Appleby asked, holding his hands palm up. 'I hate it as much as you do, but you can do one of two things; you can get on with your lives and moan and whine about the injustice of it all, your glass well below the halfway line, or you can carry on with your lives and know that some great good came of all of this.

'The man, Finn, wiped out an entire arm of the Russian underground single-handedly. His travels around the world have seen scores freed from slavery because of him.'

He sat back and steepled his fingers in front of his chin. 'I would rather see all of the good which Finn managed to achieve than think of the few who may have escaped justice.'

Another ponderous minute passed as they all thought of Finn and the things he had done, the people who were living freely because of him.

Shelby stood up then. 'With your permission then, sir,' he said, and pulled Rachels chair back as she also stood up.

Sophie, Anna, Keys and Dilger followed.

'I think we should get back to it.' Shelby finished and smiled.

\* \* \*

*Portugal.*

A huge acacia stood at the top of the cliff, its shade spreading out beneath a canopy of swaying green.

Kurshid sat with baby Delara, suckling the child as she looked out across the beaches below her and to the turqoise sea beyond.

Nim approached from behind, carrying a laden tray of cool drinks and bowls of fruit. By her side, the limping, smiling Faria carried a single jug of clear water.

Nim had been beside herself with grief and horror when she had heard Faria's, tiny voice scream out and then suddenly fall silent all those weeks ago back on the plains of *Al'Fezid*.

She and Jimi had rushed over to her, turning her over and expecting to find the worst.

The little girl had been hit in the leg, the bullet going straight through her calf-muscle.

She'd screamed and tumbled and hit her face on a fallen tree-branch and then had lain there, stunned, unable to move or speak.

After the rescue, the children had been handed over to local authorities by Shelby, but he had stated that they were still under the care and jurisdiction of the British Interpol service. He had made it very clear that the children would be returned to their proper places by agents of Interpol and no one else.

Four of the children were orphans, children with no families to be returned to, Faria being one of them.

Of all the unlikely voices to be raised to champoin the children, it had been Jimi's. "They can come with us." He had said, turning to face them as they stood in a line. "If you like, that is?"

The two boys and two girls, all the same age - seven or eight year-olds - hadn't needed to be asked twice.

Kurshid could also have returned to her village, but realised she had been gone for so long now, had changed so much over time that she thought it best for her and Delara to remain as they were. After all; she already had a family in Jimi, Nim and the children now.

'Can you see them?' Nim asked.

Kurshid pointed. 'Down there in the waves. Look!'

Jimi and the three other children splashed around in the water, throwing a bright-orange ball to one another and diving head-first into the waves to catch it.

Nim, Kurshid and Faria burst out laughing as they watched Jimi disappear under a sneaky ambush by the children, their own laughing voices floating up the cliff to the three of them.

Faria had wanted to stay in the villa today, secretly catching up on her reading in her *own* bedroom - her eyes and smile had almost filled the whole villa when she had seen it - but looking at the sea and the sand and the sun and her family she thought she just might run down the path after lunch and jump in and join them after all.

*\*\*\**

*Afghanistan*

It was cooler up here on the high slopes. The trees offered a much more comfortable place to sit and think.

Just like the place by the waterfall Salya thought.

She turned her attention to the slopes below and the little house which stood inside the low, herders wall. Her home looked as different from up here as it had felt once she had returned; different and far away.

But she knew that it was she who was different really, it was her and the way she saw the world now which was different.

Her father had noticed it, noticed her confidence and a wisdom which told him that his little Salya had indeed been strong, and he was afraid again for her now, but for different reasons.

She had caught him watching her, or he would suddenly appear when she least expected it. Even if she was out somewhere on the mountains he somehow managed to find her.

He was afraid. He was afraid she was going to leave, she could feel it. But how had he known?

She looked down at the dagger in her hand, the dagger Finn had given to her. There was a lock of his hair twined around the handle now.

'I miss you.' She said, quietly.

A rumble of distant thunder came from the cloudless sky above.

She opened her other palm and studied the small, black memory-stick which Finn had slipped into her hands as he was dying, *stay free* he had said for her ears only as he closed her hand around the stolen, *Code-8* software.

She looked at her home again, to the house where she had been born. There was still an empty space down there, a space in the shape of Rafiq.

The noise of thunder came again from high above.

Salya clutched the dagger and the gift of freedom from Finn, and looked up through the trees to the sky and wondered who it was who called down to her.

---

*

The end

## ABOUT THE AUTHOR

Well, if you really want to know about me, then read on.

M G Atkinson lives in the Cathedral city of Lincoln on the East-coast of England. His writing-life began back in the days of his childhood, but his author life only began in 2014.
When asked; "What do you write?"
Atkinson replies; "Things unique and inspired."

He is inspired by the great writers, whose names simply do not need to be listed; they are the greats.
The English language has developed and evolved for hundreds of years but the meaning of prose, the deeper understanding of the written word, is all founded upon those great writers who paved the way.
Atkinson brings all of the old-word beauty and reveals it in his modern-world prose.

His belief in words and how to use them makes him think of them as playthings, hence his favourite saying: *Words are toys; play with them and build novels.*

Printed in Great Britain
by Amazon